As he tore through the dark haze of the clouds he lost track of Thom altogether. Then suddenly the fighter burst through the bottom of a wisp of cirrus and Lanoe wasn't in space anymore.

On every side, tortured clouds piled up around him in enormous thunderheads, whole towers and fortresses of cloud with ramparts and battlements that melted away into mist every time he tried to make out details. Rivers of dark blue methane coiled and bent around waves of atmospheric pressure.

The sheer scale of it was lost on him until he saw the yacht, a tiny dot well ahead of him. It shot through a streamer of mist that arched high overhead, but the streamer was just one tiny arm of a vast storm as big as an ocean on Earth. And that was just what Lanoe could see from inside the fighter, a tiny fragment of a colossal world of clouds.

The yacht was out of place in that vast cloudspace. A mote of dust on the storm. It was still tumbling, end over end—the kid hadn't regained control. Tiny shards of debris were still pouring off its shattered airfoil, like thin smoke that traced out the yacht's spinning, tumbling path. Damn it.

At least atmospheric resistance had slowed them right down—maybe Lanoe could actually catch the kid now.

The green pearl in Lanoe's vision blinked back into existence, surprising him. The comms laser had reestablished contact.

"Thom," Lanoe called. "Thom, are you there? Are you okay?"

The kid sounded terrified when he replied. Breathing hard, his voice pitched too high. "I'm ... I'm still alive."

FORSAKEN SKIES

BOOK ONE OF THE SILENCE

D. NOLAN CLARK

www.orbitbooks.net

Copyright © 2016 by David Wellington
Excerpt from *Forgotten Worlds* copyright © 2016 by David Wellington
Excerpt from *The Lazarus War: Artefact* copyright © 2015 by Jamie Sawyer

Cover design by Lauren Panepinto
Cover illustration by Victor Mosquera
Cover copyright © 2016 by Hachette Book Group, Inc.

Orbit
Hachette Book Group
1290 Avenue of the Americas
New York, NY 10104
orbitbooks.net

First Edition: September 2016

Orbit is an imprint of Hachette Book Group.
The Orbit name and logo are trademarks of Little, Brown Book Group Limited.

The publisher is not responsible for websites (or their content) that are not owned by the publisher.

The Hachette Speakers Bureau provides a wide range of authors for speaking events. To find out more, go to www.hachettespeakersbureau.com or call (866) 376-6591.

Library of Congress Cataloging-in-Publication Data

Names: Clark, D. Nolan.
Title: Forsaken skies / D. Nolan Clark.
Description: First edition. | New York : Orbit, 2016.
Identifiers: LCCN 2016022305| ISBN 9780316355698 (trade pbk.) | ISBN 9780316355704 (ebook)
Subjects: LCSH: Outer space—Fiction. | GSAFD: War stories | Science fiction
Classification: LCC PS3603.L3568 F68 2016 | DDC 813/.6—dc23 LC record available at https://lccn.loc.gov/2016022305.

ISBNs: 978-0-316-35569-8 (trade paperback), 978-0-316-35570-4 (ebook)

Printed in the United States of America

RRD-C

10 9 8 7 6 5 4 3 2 1

For Jennifer

PART I

HOT JUPITER

Chapter One

Flying down a wormhole was like throwing yourself into the center of a tornado, one where if you brushed the walls you would be obliterated down to subatomic particles before you even knew it happened.

Racing through a wormhole at this speed was suicide. But the kid wouldn't slow down.

Lanoe thumbed a control pad and painted the yacht's backside with a communications laser. A green pearl appeared in the corner of his vision, with data on signal strength rolling across its surface. "Thom," he called. "Thom, you've got to stop this. I know you're scared, I know—"

"I killed him! I can't go back now!"

Lanoe muted the connection and focused for a second on not getting himself killed. The wormhole twisted and bent up ahead, warped where it passed under some massive gravity source, probably a star. Side passages opened in every direction, split by the curvature of spacetime. Lanoe had lost track of where, in real-space terms, they were—they'd started back at Xibalba but they could be a hundred light-years away by now. Wormspace didn't operate by Newtonian rules. They could be anywhere. They could theoretically be on the wrong end of the universe.

The yacht up ahead was still accelerating. It was a sleek spindle of darkness against the unreal light of the tunnel walls, all black carbon fiber broken only by a set of airfoils like flat wings spaced around its thruster. At his school Thom had a reputation as some kind of hotshot racer—he was slated to compete in next year's Earth Cup—and Lanoe had seen how good a pilot the kid was as he chased him down. He was still surprised when Thom twisted around on his axis of flight and kicked in his maneuvering jets, nearly reversing his course and sending the yacht careening down one of the side tunnels.

Maybe he'd thought he could escape that way.

For all the kid's talent, though, Lanoe was Navy trained. He knew a couple of tricks they never taught to civilians. He switched off the compensators that protected his engine and pulled a right-hand turn tighter than a poly's purse. He squeezed his eyes shut as his inertial sink shoved him hard back into his seat but when he looked again he was right back on the yacht's tail. He thumbed for the comms laser again and when the green pearl popped up he said, "Thom, you can't outfly me. We need to talk about this. Your dad is dead, yes. We need to think about what comes next. Maybe you could tell me why you did it—"

But the green pearl was gone. Thom had burned for another course change and surged ahead. He'd pulled out of the maze of wormspace and back into the real universe, up ahead at another dip in the spacetime curve.

Lanoe goosed his engine and followed. He burst out of the wormhole throat and into searing red light that burned his eyes.

―――✳―――

Centrocor freight hauler 4519 approaching on vector 7, 4, –32.

Wilscon dismantler ship Angie B, you are deviating from course by .02. Advise.

Traffic control, this is Angie B, we copy. Burning to correct.

The whispering voices of the autonomic port monitors passed across Valk's consciousness without making much of an impression.

Orbital traffic control wasn't an exacting job. It didn't pay well, either. Valk didn't mind so much. There were fringe benefits. For one, he had a cramped little workstation all to himself. He valued his privacy. Moreover, at the vertex between two limbs of the Hexus there was no gravity. It helped with the pain, a little.

Valk had been in severe pain for the last seventeen years, ever since he'd suffered what he always called his "accident." Even though there'd been nothing accidental about it. He had suffered severe burns over his entire body and even now, so many years later, the slightest weight on his flesh was too much.

His arms floated before him, his fingers twitching at keyboards that weren't really there. Lasers tracked his fingertip movements and converted them to data. Screens all around him pushed information in through his eyes, endless columns of numbers and tiny graphical displays he could largely ignore.

The Hexus sat at the bottom of a deep gravity well, a place where dozens of wormhole tunnels came together, connecting all twenty-three worlds of the local sector. A thousand vessels came through the Hexus every day, to offload cargo, to undertake repairs, just so the crews could stretch their legs for a minute on the way to their destinations. Keeping all those ships from colliding with each other, making sure they landed at the right docking berths, was the kind of job computers were built for, and the Hexus's autonomics were very, very good at it. Valk's job was to simply be there in case something happened that needed a human decision. If a freighter demanded priority mooring, for instance, because it was hauling hazardous cargo. Or if somebody important wanted the kid glove treatment. It didn't happen all that often.

Traffic, this is Angie B. We're on our way to Jehannum. Thanks for your help.

Civilian drone entering protected space. Redirecting.

Centrocor freight hauler 4519 at two thousand km, approaching Vairside docks.

Vairside docks report full. Redirect incoming traffic until 18:22.

Baffin Island docks report can take six more. Accepting until 18:49.

Unidentified vehicle exiting wormhole throat. No response to ping.

Unidentified vehicle exiting wormhole throat. No response to ping.

Maybe it was the repetition that made Valk swivel around in his workspace. He called up a new display with imaging of the wormhole throat, thirty million kilometers away. The throat itself looked like a sphere of perfect glass, distorting the stars behind it. Monitoring buoys with banks of floodlights and sensors swarmed around it, keeping well clear of the opening to wormspace. The newcomers were so small it took a second for Valk to even see them.

But there—the one in front was a dark blip, barely visible except when it occluded a light. A civilian craft, built for speed by the look of it. Expensive as hell. And right behind it—there—

"Huh," Valk said, a little grunt of surprise. It was an FA.2 fighter, cataphract class. A cigar-shaped body, one end covered in segmented carbonglas viewports, the other housing a massive thruster. A double row of airfoils on its flanks.

Valk had been a fighter pilot himself, back before his accident. He knew the silhouette of every cataphract, carrier scout, and recon boat that had ever flown. There had been a time when you would have seen FA.2s everywhere, when they were the Navy's favorite theater fighter. But that had been more than a century ago. Who was flying such an antique?

Valk tapped for a closer view—and only then did he see the red lights flashing all over his primary display. The two newcomers were moving *fast*, a considerable chunk of the speed of light.

And they were headed straight toward the Hexus.

He called up a communications panel and started desperately pinging them.

Light and heat burst into Lanoe's cockpit. Sweat burst out all over his skin. His suit automatically wicked it away but it couldn't catch all the beads of sweat popping out on his forehead. He swiped a virtual panel near his elbow and his viewports polarized, switching down to near-opaque blackness. It still wasn't enough.

There was a very good reason you didn't shoot out of a wormhole throat at this kind of speed. Wormhole throats tended to be very close to very big stars.

He could barely see—afterimages flickered in his vision, blocking out all the displays on his boards. He had a sense of a massive planet dead ahead but he couldn't make out any details. He tapped at display after display, trying to get some telemetry data, desperate for any information about where he was.

Then he saw the Hexus floating right in front of him. Fifty kilometers across, a vast hexagonal structure of concrete and foamsteel, like a colossal dirty benzene ring. Geryon, he thought. The Hexus orbited the planet Geryon, a bloated gas giant that circled a red giant star. That explained all the light and heat, at least.

He tried to raise Thom again with his comms laser but the green pearl wouldn't show up in his peripheral vision. Little flashes of green came from his other eye and he realized he was being pinged by the Hexus. He thumbed a panel to send them his identifying codes but didn't waste any time talking to them directly.

The Hexus was getting bigger, growing at an alarming rate. "Thom," he called, whether the kid could hear him or not, "you need to break off. You can't fly through that thing. Thom! Don't do it!"

His vision had cleared enough that he could just see the yacht, a dark spot visible against the brighter skin of the station. Thom was going to fly straight through the Hexus. At first glance it looked like there was plenty of room—the hexagon was wide open in its middle—but that space was full of freighters and liners and countless drones, a bewilderingly complex interchange of ships jockeying for position, heading to or away from docking facilities, ships being refueled by tenders, drones checking heat shields or scraping carbon out of thruster cones. If Thom went through there it would be like firing a pistol into a crowd.

Lanoe cursed under his breath and brought up his weapon controls.

❦

Centrocor freight hauler 4519 requesting berth at Vairside docks.
Vairside docks report full. Redirect incoming traffic until 18:22.

Valk ignored the whispering voices. He had a much bigger problem.

In twenty-nine seconds the two unidentified craft were going to streak right through the center of the Hexus, moving fast enough to obliterate anything in their way. If there was a collision the resulting debris would have enough energy to tear the entire station apart. Hundreds of thousands of people would die.

Valk worked fast, moving from one virtual panel to the next, dismissing displays and opening new ones. His biggest display showed the trajectory of the two newcomers, superimposed on a diagram of every moving thing inside the Hexus. Tags on each object showed relative velocities, mass and inertia quantities, collision probabilities.

Those last showed up in burning red. Valk had to find a way to get each of them to turn amber or green before the newcomers blazed right through the Hexus. That meant moving every ship, every tiny drone, one by one—computing a new flight path for each craft that wouldn't intersect with any of the others.

The autonomic systems just weren't smart enough to do it themselves. This was exactly why they still had a human being working Valk's job.

If he moved this liner here—redirected this drone swarm to the far side of the Hexus—if he ordered this freighter to make a correction burn of fourteen milliseconds—if he swung this dismantler ship around on its long axis—

One of the newcomers finally responded to his identification requests, but he didn't have time to look. He swiped that display away even while he used his other hand to order a freighter to fire its positioning jets.

Civilian drone entering protected space. Redirecting.

Centrocor freight hauler 4519 requesting berth at Vairside docks.

The synthetic voices were like flies buzzing around inside Valk's skull. That freight hauler was a serious pain in the ass—it was by far the largest object still inside the ring of the Hexus, the craft most likely to get in the way of the incoming yacht.

Valk would gladly have sent the thing burning hard for a distant parking orbit. It was a purely autonomic vessel, without even a pilot onboard, basically a giant drone. Who cared if a little cargo didn't make it to its destination in time? But for some reason its onboard computers refused to obey his commands. It kept demanding to be routed to a set of docks that weren't even classified for freight craft.

He pulled open a new control pad and started sending override codes.

The freighter responded instantly.

Instructed course will result in distress to passengers. Advise?

Wait. Passengers?

Up ahead the traffic inside the ring of the Hexus scattered like pigeons from a cat, but still there were just too many ships and drones in there, too many chances for a collision. Thom hadn't deviated even a fraction of a degree from his course. In a second or two it would be too late for him to break off—at this speed he wouldn't be able to burn hard enough to get away.

On Lanoe's weapons screen a firing solution popped up. He could hit the yacht with a disruptor. One hit and the yacht would be reduced to tiny debris, too small to do much damage when it rained down on the Hexus. His thumb hovered over the firing key—but even as he steeled himself to do it, a second firing solution popped up.

A ponderous freighter hung there, right in the middle of the ring. Right in the middle of Thom's course.

It was an ugly ship, just a bunch of cargo containers clamped to a central boom like grapes on a vine. It had thruster packages on either end but nothing even resembling a crew capsule.

Lanoe had enough weaponry to take that thing to pieces.

He opened a new communications panel and pinged the Hexus. "Traffic control, you need to move that freighter right now."

The reply came back instantly. At least somebody was talking to him. "FA.2, this is Hexus Control. Can't be done. Are you in contact with the unidentified yacht? Tell that idiot to change his trajectory."

"He's not listening," Lanoe called back. Damn it. Thom was maybe five seconds from splattering himself all over that ugly ship. "Control, move that freighter—or I'll move it for you."

"Negative! Negative, FA.2—there are people on that thing!"

What? That made no sense. A freight hauler like that would be controlled purely by autonomics. It wasn't classified for human occupation—it wouldn't even have rudimentary life support onboard.

There couldn't possibly be people on that thing. Yet he had no reason to think that traffic control would lie about that. And then—

In Lanoe's head the moral calculus was already working itself out. People, control had said—meaning more than one person.

If he killed Thom, who he knew was a murderer, it would save multiple innocent lives.

He reached again for the firing key.

There had to be an answer. There had to be.

Instructed course would result in distress to passengers. Advise?

Valk could see six different ways to move the freighter. Every single one of them meant firing its main thrusters for a hard burn. Accelerating it at multiple g's.

If he did that, anybody inside the freighter would be reduced to red jelly. Unlike passenger ships, the cargo ship didn't carry an inertial sink. The people in it would have no protection from the sudden acceleration.

Centrocor freight hauler 4519 requesting berth at Vairside docks.

The ship was too stupid to know it was about to be smashed to pieces. Not for the first time he wished he could switch off the synthetic voices that reeled off pointless information all around him. He opened a new screen and studied the freighter's schematics. There were maneuvering thrusters here, and positioning jets near the nose, but they wouldn't be able to move the ship fast enough, there were emergency retros in six different locations, and explosive bolts on the cargo containers—

Yes! He had it. "FA.2," he called, even as he opened a new control pad. "FA.2, do not fire!" He tapped away at the pad, his fingers aching as he moved them so quickly.

Instructed action may cause damage to Centrocor property. Advise?

"I advise you to shut up and do what I say," Valk told the freighter. That wasn't what it was looking for, though. He looked down, saw a green virtual key hovering in front of him, and stabbed at it.

Out in the middle of the ring, the freight hauler triggered the explosive bolts on all of its port side cargo containers at once. The long boxes went tumbling away with aching slowness, blue and yellow and red oblongs dancing outward on their own trajectories. Some smashed into passing drones, creating whole new clouds of debris. Some bounced off the arms of the Hexus, obliterating against its concrete, the goods inside thrown free in multicolored sprays.

On Valk's screens a visual display popped up showing him the chaos. The yacht was a tiny dark needle lost in the welter of colorful boxes and smashed goods, moving so fast Valk could barely track it. But this was going to work, a gap was opening where the yacht could pass through safely, this was going to—

There was no sound but Valk could almost feel the crunch as one of the cargo containers just clipped one of the yacht's airfoils. The cargo container tore open, its steel skin splitting like it was a piece of overripe fruit. Barrels spilled out in a broad cloud of wild trajectories. The yacht was thrown into a violent spin as it shot through the Hexus and out the other side.

A split second later the FA.2 jinked around a flying barrel and burned hard to follow the yacht on its new course, straight down toward Geryon.

Chapter Two

Lanoe had to lean over hard into a tight bank to avoid the swirl of cargo in the Hexus but he almost laughed as he worked his controls, throwing his stick to the left and then the right. Whoever was running traffic control back there was a genius.

He sobered up again almost instantly when he saw where he was headed next. Thom had been thrown for a loop by a grazing collision and now he was falling out of the sky. Up ahead lay the broad disk of Geryon, a boiling hell cauldron of a planet. Out of control and spinning, Thom couldn't fight the pull of its gravity. He was going to fall right into that mess.

Geryon was a gas giant, a world with no surface, just a near-endless atmosphere. From a distance it looked like it was tearing itself apart from the inside out. It was banded with dark storms, nearly black, that hid an inner layer of incandescent neon. The buzzing red light streaked outward through every crack and gap in the cloud layer, rays of baleful effulgence spearing outward at the void.

Lanoe barely had time to get a look at the planet before the yacht pitched nose first into its atmosphere. He burned after it, down into the topmost clouds. He tried to paint the kid again with the communications laser, not expecting a result. He didn't get one.

As he tore through the dark haze of the clouds he lost track of

Thom altogether. Then suddenly the fighter burst through the bottom of a wisp of cirrus and Lanoe wasn't in space anymore.

On every side, tortured clouds piled up around him in enormous thunderheads, whole towers and fortresses of cloud with ramparts and battlements that melted away into mist every time he tried to make out details. Rivers of dark blue methane coiled and bent around waves of atmospheric pressure.

The sheer scale of it was lost on him until he saw the yacht, a tiny dot well ahead of him. It shot through a streamer of mist that arched high overhead, but the streamer was just one tiny arm of a vast storm as big as an ocean on Earth. And that was just what Lanoe could see from inside the fighter, a tiny fragment of a colossal world of clouds.

The yacht was out of place in that vast cloudspace. A mote of dust on the storm. It was still tumbling, end over end—the kid hadn't regained control. Tiny shards of debris were still pouring off its shattered airfoil, like thin smoke that traced out the yacht's spinning, tumbling path. Damn it.

At least atmospheric resistance had slowed them right down— maybe Lanoe could actually catch the kid now.

The green pearl in Lanoe's vision blinked back into existence, surprising him. The comms laser had reestablished contact.

"Thom," Lanoe called. "Thom, are you there? Are you okay?"

The kid sounded terrified when he replied. Breathing hard, his voice pitched too high. "I'm...I'm still alive."

"Damn it, Thom," Lanoe said. "What were you thinking back there? There were people on that freighter. You could have killed them."

It took a long while for Thom to reply. Maybe he was just struggling to pull out of his spin. Lanoe could see his attitude thrusters firing, jets of vapor that were lost instantly in the dark cloudscape.

When Thom did come back on the line he sounded calmer, but chastened. "I didn't know that."

Lanoe couldn't help but feel for Thom. When the kid had made a break for it, when he'd stolen the yacht and run for the nearest wormhole, Lanoe had followed because he thought maybe, somehow, he could help. To the kid it must have looked like there was a hellhound on his tail. "Get control of your ship," Lanoe told him. Though honestly it looked like Thom had already done just that. The yacht had stabilized its flight, even with one damaged airfoil. The kid had skill, Lanoe thought. He had the makings of a great pilot. If he didn't die right here. "You all right?"

"I'm fine."

"Then let's think about how to keep you that way. Slow down and let's talk about this. Okay? First things first, we need to get out of this atmosphere. Let's head back to the Hexus. I can't promise people there will be happy to see you, but—"

"I'm not going back," Thom replied. "I'm never going back."

━━━━✦━━━━

It should have been over by now.

It should have been quick and painless. He should have hit that freighter dead-on and that would have been that.

Thom realized his eyes were closed. That was stupid. You never closed your eyes when you were flying—you needed to be constantly aware of everything around you. He opened his eyes and laughed.

There was nothing to see out there. Black mist writhed across his viewports. His displays were all turning red, but who cared? That was kind of the point, wasn't it?

Just fade to black.

If only Lanoe would shut up and let him get on with it.

"There's no way forward here, Thom. If I have to shoot you to stop this idiotic chase, I will. Turn back now."

"Why would I do that?" Thom asked.

"Because right now I'm the only friend you have."

"You were my father's puppet. I know you'll take me back there if I give you the chance."

"You're wrong, Thom. I just want to help."

Thom leaned back in his crash seat and tried to just breathe.

He was surrounded by expensive wooden fittings. His seat was upholstered in real leather. He couldn't help thinking the yacht would make a luxurious coffin.

Thom was—had been—the son of the planetary governor of Xibalba. He was used to a certain degree of luxury. He understood now how much of that he'd taken for granted. Nothing had ever been denied to him his whole life.

No one had ever bullied him in school—his father's bodyguards had seen to that. No one had ever said no to him as long as he could remember. But now Lanoe wouldn't just give up. Wouldn't just let him go.

It was infuriating.

Thom wondered why he didn't just switch off his comms panel. Block Lanoe's transmission. Maybe, he thought, he just wanted to hear another human voice before he ended this.

Even if he didn't want to hear what Lanoe had to say.

"I was just your father's escort pilot, Thom. I'm not here to avenge him. The Navy assigned me to work for him, but it was just a job. I never even liked him."

"I hated him," Thom replied, unable to resist. Maybe he wanted to justify what he'd done. "I always hated him."

"Well, that's in the past now," Lanoe said. "As is my job—I don't owe him anything now that he's dead. I came after you because believe it or not, I do like *you*. That's all. Please believe me."

"I can't," Thom said. "Lanoe, I'm sorry, but I can't trust anyone right now."

Over the line he could hear Lanoe sigh in frustration. "Why'd you even do it?" Lanoe asked. "Why kill him? In a year you would have been away at university. Away from him."

"You think so?" Thom said. "You don't know anything, Lanoe."

"So enlighten me."

Thom smiled at the black mist that surrounded him. He couldn't think of a good reason to lie, not now. "I wasn't going to

Uni. I wasn't going anywhere. He was sick. All that stress of his high-powered job just ate away at his heart. You know what they do, when your body gives out like that? They give you a new one."

"So he would have lived a little longer—"

"You still don't understand, do you? I wasn't born to be his heir."

When you were rich and powerful, you didn't have to worry about getting sick. You didn't have to make do with an artificial pump ticking away in your chest, or taking immunosuppressive drugs for the rest of your life. You didn't even have to worry about getting old.

No, not if you had a little forethought. Not if you could afford to have children. Kids whose neurology was a perfect match for your own.

The old man could have arranged for Thom to have an accident that left him brain dead. Then he could have his own consciousness transferred into Thom's young, healthy body. It happened all the time in the halls of power. The legality was questionable but a lot of rules didn't apply to planetary governors.

"I was designed," Thom said. "Built to be his next body."

There was a long pause on the line. "I didn't know," Lanoe said.

"He had to die," Thom said. In his mind's eye he saw it all over again. Saw himself pick up the ancient dueling pistol. Felt it jump in his hand. The old man hadn't even had a chance to look surprised. "Do you understand now? I'm only twenty years old, and he was going to steal my body and throw my mind away. Kill me. So I had to kill him if I wanted to live. And now I have to keep moving. For another thirty-six hours."

"Thirty-six hours?"

"His doctors will have stabilized his brain, even if the rest of him is dead. They can keep his consciousness viable that long. If they catch me before his brain really dies, they can still go ahead with the switch."

"Let me help, then," Lanoe said.

Thom closed his eyes again. Nobody could help him now.

He leaned forward on his stick. Brought the yacht's nose down until it was pointed right at the core of the planet. Opened his throttle all the way.

The yacht dove into a dark cloud bank, a wall of smoke thick enough to block Lanoe's transmission.

This would be over soon.

A rain of fine soot smashed against Lanoe's canopy as he dove straight down into the pressure and heat of Geryon's atmosphere. The clouds whipped past him and then they were gone and he stared down into the red glare of the neon layer.

He couldn't see the yacht—it was hidden behind that shimmering wall of fire. He spared a moment to check some of his instruments and saw just how bad it was out there. Over 2,000 degrees Kelvin. Atmospheric pressure hard enough to crush the fighter in microseconds. The FA.2 possessed enough vector field strength to hold that killing air back, according to its technical specifications. Even so, he was sure he could hear his carbonglas canopy crackle under the stress, feel the entire ship closing in on him as the pressure warped its hull. His inertial sink held him tight in his seat as the ship rocked and trembled in the turbulent air.

If the fighter was in that much distress, could the kid hold up at all? Lanoe had no idea what kind of defensive fields the yacht carried. It was possible that the next time he saw Thom the kid would be a crumpled ball of carbon fiber, tumbling slowly as it fell toward the center of the planet.

Yet when his airfoils carried him rattling and hissing through the floor of the neon layer, he saw the yacht dead ahead, still intact, still hurtling downward on a course that went nowhere good. There was nothing but murk down there, pure hydrogen under so much pressure it stopped acting like a gas and turned into liquid metal. No ship ever built could handle this kind of strain for more than a few minutes.

Lanoe didn't know if even comms lasers could cut through

the dark, swirling mess but then the green pearl in the corner of his vision appeared and he opened the transmission immediately. "Thom," he said. "Thom—is this what you want? Did we just come here so you could commit suicide?"

There was no reply.

All over Lanoe's panels, red lights danced and flickered. Lanoe couldn't do this much longer and still hope to get back to space in one piece.

He set his teeth and sped after the yacht.

Everything shook and strained and groaned. The wooden veneer on the console in front of Thom creaked and then split down the middle, a jagged fissure running across his instrument displays. So close now.

The carbon fiber hull of the yacht couldn't take this pressure or this heat. The ship's vector fields were the only thing keeping Thom alive. If they failed—or if he switched them off—it would be over before he even knew what had happened. The ship would collapse around him, crushing his flesh, his bones. His blood would boil and then vaporize. His eyes would—

A sudden loud pop behind him made Thom yelp in surprise and terror. Broken glass splattered across his viewports and yellow liquid dripped down the front of his helmet. Hellfire and ashes, was this how it happened? Was that cerebrospinal fluid? Was his head caving in?

No. No—the fizzy liquid running across his vision was champagne.

Behind the pilot's seat was a tiny cargo cabinet. There had been a bottle of champagne back there, put there by the old man's servants for when Thom won his next race. Wine made from grapes actually grown in the soil of Earth. That bottle had been almost as expensive as the yacht itself.

The bottle had been under pressure already—the added strain of Geryon's crushing grip had been too much for it.

An uncontrollable laugh ripped its way up through Thom's throat. He shook and bent over his controls and tears pooled in his eyes until his suit carefully wicked them away. He had been scared by a champagne bottle going off. That hadn't happened since he was a child.

Scared.

Fear—now that was funny. He hadn't expected to be afraid at this point. Thom was no coward. But now his heart raced—he could feel adrenaline throbbing through his veins.

He hadn't expected to be scared.

He looked out through his viewports at the dark haze ahead, at the center of the planet, and it was so huge. So big beyond anything he could comprehend.

Suddenly he couldn't breathe.

━━<del></del>━━

"Lanoe?" the kid said. "Lanoe, I think I made a mistake."

Lanoe clamped his eyes shut. There was nothing to see, anyway, except the tail of the yacht. "Yeah? You're just getting that now?"

"I'm sorry I dragged you into this," Thom said. The transmission was full of noise, words compressed down until the kid's voice sounded like a machine talking. "Something's gone wrong. Lanoe—I thought I could do this. But now—"

"That's your survival instinct kicking in. Self-preservation, right? Don't fight that urge, Thom. It's there for a reason."

"I think maybe it's too late. Oh, hellfire."

Lanoe shook his head. The kid had some guts to have gotten this far, but what a damned idiot he was. "Pull up. Come on, Thom, just pull up and get out of here."

"I can't see anything—I don't even know which way is up!"

"The Hexus. Look for the Hexus. Its beacons should be all over your nav display—latch on to them. Pull up, Thom. Come on! Don't go any lower."

"I'm trying. . . . My controls are so sluggish. Lanoe . . . I."

The green pearl kept rotating, numbers streaming across its surface. The connection hadn't been cut off. The kid had just stopped talking.

"Damn," Lanoe said. He started easing back on his control stick. Fed fuel to all of his retros and positioning rockets, intending to swing around and punch for escape velocity.

But then the kid spoke again.

"I don't want to die," Thom said.

Lanoe saw the yacht ahead of him. Its nose had come around, a little. The kid was doing his best. All of his jets were firing in quick stuttering bursts as he tried to check his downward velocity. If he could get his tail pointed down he could fire his main thruster and head back toward space.

But the nose was swinging around way too slow.

Lanoe saw why right away—it was that broken airfoil, the one he'd smashed against a cargo container. Airfoils were deadweight in space but in an atmosphere like this they were vital, and Thom was running one short. That was going to kill him.

No. Lanoe wouldn't accept that.

"Listen," he said. "You can do this. Take it easy, don't waste any burns."

"I'm trying," the kid told him.

"Get your nose up, that's the main thing."

"I know what to do!"

"I'm going to tell you anyway. Get your nose up. Come on, kid!"

The yacht had fallen so far down Lanoe could barely see it. How much longer would the kid's fields hold out? They must be eating up all his power, just to keep the yacht from being crushed. That extra energy could make a real difference.

"Thom—transfer some power from your vector field to your thrusters."

"I'll be splattered," the kid pointed out.

He was probably right. But if he didn't get his nose up, he was going to die anyway.

"Do it!" Lanoe shouted. "Transfer five percent—"

One whole side of the yacht caved in. Lanoe felt sick as he watched the carbon fiber hull crumple and distort.

But in the same moment the yacht swung around all at once and got its nose pointed straight up. Its main thruster engaged in a burst of fire and it shot past Lanoe's fighter, moving damned fast.

Lanoe's own fields were complaining. He was used to the fighter's alarms, its chimes and whistles and screaming Klaxons. He ignored them all. He sent the FA.2 into a tight spin until his own nose was pointing up, then punched for full burn.

Ahead of him the wall of buzzing red neon came and went. The clouds of soot and dark blue methane. For a split second he saw blue sky overhead, pure, thin air, and then it turned black and the stars came out.

Ahead of him the yacht burned straight out into the night, standing on its tail.

In the distance, past the kid's nose, Lanoe could see the Hexus. If they could just make it there maybe this chase could end. Maybe they could both come out of this okay.

"Thom," he called. "Thom, come in."

There was no green pearl in the corner of his vision. Lanoe came up alongside the yacht and saw just how much of it had collapsed. The whole forward compartment had imploded, all of the viewports shattered down to empty frames.

"Oh, hellfire, Thom," Lanoe whispered. "I'm sorry. I'm so damned sorry."

Chapter Three

As usual, Valk had been left to clean up the mess.

And this was a big one.

Already the synthetic voices were burbling away with demands and threats. Centrocor owned both the freight hauler he had nobbled and the Hexus itself, and he had damaged both of them. Centrocor was a poly—one of the big transplanetary commercial monopolies that owned, de facto, this entire sector and all twenty-three of its worlds. They had much more pressing concerns than asking if there had been any casualties. The fact that Valk had saved some lives here was far less important than those barrels he sent spilling out into the void.

Most likely he would come out of this with a bunch of lawsuits on his record. More important, he would probably get fired, too. Without a job—well, he didn't know what he would do then. The job was all he had.

So he sent a drone swarm out to recover the cargo containers and as many of the barrels and boxes and broken crates as they could chase down. He sent a quick message to the maintenance staff asking them to make sure the Hexus hadn't been damaged irreparably by flying debris. Then he switched traffic control over to the autonomics and logged out for the day.

He had a mystery to solve. To wit: What the hell were people doing onboard a cargo ship?

The noise was the worst of it. The cargo container vibrated like a struck bell, and every so often they would feel the pull of acceleration and be squashed up against one barely padded wall, sometimes hard enough that red spots would burst behind Roan's eyes. But the noise was worse. Booming, mechanical noises that resonated inside the container and made her teeth hurt.

She had a vague idea of what was going on. The container had come loose from the freighter somehow and they'd gone tumbling off into space. She'd thought they were lost forever until the noise started. That had to be a drone or something grabbing the container in mechanical arms. Dragging it back to safety, she hoped.

Very, very slowly. It had been more than an hour already and she had no idea how much longer it might take.

The two of them, Roan and her teacher, Elder McRae, were low on breathable air—they'd barely budgeted enough on life support to make the twelve-day trip—and the container had started to stink the first time they'd had to use the chemical toilet. There had been nothing to do during the slow journey to Geryon. They had exactly what they needed to survive and nothing more. The only illumination inside the container came from a single display foam-sealed to one wall, a flickering plane of light no wider than Roan's two hands laid side by side. It showed nothing now but the hexagonal Centrocor logo, slowly rotating as it tried to reestablish communication with the freighter's computer brain. And failing.

"How much longer?" she asked, just to hear her own voice.

"Patience is not one of the four eternals," Elder McRae replied. "Perhaps it should be."

The elder had her eyes closed. Her lined brown face barely stirred as she took one shallow breath after another. Roan envied her composure, her discipline. For years Roan had studied to come close to the kind of inner peace she saw in the elder. The woman had been like a second mother to Roan, and a great teacher.

Right at that moment Roan hated the elder's stupid face.

Which of course immediately made her feel deep shame and regret. She was forgetting her disciplines, forgetting all she'd learned—

The container lurched sideways so suddenly it was all Roan could do to grab one of the nylon loops attached to the wall, to keep herself from being thrown about like a pebble in an empty can. The elder, of course, had already strapped herself down.

The movement was followed by a new suite of noises, each louder and more ear-piercing than the last. A nasty thud rocked the container and Roan felt that they had stopped moving. Maybe they'd finally reached their destination, she thought.

Then the whole container began to spin around them, and Roan felt all the blood rush out of her head. She was certain she was going to be sick.

The Hexus had six long arms, each of which rotated on its long axis to generate artificial gravity. Valk's traffic control station was in one of the vertices between the arms, a place where he could just float and not have to use his legs.

Going into one of the arms—going into any place with gravity—meant agony. But the only safe way to pop open the cargo container and extract its stowaways was to bring it inside, into heat and air. If Valk wanted to see what was inside that container, he had no choice.

He had the drones bring the container into one of the giant spin locks, a huge drum at the end of Vairside, one of the six arms of the Hexus. He floated in beside it as jets flooded the drum with air. The walls started to rotate and then, almost gently, Valk and the container settled down to its floor. It took three minutes for the lock to match the rotation of Vairside, during which time Valk felt himself grow heavier and heavier.

The second his feet touched the floor, it began. Cramps in what were left of his feet, first. A throbbing in his thigh muscles. He became far too aware of the shapes of the bones inside his legs, felt his kneecaps grind back into place.

His suit knew what to do. It massaged his calves with custom-made rollers. Heating elements in his boots activated and warmed his aching flesh. A white pearl appeared in the corner of his left eye, offering painkilling medication.

He blinked it away.

The hospital had given him his special suit after his accident, seventeen years ago. He hadn't taken it off since. At least a dozen times a day that white pearl appeared before him, asking him if he wanted the drug. It was proven not to be habit-forming, they told him. There was no chance of chemical addiction. It wouldn't impair his ability to work.

Valk knew if he started saying yes to the white pearl he wouldn't stop. Why, when the pain would always be there? Blinking away the white pearl had become a reflex after a few years. Now it was a tiny victory every time he did it. Tiny victories being the most he let himself hope for, these days.

He gritted his teeth and waited for the pain to suffuse him. To become just part of who he was. Over the years he'd grown so familiar with it that he could, if not ignore it, at least grunt his way through it.

Eventually the spin lock reached the correct angular momentum and the big doors opened. Drones picked up the cargo container, their segmented arms straining under its new weight, and carried it into the broad, open entrance vestibule of the Vairside arm. Other drones waited their turn, big construction models that could cut the container open without damaging anything inside.

Centrocor wasn't taking any chances. If the people inside died on Hexus property the poly could, conceivably, be sued for wrongful death. It would never happen, of course. Centrocor had more lawyers than the Navy had pilots. But Valk supposed you didn't get to be a Multiplanetary Development Monopoly by taking risks.

As the drones moved in to dismantle one of the short ends of the container, Valk walked over to stand where he could get a good look inside. Steel dissolved to bubbling foam as the dismantlers did their work and then a drone with a floodlight came up to illuminate the interior.

There wasn't much to see. The interior walls of the container had been lined with soft plastic, studded with the nylon hand loops you saw everywhere in microgravity environments. There were a few pieces of life support and sanitary equipment but the cavernous interior was otherwise completely bare.

Then the stowaways came forward. An old woman and a teenage girl, both dressed in colorless but clean tunics and leggings.

Instantly a hundred Centrocor drones came swooping down on them, all talking at once.

———※※———

A fist-sized plastic drone drifted into Roan's face with a whir of ducted propellers. Manipulator arms and sensors on flexible stalks dangled from its underside. It spoke to her in a voice that wasn't human at all.

Welcome to the Centrocor Hexus.

Another one bobbed up beside her, and another until a cloud of them had gathered around her head, all speaking at once.

Please do not move while the scan is in progress.

You have certain rights, some of which you may have already waived.

How can we help you explore Vairside?

Anything you say may be used against you in a court of law.

State your language preference so we can proceed.

Please fill out these forms, which are vital for public health and safety.

You may be under arrest. Authorities will be with you presently.

Please speak or enter your Centrocor Rewards Club number now.

She winced backward, overwhelmed. She bumped into Elder

McRae, who put a steadying hand on her arm, but the teacher looked just as confused and frightened.

Then a giant in a heavy space suit loomed through the cloud, batting at the drones with his hands. One by one they moved back, away from the big man. He had to be two and a half meters tall—taller than anyone Roan had ever met. His suit gave bulk to his already wide shoulders. His helmet was up and polarized to a glossy black. She expected him to lower the helmet, to show his face, but he didn't.

"You just have to show them you mean business," he said, shoving one last drone up against the wall. It protested in a high whine for a moment, then fell silent. "Sorry about that," he said.

"Who are you?" Roan asked.

"Tannis Valk. I'm in charge of traffic here. I've got some questions for you." He leaned farther into the cargo container. "Are you serious?" he asked.

"Serious about what?" she asked. Roan didn't like this, not at all. Why wouldn't the man show them his face? "Are we under quarantine or something?"

"Hmm, what?" Valk asked. "No. Serious—I mean, where are you two from?"

It was all too much. Roan wanted to shrink back into the container, to get away from this strange man and the swarm of drones.

"Why can't we see your face?" she asked.

"I had an accident awhile back," Valk replied. "Trust me, you don't want to see what's under here. Listen, I need some answers. How long have you two been in here?"

"Twelve days," Roan said. The elder squeezed her arm again, but she ignored it. "We're from Niraya."

"You came all that way in *this*?" Valk asked. "In a cargo box? It's a miracle you made it. That freight hauler you were attached to didn't even have a human pilot. It barely knew you were alive in here. Which I'm guessing was the point, huh? You knew it was illegal to travel like this."

"When you don't have any money," Roan said, "you have to—"

The elder's hand grabbed her arm again. This time she pinched hard enough to make Roan fall silent.

"M. Valk," the elder said, stepping forward, "are we under arrest?"

The giant shrugged. The hard shoulder plates of his suit lifted and fell, anyway. It looked like an exaggerated shrug, like the gesture of a cartoon character. "That's kind of an open question. Technically you broke the law, stowing away like this. But Centrocor's interest is in limiting its liability, so maybe they don't want to start a docket on you two. If you could just tell me why you came here, and what you—"

The elder cleared her throat to quiet him. She drew herself up to her full height—a good head and a half shorter than Valk. But she got that look on her face, the one she used when Roan was being obstinate and refused to learn a lesson.

Roan lived in mortal terror of that look.

"Are you going to detain us, M. Valk? We have business here. Urgent business."

"I don't have much authority in that," Valk told her. "I can guarantee you'll be monitored until we clear this up. Your movements will be logged and you won't be allowed to leave the Hexus."

"That's acceptable," the elder said.

Valk nodded, his helmet bobbing forward, then back. It was like he was pantomiming human gestures. "Listen," he said. "If you just tell me what's going on, if you give me enough to file a complete report, we can avoid—"

"If we aren't being detained, we'll be on our way," the elder told him. Then she grabbed Roan's elbow and pushed her toward the slagged end of the cargo container and into the cavernous space beyond.

Up ahead a massive portal opened into light and noise and the unbearably enticing smell of cooked food. A four-meter-wide display hung in the arch, reading WELCOME TO VAIRSIDE. CIVILIAN REGS APPLY.

Roan glanced back and saw Valk inside the cargo container,

running one big finger across the soft plastic that lined its walls. Then the elder steered her through the portal and into the welter of sensations beyond, and she stopped thinking about anything else.

~~~~

Clean.

Way too clean.

Valk squatted down on his haunches before the life support system the stowaways had left behind. The old, old agony in his knees flared up and he had to wait a second for the red haze of pain to recede from his vision. When it cleared he studied the little unit as if it were an archaeological find.

Valk couldn't remember the last time he'd seen a water recycler so crude—it ran on actual batteries, it looked like. And the air scrubber had weld marks and sticky bits of tape all over it, as if someone had built it from spare parts.

Yet when he opened it up the filter inside was immaculate, as if it had been scoured clean very recently.

Valk gave his suit a command. A grid of tiny holes opened in the flowglas of his helmet, just big enough to let a little air through. He inhaled sharply through his nose. The container stank. Well, two people had been living inside for twelve days. He had seen chemical toilets in better shape, too. There probably hadn't been much they could do about that—but everything inside the container that could be cleaned, had been. Assiduously.

He went over to the display that had been mounted on one wall and pinged its logs. Only a few entries popped up, just standard stuff. They had used the display to communicate with the freighter's autonomic pilot. Once to let it know they were alive and it needed to be careful with them. A couple of times during the journey, they'd logged in to check on their ETA.

There were no entertainment programs on the display. No games or videos or anything to help them pass the time.

They must have spent most of their twelve-day journey cleaning and fixing things. Keeping themselves alive. How had they not gone crazy in the dark and the lack of stimulation?

Niraya. The girl had said they came from Niraya. Valk had heard of the place in a vague sort of way. It was one of the planets the Hexus served, but not a lot of traffic went through there. He patched his suit's computer into the display and looked it up.

Lines of text scrolled across the screen, giving him way more information than he wanted—climate data, historical logs, financials. He went for the quick version instead. He saw right away why he'd barely heard of the place. It was about as far from Earth as you could get and still be in human space, hundreds of light-years away in the direction of galactic center. It had been settled during the Brushfire as a colony for the followers of some minor religion or other. Centrocor had taken on responsibility for its development, and nobody had ever challenged their authority. No other poly seemed to think the place was worth conquering. In exchange for their patronage, Centrocor had built a mining concern there—though the operation had never been very profitable. Nobody was paying big money for iridium or cobalt. Niraya was dirt poor, so broke it hadn't even finished terraforming operations. Even now, a hundreds years after it was settled, it was barely fit for human inhabitation.

Well, the place's poverty might explain why the two of them had to stow away in a cargo container rather than buying passage on an actual passenger ship. And if they were adherents of some strict religious order—judging by their clothes, they weren't miners—that might explain the fanatical cleanliness.

But what in damnation would people like that want on the Hexus?

He walked out of the container and over toward the arch that led to the dubious delights of Vairside. Whatever vice or kink you had, you could get it serviced in there. The crews of passing ships and Navy personnel on leave went there to blow off steam, to gamble away their pay, to generally raise hell. It was the last place in the galaxy Valk could imagine religious types wanting to go.

Valk didn't like any of this. He didn't like mysteries, never had.

Which meant it definitely wasn't his day. While he stood there, staring through the arch as if he could see the stowaways out there, his suit chimed at him. A blue pearl appeared in the corner of his vision, telling him he had a new message from the traffic control autonomics.

The FA.2, the fighter he'd seen racing down into Geryon's atmosphere, was back, requesting clearance to dock at the Hexus. There was no sign of the yacht the FA.2 had been chasing.

Mysteries on top of damned mysteries. And getting answers meant spending a lot more time on his feet.

As if sensing his frustration, the white pearl appeared in the corner of his eye again, offering painkillers. He blinked it away.

———

Lights.

So many lights!

The Hexus must have had power to burn, to squander. Lamps on high standards lined the narrow streets of Vairside, shedding a dusky glow on everything. Bulbs burned inside every shop and restaurant. Huge signs floated overhead, blasting out light, advertising products Roan could scarcely imagine. Drones zipped by overhead shining lights down on the crowds—

The crowds! So many people, throngs of them in every winding side street, floods of them spilling out of doorways, clustering in little parks hemmed in only by wrought-iron fences. Thunder roared overhead and then a train pulled into a station, spilling out more people, as if the street weren't crowded enough. Dressed in a hundred different kinds of clothes, jumpsuits and flight jackets and paper overalls, long coats that brushed the heels of their glossy black boots, some wearing nothing but shorts, some of them were almost naked, men and women both. So many people, babbling a dozen languages, adorned in so many bizarre ways. Some had metal pierced through their noses and cheeks. Some had patterns of scars up and down their arms. Many, so many had dyed their hair unnatural colors. From the back of the train a dozen more pushed past, all falling down, holding on to each other. They wore space suits with painted shoulders, Navy people, she thought—she'd heard their suits were their uniforms, and they never took them off. They laughed and stared at her and a few gave her looks that made her blush.

Elder McRae held her tight, which was good. After twelve days in the cargo container with no gravity, now she was walking on her own feet but still she felt like she would float away, be caught by a gust of wind or the random energy of the crowds and be carried along, swept off to some incredible new spectacle.

Her head throbbed with pain, like a ring of iron had been clamped around her temples. It was the noise. The noise! Voices sounded from every corner, asking for things, promising things, whispering snatches of overheard conversations she couldn't ever follow. Voices thick with accents until she couldn't understand their words. Voices uttering oaths and curses and absurd promises. Voices using obscenities that shocked her. Voices thick with culture and sophistication, dripping with sarcasm and feigned surprise.

The smells—the smells of food and perfume that came wafting from every building, the smells of sweat and people, the smells of metal and burning fuel and chemicals that wafted off the train as it hurried off to its next stop. Smells she'd never encountered before, smells she couldn't name.

There was so much she couldn't follow, so much she couldn't understand. They passed by a shop with lights in its windows, lights illuminating a dress made of interwoven gauze strips. Roan could never see anyone on Niraya wearing something like that—even if they could afford it. But it was so beautiful. Who was that dress made for? Before she could even get a good look at it Elder McRae dragged her onward.

Past a little pond, perfectly hexagonal in shape but with flowers growing on its mossy banks. A group of Navy people stood on the far side, squatting down and jeering at some frogs that leapt from hiding. One of them drew a pistol and fired a bullet into the still, dark water, right next to a frog, making it jump to the left. The others laughed and cheered, and exchanged sheaves of money.

Roan gasped in bewilderment but they were already moving on. Past, this time, a wide yard full of little paper houses, rice paper stretched over wooden frames, just big enough to sit inside. At the center of the yard lay a pile of what looked like emaciated mannequins. A man in a vest and a round hat took money from a man in a jumpsuit, then handed him one of the mannequins. The man in the jumpsuit carried it toward one of the little houses, and even as he stepped inside Roan saw the mannequin plump out, its hips widening, breasts budding from its chest.

The elder said something admonitory Roan barely heard. She looked away and followed as the elder pulled her along another little road. They had directions, Roan knew, a map of where to go, but she couldn't imagine how the elder could follow it, not in this chaos, this wild place.

They headed up an incline toward a platform built out over the crowds. Roan looked up and saw countless other platforms above them, stretching up into the air. Which earned her a whole new shock. If she looked all the way up, as far as she could see, past clouds of drones and drifting miniblimps—up farther, past banks of lights and speakers and ventilation fans—all the way up there was a whole other world, more streets, more lights, hanging upside down. She knew they were inside a rotating cylinder, she knew about centrifugal force, but still it was hard to believe that all the people up there weren't about to fall on her. She fought down the urge to cover her head.

So much. Way, way too much.

A thrumming twang sounded right next to her and she jumped, but it was just a man pushing a cart full of flavored ices, hawking his wares by striking a tuning fork and holding it over his head. She found it hard to look away, as if the eerie sound had pinned her to the spot.

But then the elder stopped walking and Roan came up short.

She looked around, feeling very dizzy, and saw they'd reached their destination. A restaurant up on its own platform, at the top of a wide flight of steel stairs. Dark wood and hooded lanterns, everything painted in elegant floral designs. The waiters wore black vests and carried towels over their arms as they carried platters of steaming food to the well-dressed diners. Over the top of the stairs curved a wrought-iron arch inscribed THE WALRUS AND THE CARPENTER in flowing, ornate script.

A man with a little mustache and a blue monocle screwed into one of his eye sockets peered down at them over a thick paper book. "I'm afraid we're only seating those with reservations at the moment," he told the elder. Roan had no idea what that meant, but she understood his questioning, sneering look.

"We're here to see Auster Maggs," the elder said.

Instantly the man's demeanor changed. He bowed deeply and held out one arm, gesturing for them to step inside. "Of course. You're expected."

"This time," the elder said, leaning close, "let me do the talking, all right?"

Roan just shook her head, unable to think, much less speak.

So this—this was civilization.

It was nothing like what she'd imagined.

Chapter Four

When Valk arrived at Vairside's docks, the FA.2 had just set down, the air around its retros still shimmering with heat. The canopy lifted away from the cockpit and revealed the man inside. He wore a heavy suit much like Valk's own but painted with battle flags down the sleeves and legs. Reaching up to his throat the pilot touched a recessed key and his helmet rippled and then dissolved away, melting into vents in the hard collar of the suit.

Old, Valk thought. *He looks old.* He had the dark skin of a man who had spent far too much time absorbing unfiltered ultraviolet in deep space. The heavy, creased wrinkles of someone born before elastomer inoculations were invented.

His eyes were as sharp as broken glass, though, and Valk felt like their stare bored right through his polarized helmet.

Valk already knew who this man was. He'd done his homework. He pinged the pilot's cryptab anyway, a little dull square on the chest of his suit that was the pilot's only official insignia. The cryptab contained his service record and personal information. All his military commendations were in there, including his Blue Star, and Valk knew what that meant—the pilot was an ace, with more than five confirmed kills to his name. Valk used to have a Blue Star himself, until they took it away. The cryptab confirmed the pilot's name, too.

Aleister Lanoe. The most decorated fighter pilot of all time.

Valk knew the name, and the legend, long before Lanoe came to the Hexus. The man's life story read like a text from a history class. In every major war of the last three centuries, Aleister Lanoe had been there, in the cockpit of a fighter—and always on the winning side.

Lanoe had been born on Earth, back when humanity only had one star to call its own. He'd enlisted at the start of the Century War, when Mars and Ganymede had challenged Earth for owner-ship of the solar system. He'd risen to distinction in the middle of that bloody slog, through endless battles that cost the lives of half the human race. Lanoe had survived—and, eventually, prevailed. He'd been a hero then, an ace of aces. He could have rested on his laurels, perhaps. Instead he'd joined back up when Mars tried to start things again in the Short Revolt, twenty years later. Lanoe had been right there on the front lines when Mars finally gave in and accepted its status as a protectorate of Earth.

By then the first wormholes were open, and new planets around distant stars were being settled. Dozens of new systems were opened up all at once, planets discovered and terraformed and colonized in the space of only a few decades. That had been a wild time (or so Valk had heard—he wouldn't be born for another seventy-five years), an era of warlords seizing entire sectors and battles erupt-ing in space light-years away from any front. A time so chaotic that later historians simply called it the Brushfire. Earth—and Lanoe—had fought on the side of the polys, because at the time the big interplanetary corporations were the only powers capable of bring-ing peace to human space.

At least, that had been the company line. Not everybody accepted it, even when the polys were victorious, even when they set up the institutions and infrastructure that made human space a possibility, made the galaxy safe for commerce again. There had been those who didn't want to live under the thumb of the big companies. People who wanted to live free, to set up their own planetary colonies without being forever beholden to the polys.

Unfortunately their best idea of how to get that desire across was to blow up poly facilities and murder the plutocrats in their beds. The Establishment, as they called themselves, had been branded as terrorists. The Navy, including Aleister Lanoe, had been sent to root them out and destroy them. They'd been successful at capturing or killing the freedom fighters—Lanoe had won that war, too—but their victory was short-lived. A new, more organized Establishment had risen from the ashes. Instead of relying on sneak attacks and assassinations, the new Establishmentarians had mustered fleets of warships and divisions of marines. They'd seized the planet Sheol and raised their blue flag there, swearing to defend it and their right to live free.

That had been where Valk came in—he'd flown under the blue banner, on the side of self-determination. He'd been an Establishmentarian, himself.

He should have known better. It wasn't long before Aleister Lanoe and the Navy rolled in, guns blazing, to take Sheol back. The Establishment had fought like wild dogs, pushed back into a corner and with nowhere to go. They'd sacrificed thousands of lives to keep the dream going. Valk had risen to minor celebrity himself, one of the Establishment's top aces, and he'd been willing to fight to the death. But Lanoe and the polys had seemingly infinite resources behind them. Always they had more ships, more people, more money than the Establishment. It had really only been a matter of time—the grand cause had been so thoroughly doomed that the history texts didn't even call the fighting a full-fledged war. They just called it a crisis, the Establishment Crisis, as if it were destined to be no more than a footnote in the record books.

That been the last of Lanoe's wars. Humans still fought each other, of course. The polys, having achieved dominance over every human planet except Earth, had turned on each other, battling one another for supremacy. Even now Centrocor was fighting against DaoLink, and ThiessGruppe had attacked Tuonela, a planet run by Wilscon. There would always be more wars. Lanoe had resigned his commission at the end of the Crisis, though. Maybe he figured it was time to let somebody else have the glory. In the seventeen years since then, he'd lost some of his fame. His name was no longer a household word. Yet no one could take away what he'd achieved.

Lanoe's career had spanned centuries. He'd fought in hundreds of battles and won almost all of them. The man was a legend, a hero out of myth, and he hadn't got that way by being stupid.

And now Valk had to try to outsmart him.

There was no gravity in the docking facility. Lanoe kicked out of his seat and grabbed the edge of the raised canopy so he could face Valk directly. "I was told to set down here by the order of orbital traffic control. I assume that was you? The same man I spoke to when I arrived in this system?"

"Yeah," Valk said. He pushed himself over to the fighter, grabbed one of its airfoils to steady himself. "That's right. I wanted to see you for myself." He looked over the FA.2, the cigar-shaped body with its segmented canopy, the double row of airfoils, the bulky weapon pods. It had been a while, but he felt the old stirring, the *need* to fly. "I'd ask where the yacht got to, but I've had way too many people tell me to mind my business today, already."

Lanoe didn't nod. Didn't blink, either. *Cold damned fish,* Valk thought.

Valk put a hand on his chest. "I'm Tannis—"

"I know who you are," Lanoe replied. "I looked up your service record after we spoke. I have to admit I was a little surprised to find you here. Tannis Valk, the Blue Devil."

"They don't call me that anymore," Valk insisted.

"Had you in my sights once. Dogfight back in the Establishment Crisis."

"That's right. It took every trick I knew but I shook you off my tail," Valk replied.

That day, when the two of them squared off, Lanoe had tried to straight-up murder Valk. The fact he hadn't succeeded had come down to pure honest luck. Valk had been flying a fresh ship with plenty of fuel, while Lanoe had been at the end of a long patrol, running on fumes.

It was the only reason Valk was still alive.

Lanoe jumped down from his cockpit and strode over to get right in Valk's face. "We were sworn enemies, back then." He shot out a hand. "Damned good thing that stupid war is over and we don't have to try to kill each other anymore, huh?"

Valk grabbed the hand and shook it. There was no way for the pilot to see it, but inside his helmet he wore a goofy grin.

"How about I buy you a drink?" Valk asked.

The pilot's hard eyes twinkled. "It's the least you can do after refusing to let me shoot you down."

—◁▷—

Maggs took his time in the washroom.

Before the gilt mirror he slicked his hair back one last time. Took a bit of razor paper to the stubble on his Adam's apple. Adjusted the ceremonial dirk in its scabbard at his hip.

He wore a thinsuit, a dress uniform. By regs his only insignia was the gray cryptab on his chest. Since his guests weren't Navy they wouldn't be able to access the data it held, so they couldn't see his Blue Star or any of his commendations. There were other ways to indicate one's station, however. He had polished all the fittings of the suit, burnished the laurel leaves that wrapped around his collar ring. He fussed with the Velcro patch on his shoulder, hanging his gloves there just so, until the fingers hung down like the braid of an epaulet.

He put as much care into his appearance as if he were going to inspection at the Admiralty. One had to look the part.

The washroom door cracked open and a pinched little face peered inside. Maggs vaguely recognized one of the restaurant's waiters. "Your guests have arrived, sir. Thought you'd like to know."

"I'll be with them presently," Maggs said, not even looking at the fellow. He made one last swipe at a speck of dust on his sleeve, then stepped out of the washroom and out onto the restaurant's back patio.

Then he saw the Nirayans, and knew his whole effect would be lost on them. They looked like refugees from a war zone, more than anything. The girl was pretty, he supposed, though in that natural, graceless sort of way of the very young. The old woman looked like a gnarled tree that someone had draped clothes over.

Never mind. He would be gracious, as always. There was such a thing as decorum.

He favored them with a wide, warm smile, and outstretched arms. They did not get up from their seats. Ignoring the slight—most likely they'd never had to learn table manners—he pulled out a chair for himself and dropped artfully into it, one arm slung over its back.

"Shall I order?" he asked, picking up a tasseled menu.

They looked flummoxed. "You're Lieutenant Maggs?" the old one asked.

He tapped his chest with two fingers. "In the flesh. You must be Elder McRae. And this, of course, is young Roan, your assistant."

"She's an aspirant," the old woman corrected.

"I suppose we all aspire to something," Maggs said, and laughed a bit, just to break the ice. It didn't work. If anything they looked more confused than ever. He bent over the menu, careful not to let his eyes roll. It hadn't been much of a witticism but at least he was trying. "The fish here is very good. Is that all right? And whiskey for the table, since there's business to be done."

"I'm afraid I don't take spirits," the old woman said.

Maggs waved a hand in apology. "Of course, how thoughtless of me. A prohibition of your faith, I imagine."

"No," the old woman replied. "I have a genetic predisposition to alcoholism. Lieutenant—our business is rather pressing, and we came a very long way to speak with you."

"Sorry about that. In my position I have to move about quite a bit. It was just good luck I was at Geryon this week." He leaned forward a bit, to try to add a whiff of conspiracy. "I'm responsible for more worlds than just Niraya, you see."

"Of course. But given your busy schedule, then—can't the meal wait?"

"Our ways must seem strange to you," Maggs said. "But it's tradition among us to never discuss money on an empty stomach. Besides. After so many days of those dreadful meals they serve on starliners these days, surely you could both use a little fresh food." He glanced across the table at the girl aspirant and gave her a wink.

Her eyes went wide.

Still got it, Maggsy, he told himself. Funny how his internal monologue always sounded like his father's voice these days.

"We'll be down to brass tacks soon enough." He reached for the menu. "That's an old idiom that means—"

"I know it. I wasn't born on Niraya," the old woman told him.

He smiled at her. It was always important at times like this to smile. You could never let them see what you really thought. "I understand your anxiety. And I can assure you, Elder, you've come to exactly the right place."

It hurt his cheeks, but he never let the smile fade.

Valk took Lanoe through the spin lock to Vairside. "I know a little place in here," he said. "Nothing fancy. But they know to serve my whiskey with a straw."

Lanoe seemed confused for a moment but then he nodded. "You never take that helmet down," he said. "I can guess why. But you really care that much what other people think?"

As Valk headed through the broad arch he laughed. "It's not for my benefit. Come on, let's catch that train." They boarded in the rear compartment, which was reserved for Navy personnel only. The Hexus was technically a civilian station, built by Centrocor to serve its development concerns. A few years back, though, Centrocor declared war on another poly called DaoLink. Earth had sent the Navy in to fight on Centrocor's side and now the Hexus was as much a military base as anything else. Half the Navy came through at one time or another—either on shore leave, or on their way to their next deployment. Valk got a couple of stares as he boarded for the hexagonal logo painted on his shoulder plate, but nobody said anything, especially when they saw he was with Lanoe. Valk could tell when the other passengers had pinged Lanoe's cryptab because of how hastily they glanced away.

The train tracks corkscrewed around inside the Vairside cylinder, making dozens of stops, but they didn't have to go far. Valk watched Lanoe's face as the old man stared through the windows, taking in the various attractions of station life. He didn't exactly scowl at the pleasure-seekers who passed by below but he didn't look much interested in the gambling hells or the sex drone yards, either. Valk thought maybe Lanoe was not a man who gave anything away for free.

The two of them stepped off at a station on an elevated platform. It overlooked a wide lawn of real grass where Navy officers drank tea and played lawn games with their port wives. Recently it had become popular with the enlisted men, too, because they could stand on the platform and throw beer cans at the officers' servants.

"Tell me that's not where we're going," Lanoe said.

"Don't worry," Valk said, laughing. He took Lanoe up a staircase to a door made from an old salvaged pressure hatch. It hung open, one hinge rusted in place, and noise and light blasted out from inside. The place looked packed, mostly with people in space suits. A couple of them came tumbling out as they approached, tossed out by the bouncer. Valk got a glimpse of one of them, a woman with cropped hair and a shoulder plate painted with a blue and yellow constellation. He realized too late she was headed right for him, her arms outstretched. Before he could move she slammed into him and bounced away.

The pain was bad. Bad enough that the white pearl in the corner of his vision started flashing. He staggered and, much to his chagrin, Lanoe had to grab him to keep him from falling over.

"You all right?" Lanoe whispered.

"Fine," Valk said, getting back on his feet. He looked up to find the woman who had knocked into him. She and her companion were already hurrying away, but she glanced back for just a second. Maybe she felt sorry for running him over.

Except she wasn't looking at him. She was staring at Lanoe, with a look of utter terror on her face.

"Ehta?" Lanoe said. It sounded like a name.

The woman didn't respond. Her companion grabbed her by the arm and then they were lost in the crowd.

"Somebody you know?" Valk asked. The damned white pearl kept popping up every time he blinked it away.

Lanoe shrugged. "I'm three hundred years old. I know a lot of people."

The old woman refused to talk about anything but business. Before the salads had even been cleared from the table she pulled a minder from her satchel and started scrolling through old messages. "We were rather surprised," she said, "that you were willing to talk to us. I have here the transcript of our distress call to the Terraforming Authority—"

"No need to play it," Maggs said, holding up one hand. "I've heard it."

"You have?"

"I took an especial interest in your case the moment it came across my desk. Of course, the wheels of bureaucracy had to turn in their appointed rounds, and I was not able to intervene directly. The thing had to make its way through official channels."

"They said our evidence was inconclusive, and that further investigation was required," the old woman said, her hand shaking as she paged through the legalese and red tape on her minder.

Maggs had, in actual fact, seen it all. He'd been privy to several communications not shared with the Nirayans, as well. He knew that Centrocor had never heard of anything like what happened on the old woman's planet. There had been no official protocol for it. Minor functionaries had wrung their hands and wondered who they could pass the matter off to, and a few highly placed people had actually been consulted, though their contributions had been minimal. In the end a formula had been worked out, an algorithm for determining the risks and benefits of intervention. It had been decided, after much crunching of proverbial numbers, that Niraya wasn't worth it.

It would cost more to save the planet than to let it perish. Even after the inevitable lawsuits were filed. Even after insurance claims had been adjusted.

A tragedy, really.

"Further investigation," the old woman said, her lips pursed. "Dozens of people are dead, thousands at risk, and we're supposed to wait for further investigation."

Across the table, the girl reached for another slice of bread. Maggs gave her a smile and nodded at the butter. She took it as if she expected it to be snatched from her grasp.

"This is why you have a Sector Warden," Maggs said, keeping his voice low. "To catch exactly these sort of oversights." He sat up. Clasped his hands together in front of him. "I can help."

The old woman kept her face carefully composed. Clearly she didn't entirely believe him. Not yet. She hadn't been born on Niraya, she'd said. Maybe she understood a little of how these things actually worked.

"There is the question of money," he said.

Valk opened a tiny hole in the front of his helmet—not so large anyone could see inside, even accidentally—and fed the straw through it. The ice in his glass rattled as he slurped away.

As dive bars went, the place stank. There was nothing inside but some scratched-up furniture and a big display that showed nothing but ads for Centrocor products. Just then it showed a woman with gleaming teeth rubbing cream on her forearm. The view zoomed in to the microlevel to show tiny machines with serrated pincers tearing into dead skin cells. The music swelled and the view shifted back to the woman's arm, which was now as smooth as plastic.

Lanoe didn't seem to mind the blaring commercial. Nor did he seem to take much notice that half the bar was staring at his back. This was a Navy place—just about all the customers were dressed in space suits. There weren't many officers, though. Valk did a quick ping of all the cryptabs in the room and found nobody over Junior Lieutenant grade. If Lanoe shouted out the word *push-up* right now, the entire bar would have to fall to the floor.

The old pilot just sank back into his own chair, making it creak with the weight of his heavy suit, and sipped at his own glass. Staring straight forward at nothing. "We heard your story," he said, finally. "On our side of the lines. Talked about you for weeks, though I always figured it was mostly an urban legend. About how you had a full-blown flameout, your whole cockpit lit up by an antivehicle round. And yet you somehow managed to finish your mission before heading back to base."

"That's about accurate," Valk said. "Except there was a lot more screaming." He took another sip. The whiskey was cold enough to numb his mouth, just as he liked it. "As for finishing the mission, well, I'd already worked out firing solutions for two more of your ships and the fighter pretty much took them out without any help. I was too busy, what with being on fire, to tell it to stop and get me the hell out of there."

"Got our wind up, on the other side," the Commander said. "Got us thinking maybe you lot were serious about Self-Establishment. That maybe we were fighting for the wrong side." He smiled, but it was the kind of smile that could indicate anything except happiness. "Especially after we heard they fixed you up and sent you right back to the lines."

"As bad off as I was, they offered to send me home," Valk said. "Third-degree burns over ninety percent of my body. I shouldn't have lived through that. But the only thing I knew how to do was fly. So I went back. Two weeks later the Crisis was over and we'd lost."

"That how you ended up here, doing traffic control?"

"The terms of the surrender said there would be no punitive

measures taken against our officers. We were going to be rolled up into your Navy, since we were friends again. But then they stripped all of our service records. I took what work I could get."

"Our loss," the Commander said. "The Navy could use a pilot like you. Regardless of your politics."

Valk acknowledged the kindness with a brief nod. He'd learned over the years to exaggerate his gestures so people could read his meaning without having to see his eyes. "What about you, then? I heard you resigned your commission awhile back. Just walked away from what could have been a lucrative career. I heard they had you pegged for the Admiralty."

The old pilot's eyes narrowed, just a bit. Maybe because he'd had to learn how to replicate body language, Valk had made a study of it in other people. He could tell there was some pain there, buried deep. Old and familiar pain.

Well, he understood that.

"I get bored easily," Lanoe said.

"Didn't mean to pry, Commander."

That earned him a polite smile. "My name's Lanoe. And I'm going to call you Valk."

"Okay."

Lanoe raised his glass, then put it down again without drinking.

So much for Valk's plan to get the old pilot drunk. Maybe he needed to try a different tack. "That FA.2 of yours is a real beauty," he suggested.

Lanoe grinned without looking up. "For a museum piece, you mean."

Valk raised his hands in a conciliatory gesture. "No offense meant. But even when the Establishment went broke and couldn't afford new hardware, they still put me in a rebuilt FA.6."

"Nice ships, with all those gadgets. Self-repair and ammo assemblers and all that." Lanoe tilted his head to one side. "But the FA.2's never been beat for stability. Practically flies herself, so I can focus on the shooting."

"They never made you upgrade?"

"They tried, near the end of the Century War. I said no thank you. Amazing how flexible orders can be with an oak leaf on your cryptab. I guess I was just used to the smell of the FA.2's cockpit. Then when I resigned I used up my decommissioning bonus to buy her outright."

"You own that crate?" Valk had never heard of such a thing.

"They were going to scrap her. Strip her down for parts and build one of those new carrier scouts out of what was left." Lanoe shook his head. "She didn't deserve that. There's a lot of parsecs left in her."

"They do have a reputation for being indestructible. A little slow, maybe," Valk suggested, in a careful tone. "By modern standards."

Lanoe didn't seem to take offense. "I've tried to keep up with the times. I stripped out the old power plant, put in a Gôblin rotary drive. Increased the thrust about fifteen percent. Had to add some extra heat shielding in the cabin." Lanoe shrugged. "She gets me where I'm going. And I have no trouble keeping up with anything civilian."

"Civilian?"

"I've been working as an escort pilot for one big shot or another since I resigned. Easy work. I fly formation with some corporate executive's private ship—no fear of anyone attacking, I'm just there to show the Navy colors, show we're working close with the money people. A sign of respect." He shrugged. "It's a living."

"You kept up with that yacht just fine," Valk tried.

Lanoe took a deep breath. Then he picked up his glass and put his entire drink down his throat. It looked like he was about to get up from the table. "We're not just here to reminisce, are we?"

Valk considered his words carefully. "Part of this," he said, gesturing at the table between them, "is about me getting to meet a legend. I've been thinking up polite ways to ask for your autograph. But then there's also my job."

"Orbital traffic control," Lanoe said. He leaned forward. Tapped the little display in the middle of the table where you paid for your drinks.

Valk pushed his hand away. "I'm responsible for every ship that comes through this system while I'm on duty. I make sure they get where they're headed in one piece. That includes that yacht. Not to mention the freighter I dismantled so you two didn't get smeared. You forget about that?"

"No," Lanoe replied. "No, I haven't. You told me there were people on that thing." His mouth turned down at one side. "Anybody get hurt?"

"Couple of stowaways in a cargo container," Valk said. "They might have got banged up a bit, but nothing serious."

"Stowaways? Interesting."

Valk didn't like the look on his face at all. Clearly Lanoe had something up his sleeve. Something he wasn't about to share.

"I'd like to talk to them," Lanoe said.

"Oh?"

"To, you know." Lanoe made an equivocating gesture with one hand. "Apologize for nearly killing them."

"Uh-huh."

Valk wasn't done asking about the yacht, but he could see it was going to be a while before he got a straight answer. Well, introducing Lanoe to the stowaways might help resolve *their* mystery. It would give him another chance to pester them for information, at the very least. He set his glass down on the table. Then he reached over and tapped at the display, charging the drinks to his personal account.

"Let's pay them a visit," he said.

———

"You understand," Maggs said, "this is not a bribe. Earth has the Navy fighting two different wars right now, one against DaoLink, another against ThiessGruppe on a planet called Tuonela. With the fleets stretched thin, sending ships to Niraya will require a considerable outlay. Centrocor normally pays for mercy fleets but they're the ones requesting more evidence. I'll use the money to personally outfit a carrier group and we'll have this sewn up before the bureaucrats even finish filing their preliminary reports."

"I'd almost given up hope," the old woman said.

"Our lives are in your hands," the girl said. The old woman shot her an icy look but the girl's open-faced optimism lit up the table.

Maggs smiled at them both. "It's going to be all right. Did you, ah, bring letters of credit, or—"

A withered old hand reached inside the satchel and took out four black plastic chits. The old woman let them fall to the table, each with a tiny click.

Maggs couldn't suppress a tiny intake of breath, not quite a gasp. "Those are Terraforming Authority chits," he said. Each of them, he knew, would have a tiny diamond inside, inscribed with the encryption keys that would allow the bearer unfettered access to Interplanetary Development Bank accounts. No questions asked.

"When Niraya was first settled Centrocor provided us with a handful of these in exchange for an unlimited monopsony on our exports," the old woman said. "We use them to pay for yearly terraforming services."

"We were going to get some low-energy cometary impactors this year, and a new license on a strain of oxyculture lichens," the girl pointed out.

"Roan here is studying to be a planetary engineer," the old woman said.

"Quite. Let me see if I understand," Maggs said. "By giving me these chits, you'll have to cancel four years of development for your planet. Is that really what you want to do?"

"Our planet is very poor, Warden. This was the only way we could afford the price you named. It's a hardship for us, yes. If the entire population is wiped out, though, it won't matter if the planet is habitable or not," the old woman said.

"Of course," Maggs replied. He reached across the table and gathered up the chits. His hand didn't shake nearly as much as he'd expected.

Once they were safely tucked away in a pouch at his belt, he looked from one of them to the other.

"So," he said. "Will you be returning to your world immediately, or will you stay at the Hexus a few days and take in the sights?"

——————

There was a chance—maybe—that Valk could save his job. If he could file solid reports on the missing yacht and the stowaways from the freighter, he might be able to spin things so he came out looking blameless.

He had to admit to himself, though, that he was plain old-fashioned curious, too.

He pinged his computers back at traffic control and got a location for the two stowaways. The system didn't normally keep track of visitors to the Hexus—there were far too many of them for that to be worthwhile, especially since most of them were just passing through. Centrocor had a financial interest in the Nirayans, though, so microdrones had been dispatched to watch them at all times.

He'd been confused enough already that day. So when it turned out they were having dinner at one of the station's most expensive restaurants, the strangeness barely registered. For all he knew the two of them were slumming trillionaires who thought it would be funny to ship themselves from star to star in a cargo container.

Though from what he'd seen of them, that felt unlikely.

"Religious types," he told Lanoe, as the two of them caught a passing miniblimp on a high platform. This close to the axis of the cylinder, gravity was just a suggestion. They kicked off the platform and grabbed for the blimp's straps, then pulled themselves up onto the exposed seats. Valk sighed in relief as he let his legs dangle over the side. "Looked like they'd never had a bit of fun in their lives. They probably spent the whole trip here praying to their god or something."

"Hmm," Lanoe said. He seemed deep in thought.

"You'll like them, though. They're just like you—stubborn asses."

The old pilot didn't even reply. He just looked down at the platforms drifting by below, as if he expected to see someone else he recognized.

The view from the blimp could be a little disorienting. Down on the platforms, on the lower levels, Vairside felt almost like a city on an actual planet. You could forget you were inside a cylinder spinning fast enough to generate earthlike gravity. Up at the axis, though, you saw the whole thing. You could see how the walls curved up to meet you and close over your head. You could see all the platforms jutting out at crazy angles, a three-dimensional maze of buildings and parklets and the mirror surfaces of the ponds and the narrow rivers, all lit up by countless streetlights. Because Centrocor had built Vairside, the whole thing was made of interlocking hexagons, but it was only from up here that that became obvious, each little zone of vice or leisure or commerce constrained by the six other zones that surrounded it.

Their destination lay clockwise around the cylinder, about sixty degrees up the wall. Valk tapped a control pad on the arm of his seat and the blimp obligingly swiveled on its axis until their feet dangled over the roof of the restaurant. The airship vented gas and sank through a haze of advertising drones, startling a couple of bats that had been roosting underneath the machines. Lanoe tracked them with his eyes, and Valk wondered if he was working out firing solutions on them.

"Maybe I should talk to them alone," Lanoe said as they stepped down onto the roof. A spiral staircase brought them back down into real gravity.

"Not a chance," Valk told him.

They headed down onto the restaurant's platform. Valk's suit chimed and a blue pearl in the corner of his eye told him the stowaways were moving, heading out of the restaurant. They hurried down the stairs and Valk caught sight of them right away. They stood out from the crowd because their clothes were so drab and modest, compared to everyone else. When he called out to them they turned to look but then the elder's eyes narrowed. Valk knew this wasn't going to be a friendly reunion.

"Have you come to arrest us, finally?" the old woman asked.

"No, no! Nothing like that," Valk said. "Elder McRae, I wanted to introduce you to my friend here, Commander Lanoe."

"I was one of the idiots who nearly hit your freighter," Lanoe explained. "I wanted to apologize for that, and maybe talk to you about something else."

"No one was harmed, M. Lanoe. There's no need for apologies," the elder replied.

"That's very kind of you," Lanoe said. "It could have gone badly."

"One should never grow attached to might-have-beens. Now, will you excuse us? I'm afraid we don't have much time. We need to head back to Niraya as soon as possible."

"Hopefully not the same way you came," Lanoe said. He turned to look at the girl. "Aleister Lanoe," he said.

"Roan," she replied, and shook his hand.

"Just Roan?"

The girl smiled. "I gave up my family name when I became an aspirant," she replied.

Valk looked from Lanoe to the girl to the elder. He was starting to lose his patience with all this.

"I'd like to suggest a better way for you to get home," Lanoe said.

"Oh?" the elder asked.

"Will you forgive a little plain speaking? If you couldn't afford seats on a liner while coming here, I doubt you can afford them for the return journey. As I put your lives in danger, I'd like to pay off my debt to you by chartering a small starship and flying you home myself."

"That's really too generous," the elder said.

"It would let me work off some karma," Lanoe said, with a knowing smile. "It would also give us a chance to talk further."

"I'm not sure what we would have to speak about," the elder said, glancing over at Roan.

Too damn much, Valk thought. Clearly all of them were playing games and he wasn't going to get to see any of their cards. And when exactly did Lanoe become so eloquent? He'd barely said a handful of words to Valk since they'd met.

"Please," Lanoe said. "It would mean a great deal to me."

"In our faith humility precludes accepting lavish gifts," the elder pointed out.

"I assure you," Lanoe began, "as an officer of the Navy, my honor would be stained if I allowed you to be harmed on your return journey."

"Just stop this already," Valk said, softly.

"I suppose," the elder said, "if your honor is at stake, then—"

"Stop!" Valk said, almost shouting.

It worked.

They all turned and looked at him. Valk had never much cared for being stared at, but right then he was furious. "None of you are going anywhere until I have some answers. I'm going to lose my job if I don't get to the bottom of this. You," he said, looking at Lanoe, "need to tell me what happened to that yacht. And you, Elder, need to tell me why you came to the Hexus in the first place."

"We had business here, as I told you before," Elder McRae replied.

Valk shook his head from side to side. "Not good enough. Who were you meeting with? What kind of business? Answer me now or I will detain you, legal niceties or no."

The old woman looked taken aback. She raised one hand to her throat. But at least she kind of answered his question. "We were asked to keep our business discreet. I suppose, however, that you can simply consult some drone camera or other if you want to know who we dined with this evening. It was a man named Auster Maggs. His identity can hardly be considered a secret, considering his position."

Valk had never heard of him. He glanced over at Lanoe but didn't see any recognition in the old man's face. "What position is that?"

"He's the Sector Warden for all the planets served by the Hexus, including Niraya. I thought you would know such an important person, M. Valk."

Valk looked over at Lanoe, who was looking back at him. The expression on Lanoe's face spoke volumes.

"Are you sure that's who you met with?" Lanoe asked. "Your Sector Warden?"

"We had vital business with him. He was very kind to meet us at all."

Valk pinged the computers in traffic control with a simple query. Then he took a minder from a pocket in his suit and unrolled it. Displayed on its front was an image of a Naval officer, one Lieutenant Auster Maggs. Short black hair, dashing good looks, knowing sneer. "This was the man?"

It was clearly so from the elder's expression.

"Elder," Lanoe said, "I'm sorry. But I think you're mistaken as to this man's identity. Your Sector Warden—none of the Sector Wardens—ever leave Earth. They're considered too important to risk letting them travel about."

The calm look on the elder's face rippled, as the surface of a pond might when struck by a very large rock. Valk could see her attempting to regain control.

Roan, on the other hand, looked as if her jaw might actually drop off her skull.

"The money!" she said.

Chapter Five

Maggs forced himself not to reach into his pocket and touch the development chits again. They were real and they weren't going anywhere. They were the solution to a very thorny problem and the promise of moving forward.

He would still have to deal with the fact that he had deserted his post. The Navy would have something to say about that. And there were plenty of other difficulties on the road forward. At least there *was* a road forward.

He walked as casually as he could manage over to the nearest train station and up to the platform. A civilian pilot in a paper jumpsuit leaned against the railing, looking down the tracks. He turned to give Maggs the once-over and a little trickle of fear like cold water went down Maggs's spine, but he put a bored expression on his face and the pilot looked away again. When the train came, Maggs stepped aboard, avoiding the car reserved for Naval personnel. No need to run into some old chum now, someone who might remember seeing him here.

He had to get off the Hexus now, and sharpish. At the docks he would buy passage on the next liner out, headed anywhere. Of course he couldn't say as much to the ticket vendors. He took out his minder—jostling the chits in the process, good, they were still there—and looked up the departure schedule. It looked like a second-class cabin was available on a ship headed to Rarohenga. The gravity there was a bit heavy to his taste but it would do. The place was at least civilized enough that he could cash in the chits at a properly discreet bank.

The train pulled out of the station and he grabbed a hanging strap. Movement caught his eye and he turned to look. The various compartments of the train were separated by sliding glass doors. He could see into the Navy car from where he stood. It looked like a marine had tackled a Navy enlisted to the floor of the car and was beating him bloody with gloved fists. Other marines stood over the two of them, cheering and taking bets. All good fun, Maggs supposed, for the kind of psychopath who would make a career of fighting ground battles. As an officer he ought to intervene, he supposed, but that would be foolish.

"Savages."

Maggs glanced over and saw a civilian with full body tattoos and not much in the way of clothing sitting by the door. The woman had been reading her minder but now she stared at the fistfight with unveiled antipathy.

She looked up at Maggs, her mouth twisted in disgust. "Can't turn it off, can you? Teach a man to fight and that's all he ever does."

A witty retort leapt to mind, but Maggs was quite aware he was in the wrong car. The straphangers around him were all civilians. He was not, in other words, among friends. A gentler reply was in order, perhaps. *Downgrade your mix, Maggsy,* he thought. *Don't run so rich.* His father's voice, again. Dear old Dad had always been fond of pilot's argot, despite the fact he hadn't flown himself anywhere for thirty years before Maggs was born.

"The war with DaoLink will be over soon," Maggs said. "Then we'll be out of your hair."

The woman snorted angrily. It looked like she was about to spit on his boot. He would be forced to respond in the interest of honor if she did.

So he was somewhat glad when a sudden crunch drew their collective attention back to the connecting door. Someone had picked up the marine pugilist and thrown him against the wall of the train, hard enough that the entire Navy car shook. Other marines jumped to attention, their boots thundering on the floor.

The intercessor was a very tall fellow in a heavy suit with the helmet up and polarized. He bent over the enlisted on the floor, checking the poor beggar's pulse.

Behind him stood another Naval officer, also in a heavy suit. This one had his helmet down, revealing a face old and craggy— enough so it made Maggs think of the old woman he'd just fleeced.

The old man looked right at Maggs, through the door. His eyes narrowed.

Slowly he bent and touched the shoulder of the giant. Getting his attention. Then they were both looking at Maggs. Staring at him.

───※───

They'd been so damned close. They could have cut Maggs off at the next station, flanked him and had him pinned. Then the stupid marine had to go and start a fight in the middle of a crowded train car.

And of course Valk had to intervene.

It could have gone very badly—well, worse than it did. Valk might be strong enough to throw one marine around like a toy, but his buddies would have made short work of the traffic controller, and Lanoe, too. Luckily one of them had been smart enough to ping Lanoe's cryptab and notice his rank. That made them all stand aside—and in the process, Maggs caught sight of them.

The pretty little bastard clearly knew he was being followed. Through the connecting door Lanoe saw him turn and run for it, jumping over the feet of civilian passengers, shoving straphangers out of his way.

"He's moving," Lanoe said, slapping the release button for the connecting door. "You stay here—I'll get him."

"I'm not letting you out of my sight," Valk insisted.

Lanoe didn't waste breath on a reply. He hurried into the next car, pushing his way through the passengers. Some idiot tried to stop him with an outstretched arm—"Stay in your own damned car," she said—but Lanoe just twisted under the arm and bulled his way through. Up ahead he saw the connecting door to the next car was open. Well, there was only one direction for Maggs to run.

And only one more car in front of this one.

Lanoe hurried through. Thankfully the front car wasn't crowded. He jumped over a drunk who lay sprawled half in and half out of a seat, then grabbed a pole as the train banked around a tight curve in the tracks.

Up ahead he saw the door at the front of the train slide open. Grimy air burst into the train and made Lanoe's eyes water. He blinked to clear them and saw Maggs standing in the door frame, his boots right on the edge. The idiot must not have realized he was out of places to run.

"Just stand down," Lanoe called.

Valk came up behind him. Together they moved forward, slowly. The swindler lieutenant was cornered and Lanoe knew how dangerous that could make a man. He raised his hands to show he wasn't armed. "We're not going to hurt you," he said.

Maggs laughed. "You might *try*," he said.

Sheer bravado. Lanoe had seen what Valk did to that marine—Maggs was about half of the traffic controller's size. If they wanted to make this nasty, the fool wasn't going to come out of it as pretty as he went in.

Lucky for him Lanoe didn't want that. "You've got nowhere to go," he said.

Maggs glanced around him, as if some incredible opportunity were about to present itself. Then—

He was just gone.

The doorway was empty. It was as if the swindler had just vanished.

Lanoe rushed forward to the door, thinking perhaps Maggs was just hanging on to the exterior of the train. But there was no sign of him.

⟶✦⟵

Maggs held his breath—unnecessarily. His helmet flowed up around his face even before his boots touched the water, not so much as a drop getting inside. He just had time to hear someone scream before he plunged into the swimming pool.

When he'd seen it coming up, a hexagonal patch of water just a few meters down from the elevated train tracks, he'd almost laughed aloud. He'd supposed it might be dangerous, jumping from a moving train, but years out in the void had given him a certain flair for spatial relations. He'd leapt with excellent form, even avoiding a cluster of bathers at the far end of the pool.

Of course, luck was never an uncomplicated proposition. In the short interval of time between when he struck the water and when he struck the bottom, he just about had the neural capacity to realize he'd jumped into the shallow end.

His left foot struck the concrete bottom first. The rest of his weight came down on it in an ungainly fashion and he had the nauseating sensation of his bones bending in a manner for which they were not designed.

There was a crackling sound and then a bolt of white lightning shot up his leg and into his spine. His whole body convulsed and the air inside his helmet was filled with the kind of obscenities that should never be spoken in public.

The thinsuit he wore did not have room for all the medical technology a heavier suit might bring to bear. It did its best, his boot instantly inflating to cushion and restrain the twisted bones. The suit could do nothing about the growing pain.

Maggs sank to the bottom until he lay on his back, staring up through the blue water. A fellow in trunks and goggles stroked by overhead, silver bubbles leaking from the corners of his mouth. He started to swim down toward Maggs, perhaps intending to offer a helping hand. Maggs waved him away.

He just needed to catch his breath. He just needed—

The chits. Damnation, if they'd been dislodged from his pocket in the fall...but no, there they were. The water would do them no harm.

He had to get away. He had to get off the Hexus before his pursuers caught up with him. A twisted leg would slow him down, but stopping now for any reason—seeking medical attention, for instance—was out of the question.

Once he thought he could move without vomiting inside his helmet, Maggs turned himself over on his stomach and crawled to the steps that led out of the pool, mostly using his hands for propulsion. He hauled himself up and out, water streaming from his thinsuit in sheets. His helmet came down automatically.

Now came the critical trial. He stepped up onto the lip of the pool, first with his good leg, then with his bad. He could just about walk on it, if he didn't mind a little brain-melting agony.

All around the pool bathers looked up at him, some murmuring in surprise or even concern. He made a point of avoiding eye contact as he limped out of the pool area and into an adjoining hostelry.

It turned out to be a low sort of place. There was no concierge, nor even anyone at the front desk. Booking rooms or obtaining other services was accomplished by way of a kiosk set into one wall. Maggs dismissed a prompt asking him if he wished to inquire about hourly rates. Paging through the available options he finally found one that would allow him to summon transportation.

He chose the quickest option, a drone pedicab. Then he went and stood by the doorway, just inside its shadow, where he could watch the street. If he could just stay free until the pedicab arrived, he thought, he would still have a chance.

When the train pulled into its next stop, Lanoe jumped out with Valk right behind him. He stared around the platform as if Maggs would just reappear as easily as he'd vanished, perhaps with a taunting wave before he jumped on the back of a passing elephant or something even more impossible.

"If we split up, we can cover more ground," Lanoe pointed out.

Valk laughed. "You don't give up, do you?"

Lanoe shook his head. He might say the same to the damned traffic controller. "Right now, the only thing I care about is catching this guy," he said.

"Okay," Valk replied. "Why?"

"Why what?"

Valk leaned forward, his hands on his knees. It was a passable impersonation of a man trying to catch his breath. "You set off after this bastard almost before I had his location. What are you trying to prove?"

"He stole the Nirayans' money," Lanoe answered. "If we catch him in time we can get it back."

"That simple, huh? Seemed like you wanted something from them. You could have stayed behind while I ran off in hot pursuit, talked to them where I couldn't hear."

Lanoe supposed that was true. The Nirayans had information that might be useful to him. He hadn't stopped to think about that, though. He supposed he'd thought they would be more forthcoming if he'd done them a good turn.

Maybe.

"Sometimes I outsmart even myself," he said. "What about you, then? You're a traffic controller. Not a policeman, even if you act like one. Why not just let the local constabulary take over?"

"Have you seen this place?" Valk asked. "There are cops, yeah. They're what you might call risk averse. If they actually investigate a disturbance, they might get hurt in the process, and that means lawsuits, and Centrocor hates lawsuits. No, the local cops are more interested in assigning fines and penalties after the dust settles." He shook his head from side to side. "You want something like this done right, you do it yourself. My job's on the line here. I've got an actual reason to chase Maggs down."

"Any thoughts on how we do that, then?"

Valk stood up straight again, glanced around for a second, perhaps to orient himself. "Come on. This way."

He set off through a flock of pigeons that wheeled up around his legs and almost immediately settled down again. Lanoe followed, getting even less of a reaction. "Did you get another fix on Maggs?" he asked.

"No," Valk said. "Just a hunch about where he's headed."

Maggs bought a packet of sealant foam from the hostelry before the pedicab arrived, a quick-setting resin meant for patching holes in space suits. He worked the sticky goo over his cryptab until it was completely obscured. No point getting to the docks only to have some passive scanner ping him and log his identity. He didn't know if the authorities had put out an alert for his particulars yet, but he didn't want to take any chances.

At his request the three-wheeled drone took him down side streets and through a cramped alley behind a row of shops. It felt like the machine just crawled along. He wished he knew Vairside better but in the end he had to trust the drone's limited brainpower. It took far longer to reach the docks than he'd hoped, but he got there without, to his best knowledge, being spotted.

When he arrived at the portal to the big spin lock he stepped out and—thoughtlessly—directly onto his sprained ankle. The pain was worse this time, but at least once the spin lock ground down to zero he didn't need to walk anymore. He floated through into the busy docks, dodging fuel and maintenance drones and the occasional human worker.

The six arms of the Hexus met at six vertices, each of which comprised a spacious docking facility. Autonomic freighters and dismantling ships docked on the exterior, out in hard vacuum, but any ships that carried human crew or passengers were brought inside into warmth and air. Ahead of Maggs lay the berths, a honeycomb of enormous compartments in various sizes, half of them full.

Naval personnel were allowed to skip the security checkpoints and head straight to their ships. The liner headed to Rarohenga sat in a medium-sized bay halfway up the stack, serviced by a tall gantry. Maggs queried the clock in his suit and saw he still had six minutes to get aboard before the hatches were closed. Ignoring the gantry, he grabbed a passing drone and then shoved it away from himself, using its mass to propel him through the air toward the berth.

He was going to make it. He was really going to get away with this.

He checked his pocket one more time. Counted the chits as he sailed through the air. Caught himself on the edge of the berth to stop himself from flying right past.

The liner proved uninspiring. Maybe fifty meters long, its sides studded with viewports, its engines dark with carbon deposits. Its bulbous nose pointed outward toward the void and it hummed noisily as it powered up for departure. Judging by the shoddy paint job he reckoned he was in for some terrible food and even worse entertainment options over the next six days, but no matter. The liner meant freedom, freedom not only from pursuit but also from a cloud that had hung over him for far too long.

A line led from the gantry over to the main hatch, put there for the convenience of passengers unaccustomed to microgravity. Maggs grabbed the line and hauled himself hand over hand toward the hatch. He saw a flight attendant peering out at him and he smiled.

"Terribly sorry if I'm late," he called out. "I have a second-class reservation for—"

He stopped because suddenly the flight attendant ducked out of view, even as the hatch slid up and locked itself in place.

No. That wasn't acceptable. He had made it just in time. The crew were legally bound to let him board right up until the last minute. He was a lieutenant in the Navy, for hellfire's sake. He had certain rights!

"Hello," he called. "I beg your pardon, but—"

His heart stopped beating, then. His two pursuers, the giant and the old officer, came kicking around the nose of the liner, headed in his direction.

He swiveled around and saw the blast doors of the berth closing behind him.

No way out.

Lanoe grabbed a stanchion on the side of the liner to steady himself. Hand-to-hand fighting in microgravity was always tricky, and he was pretty sure that was where this was headed. From the corner of his eye he saw Valk moving to the side, flanking the swindler.

Then Maggs drew his Navy dirk from its scabbard.

Lanoe watched the serrated edge. He had one of those himself, though he couldn't remember where he'd stashed it. The blade was razor thin, made of an ultrahard ceramic that could punch right through a heavy suit and whoever was unlucky enough to be wearing it at the time.

"You really want to go down that road?" he asked.

Maggs looked up at him. The look on his face was more one of disappointment than desperation. "Hmm?" he asked. "Oh, this? I was thinking of falling on it, like an ancient Roman. The honorable thing, and all that. But not today, I think." He released the knife and let it spin in the air in front of him for a moment, then grasped it by the blade. He held it out, pommel first, in Lanoe's direction.

Lanoe moved carefully over to take it. Maggs didn't try anything stupid.

Instead the swindler's eyes flicked across Lanoe's cryptab, and then Valk's in turn.

"I say," Maggs chuckled. "The famous Aleister Lanoe and the Blue Devil. Why, I'm quite flattered."

Valk had moved up close behind Maggs while Lanoe took the dirk. "What's he talking about?" the traffic controller asked.

"I knew the Admiralty would send someone to track me down," Maggs answered. "I had no idea they would put two such tigers on my trail."

"Nobody sent us," Lanoe pointed out.

"I looked at your records," Valk added, "and I didn't see anything about the Admiralty. You're listed as AWOL, but there was nothing about bringing you in."

"Is that a fact?" Maggs asked. His face fell. "Perhaps ... perhaps they knew why I had to leave. Perhaps they—"

He didn't get to finish the thought. Valk pressed a neural stunner against the back of Maggs' neck and discharged it. The swindler's eyes rolled up in their sockets and his mouth fell open, a tiny globe of spittle drifting off his tongue.

Lanoe raised an eyebrow. "He was going to surrender peacefully," he said.

"The way he talks was giving me a headache," Valk said.

Chapter Six

When they dragged the Lieutenant into the dark room, Roan could barely look at him.

Some part of her had hoped that his face would be bruised and blackened, that the two Navy men would have beaten him. It was a terribly uncharitable impulse and she loathed it in herself at once, of course.

The tall one, the one who wouldn't show his face, shoved Maggs into a chair and then removed a small black box from the back of his head. The Lieutenant's eyes swiveled around and he closed his mouth. He looked all around him, perhaps taking in his surroundings.

Roan had been told that this place was a casino, though it was currently shut down. The tall one—M. Valk—had said that it had been a front for drug running and the owners had been arrested. It would reopen under new management in a few days but for now it was a place where they could meet undisturbed and without being overheard. It had red plush walls and it was filled with tables, each topped with the smooth gray surface of a powered-down display. Roan had tried to imagine what it would be like when it was functional, the holographic colors of the games, the bizarrely dressed people pressed in tight around each opportunity to wager, cheering or groaning as the random number generators dictated. She thought it might be nicer than the mournful silence the place showed now.

The old Navy man, M. Lanoe, walked over to Elder McRae and handed her the four development chits. She favored him with a nod and a quiet thanks. If he'd been expecting more his face didn't show it.

Having the money back was good. Roan was very grateful to the two men who had recovered it. Though it didn't really matter in the end. The one chance Niraya had possessed—the one hope—had turned out to be false.

She allowed herself to feel a crushing sense of disappointment.

"Can you talk, yet, or do you need a minute?" Valk asked.

"I am . . . somewhat recovered," Maggs answered.

"Don't try to run away. Your feet'll still be numb," Valk told him.

Maggs seemed to find that amusing. His mouth twitched upward in something like a smile. His sardonic mirth was too much for Roan, and she looked away again.

"You mind if I sit in on this?" Lanoe asked.

"I suppose you've earned it," Valk said. "Just let me ask the questions, okay?"

"Sure," Lanoe said.

Across the room Elder McRae watched the men with her accustomed calm. Roan supposed that fifty years from now, when she'd finished her own training, she might be able to master herself like that. She could see why that would be valuable at a time like this. She couldn't help herself but ask, "Is he going to prison?"

"That's what we're here to figure out," Valk told her. "Now. Let's get started. Lieutenant Maggs, I've seen your record. You've got a Blue Star, which means you're a pretty decent pilot. You're on the active list. Why are you here at the Hexus? Why aren't you off fighting in some war right now?"

"I think perhaps I should have an advocate present," Maggs replied.

"You're not under arrest. You're still in one piece. You want to stay that way, you'll answer me."

Roan glanced over at Elder McRae, expecting her to protest—
they couldn't let anyone be harmed in their presence, not if they
could help it. Their faith was one that abhorred violence. But the
elder just sat there, watching. Maybe, Roan decided, the threat was
a bluff and the elder knew that.

"Oh, all right, if that's necessary. I am on the active list, yes,
but only as a staff officer. I fought in the war between Centrocor
and ThiessGruppe, six years ago. You'll remember that conflict, of
course, because—"

"I don't pay attention to what the polys get up to. Not anymore,"
Lanoe said.

Maggs looked hurt. "Well, it was a nasty enough scrap, I assure
you. After we mopped up the insurgents in the Mictlan Cloud I
requested a transfer away from combat duty. I was seconded as an
attaché to Centrocor. The work lacks the excitement of the front
lines, but it pays better, and I had acquired certain...debts."

"What kind of debts? Gambling? Drugs? Unpaid taxes?"

"The kind," Maggs said, "that have to be paid back."

Valk grunted in frustration. "It doesn't matter. How did you get
involved with the Nirayans?"

"It's all very simple. They sent an official notice of distress to the
Centrocor Terraforming Authority. The wrong people altogether,
of course. The Authority is just a workgroup of Centrocor's planetary services division. They aren't qualified to handle this kind
of request. It wasn't about terraforming at all, you see—in fact it
was a defense matter. Because I'm an attaché between Centrocor
and the Navy, the request was passed on to me, so that I could get
the official response of the Navy. I forwarded the Nirayans' request
through proper channels, and the Navy sent it back with a funding
inquiry. Centrocor asked the Navy for an itemized estimate, and
the Navy asked Centrocor for...well. This is how it works, you
see. The giant bureaucracies that overhang our fates like constella-
tions, those faceless monoliths, are actually made of a great many
people. All of whom have jobs they wish to keep, all of whom have
tail sections they need to cover. You understand?"

"Not in the slightest," Valk said.

Maggs laughed. Roan grabbed the edge of a table and held on tight as rage burned inside her stomach.

"Action was going to cost money," Maggs went on. "And Centrocor hates spending money. So the case was just handed back and forth between the poly and the Navy. Like two marines with a live grenade, tossing it between them, not wanting to be the last one to touch it."

"But you got involved," Valk pointed out. "You grabbed the grenade and ran with it?"

Maggs sighed. "The Nirayans kept sending more and more requests for an answer to their dilemma. It was clear they were desperate. I sent them a message saying I was their Sector Warden and that I could help them. For a fee." He shrugged and one of the gloves fell off his shoulder. "As I said. I have debts."

"You lied to them," Valk pointed out.

"Well, yes. Otherwise I wouldn't be sitting here now, would I? If I was an actual Sector Warden, I would be back at the marshaling yards around Earth, putting together a carrier group." He laughed at the idea.

"Let's be clear about this, for the record," Valk said. "You don't have the power to raise a carrier group to help the Nirayans."

"No, of course not."

Roan couldn't take this. She spun around and stared at Maggs, stared him right in the eye.

He looked back, seemingly as calm as Elder McRae. There was no shred of contrition in his face.

Roan dug her nails into the palms of her hands, to keep herself from screaming at him.

"At this point, no one does. It's just not going to happen, I'm afraid. Centrocor has already made a decision," Maggs went on. "They had to do some very tricky math, but really it just came down to a risk-benefit calculation. There aren't enough people on Niraya to warrant military intervention, not in any kind of cost-effective way."

"It would cost too much," Valk said. "You're saying they asked

Centrocor for help, and Centrocor said it would cost too much to defend them."

"If you wish to put it in plain terms," Maggs said, "then...yes."

Lanoe raised a hand, like a pupil at school. When Valk nodded at him, he said, "I'm confused. Why does a planet like Niraya need a carrier group in the first place?"

"Didn't they tell you already?" Maggs asked.

Lanoe glanced over at Elder McRae but she didn't move, didn't speak.

Maggs inhaled deeply. "Why, they're being invaded, of course."

Lanoe turned to face the Nirayans. "Is that true?"

The old woman's face was a mask carved from wood. "M. Maggs asked us to be discreet. He told us that while what he could do for us was not technically illegal, Centrocor would try to stop us if they found out." She nodded at Valk. "You have my apologies for being so abrupt with you when we arrived, but we were attempting to keep things quiet."

"So what he's saying is true," Lanoe said. "You're being invaded."

"Yes," she said.

Valk shook his helmet from side to side. "But why? No offense, but from what I've seen Niraya hasn't got much worth taking. I guess...it could be a strategic move. DaoLink is taking a lot of heat from Centrocor right now. They might be trying to open up a second front, to draw forces away from their main lines."

"We don't know who the invaders are," the elder said. "I am not prone to drawing conclusions based on scant evidence."

Lanoe sat down in a banquette, the wood creaking under the weight of his heavy suit. "Will you tell us what you do know?"

The elder adjusted her hands in her lap. Lanoe suspected that for her that was the equivalent of an explosive emotional display. Well, if his planet were being invaded he supposed he would be upset, too. If he had a planet to call his own.

"I suppose there's no harm in speaking of it now. All right."

"Start as far back as you can," Lanoe said.

The old woman fished a data tab out of her pocket. "I have all of our evidence with me. I brought it in case M. Maggs should desire to review it." She plugged it into a faro table and then summoned a virtual keyboard. She tapped a key before she spoke again.

"Niraya," she said, "is a small colony, just starting out, really. Barely a hundred thousand people live there, mostly in two large habitable craters and then on a scattering of farms and animal stations." As she spoke a globe of the planet lit up above the faro table. It looked like a dirty yellow ninepins ball. "We don't see much traffic in our system. Centrocor has the monopoly on what trade there is, mostly bulk ore from a few mines." She glanced around at her listeners. "I'm sorry, this is probably more than you wanted to know, but it will become important in a bit."

Valk sat down near the faro table. "Niraya was colonized as a religious retreat, right?"

The elder nodded. "A little more than a century ago, before the revolt of the Establishment. My people—my ancestors—belonged to the Transcendentalist faith, as I do. The faith began on Earth but it became increasingly difficult to live a simple life there— modern life presents too many distractions to let one properly focus the mind. We needed a place where we could turn our faces away from worldly influence. Niraya was chartered as a place of peace, a haven for all seekers and those in need of tranquility of spirit. Few of the hundred thousand people who live there now practice any kind of organized religion, but we minister to the needs of their souls as they desire."

"You're some kind of priest, then?" Valk asked. "Niraya is a theocracy?"

The girl, Roan, rolled her eyes.

The old woman ignored her. "I'm an elder. The Transcendentalist faith doesn't have priests, or anything like that. I have devoted my life to the study of wisdom, regardless of its source. I pass on this wisdom whatever way I can. I am called an elder because I have grown old in this service. As far as theocracy, well, Niraya functions under a sort of benign anarchy. No one is officially in charge of the planet. Most of the colonists listen to us elders when it comes time to make decisions, but they are under no obligation to do so."

Lanoe lifted an eyebrow. He'd never heard of a planet that wasn't run by some bureaucracy or another. He supposed if you were small enough it wasn't worth it for your poly overlords to micromanage everything you did. Interesting.

"Sounds like a nice place to get lost," he mused.

The old woman touched her keyboard and the holographic globe began to rotate.

"Twenty-seven days ago, a spacecraft entered orbit around Niraya. We weren't expecting a freighter for weeks, so we didn't notice until it was almost upon us." A mote of light appeared above the globe, spinning around it in a tight polar orbit. The kind of orbit a weather satellite might use—or a reconnaissance probe. An orbit like that would eventually cover the entire surface of the world. "This vehicle did not attempt to contact us, nor did it respond to any signal we sent it," the elder said. "It made thirty-one full orbits. Then it released a lander, a craft massing about one and a quarter tons, which entered our atmosphere here and touched down here nine minutes later."

The mote of light split into two. The dot representing the lander came down in the midst of an empty patch of Niraya, far from either of the main craters.

"We have no video of the descent or landing, I'm afraid. Niraya doesn't have much of a satellite network and we had no cameras anywhere near this area. It's just a wilderness. We dispatched ground vehicles as soon as we knew where it had come down, but they didn't arrive for another three hours. In the meantime, the lander had moved. It progressed immediately to the nearest livestock station—just a ranch in a deep canyon, a couple of farmers and two hundred meat animals. Birds. By the time our ground vehicles arrived, nothing remained alive at the station. Three minutes later our response team was dead as well."

She turned and stared at Lanoe with a bleak expression. "We do have video of that," she said.

Roan had not seen the video before. Almost nobody on Niraya had seen it—the elders had decided not to share it publicly, for fear of starting a panic. It didn't take long for Roan to see why that was a concern.

The file the elder brought up was grainy and the color balance was off, an automatic recording from a camera mounted on the dashboard of a ground vehicle. At first it showed nothing but the inside of the vehicle's sealed cabin, just a shot of two grizzled men in heavy quilted jackets. One of them looked a little like Roan's father. They were talking but the audio quality was too low to make out what they said.

One of them tapped a key on the dashboard and the camera switched to a forward view. Roan saw two more vehicles rumbling up ahead, big utilitarian half-tracks that fishtailed and swerved as they raced across an unending landscape of slickrock and scrubby yellow vegetation. They kicked up a lot of dust as they dove into a high-walled canyon, a defile full of the haze you got in the low-lying areas where the atmosphere was thick enough to breathe.

As the vehicles headed down into the canyon Roan saw the first of the dead animals, a smear of reddish gore on the side of a narrow track. One of the men shouted something and the camera automatically panned to record the body, but the vehicle was moving so quickly it was only on-screen for a second.

The view jumped and smeared as the vehicles roared down into the canyon, hurtling around a tight curve and then braking hard as they approached their destination. For a while Roan could make no sense of the video but then it wobbled back to something approaching clarity, though the dust was still very thick.

There was more red—more blood, a fan of it sprayed across a canyon wall. The camera swiveled around to focus on the bodies of more animals. They looked like emus. Big flightless birds were the preferred meat animals on Niraya, since they could thrive in low-oxygen environments. Roan had seen plenty of emus and ostriches in her life, but few of these animals were intact enough to resemble anything but butchered meat.

Then Roan noticed that one of them had hands. Human hands. She fought back a wave of nausea.

The men in the trucks were all shouting now. Some had jumped out of their vehicles. She saw the tubes of respirators flopping from their collars, saw their heavy boots. They could be anyone she knew back on Niraya. Two of them headed down into the canyon with long rifles in their hands while a third gestured at the camera, shouting for one of his people to make sure it was recording. Roan could see his face quite clearly. There was dust in the fine wrinkles around her mouth and his hair was the color of new iron.

"Elder Mosaddeq," she said, unable to control her voice.

In the video, he grabbed one of the men by the arm and shoved him forward, deeper into the canyon. He didn't want to seem to go. There was a noise that Roan thought at first must be an artifact of the recording. With a shudder she realized it was the sound of someone screaming in agony.

The dust that obscured the view wouldn't settle. The view of the canyon ahead showed nothing, just dark shapes moving fast. The camera was smart enough to know it wasn't recording anything useful so it switched back to focusing on Mosaddeq's face. Roan wished it would look elsewhere. Mosaddeq looked terrified, and she knew he had good reason.

Roan looked up at the people in the casino. Elder McRae had turned away from the view—she'd seen it before. Lanoe sat forward with his forearms resting on his thighs, only his eyes moving as he took everything in. Valk sat nearby, fidgeting, his hands clenching and unclenching in his lap. Maggs was wholly absorbed by the view in the display. He had the decency to look appalled.

In the video, Mosaddeq began to speak.

"All dead," he said, "all of them. Tell—tell Elder Young, tell—"

The camera jumped back to the dust in the canyon. There were fewer shapes moving in there now, in fact it might just be one big one.

"—made contact at seventeen forty-nine local time, I think. Our weapons had no effect. Repeat, weapons had no effect. Garner and Ionescu are dead. We're going to try the explosives, just give me—"

The camera focused on the dust of the canyon but this time there was something to see. The lander had emerged from the murk and shown itself clearly for the first time.

It stood nearly six meters tall, towering over the vehicles. It looked like a cluster of long segmented legs with nothing resembling a head or body, just dozens of limbs that ended in sharp points. It was smeared with blood everywhere. One of the legs dragged behind it and Roan gasped when she saw it was still impaled on the body of one of the men from the trucks.

Mosaddeq didn't run. His training as an elder would keep him there, Roan knew, where he might do some good. It would keep him even from saving his own life, if there was still something he could achieve. He kept shouting orders, though Roan couldn't see anybody else in the camera view.

"Get those explosives up here! The blasting gel—get those tubes up here! Tell Elder Young—tell her we couldn't—we tried, weapons had no effect, we couldn't get—what? I can't hear you, say that again. I can't—"

The camera focused on him as his last words turned into a gurgling scream. One of the lander's legs was visible, emerging from a red hole in Elder Mosaddeq's stomach. He tried to grab the leg, maybe to try to damage it with his bare hands, maybe just because he was falling and he wanted something to hold on to.

Roan thought the camera had gone out of focus, but then water splashed on her hand and she realized she was weeping. She fought to control herself—the elder's sacrifice deserved better—but the tears kept coming.

The lander walked over his corpse, its shadow passing over his face. It didn't even slow down, just kept moving. Roan could hear every pattering crunch of its footsteps as it trod the dusty rock of the canyon floor. The camera followed it for a while, providing a good view of the thing walking away.

The camera's computer must have recognized that the action was over. That there was nothing more to see. Its facial recognition software took over, and the view snapped back to Mosaddeq's face, lying in the dust, the eyes turning to lifeless glass.

Eventually Elder McRae reached over and switched off the video.

Lanoe felt for the people he'd just watched die, but in an abstract kind of way. He'd been a warrior far too long, he thought. He knew he should be more moved, more horrified. All he could think of, though, was how to kill that damned thing. Bullets didn't harm it. He hadn't heard any explosions in the video. Did they try explosives on the thing or not? Maybe—

But Elder McRae was talking. He snapped himself out of his thoughts so he could listen to her, because she had more data for him.

"The lander moved immediately to the next livestock station and repeated what you saw there," the old woman said. "It left nothing alive. It worked its way through six more stations before it was stopped."

Lanoe grunted. "The rifles in that video—they had no effect."

"No," the old woman said. "Nor did the explosives—blasting supplies from our mining operations. As I said, Niraya is a place of peace. We're far from the wars, and there are no predators on our world. We have few weapons, and nothing particularly advanced."

"But you did kill it, eventually," Valk said.

Lanoe shook his head. Weren't they listening? "She didn't say they killed it. She said it was stopped."

The old woman nodded. "It was headed directly for Walden Crater, the place where the vast majority of our people live. Before it could arrive, it had to pass by one of our fusion plants, and we made a very difficult decision. The temperature inside the reactor averaged about a million degrees. We...dropped containment."

She tapped at her keyboard again and a new video popped up to hover in the air over the faro table. The camera view showed a stretch of canyon land where nothing moved—it could have been a still image except for a high streamer of cloud ribboning by overhead. The lander wasn't visible—the video must have been taken from a significant height, perhaps from orbit.

Without warning, brilliant scintillating light filled the image, bright enough to make Lanoe wince and look away. When he looked back the landscape had changed. Rivers of molten rock twisted across a blasted plain, the entire view shimmering under a red sky.

"There were...environmental consequences," the old woman said. "We may have set our terraforming efforts back by a few years."

Roan piped in from the other side of the room, in a small voice. "You can't pump that much heat into an atmosphere—even one as thin as ours—without causing storms. Our weather patterns are going to be unpredictable for a generation."

The old woman looked down at her keyboard. "It had to be done."

"I'm just saying it's going to cause problems," Roan insisted.

"It had to be done." The elder stared the girl down. Eventually she turned away and went to sit down in a corner.

"What about the orbiter?" Lanoe asked, maybe to clear the air.

"The orbiter?"

The old pilot arced his hand through the air as if she were asking what an orbiter was. "The vehicle that originally entered your space. It dropped its payload—this lander—but you said that part of it remained outside the atmosphere."

The old woman nodded. "Yes. Yes." It looked like she needed a second to gather her thoughts. "The orbiter was...just a shell. We sent up one of our shuttles to investigate it but they found little to report on. An empty pod, with very primitive thruster elements mounted on its exterior surface. There were no life support facilities because there was no pilot. No significant computers onboard. Clearly it was designed simply to bring the lander to us. Furthermore there was no indication where the vehicle came from or who sent it. The only thing we found inside was a communications laser."

"To control the lander, maybe?" Valk suggested. "That thing looked like a drone to me. Maybe it was taking its orders from the orbiter."

"The laser wasn't pointed at the ground," the old woman said. "It was pointed outward, toward space. That's how we discovered that our nightmare wasn't over."

⸺✳⸺

Roan rubbed at her face with her hands. She still had trouble believing that it wasn't going to stop. She'd put so much hope in Lieutenant Maggs, in his promises. None of it had been real. No help was coming.

Niraya was doomed.

The elder was still talking, though Roan barely listened. "The communications laser was pointed at an empty patch of space. No planets in that direction, not even any stars for hundreds of light-years. When we reached the orbiter it was active, sending a coherent signal. Frankly, our people were too terrified of the thing to even switch it off, at first. They didn't know if the orbiter was booby-trapped. They did eventually cut power to the laser, but not before it sent its message."

She tapped at her keyboard to open a new video file.

"The message was encrypted, and we could make no sense of it. There was one thing we could do, however. Niraya has an orbital telescope—normally we use it to track the movement of terraforming impactors and as an early warning system to watch for incoming asteroids and comets. This time we used it to track the communications laser to its destination. We found there was something out there, something that was awaiting that signal. I apologize for the poor resolution of this image, but I believe it speaks for itself."

She expanded the display until a still image filled the air above the faro table, spilling over the sides and stretching up to the ceiling.

The Navy men, including M. Maggs, got up to walk around the image, studying it from all sides.

A collection of blobbish gray shapes hung in the air there over the faro table. Some bigger than others. In general they were spindle shaped and they were all pointing in the same direction. They were fuzzy at the edges and tinged a distinct blue.

There were hundreds of them. Strung out in a loose cloud formation, the smaller blobs cluttering the front of the image, one very large shape loitering toward the back, where the resolution broke down and the image turned to fog.

A scale indicator floated near the bottom of the image. Even the smallest of those blobs was huge compared to the ton-and-a-half lander.

Roan had seen the image before, though she didn't claim to understand it. She didn't know what the Navy men were looking for as they bent under the image to look inside it or circled around it, pointing out details to each other. As far as Roan could tell there were no details to scrutinize, no profiles or silhouettes to make sense of. Her studies in planetary engineering hadn't prepared her to interpret this kind of image.

"They're all pointed the same way," Valk said. "Moving on the same trajectory. I'm thinking that rules out a meteor swarm or anything natural."

Lanoe nodded. "Moving too fast, anyway. Look at the blue shift."

"I assumed that was a color error in the image," Maggs said. "Now that you mention it, though..."

The other two turned to stare at him until Maggs backed away from the faro table, huffing in indignation.

"How fast are they moving?" Valk asked. "About half light speed?"

Elder McRae nodded. "A little less than that. Currently they're decelerating."

"That definitely rules out anything natural," Valk said.

"How far away?" Lanoe asked.

"Roughly five hundred billion kilometers," the elder said.

Lanoe tilted his head to one side, then the other. "Twenty light days, give or take. So forty-some days until they arrive. When was this image taken?"

"Twenty-six days ago," the elder said.

Valk spread out his arms to indicate the whole image. "Lanoe, am I wrong about what this is?"

"I doubt it. That first lander, the killer drone—that was an advance scout. Gathering intelligence for…" He waved at the display of bluish-gray blobs. "For this."

He glanced over at Maggs, who just nodded.

"It's a fleet," Lanoe said. "An armada."

———※———

"We believe there will be more landers like the one in our video. Or perhaps worse things. As I said before, I dislike conjecture," Elder McRae said. "I can't help but believe that this fleet intends us harm, however."

Roan pulled her legs up to her chest and hugged them. "They're going to kill us. All of us." The elder glared at her but she didn't care.

"You can't know that," Valk said. "Listen, if this is just DaoLink opening a second front, they've already made their point. Maybe that's even why Centrocor is dragging their heels. Maybe they know DaoLink is laying a trap and they don't want to just rush into it."

"It's not DaoLink," Maggs said.

Roan glared at him. He'd already dashed their hopes. Did he have to make things worse?

"You know that for a fact?" Valk asked.

Maggs shrugged. "I'd wager money on it. The war between them and Centrocor—any war between two polys—is one of propaganda as much as arms. That means everyone has to know it when you make a move. If they intended to seize Niraya, even as a ruse, they would have already issued a proclamation and half the galaxy would be talking about it. They would want to provoke Centrocor into action, and that means getting this story in the public eye."

"Okay, so maybe it's pirates or something," Valk said.

"Technically, pirates attack ships in space," Maggs pointed out. "The word you want is *raiders*. And why anyone would raid a place like Niraya—"

Valk lifted his arms and let them drop again. "Raiders, whatever! Have they tried to contact you? Maybe demanded money so they'll go away?"

The elder shook her head. "There's been no communication from the incoming fleet, of any kind. We've tried to contact them several times but there was no response."

Roan couldn't look at them while they talked about the fate of an entire planet like it was a puzzle to be solved. Instead she looked over at Lanoe. The old Navy man was still staring at the telescope image of the fleet, as if it would start moving.

He must have noticed her staring at him. He turned and looked her in the eye, but his mouth was just a hard line.

"So you fight them when they come," Valk said. "You—you buy guns, or something, you fortify your crater town."

"Peace is one of our core beliefs," the elder replied. "I'm not saying we won't defend ourselves—we have some weapons, as you saw in that video, for when there is no other choice. We'll try to fight this invasion, certainly. But you saw how ineffective our weapons were. We don't even know how to begin resisting this."

"You can't just give up," Valk said.

Lanoe never broke eye contact with Roan. He took a deep breath but he didn't move an inch. She tried to keep her face still, impassive, just as she'd been taught.

"I know some people at Centrocor," Valk suggested. "Maybe I can put in a good word for you, assuming I'm not drowning in lawsuits by now."

"Centrocor won't help," Maggs said. "I've already explained—"

Then Lanoe nodded at her.

Roan had no idea what that meant. It made a chill run down her spine, though.

"They won't," Lanoe said, standing up.

Everyone in the room turned to look at him. The sudden silence made Roan's head swim. There was something in his voice, something that demanded attention. Maybe they'd taught him how to do that in the Navy, she thought.

"But they should. Somebody should."

He strode over to where Maggs sat in his chair. "You and me," he said. "We're going to talk."

Then he grabbed Maggs and pulled him to his feet. The Lieutenant winced but said nothing. The two of them headed for the door.

"Hey," Valk said, chasing after them. "Where the hell do you think you're going with my prisoner?"

———

Lanoe shoved the swindler ahead of him, through an alley toward a big hexagonal reservoir behind the casino. It would be a great place to quietly kill Maggs and dump his body. That wasn't what Lanoe had in mind, but if the young fool wanted to think it, Lanoe wasn't going to stop him.

A narrow platform surrounded by a rusted iron railing stood out there on top of a giant outflow pipe. Lanoe put his hands on the railing and stared down into the turbid water five meters down.

Maggs was behind him, maybe two meters back.

"Go ahead and run, if you want to," Lanoe said. "Valk will have microdrones watching you, so we can catch you again."

He could almost feel Maggs fuming back there. "Honor precludes such a thing."

"Sure. Maggs. Maggs. I knew an Admiral Maggs once."

"My father."

Lanoe nodded. "I knew him as Wing Leader Maggs, first. Then I served under him when he was a group commander. I wasn't there when he died at the Uhlan Belt, but I remember when I heard about it. You inherited your commission?"

"That's right."

There was technically no shame in it. The wars had gone on for so long that the Navy's officer corps had become a veritable aristocracy, with the children of the top brass automatically qualifying for officer ranks when they came of age. Lanoe had never had much use for legacies, though. The skills you needed to fly a cataphract didn't come attached to your chromosomes.

This Maggs, Lieutenant Maggs, had a Blue Star, though. Lanoe had never heard of anyone buying one of those for their kid.

Maybe there was a chance. It felt kind of slim, but maybe.

"If," he said, "we turn you in for impersonating a Sector Warden—fraud would be a lesser charge—you'd spend ten years in the brig. Not to mention having your commission stripped and your family name trampled underfoot."

"A fate I'd avoid, at some cost," Maggs said.

Lanoe nodded. "It would hurt the Navy's reputation, too. That's something that still means a little to me. Maybe there's another way. You contracted to do a job for the Nirayans. Maybe you go ahead and do it."

"Even one possessing my skills can't shift Centrocor's hypothetical heart at this juncture," Maggs pointed out. "They've established a protocol."

Lanoe shook his head. "That's not what I meant." He leaned forward on the railing.

Maggs was quiet for a bit, maybe wrestling with Lanoe's suggestion. "You're joking," he said, finally.

Lanoe failed utterly to admit it.

Maggs shook his head. Laughed a bit. Walked a few meters away, came back.

"You're suggesting you'll keep my name clean if—and only if—I go defend Niraya. If I take on this entire raider fleet by myself. That's suicide."

Lanoe kicked at the edge of the platform. Flakes of rust broke free and twisted down into the rushing water of the outflow.

"I didn't say you would be going alone."

Chapter Seven

Caroline Ehta woke up feeling almost *good*.

She was lying in a real bed under a heated blanket, instead of in some mud puddle on a half-terraformed moon. She was naked, still a little bit drunk, and when she stretched and flexed her muscles, she felt somebody else lying next to her. Which brought back the events of the night before.

Pretty much okay.

Something had woken her, some noise in the street, she thought. She lay there in the dim room listening for it to come again. If it didn't she could just go back to sleep, which sounded fun.

This was the Hexus, where it never really got quiet. There were people downstairs in the hostel's main room, laughing and shouting at each other. Probably having breakfast. As long as none of them shot each other she could sleep through that. She could hear the repetitive *ding-ding-ding* of thumb-cymbals down in the street, which she knew meant a cart was down there selling coffee. If she really put her mind to it, she could get used to that sound and eventually drift off again.

The guy in the bed next to her snored. Well, she'd done enough garrison duty to learn how you dealt with that. She brought her left heel back and prodded him in a sensitive place. He snorted in surprise and moaned like he had a hangover. But he stopped snoring.

Unfortunately, he didn't go back to sleep. "Oh, shit," he swore. The profanity was a little shocking, even from the mouth of a marine.

"Sleep it off," she said, the words muffled because her mouth was pressed against her pillow and she didn't feel like expending the energy to turn her head.

"Oh, hellfire," he said. "Last night we didn't... Tell me we didn't—"

"Relax," she told him. He was a PBM, a Planetary Brigade Marine like herself, but he'd been raised on Adlivun, a pretty conservative planet. They still had some weird hang-ups about sex back there. "If a girl does it, that doesn't make you—"

"Oh shit," he said again. She felt him burrow deeper under the covers in shame, which made her smile.

Ding-ding-ding. The sound from the coffee cart came almost regularly enough to be background noise. If she just focused on that, on listening for the next time it came, she would be fine. She would fall back asleep and maybe not wake up until dinner.

Ding-ding-ding. Chirrup.

Ehta's eyes opened and she took a deep breath. That last sound hadn't come from the coffee cart. That was the incoming message alert. It was also, she realized at once, the sound that had woken her.

She pushed herself upright in the bed, throwing the covers back. Her bedmate, whose name was—was—best not to worry about that just then—started motivating, too. If that message was a deployment order, the two of them would have twenty minutes to report for inspection out at the docks.

"Where's my suit?" she asked.

"How would I know?" he asked, grabbing his own suit from a chair by the bed. He unzipped the back opening and shoved his feet inside. Of course he got both feet in the same leg of the suit the first time, so he had to pull them out and try again. Which meant he had to jump out of the bed and stand there, naked, facing away from her.

She admired the view for a moment. But she really needed to find her suit. It didn't immediately present itself. It wasn't lying curled up in a corner, or shoved under an end table. It was too big to be under the bed. She checked anyway.

"Seriously, where is it? You pulled it off me last night, I was too drunk. What did you do with it?"

"You think I was paying attention to that?" he asked her. He turned and she saw the long scar running down his cheek. She'd always liked men who didn't have their battle scars removed. Too bad they were deploying—there wouldn't be a chance for a reprise of last night until they next got leave, and one of them might be dead by then, given the average life span of a Poor Bloody Marine.

She went to the door of the room and threw it open. A man in paper overalls was out there, replastering a wall. She remembered seeing one of her squadmates put his fist through that wall two days ago.

The plasterer looked shocked when he saw her. She looked down. Right. Even on the Hexus, you had to wear shorts in public.

But then she saw her suit draped over the banister of the stairs. She ran over and grabbed it and hurried back into the room before the plasterer could say anything.

"Hey," M. Last Night said. "There's no deployment order. I've got nothing in my message log."

She frowned, then lifted her suit to look at the tiny display inside the collar ring. She'd gotten a message. But he was right, it wasn't a deployment order. It was a personal message.

Then she saw who it was from.

LANOE, ALEISTER (CMDR, NEF)

She dropped the suit on the floor and ran her fingertips over her cropped hair.

So much for her almost good day.

"I tried contacting some people I know in the Admiralty," Lanoe said. "I thought maybe I could get some movement there, get them to authorize an official defense of Niraya. I'm afraid it didn't work. They told me Centrocor would have to approve any intervention, and we know Centrocor has already decided to ignore your distress call."

"I'm not sure I understand how this all works," Elder McRae

said. She and Lanoe sat in a scrap of grassy park, taking a little lunch. She had been told this was one of the more respectable parts of Vairside, which meant that people kept their indiscretions to the bushes, where they wouldn't be seen.

There was no sunlight, just the ever-present glow of the lamps that ran in serried ranks along the park's winding lanes. Yet they had tea and good bread, and the grass under them was real, grown from actual seed. The elder would very much have liked to dig her toes into it, to feel how lush and soft it was, so unlike anything on Niraya.

She had been born on a world called Jehannum, where such a thing wasn't considered a luxury. She regretted she hadn't spent more time there enjoying things like grass and sunlight. In those days she would probably have been one of the libertines in the bushes.

The memory made her smile, a bit.

"I'm sorry," Lanoe said. "Are you—all right?"

"Perfectly fine," she replied. "Why do you ask?"

Lanoe shook his head. "You just had a funny expression on your face. Never mind. You were saying—you don't understand how things work."

"Yes," she said. "I know that my planet is under Centrocor's jurisdiction. And that Centrocor has refused our request for aid. But the Navy—your Navy—isn't controlled by the polys. Correct?"

Lanoe sighed. "Technically, the Navy's only mission is to defend Earth. Since nobody's attacked Earth since the days of the Short Revolt, that leaves a lot of people with nothing to do. So the mission was expanded to 'protect Earth, and Earth's interests among the stars.' We take our orders from the International League and the Sector Wardens—together, they're the government of Earth, and either group can order the Navy around. So, yes. The polys don't run the Navy. They don't have the power to give us commands. Technically."

"Technically."

Lanoe nodded. "The polys have their own militias, and before the Establishment Crisis they used to fight wars on their own. The Navy never got involved. Since the Crisis, though, the Sector Wardens have initiated a new policy. When they feel it's appropriate, they send the Navy in to fight on the side of one poly or the other. The side with Navy support always wins, so the polys work very hard to curry favor with the Wardens."

"How do they choose which poly to support?"

"Oh, they always claim there's some important reason. Maybe they'll say DaoLink was breaking interplanetary business law, or they'll accuse Wilscon of violating human rights. They have to justify military intervention."

"But you feel this isn't always the case?"

"Every time they send the Navy into some war between two polys, the Sector Wardens pick the underdog. Regardless of who was doing what evil thing, they go with the weaker side. Whichever poly is stronger, they cut it down to size. The point of it isn't to prevent human suffering or anything. It's to keep any one poly from becoming too powerful. To maintain a balance of power between them."

"So that none of them can become a true threat to Earth," the elder said, nodding. "I see. So they do all this in defense of Earth, after all."

"Yes," Lanoe said. "Unfortunately, right now the Navy is supporting Centrocor in its war against DaoLink. Which means that if Centrocor doesn't want to defend Niraya, the Navy won't get involved, either."

"I see," she said.

"Look," Lanoe told her. "I know this is rotten. I know that the whole reason we *should* have a Navy is to help people like you. I can't defend what my own people are doing, and—"

"I didn't ask you to," the elder said.

Lanoe gave her that look, then, the one people gave her when they thought she was being inappropriately stoic. Her faith had taught her to think before she felt. To control her own emotions. Those who lacked her training could rarely understand that. To them, everything was personal. Everything was about them.

"You've offered to help us. I do not require you to set the entire world to rights, Commander. Just to help me with my little corner of it."

His face went stony. "Sure," he said. "Let me tell you what I'm actually doing, then. What I think I can accomplish in the real world."

He looked back down at the minder in his hand. She knew that his suit was capable of sending messages and collecting data all on its own, but like many old people—like herself, for instance—he seemed to prefer to work with a device he could hold in his hands, a screen he could squint at. He turned the minder so they could both see the screen, and jabbed at the display with his finger.

She saw a list of names there, none of which meant anything to her.

"If the Admirals of the Navy won't help, there are still people out there who'll at least listen when I call. I've reached out to my old squadron, the Ninety-Fourth. People I know, people I can trust. They'll sign on for this mission, no question. The problem is there may not be enough of them. Even including Maggs, we may be short on pilots. Plus there's the fact that if we want to take him off the Hexus, Valk is going to try to stop us."

"I'm not sure I understand why he's even a consideration," the elder said.

"Valk? He acts like he's in charge around here, and he'll lose his job if Centrocor finds out what we're up to. Right now he's cutting me a little slack, because he knows I'm doing the right thing. But if he gets the idea he's supposed to uphold the law or something, he'll turn us in."

The elder shook her head. "No. I mean Lieutenant Maggs."

Lanoe looked up from his minder.

"I'm not sure," the elder said, picking her words carefully, "why you feel you can trust him."

The old pilot picked up a tea cup and sipped at it. "If I were you I'd probably want him drawn and quartered."

"Luckily for him, I'm not you," the elder said. "My faith teaches me forgiveness. Not out of any sense of holiness or nobility. Simply because what's done is done. He can't go back in time and convince his younger self not to defraud us."

"I guess not," Lanoe said.

"Nor would I want him to. After all, when he contacted us, Centrocor had already turned down our request. If we hadn't come here to talk to him, we wouldn't have met you, M. Lanoe. And thus we would have passed by our best hope."

"Okay."

The elder forced herself not to smile again, since it seemed to surprise him. "My question is why *you* trust him, after he's shown us who he is."

"Sure," Lanoe replied. "On the face of it, sure. I don't, is the answer. I don't trust him beyond the bounds of a very short leash. But I'm holding that leash. He believes in honor. A kind of honor, anyway, one that means he can never run away once he's been ordered to fight. His father bred that into him."

"You can be sure of that, after having known him so short a time?"

"I know his type. You live as long as I have, you see the same kind of guy come up over and over. You get to know which way they'll jump when the shooting starts. Maggs will fight, if we don't give him any other choice."

The elder had been a little surprised to learn that Lanoe was nearly twice her age, even though they looked equally weathered. People didn't die of old age, anymore, of course—medical science had taken care of that. It couldn't prevent accidents or cure every disease, though, and it was rare to meet anyone more than a hundred and fifty years old. Lanoe had survived twice that long, even though his job exposed him to nearly constant violence. He was either very, very talented at what he did, or just very lucky. Either way, she supposed she ought to respect his experience.

She couldn't deny she had doubts, though. "Someone else could replace him. Someone who hasn't already betrayed my world."

"Forgive me, Elder," he said, "but no. That's not true. I need every single pilot I can beg, threaten, or trick into coming with us. Maggs promised you a carrier group. That was…optimistic. No offense, but I'm a little surprised you didn't see through him then and there. The idea of getting a full group to protect one planet."

"I don't even know what a carrier group is," she said.

He nodded. "A carrier group is six big ships: a couple of destroyers and cruisers supporting a big Hipparchus-class fighter carrier. Each of those six ships has a crew of up to a hundred people, and the carrier holds a full wing of fighter pilots."

"We won't be able to field that kind of strength, then," the elder said.

"No," Lanoe said, fighting the urge to laugh. He'd seen entire wars where neither side could put together a complete carrier group. "In all likelihood, we won't even get a wing—that's six squads, and every squad is ten to twenty pilots. We'll be lucky to have a single full squadron by the time we ship out."

"That doesn't seem as impressive as the carrier group," the elder said. "You feel that a squadron will be enough to repel the fleet that threatens Niraya?"

Lanoe looked away from her face. "Like I said, we need every single pilot we can get."

The elder had learned a very long time ago how to conquer fear. The look on his face made her skin prickle but as she reached for the teapot her hand did not shake. She made sure of it.

Ehta vomited in a trash can on her way to the casino. It made her feel a little better. She carried hydration tabs in a pocket of her suit. A full day's water ration in a single gel capsule. She'd been a marine long enough to know they had a secondary use. She bit down hard on one to wash the foulness out her mouth before she went up and knocked on the door.

Funny. It was the first time she'd ever seen a casino closed up in the middle of the day. But then, nothing about this felt right. Still, there were some things you had to do. When Lanoe called and asked if she'd be kind enough to come see him, she had to jump to it.

She had to say the words to his face.

Whatever he wants, you just say no, she told herself. *That easy. Just, no, sir. He's not your commanding officer. Not anymore.*

The door opened and she looked up at a big guy in a heavy suit with the helmet up and polarized. It was not what she'd expected.

"I'm, uh, here for Commander Lanoe," she said.

The big guy leaned over her. Ehta was not particularly short. Still she half-expected him to pick her up and carry her under his arm.

Stow that nonsense, she thought. He was just pinging her cryptab. After a second, he stood aside and let her into a darkened room. Inside was silence. No crowd, either, almost nobody in there, just a couple of Navy suits and two civilian women. It took her a second to make out the faces.

"Ensign," Lanoe said. She recognized his voice. Of course. She'd heard it enough times over a comms laser. "Thanks for coming."

She stepped into the middle of the room. Faced him and came to attention. You didn't salute a Naval officer—most of the time you would just smack your hand against your helmet. Instead she nodded. "Sir."

"Relax. This isn't an official inspection," Lanoe said, with a little laugh. He lifted his arms as if he might hug her. If he did, she thought she might throw up again. When she didn't stand down he dropped his arms. "I was surprised to see you the other night, coming out of that bar. I believe you'll remember M. Valk."

The giant came out of the dark behind her. Damn. She did remember, now. She'd nearly bowled him over when they bounced her out of that dive. Her eyes had adjusted and she could make out faces and she was glad to see she didn't recognize anybody else.

"I'm putting something together, and—" Lanoe stopped in midsentence. His eyes flicked down, across her suit. She knew what he'd just seen. It wasn't her cryptab. Instead, he'd noticed for the first time the anchor-and-chain motif engraved around her collar ring. The insignia that marked her out as a PBM.

She took a deep breath. "Transferred, sir. Two years ago."

"You've done two years on the ground?" Lanoe asked.

She knew what he wasn't saying. Marines didn't live that long.

Their officer corps had a reputation for getting the job done. Mostly that was accomplished by throwing enlisteds at an objective until it was buried in a heap of corpses deep enough to plant a flag in. "Turns out some of the things you taught me were actually useful, sir. Keeping your eyes open, watching your tail. I've done okay."

Lanoe shook his head. "I don't want to know what you did to get transferred," he said. It was every pilot's worst nightmare, that you would screw up badly enough they would send you off to the marines. "I can help you get back in a cockpit, though. One of the privileges of rank."

"Thank you, sir, but—"

"Don't thank me yet," he told her. "I want you meet some people. This is Lieutenant Maggs. The civilians are Elder McRae and her aspirant, Roan. They're from a planet called Niraya. Ever hear of it?"

"No, sir," she said.

"I'm hoping you're willing to change that." He turned and faced the others. "Ensign Ehta—that is, Corporal Ehta now—was one of my squadmates back during the Establishment Crisis. She's a hell of a pilot, and she could really help us. Assuming she says yes."

He turned back to her with that smile. The one he wore when he asked her to fly into the jaws of death. Back in the old days, that smile worked every time.

Just tell him no, she thought. It's two simple words, one syllable each. *No, sir.*

Then she could leave. And not have him looking at her anymore.

Chunks of ice. The size of her fist. The size of her head. Trillions of them.

She realized she'd closed her eyes. That she was flashing back. Sometimes she couldn't help it. She balled her hands into fists. Squeezed her toes together. Opened her eyes.

"—fleet, we don't know whose," he was saying. She felt like there was nobody else in the room except the two of them. Her vision had shrunk down to a narrow tunnel. But she was back, in the present. Aware of her surroundings. "It's, well. It's pretty big.

We never shrank from a challenge, though, did we? Back in the Ninety-Fourth, back in the Crisis. We took what they threw at us and we prevailed."

"So we did, sir," she said.

Chunks of ice all around. She was wedged into the broken shards of her canopy. Every display she could see flashed red. One of them told her that the containment of her power plant was slipping.

She fought to stay in the room, in the empty casino. To listen. She knew she was going to lose that battle. Half her mind was back there, in the ring around the gas giant Surtur. Seventeen years ago and it was still happening, inside her head.

"—get a squadron together. It's the right thing," he said. "It needs doing."

Gloved hands pulling at her. Not gently. Both of them cramming together inside the cockpit of his old FA.2, what she always called his Jalopy. The canopy wouldn't shut—she grabbed and pulled but she couldn't get it shut. Then the crushing tug of gravity, as his inertial sink failed to compensate for the speed he poured on, getting them away. Getting them to a safe distance.

"—cataphracts. We can help these people. We can—"

She looked back, just in time to see the flash. To watch the ring, all those tiny chunks of ice, spread outward, twist and braid with the vaporizing heat, the shrapnel. And heard him breathing, his helmet touching hers, heard him breathe, and say nothing. He didn't say a word to her until she was back on the destroyer, where she dropped to the deck plates and wept, and took a real breath again, herself.

"—not strictly sanctioned. I won't lie, what we're doing breaks so many regs we'll probably end up in the brig even if we make it back. So this is strictly a volunteer mission," he said. She could see his eyes, now. Just his old, old eyes that never quite met hers, never quite seemed to really see her. After what he'd done, after what he'd risked for her, still, he always seemed to be looking at something just over her shoulder.

"I'm afraid time is tight, Corporal. I really do need an answer now."

She shook herself. Looked around the room. Everyone was staring at her, as if she'd been standing there silent for far too long. She felt blood rush through her cheeks, felt her spine curl in embarrassment. It was a feeling she had gotten pretty familiar with.

"Sir," she said.

Just tell him no. That's all.

"Yes, sir. What are my orders?"

———✦———

M. Valk had arranged for a simple room above a respectable restaurant for the elder and Roan. Perfectly acceptable, except that it was on the third floor of the building. By the time she reached the top of the stairs, the elder was out of breath.

There were therapies one could take. Tailored chromosomes that could be delivered through a drop of medicine on the tongue, elastomer-producing cells that could smooth out wrinkles and make one's skin pliable and soft. Trained viruses could repair one's frayed telomeres and reverse the course of aging. In these days, one did not need to grow old.

The therapies were cheap and widely available. Even on Niraya the elder could have her youth back, her old vigor. They could even repair the worn cartilage in her knees so her legs didn't ache when she climbed stairs.

Her faith did not expressly prohibit such things. It did frown on them. Growing old gracefully was supposed to be an elegant mode of living. There was supposed to be a kind of peace to be found in the gradual decay of the body.

The elder tried to satisfy herself with thoughts on the cyclical nature of life, on the old moving on to make room for the new. It helped a little with the stitch in her side.

At the top of the stairs she heard voices from inside the room, and the high-pitched whine of a cheap display. She opened the door and stepped inside and saw Roan hurriedly gesture to switch off the video she'd been watching.

"Don't mind me," the elder said. She was hardly about to chastise the girl for watching videos. The faith had no prescription against that, not at all.

Like most aspirants, though, Roan seemed to find all worldliness to be a sign of weakness. The girl cast her eyes down as the elder headed into the bathroom and rubbed a wet towel across her face. When she emerged, she found Roan standing at the foot of the bed, exactly like a soldier at inspection.

The elder had been an aspirant herself, once. If you wanted to become a true acolyte of the faith, if you wanted to eventually become an elder, you had to prove yourself constantly. The aspirants were almost competitive in the ways they found to be more detached, more at peace with the world.

"Sit down," the elder said. The girl did so as if it were a holy work. "Please be comfortable. This is hardly the time for discipline. Have you left this room today?"

She used a tone of voice that suggested candor was acceptable. Roan put her hands in her lap and said, "No, I—I find this place overwhelming."

"Oh, it is that. Full of temptations as well." The elder sat down in a chair, just glad to be off her feet.

"I'm doing my best to resist those," Roan said. "I understand that stimulation can lead to attachment. Attachment can lead to misjudgment. Misjudgment only ever leads to regret."

It was a catechism, more or less. An abstract version of a complicated philosophy. "Temptations can be withstood," the elder replied, simplifying things herself, but sometimes you had no choice. "There is a story from Earth, about the bad old days of religion. When men—I can't imagine a woman being so foolish— would try to prove how holy they were by sitting on top of pillars in the desert, with no food, no water, no human contact of any kind. They called themselves stylites. They would sit up there until they would go blind from the sun. Until they starved to death. People would come from miles around to look at these men and see how devoted they were to their faith. But the men didn't do good works.

Hard to minister to the poor from the top of a pillar. They didn't teach. They didn't find wisdom up on those pillars. Only horrible suffering."

The girl's eyes were wide, and not entirely with horror. Elder McRae worried she might have given Roan ideas. "Is the story true?"

"No story is ever true. You can never know all the details. How many people ever really did such a thing? I don't know. Did any of them perish up on their columns, or did they give up once they got hungry enough? It doesn't matter. The point of the story is to show that we can be too committed to our path, too devout. So that we forget that our purpose is to be in the world and make it a better place. Not to turn away from it completely."

"I'm not doing that," Roan said. "I came here, with you, didn't I?"

These children. Always so literal, always so hard on themselves. You offered them forgiveness, compassion, lenience and they rejected them—even if those were the things they craved the most. The elder had studied the human mind for decades and still there was so much she couldn't comprehend. "Let's talk about other things. What did you think of Corporal Ehta?"

Roan didn't sweeten her words. "She seemed distracted. Even ill, I thought."

"Most likely she was hungover. Marines live very dangerous lives, and they compensate by feeding their impulses when they can. They think this will make them happy, somehow. You've never been hungover, have you, Roan? No, of course not. It is the very opposite of happiness. Still, for one so clouded, she seemed willing."

"I had the impression she agreed out of a sense of duty."

"Yes? No bad thing, duty," the elder said. "Humans find structure where they can, any structure at all to organize the randomness of existence." There could be a good lesson there, the elder thought. She made a mental note to work up a teaching. For the moment there were other concerns.

"So," she said. "I am told we leave tomorrow morning, to return to Niraya. The Commander says he has an old comrade coming in, a Lieutenant Zhang, and that she will be bringing with her as many of his old wingmates as she can find. He hopes to field a dozen fighters in our defense."

"That doesn't seem like much," Roan said.

The elder shrugged. "It's twelve more than we had when we came here."

"Of course, Elder."

Elder McRae leaned her head back against the hard wood of the chair. Acceptance, she thought, was so much easier to express than to feel.

Maybe there was another teaching in that.

———✦———

A new suit was waiting for her at the hostelry, fresh from the quartermaster. One with no anchors on the collar ring. It smelled weird at first, but then she realized that nobody else had worn it before her. That was what a new suit smelled like. She checked the cryptab and saw it listed her as EHTA, CAROLINE (ENSN, NEF). Her Blue Star was in there, too. Marines weren't allowed to have those.

It looked like she was back in the Navy.

A drone waited by the window of her room. She gave it her old suit and watched it dip in the air as it accepted the weight. It flew off without comment.

Then she managed to put the new suit on. Unlike marine suits, it included a comfort garment, a cloth one-piece you put on first. Not unlike civilian underwear, except it was studded with receptacles for the suit's many hoses and cables. She ran her thumb down a tab on the back of the heavy suit and it slid open for her. Put one leg in, then the other. She didn't freak out, not very much anyway, when the seals automatically pulled tight across her back and the comfort module snugged up hard against her groin. If anything, it felt *right*, the way the marine suit never had. Pilot suits were designed to keep you warm and safe. Keep your blood circulating and your fluids balanced. The suit, she decided, had never been the problem.

Maybe she could do this. Maybe it had been long enough.

She reported as instructed to the Vairside docks just before local dawn. Zhang was coming to meet them with the ship that would take them on to Niraya. It was going to be weird seeing Zhang again. They'd been friends, in the kind of offhand way most pilots were friends. You made a point of not getting too close to the members of your wing because every time you went out on a distant patrol you didn't know which of them would come back.

Zhang was a grizzled campaigner, a survivor, much older than Ehta. Zhang was Lanoe's second in command, and she'd seen plenty of battles. It had felt almost safe to get close to her, to confide in her. Ehta had expected Zhang to outlive her—and she had, though not in one piece. In one of the last battles of the Establishment Crisis Zhang had taken a broadside from a destroyer's Mark II coilgun. It had totaled her Yk.64 fighter but after the shooting stopped they brought her in still breathing. Half of her, anyway. The lower half of her body stayed in the wreck.

Last Ehta had heard, Zhang was working as a flight instructor back on Triton. You didn't need legs to fly. They'd given her a kind of drone she could ride around on when she wasn't in a cockpit. The few messages Ehta had exchanged with her were light, breezy. But Zhang had always been like that. Cut her in half and she would make a joke about it making her more streamlined.

The last message had come six years ago. Ehta hadn't replied to it. She couldn't stand to.

As Ehta kicked off the floor of the cavernous docks and up toward the bay she saw Lanoe clinging to the edge, waiting for her. He reached down and grabbed her arm and pulled her into the bay. "She's on her way in," he said. He had a smile on his face that looked half-genuine. Maybe he was just as simultaneously excited and worried about seeing Zhang again as she was.

Maybe more.

It had been no secret that the two of them, Zhang and Lanoe, were lovers back in the day. Ehta had heard that was over—that one of them had broken things off, and it had gotten messy. By that point Ehta had already tuned out, so she didn't know the details.

Lieutenant Maggs was there, at the top of the gantry. She smelled gin on him so she stayed clear. She had never met him, nor his famous father, so he was still an unknown quantity. Valk floated next to him, impassive as if he were a drone with its speech synthesizers turned off.

The Nirayans had strapped themselves to a bench near the gantry, perhaps not trusting themselves in microgravity. They were civilians, ground folk, and thus could be safely written off. She intended to have as little to do with them as possible.

As far as she could see, as much of this stupid mission as she'd heard, their planet was doomed. Ehta was pretty sure this was just Lanoe's last hurrah. He'd retired his commission so long ago, and now, out of nowhere, he just showed up wanting pilots to join him on some crazy mission? Maybe this was just one last valiant ride before he became entirely irrelevant. It was probably a suicide mission.

Ehta had no problem with that, as long as it was over quick.

At the far end of the bay, massive shield doors slid open and air howled around them for a moment. Ehta's ears popped in the split second before the weather field activated and sealed in the bay's atmosphere. Out in the black void she could see Zhang's ship approaching.

A Peryton-class fighter tender, judging by its silhouette. It had a big shovel-shaped nose with the three-headed eagle of the Navy painted in black. A single PBW, a particle beam weapon cannon—standard Navy armament, the same the fighters carried—had been mounted on one side of the crew section, and a sensor pod in a nest of cables on the other. Six shiny new fighters rode attached to its sunken belly like wolf cubs nursing. It was hard to get a good view of them but they looked like BR.9s.

"You expect us to fly those?" Maggs asked.

Lanoe grinned. "What did you fly back in the Crisis, Lieutenant?"

"A Z.IV with a Wivern Mark II engine and woven nanotube airfoils," Maggs replied.

"I suppose being an admiral's son comes with certain perks,"

Lanoe said. "The BR.9's the workhorse of the fleet, and for good reason. Fast, strong, maneuverable. I knew Zhang would make a good choice."

The tender didn't seem to move, just grow bigger, in that funny way space robbed you of all perspective. It wasn't until its nose poked inside the bay that Ehta got a sense of its actual scale. It ran about twenty meters long and five wide—big compared to the fighters slung under it but tiny as far as Naval ships went.

It slowed as it came into the air and warmth of the bay, then ground to a halt well clear of them. Reaction gas vented from recesses along its sides and the roar of its engines whined down to a throbbing hum.

A hatch on the side of the tender slid open and a young woman kicked out and into the bay. She wore a thinsuit with a red octopus painted up and down its right side, its tentacles wrapped around her left arm and leg.

She couldn't have been more than twenty-one. Her red hair was put up in two small buns on top of her head. She had high cheekbones and a dusting of freckles across the bridge of her tiny nose. She could have been a video presenter, except for one thing: Both of her eyes were made of dull metal, with no pupil or iris. She wore small-lensed sunglasses to hide them but it didn't quite work.

Ehta had seen replacement eyes like that before, of course. Plenty of injured pilots were blinded in the course of duty. Typically, though, losing your eyes like that was a ticket out of the service. Ehta had no idea how effective the replacements were, but she knew they kept you from being a pilot on the active list.

The woman smiled and waved at them, though, as if she could see them just fine.

Lanoe kicked off the floor to glide over to her, and she reached out to grab him but instead he touched the side of the tender and pushed himself in through the open hatch, ignoring her.

The young woman looked a little hurt, but then she shrugged and bounced over to where the rest of them waited. "Your chariot awaits," she said.

Ehta shook her head in confusion. It was Elder McRae who held out a hand and introduced herself. "May I have the honor of an introduction?" she asked, as nicely as if she'd met the blind woman at a formal ball at the Admiralty.

"Bettina Zhang," the woman said, and shook the elder's hand.

Ehta swore under her breath. Then she thought to do the obvious thing and pinged the cryptab on the woman's painted thinsuit. It checked out.

"I'm Lanoe's wingman," Zhang said.

Chapter Eight

Lanoe was on the tender's bridge, checking the displays, when the woman—when Zhang—came back in. He'd figured it out by then, and felt a little stupid. "You've changed your look," he managed to say.

"This old thing?" she asked, gesturing at her face. The face that didn't look anything like Zhang's. The hair, the body, everything about her was different now. He could only think of one way that might have happened.

She'd changed bodies. Just as Thom's father had planned on downloading his consciousness into a younger frame, Zhang must have found a body donor. Traded in her old, injured self for a newer model.

He wasn't sure how he should feel about that. At the moment it made him a little queasy.

"It just wasn't what I expected to see," he told her. He stabbed at a control display to check the tender's self-diagnostic systems. The ship was ready to head out as soon as he gave the order.

"I thought you might recognize something in my posture. Or maybe the tone of my voice," she said. She tilted her head to one side and looked at him at an angle. A challenging look. Zhang used to do that, when she wanted to cut him down a notch. Which was frequently. "All perfectly legal," she said. "It's a sort of a club. You get all the neural compatibility scans and share them around, figure out who you're a close enough match with to take the transfer, to avoid psychic rejection syndrome. This body belonged to a girl who was born without optic nerves. She wanted to know what it was like to see with real eyes. I was in the mood to have legs again. So we swapped."

Lanoe stared down at the display. She'd already laid in a course for Niraya, even. Well, Zhang had always been thorough. It was what kept her alive for so long in the anarchic battles of the Brushfire conflicts that followed the Century War, long enough that they'd actually started to trust each other. And then something more.

But the woman sitting next to him smelled wrong. She was the wrong size, the wrong shape.

"Why didn't you ever message me?" she asked. "Seventeen years and—"

"You know why," he said, almost a whisper.

"I forgave you. A long time ago."

He shook his head and she let it go with a shrug. Just like Zhang would have. Zhang knew his limitations. "Can you see at all?" he asked.

"Better than you," she told him. She lifted one long slender finger and tapped one of her eyes, under the sunglasses. "Stereoscopic lidar. The only thing I can't see is colors—this body was born without the ability to see them. Even the best technology can't tell someone blind from birth what the color blue looks like. I can't tell how much of your hair has turned white."

"More than I'd like," he said. This was too much. Too much like old times—it felt wrong, somehow. He turned away from her. "I didn't find anybody else onboard. I asked you to see if you could find the old squaddies for me, but they're not here. Where's Jernigan?" The kid from Malbolge had been the best ground-strafer Lanoe had ever seen, a specialty exclusive to madmen and those with stainless-steel nerves. Damned loyal, too. "Did you tell him I asked for him personally?"

The woman scratched at her nose. Zhang's favorite evasive gesture.

"Hellfire. You're about to tell me he's dead."

"Enemy action," she said, softly.

Lanoe gritted his teeth. "What about Khoi?"

"Accident. She was testing a new class of carrier scout. It wasn't quite ready for production. That was ten years ago."

Lanoe should have kept in touch. He'd always promised himself he would, and then never gotten around to it. Too many memories, he guessed. Too much pain he'd been trying to put behind him. "Ngai? Hakluyt? Carter?" He stopped naming names because he could see the look on her face.

"Lanoe," she said, and reached over to put a hand on his arm. He didn't shake it off. "They're gone. These new wars—they've been rough on us. Earth sends us where we need to go, but when we get there, it's the polys who issue our orders. And they've got no use for Navy regs; they send us out alone against ridiculous odds, put us on extended patrols for months at a time. They figure we're like any other resource. They can always get more."

"Who's left of the Ninety-Fourth?" he asked.

"Just Ehta, and me," she told him. "And neither of us is on the active list. The squadron was . . . disbanded. I'm sorry, Lanoe. There is no Ninety-Fourth anymore."

He closed his eyes and let his head fall back against the pilot's seat.

Valk stayed in the bay while the pilots worked around him, securing the tender for its trip to Niraya. There were all kinds of supplies that needed to be stowed properly—food, fuel, cartridges for the life support system and the PBW cannon, luggage and personal effects. Spare suits, spare parts for the fighters, hand weapons.

Roan and even Elder McRae lent a hand, though they had to ask where everything went and often just got underfoot.

Valk could have helped. He'd loaded his share of craft in the past, knew how it was done. Instead he just waited by the gantry until Lanoe finally came over and asked for the one thing only Valk could provide.

"I need to load my fighter," he said. "My FA.2. You have a port restriction on it so I'm not allowed to move it."

Valk leaned over to look at the tender and the fighters clinging to its undercarriage. "Looks like there's no room. You've got a full complement on there already."

Lanoe's eyes narrowed. "There's a repair suite inside. She'll fit in there."

"That's against your Navy's regs, isn't it? Overloading a transport?"

"You know perfectly well it's done all the time. And that this isn't an official Navy operation anyway. Are we really going to fight over this?"

Valk had never been very good at playing coy. "I've got my job to think of."

Lanoe just squinted and looked away.

"I need to file my reports. I need to explain what happened and why I explosively offloaded a freight hauler right in the middle of the Hexus and cost Centrocor so much money. That means telling them about the Nirayan stowaways, and about Maggs. They'll want to know where Maggs went. If we're all very lucky, they'll find a way to blame this whole thing on him, and the rest of us get to go on with our happy little lives like nothing happened."

"I need Maggs," Lanoe said.

Valk nodded. "I get that. And I'm not unsympathetic. When I heard the elder's story, you think I didn't want to help? And I have been helping, so far. I've stood back and let you plan this suicide mission. Maybe I wanted to see how far you would get. How many pilots still owed you favors."

"Not enough. I need Maggs," Lanoe said again.

Valk laughed. "Well, so do I."

The old pilot grabbed a girder on the side of the gantry and just floated there for a second. Then he took a deep breath. "Maybe I can give you somebody else."

"Sorry?"

"Somebody else to blame the mess on. Somebody who actually was at fault, who made you deconstruct that freighter."

"The pilot of that damned yacht," Valk said. "The yacht that you won't talk about."

"Yeah. That would look better in your report than some convoluted story about Maggs trying to defraud some hayseeds, wouldn't it?"

"Sure. And if we can blame a dead guy, all the better," Valk replied. "Fewer forms to fill out. Okay, I'm interested. How do we work this?"

"I can show you. You wanted answers to a couple of mysteries. You've got half that job done. I'll show you the other half. All I ask is, once you know everything, you give us a day's head start before you file your report."

"Show. You said show. Not tell."

Lanoe nodded. "Yeah. Let me show you what's left of that yacht. So you know what happened. Then you give me a day."

"I see this yacht. Then I decide about your day."

"I suppose," Lanoe said, "that's the best I can ask for."

———

Lanoe swung himself into the tender's bridge and strapped himself into the copilot's seat. Zhang already had the command displays up, though they weren't the kind Lanoe expected. Instead of colored lights and flashing pearls, she'd brought up a three-dimensional display her electronic eyes could make sense of. Gray liquid swam across her panels, swarming up around her fingers as they danced through the preflight checklist. He couldn't make any sense of it.

She had flown the tender through wormspace to get to the Hexus. He had to assume she knew what she was doing. "Closing blast doors. Releasing weather field," she said. Through the viewports Lanoe could see a twist of dust get sucked out through the open end of the bay, out into the void. "Are we cleared to proceed?"

Valk had come into the bridge while Lanoe wasn't looking. The big guy could be damned quiet when he wanted to be—with his helmet always up, you didn't even hear him breathing. "You're cleared," he said.

Zhang released the magnetic locks on her landing gear and the tender started to drift around in the bay. She got it under control with just a couple of microburns, then eased it out of the bay, into open space. "I've got a clear run all the way to the wormhole throat," she said.

"We've got a course change," Lanoe told her. "Bring us around to face the planet."

She craned her head around to face him, her eyebrows knitting together. Another old expression he was going to have to get used to seeing on her new face. "What's down there?"

"Take us into the upper atmosphere. I'll give you numbers when we get close."

She didn't ask any more questions. The tender's nose swung around and Geryon filled up their view, all dark clouds with red light streaming up through every gap between them. She burned for a second to get clear of the Hexus, then ordered a longer burn to accelerate them down toward the hellish storms of the planet. Lanoe consulted his minder and gave her all the flight data she needed. In a few minutes he heard a faint hiss as the tenuous upper reaches of Geryon's atmosphere lapped at the hull of the tender.

A green light came up on Lanoe's console, which was still set to normal display mode. It was a call from the wardroom behind the bridge. Elder McRae's face appeared before him in a new visual display.

"I don't claim to know anything about space travel," she said, "but I believe Niraya is the other way," she said.

"Just a quick stop first," Lanoe told her. "Nothing to worry about."

He dismissed the display and looked up through the viewports again. Stacks of black clouds towered all around him, walls rising up to swallow the tender. Ten thousand kilometers away a lightning bolt jumped from one cloud to another, suffusing them both with brilliant light. The viewports dimmed as they polarized to protect his eyes.

The tender creaked and groaned as they drifted lower through the storms. Carbon soot rasped against the tender's belly as if they were running aground on a sandbar. "No vector fields on this thing," Zhang pointed out. "If we go any lower—"

"This is good," Lanoe told her. "Keep steady on this heading."

"You're the boss," Zhang said.

Lanoe unstrapped himself and climbed out of his seat. Valk moved out of the way to let him push through the hatchway into the wardroom. Everyone in there looked expectantly at him but he just nodded and headed farther back, into the repair suite where his FA.2 hung, padded skeletal steel arms holding it secure. He closed the wardroom hatch and sealed it tight.

He put up his helmet and purged all the air out of the repair suite. A hatch at the back of the tender slid open and he fought against the sudden surge of hydrogen wind. Once the pressures had equalized he moved to the hatch and looked out.

There, exactly where he'd expected it to be. Lost against the wild cloudscape, a tiny brownish dot that was steadily growing larger. A flicker of blue light danced around its main thruster.

You couldn't really say the yacht was in orbit around Geryon. It was parked too low in the atmosphere for anything like that. But its engine still had enough power to keep it from falling into the clouds, using its thrust and its airfoils to endlessly circle the planet at just below escape velocity. He'd estimated it could stay at this height for three more days before it used up the last of its fuel.

As it got closer Lanoe could see that it looked in even worse shape than he remembered. Its whole front section and cabin were crumpled in, the carbonglas of its canopy reduced to jagged shards. He took a grapnel gun from the wall of the repair suite and fired a self-adhering line down toward the yacht. It struck home and he secured his end of the line to a stanchion just inside the tender's hatch. "Zhang, you hear me?" he called.

A green pearl started revolving in the corner of his eye. "Copy," she said.

"Keep station with this craft," he told her. "I'm going down there."

"Got it."

She was a good enough pilot, he knew, to match velocities. The line that tethered the two vehicles went taut but it didn't snap. He grabbed on to it with his gloves, then fired his suit jets for a second to send him skittering down the line until his boots touched the carbon fiber skin of the yacht. The wind howled all around him, tugged at his legs and his arms, tried to grab him and pull him free. He forced himself not to look down, or to the sides, where there was nothing but endless cloudscape for thousands of kilometers, nothing but air. If he fell now it would take him hours to die, as he tumbled down through denser and denser layers of atmosphere. He would be dead long before he reached anything like a hard surface.

He could just wedge himself inside the wrecked yacht's cabin. He tugged at the broken instrument panel and tossed it out through the viewports. Kicked at the pilot's seat until it reclined and he could climb over it.

Behind the seat was a narrow cargo locker. Its hatch was closed but the lock was broken. He lifted the door away and found Thom curled up inside.

Just as Lanoe had left him.

One of the kid's hands lifted toward the faceplate of his helmet. Lanoe pushed forward until they were face-to-face, the flowglas of their helmets clinking together. They could talk as long as they were in contact, the vibrations of their voices passing through the connection. "You okay?" he asked.

"Lanoe?"

"Yeah. It's me."

The kid had a brain in his head. Back at the end of their chase, when he finally realized he didn't want to die in Geryon, Thom must have known what was going to happen. That the yacht's cabin wasn't going to remain intact. He'd just had time to wedge himself back in the cargo locker before the whole front of the yacht imploded. It had saved his life.

It had been Lanoe's idea for him to stay there until they could figure out what to do next.

"How long has it been?" Thom asked.

"More than thirty-six hours," Lanoe told him.

"So he's dead. Really dead."

"Your dad? Yeah. He's gone. Come on. Let me help you out of there."

——

There was the usual annoying wait as the repair suite hatch closed and air flooded back into the compartment. Valk waited by the interior hatch, in the wardroom, with his arms folded in front of him. Behind him the others were all talking at once, trying to figure out what was going on when none of them had any information.

Lanoe had played this one close to the vest, no question.

When the hatch did finally open, Lanoe wasn't alone—he had a smaller suited figure under his arm. He let go of his burden and the newcomer drifted into the wardroom, toward Maggs.

The swindler pushed out of the way before they could collide.

Lanoe's helmet flowed back down into his collar ring. "Everyone, meet Thom."

Gloved hands reached up to touch the quick-release catches on the side of a civilian-style helmet. The helmet came loose, then drifted into a corner near an air vent. Revealed underneath was the face of a kid with black hair and bloodshot eyes. He looked dehydrated and a little crazy. Deprivation hadn't ruined his high cheekbones, though, or the startling violet of his irises, which had to be a designer color.

The suit looked expensive. A racing model, fitted perfectly, with copper-colored wires woven into its fabric. Valk knew what that meant—the suit had its own built-in inertial sink. A safety feature, but a costly one.

The kid came from money, that was clear. What he was doing at Geryon still remained a mystery.

"I have questions," Valk said.

Lanoe nodded at him. "Step into my office."

Valk followed the old pilot back into the repair suite. There wasn't a lot of room to maneuver back there, especially not for somebody Valk's size, but both of them were used to the cramped quarters on military vehicles. Lanoe stabilized himself by grabbing a stanchion on the side of his FA.2, while Valk stayed near the hatch.

Valk listened to Geryon's atmosphere scraping along the underside of the hull. It put his teeth on edge. "Just Thom," he said. "No family name."

"For now," Lanoe replied.

Valk nodded. "So he's in trouble. I mean, otherwise why was he running like a bat out of hell when he came here? And why else would you be chasing him?"

"Yeah, he's in trouble. He killed somebody," Lanoe admitted.

"Judging by the fact you kept him alive—and out of sight—this whole time, I figure whoever it was, you think they deserved it."

Lanoe just shrugged.

"We had a deal—you were going to tell me everything."

"It happened a long way from here. Nothing to do with you or the Hexus."

Valk reached for the hatch control. If Lanoe had brought him all the way just to keep lying to him—

But the old pilot wasn't finished. "He ran away because he didn't know what else to do. He came here because I was chasing him, and he thought he could shake me. Then he decided he couldn't, so he tried to kill himself. By ramming that freighter. When that didn't work, he tried again by diving into the planet's atmosphere. He got pretty close to succeeding before he realized he actually wanted to live."

"And you owed him a favor," Valk suggested.

"No. I don't owe him anything. But he deserves better than what's waiting for him back home. So I went to the Hexus to look for a way to smuggle him out of here, to someplace nobody would look for him. I thought the Nirayans could help with that."

"That's why you wanted to talk to them without me around," Valk said.

"Sure. Of course, once I heard the elder's story—"

"You had to jump in there, too. Had to fix everybody's problems."

"They deserve help. Centrocor wouldn't do it, so somebody else has to."

Valk laughed.

"What's so funny?" Lanoe asked.

"You can't resist, can you? Somebody gets in trouble and you have to save them. Why is that, Lanoe? Why does it have to be you? This thing on Niraya—my heart went out to them, yeah, when I heard their story. But my first thought wasn't to go flying halfway across human space to single-handedly stop an invasion."

"I'm a Navy officer. A tactician. You tell me about a fleet, I immediately think of ways to fight it."

"No," Valk said. "No. There's something else. Something in you that *needs* to fix things." What it might be was beyond him, though.

"When we made our deal we didn't say anything about plumbing the depths of my damned psyche," Lanoe pointed out.

"Nope. Okay," Valk said, taking a deep breath. "Here's the thing. If I want to save my job, I need to bring in the evildoers. Which means Maggs and this Thom. We're going to turn around and go back to the Hexus, and I'll take my prisoners off this tub, and then you can go to Niraya with your squaddies and save the planet. That's our deal."

"I asked for a head start," Lanoe pointed out.

"And I said we would see."

The old pilot's eyes narrowed.

"Yeah," Valk said. "I bluffed you. Sorry about that. I figured if I gave you enough slack, you'd show your hand."

Lanoe touched a recessed key at his throat, activating his suit's communications rig. "Zhang," he said, "set a course for the wormhole throat. Burn at will."

The two pilots stood there staring at each other until she replied.

"My board's not responding," she said. "I've been locked out."

"Understood," Lanoe said.

"Sorry, that was me," Valk pointed out.

He was so damned hard to read, when you couldn't see his face. Lanoe fought to keep himself from flying at the big pilot and smashing in that polarized helmet.

"Every ship that comes through the Hexus is under my authority," Valk said. "Including this one. I can seize control from the pilot whenever I deem it necessary. Did you really think I would come onboard without a couple of safeguards?"

"Let us go, Valk. You can take one of the fighters and fly it back to the Hexus. Give us that day's head start I asked for."

"If I go back there," Valk said, "without Maggs and Thom, I'll be fired. I've got nothing left but my work, Lanoe. It's not going to happen."

Lanoe did leap at him, then. At least he started to.

Valk pulled a nasty-looking pistol out of a pocket of his suit and pointed it at Lanoe's chest. It was a microwave beamer, fully capable of cooking Lanoe alive inside his suit.

"You're out of luck, old man," Valk said. "The hatch behind me? I've got it sealed. No way your friends are going to burst in here and save you. I hate that it came to this, but I'm out of options."

Lanoe pushed himself backwards, away from the gun. Not that it mattered. In the tight confines of the repair suite there was nowhere to run. He couldn't fight his way out of this.

Which just meant he had to think.

"You've got one more option," Lanoe said, before he'd even thought of what it might be.

"Oh?" Valk asked.

"Yeah," Lanoe said. "Yeah. You can come with us."

"I beg your pardon?"

"We have more fighters than we need. What we don't have is pilots. You were the Blue Devil once. You can come to Niraya. Fly with us. Fight with us."

Valk leaned his head back and laughed.

Lanoe frowned as he waited for the big pilot to get over it.

"I take it the answer is—"

"Yes," Valk said.

"Yes?"

"Yeah. I'll go with you. Honestly, you old bastard, I've been waiting for you to ask. I was starting to get offended."

Lanoe lifted one eyebrow in surprise.

"It's a suicide mission. Lanoe," Valk said, "seventeen years ago I was a warrior, just like you. I fought for a losing side. I lost more than most. Now...well. I've been waiting ever since for somebody to give me the order to die."

He put his gun away and called up a command panel that floated in front of his hands. He tapped a virtual key and the panel disappeared.

Over the comms, Zhang said, "Lanoe, my board just came back."

"My previous order stands," Lanoe told her.

"All hands, grab something and hang on," she said. "Next stop Niraya."

PART II

SUB-EARTH

Chapter Nine

Thom couldn't sleep.

He never wanted to sleep again.

While he'd waited inside the wrecked yacht for Lanoe to return, he'd had to ration his life support resources brutally, restricting his intake of oxygen and water to the bare minimum. His suit had kept him unconscious for all but a minute every few hours, just long enough to make sure the yacht hadn't drifted too low into Geryon's punishing atmosphere. He'd phased in and out of awareness until he couldn't sense the time passing, until it had felt like an eternity down there.

Now that he was out, alive and free, he fought for every moment of wakefulness he could get.

The pilot—her name was Zhang—had announced that it would take sixteen hours to make the trip to Niraya, wherever that was. Lanoe and his Navy friends had taken that as their cue to climb into bunks and catch some sleep. Lanoe had told him that was standard practice for Navy pilots. They spent all their time on standby, waiting to go out on long patrols or running endless drills, so whenever they had a chance to get uninterrupted rest they took it. They snored now inside their bunks, turning over in their dreams, while Thom sat in the darkened wardroom alone.

He spent the time staring out a narrow viewport, watching the luminous fabric of wormspace flow by. He'd always thought it was beautiful in a dark sort of way, the twisting, kinked walls of the wormholes, the silent wailing of the pale tunnel walls, the ghostly spears of radiance that lashed out toward the ship like phantom claws snatching at you, only to evanesce away into nothingness before they could connect. Once they passed through a junction where two wormholes crossed, and there the walls positively blazed with bluish-gray light.

He knew a little of the physics of it. Wormholes were inherently unstable, and if given their way they collapsed as soon as they formed. The wormhole throats that humanity had found near its stars kept the tunnels from imploding by putting stress on the fabric of spacetime, which protested by shedding endless photons and antiphotons that combined and annihilated each other as soon as they were created. The shimmering, spectral light was the result of all those tiny explosions.

Thom didn't spend much time thinking about science, though, as he watched the wormhole burn all around him. Mostly he thought about what was going to happen to him next.

Not that he had much to go on. Lanoe had promised to keep him hidden until his father was properly dead. That time had come and gone. It was clear that Lanoe didn't intend to turn him over to the authorities now—but what the old pilot had planned for him next remained a mystery. Thom's fate was entirely in Lanoe's hands.

He didn't like that much. He had a whole life ahead of him now—his own life, free and clear. He'd never really considered what he might do with it before. Starting out as a hunted fugitive didn't sound like a good plan.

A sudden jolt of panic shocked him out of his thoughts as he heard someone moving behind him. He turned around and saw a panel door opening at the far side of the wardroom. Just the door that lead to the sanitaries, of course. Someone had woken up and needed to pass water and he hadn't heard them go in there.

He dropped his eyes when he saw it was the girl, the civilian. He started to turn back to the viewport but then he felt the air move as she kicked across the compartment toward him. She grabbed a stanchion by the side of the viewport and stared out at the wormhole with him.

He studied her reflection in the carbonglas of the viewport. She was his age, maybe a year or two older, with undyed hair that floated around her cheeks. Her breath clouded the carbonglas and she wiped it away with the coarse fabric of her sleeve.

"It's so eerie," she whispered.

Something in her tone made him frown. "You've never seen wormspace before?"

"That's a terrible name for this," she said, as the phantasmagorical light washed across her nose, down her cheek. "It makes me think of graves. No. No, I haven't seen it before. On the way to the Hexus, we—well, we didn't have any windows. I'm sorry. I didn't mean to disturb you."

"It's all right. I couldn't sleep," he told her. "My name's Thom."

"Yes, I know," she said. She seemed entranced by the view. Thom tried to remember the first time he'd seen it, and couldn't. His father had traveled a lot and had started taking Thom with him from an early age. Most likely so that if he had an accident while away from Xibalba he would have his backup body there and ready for the transfer. As a result Thom had visited half the worlds of human space.

"What's *your* name?" he asked.

In the 'glas her reflection scowled. Had he offended her? "It's Roan," she said. "Do you often have trouble sleeping? Typically that's caused by unresolved guilt feelings."

"I'm just not tired," he told her. In the 'glas her eyes were locked on his face. Suddenly that was unbearable.

"I know a meditation technique that—"

"I'm *fine*," he said, pushing back from the viewport. He grabbed the side of a bunk and pulled himself inside it.

She turned to face him. She was silhouetted in the viewport so he couldn't see her eyes. "I was only trying to help," she whispered.

One of the Navy people—Lieutenant Maggs, Thom thought—curled around in his bunk to glare at both of them. His eyes were very red. "Is a bit of peace too much to ask?" he demanded.

Thom ignored them both. He turned around in the bunk so he was facing the wall. He'd never felt more alone.

———

Maggs couldn't sleep.

Not with the *children* creeping around and talking in what, in their youthful ignorance, they no doubt thought were low whispers.

Not with the pain in his leg. Though truth be told, it was more a discomfort than a pain. The old Commander had forced him to trade in his dress uniform for a pilot's heavy suit, which had rather excellent equipment for handling sprains and an exquisitely stocked reservoir of painkillers. He'd come to quite enjoy the cocktail made by mixing good old-fashioned gin with the white pearl that sporadically appeared in the corner of his vision.

The main reason he couldn't sleep, however, was that there was work to be done. Rather delicate work, that would benefit from being completed unseen.

He waited a decent interval after the children finally went to bed. Then he waited a bit longer, just to be safe. Only when he was sure that everyone was snoring did he begin to extricate himself from his bunk.

Now's the time, Maggsy, his father's voice said in his head.

He'd come to believe that he heard his father talking to him because he was finally accepting adulthood and his responsibilities. That he was beginning to step into dear old dead Daddy's polished boots. Yes, that had to be it.

Strafe-dive while the beggars are downwell, the voice said.

Maggs quite intended to comply. He pushed himself along the wall to the hatch to the repair suite and opened it quietly, then slid it closed again when he was through.

Lights flickered on all around him as he squeezed into the small compartment. The bloody Commander's famous if rather pathetically antiquated FA.2 sat there in the skeletal metal arms of a restraint cradle, its canopy polarized, its engine ticking away as if it were asleep, too.

Now came the rather tricky part.

Not much could happen onboard the tender that passed notice up on the bridge. When he'd opened the door to the repair suite, no doubt a light had appeared on some console up there. He assumed that the blind Zhang wouldn't notice that. If one attempted to release the restraint cradle, however, it would surely come to her attention.

Unless one knew how to spoof the logging scripts.

Maggs had a certain aptitude for systems. One needed those skills to be a confidence man in a world where computers watched everything. Over the years he'd accumulated a nice bag of tricks and hacks.

He opened a display on the repair console and called for root access. Everything was encrypted but just to Navy standards, which were woefully behind the stuff Centrocor used. The system's security features offered him only a token resistance. He found the modules he wanted and switched off automatic logging, then keyed to release the restraint cradle.

The metal arms folded back and the FA.2 drifted a bit, suddenly loose inside the repair suite. All well and good. The next step was to open the rear hatch. He pumped all the air out of the suite first so it wouldn't howl as it exploded out into the void. His helmet flowed up around his face as the suite's air sighed away. Once it was all gone the hatch slid open silently, letting the ghastly light of wormspace flood inside.

So far no alarms had sounded. No one had called down from the bridge asking him what in damnation he thought he was doing.

Almost done. He just had to climb inside the FA.2 and back delicately out of the hatch. Once he was clear of the tender he would be home free. He could pick the wormhole of his choice and make good his escape.

Using handholds on the side of the repair console, he maneuvered himself over to the cockpit of the FA.2. Rather distasteful, honestly, to have to run away in such an old crate. Still. When he arrived at his destination perhaps he could sell the thing to a private collector. That might go a ways toward paying off his debts—or at least the one he always thought of as the Debt.

A single recessed key would open the canopy. He reached for it, knowing it was all smooth sailing from here.

Then, of course, his father's voice had to speak to him again and ruin everything.

Well done. Though I'll admit I never thought of you as a quitter, Maggsy.

Now that, Maggs thought, was more than just a bit unfair.

He clamped his eyes tight and winced until the voice stopped echoing in his skull.

This had to be done. There was the Debt to be thought of. He touched the canopy release key.

And found Commander Lanoe sitting in there, smiling at him.

Maggs nearly shrieked in surprise. Such a thing was quite beneath his dignity, of course, so he fought down the impulse.

"I've spent so much of my life in this cockpit," Lanoe said, as if they'd just met by accident and were having an idle bit of chat. "Sometimes, when I can't sleep, I come in here and curl up. My squaddies used to know if they couldn't find me they should look for me here. Funny, isn't it?"

"Hmm?" Maggs asked.

"How predictable people are," Lanoe told him.

"Right. Well," Maggs said, struggling with words, "here we are."

An officer never begs for mercy, the voice in his head said. Maggs found himself fully in accord with Dear Dead Old Damnable Daddy, for once. Lanoe could toss Maggs out of the rear hatch just then, let him drift forever in wormspace, and Maggs wouldn't give him the satisfaction of screaming.

"What do we do now?" he asked.

"We go back to sleep," Lanoe told him.

"We—ah—"

"I'd appreciate it," Lanoe went on, "if you would reactivate the restraint cradle on your way back to the wardroom. I'd prefer not to get up and do it myself."

"Certainly," Maggs said.

The canopy swung shut again between them, hiding Lanoe from view.

———

Thom finally managed to sleep, for about half an hour.

Then the wardroom lights came on and Zhang's voice spoke to him through a speaker mounted in the wall of his bunk. "Realspace in about ten minutes. Thought you might like some new scenery to look at."

All around him the others rose, stretching their arms, swishing hydration tabs around their mouths. Lieutenant Maggs even stripped off a sheet of razor paper and swiped it across his smooth chin and cheeks. Just like that it was morning.

And just like that, they left wormspace behind, and emerged from the throat at Niraya. Displays lit up all over the wardroom showing charts and database entries on the local system. The tender's viewports were all polarized down to total opacity, so the displays were the only thing to look at.

The planet circled a red dwarf star only about half the radius of Earth's sun. Keeping a wormhole throat stable near a gravity well that shallow was tricky—the throat had to be positioned almost inside the star's atmosphere. The tender didn't waste its time getting away from the star—if the star flared up while they were still close it could vaporize them, and red dwarfs were known for their volatility. Zhang poured on the velocity and soon the star dwindled behind them in the display until they could see its full disk.

It wasn't actually red, of course. More of a rich orange. Ulcerous black spots covered a good portion of its surface and a long, arching prominence jetted from one side, cascades of plasma rising and then falling back toward the shimmering skin of the star.

"Cintamani," someone said, from behind Thom's shoulder.

He spun around, a little startled, and saw the old woman he'd met the night before. He knew she was an elder something but he couldn't remember her name. She was smiling, a kind smile, but her eyes were sharp enough to cut through him.

"Is that—I mean, is that the star's name?"

"It's the name Centrocor gave it when they discovered this system," she said. "It's a name from the ancient myths of Earth. Niraya—the name of my world—is the name the same people gave to the land of the dead."

"The underworld," Thom said. "My planet, too. I mean, it's called—" He stopped himself. Lanoe had said he should be careful what he told people about his past. If he was going to have a life after what he'd done, he needed to distance himself from Xibalba and what he had been there. "It's named after a mythic underworld, too."

She nodded. "When the first explorers passed through the first wormholes, they went seeking earthlike planets, and were disappointed. They found worlds like Venus, or Mars, instead—worlds that were frozen and dry, or with toxic atmospheres, worlds that were uninhabitable, sterile, dead. In their despair they named the worlds they found after hells and purgatories." She shrugged. "In time, terraforming makes any world habitable, but names persist. I take it you've never been this way before. Few people come to Niraya unless they intend to stay."

She fell silent, then, though her eyes never left his. It got creepy very fast. He looked away and muttered, "I'm sure it's a nice place."

"It's what we need. What sustains us," she told him.

He couldn't shake the thought she was after something. Why else would she single him out like this, engage him in conversation when they hadn't even been properly introduced? Thom had never truly fit in anywhere. He'd been socially awkward his whole life, probably because traveling with his father he'd never had a chance to make lasting friendships. Even he knew, though, that the old woman wouldn't stare him down like this unless she expected him to say something.

He picked the least innocuous topic he could think of. "Roan was born on Niraya, right?" he asked.

"Yes. I imagine she thought she would spend her entire life there. Until we went to the Hexus she'd never seen anything of civilization. That was a great deal of temptation to experience all at once. She must make her own choices in life, though of course I hope she'll choose to stay with her studies and her devotions, and follow the path that leads to her becoming an elder someday."

"I'm, uh, I'm sure she will," Thom said.

"If she can renounce worldly things, she has a good chance." Another warm, comfortable smile. The woman's eyes hadn't changed a bit. "Forgive me for talking your ear off, young man. I'm just excited to be going home, back to where things make sense."

"No problem," Thom said.

She pushed off the wardroom wall and went to join the pilots who were gathered around a new display that had just opened up, this one showing Niraya itself. Thom lingered behind, wondering what that was all about. He knew better than to think the woman was just making conversation. She must have seen him talking to Roan while everyone else was asleep. Was she worried he was going to—oh, no, it couldn't be. He hadn't even thought of such a thing. And anyway, he had pretty much ruined any chance he had of getting to know Roan the way he rebuffed her.

He shook all such thoughts out of his head and went over to the new display.

～✦～

"We'll make landfall in three hours," Zhang called over the speakers. "This is imagery from a weather satellite in orbit around Niraya."

Maggs couldn't see a damned thing. The others were all elbows and feet and ambition to get a look. After the rather bad showing of the night before he figured he'd keep his head down, but still. He maneuvered himself around as best he could.

By craning his head around Ehta's altogether too muscular thigh he could just make out the display. Niraya, as it turned out, was a yellowish-gray sphere with a thin skin of blue hazy atmosphere. A single curl of white cloud cast a deep shadow on the bright surface. Long cracks stretched in every direction like a cobweb of ravines and canyons, broken only by bright round patches that must be old, weathered craters.

Two craters near the terminator line, the border between the night and day sides of the planet, stood out for the patches of dark green at their bottoms. One had the square patchwork of agriculture as well. No sign of human habitation was visible from this height, but Maggs could clearly make out a whitish stretch that glittered in the scant sunlight. That, he thought, must be where they'd dropped containment on their fusion plant, to melt the murderous drone. The heat of the explosion would have turned the rock beneath to glass.

"This is it," Lanoe said. "This is the place we've come to protect. There's a hundred thousand people down there and they're counting on us."

On the display the planet didn't appear to be rotating at all. It hung there in its spherical immensity, silent and bright, while the twist of cloud turned with aching slowness, its shadow washing over those endlessly branching canyons, touching them with darkness then moving on without a sound.

The gathered pilots and Nirayans studied the world with a hushed intensity, all of them looking as if they wanted to memorize every detail of the surface. Maggs supposed it was hardly surprising. Even for veteran travelers, it wasn't like you saw a new planet every day. The boy, Thom, floated by the display with his mouth open. The Nirayans watched it with their features hardened to masks of reverence.

Maggs drew his own conclusion. *Bit of a pesthole,* he thought.

Chapter Ten

Zhang put the tender into a parking orbit around Niraya and then headed back to the wardroom, where Lanoe was hunched over a display. She couldn't, of course, see what he saw. The girl whose body she'd traded for had no optic nerves, and her brain as a result had never learned to process visual information. Zhang's lidar eyes could make out solid objects but not holograms or visual displays.

There were ways to compensate. The tender's controls were all forwarded to her suit, so she called on its computers to bring up the kind of display she could use. One of the wardroom's smaller displays switched on and generated a matrix of beams of infrared light at various frequencies. Though she couldn't see the light it gave off she could feel it as warmth on her skin. She dipped her hand through the infrared array and felt where it was warmer, where it grew cold. She'd had time enough to practice the technique and soon she had an idea of what the others saw on Lanoe's big display.

Not that it told her much. Just crude shapes, hundreds of them, like a cloud of gnats circling around a giant beetle. "What is this?" she asked.

Lanoe turned to face her. His eyes were flat black and unreflective— just like those of everyone else in her world. She remembered how hard they could look, in the old days, when he was carrying out a briefing or giving orders. How soft they got other times. "This is trouble," he said.

"This is the best image you have of the enemy fleet?" she asked.

"Updated since we arrived. Some of the elements have changed position. The smaller ships here are moving up, on a course headed right for Niraya. The bigger ships are hanging back."

"Makes sense," Zhang said. "They're sending in their fighters to screen their advance, keeping the big ships safe from direct assault."

"Sure," Lanoe said. "Perfect sense. If you know you're facing an opposing fleet. I was hoping that we would have the element of surprise here. Their original lander—their advance scout—didn't meet any real resistance. I was hoping they would assume the planet was undefended. But they're being careful, the bastards."

"Never count on your enemy's stupidity," she said. "A very wise and old man once taught me that."

"Never rush in where you don't know what the enemy's thinking, either," Lanoe said back.

Zhang nodded. "This image is next to useless. I'm assuming these little ships are fighters, but we don't know what kind or even how many there really are. And this big thing in the back—what in damnation is it?" It was hard to get a sense of scale from the crude image, but it had to be much, much bigger than any carrier Zhang had ever seen. Bigger than a lot of space stations. "We should send out a deep picket."

It could be hard to read people's expressions when you couldn't really see their eyes. Zhang had known Lanoe for a long time, though, and she could tell by the way the right side of his mouth curled up that he was annoyed.

"Great idea," he told her. "I was just asking for volunteers for that exact thing when you deigned to join us."

Zhang had to admit that stung. Back in the glory days she'd been Lanoe's good right hand. The two of them had never stood on military protocol. Few fighter pilots did—it wasn't like you could take time-out to use proper forms of address when you were shouting updates back and forth in the middle of a dogfight.

"I'll go," Valk announced, from the other side of the wardroom. She had no trouble reading his body language, since he didn't have a face to read. He was as eager as a puppy who'd been offered a scrap of chicken.

Deep picket duty wasn't exactly the kind of posting pilots squabbled over. It meant spending days out there in the void, with no one watching your six—and nobody to talk to, either. The kind of work that was both insanely dangerous and mind-crushingly boring.

"I don't do well on planets," Valk explained. "Gravity and me had a falling-out a while back."

Lanoe nodded. "Sure. Thanks. The rest of us will go down to Walden Crater—that's the local capital—and figure out what we can expect in the way of ground support. Maggs, I'm counting on you, there."

The lieutenant hadn't been paying attention. He looked around as if he'd forgotten where he was. "I beg your pardon?"

"Elder McRae tells me we're going to have to meet with all the planetary bigwigs. Convince them we actually have a chance at saving their skins. Before anyone asks, yes, I pointed out they don't have a lot of other options. Sometimes, though, you need to play nice. If we can get the Nirayans to think we're the right sort of saviors, they'll work with us on building static defenses and intelligence gathering. We can use all the help we can get. I've heard you talk fancy enough, Lieutenant, to assume you're pretty good at it."

"What do you want me to do?" Ehta asked. She was chewing on her fingernails. Well, everyone got nervous before a new deployment.

"Take a look at our new crates. Make sure they're all in working order, ready to head out as soon as I give the word." He ducked his head a little and glanced over at Zhang. "I'm sure they're fine," he said.

They should be. Zhang had already checked them herself, back when she'd requisitioned them. Technically, *stolen* was probably the more accurate term, since she hadn't gotten proper authorization from the quartermaster corps to take the fighters. But she knew they were in good shape. She had brought nothing but the best, for Lanoe.

"I'll just fly the tender, then," Zhang said. "If we're handing out assignments."

He looked away. It took her a second to realize he was failing to meet her gaze.

Okay, she told herself. *Okay, let it lie.* It had been years since they'd seen each other. It wasn't like they could just go back to the way things were as if nothing had happened. She hadn't expected this much awkwardness but... *Give it time.*

She refused to accept that the thing they shared, the relationship they'd never quite given a name, was broken beyond repair. He would come around.

Valk headed out through the rear hatch of the tender. When you spent your whole life with your helmet up, you didn't much notice the transition from air and heat to the cold of the void, except that everything got very, very quiet.

Valk didn't mind a little quiet.

Pilots had a special fear of the void. Of being sucked out of a hull breach into space, out where you could just fall and fall forever. Back when Valk still had a face people could look at without cringing, he'd felt it like anybody else—he'd had the same dream every pilot had, the dream where you were walking on a black floor and suddenly there was no floor, there was nothing beneath you at all. Those dreams had woken him in sweat and panic.

He didn't get them anymore.

It was no real difficulty for him to move along the outside of the tender, using stanchions placed just for this purpose, until he reached the nearest of the BR.9s. He clambered over the tiny ship, getting to know its shape, looking to make sure it hadn't been damaged on the journey from the Hexus. In the reflected light of the planet it was sleeker, prettier than Lanoe's FA.2, with four swept-forward airfoils that looked like the curved blades of scimitars.

The canopy was all one piece, unlike the faceted eye of Lanoe's fighter. He touched the recessed key that opened it up, expecting it to swing up on a hinge. Instead it melted back into hidden grooves, flowing like dark water until it was gone completely. Just like the fancy flowglas of Navy helmets.

Valk swung himself into the cockpit and automatic straps wove across his chest. The canopy flowed up around him, sealing him in, and a dozen bright panels came to life all around him. He set one to run a diagnostic program, then dismissed three more, since he didn't need weapons at the moment. One of the panels he'd never seen before—apparently it let you tune your vector field manually, directing field strength to where you thought you might need it the most. That could come in handy.

The fighters Valk had flown for the Establishment had been obsolete even before the Crisis began, and Navy technology had developed a fair bit in the seventeen years since they took away his Blue Star. This picket duty would be good for him, if only to help him catch up on what a cataphract could do, these days.

A green pearl appeared in the corner of his eye. Just the tender checking in, establishing a link. He acknowledged and set his comms panel to automatically retain that connection. Then he touched another panel to release the magnetic clamps that held the BR.9 to the tender's belly.

He thought of what he might say to the other pilots. *See you around. Don't forget me while I'm gone.* All of it sounded forced in his mind's ear. He didn't feel any real connection to these people—another reason why he'd volunteered for this lonely duty. So instead he said nothing, just pinged to let them know he was moving. Then he brought up the flight controls and set up a ninety-second burn that would take him out to the edge of the system.

Out into the void.

━━━✦━━━

The tender had been designed to support cataphract-class fighters in theater—carrying out repair and resupply missions in deep space, dodging antivehicle fire and flak fields, swooping in to grab wounded fighters and carry them back behind the lines. In the vacuum it was fast and maneuverable. In a planetary atmosphere it handled like a brick. It had no airfoils, so Zhang had to bring it in on positioning jets and a very light touch on the stick.

She brought them in hot but not too hot, skimming the atmosphere to shed some velocity, pulling long serpentine banks for stability. Through the wardroom hatch she could hear the others cursing as gravity pulled them to the floor and inertia made them grab for stanchions.

The ground below sped by until even her lidar eyes registered nothing but a blur. Up ahead she saw the rim of Walden Crater, a gently curving wall fifty meters high. She goosed the engines just a bit to clear a big dish antenna, then let the tender drop like a stone toward the landing field just inside the rim. She pinged local traffic control only to find there wasn't any. They must get so few spacecraft coming to Niraya they didn't need to worry about midair collisions.

Using her positioning jets as retrorockets she set down gentle as a lamb, all four of her landing struts making contact at the same time. Then she powered down the engines and stepped through the wardroom hatch. Lanoe gave her a gruff nod, which all things considered was pretty good praise.

"I'll go and get the fighters unlimbered," Ehta said, rushing past Zhang. She headed for the sanitaries rather than the exterior hatch, and Zhang could clearly hear her vomiting inside the tiny compartment.

"Was I that rough?" Zhang asked.

The Nirayans—the old woman and the girl—looked a little shaky, but Maggs just shrugged. "Were this a combat zone, I would have considered that a cakewalk," he told her. "But then again, it's been a long time since any of us saw combat."

Zhang went to the sanitaries door to ask if Ehta was okay, but Lanoe shook his head.

"Let her be," he said. "We've got things to do. She can take care of the fighters while we're gone."

They left her in the tender. The elder person, the old Nirayan, called for ground transportation on a comically antique minder while the three remaining pilots—Lanoe, Maggs, and Zhang herself—stretched their arms over their heads and stamped their feet. It could take a while to get used to gravity again, even after less than a day without it.

The kid, Thom, just skulked around the side of the tender, looking like he wanted to be anywhere else in the world. Zhang had no idea what his story was—Lanoe wasn't exactly confiding in her yet. She supposed she would find out when she needed to know.

"There will be a vehicle waiting for us at the field gates," the elder said. The young local, the girl Roan, ran to grab the elder's minimal luggage and soon they were all bundling out of the exterior hatch, onto Nirayan soil for the first time.

Lanoe got about three steps before he had to say something. Zhang smiled to herself, knowing how he was—when they'd made him a squadron leader, he'd fought it bitterly, saying he was not the kind of pilot who watched after unruly children. Ever since that day he couldn't help himself. He barked orders and handed out duties like a born officer.

"We're going to be polite, but firm," he said. "I want—"

Zhang didn't get to hear what he wanted. Before he could finish his thought, his helmet flowed up around his face, cutting off his words.

Zhang's own helmet went up a second later. She looked over and saw Maggs looking confused behind clear flowglas—his helmet, too.

Lanoe scowled and punched the key on his collar ring that retracted the 'glas. He stared at the elder as if she'd tricked them into landing on some airless rock instead of a habitable planet.

It was Roan who explained, however.

"When we first settled Niraya," the girl said, "there was barely a millibar of atmospheric pressure, and most of that was carbon dioxide. The first elders had to live in domes. We've been working hard ever since to give the planet an oxygen-rich atmosphere but it's still pretty thin. I think your suits are responding to that."

Zhang realized how heavily she was breathing, sucking in big lungfuls of air just to get the oxygen she needed.

"It's better here in the crater," Roan said. "We're a hundred meters below the surface datum. Up on top you need a respirator but down here—well, you'll get used to it, if you stay awhile."

The elder started off at a brisk pace toward a low building in the distance. "It's good to be home," she said.

———✦———

No up, no down. Nothing in every direction.

The peace of it—that was what Valk had missed, these last seventeen years. Since the last time he'd sat in a fighter's cockpit.

The utter, perfect silence of the void. Once his engine cut out, he could sense only the slightest vibration trembling through his seat. No gravity to pull at his aching bones. No comms coming in, no red lights on his panels. He let the emptiness come inside his head, let the nothingness drive out all the bad memories, all the social anxieties. You couldn't even feel lonely, at least Valk couldn't, when the nearest human being was a hundred million kilometers away.

Some pilots cracked when faced with deep picket duty. With the long, slow hours when nothing at all happened, and they were left alone with their thoughts. Others worked themselves into a lather, trying to stay sharp, stay ready for a threat that might never come. Valk knew the trick, though. There was no time out there in the deep black, no proper way to measure it, anyway. If time stopped, everything else could, too.

Niraya had shrunk to a yellowish dot well behind him. Even the red dwarf looked like nothing more than a very bright star. There were other planets in the system but they were too far away for him to make out. A few comets and stray rocks ambled across the system on long, slow elliptical orbits but they didn't bother him.

Somewhere out there was the enemy fleet, days away still. He was out here to make sure they hadn't sent any scouts racing ahead. He had a secondary mission, which was to map the system and inventory all the places that would make for good cover, places to make forced landings, places that would serve as hunting blinds. That didn't take much of his attention, though.

The BR.9 had a little hatch recessed into its belly. He touched a control and it slid open, revealing a compartment full of microdrones. Tiny satellites, in practical terms—twenty of them, about the size of a human thumb. Each microdrone carried a camera eye and a radio transceiver and a low-energy ion thruster. Valk touched another control and they shot out of their compartment, each headed in a different direction. They would take up wide orbits around the red dwarf, spreading out to create a scattered array of eyes that would miss nothing. The cameras they carried weren't a match even for Niraya's outdated space telescope, but working in concert there wasn't a part of the system they couldn't observe in minute detail. When the enemy fleet arrived, the microdrones would provide Lanoe and his pilots with real-time imagery and telemetry data. Hopefully with that kind of intelligence they could avoid any nasty surprises.

The drones moved fast getting away from the fighter. Valk saw a flash as one of them caught a stray beam of light, and then nothing. He checked to make sure they were broadcasting on the right frequency, and that was it. The end of his secondary mission.

Back to his primary role. He touched his engine controls and the fighter thrummed to life. He programmed a ten-second burn that would take him on a long arc across the orbit of a gas giant planet, out farther into the dark far corners of the system, then slowly circle back toward Niraya. It would take him more than a day to get back, assuming he didn't find anything. If there were enemy scouts in the system already, he might get to stay out longer.

The burn hurt. His inertial sink protected him from most of the acceleration, but it was designed for normal human tolerances. Since his accident, any kind of sudden motion gave Valk new pains to endure. But that was all right. He blinked the white pearl away from his vision and let the hurt flow through him.

In his Zen state, he could imagine that the pain was just light, greenish-white light that flowed up through his legs and out through his spine. He was at one with the void, at one with the universe. There was nothing out there. There was nothing inside himself.

Pilot distress detected, a synthetic voice whispered in his ear. *Would you like to adjust inertial sink settings?*

He opened his eyes. He hadn't realized they were closed.

A new panel had appeared before him, one with a bewildering number of options for customizing the BR.9's various systems.

Back during the Establishment Crisis, he had flown crates that were welded together from spare parts, obsolete fighters with secondhand engines jammed in where they didn't belong. Piles of junk that could just barely keep a human being alive long enough to fire a gun or two.

This fighter, though, this BR.9 that Lanoe had given him—it was brand-new. Straight out of a factory yard, with all the bells and whistles the Navy, backed by poly money, could think up.

He could adjust the inertial sink so it would keep him from hurting himself every time he triggered a burn. The idea that you could do that had never occurred to him. You could adjust the lumbar support of the pilot's seat. You could change how your displays popped up, change the tones your alarms used—you could change everything.

He spent a good hour just paging through the options. And then he found the entertainment settings and his jaw dropped.

Music from a dozen worlds—videos from the studios on Mars and Patala—hundreds of games and applications for learning new languages or brushing up on your math or your Navy regs.

Valk laughed out loud.

Back in the Crisis his patched-together FA.6 never had a damned *entertainment system.*

Enough with this Zen nonsense—if he was going to be stuck out in the dark for twenty-four hours, how about a little music? He punched in some Martian Ska and a horn section blasted its way through his ears and soon he was singing along at the top of his lungs.

"My baby's got a brand-new dress! My baby's hair's all in a mess!"

Even the microdrones were too far away to notice how badly out of key he sang, and that was just the way Valk liked it.

———————

The crater wall rose all around them like a mountain range that stood over the town in every direction. As the little ground car zipped along the streets Zhang couldn't not see it—despite how much else there was to take in. She was in the back, on a seat that faced backward, her feet dangling above the semipaved road. Roan sat next to her, pointing out anything she thought Zhang might find interesting. "That bunch of pipes there is the top of our reservoir," the girl would say. "We can't just dig wells—there's no aquifer here—so we recycle every drop. Oh, and over there is the school I went to when I was younger. My teachers were all elders—look, there, that's the Meeting Hall, that's where we come together to debate anything that affects the entire community."

Zhang nodded and smiled but paid very little attention. She was more interested in the houses and side streets they drove past, the little scenes of life she caught as mere glimpses as they passed by. Children playing with a ball in a big, fenced-in yard, chickens running in crazy circles around their feet as they rushed back and forth. Old men drinking tea in a café with a dusty awning. Laundry hanging from lines between houses to catch the sun. The serious face of a dog staring at her from an open doorway.

Did people really still live like this? It was hard to imagine. Zhang had been in the Navy for so long she could barely remember her own childhood, back on Earth. Even back then, more than a hundred years ago, the streets had always been deserted, certainly no children out there where they could be hit by the traffic. Her young life had been contained inside the concrete tower blocks two, three hundred stories high.

There was only one building in Walden Crater more than two stories tall, and that was their destination. It didn't take long to reach.

"It's just called the Retreat," Roan told her. "It's where the elder and I live and study."

Zhang's first impression was of a pyramid, or a ziggurat, a pile of stone tapering as it rose to a narrow, flat top. Its surface wasn't smooth, however, but intricately, elaborately worked, with no sense of order or restraint. Rows of columns held up square blocks of foamcrete studded with perfectly square windows. Elaborate gargoyles perched on top of glass solaria. Rather tacky stringcourses ran along the tops of rooms fronted with elegantly minimal paper screens. Taken as a whole the building looked wild, like maybe it had grown that way naturally. If one was feeling generous. Zhang tried not to think of it as a jumbled mess.

"It was just a basic dome when the planet was settled," Roan explained. "But each aspirant is expected to add something of their own to the structure. A new room, or just a statue, or maybe they fix the plumbing or update the electrical system. You work on your contribution the whole time you're studying and then when you become an elder you live inside something you built with your own hands."

"You can just build whatever you like?" Zhang asked, as the ground car pulled up in front of a humble little doorway.

"It's important to make your own choices," Roan said. "To express your true being. Maybe it helps you purge the chaos from your self, or maybe you find peace in the work. It's different for everybody, I guess."

Well, that explained the combination of architectural styles, anyway. "Where's yours?" she asked.

Roan looked down at her hands where they lay folded in her lap. "It's not very good," she said.

"I want to see."

The ground car had stopped and the others were piling out, headed in a group toward the door. Roan jumped down and led Zhang around the side of the building to show her a point on the structure near the top. The wall there was simple concrete with a single tall, narrow window that didn't look quite straight.

"I'm still learning," Roan said. "I have years yet to get it right."

"It looks—sturdy," Zhang said.

"You don't need to coddle me," Roan said. "When people lie to preserve the feelings of others, they harm everyone involved. I know it's terrible."

Before Zhang could say anything more, the girl led her back around the building to rejoin the others. Together they filed inside, through a long corridor that led straight to the heart of the Retreat, a massive room with a high, domed ceiling. Long structural members arced like a steel cobweb overhead, dividing the dome into hundreds of triangular panels.

The space beneath the dome was cold and drafty but some effort had been taken to make it cheery. A long banner—which Zhang couldn't read—hung across half of the big chamber, while underneath it a small stage had been erected. A couple hundred chairs had been set up before the stage, only a scattering of them filled with people, who turned to stare at the pilots as they came inside. To one end of the stage a band with acoustic instruments played a jaunty tune. One of them was seriously out of key, which made Zhang smile.

A welcoming ceremony. *How quaint,* she thought, if a little pathetic. The turnout, for one thing, was almost insulting. She didn't let those thoughts linger, though, instead scolding herself when she remembered how little these people had. They'd clearly done their best.

Then she noticed a long table on the other side of the stage, laden with bowls and platters, all of them heaped with steaming food.

Free grub, she thought, which to a warrior like her always covered a multitude of sins.

"I don't understand," Roan said. "Where is everyone? This place should be packed. Don't they understand how important it is that you're here?"

"Maybe they'll show up later," Zhang said. "I mean, we just got here ourselves. It'll take time for them to know there's something to see here."

"No, they should already have arrived! Everyone on the planet knew about this ceremony, well in advance," Roan replied. "We sent a message from the tender as soon as we left the wormhole throat, to say we were on our way."

"You did *what*?" Zhang demanded.

It looked like Lanoe had heard it, too, as he chose that moment to stomp over toward them, murder in his eyes.

Valk was on his ninety-fourth game of Centrocor Challenge when the microdrones started pinging him.

It was a dumb little game where you tried to match colored hexagons before they tessellated across a rotating spheroid. There was nothing much to it but he found he couldn't stop playing—there was always at least one more match, and if you got six in a ring the game made a soothing chime sound. At first, when the ping came in, he thought he'd unlocked some kind of secret combo.

A new display opened near his right hand, though, and he grunted and looked over to see what was happening. His game kept running without him and the hexagons completely covered the spheroid. The game screen flashed and asked him if he wanted to reset the spheroid for only six virtual diamonds.

He wasn't about to spend real money on virtual gems. He dismissed the game panel and brought the new display over in front of him. The microdrones wouldn't achieve their best configuration for days yet, but already they had mapped the local volume of space and were sending him imagery. The display showed a simplified map of the system, out to about ten astronomical units.

Niraya wasn't the only planet circling the red dwarf. There were three others, all ice giants well outside the habitable zone. Valk was supposed to see if any of them would be useful from a strategic perspective. One of them looked promising—if you drew a straight line between Niraya and the encroaching enemy fleet, the outermost of the big planets was only a few degrees of arc off of that line. The planet might make a good place to stage an ambush.

Otherwise most of the system was just empty space. A thin belt ringed the star, out at about two AU, but nothing there could properly be called an asteroid. Just dust and ice, mostly objects no larger than Valk's fist. More of a hazard to navigation than anything useful.

The microdrones had turned up a few comets and big rocks on long elliptical orbits—at best, places to set down in an emergency. None of them were in great positions.

The most interesting thing on the display, however, was almost too small to see. Valk magnified the view again and again until he had a useful image, and even then it was just sixteen bright dots that flickered with reflected starlight. The dots were moving fast, though—really fast, two and a half thousand kilometers per second. That was nearly one percent of the speed of light. Nothing natural moved that quickly.

The dots were spread out across a staggered line, as well. They looked almost like they were flying in formation.

Valk checked their trajectory and took a deep breath. Yep. Just as he'd expected. They were headed straight for Niraya.

It looked like the fleet had sent advance scouts after all. He punched for a new burn to intercept, a six-minute burn that would bring him close to matching their velocity. The adjustments he'd made to the fighter's inertial sink worked perfectly—this time there was no pain at all as the fighter's engine roared and pushed him hard back into his seat.

Chapter Eleven

Lanoe fought for control over his emotions. He very much wanted to explode, just then. It was perhaps not the best possible time.

"It is not commonly accepted conduct," he said, in a deep, growling voice, "to broadcast troop movements in a time of war."

He had to hand it to the elder. The old woman didn't wince. "I'm not a soldier. I'm not aware of such things."

"The enemy is, in all likelihood, monitoring every communication that gets transmitted in clear, anywhere on this planet," Lanoe went on. "If I were them, I know I would. From now on anything you say about us—anything—needs to be encrypted. Better yet, don't transmit at all."

"That will limit my ability to—"

"We had—perhaps we had—some element of surprise before," Lanoe went on, ignoring her. "The enemy didn't know we were coming. They didn't know this planet had any space-based defense. Now, thanks to your little slipup, they know the Navy has gotten involved. Can you see how that compromises our mission?"

"Yes, of course I can. I understand what I did wrong, Commander. I think we can move on to other matters, now. Perhaps, for instance, we can go in and greet the people whose lives you have agreed to protect."

Lanoe looked over at the banner strung over the stage. It read

WELCOME HEROES, which irritated him. They hadn't done anything heroic yet. He grew even more angry when he saw the mostly
empty seats in front of the stage. He started to form a response
to the elder's suggestion—something that would blister the elder's
ear—but he knew he needed to get this over with. He stomped
across the concrete floor of the dome, not particularly caring if anyone followed. When he reached the stage there was a polite smat-
tering of applause, and then the band stopped playing.

Up on the stage he stared down at the Nirayans, a group of people in
dress as varied as the décor of the building looming above them. Some
wore the simple tunics and leggings of the Transcendentalists. Others
wore Centrocor uniforms or work clothes—coveralls and chunky
boots. A delegation of three people were dressed in elaborate robes and
wore high furred hats of a type he'd never seen before. The eyes of this
last three looked glassy and confused, as if they were on drugs.

All of them stared at him like an exhibit in a zoo.

Great, he thought. *The adoring public.* It wasn't the first time in
his career he'd been called on to address a group of civilians, but he'd
never gotten used to doing it. He supposed he should say something.

"Thank you for coming," he told them. There was no microphone to speak into, but the weird acoustics of the dome made his
voice echo. "I'm Commander Aleister Lanoe. I represent the Navy.
My pilots and I are, uh. Well. We're going to do our best on your
behalf. We have been thoroughly briefed on the local situation and
we have every, um. Sure. Every confidence that we can bring this
crisis to a speedy and . . . safe resolution."

He looked down into a few dozen pairs of very wide eyes. It was
hard to think with them staring at him like that. Hard to know
what to say.

"I guess . . . I guess, well. Okay. Any questions?"

Everyone started talking at once, shouting out so many different
things he couldn't make sense of any of them. A tall woman in a
Centrocor uniform jumped to her feet and bellowed loudly enough
to be heard above the din. "I want to be evacuated immediately,"
she insisted.

"Sorry?" Lanoe asked, completely lost.

"I'm a Centrocor employee. The poly has a responsibility to people like me. I've worked for the mining concern here twenty years, and there isn't a single black mark on my record! I want to be relocated to the Hexus or some other safe poly installation immediately, and that goes for my entire staff as well."

"I don't know if . . ." Lanoe said, trying to think of a polite way to tell the woman to sit the hell back down and shut up. "How many staff do you have?"

"I have thirty-four hundred people working in seventeen mines. They'll need to be relocated at least for the duration, so you're going to have to find billets for them; they'll need food allowances and per diem expenses for each day we have to be away, not to mention indemnity for the lost time and productivity."

Lanoe gave her a tight smile. What she wanted was impossible, of course. They could maybe pack twenty people in the tender, if they were all friends. Even if they made daily trips back and forth to the Hexus it was never going to happen in time. He started to open his mouth to say as much, but then someone behind him cleared their throat in a particular way. Not particularly loud, just . . . authoritatively. Lanoe swung around and saw Maggs standing there.

"Excuse me, everyone," he said. "I," and he placed one hand, fingers splayed, across the cryptab on his chest, "am Lieutenant Auster Maggs."

The tangle of voices quieted down almost instantly. Every eye present focused on Maggs as he smiled and nodded at various people in the audience as if he already knew them personally. He came back around to the tall woman, the mining administrator, and his smile grew an extra notch wide.

"We'll get to your people in just a moment," he told her, with a sly wink. Lanoe was surprised to see the tall woman's mouth twitch in the suggestion of a smile. "First, though—friends, seekers, you look troubled."

He stepped down off the stage and walked over to the people in the robes and furred hats. They stared at him like a tiny bird staring into the eyes of a cobra. "We," the shortest of them said—his hat was especially tall—"have been chosen by lot to represent the Church of the Ancient Word."

"I could tell you were a holy man," Maggs said. "Tell me, Father, what's your name?"

"Oh, well—I'm not—we prefer not to use titles like 'father' or even individual names," the representative of the church said. "The greatest enemy of spiritual development is the ego, after all."

"I've tried so hard for so long to come to an accommodation with mine," Maggs said, with an apologetic simper. "Tell me. What brought you here today?"

"We—well, that is, the church, as a, a communal, that is to say, a nonhierarchical body—"

Maggs nodded in sympathy.

"We resolve that we oppose violence in all forms. We understand that the defense of the planet may involve some—some—some danger. But we've come to petition you to try not to...to..."

"Please," Maggs said, resting a hand on the man's shoulder. "I'm listening."

"We'd like you not to kill anyone. If that would be. That is. Possible."

Maggs closed his eyes and bowed his head as if he were praying with the man. "We're Navy pilots. We do deal in aggression, it's true. But we're not butchers. I promise you, we'll keep the bloodshed to an absolute minimum."

The church man looked up at Maggs the way a teenager might look up from the first row of a concert hall at a pop star.

"Now," Maggs said, "I know everyone here today had a very good reason to come. You all have pressing concerns and believe me, we know how important this situation is, how it affects each one of you. I give you my personal promise that we'll hear you all out, on an individual basis." He started to climb back up on the stage, but before he got there he turned back and aimed a big smile right at the mining administrator. "Especially with you," he said.

Lanoe was too far away to see if the woman blushed or not, but she definitely looked away with an embarrassed smile.

"First things come first, though," Maggs said. He gestured broadly at the table with all its platters and dishes, as if he'd made all the food with his own two hands. "And first—we eat!"

The people in the chairs, the ones who'd been so full of questions and demands before, laughed in unison. Then they got up and started to form an orderly line in front of the food table.

Zhang went over there as well. While Lanoe watched from the stage, she started talking to the people in the line, smiling and shaking hands and laughing at jokes. Just like that—as easy as that—the welcoming ceremony was over. At least the part where Lanoe had to give a speech.

He would admit to himself he was distinctly relieved. He stepped over to Maggs to find out what had just happened. "Where did you learn how to do that?" he asked.

"My sainted father was in the Admiralty," he explained. "He was constantly at some public relations work, you know—pressing the flesh, scratching backs. He taught me a very important lesson."

"What's that?"

"When dealing with a crowd," Maggs said, "you separate them into two groups. Those who are insane and those who are simply indignant. You put the latter bunch aside—give 'em time, he always said, and their jets will cool down. Anger goes away, but crazy never does. So you deal with the madmen first."

"Hellfire," Lanoe said. "I knew we brought you for a reason."

~~~

Valk wasn't sure what to do.

His microdrones showed him the enemy ships in high resolution. Sixteen of them. Fifteen had spherical segmented metal hulls with just the pits of maneuvering jets showing on their surfaces. They matched exactly the imagery he'd seen of the orbiter that first attacked Niraya. He had no doubt that inside of each of them was a killer drone made of nothing but legs ending in sharp claws.

The sixteenth craft was different, elongated, its surface complicated by pipes and cables and studded with spikes that had to be the barrels of weapons. Some kind of defensive escort for the orbiters, clearly, but the configuration made no sense to Valk. The enemy interceptor had no airfoils and it was three times the size of his BR.9. Too big to have a vector field onboard, far too small to function like a Navy destroyer. It wasn't like any kind of ship he'd fought before.

Normally the role of a deep picket was to observe and report. Valk filed all the imagery he had and shot it off toward Niraya, earmarked straight for Lanoe. His job should have been over at that point—he should have veered off and headed back to base, so a full patrol could come out and take care of this threat.

The speed of light was a problem, though. Valk was ten light-minutes out from Niraya. If he asked for Lanoe's orders it would take at least twice that long to get a reply—his signal had to travel all the way to the planet, then Lanoe's response had to travel all the way back. As fast as the orbiters were moving, twenty minutes was far too long to wait. If those orbiters reached Niraya before Lanoe could scramble a patrol, they would drop their landers—and people would die.

The obvious answer was for Valk to take the initiative and kill these things himself. It wasn't a great option. His tactical position was lousy—he was alone and he had no cover to speak of.

He would just have to fall back on the oldest trick in the book.

He leaned on the BR.9's stick and swung around until his back was to the red dwarf. Maybe the orbiters and their escort wouldn't see him as he came screaming out of the sun. He armed his PBWs and readied the cannon that launched his disruptors and antivehicle rounds. He cranked the sound system until an extended drum solo drowned out every nonviolent thought in his head.

His weapons panel flashed an amber light at him and he looked down to see he had a firing solution on three of the orbiters, even though he was still fifteen thousand kilometers away from them. Bless Navy optimism, he thought—at that range, even PBW fire would take five seconds to reach the orbiters. More than enough time for them to dodge. He held off for three more seconds—counting them down against the beat of the music—then squeezed the trigger built into his control stick.

His twin PBWs fired simultaneously. Beams of protons lanced forth, the BR.9 spitting fire in two flat streams, even as Valk hurled himself straight at the line of enemy ships. Two seconds to impact and he watched the targeted orbiters, knowing they would move, knowing he'd wasted his opening shot. One second to impact and they—they didn't move. They weren't evading.

Had his trick really worked? Could they not see him approaching against the disk of the sun?

Zero seconds to impact.

His cannon fire ripped through the hull of one orbiter, then the other two a microsecond later. Metal boiled and vaporized in the dark, as the orbiters were reduced to debris and slag.

He wasted no time congratulating himself. He cut all thrust, then punched for maneuvering jets to swing himself around until he was flying backward, the line of orbiters receding in his forward view.

Amber lights on his weapons panel. New firing solutions available. He let fly another volley of particle beams from close range, watched the orbiters sizzle and pop. As easy as cracking eggs with a hammer.

And still the orbiters didn't respond. They didn't turn off from their course, didn't veer away from him. They were holding steady on their established trajectory, still screaming down toward Niraya at a thousand kilometers a second.

The interceptor, on the other hand, started to turn. Brought its nose around to face him. He saw its weapon spikes start to glow.

Well. Finally something that made sense.

━━━✳━━━

The ceremony went on for what felt like hours. Lanoe spent most of it picking at a dish of noodles and thin, gray vegetables that tasted like nothing at all. He didn't care much about the food. He was just glad that everyone seemed to be ignoring him. The locals were much more interested in talking to Maggs and Zhang.

The swindler was in his element. He grasped hands and smiled when appropriate, or turned his face grim and respectful when some religious nutcase whispered conspiracies at him over a glass of watery fruit juice. Maggs never seemed to get tired of the attention.

Just watching him go tired Lanoe out. So he turned to watch Zhang instead. She might not have Maggs's effortless grasp of social niceties, but she had always been better at this sort of thing than Lanoe was. She seemed to be following Maggs's lead, playing the slightly more sober counterpoint to his charismatic presence. Those few people who looked as if they'd seen through Maggs's manufactured cheer would turn to her looking for more serious answers, and she was always there, ready to provide.

He had no idea what to think about Zhang. He had a very hard time remembering it was even her. The new body she wore was not exactly difficult to look at, but it still made his head hurt. He remembered every inch of Zhang's old one, every scar, every freckle, every—

Better not to start thinking like that. The new Zhang was a fifteenth his age. If he started wondering what remained between them, it could get very weird, very fast.

He made a point of not watching her too closely. Of not thinking those thoughts. Anyway, it wasn't like there was a point to them. The last time he'd seen Zhang she'd been in a hospital bed, wired up to a dozen machines. She'd screamed at him to leave, to just leave her alone. And he had.

For seventeen years. Even for someone as old as Lanoe, that was a long time to let things fester.

Which just left him with Thom to watch. He'd worried that as soon as the kid was back in human society again he would start blabbing about what he'd done, about how he was responsible for his father's death. That wasn't going to help anybody.

But instead Thom just lingered in the back seats, far from anyone else. Looking glum and angry. Well, that was better than the alternative. Lanoe joined him as soon as he could—at least it was peaceful back there.

"Staying out of trouble?" he asked.

Thom gave him a look that was less angry than resigned. "I can't ever go back, can I? I'm going to spend the rest of my life here. On a planet with basically no atmosphere."

Lanoe sat down next to him. "We'll figure something out," he said.

Meaning yes. Thom was going to have to stay here—the last place the authorities would look for him. He would spend the rest of his life on Niraya.

But Lanoe knew that wasn't what the kid wanted to hear, just then.

Thom tilted his head back to look up at the painted triangular panels of the dome. "Okay. I mean, I know you know best. I'll do what you say. So give me my orders."

"Huh?"

Thom looked at him and his face was set in an expression of grim intent. "If I want a life, any kind of life, I need to do what you say. I understand that. So just tell me what to do."

"I already did. Keep your head down. Don't talk to anyone."

"Maybe I can help out, here," Thom said. "Help...you know. Defend this planet, I guess. I mean, I can do something."

"I'm not sure what," Lanoe said. Thom didn't exactly have a lot of useful skills. He'd spent most of his youth learning how to fly yachts and which set of clothes were appropriate for which sort of party. "But okay. That's a good attitude."

"Thanks, I guess," Thom said. With just a little sarcasm.

"We'll find you something to do. Maybe you can be our good-will ambassador."

Lanoe knew he deserved the nasty look that earned him.

"It's a serious job," Lanoe told him. "You see how few people there are here? You know why that is?"

Thom shook his head.

"It took me a while to find out. The elder and her church,

whatever, back when the lander attacked, gathered up the most important people on this planet—the head of Centrocor's mining operations, the leaders of the other churches like those guys in the big hats. They briefed them on what was happening, that the planet was being invaded. Then they all agreed not to tell anybody else."

"What?"

Lanoe nodded. "The people in this room are the only people on Niraya who know they're being attacked. The vast majority of the population has no idea. Does that sit well with you?" Lanoe didn't wait for an answer. "I don't like it at all."

"So you want me to...what? Tell the rest of them?" Thom asked, looking terrified.

Lanoe shrugged. "No. Not yet, anyway. For now—we play it their way. It's their planet, right? They get to decide, I guess."

"But the people—they have rights," Thom insisted.

Lanoe shrugged. "I'm no politician. Nor an ethicist. Not my job. For now, just get to know the people here. Get them on our side. This planet was settled by people who wanted to get away from things like the polys and the Navy. They're not going to be thrilled we're here, even if they need us. Maybe having a civilian to represent us is a good idea."

"You want me to be a politician for you," Thom said.

Lanoe considered that. Well, if Thom got to know Niraya better, maybe it would go easier for him, since he would probably never leave it. Maybe he'd even get to like the place. "I guess so."

"Okay. How do I do that?"

Lanoe had to admit to himself he hadn't the faintest idea. "We'll figure that out as we go along. For now, if you really want something to do, head back to the spaceport," Lanoe said. "Help out Ehta, if you can."

Thom just nodded.

Lanoe would have said more but just then Elder McRae gave him a little wave. Time to talk about important things. "We'll keep you busy," he said.

Thom just nodded, his eyes on the floor.

The elder had gathered the other pilots. Maggs was still making apologies and shaking hands as the elder led them out of the dome and up three stories to her office. There was no elevator, of course. The three Navy officers were out of breath before they'd climbed a single flight of stairs, but the elder looked fresh and ready to talk when they arrived.

Graceful, thin columns rose to a vaulted ceiling in her office. A central area floored with perfectly fitted flagstones led to four arched alcoves, one of which was used for the door that opened onto the stairs. Of the other three, one had a broad window with a view of the crater and the town and one was stuffed full of book-shelves containing actual bound paper books—which would have been surprising except they looked so appropriate in this place. The last alcove contained a narrow camp bed made up with crisp white sheets. Evidently she slept here as well, at least part of the time.

The central space contained a desk with a display top and a couple of straight-backed wooden chairs. No art, no carpeting, nothing to distract or divert. It felt chilly, even though Lanoe's suit automatically compensated for the local air temperature.

The girl, Roan, came in behind them with a pot of hot water and some cups, in case anyone wanted tea. No one did. Roan set the pot down and went over to the bookshelves, then produced a brush and started dusting the old volumes.

At the desk the elder summoned a virtual keyboard to bring up the latest imagery from the space telescope.

"Not much change," Lanoe said, nodding at the display. "They've advanced their fighter screen some more. Well, now that they know we're here, they would, wouldn't they?"

He glanced up at the elder as he said it, but she didn't react.

"Two weeks before that big ship arrives," Lanoe said, pointing at the largest blob, the one they thought had to be a carrier. "We're going to have our work cut out for us. We'll need to run con-stant patrols to deal with their fighter screen. Meanwhile there'll be plenty of work to do on the ground. We'll need intelligence—imaging from the space telescope we've got, and Valk will put down a microdrone network, but we need more than that. We also need to get a supply train going—fuel dumps and ammo caches, repair facilities, food and consumables for five pilots. Zhang, you can handle the logistics, right?"

"Absolutely," she said, a little too perkily. "Anything you need."

"Maggs, you've already proven you're our best civilian liaison. We need every engineer on this planet working for us."

The elder inhaled sharply. "I'm sorry, why is that?"

Lanoe stared at her. "There are five of us. There are hundreds of ships in this fleet. We need every bit of help we can get. I can put your people to work building static defenses—orbital guns, specifically—but there'll be lots of things we need built. Ground stations and more telescopes. We definitely need to improve your communications grid."

"I don't know," the elder said. She shook her head. "That sounds like it will cost a lot of money. We don't have any. Also, we'll have to work with the miners to organize such things, and relations between the Retreat and Centrocor have never been cordial. What you're asking—"

"You want your people happy, or alive?" Lanoe asked.

To the elder's credit, she didn't snarl or flinch or anything. She just stood there looking placid.

"I asked you a question," Lanoe said.

If the room had felt psychologically chilly before, suddenly they were all at risk of emotional frostbite.

"I didn't feel it required an answer," the elder replied.

Lanoe grabbed the edge of the desk with both hands. "Am I the only one here who understands how serious this is?"

"No," Roan said, stepping forward. "You don't get to say that. This is our planet, not yours. You can't possibly understand—"

"Roan," the elder said. There was steel in her voice.

The girl bowed her head and stepped back.

"You'll have the help you ask for," the elder said. "It will, however, take a little time to organize our efforts. Civilian efforts."

Lanoe nodded, his fingers beating on the desk like a drum. "Time," he said. "Lady, you don't *have* any."

His cryptab throbbed against his chest. He had a new message. He started to swipe it away angrily, then noticed it was from Zhang. *COMMS FAILURE IN REAR RECTENNA.*

Lanoe seethed but he understood what she meant. The two of them had set up a code, back when they were commander and second in command. The message she'd sent, properly decrypted, meant *you're talking out of your ass.*

He looked over at her and saw her nod at the door. "Excuse me," he told the elder. "I need to confer with my second in command."

The elder didn't seem too put out.

Out in the hallway Zhang waited for him. "Don't even start," he told her.

She ignored his orders. "What's wrong with you? Why are you treating her like that? Just because she's about as emotive as a brick wall doesn't mean you can vent your frustrations on her."

He glared for a while. He rubbed at his scalp.

"Civilians," he said.

She nodded, as if she understood.

"That bunch who came to meet us—making demands, like we weren't here to save their stupid asses. And then she starts talking about time. You know how well I do with public relations."

"Lanoe," she said, very calmly, "I'm going to remind you of something now. It was your idea to come out here and help these people. Yours. You want to tell me why you wanted to do that, when you clearly don't even like them?"

He bit off what he wanted to say to that.

"Fine, don't tell me," she said. "But look. You have *some* reason to want to help them. It seems counterproductive to me to tear their heads off, now."

Damn it.

Hellfire.

She was right, of course.

Good old Zhang. Always watching out for him. The new body hadn't changed her that much, apparently.

"Okay," he said.

"Yeah?"

"You and I are going to have to have a long talk at some point," he said, the same way he might tell his squad they were about to be inspected by a visiting admiral. An unpleasant chore nobody looked forward to.

It made her beam at him. Like that was all she ever wanted from him.

Seventeen years he'd stayed away, not even sending her a get-well message when she was stuck in the hospital. Now she was acting like no time had passed at all.

He didn't get it.

"Let's go back inside. Maybe apologize, or something," she told him.

"Ha." He started to say more but then his cryptab throbbed again. Another message. "I've got something coming in from Valk," he told her.

"Yeah?"

"Yeah," Lanoe said. "I think he just started our war for us."

———

Valk had a secret.

He pulled the BR.9 around into a corkscrew roll, accelerating away from the enemy interceptor. It lumbered after him, just starting to gain speed. It was a lot bigger than he was, and all that mass would take some time to get turned around. But there was no question now—it was coming for him.

Valk's secret was that he was only a middling pilot.

Oh, he'd been the leader in his squad. But that wasn't saying much. Even in its early glory days the Establishment had been lousy at training its pilots. Many of them died before they even got their flight certificate. Those that made it to the front lasted, on average, three missions before getting killed.

Valk had got his Blue Star by luck, mostly, by staying alive long enough to catch fighters that were low on fuel or had already been damaged. He'd come close to dying way too many times, and always by his own fault. Even his accident had happened because he wasn't looking behind him, hadn't even seen the AV fire coming his way. Somebody high up in the Establishment's ranks had heard his story and had created the Blue Devil nickname because at the end, right before the grand idea fell apart, they'd needed propaganda victories as much as material ones. They'd created the myth of the pilot who refused to die before finishing his mission.

They'd had to bully him back to the front. He'd wanted to die, had thought he had a right to that. But the grand cause wanted a hero instead of a martyr.

As the enemy interceptor came for him, out there in the dark far from Niraya, he had only one thought in his head: *oh damn oh damn oh hell.*

The weapon spikes on the interceptor's spine recoiled visibly as it opened fire. The corkscrew roll saved him—the projectiles passed to his left and his right, above and below him, none of them connecting. Behind him the interceptor's thrusters belched fire as it sped after him, not even bothering to match his roll, just flying up his six as straight as an arrow.

Valk snapped around in a rotary right and burned away at a sharp angle, thinking he would flank the interceptor. He had the advantage in speed and maneuverability.

The interceptor had more guns than he did. They bounced and shook as it spread rounds all across his course. One of them came close enough that a panel lit up inside his cockpit, his computer having analyzed the projectile. A kinetic impactor—basically a lump of dense metal. The interceptor might as well be shooting cannonballs at him.

Of course, as fast as he was going, if he ran into one of those it would tear a hole right through him. His vector field would deflect anything but a direct hit, but if even one shot got through it would kill him.

It would be easy enough to break off, to pull some quick snap turns and burn for Niraya. That would mean abandoning his attack on the orbiters, though—which had been the whole reason why he'd started this fight.

He was going to have to close and engage. No choice.

The interceptor kept firing, nonstop. How many of those impactors could the thing carry? Valk swept in toward his enemy, wiggling his stick back and forth, jinking so the interceptor couldn't get a solid firing solution on him. A kinetic impactor smacked off his vector field and he felt the BR.9 thrum like a violin string but a quick check of his systems panel showed no significant damage. The interceptor was close now, filling up his viewports with its lumpy, dark shape. It showed no lights at all but that didn't matter. Valk's sensors had painted the thing stem to stern and he could see it just fine on his displays.

He readied an AV round—the same kind of projectile that nearly killed him and made him famous—and told his computer to work up a solution. He knew the algorithms it would use. It would sweep the interceptor with millimeter wave scanners that could see right through the enemy craft's hull. If it found any significantly large cavities inside—for example, the pilot's cockpit—it would find a way to put his AV round right inside that space. The AV would breach the hull and then explode in a jet of superheated metal inside the cockpit, incinerating any organic material it touched. Like, for instance, the pilot. A bad way to die, but Valk didn't waste any sympathy on this bastard.

While the computer worked on its solution, Valk focused on staying alive. Impactors zipped past him on every side. There was no human way to predict where the next one would be. Valk could only trust to intuition and luck. He swiveled around on his long axis until the interceptor looked upside down in his viewports and then punched for a quick Z-burn, simultaneously pulsing his engine. The effect was to throw the BR.9 into a tight loop, getting him out of the way of the enemy's fire and giving the computer time to think. As he swung around in space, he trained his PBWs on the interceptor and loosed a volley of shots at it. All of them went wide. He'd known they would, but had hoped they would make the interceptor's pilot keep his head down.

The impactors came on just as fast and as thick as ever. Valk saw one approaching—actually saw it as a shadow looming dead ahead—and twisted out of his loop just in time to avoid it.

A blue pearl appeared in the corner of his vision. The computer was done finding its solution. He reached for the trigger to launch the AV—but first he actually looked down at his weapons panel.

No cavities detected. AV fire not recommended against target.

What? That was—that couldn't be right. There were no hollow spaces inside the interceptor's hull? None at all? That would mean there could be no cockpit in there. That made no damned sense at all. Though if the computer had told Valk that the enemy ship was just a hollow skin full of impactor ammunition, he supposed he might have believed that.

Working fast, he took his AV offline and switched to a disruptor. No need for a firing solution this time—he would just need to get close, and be lucky.

The interceptor hadn't just sat there dead in space while Valk flew circles around it. Whether or not there was a cockpit in there, somebody onboard was smart enough to figure out that Valk was trying to edge his way back toward the orbiters. They'd brought the interceptor's nose around and moved to keep him from the defenseless targets. Now they turned again, to face him head-on. Because the interceptor was longer than it was wide, that meant giving him a smaller target. It also meant that the distance between them was shrinking at an alarming rate.

Valk burned away from the interceptor, straight out into the void. Just as he'd expected, the interceptor followed him, pouring on speed to catch up with him. The spiky guns kept belching out impactors the whole time. Valk kept his acceleration low, just enough to keep ahead of the oncoming juggernaut. What he was about to try would take some very careful timing. It also demanded from the gods that the interceptor didn't fire an impactor right up the funnel of his main thruster.

As if thinking made it so—or nearly—the BR.9 shook just then as a near miss tore through its vector field. A noise like a gunshot echoed through the cockpit, deafening Valk until he couldn't hear his music anymore. He let out a scream he couldn't hear and looked down at his displays. One of his airfoils was gone, sheared off by an impactor hit.

Well, out here in space he didn't need them.

Just hold on. Don't panic and run. Let him come to you, Valk told himself.

Behind him the interceptor blocked out half the stars. It was right on his tail, barely five hundred meters back. Three hundred. Impactors hit his vector field so often now the whole fighter shook and groaned.

One hundred fifty meters. Now.

Valk stabbed at a virtual key on his flight display. The fighter's positioning jets fired and the BR.9 spun around, the stars in Valk's viewport blurring as he swung around to face the interceptor. The jets fired again in the opposite direction to stabilize him and he was flying backward.

He didn't even look at his displays. He brought up a virtual Aldis sight, just a glorified set of crosshairs superimposed on his canopy, and focused on a likely spot on the interceptor's right flank. Two bulbous pods met there, with a small gap between them. Valk gave his computer a second to firm up the shot, then squeezed his trigger.

The disruptor round was a lumpy rod about a meter long. Most of it was solid carbon, dense and hard as diamond. Studded inside the rod were hundreds of small but very powerful explosive charges. They were timed to explode in series, each of them going off a millisecond after the one before it.

The disruptor dug through the interceptor's solid bulk, tearing the enemy craft apart as it wormed its way through. The carbon rod turned to shrapnel that tore the interceptor apart from the inside.

The interceptor's guns kept firing, impactors whizzing past Valk in a steady stream. He felt cold dread grip his stomach and he was certain, absolutely convinced, that the interceptor had some way of shrugging off his disruptor just like it had proved immune to his AV round.

But then something inside it—maybe its fuel tank, maybe an ammunition magazine—exploded, and the whole ship blossomed outward in a spreading ball of fire that turned dark and dissipated almost instantly. Pieces of the interceptor flew off in every direction. Stray impactor rounds formed a cloud all around it, glittering in Valk's lights.

Inside the BR.9's cockpit, Valk had stopped breathing. He watched the interceptor's pieces spread outward, tumbling and twisting, until he couldn't hold out any longer.

He drew a breath.

He'd made it.

Chapter Twelve

I t was hard to make small talk when you couldn't tell anybody where you were from. Or who your family was. Or, for that matter, why you'd been dragged out of a wrecked yacht hidden inside a gas giant and lugged along as deadweight to the middle of a combat zone.

Thom did his best.

"Lanoe said you were in the marines," he said.

Ensign Ehta didn't seem to have heard him. At least, she didn't reply. She punched a virtual key on her wrist display instead. The magnetic winch on the side of the tender whined and groaned and another fighter detached from the undercarriage. A telescoping crane arm reached out and gently deposited the fighter on the ground.

Thom tried to help, steadying the fighter as it touched the concrete, trying to keep it from wobbling. Of course, if something went wrong and it tipped over, the fighter would crush him, even in Niraya's low gravity. So Ehta had to keep an eye on him as well.

"Is it true? You were a marine?"

"Yeah," she said. She walked around the fighter, checking it for damage. Her wrist display flickered and chimed as it ran a diagnostic on the fighter's systems.

"You must be pretty brave," Thom suggested.

She glanced up at him. He couldn't read her eyes.

"You hear stories," Thom said. "You know. I saw a newscast on the battle at Nergal last term. We thought there had to be some kind of rounding error when we saw the number of casualties."

She picked up a tool, something with a light on the end, and swept it around inside the fighter's main thruster.

"It wasn't an error, though, was it? You really lost five thousand troops in one day?"

"More like in a minute," Ehta said. She switched off her wrist display. "The marines fight on the ground. Ground's a bad place to be when the Navy's in orbit." She shrugged, then peered down the barrel of a particle beam cannon.

"How does something like that even happen?"

She looked down at the tool in her hand. Then she set it carefully on a ground cloth and sighed. "If I tell you, will you be quiet and let me work?"

"I'm—I didn't mean to—"

She tilted her head to one side, ignoring his stammering apology. "There was a lot of fighting around the main refinery yard on Nergal, lots of DaoLink insurgents but they were low on supplies and we were about to break through." She shrugged. "DaoLink had a cruiser in a polar orbit, though. It opened up with its seventy-fives—that's a kind of gun with a seventy-five-millimeter bore. Fires about six thousand rounds a minute, though that's misleading, because it only carries enough ammo to discharge for ten seconds at a go. Anyway, they had a whole battery of those guns and they opened them up all at once. Blew up the refineries, but I guess they figured it would be cheaper to rebuild them than to surrender them."

Thom made a conscious effort not to let his jaw drop. "But all those people—they just—just killed thousands of marines to—"

"Well, see, marines are even cheaper than refineries," she pointed out. "There's a lot of people on Earth and Mars and Ganymede and not a lot of jobs since the polys got enfranchised. So you can always get more marines."

She closed her eyes for a second, as if she were remembering that day. Slowly a smile curled across her mouth. "Nergal," she said. "Real pretty."

"It...was?"

"The fighting was actually on one of its moons. Nergal was up there in the sky. It's a gas giant, a hot one like Geryon—you saw Geryon pretty good, I guess."

"More of it than I would have liked."

She nodded, but she wasn't looking at him. "Well, this one had rings. That close to the star, they weren't ice rings, though, like Saturn's. Ice would have just sublimated away. These rings were made out of rock, so hot it was molten. The rings glowed, like a ribbon of fire floating around this big dark planet." She opened her eyes and looked at him. "Pretty."

Thom had no idea how you could think about the scenery when so many of your friends and comrades were getting blown up from space. How much violence and death did you have to witness before it was less noteworthy than the view?

He'd wondered the same thing about Lanoe, though in the abstract. He knew Lanoe was a highly decorated pilot. That he'd fought in more battles than Thom had even learned about in his history classes. You'd think that would leave some kind of mark on somebody. That you would just be able to tell.

Instead, back when he worked for Thom's father, Lanoe had just seemed like a quiet old man. It wasn't until Lanoe had chased him halfway across the galaxy that Thom had realized there was more to him. That he had depths Thom couldn't even begin to fathom.

Being around all these old people with their stories, with their decades or centuries of experiences, made him feel ridiculously young. Unproven. His father had always kept him away from any kind of danger or excitement. His life had been one of unrelenting boredom, relieved only by the occasional yacht race.

He wondered if he was ever going to have a chance to make something of himself. Lanoe had brought him to Niraya, he knew, because it was the last place the authorities would think to look for him. But did that mean he was going to spend the rest of his life, there?

Hellfire, he hoped not. The air was so thin he could barely breathe. The gravity was lower than he was used to and that was annoying every time he tried to walk straight. It was cold, too, near freezing even with the local sun riding high in the sky.

"You must have seen a lot of things nobody else ever will," Thom said. "I mean, I've seen a bunch of planets, but typically just the spaceports and some hotels and—"

"Kid," Ehta said, "I've got work to do here, you know?" She tapped at her wrist display and small hatches opened on the sides of the unlimbered fighter. One after another she yanked out long, rectangular slabs of metal that Thom knew were fuel and ammunition cartridges. She laid them carefully on a sheet and started rubbing at them with her gloved fingers. He had no idea what she was trying to check.

He waited until he couldn't stand it anymore. The not talking. "I'm sorry if I bothered you," he said.

She sighed and looked up at him. He couldn't take the expression on her face. He could imagine what she was thinking. He was just a kid, some stupid rich kid Lanoe had taken a shine to for some reason she couldn't guess. Meanwhile she was a pilot and a Navy officer doing vitally important work that could save lives.

"I'm sorry," he said again. He turned away. He would have run off, if he'd known of anyplace to go. "I'm sorry I'm in the way. I'm sorry I'm so useless."

"Kid," she said, "relax. Just...relax. And shut up."

His cheeks burned with shame. He was about to say something more, make another apology, except just then her wrist display started chiming and she looked up into the sky. He turned to look as well, and saw something small, moving fast, headed in their direction. It quickly revealed itself to be a fighter—a BR.9—coming in for a landing.

"Valk's back," Ehta said. "Early." She glanced at her wrist. "*Really* early."

Her display chimed at her again and Lanoe's face appeared floating above her wrist. "Ehta?" he said. "When Valk lands, get him over here to the Retreat as quick as you can. We've got a lot to talk about."

By the time they reached the elder's office, Ehta was gasping for breath. She was gratified to see that Thom was in just as bad shape—she'd thought she was getting old.

Valk never even slowed down. He hadn't lowered his helmet, of course, so he had plenty of oxygen. He hammered on the door like he owned the place and hurried inside. Ehta gave Thom a look and headed in as well.

Inside, the elder and the other pilots were huddled around a desk, deep in conversation with a tall woman Ehta didn't recognize. She had black hair cut to fall around her ears and she wore civilian clothes that were less than a decade out of date, so for this planet she looked pretty hip. "This is M. Derrow," Lanoe said, pointing at her. "She runs the mining operations for Centrocor. She's an engineer." He looked up at Valk. "You have it?" he asked.

"Yeah," Valk said.

When he'd landed at the spaceport, he was carrying something big and heavy in his arms. He'd been in too big a rush to get to Lanoe to show it to her on the way over. Now he dumped it onto the desk with a clang. Powdery black residue scattered across the display top.

Ehta joined the general throng, trying to get close enough to see what it was. Not that it was easy to tell. The object had been heavily damaged, cut up by a particle beam by the look of it. It was about as thick as Ehta's thigh and scorched black until whatever color it had been originally was gone. One end of it was just a mass of severed wires and cables. The other tapered to a savagely sharp point. Like the claw of some giant robot wolf, maybe.

"Do you recognize this?" Lanoe asked the elder.

The old woman studied it carefully before she replied. "Yes. It looks just like one of the legs of the lander that killed my people."

Lanoe nodded. Clearly that was what he'd expected to hear.

Ehta had barely glanced at the video of the killer drone attack. She remembered seeing a claw like that protrude from the chest of the dead elder in that video, though. She shivered a little.

"This time they sent fifteen of them, with one interceptor as an escort," Valk said. "I've got video and my fighter's logs to look at, if you want."

Thom reached out one finger to poke at the exposed wires.

"Leave that," Lanoe barked.

"I just thought—"

"We don't know if it's safe," Lanoe said, his voice softening a little. "Roan," he said. "Can you do me a favor?"

The Nirayan girl looked surprised. "Yes, of course," she said.

"Take Thom somewhere and get him something to eat," Lanoe said.

Ehta could see Thom winding up to protest, but the look on Lanoe's face was pretty clear. This wasn't a conversation for unauthorized civilians. The kids left the office together without any more fuss.

"This isn't for public consumption," Lanoe said, gesturing at the thing on the desk. "Okay? M. Derrow—when Valk told me what he was bringing back, I knew we'd want an engineer's perspective. That's why we called you in here."

Derrow nodded uncertainly. She stepped up to the desk and took a long, thin probe out of one of her pockets. Then she looked at Valk and Ehta as if she'd suddenly realized there were strangers in the room. "I'm, uh, that is—I'm an administrator, mostly. I have a desk job. It's been a long time since I actually did any fieldwork."

"You're saying you can't tell us anything?" Lanoe asked, looking angry. He never did have much use for people who wasted his time.

"If I may," Maggs said, leaning in. He smiled at the administrator and she glanced away. *Uh-ho,* Ehta thought. Maggs was already working his magic. "We need to keep this at the very top level. Tip-top. That's why we wanted a woman of your...standing to give it the eye."

"Well…" Derrow said. "Let's see." She touched the claw with her probe in a couple of places. "Pretty bad scoring. This damage—it looks like maybe some kind of laser cutter did this?"

"Particle beam," Valk said. "My, uh, particle beam."

"Ah." Derrow squatted down to get a better look at the ragged end. She stuck her probe into the stringy mass there, then took out a pair of pliers and grabbed one of the strands. She gave it a good tug as if she was trying to pull it out.

Instead, the claw spasmed and thumped against the desk, its point digging a deep gouge out of the display top. It started flopping its way across the desk until Derrow let go of the pliers.

Instantly it fell back, inert again.

"Is that thing alive?" Zhang asked. "*Was* it alive?"

"No," Derrow told her. "It's all metal. Lightweight alloys but nothing all that exotic. This was built, not born. Though it's not a design I'm familiar with. These wires," she said, touching the strands with her probe again—Ehta flinched in case the thing came back to life, but it didn't—"are designed to act like muscle fibers. You pull on them and the whole limb contracts or flexes."

"A drone," Lanoe said. "We knew that already. But you say this is new to you. Maybe some kind of new technology? Something DaoLink cooked up in a lab, maybe, and they needed to test it so they sent it here to see what it could do?"

"No," Derrow said. "No. This isn't new technology at all. In fact, it's pretty archaic. The concept goes way back, but this implementation is crude compared to modern myomechanicals—plastics with selective elasticity that make this look like a child's toy. If Centrocor has that tech, so does DaoLink. This is antique. This," she said, looking distinctly unimpressed, "would rust if it got wet."

"I don't understand," Lanoe said. "Why would they send old technology here?"

Derrow shrugged. "It's cheap? Disposable?"

Zhang leaned over the claw, studying it with her metal eyes. "Is there any indication who built it? Any, I don't know. Serial numbers? Maker's marks?"

Derrow used her tools to turn the thing over, study it from all sides. "Nothing like that."

Valk turned to face Lanoe. "There's something else. I tried using an AV on the interceptor, but my sensors couldn't detect anything like a cockpit onboard. No cavities large enough to hold a pilot at all."

"So the interceptor was a drone, too," Lanoe said. He looked confused. It was hard to see the difference in that wrinkled face between confusion and anger, but Ehta had known him long enough to tell. "Remotely piloted, maybe."

Valk shook his head from side to side, an exaggerated gesture for a man with no face. "No way. My scans were thorough—there were no other enemy craft in the system, and the rest of the fleet is still light-days from here. The interceptor was slow, but it was tracking me in real time. No way a remote pilot could fight like that. The battle would have been over before they even knew it was happening. The interceptor was relying on its onboard computers."

"No. That's impossible," Zhang said.

"Um," Derrow said, "can I ask why?"

Zhang folded her arms and lifted her left shoulder in a kind of noncommittal shrug. "You don't let a computer fly a warship. You just don't."

"Humanity," Lanoe said, "has made a lot of mistakes with our technology. But we don't make the same one twice. We dropped atomic bombs on ourselves once, and never again. We turned one planet into gray goo with nanotechnology. Never again. We don't build artificial intelligences smarter than a mouse, and we will never, ever make a computer that smart and give it weapons. They tried it in the early days of the Century War and—well. It took a lot of us to fix that mistake."

"Then how do you explain this?" Derrow asked.

"I'd love to hear suggestions," Lanoe replied.

Ehta surprised even herself when she cleared her throat.

"Maybe," she said, "I, uh. Have one."

Though she knew they would scoff when they heard it.

Thom stomped down the stairs, with Roan following close behind. He couldn't believe Lanoe would just dismiss him like that. Lanoe had saved his life—and risked so much in the process. Now he was just going to dump Thom on this backwater planet and leave him to do...what? Nothing. Worse than nothing—he had to be looked after, tended to. Lanoe was treating him like a liability.

Well, he might be just that. If the authorities ever found out that Lanoe had helped Thom, they could arrest him as an accessory to—to—

He couldn't bring himself to even think it.

"There's a refectory downstairs," Roan called after him. "I don't know if you were actually hungry or not, but..."

He turned around on the steps. Even walking down the stairs had left him out of breath, and now a surge of anger swept through him, pure unfocused, frustrated wrath that made his head swim. Why had Lanoe saved his life at all, just to bring him to this place that wasn't even habitable? He thought of about a dozen choice comments he could make, barbed witticisms to direct at the girl's bland, impassive face. She was already angry at him, like so many other people. Why bother even trying to be social?

Because she was the only person on the planet, maybe, who would actually talk to him. If he was going to spend the rest of his life here, he needed to start making connections. Friends.

He stopped himself before he could say anything nasty. Leaned against the wall and just breathed for a second. Then he nodded to himself. "Roan," he said, "you and I got off on a bad foot. Last night, I mean, on the tender."

She nodded but didn't say anything.

"I guess I'm—I'm very sorry, if I was...if I was abrupt."

"I've already forgiven you," she said. She came down the steps until their faces were level.

"You have?"

Cold as it was on the stairs, everywhere on the planet, he could feel the heat radiating from her body.

Was it possible that she didn't hate him? He'd just kind of assumed that he'd already ruined his chances for finding a friend his own age here. But maybe—

"The faith teaches us not to hold on to resentment."

"Oh," Thom said.

"The elder says that attachment to a slight is like clutching a venomous snake to your breast and hoping your enemy dies."

"Oh," he said again.

"So *are* you hungry?" she asked.

"Not—not really."

"Then what do you want to do? Other than run off in a huff?"

Thom inhaled sharply through his nose. Was she making fun of him? No, he could see in her face that she didn't mean anything by it. In fact, what she'd said . . . was kind of funny.

He smiled, and started to laugh, but then just shook his head. He needed all the breath he could hold on to. "I guess I want to do something meaningful," he said, at last, when he could think clearly.

"You want to work," she said, nodding. "Good. Work is an excellent method for handling confused feelings."

Thom rolled his eyes. "I didn't mean I wanted to dig irrigation ditches or anything. I'm supposed to be some kind of goodwill ambassador here. I have no idea what that means, or how to do it."

"I know a place you could start," she said.

Everyone stepped back so that Ehta could approach the desk and the black claw lying there. She squatted down next to the desk and studied it from a different angle, but it didn't reveal any great secrets to her.

She looked up at the elder. "You say you've been trying to communicate with the enemy fleet this whole time, and there's never been any response."

The elder nodded.

She turned and look at Lanoe and Zhang. "The fleet that's coming at us from the wrong direction. If it came through the local wormhole throat, it would be coming out of the sun. Instead, it's headed inward from deep space. As if it didn't use a wormhole at all."

Lanoe frowned. "Which is preposterous. You can't travel faster than light without using a wormhole."

"So how did they get out there?"

Lanoe shrugged. "There are thousands of passages in worm-space, plenty more than have ever been charted. Maybe there's a wormhole throat out there, just outside the system."

Ehta shook her head. Instead of refuting him, though—he was her commanding officer—she turned and looked at Derrow, the engineer. "This technology is nothing like what you would use, right? You were trained to build things."

"I was," Derrow admitted, as if she were being cross-examined in a courtroom.

"You wouldn't build like this. If you were designing a killer drone, you wouldn't use this technology, that's right, isn't it?"

Derrow gave an acquiescing shrug.

Ehta nodded. "I know this is going to sound crazy. But—"

"Oh, do be serious," Maggs said, interrupting.

Ehta tried to stare particle beams at him, but he just shrugged off her look.

"You're going to say that we're fighting aliens," he said, and laughed.

"Maybe they don't communicate because they don't know our language. Maybe they don't even have what we would consider a language. Their technology is different, the way they fly between stars is different—"

"Ensign," Maggs said, in the way only a lieutenant could. "You're downright cracked. Humans have been exploring the galaxy for two hundred years. In all that time, we've never found anything with better conversational skills than an amoeba." He turned and gave Derrow a smile. "A superstitious crowd, fighter pilots," he told the engineer. "They tend to pass around conspiracy theories the way some people pass on a cold."

"It fits all the data we've got," Ehta pointed out.

"Except the biggest data point of all, which is that aliens don't exist," Maggs said. "Are you really going to waste our time with this nonsense?"

"Let her talk," Zhang said.

Ehta nodded her thanks. And then found that most of what she'd planned on saying had fallen right out of her head. Maggs had shaken her confidence in her idea, but she knew there was something there.

Maybe if she tried a different tack. "You've been operating under the premise that this is DaoLink attacking Centrocor in some new, impossible way," she told Lanoe. "But would DaoLink send armed drones against another poly? I know they think they're untouchable, but are they really that stupid?"

"I wouldn't put much past a poly," Lanoe said.

"Maybe," Ehta admitted. She could feel herself deflating. If somebody else would agree with her, anybody—

"I saw those things, out there," Valk said. "I killed a bunch of them."

"And?" Maggs asked.

"Could have been aliens. They didn't act like human ships, I'll say that much."

Ehta could have kissed the giant right then and there. If his helmet wasn't up. And assuming he had lips underneath it.

"For the sake of argument," the elder said, "let us presume M. Ehta is correct."

Maggs sneered, but nobody spoke against the elder.

"How does it change things?" the old woman finished.

Zhang blew a long breath out through her cheeks. "We still have to fight them. Alien or poly."

The elder nodded. "Then perhaps we should focus on that."

"Sure," Lanoe said. He turned and looked at his pilots. "We'll start patrols as soon as we can get the fighters off the ground."

Ehta's blood ran cold. They were supposed to have weeks yet. Days at the very least. Valk had run across an advanced group, a vanguard, but—

"Whatever they are," Lanoe said, "they still want to kill us. We need to stop them."

Thom stepped out of the ground car and looked around, not knowing what he had expected. It certainly wasn't this. Roan had driven him out into the town, through streets lined with low brick houses. They'd finally pulled up in front of what looked like a very large shed made of corrugated metal. A couple of ground trucks stood in a lot to one side, and he could hear heavy machinery rumbling inside.

"Where are we?" he asked.

Roan pulled a plastic crate out of the back of the car and handed it to him. "This is an animal feed factory. About two hundred people work here."

"Okay," he said. "But why are we here?"

"Part of my work as an aspirant is in community health outreach. I'm here to inoculate the workers today."

"Okay," he said again. "But why am I here?"

"You're a goodwill ambassador. You said you didn't know how to do that. Well, I assume part of it is meeting Nirayans and talking to them, right? So here's your chance to meet about two hundred of them."

"Okay," he said, wondering when he would start to understand.

She led him inside the building, into a cavernous space filled with heavy milling machines and old-fashioned looking conveyor belts. Workers in paper coveralls and facial masks poured out ingredients from colorful plastic drums or sorted through the pebbly feed as it came out of the drying beds. Some of them waved at Roan as she passed. She took Thom through to a suite of offices at the back of the factory floor, just a couple of simple rooms with desks and chairs pushed up against the walls. Together they set up a folding table and some chairs, then unpacked the crates she'd brought from the Retreat. They said little as they worked at sterilizing the room, sweeping its corners with ultraviolet lights and filtering the air through a semipermeable membrane. When that was done she took out a bottle and a brush sealed in a plastic envelope. "Hold out your hands," she said.

He did as she asked. She unwrapped the brush, then swirled it around inside the bottle, which looked mostly empty to Thom. "This is a viriphage culture," she said. "It's a bacterium we brew up in our infirmary."

He started to pull his hands away as she daubed at them with the brush. "Hold on—"

She actually let out a little sigh. It was the most emotion she'd displayed since he met her. "It doesn't affect human cells. The bacterium eats specific viruses that cause contagious diseases. Things like influenza and tuberculosis. This will actually make you healthier than you were before."

He nodded and let her finish, coating his hands front and back with just a tiny film of sticky residue. She did her own hands next. "Now whenever we shake hands with somebody, we'll inoculate them at the same time."

"Oh. You still worry about diseases like that here?"

She didn't sigh, but he thought she might have gritted her teeth a little. "Where you're from, most likely there's some incredible high-tech way of protecting people from getting sick. Here we have to use the old ways."

Thom shrugged. He'd never bothered learning anything about medicine. He'd been genetically engineered from the chromosomes up and had never had so much as a sniffle in his life so far. "How often do you have to do this?"

"New strains of viruses come along all the time," she said. "We try to inoculate everybody in Walden Crater at least twice a year. I'm here this week; next week I'll head over to the farmer's market. It's this or deal with an inevitable epidemic."

"I guess that makes sense."

"Yes. Now. Are you ready to meet your public?"

"I...guess so," Thom said.

"Good." She unrolled a minder on the table and tapped out a message. Soon the factory workers started filing in one at a time.

There was a little more to it than just shaking hands, though they made sure they did that as often as possible. Roan's minder contained full medical records for everyone they met, and she asked them if they needed anything else while she was there.

Their first patient, a middle-aged man named Alek, asked about back pain. "It gets pretty bad, leaning over the belt all day," he said.

"There's an exercise routine that should help with that," Roan said, reading off her minder. "I'll send you the details."

He didn't seem thrilled by that—maybe he was expecting some drugs or something—but he nodded.

"How do we handle payment?" Thom asked.

Alek and Roan both stared at him. "Payment?" Roan asked. "For what?"

"For...this," he said. "You just do this for free?"

"Of course we do. This is about protecting all of us. Why should anyone have to pay for something that benefits everybody?" Roan asked. "I'm sorry, Alek. He's not from here. In fact—he's come to Niraya specifically to talk to people like you."

Thom nearly fell out of his chair. But that was right, wasn't it? A goodwill ambassador was supposed to talk to people. Get them on Lanoe's side.

"Ah, yes," he said. "I represent the—the Navy," he said, trying to think in a hurry. Trying to remember what he was allowed to say. He wasn't supposed to mention the invasion fleet, he knew that, but he figured it was okay to talk about things that had already happened. "I'm sure you've heard the news about the drone that landed here and killed those farmers," he said.

"There's a drone killing farmers?" the man asked. "Drones aren't supposed to do that! What are you talking about?"

"It's—it's been destroyed," Thom said. "I'm sorry, I thought you would have heard about this on the news videos."

"I don't bother with that kind of thing," Alek said. He rubbed at his face, then stared down at his hands. He rubbed them together, perhaps feeling the slight stickiness of the viriphage film. "It's just a lot of religious stuff, usually. Oh hellfire. Drones are attacking people, and you're going to start charging us for health care? What's going on?"

It took Roan quite a while to calm the man down. Eventually he left but he didn't look very reassured.

"That could have gone better," Thom said.

Roan didn't meet his eyes. "Maybe so."

"I'm sorry," he said. He couldn't believe what a damned mess he'd become. Ever since he'd—ever since he'd shot his—since he'd run away, nothing had gone right, he'd just made one stupid mistake after another. "I'm—I'm just sorry. I assumed everyone knew about the drone attack, at least, if not the invasion fleet."

"The Retreat has made information about the attack publicly available, but not everyone bothers to keep up with events outside their own neighborhood," Roan said.

"But—how could they not all be talking about this? I mean, they must have broadcast that video you have, the one of the lander attacking the bird farm." Thom had seen the video onboard the tender before they landed—Lanoe had made them all watch it and study the telescopic imagery of the approaching fleet.

"Actually, no," Roan said.

"What?"

"The elders published a considered, text-only report about the attack. As for the video, they held it back. They decided that it might...demoralize Nirayans to see that. It's very graphic."

"Yeah. It is. And people should see it, anyway. They should know what's coming for them."

"Why?" Roan asked. "So they can be terrified of something they can't do anything about?"

"If it were me, I'd rather know what was coming," Thom said. "Can you honestly tell me you'd prefer to be kept in the dark?"

"My opinion isn't important," Roan said.

"It is to me," Thom said. "Come on. What do you really think, Roan? That holding back that video was the right thing to do?"

"I can see both sides," she said, turning her head away from him. He could tell she had her doubts. Still, when she spoke again, it sounded like she was handing him an official line. "We've done what we can to defend Niraya, by bringing Commander Lanoe and the other pilots here."

Thom stared at the side of her head for a long time, trying to think of what to say next. Maybe he was starting to understand why Lanoe thought they needed a goodwill ambassador. Maybe there was actually something of value he could contribute.

"Call in the next patient," he said.

"Thom, please, don't make this difficult."

He kept staring at her, even though she wouldn't look at him.

"Call them in," he said.

A young woman came through the door, though she didn't close it behind her—as if she expected she might have to run away.

"Is it true?" she asked.

"I beg your pardon?" Roan asked.

"I just heard—the Navy is attacking farmers," she said.

<hr />

"It's like it's my birthday three months early," Maggs said, though Ehta couldn't tell if he was being sarcastic or not.

On the concrete of the spaceport the BR.9s lay sitting in a perfect little row, their airfoils nearly touching. Lanoe stood to one side by his FA.2, his arms folded behind his back. The way he stood when he was trying to look like a proper commanding officer.

"Pop 'em open and have a look," he said to the gathered pilots. "We start patrols in an hour. For now just get used to your new crates."

There were more than enough to go around. Valk went immediately to the BR.9 he'd already used against the enemy fleet. One of its airfoils was broken but the jagged edge had started to turn soft and furry. The BR.9 had a self-repair function that would have the airfoil good as new in a few days. "You mind if I stick with this one?" he asked.

"Be my guest," Lanoe told him.

Zhang went next, beaming from ear to ear as she rushed forward to claim her fighter. She lowered her canopy and slipped inside. She fiddled with the displays until they looked like they flowed with gray liquid—the kind of displays her artificial eyes could see. She didn't waste any time getting to the customization screens, moving the cockpit seat forward, adjusting the running lights. Then she found the screen for the fairing lights and she squealed with glee.

Running along either side of the canopy of the BR.9, all the way back to the main thruster package, there were two curved sections of hull armor that weren't pierced by vents or studded with equipment. Normally these twin fairings were a dull gray color, but they were embedded with chromatic filaments. On a command from the cockpit they could be made to flash various colors in varying levels of brightness. The idea was to allow pilots to light them up to indicate they were in distress, or to set them to the colors of their respective squadrons, or even use them to send coded messages back and forth during battle. Some bright pilot many years ago had realized, however, that you could program them to display pretty much any image you wanted. Back during the Establishment Crisis it had become a cliché for pilots to decorate their fighters with tiger stripes or slavering jaws full of teeth. It had become one more thing for Navy pilots to compete over—who had the most creative or shocking or aesthetically pleasing fairing art.

There was no real question what Zhang would choose. She tapped away at the controls and soon red tentacles wove and twisted across her fairings, just like the arms of the red octopus that decorated her suit. Ehta remembered that Zhang had always changed her fairing imagery every few years but once she had a motif she stuck with it.

"The irony, of course," Maggs said, leaning over to whisper in Ehta's ear, "is delicious, a blind woman getting so excited about fairing art she'll never see."

Ehta brushed him away like a fly. "Everybody else will see it; that's the point."

"Hmm." Maggs went next, picking the closest BR.9 to him. He climbed into the cockpit and went immediately for the customization panels. His fairings rippled and furled like flags snapping in a strong wind, showing first the triple-headed eagle of the Navy, then the green and black standard of the Admiralty, and finally a flag showing a red shield with crossed lightning bolts. She figured that last one must be his only family crest—she knew his father had been some kind of top brass, and the Navy let people like that have all the trappings of ancient aristocracy.

Valk shook his head—a gesture that included his shoulders, since nobody could see his head through his polarized helmet. He turned toward Lanoe. "What art are you going to fly, boss?"

"My FA.2 doesn't have customizable fairings," Lanoe explained. He didn't seem to feel particularly left out. "I go to war with a blank shield. But you go ahead, pick something."

Valk didn't even climb into his cockpit, just leaned over and started tapping away at the panels. His fairings lit up a shade of blue Ehta recognized at once. A pattern of black stars, galaxies, and nebulae drifted across the blue field.

"Oh, I say, that's a bit over the line," Maggs insisted, still nestled inside his fighter's cockpit with the canopy down.

Valk had chosen the campaign colors of the Establishmentarians. Well, he had fought for them. Though Ehta could imagine less incendiary designs he might have picked. She, Zhang, and Lanoe had all fought against the Establishment—and lost a lot of friends to their attacks.

"Commander," Maggs said, "are you going to let him get away with this?" Without waiting for an answer, he turned to face Valk. "You know you lost that war, don't you?"

"You wanted the Blue Devil," Valk said, though it was hard to see who he was addressing. "You got him."

"Sure," Lanoe said. "Maggs, I don't know if you've figured this out yet, but this isn't an official Navy mission. Valk's colors can stand."

Maggs muttered something, but not loud enough that Ehta could hear it.

It didn't help that her ears were ringing. Or that her heart kept skipping beats. She knew what was coming next.

"Ensign," Lanoe said, "I believe it's your turn."

She nodded without looking at him. She couldn't stand to look at him, just then.

"What design are you going to use?" Zhang called. "Remember that one you had at Eblis? That fractal thing that if you looked at it hard enough you realized it was made of grinning skulls?"

Oh, she remembered. Ehta had no trouble remembering things. Forgetting was the hard part.

She forced herself to walk past Maggs to the next fighter in the row. Its canopy was polarized and it stared at her like the eye of some cyclopean insect. Her mouth was suddenly full of saliva. She choked it down, then reached over and tapped the recessed key. The canopy melted and flowed down into vents along its rim. Revealed inside was the cockpit, with its complicated seat and its dead displays.

"Is there a problem with that one?" Lanoe asked. He was standing right behind her. She hadn't seen him come up, and she jumped a little.

"No, I checked them all out myself. They're all good," she said. She grabbed a handhold on the edge of the cockpit and tried to lift her foot up to step inside.

Her foot might as well have been glued to the concrete. It wouldn't move.

She had been putting this off ever since Lanoe contacted her, back on the Hexus. She'd gotten this far mostly through denial. She'd known perfectly well that eventually she was going to have to do this, but always it had seemed like that was something far off in some dreadful future. Now the day had come.

She tried lifting her other foot. It came up, but not far enough.

"Ensign?" Lanoe asked. Not unkindly.

She thought about turning around, facing him and telling him what was wrong. Telling him everything. But she couldn't do that. She owed him. She had to—

She closed her eyes. Her head rang like a bell. She couldn't open her eyes. She felt something hard smack against the side of her head and she realized she must have collapsed.

"Get a medkit!" she heard Zhang say.

"Watch out!" Maggs shouted. "I think she's going to—"

Ehta's stomach heaved. She didn't know if she threw up or not. She finally managed to open her eyes and saw boots all around her. She was lying flat on the ground. They were all looking at her.

Her whole body shook as she sat up on the concrete. Zhang came toward her with a spray hypo, but Ehta just shook her head. She looked over at Lanoe.

She could see in his eyes that he knew. He knew.

She pulled her knees toward her and wrapped her arms around them. Tried to breathe. Just tried to stop shaking.

Chapter Thirteen

I didn't get busted down to the marines. I volunteered."

Zhang leaned forward, her hands reaching for Ehta's. Ehta refused the consolation.

They were sitting with the elder in the old woman's office. Ehta had been unable to talk out at the spaceport, barely able to breathe. Zhang had brought her here because she thought maybe the elder could help. She was supposed to be some kind of counselor or something, at least as Zhang understood it.

The elder had barely spoken since they arrived, however. She just sat behind her desk, her hands palm down on top of it. Occasionally she nodded in sympathy, but that was it. It looked like it was up to Zhang to make sense of what had happened.

She shook her head. "I don't understand. The marines? But that's so *dangerous*. Marines get killed all the time. I'd think if you were afraid to fly, then—"

Ehta's eyes blazed with anger. "I'm no coward!" she said. "I just can't do it anymore. I can't get back in a cockpit." The anger dissolved abruptly and she rubbed at her eyes with her fingers. "I'm so sorry, Zhang. I'm so sorry."

The elder took a box of tissues out of her desk, but Ehta ignored it.

"Tell us what happened," Zhang said. "How this began."

"You think that'll help?"

"I need to understand."

Ehta nodded, but she wasn't looking at either of them. "Okay," she said. "Okay."

She took a breath. Blew it back out. Zhang sat back in her chair, ready to listen.

"It started a couple of years ago. I couldn't sleep. I would lie down and close my eyes and I would be back in my cockpit. Running through checklists, making sure everything was working. It was fine, just distracting. I was flying two, sometimes three patrols a day back then, and I thought it was just like when you look at the sun and afterward you see spots. Just, like, a residue of the day. It didn't stop, though. It was every night. When you don't sleep for a long time, it gets to you. You get forgetful. You drop things, like, little things, you pick them up and they just slip out of your hands. It's annoying. But you keep going. You have to keep going, so you just... You don't stop.

"At night, when I really, really wanted to just sleep, I was still going through those checklists. Except then red lights kept coming up." She glanced briefly at the elder. "That means something's wrong. Something's broken, or you're out of fuel or ammo, or you can't get a comms signal... whatever. Red lights are bad. And there were more of them every night.

"Sometimes, I would play out one of my patrols in my head. Go through every part of it, thinking through what I did right, what I did wrong. A lot of the time, I just didn't know which was which. And always there were more red lights, and I got more and more tired... I was getting nervy, and I knew it, but I had to hold on. Always there were more patrols. They bumped us up to four a day at one point. I had to eat in my cockpit because there was no time for it back at base. The only time I wasn't in my fighter was when I was supposed to sleep.

"Then one day I went to the hangar to start a patrol and it just came to me, like this amazing idea. It's funny—at the time, I thought I was the first one to think of it. If I was sick, I didn't have to fly. So I made myself throw up. They took me away to the infirmary and the doctor there barely even looked at me. He tested my vitals and gave me a pill. I threw it away—I knew I didn't need it.

"What I'd needed, what I'd gotten, was time. A little time when I wasn't on patrol. Just skipping that one mission, it felt like enough. I was mostly okay for the rest of that day. I flew the rest of my patrols and it was fine. And that night there was one light on the board in my head that wasn't red. Just one. But by then, that was a victory. Something had *worked*.

"The problem was, the brass knew about malingerers. They knew, the second time, the third time I made myself throw up, they knew I was faking it. They let me get away with it for a week, until one day I skipped two patrols. That was half my workload, and that was too much."

She looked across the desk at the elder. Zhang could see by the way Ehta scrunched up her face, her mouth twisted over to one side, that she didn't think the elder could understand. Well, maybe that was true. If you weren't a pilot, if you'd never flown a bad patrol, and then another one, and another...

"Pilots get nervy. They call it 'getting the wind up,' which is an expression I will never understand. There was no wind in my cockpit. I didn't feel crazy. I didn't feel sick, just so very tired.

"They told me I *was* sick, though. Sick in the head. But lucky me! There was a treatment for what I had. They would go into my head and find whatever it was that had gone wrong, the wires that got crossed or whatever. The specific neurons that were keeping me from sleeping. The problem, they told me, was that I was making the wrong connections in there—attaching memories of flying to the wrong kind of emotions. The connections are carried on your dendrites, the, like, the branches that spread out from one neuron to another. So they would use a tiny little laser to burn off the bad little dendrites but leave the body of the neurons intact. I wouldn't miss a few diseased dendrites, would I? Of course not.

"I actually, you know, for one second I was actually excited. Just so happy. They could fix me like a broken airfoil. Make me okay again. Let me sleep.

"Then I met another pilot, a guy who'd had this procedure. He was all right, sure. You could have a conversation with him, even joke around. He flirted with me and we talked about old battles. Just like any other pilot. The whole time, though, I could see right through his eyes. Like they were made of glass.

"I could, you know, I could see right inside his head, maybe because he and I had the same damage. I don't know. But I could look inside his head and there was nothing in there. Nothing but engine and weapons panels, and PBW tracers bouncing back and forth. I looked up his flight record. He'd gotten more kills since his procedure than he'd had before it, lots more. I looked at recordings of his fights and I could tell. That wasn't a man in that cockpit. It was—it was something they'd made, something they'd put together in an operating room. It could fight, it could fly. But it wasn't him anymore. All that other stuff, the flirting and joking and everything—he was doing that on autopilot. Inside his head he was still flying, even when he was talking to me. He was *always* flying.

"They hadn't fixed him at all. He was even more broken than I was. They just made him stop caring about how broken he was."

Zhang tried not to shiver. She'd met pilots who'd had that procedure. She'd fought with them. They fought hard, but never for very long. They started taking bad risks, because they just didn't care— they'd lost their fear. And so they died, because they couldn't get scared enough to run away when everything went wrong.

"The treatment wasn't voluntary," Ehta said. "I needed to fly, according to the brass, so I was going to get treated whether I wanted to or not. But I couldn't do it. I just couldn't.

"So instead, I asked for a transfer. I volunteered for the marines."

Zhang pursed her lips. "Who was commanding the Ninety-Fourth at that point? Rannegan?"

"No, he died at Asmodeus. It was Genet."

Zhang nodded. "I knew her. Trained her, in fact. Decent woman. I imagine she wasn't pleased when you transferred."

"She tried to stop me. But there's a regulation about that. They need marines, more of them all the time. If you volunteer, nobody can stop you—not your parents, not your planetary governor. Your commander doesn't stand a chance."

The elder leaned forward. "When M. Lanoe asked you to volunteer for the current mission," she said, "you said yes before you'd heard the details. Did you know he wanted you to fly again?"

"There's only one kind of mission Lanoe does. I knew," Ehta replied.

The elder nodded. "You could have said no. You could have told him all of this, back then."

"If you're going to say I've let down the squad, or I've let down your damned planet, save your breath, lady," Ehta said, angry again. She was cycling through moods very rapidly—Zhang didn't imagine that was a good sign.

"I simply wish to know," the elder went on, "why you accepted a mission you knew you couldn't perform."

"I didn't know if I could do it or not," Ehta replied. "It's been a couple of years. In the marines, I never had trouble sleeping. I thought maybe it would work again. That I'd gotten over it. I was lying to myself, of course. But I owe Lanoe so much. I owe him this huge debt, so I guess—I wanted to believe it."

She covered her face in her hands.

The elder looked over at Zhang. "Perhaps," she said, "we should give M. Ehta some time to compose herself."

Zhang nodded and got up from her chair. The elder took her out into the hall and closed the door. "I assume you've seen this before," she said.

"It happens," Zhang said. "More often than the Navy likes to admit. What we do—the missions we fly—human brains didn't evolve for that kind of work. There's so much to keep track of, so many things going on at once, and if you make one little mistake you're dead. We all feel it—what happened to her, we all go through that." She shook her head. "Everybody handles it differently, but—her story doesn't surprise me."

"I was asked to speak with M. Ehta and to offer my opinion on her mental state," the elder said. "I'm not a psychologist. I counsel to the faithful, but mostly that means helping aspirants find their path, or at most helping two miners keep their marriage together. I have no formal training in the treatment of stress trauma. I don't think I need to be an expert, though, to make a prognosis here."

Zhang nodded, her face very tight and controlled.

"That poor woman is never going to fly again," the elder said.

Dozens of compartments had been cunningly constructed inside the walls of the tender, places to stash extra ammunition and fuel, food, and consumables, not to mention actual luggage. It took Maggs the better part of an hour to find what he sought—a toolkit that contained a rotary cutter. He shoved the rest of the equipment back in the kit as best he could, then headed back out into the light and what passed in this desolate place as air. Valk and Lanoe were out there deep in conversation, no doubt discussing the fate of young Ensign Ehta. He ignored them and leaned against the side of his fighter. The rotary cutter spun up with a satisfying whine as he engaged its motor, its diamond carbide cutting wheel sparkling as it spun faster and faster.

Just the thing for trimming his fingernails. He was almost finished when Zhang returned, sans ensign.

"Where is she?" Lanoe demanded, his voice lowering into a growl.

"She's in the elder's office. You're not going anywhere near her," Zhang told him.

"Is that right?"

She put a hand on Lanoe's chest, just above his cryptab. *A tad familiar with her commanding officer,* Maggs thought, in his father's disapproving voice.

One hears things, he replied, under, as it were, his mental breath.

"She's got a bad case of nerves. She thought she had it under control, but she was wrong. How many times have you heard that story?" Zhang asked.

Lanoe turned his face away in disgust.

"Don't," she said. "Don't even start. That woman worships you, you know that? She only made it this far because she didn't want to disappoint you. The very last thing she needs is a lecture."

"Sure. And the last thing I need," Lanoe said, looming over the little slip of a blind girl like some ogre in a reality play, "is a twenty percent reduction in my force. You understand what this means, don't you? We had five pilots to face an entire fleet. Now we have four."

"Then we'll just have to make do!" Zhang said.

Lanoe stared down at her with eyes not entirely dissimilar to the cutting wheel in sharpness and steely glint.

Zhang's eyes were of course made of metal, and it was difficult to read their expression. But Maggs could see from the set of her shoulders she wasn't about to back down. *Well, good for her,* he thought, then patted himself on the back—mentally, of course, as such a thing would be dangerous while holding a cutting tool—for his charitable estimation. *Anyone who can stand up to that bully deserves a bit of respect,* he decided.

It took positively ages, but eventually Lanoe gave in. "Fine," he said. "She can run ground control. Right now you and I are heading out on patrol."

"Us?" Zhang asked, a trifle gobsmacked.

"Valk just came back from a deep picket; he's earned a little rest," Lanoe pointed out.

The giant pilot stood up straight, having heard his name. "Actually, I'd be happy to—"

"He's going to rest, because I ordered him to," Lanoe said, never looking away from Zhang's metal eyes. "As for him," he said, pointing one gloved finger right at Maggs, "he's got work to do planetside."

"Do I?" Maggs asked, quite surprised.

"I saw the way you and that engineer were together," Lanoe said. "I'd call that a positive rapport. I want you to get her on our side. If we're out a pilot, we need to make up the shortfall somehow. Get the engineer to agree to build some ground-based weapons for us. Understood?"

"Oh, aye, aye, Commander," Maggs said.

Lanoe gave him a curt nod. Then he tapped the key at his throat that raised his helmet. "Besides," he said to Zhang, "you and I are supposed to have a talk. Well, we've got hours of flying time to log, so this should give us a chance."

He stormed over to his FA.2 and strapped himself in. Within seconds he had lifted off the ground and was receding into the upper atmosphere.

Zhang stood where she was for a moment longer, her head bowed, but her shoulders still high. Then she let them fall. Nothing more, but on a body like that such gestures spoke volumes. She went to her BR.9 and readied it for takeoff.

"Maggs," she called, before she left. "Nobody's going to begrudge you a little fun. But don't do anything that's going to come back and bite us later."

How deeply insulting, Maggs thought to himself.

What he said was, "I shall be the soul of propriety."

Zhang didn't bother to comment. Before he could say anything else she was up, up, and away.

Once they were gone he turned to see if Valk had any comments—people so often did, nosy bastards. But the giant had climbed inside his own cockpit. "I'll rest better in orbit," he said. "If anybody asks where I am—"

"They can simply do a search for your cryptab," Maggs said. "I'll be busy with other matters."

Valk didn't even bother to perform that gruesome bow he used in place of a nod. As quick as the others had gone, he took off for space.

Which left Maggs the only fighter pilot *mens sana* on the planet.

That had possibilities.

He considered—and not briefly—jumping in his fighter and just lighting out for the wormhole throat. He could be away before anyone noticed, away from this rotten planet and this suicidal mission.

He told himself that he would not do so, because he was a man of honor and he'd been given orders to carry out. The real reason—which his father's voice was perfectly happy to remind him of—was that he knew Lanoe would just come haring after him to bring him back.

Anyway. Carrying out his orders didn't need to be such an onerous task. It had its own compensations, in fact.

He took a minder from his pocket and unrolled it across the fairing of his BR.9. The local directory was quaintly small and it didn't take long to find Mining Administrator Derrow's address. He pinged her and she answered almost immediately. On the screen he saw a view of her from just below chin level, which allowed him unfettered visual access to the interiors of her nostrils. He gave himself credit for not letting his smile falter one bit.

"Something I can help you with, Lieutenant?" she asked, once they'd exchanged the usual pleasantries.

"I certainly hope so," he told her. "All my fellow pilots are away at the moment. It's just me down at the spaceport, which means I'm in terrible danger."

"Oh?" Her eyes widened and he could tell he had her attention.

"Yes," he said. "The danger of eating dinner alone."

━━━✦━━━

Lanoe didn't say a word for the first hour of their patrol.

He'd burned hard to get away from Niraya, and Zhang had to strain her engines just to catch up. Once they'd matched acceleration she took up a station-keeping formation with him, never getting closer than ten kilometers to his FA.2. She could just make him out as a fast-moving dot on her left.

Out there in the void, there wasn't much else for her to look at, though. Her cybernetic eyes couldn't make out the stars. Far away as they were, they were just points of light in a backdrop of darkness—and her borrowed brain didn't really understand either of those concepts. To her space wasn't black. It just wasn't there.

Their course took them on a long, curving path out toward the distant enemy fleet, though she knew Lanoe would turn back long before they got that far. He was worried that they might see more incursions like the one Valk had found—more landers, more interceptors. So far the network of microdrones had found nothing, but years of war had taught both Lanoe and Zhang not to put all their faith in imagery and intelligence.

Lanoe kept his engine burning long after they'd left Niraya well behind. The two of them passed through the belt of dust Valk had told them about. Zhang saw nothing, really—the rocks that made up the belt were too small and too far apart for that. One grain of dust did smack into her vector field in a sudden burst of heat but it happened so fast she didn't even bother responding to the warning on her console.

It was enough to get Lanoe talking. "You okay?" he called.

"Just a bug on my windshield," she said.

"Sure. How does it feel, being out here?"

"Flying a patrol, you mean? Lanoe, I never stopped. I've trained more cadets than you ever had in your squadron. Part of that was just this kind of work. War games, anyway. This feels fine. It feels like I'm right where I belong."

"In that—your new body, I mean."

"I'm *fine*," she said. "I should be asking you all this. You're the one who retired."

She knew it was the wrong thing to say as soon as it was out of her mouth, but once you sent a message by comms laser, you couldn't exactly call it back. When he didn't respond for a full minute, she pinged him just to make sure he hadn't cut off their signal link.

"You said we were going to talk. I get that it's a chore for you," she told him. "It's not like we have much else to do right now, though."

"Sure," he said.

She waited for him to say more. A fool's errand, of course. He was going to make her start. "There's a lot of ground to cover. It's been a bunch of years."

"Yeah."

"But I'm guessing the big problem is my new body. You aren't used to me looking like this. I get it. The last time you saw me,

I didn't have any legs. But it's still me in here. My memories, my training, my feelings—none of that has changed."

"I get that."

"Do you?" she asked. She touched her stick and banked over a little until she was closing the distance between them. "The way you look at me—okay. This body is young. It's very young. But I didn't choose it. I was on a list and this was the first body that came available."

"How does that even work? This girl, the one with no optic nerves. She's in your old body now, right? The one I remember. Is she going to live like that for the rest of her life?"

"It's a temporary swap," Zhang told him. "Just until one of us decides we want to switch back. I talk to her occasionally and she tells me there are still plenty of things she wants to see. She loves having eyes for the first time. Just like I love having legs again. So far we're both happy with how it worked out."

"What if you die out here?" he asked.

"That's a risk you accept when you go on the list."

She could imagine him shaking his head. Trying to grapple with it all.

Maybe she needed to give him some space.

"If you can't get past this, then maybe somebody else needs to be your second in command," she said.

"Come on—"

"Not that there's a lot to choose from. Maggs is definitely not right for the job. You and Valk seem to get along, though."

"He's not a people person," Lanoe pointed out.

"I've noticed that."

"And," he said, as if he were admitting something deeply disagreeable, "you're still a pretty good wingman. Back in the elder's office, when I started talking to her like a problem cadet—you reeled me back in. Just like you used to."

"Somebody had to," she suggested. "Okay, I'll keep the job, since you asked so nicely. But we were more than just squaddies, before. We can't just ignore that."

A collision detection warning sounded inside her cockpit. She ignored it—but Lanoe must have heard it as well.

"You're slipping left," he told her. "You need to correct your course."

"No, I don't." She tapped the throttle and then hit her maneuvering jets to swing herself around on her long axis. When it was done she was only a few meters from Lanoe's fighter. Flying upside down, from his perspective, and just above him. She drifted a tiny bit forward until their canopies were almost touching, and she could look straight up and into his cockpit.

She saw him through four layers of glass—two canopies, two helmets. Her lidar eyes were almost up to the task. The image of him she received was washed out, a little indistinct. He looked like a ghost down there. Maybe like what a memory would look like if you put it under a microscope.

But then he looked up at her and their eyes met.

"I'm still the woman you proposed to," she said.

"Which means you're still the woman who said no," he answered.

><

The sun hadn't moved a millimeter in the damned sky.

Maggs kept glancing up at it, daring it to move while he wasn't looking. Still it hung there more or less exactly just about overhead.

He pulled up a display on his wrist and pinged the local time server. "Bloody bones," he said. The sun wasn't going to set for another three weeks. The night would be twice that long.

He made a mental note not to be here when it fell.

"Did you say something?" Derrow asked, from the kitchen.

He let the curtains fall back over the window—now he knew why they were so heavy—and stepped through the archway that separated the two halves of her apartment. She was stirring a pot of noodles, glancing back at him over her shoulder.

Getting a home-cooked meal out of her had been a bit of a coup. There were restaurants on Niraya, of course, though none that

Maggs would have eaten in on a bet. He'd made a big show of lay-ing his cards on the table, telling her that he was under orders from his CO to talk business tonight, that they ought to head some-where with a bit of privacy. She'd seen right through his tale, of course—just as he'd meant her to. But here they were.

"How do you know when it's time to go to bed?" he asked.

She looked the tiniest bit shocked. "Is that a riddle?"

He pointed upward, through the roof. In the general direction of the sun.

He was pleased to find it didn't take her long to get it. "Oh, you mean with how long the days are? We've developed a simple but efficient system for ordering our daily schedules. A real triumph of local engineering."

"Oh?"

She gave him a sly smile. Then she tapped her kitchen coun-ter, calling up a display there that showed local time. "It's called a clock," she said.

He laughed and leaned up against the wall. It had been a pleas-ant surprise to find that Derrow thought this planet nearly as unin-spiring as he did himself. She had a rather nice laugh, too.

"There's beer in the fridge," she told him. "Imported, I promise."

"That must be expensive," he said. He bent over the refrigerator and found the promised bottles, and behind them—*aha*—a glass jug full of vodka. At least, someone had written the word VODKA on the bottle in black grease pencil. "Hate to waste the good stuff. How about we stick to this?" He held the jug up at an angle and raised an eyebrow at her.

"You sure?" she asked. "That's local. We have a still out at the refinery we made out of surplus equipment. Don't tell Centrocor."

He explored her cupboards until he'd found two pony glasses. He gave them each a generous splash, then handed her a glass. Clinking his against hers, he said, "Here's to the poly who watches over and protects us all."

She looked down at her glass. "Except when they don't."

"Precisely," he said, and took a sip.

Bracing was one word that came to mind. *Industrial effluent* was another. It made his eyes water a bit but he nodded appreciatively and set his glass down.

Derrow knocked hers back with barely a grimace, then held it out for another go. He laughed again and poured, though he said, "Don't get too far ahead of me. We have plenty of actual work to discuss."

And so they did, over bowls of noodles. The food was atrocious but she barely glanced at her bowl as she shoved the carbohydrates into her mouth. Her eyes were on a minder she had unrolled across the table. The display there showed a slowly rotating schematic of a basic rail gun. He had downloaded it from the Naval archives. A legend at the bottom of the display insisted the plans were only to be looked at by an officer of the Neddies, the Naval Engineering Division, but the encryption on the archive had been laughably easy to defeat.

He watched her as she studied the display. Her black hair had been cut just below her ears, which exposed her long, tanned neck. Her eyes were clear and rather bright, and if her chin was a little weak he didn't suppose it was a deal breaker.

She caught him looking and speared him with her gaze. Then she raised one eyebrow.

He made a point of looking decorously away.

"The principle's nothing special," she said, poking at the schematic to make it turn faster. "Just a mass driver with a ramped-up output." She frowned. "There's some fiddly stuff over here you need to keep the rails from melting every time you fire. But yeah, any half-competent engineer could put one of these together."

"We need a bit more than just one," he said.

"Lucky for you, I'm more than half-competent," she said, and smiled at him.

It was one of those kind of smiles. Business wasn't quite done, though. "How many do you think you could put together in the next week?"

He could see in her eyes that she thought that was a ridiculously short amount of time to build a gun capable of shooting spaceships out of orbit, but she didn't say so. Instead she bit her lip and inhaled slowly, taking in extra air to cool her overclocked brains, perhaps. "I'll have to work up some schedules, make sure we have the right materials, or, because we won't, find materials that can be substituted for what's listed here. I'll need to get my teams sorted out, find the best people from each of my workgroups... It's not the kind of project where I can just give you an answer tonight."

"Oh," he said, "I can wait until morning."

Her mouth pursed as if she was trying to hold back a gasp. "I'll work up a proposal, a budget, start on a schedule," she said, never quite looking directly at him. "I don't know where to send it, though. Where are you and your friends staying?"

She could, of course, have sent the information directly to his electronic address. No need to have it couriered over. "We haven't worked that out yet. I suppose we can always bunk in our tender, if we have to. The accommodations are a bit... rough."

"Maybe I can help with that, too, sort out a place for you to billet."

He lifted one shoulder in a desultory shrug. "Shouldn't be too hard. I'm the only one who needs to find a place to sleep tonight. You're very kind, M. Derrow."

"You need to start calling me Proserpina," she said.

"Auster," he replied, holding out his hand.

She took it in both of hers. Without releasing it, she got up and moved around the table until she was standing over him. He tilted his head back to meet her gaze and she leaned closer and then her lips brushed his, quite tentatively. When he didn't try to escape she went for a much more elaborate kiss.

Then she pulled back and returned to her seat. "I just wanted to get that out of the way," she told him. "I've been waiting for it this whole time and it was distracting me, thinking so much about it."

"Forthright," he said. "Commendable." He reached for the vodka.

"Now," she said, "let's get back to this." She unrolled the minder again and started poking at the schematic, pulling the virtual gun there to pieces to see how they fit together.

———✦———

Zhang remembered when Lanoe first asked her to marry him.

They'd been in a bunk on a destroyer, a coffin-sized and -shaped room just big enough for one person to lie down in, with a display at one end and a fan at the other and not much else. Neither of them had cared that it was cramped.

She remembered the beads of sweat that floated around them, gently gravitating toward the fan. She had stretched out as far as she could and when she was drifting off to sleep, her face buried in his chest, he had said it. Very quietly.

Marry me.

She had smiled against him, wanting to laugh but lacking the energy. He was making a little joke, she thought.

The second time they'd been standing on a ridge on a moon. She forgot what planet it circled but it was a gas giant banded with white and green, with storms like staring eyes that pulled themselves apart as you watched. It filled half the sky.

The ground below them, ammonia ice as hard as steel, was littered with the wrecks of a dozen fighters. They'd lost half the squad that day but they'd won. They'd won the battle.

You and me, he'd said. We quit this, go find a planet someplace warm and I don't know. Start a farm. Get married and have babies.

All she remembered thinking that day was that they'd won. That the battle was over and the Establishmentarians were beaten, shoved back from another star system, and the two of them— they'd made that happen. Why would they ever want to stop flying? Why would they ever stop fighting, when it was so glorious?

After that it was a joke between them. *Marry me.* He'd said it when she flew rings around some poor half-trained idiot, when she fought her way through a bad line of carrier scouts. *Marry me.* When she figured out how to scam the computers so they got double rations of beer. *Marry me.*

Maybe those times didn't count.

The last time did.

She'd been so high on painkillers she could barely speak. She knew there was something wrong, really, badly wrong but all she could see was the pattern of threads in her white sheets, the weave of the bandages on her arms. The bubbles in the tubes that stuck out of her belly below her navel.

Marry me now. While we're still alive. Please, Zhang.

She had looked at him, stared at him, until he came into focus. Until she understood what he was saying.

Until she remembered what had happened.

"I don't have a—" she'd wheezed. "There's nothing down there," and she'd cried, and he'd held her hand tight, even though it was broken. "I can't—" She didn't have the breath to say it. What would marriage even mean? She'd forced herself to think it through. No sex. No babies. Not with what was left of her.

Just marry me. I'll take care of you.

"No," she'd said. But he kept asking.

Until she screamed at him and threw things and swore bloody oaths that if he ever asked her again, if he mocked her like that again—

She opened her eyes. Her new, cybernetic eyes. Let go of the memories. Looked up at him, at the shadows and lines, the planes that made up his face.

"Is that why you came?" he asked. "To tell me why you said no?"

Or maybe to say yes this time. He didn't say that. He wasn't proposing now.

That was okay. Her answer wouldn't have changed. "Maybe," she said. "I wanted to see you again; that was the only real thought I had." She smiled up at him. "Irascible old bastard that you are, I missed you. But okay. I'll tell you why I said no."

He was silent, his eyes locked on hers. His face might have been computer generated for all the emotion it showed.

"I said no because it wasn't me you wanted. You just wanted out."

He growled at her. "You don't know what I was thinking."

"When you retired, there was some talk. Actually, a lot of talk. You were a celebrity back then, in Naval circles. There were so many rumors. I was still in the hospital at the time, and even I heard them. You'd lost your nerve. You'd punched an admiral in the nose because he gave you orders you didn't like. You were a secret Establishmentarian."

"Hogwash," Lanoe said.

"I know. I know it was all nonsense. You never lost your nerve. But you lost something. You didn't want to fight anymore."

"I get bored easily," he said.

"Don't lie to me," she told him. "Keep your secrets if you want, but don't kid me along, Lanoe. Not after what we used to be."

He actually did what she asked, for once.

He kept his mouth shut.

"I knew, from the very first time you asked for my hand, what it was you were looking for. An excuse to get out of the Navy. You wanted me to give you that excuse, and I wouldn't."

"I'm still technically on the reserve list," he said. "And look where I am now. In a fighter, looking for somebody to shoot."

"Sure," she said. His favorite word. "You want to tell me why?"

"Why what?"

"Why," she said, "*you're* here. Fighting somebody else's war for them."

He sighed. Looked away from her, his eyes tracking across his panels. Maybe he hoped that a wing of enemy interceptors would suddenly appear and save him from having to have this conversation.

"Maggs said something to me once," he told her. "He said he had debts. The kind you have to pay back. I've got debts, too."

"What kind?"

"The kind you never can pay back. I killed a lot of people, Zhang. I killed so many people in all those wars. Pilots, marines, people who were just on the wrong damned cruiser when I happened to have a disruptor left. So many who never even saw me, because I killed them before they knew I was there."

"You're here to make up for that?"

"No. Like I said, you can't pay off that debt. For a long time I thought I was just damned. Irredeemable. Still kind of think so, but I know that doesn't let me off the hook. I see people in trouble, I have to help them. That's why I went chasing after Thom. It's why I helped the Nirayans get their money back when Maggs robbed them. I can save a hundred thousand people here, which is a lot more than I ever killed. It still won't make things right. But it's something."

"Hellfire," she said. "Lanoe—I'm so sorry you feel that way. You—"

"That's it. That's all I'm going to say. The last thing I need right now is to spend this entire patrol talking about our feelings."

She saw his hand move over his control stick. The FA.2 veered away from her, off into the nothingness. It would have been easy enough to follow, to pull back into formation with him, but she didn't.

She knew him. Knew him well enough to understand when he needed to be left alone.

She knew him well enough to know when he was lying—not to her, this time, but to himself.

<hr />

Maggs woke to a flash of delightful skin as Derrow—*Proserpina, please,* he thought, *we've been properly introduced now*—clambered over him, her thigh brushing his cheek and then her foot in his face. She laughed as she stumbled off the bed and hopped over to a chair on the far side of the room. "Sorry about that," she said, though she didn't look one bit sorry. Her tangled hair bunched up on one side of her face and her makeup was deliriously smeared.

Enticingly so, actually. He lunged across the sheets, grabbing for her hip, intending to pull her back down with him, but she danced away. She pulled on a *yukata* that hid absolutely nothing and sat back down in the chair.

"I've been thinking," she said.

"I'm deep in thought myself just now," he said, leering at her.

His vanity did not suffer overmuch. Her eyes ran up and down his long leg where the sheet didn't cover it, and he knew she was very close to coming back to bed. She grabbed a minder, though, and unrolled it across her thighs, which was a damned shame.

Clearly she was one of those people who did their best work first thing in the morning. And by best work, it was not to be assumed that he meant—

"If we clad the upper part of those rails in phenolic plastic," she said, "that would help with the heat profile. Though it won't be enough."

The guns. The bloody damned guns. He reached for the bedside table and called up a display. The bloody damned guns at seven o'clock in the morning.

"Let me see," he said, climbing out of the bed. His leg was still giving him trouble—when he wore his heavy suit he barely noticed it, but it would take time for it to properly heal. He hadn't had any painkillers since the night before, either, though there was probably enough rough vodka in his system to compensate.

Still, he was limping by the time he reached her.

"Oh, you poor, brave man. Sit down," she said, patting the floor between her feet. He nestled in and she ran a hand through his hair while he found a way to get comfortable. He reached up a hand behind him to touch her but she batted it away.

"The power input is tricky, especially with our grid running at seventy-five percent capacity," she said. Engineers, he thought. He'd met enough of them in his life to know the type. Give them a problem, a puzzle, and they would never be happy until they'd solved it. And then once it was done they weren't happy until they had another problem to sort out.

It looked like sex was going to have to wait. Maggs began to think about breakfast, instead.

"Plus, I have no idea what we'd use for projectiles. Niraya burned through its radioisotopes a long time ago, so there's no source for the depleted uranium to make these slugs. The hardest part, though, is going to be convincing people we need to do this."

That struck an odd note for Maggs. "Your planet's being

invaded. The threat of imminent demise won't be enough to moti-vate them?"

She clucked her tongue. "It's not that simple. I know a little about what's going on—just a little. I've seen the video of the killer drone. But the elders won't release it to the general public. They say it would be bad for morale."

"It is hard to watch," Maggs said.

Derrow looked right at him. "It's the only evidence we have, though, that this is even happening. For your average Nirayan, all they know is the power grid's gone wonky. There weren't any lights flashing in the sky. The drone was destroyed before any of us actu-ally got to see it. People are scared, but they don't know why. They know something's going on but they have no idea what."

"I can assure you, the enemy fleet is real. The threat is real."

"But we don't know anything about it."

"Sadly, we pilots are sharing the same boat, with scant more oars," Maggs said. "We're still a bit mystified as to what we're fighting, ourselves." He smiled to remember the conference of the severed claw. "Remember when Ehta thought it might be—ha—aliens? That's the best theory we've had so far."

She did not smile or laugh. "You don't think...?"

"No, M. Derrow. I do not believe we are fighting *aliens*."

She let out a long sigh. Clearly she was relieved to hear him say it.

Which got him thinking. Maybe there was something here, an angle. He doubted very much she believed in aliens—she was far too levelheaded for that. But perhaps if he planted just the right seed...

Too devious for your own good, his father reproved him, in his head.

Devious, he thought, was another name for clever.

"Mind you," he said, picking his words carefully, "if it *were* aliens—" He laughed at the thought. Positively scoffed at it. Best not to lay that on too thick, though. "I mean, if it were, we'd be right out of luck, wouldn't we? That's an unknown quantity pretty much by definition. We're trained to fight other humans, not tentacled monstrosities from beyond. We wouldn't even know how to fight something like that."

"Hmm," she said. She was silent long enough that he began to wonder if he'd pushed too far. He turned his head around as far as he could to look up at her face and caught her brooding. Once she realized he was looking at her, of course, she shook it off.

"But I can assure you, I have one hundred percent confidence, the enemies we're fighting are as human as you and me."

"Fair enough. Now. As for your guns—I'm looking at these power spikes on this graph here," she said, showing him something on the minder he didn't even try to recognize. "That's a magnitude greater than an iron projectile ought to be able to withstand. We need to think about high-density polymers instead, something so rigid it'll take that kind of acceleration..."

Lanoe kept them out on patrol all night, until Zhang was sure he was just daring the enemy to come attack them. They linked their controls so that they could take turns getting some sleep—though she was convinced he was less tired than that he just didn't want to talk anymore about *feelings*.

Well, he'd always been that way. She had, too, back when they were together. It was one reason they'd gotten along so well. She knew now that she had been running away from a lot of things—doubts, insecurities, the usual stuff. It was only after she'd lost her legs that she'd been forced to actually figure out who she was and what she intended to do with the rest of her life.

For a man like Lanoe, maybe that moment of decision never had to come. You do the same job for centuries, literal centuries, and maybe you get defined by it whether you want to be or not.

While she listened to him snore she had plenty of time to think about such things. And then more time to just be bored. And still more time, which she spent actually doing the job that had brought them out here.

Valk's microdrones had charted the system down to every rock bigger than a house. The space telescope in orbit around Niraya was slowly building up a better picture of the enemy fleet, though it wouldn't have true imagery until long after it was no longer required. By then the fleet would be defeated—or everyone on Niraya would be dead.

Still, every bit of intelligence they could gather was useful. Zhang's BR.9 had its own sensors and she kept them sweeping the void, looking for the telltale signs of invaders. Any object moving at faster than the escape velocity of the system. Anything that changed course in a way that couldn't be accounted for by gravity. Anything denser than iron, and especially any flash of light that couldn't be explained by natural causes.

She found only one thing worth investigating, and even that was a stretch. She let Lanoe sleep until he woke up on his own and asked if she'd detected anything.

"Maybe," she told him. "It's almost certainly nothing."

He almost growled as he replied. "We can't afford to make mistakes out here."

She nodded to herself. He was right—though investigating her anomaly would take them well off their course, and probably extend the patrol by hours yet. That was the thing about patrols like this. They took forever, and ninety-nine times out of a hundred they turned up nothing.

That hundredth time, of course, you found somebody and they tried to kill you.

"Just a light flash," she said, "on one of the moons of the ice giant. The profile was a little odd, it lasted just a couple of microseconds too long. Otherwise I'd say it was a meteor impact."

"Did it repeat?" he asked.

"No," she said. If it had, that would be a clear sign that something was going on. Meteors very rarely struck the same place twice. "I've already worked out a minimum energy course correction that would take us over that way, bring us in about ten thousand kilometers from the moon. Any closer than that and we'll burn a lot of fuel."

"I've got plenty," he told her. "How do your tanks look?"

"Fine," she said, with a sigh. It looked like they were doing this.

According to her charts, the local name for the ice giant was Garuda. It was the farthest planet out from Niraya's star, about as far out as Earth was from the Sun. Roughly the size of Neptune, though less dense and considerably warmer—its top layers of clouds were just below the freezing point for water. It had a system of rings, like Saturn, though these were thin and made of dust rather than ice. They would be all but invisible to normal human eyes—even Zhang's lidar eyes could barely make them out.

The planet had twenty or so moons, most of them a hundred kilometers across or less, not big enough to be spherical. There were four exceptions. Three were ice balls that, judging by their density, were just globs of water covered by an icy skin, with no real cores at all. The fourth and farthest from the planet, called Aruna on her charts, was made of dense rock, three thousand kilometers in diameter. It even had an atmosphere of methane and nitrogen—thicker than the air she'd breathed on Niraya.

The light flash had come from the surface of Aruna. One of the microdrones had caught the flash just on the limb of the moon, a bad angle for imagery—Zhang had studied the recording but could barely make out the flash even after the display adjusted the image into something she could see with her lidar eyes.

The two of them swooped in toward the moon, burning a lot more fuel than Zhang would have liked. Especially since a lot of that time they flew backward, thrusting against their own velocity. Unless they slowed way down they would just shoot past Aruna too fast to even get a good look.

As it stood, if they did one quick orbit of the moon and found nothing, they would have enough fuel to make their way back to Niraya—if they canceled the rest of their scheduled patrol. If Lanoe wanted a better look than one orbit could provide, they might end up limping home.

Garuda grew swollen and fat as they approached, until it filled three-quarters of her view. Aruna swung into view from behind that turbulent cloudscape, dark because she'd tuned her displays to show density. "Lots of iron down there," she told Lanoe. "That's going to block most of my sensors. You see anything yet?"

"No. I want to do some close contour chasing, bring us in nice and low," he said.

"You're the boss." She adjusted her trajectory again, burning still more fuel.

Pilots always felt a moment's disorientation when they transitioned from flying free through limitless space to actually flying over a solid surface like a moon or a planet. Suddenly "up" and "down" meant something again—so even though the moon could claim less than ten percent of standard gravity, its pull was real, something she had to compensate for. Zhang kept a light hand on her control stick as she raced along by Lanoe's side, hopping over spiny mountains, dropping like a brick into the deep basins of fresh craters.

The terrain flew by below them too fast for human eyes to make out much detail. Zhang's eyes weren't limited by human biology, though, and she saw how the ground had been stretched by gravity, cracked wide open in deep fissures. Jagged, almost serrated ridges of stone jutted up from plains lined with long furrows. Geologically fascinating, she was sure, but that wasn't what they'd come for.

"The flash came from inside a crater just over the horizon," she told Lanoe. "If there's something there, we'll see it in—mark—ten seconds. Nine."

She let the rest of the countdown pass silently. She'd already convinced herself there would be nothing down there. The flash had been some random bit of rock pulled out of the sky by gravity. For it to be visible from so far away, the impact must have created a serious shock wave in Aruna's atmosphere. It might have made the whole moon ring like a bell with seismic tremors. But it was meaningless to them, a waste of fuel to investigate, a waste of time to—

"Oh," she said, as the crater came into view.

It wasn't like the others she'd seen. It was much deeper, for one thing. And its interior walls weren't smoothly curved like a normal crater's. Instead they were cut into broad terraces, forming a series of concentric rings. From above the crater would have looked like a bull's-eye. From their low vantage she could see how deep the inner rings sank, until they formed a round pit gouged out of the moon's side.

Things moved down in that pit. Things with lots of legs and no heads. They sank their appendages deep in the rock and tore it asunder, raising clouds of dust that billowed out in long plumes.

The outermost ring was wreathed with complicated machinery, kilometers of pipes and wires stringing together domes and cylinders and high towers crowned with their own writhing, segmented arms. She couldn't help but think they looked like sea anemones, their long limbs waving in some unseen current. Vapor and smoke puffed from their ends without any pattern she could see.

"That's no crater," Lanoe said. "It's a strip mine."

Chapter Fourteen

A line of red pearls appeared in the corner of Lanoe's vision. He pulled up his sensor board and saw heat sources warming up all around the crater's rim—especially on the side nearest to the two fighters. "They've seen us," he said. "Those towers around the rim. Do they look like antivehicle batteries to you?"

"They don't look like anything I've seen before," Zhang replied. "I'm still going to say yes."

"No point in being sneaky, then. Break left," he said, and pulled his FA.2 into a wide bank to the right. He didn't need to look over to see Zhang headed in the opposite direction—they'd done this a thousand times before. She knew the drill.

He kept low, skirting just outside the crater rim, ready to drop behind it when things got too hectic. Inside the crater the towers with their crowns of slowly waving arms grew hotter and hotter. One of them craned its top around as if it were looking right at him, and a plume of dazzling red fire spurted from its arms. Plasma, he thought; the thing was shooting plasma at him. The stream moved fast but Lanoe was far enough away that he had time to duck behind the rocky wall of the crater before it struck.

Above him rock exploded in a shower of incandescent lava as the plasma hit the crater wall. A few drops of molten rock spattered down onto his vector field and were deflected harmlessly, but the temperature readings on his sensor board were ridiculous. For a millisecond there the rock had burned hotter than the surface of a good-size star.

Getting plasma that hot that fast required an enormous amount of power. He wondered if there was a way to make use of that datum. In the meantime—

Using his airfoils, he swung upside down into a tight barrel roll that let him just peek over the crater rim. The tower's arms hung flaccid now, spent, but he didn't want to give them a second chance at shooting him—if that plasma hit him it would overwhelm his vector field and roast him alive. He lined up a shot with his PBW cannon and poured fire into the tower, just below its crown, where it was held up by a framework of skeletal girders.

Accelerated protons tore through the steel supports. The tower crumpled over on its side and went down, falling with glacial slowness in the low gravity of the moon.

All that before he completed his barrel roll, taking him back down below the rim of the crater. "Those towers go down easy," he told Zhang, "but there are a lot of them—I counted at least a hundred. And I'm guessing they won't let us just walk away now. The second we pop our heads over the side of the crater they'll start shooting again. We're going to have to take out this facility before we can get away."

"I have my doubts about the veracity of that statement," Zhang said.

Lanoe smiled to himself. When she talked fancy like that, it was meant as a gentle jibe. If she'd really disagreed with his assessment she would have said so with a lot more cursing. *Good old Zhang,* he found himself thinking.

"You have a brilliant plan here, boss?" she asked him.

"Maybe. Those towers can't be generating that much heat on their own—they're too skinny. There has to be a central power plant here. If I can slag that, all the towers will go silent. I've got a full rack of bombs. You've got the better sensor package."

"You always did know how to give a lady a compliment," she replied.

He laughed. "On our approach, did you get a decent map of this place? See anything that looked like a fusion plant, or maybe some big geothermal loops?"

"Let me run an object recognition algorithm on my imagery," she told him. "But tell me something—if it's inside the crater, how do you plan on getting to it without getting fried yourself?"

"I guess I'm going to need someone to draw their fire for me," he told her. "Zhang—this is going to be dangerous."

"I didn't join the Navy for the retirement package," she told him.

He nodded to himself.

Good old Zhang. He tried not to think about the fact that good old Zhang was wearing the body of a twenty-five-year-old, a body she was supposed to give back to its owner. That kind of thing might stop him from sending her in on such a risky mission.

The two of them circled the outside of the crater, staying well below the rim, picking up speed. When they did this stupid thing they needed to be moving *fast*. Zhang linked her controls to Lanoe's, basically letting him fly for her. As they bobbed up and down, barely clearing the boulders and jagged hills that littered the ground around the crater, she had plenty of chances to regret that decision, but she needed her hands free.

Her computer had good video of the inside of the crater, taken during their approach. It had broken that feed down into still images and studied them until it had identified every structure inside the crater, every building or piece of enemy machinery. It used a pretty good algorithm, but the computer wasn't smart enough to understand what it was looking at—that was up to her.

Her infrared displays flickered through hundreds of magnified images, blown up details of the structures her sensors had mapped inside the crater facility. She studied them not with her eyes but with her bare hands. She'd become so adept at it that it felt like she was touching the holographic pictures, feeling the rough textures of the enemy machinery, swiping through dozens of them a second.

None of it looked like anything she'd seen before. There were bulbous shapes like clusters of mushrooms, long filamentary nets like spiderwebs. When the crowned pylon shapes of the towers came up she flicked them away in annoyance. There had to be something there, something that could generate all the power a facility like this needed. She found a couple of weird structures like weathered stones, or maybe like pieces of coral—irregularly shaped and riddled with holes, but no, a power plant should be giving off incredible amounts of waste heat, and the spongy structures were ice cold.

When she finally found it, the power plant was the most normal thing she'd discovered so far. A nest of thick tubes that plunged down into the central pit. They gave off so much heat they nearly scorched her fingers.

"Got it," she said. "It's geothermal. Right in the middle of the crater—you're going to have a devil of a time getting in there." She sent a copy of the image to Lanoe, then pulled her gloves back on and grabbed her control stick. "I'm breaking our link now. You ready?"

"I'm ready," he called back. "Start your run anytime, and I'll duck in once you've got their attention."

Zhang nodded to herself. No time like the present, right? Even if it meant there was no future.

She pulled back hard on her stick, angling it just a touch to the left, at the same time firing her maneuvering thrusters so that she shot upward, over the crater rim, in a long, twisting corkscrew, giving the towers something to shoot at while making herself as tricky a moving target as possible.

The towers responded instantly, just as she'd expected they would. Crowns of segmented arms twined together and bright tongues of fire licked upward at her, plasma streaming past her canopy as she twisted away from it. Through her vector field, through her canopy and the flowglas of her helmet, still she felt the intense heat on her face, felt it make the fine hair on her nose curl up. She threw her stick over to the right and shot out of her corkscrew, then dove toward the crater at a shallow angle, less than a kilometer over the tops of the towers. More and more of them turned to point their arms at her, and suddenly a dozen plumes of superhot plasma came arcing up toward her at once, converging on her location.

She wanted desperately to crane her head around and look for Lanoe, make sure he was safely inside the crater and well into his bombing run. There was just no time, though. The plasma raced toward her and in a fraction of a second it would reach her. That much heat would vaporize her fighter even on a near miss.

So before it arrived she pulled the oldest trick in the book. She knocked her stick hard over to the right and made a ninety-degree turn, her BR.9 shuddering with the strain but obeying her command. Then she pushed herself into a flat spin, stalling on her airfoils in the thick atmosphere of the moon. Her fighter twisted on its long axis until the crater and the planet in the sky switched positions over and over again, until she had to look away from her canopy so she didn't get dizzy.

Above her the plasma streams converged and billowed in a fiery cloud that threw long shadows across the enemy facility. She had a moment to look down, and saw Lanoe moving over the face of the crater. Like a bat out of hell he shot across the strip mine, mere meters off the ground. She saw something else start to move down there, something with long legs and not much else—

But there was no time to worry about him. More streamers of plasma arced toward her, and she had to twist away again, just ahead of disaster.

Lanoe dodged around a big structure like a cluster of domes wrapped in a cobweb, then jinked back to the straight line of his bombing run with one smooth motion. Up ahead lay a great twisting plain of pipes and tubes. The ground fell away beneath him and he dropped hard over the clifflike wall of one of the inner terraces. Not far now—he could see the big pit up ahead, the hole the enemy had dug into Aruna's side. Mining drones like spiders with hands scuttled in and out of the pit, dragging chunks of rock bigger than they were, headed for what might have been a conveyor system.

None of it made sense. He'd ground-strafed his share of bases and spaceports in his time, bombed bunkers and factories and yes, even mining facilities and none of them had looked like this. The weird machinery all around him ran on principles he couldn't fathom.

Not that it mattered in the slightest. On the far side of the pit lay the thick looping pipes of the power plant, so hot they glowed with a visible sheen. All he had to do was get over there, drop his bombs, and streak away before anyone managed to kill him. Easy.

Hang in there, Zhang, he thought. *Not long now.*

He scowled and tried to shove those thoughts out of his head. Zhang knew what she was doing—how many times had they run an assault like this together? How many scrapes had they pulled each other through? She had her job to do, he had his, and if he started worrying about her safety it would just distract him.

At these kind of speeds, that would get you killed fast. He had to concentrate, had to pull this off flawlessly. Whatever the enemy was mining here, he couldn't let them have it. Destroying this place might weaken the enemy—at the very least it would annoy the fleet's commanders, which was more than worth the cost.

Something hunched and twitchy moved in his peripheral vision, far enough away he could barely make it out. He called up a magnified view and moved it to one side of his canopy so it didn't block his line of sight. A forest of tall pipes lay just ahead of him, each pipe ending in a fluted mouth that pointed at the dark blue sky. A communications array? A pump for exhaust heat? It didn't matter—he didn't want to fly over those yawning mouths. He zigged around them, then zagged back, and only when he was fully clear did he spare a glance at the magnified view.

At first he thought it showed one of the mining drones, except this one didn't have hands. Then he recognized the cluster of conjoined legs for what they were. It was a killer drone just like the one that landed on Niraya. The mining drones were no larger than big dogs but the lander was the size of a house. As low as he was flying it would be able to reach him from the ground. It would be easy enough to pull back on his stick and gain some altitude, get clear of the drone's stabbing legs—but if he did that, he would expose himself to fire from the plasma towers. He had to stay low.

And the drone was moving toward him—fast.

He'd seen the video of how those things killed. He'd seen people impaled on their pointy legs. He had no idea if it could pierce his vector field with those claws, and no intention of finding out firsthand.

He pulled up a virtual Aldis sight and laid the crosshairs right on the lander, near its top, where it was thickest. The things were bulletproof, he knew that much, but Valk had been able to carve them up with his PBWs. Lanoe waited for the best firing solution, then pulled the trigger.

The lander lurched to one side as the particle beam sliced through a dozen of its legs. It tried to stay upright, tried to find some ways to balance on the limbs it had left, but even in the moon's low gravity it couldn't manage. It fell over slowly, legs still twitching and stabbing at the ground.

Which should have been fine, just fine—except a red pearl appeared in the corner of Lanoe's vision, telling him his computer had detected a new threat.

He didn't need a magnified view to see it coming. Up ahead, just off to his left, a hulking edifice squatted on the crater floor. A giant heap of coral or pumice, full of holes. Dark shapes squirmed inside those holes, squeezing themselves out through apertures that should have been too narrow to allow it. One by one landers spat out of the structure, tumbling over each other in their hurry. They took a second to find their best footing, but once they were upright they came scurrying forward in great leaps and bounds. Four of them—five—maybe a dozen.

All converging on his position.

Zhang twisted and turned, always staying one step ahead of the plasma streams. She was high enough above the crater now that the towers could barely track her—as soon as they fired she was banking away, flipping around on her long axis and accelerating into a new spin. She could have kept up those evasive maneuvers practically indefinitely—at least until she ran out of fuel—without being hit.

Of course, the towers didn't need to get a direct hit to kill her. The heat from all that plasma lingered in the moon's atmosphere. If Zhang could have seen it, she knew the air around her would be shimmering. She knew for a fact she had started to sweat inside her suit. With all the heat shielding both her suit and her fighter possessed, it had to be five hundred degrees outside her canopy.

The heat played merry hell with her aerodynamics. All the new heat fought with the moon's cold air and suddenly she was being tossed around by hurricane force winds. Her airfoils had to change shape, growing longer and thinner as they bit into the methane wind, trying to gain traction. Her turning radius suffered and her aerobatics grew sluggish and difficult. All while her fighter's cooling system struggled to keep her from roasting to death.

Not that it mattered to her, just at that moment—she was far more worried about Lanoe. She had to force herself to keep watching the plasma towers, because what she really wanted to do was look down and see if he was all right.

Well, she told herself, if he was alive he was fine. And if he was dead, she had no reason to keep up this crazy ballet. So she had reason to look for him, occasionally.

Protocol for this kind of assault included radio silence—you did not chatter to each other while both of you were so busy. She couldn't call him up and ask him if he'd been killed or not. Instead she told her computer to track movement down in the crater and let her know if it stopped.

She was not prepared for the data it gave her—that the entire crater was moving. Crawling with drones.

She twisted around a streamer of plasma so intensely hot it knocked out some of her cameras, then she dove right through a patch of clear air before the towers could fire again.

Below her Lanoe stayed on the course of his bombing run, his trajectory as straight as an arrow. Not long now, no matter how this played out.

———

Spidery arms lanced at his canopy. Drones leapt toward him, getting impossible hang time in Aruna's low gravity. Lanoe's trigger finger was sore from firing his PBWs so often as he tried to chew a way through to the geothermal loops that were his target.

The FA.2 was a lot faster than the drones. As he passed them by some tried to give chase, only to fall away in his rear displays. But others kept appearing before him, looming into his path so he had to hop over them or weave around them. The actual landers, the six-meter-tall killers, were rare but they were his biggest concern. The smaller mining drones were mostly just a nuisance. They could jump at him but he doubted they could get through his vector field.

Still, he had no desire to find out.

They obscured his forward view. They smacked into his airfoils and made his whole fighter ring as they were tossed away by the speeding fighter. Every impact knocked him a little this way, a little that way—always off course. Maybe that was the whole point of them swarming him.

Then one jumped straight onto his canopy and stuck there, its hands clutching hard at the carbonglas, its legs pulling back for striking blows.

One of those claws came down hard, just half a meter from Lanoe's face. The point smashed into the carbonglas and dug in with a terrible screeching sound and for a moment Lanoe thought it was all over, that he was dead.

But the canopy held. It was made of strong stuff, the best the Navy could provide, reinforced by the intangible armor of his vector field. The claw couldn't get through. It had left a pretty deep mark, but it hadn't broken through.

He breathed a sigh of relief. He wasn't out of the woods yet, though.

With the drone obscuring his canopy he could see nothing—if anything was right in front of him, he knew he would plow right into it and his bombing run would end very quickly and very anti-climactically. He had to get the mining drone off his canopy.

Only one way to do that.

He was flying ridiculously low—barely a meter away from scraping his undercarriage on the crater floor. He called up the panel that controlled his maneuvering thrusters and tapped in a very complicated series of burns.

Then he pushed his stick forward as hard as he could.

His various jets and thrusters all fired in carefully timed bursts, keeping him from just crashing headfirst into the ground. Instead, the FA.2 rolled forward in a somersault, ass over teakettle, without actually losing a millimeter of altitude. He didn't so much as brush the ground.

The mining drone on his canopy wasn't as lucky. It scraped along the ground for a fraction of a second before disintegrating into a cloud of broken metal claws. Lanoe watched the debris tumble and bounce off the ground behind him—then watched the sky roll past above him, a sky like a mirror broken by streamers of plasma—then watched the facility come back into view before him as the fighter completed its flip.

He could see just fine, now.

And what he saw cheered him—the central pit, the deepest part of the crater, lay just ahead. In a few seconds he was going to reach the loops, the power plant that kept this place running, and he would release his bombs, and—

Right in front of him four of the big landers stood up on their many legs, forming an impenetrable wall.

Streamers of plasma cut through the air left and right, far too close. The sweat on Zhang's face dried as fast as it came, leaving a crust of salt on her cheeks and nose. She felt like the blood inside her skull was starting to boil.

Still she leaned on her stick, the nose of her BR.9 pointed straight at the ground. Her airfoils pulled her into a tight spin that was just enough to keep the towers from getting a solid lock on her. The more altitude she lost, the greater the danger that one time, just one time, a shot would get through.

She had her orders. She didn't care—Lanoe was down there, waggling back and forth in distress as he tried to avoid slamming into a wall of drone legs. She started firing long before she could actually see the drones with her cybernetic eyes, giving the computer free rein to pick its targets.

Superhot plasma washed across her canopy, but it was an old shot that had already started to dissipate. Just hot enough to give her a nasty sunburn. She knew this because she didn't vaporize in a puff of carbon.

Then she was through, below the crowns of the towers, and they stopped shooting. Most likely they didn't want to damage their own facility, but she didn't care—any respite was welcome. She saw the four landers below her, saw her PBW shots go wide, splashing against the dusty surface, making tiny, useless craters.

Computers never could shoot worth a damn. She grabbed back manual control of her cannon and stabbed at her weapons panel. Virtual sights were useless to her—she couldn't see them—but Zhang had been shooting PBWs since she was a teenager, and that was a very, very long time ago.

One target. Two. Three. Four. She yanked her trigger again and again, moving on from one target to the next without even checking to make sure they were down. They fell, but with painful slowness, and she could only watch as Lanoe shot right between two of them, two killer drones that hadn't finished dying yet. One of them made a halfhearted stab at the FA.2 but it was through and clear well before the blow landed.

⟞✦⟝

Good old bloody old Zhang. Lanoe wanted to whoop in joy.

She dropped down beside him, flying just off the edge of his left side airfoils, and he could see her through her canopy, see her wink at him. He gave her a cheery wave and then bent back over his controls.

The FA.2 raced over the innermost of the concentric terraces and then, suddenly, there was nothing beneath him, nothing but the deep pit. A floating display near his knees showed him what was down there and the vision cut through his ebullient mood. He couldn't see the bottom of the pit—the whole thing was full of spidery mining drones, their hands still plunging into the moon's rock and tearing loose pieces of ore, as if nothing at all were happening above them.

He tore his eyes away from them and saw the giant loops of the power plant before him, pipes so thick he could have flown down them if they were empty. He called up a virtual bombsight and let his computer find the weak points in the loops, the spots where they were hottest, the places where they'd been bolted to the side of the pit.

The bomb rack on the belly of the FA.2 was full of very smart, very tiny munitions that could glide to their targets without any human help. Lanoe tapped a virtual key and they all fell away at once. His fighter bobbed upward, ten meters up—high enough to draw fire from the plasma towers. He ducked back down before any of them got any ideas, then banked hard—*hard*—to get away from the pit.

He had a feeling it was about to become a very hazardous environment.

The pipes he could see were only the top and smallest part of very, very long shafts sunk into Aruna's fiery innards. They pumped magma up toward the surface and used the heat of the molten rock to generate power. The magma lost ninety percent of its heat when it reached the top of that column, turning almost solid. That cooler rock slurry was pumped back down toward the core, where it could be heated again and brought back up in an endless loop.

All of which simply meant that the enemy had been foolish enough to put a bunch of pipes full of red-hot pressurized magma right in the middle of their mining facility. It didn't take much for Lanoe's bombs to crack those pipes wide open so they spurted endless gouts of lava all over the complex.

The spidery drones down in the pit didn't have heads, much less eyes to look up and watch as the lava came showering down on them. Some of them managed to scuttle out of the pit before they were swept away. But not many.

Meanwhile, all over the complex, the power supply just suddenly...disappeared. Lights went out. Conveyor systems stopped moving.

In the base of each of the plasma towers, magnetic fields collapsed, magnetic fields that had been holding in enormous quantities of high-temperature ionized gas.

Almost in the same instant, every single tower in the facility turned into a Roman candle, explosions blasting apart their girders, sending the twined arms of their crowns pinwheeling away across the moon's skin. Debris blasted across the crater like an endless hail of bullets, smashing equipment, blasting drones to pieces.

And at the center of the complex the lava kept bursting from the broken pipes. It filled up the central pit until it was a cauldron of orange glowing soup, then spilled out over the rim and filled the innermost terrace as well, the biggest volcanic eruption Aruna had ever seen.

High above, Lanoe and Zhang burned for orbit, so they could watch it all happen without getting incinerated themselves.

Chapter Fifteen

The elder had asked Roan to look in on M. Ehta and see how she was getting along setting up a ground control base. So she checked a ground car out of the Retreat's motor pool and headed out to the edge of Walden Crater, to where an impossibly long staircase doubled back and forth up to the very lip. By the time she reached the top she was panting for breath, even though she'd been born on Niraya and was used to its thin air. She leaned against a steel railing until the black spots stopped swimming in front of her eyes, then walked around a squat concrete building to where a field of huge radar dishes sat rusting in the sun. M. Ehta was down among them, unreeling a spool of cable. "Half of these aren't even hooked up," she said, when she saw Roan approach. "It took me a while to figure that out. I spent most of my morning clearing rats out of the main building."

Roan shrugged in apology. "This place used to keep us in touch with the farms out in the canyons," she said.

"Used to? You lost interest in what they had to say?" M. Ehta asked. "I suppose herders aren't known for their sparkling conversation."

Roan looked away. "Those were the stations where the people were murdered by the killer drone. Most of them. The rest were abandoned after we sacrificed our fusion plant to stop the massacre."

M. Ehta at least had the decency to drop her eyes. "I didn't know," she said. "Here. Hand me that cable crimper."

Roan looked and found the tool lying on a cloth a few meters away. For a while she helped M. Ehta hook up the maze of cables linking the dishes together. It took some mental effort to keep the snarled network straight in her head, but physically it wasn't too demanding. When it was done they headed back to the control building, a concrete box full of spiderwebs and machinery so old and dusty it looked antiquated even to Roan's untrained eye. M. Ehta plugged a minder into the main console and through a broad window they watched the dishes turn on rusty pivots, creaking and groaning until they all pointed straight upward.

"There," M. Ehta said. "Now I can talk to anybody in the system." She called up a series of displays from her minder, none of which showed any data Roan could understand. "See what's going on."

"You're going to coordinate the defense?" Roan asked.

M. Ehta snorted. "Hardly. That's Lanoe's job. I just keep an eye on the skies, you know? Watch out for trouble, let them know if I see anything coming in. For all the good it does anybody."

Roan was confused. "You make it sound like that isn't important."

"Let's say I actually spot an incoming wing of landers, right? Except they're out at the edge of the system. Light and radio waves can only travel so fast. It takes twenty minutes for that information to get to me. I forward on the sighting, and Lanoe gets to hear about it twenty minutes after that. I've never heard of a dogfight that lasted forty minutes. In the time it took me to ping him and warn him of trouble, he'd already be dead." M. Ehta pulled her gloves off and threw them down on a console in disgust. "This isn't a real job, kid. This is exile, for the pilot who can't fly."

Roan could sense the woman's frustration and anguish. Roan had been trained in disciplines of compassion and forgiveness, and her immediate reaction was to reach out, to comfort. But when she opened her mouth, something else entirely came out, unbidden.

"Why did you come here?" she asked. At least her tone of voice made it sound more like curiosity than anger.

M. Ehta just turned a tired-looking eye at her and said nothing.

"Why did you tell M. Lanoe you could fight? You must have known—suspected, at least—what would happen when you tried to fly again. You must have known! But still you came here. You've endangered us all."

"That's how you figure it?"

Roan shook her head. Better to just let this go. She couldn't help herself, though. "If you'd told M. Lanoe back at the Hexus, he could have found somebody else, some other pilot to take your place, someone who could fight."

M. Ehta nodded slowly. Then she leaned back in her chair until its springs squealed and it slipped an inch across the floor. She put her hands to her eyes and rubbed hard at their sockets. "Let me tell you something about Lanoe," she said, finally. "You have this idea he's some kind of demigod. That he's going to save your planet with one arm tied behind his back. And yeah, in his day—he was red hot. The best pilot who ever lived. But people get old, kid. People lose their touch."

"What are you talking about?" Roan demanded.

"I lost my nerve, sure, that makes me some kind of freak to you. He lost—something else. They still tell stories about him but every story ends the same way. 'I wonder what happened to him?' 'Why did he stop fighting?' His squadron doesn't exist anymore. His rank's straight-up vestigial at this point—I doubt if he went to the Admiralty anyone would even stand to attention for him these days, even if they recognized him. Long before you met him, his star was already falling."

"He's a good man. He helped us when nobody else would."

M. Ehta nodded. "Sure. But when he put out the call for other pilots to come, the only people who would even consider it were the ones who owed him bad, or had no choice. If I didn't come, nobody would have taken my place."

"You don't care. You don't care about Niraya. Or us. The people who live here."

M. Ehta just shrugged. "Not my job to care. I just follow orders."

Roan shook her head and got up to leave. "If we're done here, I have some other duties to see to."

The pilot just waved her away.

She headed back down the endless staircase, gasping for breath all the way. It wasn't lack of oxygen that had her in such distress, though. It took all of her training to regain her composure so she could drive.

She had one more errand to do. Elder McRae had tasked her with helping all of the offworlders, as requested. It wasn't a difficult assignment, since most of them seemed happier flying around in space than spending time on the planet they were supposed to defend. At least one of them actually seemed to care about the people of Niraya.

Not that he was much use. She pulled up in front of the Retreat and found Thom waiting for her, a tentative smile on his face. "Thanks for driving me around," he said, once he was in the car and had his safety belts on.

"I live in service to my faith and my people," she said. She knew it sounded almost sarcastic, but it was a mantra that had gotten her through plenty of unpleasant duties before.

Thom might have been forgiven if he'd chosen to just give up on his role as goodwill ambassador, after the disaster at the animal feed factory. He'd left there having convinced half of the staff that the Navy was carrying out biowarfare experiments on Niraya. Roan had not expected him to ask for her help again—but here he was. Maybe he thought he could turn things around. Maybe he thought that if he actually convinced some people the Navy was on their side Lanoe would respect him. Or at least notice.

It was a fool's errand, but Roan had to admit it was nice being around somebody who actually thought the pilots had a chance.

In spite of his poor showing at the factory, or perhaps in hope of repairing some of the damage, the Retreat had organized a public meeting so Thom could address people directly. Not at the Retreat itself, of course—the elders didn't want to be directly involved in Thom's mission. Instead the Christian Gnostics had agreed to let

him speak from the pulpit of their church. After the Transcendentalists and the Church of the Ancient Word they were the third
largest of Niraya's communities of faith, representing thousands of
people. No one really expected much of a turnout, but the chance
to be heard seemed to galvanize Thom. Maybe a little too much.

"I'm worried I might be sick," he said, as she drove him through
town.

"I'm barely driving fifteen kilometers an hour," Roan pointed
out. They had to keep the speed down to avoid a herd of ostriches
being driven through the central square. Dust and stray bits of
down fouled her windshield and she triggered her wipers—the
only use they had on a planet where it never actually rained.

"It's not motion sickness—I just. I've never really, you know.
Spoken in public before. My father," he said, then suddenly fell
quiet. He was staring at her. She took her eyes off the road just long
enough to glance over at him.

"What about your father?" she asked.

"He's...He was a politician. He used to talk to crowds all the
time. I would stand up on a platform next to him and watch and
smile, but that was it. I was always amazed at how he could just
look out at a sea of faces and not be petrified wondering what they
were all thinking."

"Maybe it's genetic," Roan pointed out. "Maybe you'll be a
natural."

"If I don't puke all over my podium," he said.

Despite herself, she laughed. Which made him smile. It felt good
to be able to help someone like that, she had to admit.

She pulled up in front of the church, one of the bigger structures
in Walden Crater, and together they watched the entrance for a
while in silence. The church was shaped like a giant seashell lying
on its side, its spirally curling walls glistening like mother of pearl.
Roan had no idea why they'd chosen that shape—there were no
seas on Niraya, not so much as a lake, and she doubted most Nirayans even understood what the church was supposed to represent.

The opening of the shell, where whatever cyclopean sea-beast that once lived inside it would have poked its head out, was filled in with stained glass and a huge Gothic arch through which people were streaming inside.

Lots of people. When Elder McRae told her about this meeting, she'd assumed that maybe a dozen or two of the curious would show up. Judging by the line to get in, it looked more like hundreds. Word must have spread—the workers at the factory must have told everyone they knew about the Navy's arrival. Roan hadn't expected anyone to really care, since Nirayans tended to be uninterested in anything that happened outside Walden Crater. Clearly, she'd been wrong.

"We're supposed to use a back entrance," she said, and started the car up again before Thom could be ill inside her vehicle. She drove around to the back, which was mercifully clear of people, and together they stepped in through a small gate. Inside a man wearing a tunic with a high collar was waiting for them. He had a long but perfectly groomed beard and wore a kind of flat hat with a tassel on one end. "Welcome," he said, raising his hands up as if he were surrendering to them. "I'm Patrus Ogham. We're so glad you could come."

Thom shook the man's hand and the three of them headed to a small space behind the pulpit. "Not much of a greenroom, sorry," the Patrus told them. "This is where we don our vestments before going out to preach."

The walls of the little room were covered in intricately carved wooden panels, stained black. Over their heads stone statues battled each other across the ceiling, some with beautiful human features, others twisted and deformed and demonic. For a Transcendentalist like Roan it was positively grotesque.

"Whenever you're ready," the Patrus said, his eyes shining as he smiled at them.

"I can't go out there with you," Roan told Thom. "I'm not here in any official capacity."

He just nodded and stared at the door to the pulpit. From beyond they could both hear the hissing sound of many people in hushed conversation.

"Roan," Thom said. "Roan, hold my hand."

"What?"

He didn't look at her. He was staring at the door. "Just—just squeeze my hand, once. It'll help. Please."

She reached down and took his hand in hers. It felt damp and weak, as if he could barely hold on to her fingers. She wrapped both her hands around his and gave it a good squeeze. It felt like the least she could do.

The effect on Thom surprised her. He seemed to stand up taller and his mouth set into a bright smile.

The Patrus cleared his throat.

Thom nodded, once, still not looking at her. Then he stepped through the door. Roan got just a quick look out at the audience and saw that the church was packed to capacity, people even standing in the aisles between the ranks of pews. All of them come to hear what Thom had to say.

There was a great roar of excitement, though no applause, and then the Patrus closed the door behind Thom and shut off her view.

By the time they reached the ice giant's moon, Valk was more than ready to set foot on solid ground again. As much as he hated gravity it would be better than spending more time in the tender with his two passengers.

He'd been alone up in the pilot's seat, while they'd stayed back in the wardroom for the six-hour flight. The bulkhead that separated the two compartments was thin enough, though, that he'd heard every word as Maggs tried to convince Derrow, the mining engineer, to join the zero-g club.

Meanwhile Derrow had done a very poor job of hiding the fact that she felt spacesick. Otherwise she probably would have gone along with Maggs's idea. Well, thank the devil for small mercies, Valk thought.

By the time the moon came into view, partly eclipsed by the ice giant, he'd had enough. He called them both up to the bridge and let them have a good look. Together the three of them watched the moon turn, a bluish-gray sphere pocked with craters. A sliver of blue haze was visible on its limb, and white clouds swirled across nearly a quarter of its visible surface.

"Yeah, that's Aruna," Derrow said. "Funny, though. When we set up the mining colony on Niraya, we looked at this place as an alternate location. We logged a lot of video. I don't remember seeing any storms that big."

Valk checked his instruments. "Well, you're going to see a lot more of this one. Our rendezvous point is right in the middle there."

Derrow scowled at him. "At some point am I going to find out why you dragged me out here? Or is that still a military secret?"

Valk shrugged. "You know as much as me." Lanoe had called him while he was sleeping in orbit around Niraya. He'd said to bring Maggs and the engineer as fast as he could, but that was it.

"Perhaps," Maggs said, "they shot down an enemy craft and they want you to take a look at it."

To Valk, Derrow didn't seem all that enthused about the prospect.

He brought the tender down carefully—it handled like a brick in any kind of atmosphere, and the storm didn't help. They flew down through increasingly dark and foreboding clouds until he had to fly by instruments. Even when they cut through the lowest cloud deck and back out into clear air, it was nearly pitch black outside. Rain slapped against the viewports, sluicing away in long, fat rivulets that turned to steam as Valk watched. "That's weird," he said. "It's a hundred degrees out there." He was used to moons being cold and icy.

"That's way too warm for Aruna," Derrow agreed. "It should never get much above freezing."

Through the murk Valk could just make out a V-shape of landing lights down on the ground. He brought them in slow and steady, then touched down with a sickening lurch. His instruments told them they'd landed on a shelf of rock high on the inner rim of a big crater. He pinged for Lanoe's cryptab and found it less than a hundred meters away, though he couldn't see anyone through the viewports.

By the time the three of them clambered out of the airlock—
Derrow in a civilian suit that sagged around her waist and ankles—
Lanoe and Zhang had come up to meet them. Zhang waved and
Valk headed over toward her. The white pearl flashed in the corner
of his vision, but just for a moment. The gravity here was a tenth
what he was used to, and his legs barely ached.

"Sorry about the weather," Zhang said. "That was our fault. Can
you see anything in this?"

Valk looked around. The rain slashed at the soil around his feet
and sent up little puffs of vapor wherever it hit. He wondered if it
was more than just water. Deep fog cut off most of the light, but he
could make out a dull red glow in the distance, in the direction of
the center of the crater.

"It's still molten down there. Try switching your helmet to
low-light mode."

Derrow must have figured that out before she was told, because
before Valk could even switch the optical filter of his helmet, the
engineer started swearing.

"What is this? A city? Who built it?" she demanded.

"Our enemy," Lanoe told her.

Valk could see it now. The crater was filled with jagged edges
and right angles, as well as curves unlike anything found in nature.
A vast ruin, half of it melted down to slag, half still standing—
buildings and machines and structures he couldn't identify. And
right in the middle, a pulsing soup of brilliant light. That red glow
he'd seen was blinding in the enhanced view, a coruscating mass of
heat and heaving motion.

"What is that?" Maggs asked. "A—what do you call it, a caldera?"

"No," Derrow said. "There's no history of volcanism on Aruna—
I did a geological survey myself. I mean, I was just working from
distant imagery and some computer-guided models, but...no.
This isn't a volcano. You guys did this."

"Sure," Lanoe said. "You figured it out. But that's not why we
brought you here. We melted a bunch of their stuff, but there's enough
down there still standing that we have a chance to learn something

about them. Maybe something crucial. I'm sorry, M. Derrow. I know you have work back home. But we desperately need your eyes on this."

Maggs turned to look at Lanoe, then. "And why, pray tell, was it so important that I come out here as well?"

"Because," Lanoe said, "we just took away one of the enemy's most important assets. Something they can't just let us have for free."

"We're expecting an attack," Zhang said. "In retaliation. Or maybe just so they can get their colony back. Either way," she said, and shrugged, "they're going to come at us here, soon, and extraordinarily hard."

Patrus Ogham made tea for Roan while the two of them waited in the little vestry behind the pulpit. Neither of them spoke. They were far too busy listening through the door, listening to Thom give his speech.

Thom made a good start of it. He introduced himself as a special envoy from the Navy, sent to talk about the defense of Niraya and how no one should give in to fear, about how some of the best pilots the Navy had ever produced were at that moment fighting to keep Niraya safe.

Roan could hear the occasional cough from the audience. She heard someone out there yawn, as Thom kept talking about M. Lanoe's qualifications. About how the fighters they'd brought carried the most advanced technology that Earth's military had ever created. About how he truly believed that they were going to protect Niraya and keep everyone safe. Then he fell silent. He just stopped talking.

Someone started to clap then, halfheartedly, because they must have assumed Thom was done. That he had nothing else to say.

It turned out that wasn't true.

"That, uh." He paused for a very long time. Maybe he was drinking water. Roan wished she could see him. "That sounded like a press release, didn't it?" he said.

There was polite laughter from the audience.

"The thing is—I've been told what I'm allowed to say," Thom went on. Roan glanced over at Patrus Ogham. The Patrus had tilted his head to one side as if he was suddenly very much interested in hearing what came next.

"I've been told what I'm *not* allowed to say. I guess." Roan had been trained in reading people. In understanding what they said emotionally, in addition to what they said in words. She heard Thom's voice rise nearly half an octave, heard his words catch in his throat. He was frightened, she thought. Terrified of what he was going to say next.

"No," she whispered. "No, you aren't supposed to—"

Patrus Ogham hissed at her to be quiet.

"For instance, I'm not supposed to tell you that the danger isn't over. That there's an entire invasion fleet coming toward Niraya right now. Hundreds of ships, maybe, and we don't even know who sent them. We do know that by the time they reach this planet, they'll be—"

He might have said more, might have given more details, but just then people in the audience started shouting questions at him. First just a few, one at a time, but soon they were bellowing over each other to make themselves heard.

"What?"

"What are you talking about?"

"Invasion? You mean they're—"

"How many ships?"

"Is it DaoLink? Is DaoLink coming to attack us? Is it—"

"How long before this fleet gets here?"

"Well," Thom said, and for a moment he could be heard over the shouted questions. "That's a complicated thing to figure out. It's dependent on how hard the enemy fleet decelerates, and what kind of assets they choose to deploy in their final approach—"

They didn't let him finish. The crowd was roaring now, exploding with questions.

"Who sent this fleet? Was it one of the polys?" someone shouted, and a dozen voices chorused in with "Here, here," and the like.

"At the moment we haven't determined—"

"It's God's judgment!" someone screamed. "The faithful will be tested, and the unrighteous laid low!"

About half the crowd seemed to agree with that statement. The rest hissed and booed and shouted for the fanatic to shut up.

Over his teacup, Patrus Ogham made a show of wincing in distaste.

Thom's voice didn't crack as he responded. "There's no sign this is anything but a fleet of conventional spacecraft," he said. "There's no reason to think there's a spiritual motivation for this attack."

"But then why come against Niraya? We've got nothing to steal," someone in the audience pointed out.

Someone else shouted loud enough to drown out the murmuring crowd. "It's the polys, probably Centrocor. They want to drive us off so they can strip-mine the whole planet!"

"Are you stupid, or just naive?" someone else bellowed. "Centrocor already owns this place, down to the mantle. This isn't an invasion fleet, it's a new wave of mining ships and police, here to make sure we don't—"

"Obviously it's DaoLink; they're fighting Centrocor right now, or don't you watch the news videos? Don't you—"

"Angels light and dark have bodies material as well as spiritual—"

"If it's Centrocor, then why is the Navy fighting them and—"

It became difficult to hear any given voice after that, as the crowd shouted and screamed and laughed, the religious sneering at the more practical, the paranoid insulting the few voices of reason out there.

Roan watched the door to the pulpit, expecting Thom to come bursting through, perhaps in tears.

But he didn't. As the argument lowed and bellowed and echoed until the walls of the church shook, Thom stayed out there, a focus for it all. Maybe hoping they'd eventually settle down, that he would get a chance to speak again. Roan hoped that was true—she found herself silently rooting for him, desperately hoping that he was okay.

The other possibility, of course, was that he had frozen in fear. That he stood out there paralyzed and swaying on his feet, unable to handle the barely contained animus that filled the church.

For the better part of an hour, the door stayed closed. Roan's anxiety only increased. She was truly worried about him, she realized, this dumb boy from another planet whom she owed nothing, whom she barely knew. Despite herself, despite her training—despite the fact that he'd just gone against the collective will of the elders of her faith—she cared. Maybe it was just a normal human feeling, basic empathy for someone who must be suffering. Yes. That must be it.

In time the roaring settled down to an uncomfortable din. Either the people out there felt like they'd made their various points, or they had just run out of steam. Either way, eventually it grew quiet enough for Thom to speak again.

"Thank you, everyone, for your comments and questions," he said. The babble didn't stop. "I hope you found this worthwhile. Good night."

There was no applause. The crowd seemed to have forgotten Thom was there.

The door opened and he stepped through. He looked pale and shaken and he didn't waste any time sitting down. The Patrus poured him a cup of tea.

"I'm...sorry," he said, finally, looking at the holy man. "I don't think that's what you expected to happen when you agreed to let me speak here."

The Patrus raised one eyebrow. "No?"

"I thought maybe...Well, I expected it to go differently."

"My child," Patrus Ogham said, reaching over to pat Thom's hand, "you did fine. Absolutely fine."

"I...did?"

The Patrus nodded gleefully. "Nothing like a good threat of divine wrath to bring 'em in to church. I daresay we'll double our normal attendance at our next service. And more congregants means heavier collection plates. This went splendidly, as far as I'm concerned."

Thom had nothing to say to that.

Awhile later, when the church had emptied out, Roan drove Thom back to the ground control station where he was staying with Ensign Ehta. He didn't say much on the ride. She forced herself not to keep glancing over at him, to see if he was okay. Clearly he just wanted to be left alone.

When they reached the bottom of the stairs leading up the crater wall, she switched off the ground car and released her safety belt, then turned in her seat to look at him. It was time. There was something that absolutely had to be addressed. "You weren't supposed to tell them about the fleet," she said.

"I know."

She shook her head. She knew better than to chastise him. That wasn't the way of the Transcendentalist faith. You accepted what had happened and moved on, looking for ways to do better the next time.

Sometimes that was hard to keep in mind. "You were told, specifically, not to mention it! Thom, what were you thinking?"

"I thought they had a right to know."

"Even if it fills them with anger? Even if it leads to wrath?"

What he said surprised her. "They're scared," he told her.

"They sounded pretty wrathful to me."

He shook his head. "That's just a side effect of the fear. They're terrified of what's going to happen to their planet. Well, you can hardly blame them for that. But it's more than that. They're scared because they don't know. They don't know what's coming. They don't even know what we're doing about it—and I can't make them see it. I'm just not that good an orator. Hellfire, they don't even know what the enemy looks like, because they've never seen that video."

"The elders are worried that if they see it, it'll start a panic," Roan pointed out.

"Maybe," Thom said. He shook his head. "Maybe it would. And maybe that's what they need. Right now they're just confused and scared and I didn't help with that. It looks like all I did was give them a chance to vent."

"Maybe," she said, "just maybe, you should let wiser heads make decisions like this. Let the people who know this planet and its people choose what information to release, and what to hold back."

"Okay," he said. "If you can tell me I did the wrong thing, and mean it."

"Thom, that isn't what we believe. We hold to the four eternals, which include—"

"No. Don't give me dogma. Give me your real opinion. You think I did the wrong thing? I want to hear it. Not what your faith would say. Not what Elder McRae wants you to say. I want you, Roan, to tell me how you feel."

"I can't—"

"Yes, you can."

She'd intended to say that she couldn't extricate herself from the faith, because she belonged to something larger than herself. That she had duties that precluded her having a personal opinion in this matter.

Even in her own head, it sounded like an evasion.

"Tell me people don't have a right to know what's going to happen. Tell me that, and mean it, and I'll...I'll apologize."

Roan rolled her eyes. "I think you should get out of my car," she told him.

Which for some reason, some unguessable reason, made him smile. Then he said something that truly surprised her.

"Can you do me a favor?" he asked.

Now? He was going to ask her for something now? But of course the faith believed in service. She fought back the urge to sigh. "If I can," she said.

"I want to set up another event like this."

"Really?" she asked.

"I have to try again," he said. "Please. See if the Retreat will let me talk to the—the Church of the Old Word?"

"Ancient. The Church of the Ancient Word," she corrected.

He turned and flashed her a smile. In the dim cabin of the ground car, his eyes caught some light off the dashboard perhaps, and they flashed at her. She saw, perhaps, why Lanoe had chosen Thom to be his goodwill ambassador. The boy was very good looking, for one thing. For another he had a sort of easy charm, a charisma about him. You could sense it. If he'd chosen to go into politics, he probably would have done very well. Assuming he learned how to give a speech.

"I'll do what I can," she said.

"Thanks," he said. Then he fumbled getting his door open and jumped out of the car.

She watched him climb the stairs toward the ground control station. Once he was gone, she sighed a little to herself. Then she switched on the car and drove back to the Retreat.

⤙⤚

The tender flew long, slow circles over the crater, the sensor pod on its side tilting this way, then that. Zhang had taken it up as soon as the others arrived, to scan the structures of the mining facility for any sign of motion. High above the clouds Lanoe's FA.2 hung in a stationary orbit, ready in case the enemy had any nasty surprises lurking up in space.

Down on the ground Valk kept his eyes open, watching out for any drones that might have survived the apocalypse in the strip mine. He had a heavy particle rifle swinging at his side, which made him feel a little better about the job he'd been given. He had to stop every so often and pour out the rainwater that filled the barrel, but he was pretty sure the weapon would still function.

"Over here," Derrow said. Her voice quavered with anxiety but so far she'd been all right. She pointed at a structure that looked to Valk like a giant sponge, shapeless and riddled with holes. It stood maybe twenty meters high, and three times that wide. The three of them headed over, careful where they stepped. The ground here was webbed with cables and pipes, some so small you didn't see them until you tripped over them.

Up close the structure looked like it was made of lace. Around the big holes were countless smaller ones, and around those were tiny holes the size of pinpoints. Kind of like foamsteel, except the pattern wasn't random. Fractal, maybe. "You have any idea what this is?" Valk asked.

Derrow shrugged. "All that empty space probably makes the building really light. Cheap on material costs, too. It makes sense, but—I've never seen anything like it."

Valk reached up and punched the side of the structure. It dented in without much effort at all. Dented, but didn't break.

"I'll remind you," Maggs said, "Lanoe saw a half-dozen landers come squeezing out of a structure like this. What if one of them was still in there?"

"Then I probably just woke it up," Valk told him. As soon as he'd said it, though, he felt bad. Teasing Maggs was one thing but he didn't need to scare Derrow. "Relax. Lanoe and Zhang already knocked out all the landers and worker drones." At least, they claimed to have done so.

Valk stuck the rifle's snout inside one of the big holes. A lamp on the weapon's receiver lit up and swept across the opening but Valk could see nothing but shadows inside. "Let's take a look," he said.

"By all means, you first," Maggs said, with a laugh.

"We need to see," Derrow said. It sounded to Valk like she was trying to convince herself. She looked to Valk and through her face-plate he could see her sweating. It was hot out here but he imagined her suit was compensating just fine.

Okay, then. He put a hand up on the edge of the hole and pulled himself up inside, wriggling around to get his bulk through the aperture. That hurt, a little, but not enough to make his suit offer him painkillers. The hole must have been designed to be just big enough for a lander to squeeze through, he decided. Well, the landers were just machines, and probably didn't worry too much about comfort.

After he'd pushed about a meter forward the hole opened up into empty space. It was pitch dark in there. He could hear a steady dripping, most likely from rain finding its way inside. He summoned a

display on his wrist and held his arm up so the light would illuminate the interior.

Maybe he'd half-expected to find a lander towering over him,
its legs raised to impale him on metal claws. In that he was disappointed. What he did see, though, was weird enough.

The interior of the structure was open and empty, a mostly
spherical chamber more than fifty meters across. There was no distinction between walls, floor, or ceiling—the inner surface curved
seamlessly all around him. That surface wasn't flat, but instead
lined with ribs that converged at either end of the space. He felt like
he was inside the hollowed-out rind of some colossal piece of fruit.

The endless pattern of holes made the thing feel rotten or maybe
skeletal, and all that empty space was just eerie. Rainwater fell in
a steady stream from the upper portion, only to leak out again
through holes in the floor before it could collect.

He got the impression this was a place human beings were never
supposed to go.

Derrow clambered up beside him and he reached out a hand
to help her. Maggs brought up the rear and once he was inside he
climbed a ways up one of the ribs, using the holes as fingerholds.
Just showing off, Valk assumed, but then he saw what Maggs was
after. The interior wasn't as featureless as he'd thought. Maggs had
found a thing like a floppy segmented worm hanging from one of
the smaller holes. He batted it back and forth, and luckily for him
it didn't come to life and attack him. "What is this?" he asked.

Valk looked around and soon saw others just like it, dangling
lifelessly from holes spaced evenly around the interior.

Derrow went over to one that she didn't have to climb to reach.
She stared at it for a long time before answering. "A hotpoint, I
think. The drones...live inside these things, right? This is a kind
of barracks. That's our hypothesis? I think this is how they recharge
themselves." She dropped the wormy thing and ran her glove along
the curving edge of one of the ribs. "Okay, I need to not think about
dozens of those things crammed in here like sardines, writhing
against each other. I need to think about something else, right now."

"I have a suggestion," Maggs said, with an unmistakable tone in his voice. Valk expected her to snarl at him and tell him now wasn't the time but instead she laughed.

"I'll bet you do," she said.

"Yeah," Valk told them both. "Come on, there's nothing else to see here."

The three of them climbed out through one of the big holes, back into the storm. Valk was almost glad for the rain that lashed across his helmet, as if it were washing him clean.

Their next stop was a sort of pylon about two hundred meters away. They shuffled over toward it in the low gravity, careful not to launch themselves off the ground with anything like a confident step. The pylon was a lot less creepy than the barracks, or at least it looked more like something a human would build. It was triangular in cross section and rose about thirty meters off the crater floor. They craned their heads back to see its top, a bulbous sort of pod from which dangled dozens of short arms.

"Communications?" Maggs suggested.

Derrow shook her head and pointed at a column of thick pipes running up the pylon's side. "No. This is a cracking tower. I mean, it's not how I would build one, but...the process is pretty fundamental. We use something similar at the mines back on Niraya. It's for distilling heavy chemicals down to smaller compounds."

Maggs looked over at Valk, who just shrugged. Their job wasn't to understand what she said, just to keep her safe while she looked at things.

There was no way inside the cracking tower, so they moved on. Ahead of them the crater floor gave way at a massive and abrupt cliff. Looking over the side Valk could see the next level down, about half a kilometer below him in the murk. There was no way to get down without jumping so they turned aside and headed toward a very large structure they could just see in the distance.

As they approached it took on an oblong shape, though not as round as the barracks they'd first explored. One whole side of it was open to the elements, which made Valk think it looked like a hangar or something. It was hard to tell from a distance but it was clearly gigantic in size, maybe half a kilometer long and half that wide.

The pipes and cables that crisscrossed the ground lifted into the air near the big structure and draped over it like the strands of a spiderweb. Close up he could see they wrapped around the structure like they were enclosing it in a cocoon.

Their was no sign of a door or hatch in its exterior walls so they walked around to the open side. Darkness filled the cavernous space within. Well, that made sense—Lanoe had cut all power to the crater's structures. Valk couldn't shake the thought, though, that even when this place was fully operational it would have done its work in darkness. Neither the killer landers nor the interceptor he'd fought had anything like eyes, after all, so why would they need lights?

As they stepped inside out of the rain Maggs took a Very pistol out of a pocket of his suit. He loaded two flares inside, then fired them up high, into the open space of the structure. They lit up as soon as they left the barrel, then deployed rotors at the top of their arcs so they could hover in the air. The reddish light they gave off filled the giant space with a slowly coruscating glow, almost as bright as daylight back on Niraya.

What they illuminated looked to Valk like a hundred thousand braids of hair hanging down from the ceiling, long and ropy, some coiling on the floor, some hanging free. He hadn't the slightest clue what he was looking at, though something about the braids seemed familiar.

Together the three of them moved through the forest of hair, careful not to touch any of the hanging plaits. Valk quickly realized they were bundles of metal wire, not actual hair, but he still didn't want to get anywhere near them.

Deeper inside the hangarlike space were machines, some of which Derrow could identify as wire swages—devices for taking thick wire and making it thinner. Other machines just made her shake her head. At the very center of the giant structure several massive shapes hung in the shadows. Maggs sent a command to his flares, moving them forward to light up more of the space.

That was when Derrow screamed.

Valk didn't blame her. He'd seen the video, same as she had. A dozen landers—all legs and claws—hung from the ceiling, motionless but instantly recognizable as the machines that had killed all those Nirayan farmers.

One of them had a leg that had been flayed open, the skin parted and the bundle of wires inside exposed. That was why the hanging wire had looked so familiar—he'd seen it before when she'd examined the claw back at the Retreat.

When they'd all had a chance to calm down—when the landers failed to come to life and kill the three of them were they stood—Maggs asked, "Is this a repair shop? Were they trying to rebuild the ones Lanoe killed?"

Derrow took a step backward. Her hands were out in front of her, as if she could ward off the killer drones. "I don't think so," she said. "I think...oh, damnation."

"Tell me," Valk said.

"I don't think this crater was just a strip mine," she said. "I think this is a factory. I think this is where they make those things."

❧

After he'd addressed the Gnostic Christians, after he'd revealed the existence of the invasion fleet, Thom became a minor celebrity on Niraya. Roan—who had been assigned to help him however she could—arranged chances for him to speak with the Gospel of the Fallen Star and the Church of the Ancient Word. The Centrocor mining concern asked if he would present them with a formal statement on behalf of the Navy and he said he would give it his best shot. Local media got interested as well, sending a reporter out to interview him. They chose to do it at the ground control station, the closest thing the Navy had to an official base on Niraya.

Roan went along, because Elder McRae wanted her to be present whenever he spoke. The elder, of course, refused to show any anger or displeasure at his revelation of her secret, but it was clear she was deeply concerned with how the news would affect the people of Niraya. Perhaps she thought that Roan would keep him from making things any worse.

Roan tried to focus on her responsibilities to the faith, but instead found herself more worried about how Thom was handling the demands the people put on him. The day the reporter came he was very nervous before he spoke. He didn't ask her to hold his hand, this time. Maybe he was just getting better at public speaking. Roan went and sat with Ensign Ehta, who, having nothing else to do, had decided to watch from a corner of the room.

The reporter was a woman of maybe thirty, well dressed for a Nirayan. She had a camera drone that floated around behind her left shoulder, capturing everything for the record. "Thanks for agreeing to this," she told Thom, as she made a big show of setting up—unrolling a minder on the table between them, adjusting the center's lighting to get the best shot. "Before we begin, I want to ask you—just for my personal information—how much danger you think we're in. Is the Navy up to stopping this fleet?"

Roan could see what was happening—the reporter was hoping to catch him saying something meaningful while he thought they were off the record. Roan wanted to wave her hands in the air and warn Thom to hold his tongue, but it turned out to be unnecessary.

Thom just gave the reporter a warm smile and nodded at the camera drone. "You're already recording," he said.

"Hmm?" the reporter asked. "This thing? Oh, it's always on, to catch any good B-roll for when I edit this piece."

Thom nodded. "Well, to answer your question—I have every faith in the Navy, and especially in the commander of the local force, Aleister Lanoe. If anyone can keep the enemy at bay, it's him."

"What can you tell me about the enemy we're fighting? There's a lot of contradictory information out there. Some people claim it's a fleet of ships sent by one of the polys, probably DaoLink. Some say it's a swarm of angels descending to purify Niraya."

Thom's smile turned up a little at one corner, just enough to indicate he didn't take the idea of divine intervention seriously. "I can't say much about who sent the fleet, because honestly, we just don't know yet."

"You don't even know who you're fighting?"

"We do know a few things. The fleet didn't come through the local wormhole, and so far we've seen that they rely heavily on drones to fight for them rather than engaging us personally. I know there are a lot of people on Niraya who choose to live nonviolent lives, and I want to assure them that so far there's been no blood spilled. We hope to keep it that way."

"Hold on," the reporter said. "Drones?"

"That's correct," Thom said. Did he look a little put out? Roan could guess what he was thinking—that if the Retreat would release the video of the first attack, he wouldn't have to explain this.

"Drones, like this one?" the reporter asked, gesturing at the machine that hovered behind her. "I've never heard of an armed drone. Drones don't kill people."

Thom smiled through gritted teeth. "It's actually illegal for anyone to put a weapon system on a drone. The penalties are considerable. But I assure you, whoever this enemy is, they've done it. The machines they're sending against Niraya—"

"And again, you don't know who 'they' are," the reporter pointed out.

"Yes. I mean, no, we don't know."

"It seems you don't have much in the way of actual information to give my viewers."

Thom started to shrug, then seemed to catch himself. His smile was plastered on at that point—Roan could see his lips starting to twitch. "There's a great deal that's unknown. We do know that Niraya is in serious danger."

"From killer drones," the reporter said, again.

"The people of this planet need to know that," Thom told her. "They need to understand what's going on. It's my job to tell them what we do know. And to reassure them that we're fighting on their behalf, giving it everything we've got."

"How is the Navy doing that? What can you tell us about the

fighting? Have Commander Lanoe and his pilots attacked this enemy directly, yet?"

"I—I can't comment on actual engagements—"

"Yet another thing you can't tell us. Or won't."

Thom looked away from her, away from the camera. Even to Roan he looked shifty and defensive. This wasn't going well.

"I'll share any information I can," he promised. "I'll answer any questions."

The reporter nodded and made some notes on her minder. "You recently addressed the Christian Gnostics," she said.

"That's correct."

"Was there any reason why you went to them first? You aren't a religious man yourself. I mean, not as far as I could turn up in my research."

Thom's eyes went wide, shining under the lights. Roan winced to see how scared he looked. "You did a background check on me?" he asked.

"Of course. That's part of my job. I wanted to make sure I knew what questions to ask. It wasn't easy, though. For one thing, you're not listed anywhere in any Navy database."

"No—I . . . no," Thom admitted.

"You aren't in the Navy at all, are you? Unless"—and the reporter laughed at the idea—"you're some kind of secret intelligence officer or something."

"No, no," Thom said, "I'm not in the Navy. But Commander Lanoe asked me personally to be his liaison to the people of Niraya."

"An interesting choice, since—and honestly, I'm embarrassed by this. I mean, I think of myself as being good at my job. But I couldn't find any records about you at all. Nothing. I've never seen anything like it. You and your Naval associates came here from the Centrocor Hexus, but their records don't show you being there, ever."

"I met up with the pilots near the Hexus, but I never actually set foot on it," Thom said. "Listen, forgive me, but I don't see why talking about me is relevant. I'm here to discuss the invasion."

"Of course you are," the reporter said. Then she rolled up her minder and sat back in her chair. "Except you have no actual information to pass on. What do you want to talk about? Not yourself. Not the Navy's plans. Do you want to discuss Commander Lanoe? Do you want to tell me why, if we're actually under attack, the Navy sent a man who's been retired for seventeen years?"

"This interview is over," Thom said.

"If you like," the reporter said, as if it meant nothing to her. She packed up her things and left without another question.

When she was gone Ensign Ehta came over and thumped Thom on the back. "Good job, kid," she said.

"What?" Thom asked, wheeling on the grounded pilot.

"You kept your mouth shut." Ehta nodded happily. "Never saw the point of public relations myself. Don't know why people have so many damned questions. I mean, they should just let the Navy do its job, right? Stay out of our way."

Thom shook his head. "That's pretty much the opposite of what I'm trying to do here. I want the people of Niraya to support you, not pretend like you don't exist."

Ehta shrugged expansively. "In that case—damn. I guess you messed up."

Thom stormed out of the ground control station and down the stairs toward the crater floor. Roan chased after him, having no idea what to say. When she finally caught up to him at the bottom of the stairs he turned and stared at her with wild eyes. Then he grabbed her and pulled her into a tight hug.

She tensed up, unsure of what was happening. He was very warm, and she could feel how skinny he was under his stylish clothes. Roan couldn't remember the last time someone had hugged her. What were you even supposed to do? Eventually she put her arms around him and patted him, gently, on the back. He released her, then, to her immediate relief.

"Sorry. I just needed that," he told her. "I needed to hold somebody who doesn't hate me. I hope it's okay. I mean—it's not against your beliefs, or anything, to hug someone."

"I don't think there's anything about hugging in the Four Eternals," she told him. She surprised herself by laughing a little. Maybe just a release of nervous energy. "I guess I just wasn't expecting it."

He nodded and pulled away from her.

"I can't do any more interviews," he told her. "Not if they're going to ask about my past. And when I talk to the churches, I just make them think their gods hate them or something. What am I even doing here, Roan?"

"Your best," she said.

"It's not enough! After this—after this mess, they're going to think they're being attacked by cute little *robots*. I'm just making things worse. If they could see that video, maybe—but your elders won't let that happen. It's like they're happier with the people on this planet being misinformed and ignorant. It's as if they prefer it that way."

"They're just trying not to scare anyone," Roan said, but she wasn't sure if she believed that anymore herself. "Look, Thom—"

"I can't do anything right, can I?"

"Thom, it's okay," she tried, desperately wanting to soothe him. Because clearly it wasn't okay at all. Yet she couldn't think of what else to say. "It's going to be okay."

He dropped into a chair and chewed on his thumbnail. "I know what we have to do," he told her.

"You do?"

"I need to talk to the elder. I need to ask her for something."

Chapter Sixteen

Thom paced back and forth in impatience while Elder McRae studied a minder at her desk. She flipped through several pages of reports without so much as a sigh or a raised eyebrow. When she finally looked up at him her face was a dispassionate mask.

"It appears," she said, "that you've had an effect, at least."

Thom stared down at his boots. "If anything I've made things worse."

Just after his video interview went live, news had come in that a pair of Christian Gnostics had been attacked by a much larger group of Centrocor miners. Apparently the Gnostics had been preaching at the entrance to the mining concern—imploring the miners to repent and convert before God destroyed Niraya. The Gnostics must have been pretty strident in their appeals, but that hardly justified the savagery of the attack—both of the preachers were in the hospital now, one with broken ribs. "I got some people hurt, frankly," Thom said.

"An isolated incident," the elder said. "The Centrocor administrators acted quickly to arrest the attackers. They assure me there will be no further violence."

Thom rubbed at his eyes with the balls of his thumbs. "Before, the people of this planet were confused about what was happening. Now they're fighting about it."

The elder nodded. "Perhaps not what Commander Lanoe was hoping you'd achieve."

"You didn't want this, either," Thom said. "I'm sorry—I know you didn't want news of the invasion getting out. I know I went against your wishes."

"We all choose our own path."

Whatever he thought of the elders and the Retreat—and his estimation of them had sunk pretty low—they weren't cruel. No, they weren't despots. They didn't run Niraya with an iron fist. Instead they seemed to treat anyone who wasn't a member of their faith like a child who needed to be carefully and kindly supervised.

Even now, even after he'd defied her, he knew that Elder McRae wouldn't chastise him. She wouldn't punish him. He thought maybe he'd prefer it if she did. At least then someone would be giving him guidance, instead of just forcing him to live with his own doubts. He'd tried to contact Lanoe, to at least see if the old pilot approved of what he'd done, but Lanoe was too busy to talk.

Thom had never felt so alone. He shook his head, mostly because he couldn't believe what he'd gotten himself into. "I think I made the right decision," he said. "I wish I could know for sure."

"It's impossible to say. In the faith, we try not to think about hypotheticals," the elder told him. "Instead we focus on realities. Tell me, what do you want to achieve?"

"I'm hoping I can turn things around," he told her. "I'm hoping I can at least dispel some of the weirder conspiracy theories. If the people knew they were being attacked by drones—machines, not supernatural creatures—then at least some of the anger would be allayed."

"Are you so sure?" Elder McRae asked. "You might be surprised at how the religious mind works. The Christians have a saying— that their God works in a mysterious fashion, something like that. They might very well see the drones as the instruments of their deity's judgment." She smiled at him. "I should know what faith can do when married to a little imagination. I've made similar leaps in my own thinking."

"You need to make an official announcement. Tell people everything you know. When I tell them all I do is start rumors and urban legends. They'll believe it, coming from you. They have a right to know."

The elder didn't even look up. "It's been discussed. A decision has already been made," she said.

In other words the Retreat wasn't going to do anything. Thom couldn't believe it. All those people on Niraya, thinking they were safe—he stepped forward and leaned on the desk. "At least give them some idea of what's going on! You have the video. The video of the lander attacking the canyon farm. If you released that video, let people see what's coming for them, it might—"

"Out of the question," the elder said, before he could even finish.

"But why?" Thom asked. "What are you afraid will happen if people see it?"

The elder folded her hands in her lap and closed her eyes for a moment before answering. "Panic. Rioting, perhaps. Further violence. I'd think that's the last thing you'd want."

"You don't think these people have a right to see it?" Thom demanded.

"I try to take a longer view, in my decisions," the elder told him. "Consider the possibilities. There are two, yes?"

"Only two?"

"Indeed," Elder McRae said. "One. Commander Lanoe and his pilots will repulse the invasion. At which point that video will become a matter of historical curiosity. Two. They will fail. Everyone on Niraya—including you and me—will die, and quite soon. In what way do you think it will improve the last few days of this planet for the people to be terrified by that ghastly video?"

Thom stared into her eyes. They were completely unreadable—this was a woman who'd spent half a lifetime learning how to control her emotions. To keep herself calm no matter what.

No matter what.

"You don't think they can do it," he said, very softly.

"I don't like to make predictions."

He shook his head. "No. You've thought it through. You think Lanoe will fail."

"I've said all I will on this matter. Now. If you have any other business...?"

He might have said more, except just then there was a clatter of noise outside the door, and then a curt knock. Roan had been waiting outside—now she stepped into the office and nodded at the two of them. "Ensign Ehta is here, Elder," she said. "She'd like to speak to you."

"Of course," the elder said.

Ehta came in puffing for breath and red in the face. Clearly she'd come from the ground control station in a hurry. At first she couldn't even speak.

"Roan, get her a glass of water, please," the elder said.

When Ehta had recovered a little, she dropped into a chair, heavily enough to make it creak. "New imagery," she said. "The enemy fleet...It's...maneuvering." She tapped at a virtual keyboard on her wrist and a holographic display appeared in front of her, showing the same gray blobs they'd all seen before. They had come into better resolution now, so that their actual shapes could be made out, though without much in the way of detail.

The biggest ship, the one they called the carrier, was still mostly a big ovoid blur though now spiky projections were visible on its forward end, long spires that looked like the frill around a lizard's neck or, if one were feeling gloomy, perhaps like teeth.

The smaller line ships—what Lanoe had suggested were destroyers—had taken on shape as well. They looked like twisted horns or jagged triangles.

Around them the smallest ships moved like a cloud of gnats, still just flecks of gray with no visible shape.

"They're decelerating," Ehta pointed out. "But not as quickly as they were...I know the, the"—she waved a hand in the air—"the mechanics of it are kind of hard to grasp, but that means, basically—they're coming on faster than before."

The elder got up from her desk and came over to study the projection from various angles. "What about their trajectory? Has that changed?"

Ehta shook her head. "No. They're still on a course directly for Niraya. Well—most of them are."

Thom frowned. "Most?"

"There were eight of those...destroyer things," Ehta said. "In the first image. I counted them. There's only seven there. I went looking for the other one. It's moving toward the ice giant, toward that moon where Lanoe went. I'm guessing it's been sent to take them out."

"There's only four of them there, four ships against that thing," Roan said, her eyes very wide.

Ehta shrugged.

Thom glanced over at the elder. "Lanoe can handle it."

"We can hope so," Elder McRae said. "How long before the main fleet arrives here, at Niraya?"

"Less than a week," Ehta said.

All of them were too stunned to speak after that. Thom had known this was coming—known the fleet was on its way. But that had always been an abstract sort of idea before, something that would happen in some nebulous future.

Now it was real. Now it was breathing down their necks. Less than a week before everyone on Niraya died. The elder, Ehta, himself. Roan. He looked over at her face but couldn't see anything there except that she looked scared. *Well,* he thought, *she should be.*

He shook his head and headed for the office door, intending on—actually, he had no real idea what he intended to do next. He just wanted to get away from the specter of apocalypse in the office.

When he was out on the landing he heard the door open again behind him. He turned, hoping to see Roan there.

Instead he saw Elder McRae.

Her mask had slipped, just a little. He could see something similar to fear in her eyes. Concern, maybe.

"Thom," she said. "I'd like to ask for a favor."

He stopped where he was and just waited for her to go on.

Clearly she had no desire to rely on him. She didn't trust him. But she needed something.

"I'd prefer if this news wasn't shared outside of my office," she said.

"You want me to help you keep your people ignorant," he said.

If she was offended by being spoken to like that, she didn't show it. "The last thing this planet needs is fear-mongering," she told him.

He smiled. How he would have liked to tell her to go to hell, just then.

Too bad she was going to get what she wanted. "Information on enemy movements is one of those things Lanoe doesn't want broadcast," he said. "You're not the only one who believes in secrets."

Maggs crawled into one of the bunks in the tender's wardroom. He'd been walking for hours and needed a bit of a lie-down. The other pilots clustered around a large display while Derrow— Proserpina, he corrected himself—went over what she'd found.

"This place has been operational for a while," she said. "Just going on how elaborate it was, how much they built and how much they dug, I'd say they were here on Aruna long before they sent that lander to Niraya."

"Maybe this place was what they wanted all along," Valk pointed out. "Killing all those Nirayans was just like posting a 'no trespassing' sign."

"Sure, maybe," Lanoe said. He turned to face all of his attention on M. Derrow. "Did you find any indication of who built it?"

"We found no trace of any living, organic creature anywhere we looked," she said. "We explored about sixty structures in total and I'm confident in saying there were no living things in this facility, even before you blew it up."

That got a few laughs. Well, Proserpina was a midlevel Centrocor manager, a job where you needed to know how to give a presentation.

"The whole place was automated. If I'm correct, it was built by machines, too, with no human supervision. That's against every protocol I know. If there's even one bad line of code in its instructions, a drone will mess up a project every single time. You need at least one person to supervise them, to debug them when it's necessary." She threw up her hands. "But that's what we found here. Unsupervised machines."

"Which fits with everything else we've seen," Valk piped in. "That interceptor I fought didn't have a pilot. The landers are autonomous, too."

"Forgive me," Lanoe said, "I know you're a miner. But I don't imagine it takes a lot of code to teach drones how to dig up rocks."

If Proserpina was offended she didn't show it. "Sure, I guess. But there was a lot more going on here than just grubbing for ore. I know a strip mine when I see it. But I know a factory, too. There are assembly sheds like the one we found all over the crater. Some of the other structures are machine shops and forges... The mine is just there to provide the raw materials. Everything in this crater is here for one purpose, to make more of those landers."

"Why weren't there more of them when we arrived, then?" Zhang asked. Zhang did most of Lanoe's thinking for him, as far as Maggs could tell.

"Because of these things," Proserpina said, and changed the display. From his vantage Maggs could just see it showed video of the spongelike structure they'd investigated. "You thought these were barracks. And yes, they house the landers when they're not in use. When I went inside this one, though, I saw the interior was really robust for such a lightweight structure. That got me thinking. You see these ribs on the inside? You don't need those if you're just building a house, especially not on a moon with so little gravity. It's just overdesigned for that purpose. But then I realized where I'd seen a design like that before. This isn't a barracks, it's a cargo module."

"What does that mean?" Lanoe asked.

"They build the landers here, stuff them in these modules—so they can ship them someplace else. Back to the fleet, maybe. Or... Look, I don't want to speculate too much."

"Go ahead," Lanoe told her.

The engineer nodded. "Maybe they were going to ship these to Niraya. Maybe this is where they're assembling their invasion force."

None of the pilots had anything to say to that.

Proserpina let the silence draw out for a moment before she went on. "This is manufacturing on a huge scale. Everything in this crater was designed to build those landers. Because it's all done by machines there's no need for any real infrastructure—no communications, no living quarters, no food or water supplies. Just factories. I couldn't even identify any purely defensive structures."

Lanoe snorted. "They put up a damned good fight if that's the case."

Proserpina shook her head. In the low gravity her hair swung around her cheeks in a way Maggs found decisively fetching. "I said purely defensive. From what you told me, you were opposed by a bunch of landers and workers that just slowed you down a little."

"What about the antivehicle towers?" Zhang asked. "They nearly fried me."

"Those weren't designed to shoot you down. Those were smelters—they used the high-temperature plasma to melt down the ore and burn out any impurities. They could be used as weapons by venting that plasma in your direction, but as weapons go they were incredibly inefficient. If they'd managed to kill you or drive you off, it still would have set them back by months to lose all that plasma."

"Sure," Lanoe said. "That's interesting. Moot now, though. My main question for you right now is who built this place."

"Hard to say. There were no poly logos anywhere in the structures I saw. That's not how Centrocor operates—they put their hexagon logo everywhere they can."

"So it was DaoLink?" Zhang asked.

"Well..." Proserpina chewed on her lip. "Maybe. I mean, I can't rule that out a hundred percent. But...I don't know. This technology, it just isn't something I've seen before. Machines building the machines to build more machines."

"Some kind of new technology," Zhang suggested. "Something

they're testing out. It makes financial sense, right? If everything's done by machines then you don't need to pay any workers. I can definitely see a poly thinking that was a good idea. No salaries, no health care, no food costs, even."

"Damned polys," Valk said. "That's exactly their kind of thinking. And they know it's going to be unpopular, so they experiment with it out here, where nobody's looking. No logos because if something goes really wrong, then it can't be traced back to them. They don't care about people, they never have, why, back in the Crisis—"

"Enough Establishment rhetoric," Maggs said.

Valk turned to stare at him—at least, Maggs assumed that was what he was doing. Faceless bastard.

"Why attack Niraya, though? If they had what they needed out here on Aruna, why send that lander to kill the farmers?"

"If this is new technology the polys have created," Zhang pointed out, "maybe they sent it here to test it."

Proserpina threw her hands up and shouted, "Enough! If you can stop hypothesizing for a second, I have more to say. You dragged me all the way out here; the least you can do is actually hear me out."

"Sure," Lanoe told her. The others nodded. Maggs gave her one of the warmer smiles in his stock.

"Thank you," she said. She bent over the controls of the display and brought up some new images. Tomographic cross sections and millimeter-wave deep scans of the machinery they'd found in the factory.

"Everywhere we went in the crater, I could figure out what this stuff did pretty easily. Nothing here was designed to be pretty, or user-friendly, or anything like that. It's basic machinery, designed to work and nothing else. That made it easy for me to see exactly what everything did, and how it was done. Except there were a couple of places where I looked at a machine and it was just…wrong."

"Wrong how?" Zhang asked.

"I don't want to get technical here, but there are some basic principles of engineering, some really bedrock stuff, that don't appear anywhere in the crater. No wheels, for instance."

"What do you mean?" Lanoe asked her.

"I mean nothing in this crater has wheels. It all has legs instead. Here." She adjusted the display. "You see this line, this was a main route from the pit mine to the nearest smelter. All the ore they dug up had to be carried along this line. It's a road, a good, flat, gently graded road that makes perfect sense. But there are no trucks on that road, no trains. Every piece of ore was carried from pit to smelter by a worker with a bunch of legs. That makes *no* sense. It shows up in the factory, too. There's no assembly line in there, because that would mean conveyor belts, and a conveyor belt is just a fancy application of the wheel."

"I don't understand," Zhang said.

"Whoever designed this facility," Proserpina told them, "didn't want to use wheels. Or didn't know how."

The pilots stared at each other, and it was clear to Maggs they weren't getting it.

He'd already twigged to where this was going, though.

And he quietly, if secretly, approved.

"The funny thing is, there are rotary elements all over the place. Centrifuges, pulleys, lots of things. But no wheels at all. Just legs."

Lanoe nodded. "That does seem strange," he said.

Proserpina sighed. "Look. If this is the polys...there had to be some human involved, somewhere. The machines build the machines all the way down, fine, but there had to be a prime mover, a human engineer who designed the first machine. And I guarantee that engineer would know about wheels. This only makes sense if that first engineer had no idea what a wheel was, like maybe they grew up in space or they evolved on an ocean planet or a gas giant with no surface—"

"You're saying the machines weren't designed by a poly engineer," Zhang said, very carefully.

"I'm saying they weren't designed by a human engineer," Proserpina replied. Clearly she knew she was fighting an uphill battle. Her stance changed, her shoulders coming forward, her head back. As if to fend off a blow.

She let them all stand—or recline, in Maggs's case—there in silence while the import of her words sank in.

"It's time," she said, eventually, "to talk very seriously about aliens."

<hr/>

It was cold in the dome at the base of the Retreat. The air didn't move but it sucked the heat right out of him. The flagstones were hard on his knees where he knelt on the floor.

Thom had never prayed. His father had thought religion was for the feeble-minded, and Thom had grown up thinking only the things of the material world mattered. He didn't pray now, either, but instead he turned his thoughts toward Lanoe, so far away.

I've let you down. You risked so much to save me, he thought. *You shouldn't have. You should have let me die in Geryon. Rather than just delaying the inevitable.*

Warm hands on his shoulders. A soft voice in his ear calling his name. He lifted his head and looked behind him and Roan was there. He could see in her face that she was worried for him, that she could see how much he hurt.

She knelt down beside him. "The first elders, the pioneers who were the first people to live on Niraya, all lived inside this dome," she said, as if she were a tour guide filling him in on local folklore. He didn't mind. It was a break from being stuck with his own dark thoughts. "There was no breathable air outside at all. They lived in here with some animals and a lot of plants. They studied and meditated and worked tirelessly. They died in here."

"They were that desperate to get away from the rest of humanity?" he asked.

"They *believed*," she said. "They believed that this planet could mean something. Look up."

The dome itself was made of steel girders framing hundreds of triangular panels, each a meter or so on a side. "That used to be glass up there," Roan said. The panels between the supports had been plastered over long since. Each section had been painted, though each one, it seemed, in a different style or color palette. A few of them were blank. "Every time an aspirant becomes an elder," Roan said, her voice hushed with reverence, "they paint one of those."

Thom studied the panels, though there were so many and they were all so different none of them really stood out. He saw one that showed a figure in an old-fashioned baggy space suit standing at the rim of a canyon. Another was a pattern of concentric circles, each densely figured with the shapes of tiny human embryos. Some were just swatches of color, deep rich blues or simple, pure yellows.

"Look, do you see that one? It's always been one of my favorites," she told him. He followed her finger to see where she was pointing. The panel was barely touched, its plaster unpainted except that in the middle of the space, in simple lettering, was written the legend IT WILL BE GREEN.

"You're going to paint one of those, someday," he told her.

But she shook off his assumption. "Not every aspirant makes it to elderhood. It's a hard road and it's not for everybody." She looked more wistful than disheartened by the prospect. "I've been studying to be a planetary engineer," she told him. "I've learned all about how you can change a planet, change its chemistry at the most basic levels, to make it more livable. How you can drop comets on a planet to give it more water, and what plants are best for generating oxygen. I always knew, though, that no matter how hard I worked or how much of my life I gave to it, I wouldn't live to see Niraya turn green. The elder who painted that panel," she said, "knew the same thing. But he or she kept working. They kept working because they believed in the future."

He reached over and took her hand. She stared down at it for a moment, and he saw her mouth fall, saw her shoulders slump. He thought maybe she was going to pull away. He was—attracted to her. Maybe that was the wrong word for it. He was drawn to her. She was his only friend on this planet, the only person who'd

shown him any sympathy. Of course he was going to develop feelings for her.

That didn't mean she would feel the same way, though. It didn't
mean she would feel anything. He loosened his fingers, in case she
wanted to pull her hand back. She didn't, though. She just left her
hand in his, let it be.

He drew so much comfort from the touch, so much peace. He
almost didn't want to break the spell and end that moment. He had
to tell her something, though. Truth was important to her. Honesty. He had to tell her what he'd discovered.

"Elder McRae thinks Lanoe will fail," Thom said.

Roan nodded. "I heard the two of you talking. I know you disagree with her, though."

Thom wasn't sure if that was true, anymore, but he said nothing.

"Can I show you something?" she asked.

"Aliens," Lanoe said.

Maggs considered himself a bit of an expert of reading people.
He had made quite the study of the way a person's tone of voice
could give them away, even when they said the most mundane of
things.

In this case, he determined that Lanoe a) had dismissed the idea
before as not worth thinking about; b) was now still very uncomfortable with the idea; and c) very much wanted someone else to
scoff at the idea and tell him it was nonsense. From which one
could draw the inescapable conclusion that he d) was starting to
believe it.

Normally Maggs would have been happy to squash the idea.
It was after all preposterous—when the smoke cleared, it would
be revealed that this was all some new black project run by the
polys, that there was a perfectly logical solution without the need
for resorting to fairy tales and the supernatural.

Just then, however, Lanoe believing in little gray men served his purpose.

So he stayed quiet.

After all, there were others more than willing to speak.

"I've spent my whole life thinking we were alone in the universe," Zhang said. "I don't know—"

"Just because we haven't met any aliens before doesn't mean there aren't any," Valk pointed out. "We've settled less than a hundred planets, right? How many planets are there in the galaxy? Billions? We could easily have just missed finding them before a dozen times."

"I get that," Zhang replied. "Sure. It's a big galaxy. But if there are aliens, whole space-faring cultures of them out there—maybe we wouldn't have met them in person by now, but surely we would have heard something. Some radio signal, some video broadcast of a situation comedy starring a guy with four eyes and two heads. Some chatter between their ships...anything."

"Maybe we just don't communicate the same way they do," Valk pointed out. "Look at this bunch. We've been trying to contact them by radio ever since the first lander put down on Niraya, and nothing. Not a word from them. Maybe we've just been trying the wrong way—maybe they communicate by telepathy instead of talking. Or maybe they communicate with smells, or radioactivity, or—"

"Stop, both of you," Proserpina said. "Just listen to me for a second. Let's say they are aliens. What does that mean?"

"It would mean we have no idea how to fight them," Maggs put in. "And let's be honest, that's exactly what we've seen so far. Valk nearly got killed using the wrong ammunition against them. Lanoe and Zhang thought they were fighting antivehicle guns that turned out to be smelters. All of our training is in how to fight other humans."

"We've done all right so far," Lanoe said. "Valk took out that interceptor. We smashed this place just fine."

Maggs shrugged. Best not to overplay his hand.

"You wanted me to build you some guns," Proserpina said. "Rail guns. Auster—M. Maggs, I mean—showed me the schematics. Do you know if those will even work against alien ships?"

"No," Lanoe admitted. "Though it seems likely. This bunch don't have the wheel, you said. They don't seem to have vector fields, either. You said their technology was all cheap and disposable. I'm guessing that doesn't line up with being immune to rail-gun shot." He looked around at his pilots. "Aliens. Sure. We'll run with that thought for now, until it gets proved wrong. That just means we need to keep our eyes and our brains open. We need to learn some new tactics. M. Derrow, I want to hear your thinking about that."

"Me?" Proserpina asked. "I don't know anything about fighting."

"You've got a better idea than any of us what the enemy's made of," Lanoe told her. "If there's a weakness there, something we can exploit...anything, I want to hear about it."

She sat down for a while to think. The others kept silent, as if they didn't want to disturb her mental processes.

"Well," she said, finally, "there's the fact that all we've seen is drones."

"Go on," Lanoe said.

"Like I said earlier. You can't just let drones do their own thinking. They're not smart enough to know when they've got something wrong. Say—just as an example—say you have a drone and its job is to clean a certain stretch of hallway. It's very good at it, it gets every little speck of dust, disinfects all the doorknobs, picks up any trash. But it's only as good as the person who programmed it. If that person made a mistake, or just left something out, the drone will eventually screw up. It'll clean the floor so hard it wears a hole through it. Or it'll pick up what it thinks is trash but is actually somebody's pet dog."

Zhang, at least, laughed at the thought.

"Because, see, it doesn't know any better. The programmer didn't tell it that a dog isn't trash. Or that the purpose of a floor is to not have holes in it. So when the drone does something unexpected like that, the programmer has to come in and fix the program. Refine the instructions. The drones here on Aruna achieved something amazing, all on their own—they built a factory to make more drones. That's great programming. But if there was a zero somewhere in that programming that should have been a one, somebody conscious and self-aware will need to come fix it."

"An alien," Valk said. "One of the aliens needs to be close by to make sure the drones stay on-task."

Proserpina nodded. "It makes sense to send drones in to do your fighting for you, I mean, we all know how that goes wrong, but from one perspective it makes a lot of sense. You don't have to endanger yourself. You don't have to feel guilty if some of your drones get destroyed. You'd need to be close by, though, just in case."

"So what's your suggestion?"

She waved her hands in the air. "Look, I'm no fighter, I said that. But I think I understand that programmer, a little. I understand that they chose to send drones instead of doing their fighting themselves. So my suggestion is that you find the programmer. You find them and threaten them and I bet they would surrender on the spot. They're willing to throw away countless drones, but not themselves."

Lanoe nodded. "Sure. And I bet I know where they are."

"The carrier," Zhang said. "That really big ship we saw in the space telescope imagery. That's why it hangs back, at the rear of the fleet. And why it's different from all the other ships."

"That's where I'd want to be, if I was soft and squishy and all my troops were robots," Valk said.

"A wonderful analysis, Proserpina. Of course," Maggs said, "we'd have to find a way to get to that carrier. Through all the line ships and fighter escorts and whatnot. With just four of us."

"I never said it would be easy," Lanoe replied.

Roan signed out a ground car and drove them to the far edge of the town, to where a long ramp led up through a lava tube and through the wall of the crater. It was dark inside the tube, the car's lights illuminating the road ahead of them only a little ways. In the gloom she and Thom glanced at each other. Neither of them said anything.

They emerged into dazzling sunlight on a plateau just below the crater's rim. He could see for kilometers in every direction—he saw the labyrinth of twisty canyons that covered most of Niraya's surface, and realized he'd never been out there before, out where the air was too thin to breathe and people were few and far between. Strange to think that there was an entire planet beyond the little town. A whole world.

Roads headed off in various directions—to the mining concern in its other crater, kilometers away. Toward farms in distant, deep canyons. A narrow track, barely a path smoothed through the rock, led north, and it was this way Roan took.

The path headed down into canyons, walls of rock soaring up over them. It was all slickrock, solid stone carved by wind, except for the occasional tiny patch of dusty yellow plant life. Nothing stirred among the fallen scree of boulders and broken rocks—there were no animals out here at all.

Occasionally the walls of the canyon would come together in a dramatic arch that made the sun flicker as they sped by underneath. Roan pointed out her window once and he saw a place where the rock had weathered down to a cluster of hexagonal columns, shiny and smooth as glass, like the pipes of a church organ. Mostly Thom was only aware of the silence, of the incredible hushed feeling of Niraya, as if the entire planet were holding its breath. The ground car's engine made almost no sound at all, and the air was too thin for any more than a puff of wind. If Roan hadn't been sitting next to him, bouncing around in her seat as the big balloon tires took the rough terrain, Thom might have panicked, alone as he was in that desolate place. As it was he just felt like the two of them were the last two people in the universe.

The canyon floor started to rise through a series of long switchbacks. The walls on either side receded and they came up onto another flat stretch of land, a scratched-up plain of rock and sunlight. Roan drove another kilometer or so until Thom saw a long, low mesa climb over the horizon.

She switched off the engine and coasted to a stop. He couldn't see why she'd chosen this particular place to end their journey, but he didn't protest. She reached across him and opened a compartment in the dashboard. Taking out two respirator masks, she put one over her face, then showed him how to do the same. "We're walking from here," she said.

The ground car's cabin had been pressurized. When they stepped down onto the naked rock, the air pressure was so low that Thom felt his skin tighten as his pores closed, a natural response to the lack of air. The respirator sprayed water across his nostrils so they wouldn't dry out and crack.

"Be careful where you step," she told him. Then she set off at a quick pace, walking toward the mesa. Thom followed after her, watching her weave around a patch of ground that was slightly bluer than the rest. Ahead the rock was speckled with bright yellow and deep black.

Lichens. He understood the principles of terraforming, and he knew that lichens were used on planets that could just barely support multicellular life. They needed very little water to survive, and they gave off a surprising amount of oxygen. If you could grow enough of them on a planet like Niraya, they would eventually give you a breathable atmosphere.

The lichens came in a dozen different muted colors and a hundred different shapes, from simple black spots on the ground to feathery masses like green dust bunnies gathering in the cracks of the slickrock. Roan was very careful not to step on any of them—they must be very delicate.

Thom did his best to do the same. He watched his feet and tried to match her stride. His respirator hissed and snored against his face but very quietly and the only loud sound was the crunch of his boots on the dusty rock, the repetitive thuds of his clumsy footfalls. He fell into a careful sort of rhythm of walking and so it was jarring when Roan grasped his arm to make him stop.

The mesa had snuck up on them when he wasn't looking. Now it was right before them, a wall of stone thirty meters high that ran off in either direction for what seemed like forever. It presented a craggy face to the sun that hung motionless in the sky behind him.

Every square centimeter of that wall was covered in lichens. Huge, concentric rings of them, dozens of meters wide, black and purple and a frosty pale green. Where the rings touched they joined together in trefoils and looping curves, some of them forming broad patterns bigger than the ground car behind them, bigger than he could take in. They had a slightly furry texture that rippled in the tenuous breeze, until the whole wall shimmered and coruscated with trapped light.

It was...beautiful. So incredibly beautiful.

"I come here," she said, "when I can't find peace anyplace else. I think about how this happened, about how long it took for the lichens to colonize this wall. Season after season of growing and then quieting down during the long nights, then growing again when the sun came back." She sat down with her legs folded and he joined her, sitting close enough that their knees touched.

He nodded, his eyes never leaving the shimmering spectacle before him.

"What do you see?" Roan said, whispering, as if even a raised voice here could harm this precarious ecology.

"Raindrops," he said. "Raindrops falling on the surface of a pond."

A funny little smile crossed her face, never quite settling down. "It doesn't rain here," she said. "I've never seen rain."

A strand of her hair fell down across her nose and the top of her mask. He felt a very strong urge to reach over and brush it away, but he didn't. She left it there for a long minute, then reached up and moved it back into place herself.

"When I first met you," she said, "I thought you were just some useless pretty boy from some decadent world. A social parasite."

He laughed, though he knew she was serious. And not entirely incorrect. His life so far had been a privileged one. Compared to the lives people lived on Niraya, his had been an uninterrupted pageant of luxury.

"When Lanoe asked you to be his goodwill ambassador, I

thought he was just making busywork for you. But you took the job seriously. When you spoke to the Gnostics, when you tried to do that video interview...I saw something new in you, Thom. I could see you really wanted to save Niraya, while everybody else—the pilots, the elders—they'd already given up. You hadn't even seen this," she said, gesturing at the shimmering lichens. "You didn't know this place could be beautiful. You wanted to help anyway. Thom, you can't give up now."

He looked down at his hands. "Everything I do goes wrong. I've managed to piss off everybody. Even Elder McRae."

If she was shocked by his obscenity, she didn't show it.

"You know how this planet got settled," she told him. "About the original elders, and how they wanted to choose a life for themselves. A spiritual life. That's a good story. It's an old one, though. There are a lot of people who didn't choose this place. They were born here, and had no place else to go."

"People like you," he said.

"People like me, yes. For most of us this is the only planet we've ever known. The only place where we know how to live. Even if we could leave, if there were some way to escape what's coming, where would we go?"

Thom shifted uncomfortably, because he wasn't sure what she was really asking. "Roan, I can't leave now, either. I owe Lanoe too much."

She shook her head. "I didn't think you would. I just...If I only have a couple of days left to live, I want to know we'll keep working, keep fighting, because if we just stop, if we just sit here and wait for the end, I know I'll go crazy with fear."

For a while she was silent. Thom listened to their respirators hiss and kept his own thoughts to himself. He wanted to reassure her, to tell her Lanoe would save them, but he knew it would just sound like an empty promise now.

Eventually she spoke again, maybe just to fill up the silence.

"I was born in one of the canyons, about a hundred kilometers from here," she said, finally. "My father wasn't cruel, but he was very religious. He belonged to a fundamentalist sect that held that God created man, but woman was kind of an afterthought. There was no point in educating me because I would never be smart enough to be useful. The most I could hope for, he believed, was to marry a farmer and make babies. Preferably male babies."

She turned to look at him, maybe to see if she'd shocked him. He didn't know what to say—it sounded horrible.

"I ran away from home when I was twelve. I went to Walden Crater because I thought that everything was bigger there, brighter and better and you didn't have to wear a respirator every morning when you went out to feed the emus." She laughed a little, amused by her own distant naiveté. "I found out pretty quick I wasn't made for town life. I had no skills, I didn't even know how to read or use a minder. The only real option I had was to join one of the churches. They'll take anybody. I thought the Transcendentalists were appealing because they never seemed to get angry or sad." She shrugged. "It was that or the Gospel of the Falling Star, and they... Well, that wasn't my path."

Thom nodded. "I got a request from them to attend something they called a Darkness Mass. I have no idea what that means, but it sounded kind of sketchy."

"You've got good instincts. They do their rituals...naked," she said, whispering the last word. He laughed and, surprisingly, she did, too. "They call it 'going skyclad.' They dance in a big circle, around a fire. That's what they consider religion." She shrugged. "They think it makes them free. Everybody wants to be free. In the Retreat, the elders talk all the time about choosing your own path. About making your own decisions. But it's a lot of nonsense, Thom. We don't get a lot of choices in life. Not really. That's what makes them so precious."

"Is that why we're here? To talk about choices? You want me to choose to keep fighting, right?"

"I brought you out here because I want you to help *me* make a choice," she said. "A big one. I need to decide whether I want to stay with the faith, or leave it forever."

"That sounds pretty drastic."

"Yeah," she said, with a sigh. "I don't know what I would do without the Retreat. It's been my home for almost half my life. It's been my calling, and my refuge. The elders have been very good to me—they taught me so many things."

"You've worked really hard for them," he said. "Paying back that debt."

She looked at him for a while, just watched his eyes. "The Retreat talks a lot about personal responsibility and being centered. But they've changed, I think. Gotten hidebound. You asked me awhile back whether I thought people had a right to know about the invasion fleet, and I put you off."

"Your faith wouldn't let you answer the way I wanted you to," Thom said.

Roan nodded. Then shook her head. "I didn't want to answer at all. Because it meant making a hard choice. The answer, of course, is yes. People have a right to know what's going to happen to them. Of course they do. But saying that makes me question so many other things."

"Roan—"

"I'm beginning to think it isn't the faith that deserves my loyalty. I think it's Niraya itself I believe in."

"You sound like you're trying to talk yourself out of something. Or into something. I can't tell," he said. "Why don't you just tell me what's going on here?" he asked.

"Okay. Do you remember, before, when Elder McRae followed you out of her office, when she asked you to not tell anyone about the fleet advancing on Niraya?"

"I do."

Roan took a deep breath. "She left her personal minder sitting on her desk. While she wasn't looking, I cloned its memory to my own minder. I copied everything."

"Wait—you did what?"

"One of the files I copied was the video. The video of the lander attack. The one you think everybody should see."

"Oh," he said.

"I can let everyone on Niraya see that file. Tell them the truth. Of course, if I do, it means the end of my time with the faith. They'll kick me out of the Retreat and they'll never let me back in." She took a deep breath that made her respirator cloud up. "I'm going to do it, Thom. I'm going to do it anyway. It's the right thing to do."

The look in her eyes was anything but certain. Had she brought him out here to ask for his advice? Or did she want him to talk her out of this?

He tried to think it through rationally, calmly, like a Transcendentalist would. "You'll lose everything. You shouldn't have to be the one to do this. It should fall on somebody else."

She frowned. "I wish it could, Thom. But we have so little time left. It seems pretty likely," she said, "that everybody on this planet is going to die soon. I need to do this now or not at all."

"If you show everyone that video, maybe they'll just panic," he said.

"But that'll be their choice. They'll get to determine how they want to spend their last days for themselves. Yes," she said, nodding to herself. "I have to do this, Thom."

"Then..." He stopped, unsure what to say next. "Then," he tried again. "Then I want to help. I want to do this with you."

She nodded. All her training, all her discipline couldn't hide the look of gratitude in her eyes. She climbed to her feet, careful not to step on any lichens. "Okay," she said. "Let's go."

"Where? How do we start?"

"Back to the car, first. After that...we'll figure it out." She started walking and he got up and followed her, careful to only step where she did. Careful not to hurt her planet.

Knowing full well that what he was about to do might make it tear itself apart.

Maggs and Valk unrolled a giant Mylar tent across the sodden rock of the moon. In the low gravity it was easy to prop it up, to make a shelter from the rain. A shelter big enough to cover one of the half-constructed landers, as well as Proserpina and her equipment. A silver roof that billowed in the poison wind and made a sound like a thousand snare drums pattering away as the rain struck its top side.

As soon as the shelter was erected she moved in quickly to perform something rather like an autopsy. Maggs stood back and watched, fetching her tools as she requested them.

It was insufferably boring, of course. He could only watch her cut the skin away from the tangles of wires for so long before his mind began to drift. He watched her instead, his delightful engineer. Watched the way her body moved as she tugged at the metal braids, as she bent over to dig inside its mechanical entrails.

She put her foot up on one of its legs and leaned deep inside its carcass with a pair of pliers. She got hold of some hidden component, then pulled hard to get it loose. It fought her: She had to apply more and more leverage.

When it finally came loose, it did so all at once and in the low gravity she flew backward, launching herself off the ground.

Maggs jumped after her, getting his arms around her and bringing them both thudding back to the soil in a heap of limbs, with her on top. She struggled around until she was almost facing him, then held up her prize—a little bauble of brass and silicon, nearly crushed between the jaws of her pliers.

As she moved across him, trying to get back to her feet, Maggs pulled her closer until she laughed. "In such a hurry to get off of me?" he asked.

She shook her head inside her helmet. "I need to get this in a millimeter-wave scanner," she said.

"You need to take a break. You've been working for hours now."

She struggled away from him and he let her go. "Later, maybe." She gave him a longing look. "Okay, definitely. But later." She hurried off to a pile of cases that held her tools and her computers. She didn't even offer him a hand to help him get back up.

Though hardly given to intensive self-examination, Maggs knew he was a vain man. He possessed no pretensions otherwise—false modesty in his esteem being a quality more loathsome than the breath of vipers.

So he took some offense that his charms weren't enough to penetrate her defenses. Still. He needed her, for his latest scheme. She was, not to put too fine a point on it, the linchpin holding everything together.

A war's not won the day it breaks out, his father's voice said inside his head.

Patience, in other words. For now he would bide his time. He went back to watching her work, as she bent over some arcane bit of computer equipment, watching numbers crawl across a screen. Eventually, they stopped. And then she nodded to herself. Clearly she'd found something. She called Lanoe over and he came running, bouncing high over the wreckage and the rubble of the facility.

"How's it coming along?" the old bastard asked.

"Slowly," Proserpina said. "But I've got something now. You asked me to take this thing apart and see what I could tell you about its brain."

"Sure," Lanoe said.

"It doesn't have one."

"I don't understand."

She nodded and took the bauble out of the millimeter enwidgetizer or whatever the instrument was called. "It doesn't have any kind of central processor. Its logic elements are spread throughout the body, more like a nervous system than a central brain. There are animals back on Earth that operate like that—really primitive stuff, starfish and sea cucumbers and things like that."

"Have you ever seen a drone with that kind of hardware before?" Lanoe asked.

"Not one made by a human being. Look, here," she said, and brought up a display. It showed a simplified view of a lander, a cluster of legs joined together at one end. Glowing lines spread through each leg in a pattern like veins or the branches of a tree. "This shows the electronic components inside the thing. Like the nerves in your arms, they ramify outward until they reach the skin. You've seen how the things don't have anything like eyes."

"I thought maybe the cameras were just hidden," Lanoe said. "Or microscopic."

"No," Proserpina said. "These landers are blind. They operate almost entirely by sense of touch. The entire skin seems to be one big haptic sensor, and it's very sensitive. They're deaf and blind but if they touch something as smooth as glass it probably feels like sandpaper, because they can detect incredibly fine textures."

Lanoe frowned. "When I was flying over this crater they definitely knew I was there. They didn't have to touch me to react to my presence."

"No, because there's another kind of sensor in that skin. One it took me a long time to identify, because I've never seen anything like it. I'm still not sure how it actually works. It picks up coronal discharges from objects composed of carbon and water."

"I don't know what that means," Lanoe said.

Proserpina held the bauble up to the light and turned it slowly so it glittered. "I'll give you the short version. It's a life detector. Somehow it picks up the presence of living things anywhere nearby. Even if they're hidden behind a wall, or inside a fighter, or whatever."

"Neat trick," Lanoe said.

"Tell me about it. This thing—it confounds me. It's so simple, so basic in design, and yet it has that sensor onboard. Something I don't think humans could invent if we tried, it's so advanced. Which leads me to my next point."

"Go ahead."

She turned the bauble over and over in her gloved hands. "I tried taking a look at its programming. No luck there—it's not any kind of code I've ever seen. Well, I expected that. But it doesn't even read right. It doesn't even think in binary; instead it's like base fifteen or something crazy like that…Sorry, I know, too technical, and it doesn't really matter. What does is this. I can't read this drone's code, but I can the shape of the programming, the file sizes, stuff like that. And what I found is crazy. Just a few lines control the whole thing—just a single, dirt-simple program. I can make an educated guess what that program is."

Maggs suddenly found himself paying attention. Was it possible that he even cared? Unlikely, but he wanted very much to hear what she said next.

"Walk around in circles," she said. "Look for anything living. If you find something living, stab it until it isn't living anymore. Repeat."

When they arrived at the ground control station, Ensign Ehta squinted at the two of them. Thom had the idea she'd been asleep when they arrived, napping in her chair. The minder in front of her displayed the gray shapes of the enemy fleet, just as he'd seen them before. "Something up?" she asked them.

Thom opened his mouth to speak but Roan beat him to it.

"The elder wants to know if there are any updates on the fleet."

Ehta nodded and rubbed at her face. "Well," she said, "I've been tracking that big line ship headed toward Aruna. It's definitely sticking to its course. Lanoe and them are going to have a nasty fight on their hands."

"Do you think they'll win?" Thom asked, leaning over the display, trying to wring some new information out of the gray shapes.

Ehta laughed. "That's what cataphract fighters are made for, kid. Fighting line ships. Of course, it doesn't always work."

"They'll make it," Thom said. "They have to."

Having received the update, they had no reason to stick around. Thom knew they couldn't proceed with Ensign Ehta there, but he had no idea how to get rid of her. Roan went over and examined a rack of equipment, while Thom just stood in the middle of the room. He realized how sweaty his hands were and he shoved them in his pockets. He caught himself staring at Ensign Ehta, and tried to look away. When he looked back she was staring at *him,* with a sly look on her face.

"You two, huh?"

"What?" he asked, a little too quickly. His voice a little too high-pitched.

A mischievous smile played across her face. "I suppose it's no great surprise."

"It isn't?" Thom asked.

"Hell, kid. I remember when I was your age. And the two of

you've been thick as thieves the last couple of days. It's the oldest story in the world."

Thom's mouth wouldn't seem to close properly. He had no idea what she was talking about. When he looked over at Roan, though, he saw she was blushing bright red.

"Yeah, yeah," Ehta said, rising from her chair. "You throw two young people together, they're bound to at least start thinking about it. Well, I'll tell you what. I'm not exactly necessary to the cause here, right now. Nobody's going to notice if I step away from my post for . . . an hour, say?"

"I don't—I mean, that would be—"

The Ensign held up her hands for peace. "Never let it be said I stood in the way of young love, right? Just make sure to clean up after yourselves." She made a point of meeting Thom's eye. Then she gave him a knowing wink, and left without further comment.

Once she was gone, Roan moved over to the console. She turned around and faced Thom. "She thought we were—that we came here to—"

Thom nodded. "Listen, it got her out of the way, right? Let her think that. For now, anyway. We need to focus."

There was no arguing with that. Roan unrolled her minder on the console while Thom studied the controls that moved the big comms dishes outside.

Having the video file in their possession wasn't enough. The Retreat controlled all network traffic on Niraya, and if they'd simply tried to share the video to everyone in the directory, the Retreat's censoring software would have seen it instantly and stopped it from going out. No, they needed to broadcast it directly, with a signal strong enough to make sure it was picked up by every minder and display in Walden Crater.

The ground control station's dishes were capable of sending a signal like that to distant planets. It was more than strong enough for their purpose.

Once they were sure Ehta would be far enough away that she wouldn't see the dishes moving, Thom rearranged the array until it was pointing inward, toward the crater. The dishes groaned and struggled to realign themselves. One froze in place, still pointing straight upward. It didn't matter—they still had more than enough signal strength.

Roan had the video ready to go. She turned on a microphone and got ready to introduce it. Before she started, though, she looked over at Thom, her eyes locked on his. She needed to know he was still sure. That he still wanted to do this.

It meant more trouble for him, more people to get angry with him. Thom was certain it wasn't what Lanoe had intended for him to do, back when he'd made Thom his local liaison.

He nodded without hesitation. He reached over and tapped a virtual key to start the broadcast.

Roan stared at the microphone for a second as if she thought it might bite her. Then she began. "Um. Hello," she said.

The one thing they'd forgotten to do was to think of how to introduce the video. What to say. In the end Roan kept it simple.

"This is going out to everybody. Everybody we can reach. What most of you know, I think, is that Niraya is under attack. What you don't know is who's attacking us. The video we're about to show you is going to be tough to watch, but it'll give you some information. What you do with that information is up to you."

She tapped the face of her minder and the video started to play. She turned away from the display as if she didn't want to see it again.

On the control board, every indicator was green. The signal was strong, and it would blanket the entire crater.

They let the video run to the end. Then they switched everything off. Roan rolled up her minder and held it tight in her hands.

"It's done," she said.

━━━━✦━━━━

Zhang had been out in the tender all day, up above the clouds. When she returned she went straight to Lanoe and the two of them whispered together, for far longer than Maggs strictly liked.

He was under the Mylar tent, relaxing in a folding camp chair at the time. The moon's gravity was pitiful but still, indolence was a habit he'd always cultivated.

"What do you think is going on?" Valk asked. The giant paced back and forth, stomping out from under the tent to get a better look at Lanoe and Zhang, then stomping back into the shelter. Rainwater dripped from him, big, fat drops falling slowly to the ground in the low gravity so that it looked like he was sweating through his suit. Proserpina looked up in annoyance as some of the rain got on her oh-so-fragile equipment. "Did she find something up there?"

"I'm sure," Maggs said, letting his head roll from side to side, "they'll inform us when they think we need to know."

Proserpina frowned as she looked between him and Valk's black polarized helmet. "Lanoe said something about a counterattack, earlier."

"Maybe that's it," he said, and feigned a yawn. He looked over at Valk. "If you're going to keep stalking back and forth like an exhibit at a zoo, perhaps you could do it somewhere other than my field of vision."

Valk stopped pacing. Instead he folded his arms and bobbed up and down like he needed to urinate.

One of the great compensations for the dreariness of Naval service, Maggs had always found, was that your suit took care of such things without ever requiring you to think about them. He frowned at the big fool, then went back to his studied attempt at expending no energy whatsoever.

Alas, it was not to be. Lanoe and Zhang finished their tense discussions and together they came into the tent. "Time to pack up," Lanoe told Proserpina.

"I think I might be getting somewhere," she told him. "Can you give me another hour? I've almost got the power system in this thing figured out."

Lanoe shook his head. "No, sorry. You're going home."

Valk stopped moving. He was as still as a very tall statue.

"We expected the enemy to send a massive force this way as soon as they realized their facility was offline," Lanoe told them all. "I've had us camped out here so we would be ready to face that. Funny thing is, they didn't take the bait."

"Not on our timetable, anyway," Zhang said.

Lanoe nodded. "They dispatched one of their destroyers this way. It's moving slower than I thought it would, though. Being cautious. Most likely it's scanning the moon right now, trying to figure out what happened, from about a half an AU out. At its current speed it'll take a couple days to get here—days we don't have. The main fleet is still moving toward Niraya, and they'll arrive within a week. If we wait here for the destroyer to arrive, we put everything at risk."

"I'm guessing that you've got a different plan," Valk suggested.

"Sure," Lanoe said. "We're going to take the fight to them."

For a moment the rain pattering on the tent was the only sound, as all of them considered what Lanoe's words meant.

If no one else wanted to, Maggs figured he would be the one to make it clear. "We're going to face down a destroyer with no ground support. Out here about as far from Niraya as we can get. Just the four of us."

"No," Lanoe told him. "Three of us will head out there in our fighters. The fourth will take M. Derrow home in the tender. It means fighting this thing at less than full strength, but we can't risk just leaving her here alone."

"That's very...kind of you," Proserpina said.

"I need you back on Niraya, getting the engineering crews ready to build me those guns," Lanoe told her. "Maggs," he said. "I assume you want to be the one to take her back in the tender."

Oh, now, that was rich. On the face of it, of course, it made sense. Everyone knew that he and Proserpina had a special sort of understanding, and maybe Lanoe just meant Maggs would want to make sure she was safe. Or, on the other hand, he could be impugning Maggs's honor.

Well, it would certainly be the prudent thing to do, to simply say yes. The Navy handbook probably listed some carefully worked out equation on what the chances were of three fighters taking out a destroyer on their own, and the percentage was probably on the low side.

But if Maggs did the prudent thing now—

You've never been a coward, Maggsy, his father's voice told him. *Now's your chance to show 'em all up.*

Indeed.

"No," he said. "Send Valk."

"Me?" the big pilot asked.

"Yes, you," Maggs told him. "You've already gotten your taste of glory. I haven't fired so much as a shot in this fight yet. It's my turn."

Lanoe shrugged, as if it meant nothing to him either way. "Fine. We'll get extra fuel and ammunition cartridges from the tender, then leave as soon as the fighters are ready. Valk, why don't you help the engineer with her stuff?"

It was exceedingly hard to tell, but Maggs thought the big freak looked like he wanted to protest. Eventually, though, his shoulders sagged and he went to pick up one of the equipment boxes.

"Permission to say goodbye to the engineer, sir?" Maggs asked. "Seeing as I may not return?"

Lanoe just waved in assent. He was already headed off toward his FA.2. Maggs went over to Proserpina and put a hand on either of her shoulders. "No time for a proper farewell," he told her.

She looked confused and scared. Which of course just meant she'd been paying attention.

He slid his hand down to her wrist, then summoned the display there. On the floating panel that appeared he tapped a few virtual keys until he'd established a radio frequency only the two of them could hear.

"Forgive me for taking the liberty," he told her. "There's something I need to say in private before I go—"

"Auster," she said, "please don't. I know you're going to tell me you love me or something, but that feels like we're never going to see each other again."

He fought back the urge to laugh. He was fond of her, definitely, but they were hardly sweethearts after one very pleasant night together. "Listen to me," he told her. "This is very important. I've been holding it back while the others were around, but you need to hear it and this might be my last chance."

"Oh, all right, just say it," she told him. Her eyes looked curiously hopeful.

Well, he'd already done the groundwork there. No need to go over the top. "The first time we met, back at that welcome ceremony at the Retreat," he told her, "you said something to me."

Her face clouded as she worked it through. "Back then? You mean the very first thing? That was some kind of request for evacuation or...or whatever. I was acting as the ranking Centrocor employee back then. I didn't actually expect a serious response—"

"I understand. But you've seen something, now. Something of how bad our chances are. Listen to me, Proserpina. I don't want to think what's going to happen on Niraya if we all die out here. Valk on his own won't be able to fight off the entire fleet. You have a chance, right now. Just a little bit of time. Start making that demand again—seriously this time."

"I don't know..."

"I do. There has to be a backup plan. Send a message to Centrocor and have them send enough ships to at least get you and your employees out of here." He pulled her into an embrace. "I can't stand the thought of you getting hurt."

"Auster—we both know it won't work. Centrocor has already written this planet off. Including all of its employees. They'll never send that many ships all the way out here, at least not in time."

"Convince them, then. Or if you don't think you can rely on your employers—and if I'm being completely honest, I think you're right about that—well. Get somebody else. Get cruise liners to come and pick you up. Call in some freight haulers, whatever it takes."

"That would cost an enormous amount of money," she pointed out.

"Money? Hmm. I hadn't thought of that," he said.

Sometimes the biggest lies were the easiest to tell.

—✦—

They'd broadcast the video.

"What do we do now?" Roan asked.

Thom could only shake his head. He pulled her close into a tight hug. He could feel her trembling. He was shaking, too.

"My whole life," she said. "All those years at the Retreat. That's gone, now," she told him. "I know we did the right thing, but—"

"We did the right thing. That's all that matters."

She buried her face in his chest. "Thank you," she said. "Thank you for helping me with this. I don't think I could have done it alone." He half-expected her to start crying. Instead, she just shook in his arms, as if she were cold. He rubbed her shoulders to warm her up, even though he knew that wasn't what she needed, just then.

He never planned on kissing her. It wasn't something he thought out. He just pressed his lips against the top of her head, and that felt as if he was still comforting her, as if it was part of the hug. When she turned her face to look up at him, he bent down and touched his lips to hers. That was all.

Because he was who he was, immediately he second-guessed it. "I'm sorry," he said. "Maybe that wasn't appropriate."

"I didn't push you away," she told him. "Thom—I know, I mean. I've seen the way you've been looking at me, recently. I know you have feelings for me."

He hadn't gotten so far as to figure that out for himself. He knew he'd been drawn to her, but he hadn't considered much more than occasionally holding her hand. "Maybe it's like the Ensign said. You put two people together—"

"I'm not supposed to respond," Roan told him, as if he hadn't said anything. "As an aspirant, I'm not supposed to form attachments with people. It can cause problems with my studies. With my finding my path."

"Oh," he said.

"So I couldn't respond. Or say anything, before. But now—I've turned away from the faith, haven't I? I'm not an aspirant anymore."

"Does that mean...?"

She shook her head. "I don't know what it means. Not yet. Maybe you should kiss me again. Maybe we can just try that."

He leaned down and kissed her, more seriously this time. He felt her body move against his, felt her relaxing into the kiss. That seemed like a good sign. She put an arm around his neck, pulling him down, closer to her.

Thom might have come from a more sophisticated planet. He might have grown up in a decadent culture that didn't practice much in the way of self-restraint. In point of fact, this wasn't the first time he'd kissed someone. It was almost the first time, though, and he didn't know how to proceed much better, he imagined, than Roan did.

Except he did know one thing. He knew Roan believed in honesty—whether she was a Transcendentalist or not, she'd always sought the truth.

Gently, he reached up and took her arm off his neck. Pulled his face back so he could look her in the eye. "Roan, you told me your life story. You don't know mine," he said.

"Later," she said. "You can tell me later."

"No, you have to know. Once you hear it I don't know if you'll want to spend time with me anymore."

She stared at him with sad eyes. "Thom, please."

"I'm a murderer," he told her.

That was enough to make her pull away. She moved to the far side of the room, her eyes never leaving his face. "What does that mean?" she said.

"It's...complicated."

"No," she said. "No. You can't say that and not explain."

"I want to, I just...I don't know how to tell you."

She waited him out. Staring at him the whole time. So he forced himself to find the words and tell her the whole story. About his father and how he'd discovered why he'd been born. About how heavy the gun had felt in his hand and how he didn't even need to think about it, about how easy it had been to pull the trigger, how he'd only started having doubts after the fact.

About how he'd run away, and how he'd tried to kill himself, and how he'd found he couldn't. How he'd begged for Lanoe's help.

About how he'd come to Niraya, and how he'd met her.

He wanted to say more. He wanted to talk about how much she'd come to mean to him, and how he was telling her this only because he trusted her, because he respected her and needed her to know the truth. Once he'd stated the plain facts, though, everything else just died on his tongue.

She didn't look away. She didn't scream at him, or cry, or anything like that.

Instead a calm as cold as ice came over her face. She looked almost bitterly amused. "You thought that now was the right time to tell me this."

"It was him or me, Roan," he said. "You have to see that."

She twisted up her lips, as if with deep thought. "I have no idea what to do with this information," she said.

Then she walked past him and out the door. He started to chase after her but she shook her head and glared at him until he backed off. She hurried down the stairs to her ground car and then she drove away.

Afterward he could do nothing but stand there wondering just how stupid it was possible for a human being to get.

Eventually Ensign Ehta came back.

"So?" she asked, raising her eyebrows.

He pushed past her and left the station. Headed down the stairs. He was nearly at the bottom before he realized there was nowhere, nowhere at all on this planet, for him to go.

Chapter Seventeen

Up ahead of Lanoe, Maggs's fighter blazed in the dark with its scrolling coat of arms, and Zhang's red tentacles writhed across her fairings. His own FA.2 showed no lights at all, though not for the purpose of camouflage—he just wanted to conserve battery power.

He had no idea how long this would take. If it was even possible.

In a career as long as Lanoe's, it was inevitable he would run up against destroyers—in fact, he'd taken his fair share down in battle. Though always with heavy support from ground batteries or with a wing of fighters screening his advance. He'd never even tried such a foolish thing with just a depleted squadron like this.

Added to the desperation of the plan was the fact that he had no idea what an alien destroyer's guns would be like.

Derrow had finally convinced him that this was no human enemy they faced. There just wasn't a better explanation for how weird the enemy drones were, how unlike human ships they were—they had to be aliens. The thought didn't help his mood.

"This is our big chance," he told the other two. Though he thought maybe he mostly said it to convince himself. "They were dumb enough to expose one of their principal assets. We take this destroyer away from them, and the entire fleet is weakened. Maybe compromised."

"Indeed?" Maggs asked. "May one ask how?"

"Derrow said there needed to be programmers in this fleet, somebody to correct the machines when they go wrong. If one of them is onboard this destroyer and we can take them hostage, maybe we can force the rest of the fleet to back off. We could end this whole war right now, right here."

"There were a fair number of assumptions in that speech," Maggs pointed out.

"It's a chance we won't get again, and it's worth it just for that," Lanoe told him. He would have liked to tell the swindler pilot where to stow his doubts, but just then he needed Maggs more than he needed the satisfaction. "Zhang, how's your imagery coming along?"

"I've got good video but it doesn't tell me much," she said.

A display popped up in front of Lanoe, a video image of the destroyer in flight. They'd already determined the basic silhouette, a kind of twisted horn shape about two hundred meters long that looked like no human spaceship ever built. There was more detail now, showing a hull studded with machinery or crew areas or who knew what, so tightly packed it made the destroyer look like it was covered in barnacles.

Lanoe studied the image, looking for guns, trying to get an idea of its capabilities, but couldn't make out any details that made sense to him. One thing did stand out—near the nose of the destroyer the overall shape was broken by a jagged patch that ruined the ship's tapering curve. "Huh. Does it look to anyone else like somebody took a bite out of this thing?"

"Maybe it was hit by a meteor," Maggs suggested. "Perhaps that explains why it's taking its time coming toward Aruna. Maybe it's damaged, even critically. Oh, wouldn't it be wonderful if it turned out the thing we're chasing had gone ahead and gotten itself killed before we arrived? If it was just a dead hulk?"

"You really think that's a possibility?" Zhang said.

"Not should my life depend on it. Which in all likelihood it does," Maggs replied. "When it comes to cosmic jokes, typically I find myself the one being laughed at."

Lanoe frowned. "We can't afford to assume we know anything here. We go in expecting a massive response—watch our for anti-vehicle fire, for flak, for escorts... Just keep your eyes open."

"Oh, aye, aye, Commander," Maggs said, with a sneer in his voice.

"And keep the chatter down," Lanoe told him. "Communications by laser only from now on." He switched off his radio panel before Maggs thought of anything else to say.

He got only a moment of silence, though, before a green pearl appeared in the corner of his vision. He saw it was Zhang contacting him and opened a private channel.

"What do you need?" he asked her.

"Just checking in. Seeing how you're really feeling about this."

"Like it needs doing," he replied.

"Listen—I'm just going to put this out there. If we don't come back from this, we're leaving Niraya in a real lurch," she pointed out. "Valk's a legend but he can't handle the defense on his own."

"If we can't take down one destroyer with three of us, there's no point tackling the entire fleet with four," he told her. He knew better than to think she was questioning his tactics. Back when she'd been his second in command, Zhang had always made a point of playing devil's advocate just before a big offensive. She didn't do it because she doubted him, but because she wanted to make sure he'd thought through all the angles.

Knowing her motivation made it slightly less annoying.

"What do you think about Maggs? Is he up for this?"

"He's got a Blue Star. And we're about to find out how he earned it. I know you'll be watching him like a hawk, so I'm going to just pretend I have full confidence in his abilities."

Zhang laughed. "You're finally learning to delegate."

"Guess so."

"Okay. Just one more thing. If we do make it out of this... if we get back to Niraya."

"Yeah?"

"I want to buy you a drink."

He couldn't help but smile, since she couldn't see it. "After that long talk we had about feelings, you're thinking we should see what's left of what we had, huh? Figure out what we are to each other now."

"I'd like to give it a shot," she told him.

He could hear in her voice how serious she was, how much she really wanted to try to patch things up. It had been seventeen years, and things had been ugly between them even back then. He had no idea how he would respond to her now, if they were actually alone somewhere with their helmets down. He had no idea if he could really get past seeing her in a new body. A body a tiny fraction of his age.

Still. A good commander knew when to let his people unwind.

"Sure," he said. "It's a date."

The green pearl winked out as she cut the connection.

—⟶—

It was folly to think that the destroyer wouldn't have any escorts. Zhang released a cloud of microdrones dedicated to scanning the local volume of space and it wasn't long before she'd spotted what she was looking for.

She opened a connection to both Lanoe and Maggs. "I've found their pickets," she said. "They're spread out on an arc about ten kilometers long."

"How many?" Lanoe asked.

"Sixteen. The same number Valk found back when we first came to this system. My imagery's pretty blurry but it looks like one big one and fifteen small craft, just like he saw."

"The same composition?" Lanoe asked. "An interceptor and fifteen of those unarmed orbiters?"

Zhang chewed on her lip. She wasn't sure what to make of her sensor data. "The big one's definitely an interceptor, just like the one Valk fought. The little ones, though—they're smaller than the orbiters he described." She sent the imagery over to the other two pilots. "Smaller than we are, even. I don't know what to make of that shape." In the image the small craft were just a couple of lumpy pods mounted on a skeletal frame. "I think that pod at the back is a thruster unit. The one at the front might be a gun."

"Best always to assume one's foe is armed," Maggs suggested. He sounded bored. Flying through empty space for hours along a preset trajectory could take its toll, Zhang thought. She hoped he would sharpen up once the shooting began.

"Scouts," Lanoe said.

Not all fighters were created equal. The cataphracts like Zhang's BR.9 and Lanoe's FA.2 were multipurpose assault craft, equally good at bombing runs and raids on line ships and dogfighting. There were smaller craft, though, called carrier scouts, used solely for escorting line ships. Fighters stripped down of everything non-essential, holding just enough fuel for quick jaunts and just enough ammo for a few minutes of fighting at a time. They tended to be underpowered, so much so they couldn't even mount vector fields—and as a result, they tended to get picked off like flies in any real battle. Cataphract pilots tended to sneer at carrier scouts, though it took a special kind of mad bravery to fly a scout.

"Looks like," Zhang said, "though I don't think we should take anything for granted right now."

"Sure," Lanoe said. "What's their trajectory look like?"

"They're headed toward us, though on a long curve," Zhang pointed out. "Maybe trying to flank us. I think it's safe to assume they've already noticed us. Using those life-detecting sensors Derrow showed us, I guess. Orders, Commander?"

"You two get on either side of them. I'll hang back a little and catch whatever you miss. Take these things down fast—we're not far from the destroyer now, and if it starts firing flak at us we want to be able to get out of the way."

"My pleasure," Maggs said, and surged ahead.

Zhang cursed under her breath and chased after him, Lanoe dwindling behind her until he was just a point on one of her displays, a tiny flicker of warmth under her fingers. She poured on the speed and hit her maneuvering jets, her inertial sink pulling her firmly but gently back in her seat.

Up ahead Maggs had pulled into a tight corkscrew maneuver, starting his attack run already, well before they reached the enemy. It was a ridiculous waste of fuel and she wondered, not for the first time, if maybe he'd bought his Blue Star—or used his famous father's influence to get it. She knew nothing of the man or his record, only what Lanoe had told her. Which was mostly that she needed to watch his every move.

The enemy ships appeared on her displays first, then as tiny dots she could just make out in the gray distance. One small advantage of her cybernetic eyes—because she couldn't see the stars, the enemy ships stood out like the only objects in the universe. They were strung out on a line, each one keeping an exactly equal distance from the one on either side. The slightly larger dot had to be the interceptor, keeping station at the left end of the line.

Soon she had crisp imagery and she got a good look at the scouts for the first time. Their design was dirt simple and ugly. The gun pod at the front was spherical, its curved shape broke only by a tiny aperture that made the pod look like an eyeball. A thin skeletal frame extended from the back of the pod to connect to a lumpy thruster unit that looked almost porous because it was covered in dozens of tiny maneuvering jets. No human engineer, Zhang was convinced, would ever build something so awkward and mercilessly utilitarian.

Maybe alien engineers had different priorities. Maybe all they cared about was making the little ships lethal. *Well*, she thought, *only one way to find out.*

Maggs reached them first, still spiraling madly at a speed that would have crushed him into paste if not for the inertial sink in his fighter. He was coming at the enemy from the right, so Zhang curved in on the left in a broad arc, keeping well clear of the line to come at them from the side.

The enemy ships started firing before either of them was in range. The interceptor pumped out kinetic impactors, big chunks of metal, just like Valk had said. The scouts belched plasma fire, just like the foundry towers back on Aruna, though her sensors told her this plasma was a lot less energetic. She did the math in her head, because she knew in a second she would be right in the path of those guns. The plasma fire would only be effective at short range, but the scouts wouldn't need to score direct hits. Much like with the foundry towers, even deflected shots would heat up her BR.9 until she was roasted in her cockpit, until the blood in her skull boiled and turned to steam.

Best not to get hit too many times, then, she thought.

This was going to be a tough fight, the two of them against sixteen. Zhang braced herself and punched her throttle, readying herself for the barrage—

"Mind if I take this dance?" Maggs called, startling her.

Before she could answer all hell broke loose.

Maggs came in fast, tightening his corkscrew until he was almost spinning on his axis. His twin PBW cannon flashed wildly, almost hypnotically, and one scout then another was sliced in half, their plasma pods rippling and melting like candle wax as they overheated.

The other thirteen responded instantly, breaking their formation and spinning away each on a different trajectory, some looping high over Maggs, some slipping underneath him. They moved with speed and agility Zhang could barely believe, turning and pivoting until she couldn't follow them, until they were just flickering points on her display. Their plasma guns twisted around in their mountings, their fire lancing out at Maggs a dozen times a second. Zhang thought he was done for as they swarmed around him like a cloud of deadly gnats, as fire washed over the flanks of his BR.9.

But it turned out she'd been wrong about Maggs.

His fast corkscrew approach hadn't just been for show. At that speed even a computer couldn't track him. The scouts were incredibly maneuverable, but it seemed all they could do to keep out of his way.

Sometimes not even that. His PBWs scored another hit, and then a fourth. The scouts folded up like they were made of sticks and cheap glue. He struck a fifth scout, his fire carving a line through its eyeball-like gun pod, and the thing just exploded, metal scrap jetting outward in every direction, the plasma inside burning as hot as the surface of a star for a millisecond, expanding in a vast shock wave that was gone before Zhang could even register its existence.

He cut the sixth one in half, its thruster and its gun pod spinning off in opposite directions, both quite dead.

The seventh twisted and darted away from him, only to collide with the eighth, neither of them surviving the smash-up.

Half the picket detail gone and Zhang hadn't even properly engaged yet. She made a mental note.

Maggs had not bought his Blue Star. He'd earned it the old-fashioned way, by being a hell of a pilot.

Zhang's vector field throbbed all around her then and she had to stop thinking about anybody else. A kinetic impactor had just come within centimeters of tearing her to pieces.

The interceptor was right on top of her.

Though less emaciated-looking than the scouts, it was still ugly as sin, a shapeless, lumpy design studded with spiky guns. It seemed to fire in every direction at once, its impactors streaking outward on random trajectories. Valk had described the never-ending assault of projectiles but she hadn't understood what he meant until she saw it for herself. It didn't seem to be aiming at all, just lobbing rounds at everything in its local volume.

She readied a disruptor round, then slewed around it in a wide, careful arc, keeping her nose pointed at the interceptor as she raced past its flank then around until she could see the hot exhaust of its thrusters. Her weapons panel chimed and queued up messages as the BR.9 worked desperately at finding a good firing solution.

She swiped the display away, instead locking her weapons to fire straight ahead. Then she brought her nose around to line up perfectly with the interceptor's glowing main thruster.

An impactor bounced off her canopy, rattling her bones. Warning chimes sounded from her damage control board.

She ignored them. Burned to stabilize until she felt like she was hanging motionless in space, the interceptor rotating slowly in front of her. Flexed the fingers of her hand, then wrapped her index finger around the trigger on her control stick.

Zhang fought by one simple edict: Never waste ammunition.

One shot, one kill.

She waited until she could look straight down the interceptor's main thruster, into the hot core of its engines. She wasn't thinking at all, she was just there, an extension of the fighter's weapons. When she squeezed the trigger she felt nothing.

The fighter lurched almost imperceptibly as the disruptor round jumped free. The tiny shock was enough to bring her back to herself and she slammed her control stick over to one side even as she punched the throttle, sending her veering off to the side, well clear of the interceptor.

Her disruptor detonated deep in its belly. It seemed to blur in her displays as it vibrated with the chain of explosions. Then some store of fuel or ammunition inside it cooked off and it blossomed into a vast cloud of heat and debris. Zhang's boards all chimed at her for a moment as she was buffeted by the shock wave, but her vector field held and the warning signals went silent one by one.

Zhang felt a smile creep across her face. She'd won. She'd beaten the bastard and she was still alive and—

Then a scout swung through her view, its gun pod staring right in through her canopy. Her eyes showed her an infrared view of the thing and it was bright, blindingly bright as it belched plasma across the front of her BR.9, searing heat pouring into her canopy until sweat coursed down her face and she was certain this was it, that she'd made her last mistake, that she was dead—

But as quickly as the heat came, it fell away. Ahead of her the scout had been torn to shreds, reduced to ragged jetsam that twisted away into nothingness.

A sleek shadow raced across her view, so fast she barely noticed. Maggs, in his own fighter, coming to her rescue.

She scanned the local volume of space and found none of the enemy left. The scout that he'd just blown up, the one that nearly killed her, had been the last of the fifteen. He'd destroyed them all while she took out the interceptor.

She opened a communications link. "Nice shooting," she said. "Thanks."

"Entirely my pleasure," he told her.

Maybe he wasn't such a bad sort after all, she thought. She'd met enough pilots in her time—trained enough of them—that she knew there was a certain sort, a kind who were insufferable in the barracks room but once they were out on the field they found their true selves, their nobler natures, and—

Lanoe was calling her. "If the two of you are done showing off," he said, "you might want to look at the destroyer and see what it's doing. Then maybe one of you can explain it to me, because I haven't got a clue."

Lanoe's display showed the twisted horn of the destroyer at a high level of detail now, the imagery built out of a composite of different views from various microdrones and his FA.2's own sensors. He could make out the ragged scar near its nose quite clearly, enough so that he could tell it wasn't a rupture in the destroyer's hull. There was no sign of actual damage, no visible scorch marks or stress fractures. It was as if the ragged gap were part of the destroyer's design, a normal feature of its shape.

Which just made it stranger that a cloud of debris was twisting away from the gap like a billowing pillar of smoke.

"Maybe we were right after all," Zhang said. "Maybe it did get hit by a meteor or something and now it's breaking up."

"Maybe," Lanoe said. He couldn't get past the overwhelming feeling of dread he felt, though. The feeling that the enemy was surprising them once again.

Especially when a second burst of debris erupted from farther back along the destroyer's flank, a whole new cloud billowing from its side.

"No," he said, because suddenly he knew exactly what he was looking at. "No, it can't be..."

He tapped at a virtual keyboard and magnified the view until it grew rough and pixilated, until he could just make out individual pieces of the debris cloud. And saw exactly what he expected to see.

"Fellows," Maggs called, "not be an alarmist, but is that smoke plume...turning? Rather heading in our direction, I think."

Lanoe shared the magnified view with the other two pilots. "That isn't debris," he said. "Those aren't chunks of the destroyer falling off. Those are scouts being launched."

A third column of them came boiling off the destroyer, a jet of tiny ships pushing toward them. Every single piece of "debris" was a scout breaking away from its perch on the destroyer.

Which wasn't, in fact, a destroyer at all. It was a carrier. The entire skin of the enemy ship was covered in scouts and interceptors and now all of them were deploying, headed straight for the three human fighters.

"Spread out!" Lanoe said. "We've got incoming!"

Dead ahead, along an arc fifty kilometers wide, the entire sky was full of enemy craft. Every single one of them accelerating in Lanoe's direction.

※

Zhang played her hand over her tactical display again and again, trying to get a grasp on what they faced. There was just too much information to process there.

Her eyes might be artificial but they showed her it was all true. Hundreds of enemy ships, maybe thousands.

Maggs had made short work of fifteen of the scouts, but she doubted he could handle these kinds of numbers. She knew she couldn't. The only smart thing to do now, the only course of action that made any sense, was to turn around and burn for safety. Get as far as possible from this cloud of ships and keep going.

"We can swing around behind Garuda, put the ice giant between us and them," Maggs said. "Buy ourselves some time. Those scouts can't have a very long range. If we can just get out ahead of them, we can make it out of here."

"There are interceptors in there, too," Zhang pointed out. "It looks like maybe as many as one in sixteen. We know the interceptors are capable of interplanetary distances. But I'd rather fight a running battle with those than take on all these scouts."

"I concur," Maggs told her. "Perhaps our redoubtable commander will be kind enough to give the order to break contact."

There was no response. Zhang could hear her heart beating in her throat.

"In your own good time, Commander," Maggs said.

Lanoe was still there. Zhang's communications panel said as much.

"Negative," he said, finally.

"Please confirm that last communication," Maggs asked.

"I said negative. We are not going to cut and run. If we can't handle this, there's no point in heading back to Niraya—that just amounts to giving up. You want to be the one who tells Elder McRae 'sorry, we tried to save your planet but it was just too hard'?"

"Actually? I'd be happy to," Maggs said.

"No," Zhang said. It was her job to back Lanoe up. As his wingman she had to enforce his orders; that was just part of the job. Plenty of times before she'd done so even when she disagreed with him, because when you were in the Navy, it wasn't your job to debate orders.

This time, though, she did it because he was right.

"No," she said again. "We stand and fight. He's right, Maggs. If we give up now we'll never have the nerve to try again. I don't like the odds here, three against . . . who knows how many ships. But we didn't come out here on a pleasure cruise."

"Spread out," Lanoe said. "Stack 'em up. We all know the drill."

And they did. Zhang had been in bad scrapes before. The 94th squadron under Lanoe's command had taken on plenty of fights where they were outnumbered. Lanoe had always gotten them through. These odds might be an order of magnitude worse than usual, sure. But she would fight and die by Lanoe's side if that was what he wanted.

On the plus side the destroyer—she didn't know what else to call it—didn't appear to have any heavy guns. And the scouts and interceptors didn't have vector fields.

Which was a little comfort, though not much, as the volume around her started filling up with kinetic impactors and plasma bursts.

In a massive battle like this all the rules went out the window. Should you go in screaming, at full throttle? It made you a moving target, which made you harder to hit. It also meant you were more likely to run headlong into an impactor or a piece of debris, which could end your fight right there. Did you take your time lining up shots, so you didn't waste ammunition? Then again, there were so many targets that even wild shots had a chance of hitting something.

The hardest part was keeping an eye on your squadmates, to make sure you didn't shoot one of them by mistake. Or collide with them at ten thousand kilometers a second.

Zhang twisted around in space, not so much corkscrewing as maneuvering by instinct, dashing into the cloud of scouts, banking hard as their engines lit up, as they tried to track her. She swiped away her targeting board—it couldn't keep up with all the things she needed to shoot. She held down the trigger on her stick and spat particle fire at anything that moved.

All around her scouts fell apart in pieces, or burst into flame as their fuel supplies caught. She saw one jink around to get a shot at her, only to fly right into a kinetic impactor. She didn't bother to laugh—she didn't have time.

High above her Maggs dipped in and out of the cloud, refusing to let the scouts surround him. A good strategy, one she wished she'd thought of. Where was Lanoe? There—she recognized the thermal signature of his FA.2's main thruster. He was plunging straight through the cloud, barely bothering to waggle back and forth. She saw his vector field sparkle with heat as an impactor grazed off his canopy, and couldn't help herself—she gasped a little.

"Boss," she said, "you have a plan here?"

"Give me cover, if you can," he said.

She swung around to follow him, blasting apart a scout almost as an afterthought.

There were no pilots in those scouts or interceptors, Lanoe knew. It made it easy to shoot at them. It also made them disposable. The enemy didn't care how many of its ships were lost here. All it cared about was killing humans.

Even in the darkest days of the Century War, when Earth had fought Mars and Ganymede for control of the solar system—when it seemed like the entire human race was at war with itself—even then, there had been a certain fellow-feeling among pilots. You hated it when you saw an enemy get hit by antivehicle fire, because you knew what an ugly death that meant. If somebody ran out of ammunition or fuel maybe you just let them go, a weird kind of professional courtesy offered to someone who'd had you locked in their sights a moment before.

This wasn't that kind of fight.

Lanoe kept his PBWs blazing. He swatted away the enemy scouts like flies, not caring if he cut them to pieces or blasted them into slag. He didn't so much as pause to make sure they were out of the action before moving on to the next enemy. Interceptors wheeled around to face him, their spiky guns belching out an impactor every second. He didn't waste disruptor rounds on them, just hosed them down with particle beams and rushed past them, deeper into the cloud.

It grew thicker the farther he went. Scouts crowded his view. He stopped trying to aim. He was more interested in punching his way through. Getting closer to the destroyer, the big prize.

He didn't have time to analyze imagery and sensor data, but he could see the mass of the big ship up ahead and he could see how it had changed. From a distance it had looked almost smooth, like a thing with a real hull. Now it looked like it was dissolving in acid, its edges rough and chipped, any kind of real shape lost until it was just a formless blob of metal in the dark. Each scout or interceptor that leapt from its back left it smaller and less threatening, but he had to know.

The engineer, Derrow, had said there needed to be a living, thinking commander nearby in case the enemy drones went off-program. Maybe they were on the destroyer, coordinating the whole battle. If he could get through, if he could strike down the enemy commander, maybe Zhang and Maggs didn't have to die here today.

Maybe.

For his own life he gave little thought. That was the only way he'd survived so long, gotten so many medals. If you went into a battle expecting to live through it, you made bad decisions, you gave up opportunities. On the other hand, if you went in expecting to die you probably would. The key was to put yourself aside, to think of yourself only as part of a squad.

Some days he was better at that mental shift than others. This time he was ready. This time he would achieve the impossible middle state of grace. Or so he told himself.

———⚔———

Zhang dove after Lanoe, weaving back and forth to avoid debris, ignoring impactors unless they were right in front of her. She carved up scouts as they raced after Lanoe or as they came tearing through space right after her. She took bad chances.

Still she couldn't keep up with Lanoe. He barely veered aside from a head-on collision with an interceptor. His maneuvering jets stuttered as if he was trying to conserve fuel, probably the dumbest thing you could do in a battle like this.

She knew he wasn't dumb. He was headed for the destroyer and he wouldn't be turned away from his goal, that was all.

Don't get yourself killed for nothing, she begged him, the words getting no farther than her head. She wouldn't say them aloud, certainly wouldn't message him with such trivial sentiments. She couldn't help but think them, though. *Not now, please. Not when we're so close to starting over.*

She did her best to keep the cloud from all falling on him at once. She blazed her way around him, keeping his tail clear, shouting in defiance as the enemy ships ganged up on them and came pouring down in formation from on high. She waggled her stick, let her PBWs play over the enemy ships as if she could paint the bastards with her guns. They burst apart or went spinning away or just fell silent and drifted off by the dozen, but still more of them came at her, more of them flocked toward Lanoe.

An impactor struck the side of her thruster unit, hard enough to press right through her vector field. Her bones were wrenched around inside her flesh as her inertial sink tried and failed to absorb the shock. Her engine board started screaming at her, warning her that she was about to lose all her secondary thrusters.

She bit her tongue to keep from shouting for help. Maggs was still out at the edge of the cloud, picking off enemy ships. Lanoe was surging ahead of her, getting farther and farther away. Neither of them could afford to turn aside and come to her aid.

So she let herself fall back, let her engines rest and cool as their autorepair systems came online and tried desperately to prevent any further damage.

Still the enemy came at her, relentless, never-ending. Her weapons still worked just fine. She never stopped shooting.

———————

Lanoe was nearly through.

Plasma fire washed over his FA.2 and his cockpit turned into a sauna. Then a furnace. Impactors bounced off his vector field left and right, throwing him back and forth like a toy boat in the middle of a flash flood. He kept his touch on his stick very light, just compensating for the battering, just maneuvering enough to keep from colliding with anything big and hard.

His eyeballs dried out in the heat and his eyelashes started to curl up and singe but he refused to blink. The skin of his hands cracked and bled as the heat mounted, but he kept them on his controls.

The destroyer lay right ahead of him, only seconds away. He expected the scouts and interceptors to come flocking after him, to throw everything they had at him to keep him clear of their mother ship, to defend it at any cost.

But then the other thing happened. The thing he hadn't expected.

Which was exactly how every battle went, but it surprised him every time.

It was like he'd been flying through clouds and suddenly they'd parted, dumping him out into clear air. The scouts and interceptors pulled back, spinning around to face Zhang and Maggs instead. He'd thought they would defend the destroyer to the last—instead, they let him through as if he'd crossed some imaginary finish line, as if he'd already won the race and he wasn't worth chasing anymore.

A single interceptor launched from the side of the destroyer, burning past him like he didn't exist. He fired a disruptor into its hull at point-blank range and it didn't even react, just kept to its preordained trajectory even as its stocks of fuel and ammunition cooked off and blasted it into pieces.

He let it die unwatched, his interest in it voided by what lay ahead of him.

The destroyer, half the size it used to be. Practically undefended.

If they were going to let him have his prize, if they didn't feel it was worth protecting, so be it. He was still going to blast the hell out of it.

≺━━

Zhang's engine board chimed to tell her she still had power in her main thruster. Chimed again to say her maneuvering jets still functioned. Then it blared a warning Klaxon and she knew she was in trouble.

All of her secondary thrusters were down, and heat was building up in her fusion reactor. Not so fast that she was about to turn into a giant, glorious fireball. But if that heat level rose unchecked, it would eventually melt right through the insulating layer of shielding that separated her cockpit from the reactor. She wouldn't need enemy fire then to burn her to a crisp.

It wasn't an immediate problem, but every time she used her main thrusters, the heat would rise exponentially. Her main method of avoiding the worst of the enemy fire—maneuvering at speed—would be the thing that killed her.

If she didn't keep moving, the enemy would swarm all over her and they would finish her off with plasma fire. Either way she would die in agony.

Her only chance was to conserve her thrust, to fly smart instead of fast. She brought her engine board around in front of her and studied her options, all while keeping her eyes on the enemy scouts that wheeled and darted around her. She still had her maneuvering and positioning jets, the tiny thrusters in the sides and nose of the BR.9 that allowed her to turn and brake. She could use those as much as she liked—except they ran on their own fuel reservoirs and those were limited. You weren't supposed to use maneuvering jets as your main source of thrust.

For a few minutes, though, they might be enough. As a scout dove down toward her from on high, she punched for a hard burn that sent her spinning away. The scout rushed past her and she blasted it apart with PBW fire as it passed. Up ahead an interceptor had filled the local volume with hurtling impactors. She twisted around on her positioning jets and watched as one of the deadly rounds zoomed past her canopy. She cut a hole in the side of the interceptor, then fired one of her few remaining disruptors into the cavity she'd made. It was gratifying to watch the interceptor burst apart from within like a rotten fruit, but she had little time to congratulate herself—three more scouts were headed her way on different trajectories, all of them headed to intersect right with her position.

Come on, Lanoe, she thought. *Give us a miracle here.*

Her communications board chimed at her, telling her she had an incoming message. It wasn't from Lanoe, though—it was from Maggs.

"Not to be a wet blanket," he said, "but I think I'm rather desperately in need of help out here. Anyone?"

She had no idea what to tell him. She had her hands full already.

Chapter Eighteen

Nothing. No response at all.

It looked like Maggs was on his own.

At the start of the fight, when he'd come screaming in on a high-power corkscrew and laid waste to his first fifteen scouts, he'd felt iron-bound and invincible, an angel of destruction bent toward hell on a trajectory of pain. He'd forgotten, in the years since he'd been on active duty, how splendid it felt, just how fun, to sweep through one's enemies with a truly graceful attack run.

Then the sheer magnitude of the battle had overwhelmed him, and he'd very quickly stopped enjoying himself. As he wove and darted through the outer limit of the cloud of enemies, racking up kills, he'd avoided the worst of the enemy's attacks but by sheer law of probability some of them had gotten through. One impactor after another had clanged off his hull. Sprays of plasma fire had washed across his canopy, blinding him with their incredible, dazzling light.

No, this wasn't fun at all. Especially with all the red lights flashing at him.

Every one of his boards showed significant damage. His engines were battered and bruised and their output had dropped to half of optimum. His supplies of ammunition were running dangerously low—he had but two disruptors left to his name, and even his PBWs were running short. Life support was critical and even communications had seen better days. He wasn't sure if his call for help had been received or if it had even gone out.

One more bad hit, one more damaged system, would do for him, and he knew it.

In his head his father's voice kept up a nonstop stream of advice.

Keep your nose up, Maggsy—keep turning, think in three dimensions. Keep your mind on your six, but not so much you forget to look forward. Don't just spray them down with your beamers; pick your shots. You can afford to lose your airfoils, so turn into those blows you can't avoid, let your wings take the brunt.

All very good advice, he was sure. None of which was new to him. Maggs had learned to fly and fight long before he'd set foot inside a cockpit. At his father's knee he'd absorbed all this advice a hundred times over, as Dear Old Dad regaled Maggs *enfant* with tales of epic dogfights and desperate encounters at the rim of some far-off system, all from the comfort of an armchair at the Admiralty. Maggs had, not unlike a sponge, absorbed every word, memorized every stratagem, every tactic.

In fact, once he'd reached his majority and entered the Naval ranks himself, the hardest part of his education had been unlearning half of what his father had taught him—figuring out which bits of advice were still valuable and which had been made antiquated by advances in technology, or which he'd misinterpreted from lack of practical experience.

Still, father's legacy had kept him alive. Heeding that paternal advice brought him his Blue Star and made him a bit of a hero, hadn't it?

Do remember to pivot, and keep your trajectory clear, the voice in his head told him. *Don't forget the rotary, the best trick you've got. A snap turn's better than a vector field, when you're down in the slot.*

Though perhaps the best piece of advice of all had been this: *A hero is a fellow that learned on day one how to duck, and on day two when to do it. Courage and resourcefulness ill behoove a dead man.*

Two interceptors were closing on him, their guns already belching out impactors. They didn't seem to care when their fellow scouts ran right into their lanes of fire—they were happy to blow away their own scouts, if it meant getting a shot off at a human pilot. Maggs eyed his ammunition board, saw his last two disruptors showing green lights all across their status displays. They were ready to fire. Once they were gone, though, he'd have none left.

He checked the interceptors again, plotting their trajectories. They were set to converge on a spot a few kilometers in front of him, though of course the bigger enemy ships were smart enough not to actually collide with each other. They would correct at the last moment and just miss one another and then they would bank around, double back on him where they would have a good view of his tail.

The thing about this enemy, though, unlike every human foe Maggs had ever faced down, was its predictability. The alien drones were fast and they could appear to be clever but only because they were running some algorithm, some deep-seated program. If you could guess that program's next move, you could play the enemy ships against each other. It just took a bit of gray matter, a little application—

There.

Maggs twisted around and brought his nose up until he was burning away from the interceptors. The big, spiky ships poured on their own fuel until they were arcing up to meet him—they wouldn't let him get away so easily.

Too bad an entire cloud of scouts was already swooping down toward him. Too bad for the interceptors, anyway.

The scouts tried to bank out of the way but they weren't quite fast enough. The interceptors tried to jink but they had to fight their own momentum, and they would never be as nimble as Maggs and his BR.9. Some of the scouts managed to get away. Others plowed right into the interceptors like insects smacking into the windshield of a ground car. Their spindly bodies folded and twisted as they struck home, their fuel tanks igniting silently in the void.

One of the interceptors broke in half under the weight of multiple collisions, its thrusters sending it rolling off into darkness.

The other interceptor was damaged but kept after Maggs, listing a bit but still blazing away with its heavy guns. Impactors flashed past Maggs's canopy like fat shadows, coming fast and thick. One creased his left-side fairing and it burst in a shower of sparks, adding a new red light to his damage control board.

Maggs stood on his throttle a moment longer, then yanked it back to zero as he shoved his stick over to the side. His BR.9 rolled hard to the left and the interceptor flashed past him until he could see the glow of its thrusters.

The interceptors were too big and too heavily armored to be killed by PBW fire—under normal conditions. There was no armor inside their thruster nozzles, though. Maggs brought up a virtual Aldis sight and let his computer find the perfect firing solution, let his finger hover over his trigger, waiting...waiting...now.

His particle beam lanced straight through the interceptor's engines, carving the bastard like a roasted goose. There wasn't much to see—all the damage was internal—but the interceptor's guns stopped firing. A moment later its thrusters cut out as well.

Maggs would have preferred to see the thing explode in the dark, but he would take the kill he could get.

He looked around for the next target, the next dogfight. With his free hand he reached for his comms board again. Zhang wasn't responding—maybe she was dead. He refused to believe he'd outlived the famous Aleister Lanoe, though.

"Commander," he called, "do we have an actual plan, here? Or do we just keep fighting till we die? I'm just working on my social calendar, you see."

Bravado was another thing he'd learned from Dear Old Dad. It was so much more decorous than screaming in terror.

———————

Green pearls queued up in the edge of Lanoe's vision, calls coming in from Zhang and Maggs that he didn't have time to answer.

He needed every ounce of concentration he could get, at that particular moment.

Scouts and interceptors kept launching from the sides of the destroyer, which had shrunk to nearly a third of its original mass. Lanoe watched it like a hawk, waiting to see any sign of the line ship underneath all those ancillary craft, especially keeping an eye out for anything resembling a crew section.

He wasn't just biding his time while he watched, however. The emerging scouts and interceptors paid him no attention except to swoop out of his way as they hurried toward the cloud of their fellows beyond, out where Zhang and Maggs were. The enemy didn't spare a shot for Lanoe, as if he were some neutral third party they didn't have to worry about.

He made them pay for that mistake. As soon as they were clear of the destroyer—sometimes even as they emerged—he tore them apart, racking up kill after kill after kill. He imagined Maggs would find it all terribly unsporting.

Lanoe didn't give a damn.

Some glitch in the enemy's programming, some misplaced variable in its algorithm, had given him a chance to take out a vast number of ships before they could attack his squadmates. He would thin the herd as much as he could, until the enemy realized its mistake and came for him.

If that happened, of course, he wouldn't stand a chance. He was in far too close. In a moment a hundred scouts would be on him and they would turn his FA.2 into a cloud of vaporized metal before he even started to evade.

He flew a tight course around and around the destroyer, looping down under its belly then up over its top decks then back around for another pass. This must be what an apex predator felt like, he thought—the lions of the plains of Africa, killer whales in the polar oceans must have felt like this before humans came along and beat them at their own game. To pick one's targets secure in the knowledge of one's own inviolability. It was almost boring.

The green pearls kept spinning. He let one call through, then the other. Listened more to the tones of his squadmates' voices than the actual content of their words. Zhang was in trouble, he could tell—she put a brave face on it but there was an edge of fear there, a certain clipped bite in her voice that he knew all too well.

He still didn't know how to really read Maggs, but he was certain the swindler was in bad shape, too. He'd given them a mission far above and beyond what two fighter pilots should be expected to accomplish and he knew it. Desperately he wanted to turn away from the destroyer, burn back toward the cloud and come to their aid— but he knew he was far more useful to them where he was. Every scout and interceptor he took down here was one less they would have to fight. The work he was doing was the only chance they had.

Ahead of him two interceptors jumped into space at the same time, huge and dark and lumpy. He'd used up his disruptors long before then but he'd figured out the trick of taking the big ships down with just PBWs, found all the sensitive spots in their thick hide of armor. The thrusters were good, but hard to get at. Far better to rake fire across their sensor pods. The hard part was finding them, as they were nestled deep between two ranks of guns on the interceptors' flanks. Once you blinded them, though, the interceptors would just fly off in a straight line, headed for nowhere, unable to find targets to shoot at. Like the machines they were, they had no idea what to do when their programming broke down, and thus they did nothing.

Scouts, of course, were a lot easier. One good shot and they broke in pieces. Lanoe made a point of taking careful aim, but only so he wouldn't waste ammunition.

Meanwhile, below him, the destroyer grew leaner and leaner as its cargo of drone ships launched toward oblivion. And still no sign of what Lanoe desperately wanted to find.

NO CAVITIES DETECTED, his computer kept telling him. MILLIMETER-WAVE ANALYSIS: NO RESULT. MAGNETIC RESONANCE ANALYSIS: NO RESULT.

If one of the aliens were inside that thing, Derrow's hypothetical programmer, they were buried deep.

Boards flashed at him. Red pearls spun in the corners of his vision. Alarms blared.

Maggs couldn't pay attention to any of them. All he could see was the divot in his canopy.

He'd flown right into a kinetic impactor, straight into a head-long collision with a chunk of metal the size of his fist. He must have caught it at a slight angle, because it hadn't just torn through the canopy, his body, the seat behind him—instead it had bounced off, ricocheting out into the void. The impact had been powerful enough, however, to leave a finger-long dent in the carbonglas of the canopy.

Carbonglas was nigh-on indestructible. It could be crushed under hundreds of tons of weight, subjected to temperatures higher than the surface of a star, and not even get scratched. Even particle beams could do little more than mar its shiny surface.

The impactor could have cleaved right through it like a hot knife through a ripe tomato. The fact that it hadn't—the fact that Maggs was still alive—came down to pure, incorruptible luck.

Another hit on that same location—even a near miss—would crack the transparent material, he knew. The canopy would shatter. Shards of jagged ultrahard material might come scything for his face. Or it might just explode outward, leaving him relatively unharmed—but also completely exposed to the void. And enemy fire.

When you stare Death in the proverbial eye socket, his father's voice told him, *that's the moment you see how empty it is.*

He'd never really understood that lesson until now. Maggs realized, with a start, that he'd never really been afraid of dying before.

It wasn't an experience he could recommend. He heard a weird, low throbbing alarm from somewhere nearby, though it was nothing like the alert tones his boards normally used. It was enough to make him look at his displays, which was enough to break the hypnotic spell of the divot.

When he couldn't find the source of the thumping, he blinked away the last of the cobwebs because he realized what it was. That was the sound of his own heart thundering in his chest.

He fought for control of himself. Found the steel that laced his blood, the steel his father had given him. Wheeled around just as three scouts came tearing through space at him and, with one rapierlike blast of particle fire, cut all three of them to pieces. He needed to pay attention.

If he died out here—if he died anywhere, frankly—certain debts would go unpaid. That was unacceptable.

For a good minute he did nothing but kill. Like an alchemist he transmuted this new fear into pure, cold, high-toned rage and fought like a maniac, scouts falling before him so fast he thought perhaps he could win this battle single-handed if he could keep it up. Yet something cold and thick had clotted inside his heart and it started to drag him down. Adrenaline curdled in his veins and he felt like he wanted to weep.

That was when he saw the trap. When he realized just how clever the alien drone ships could be, if you gave them half a chance.

The scouts he'd been cutting down must have been a screen, a ruse thrown at him so he wouldn't notice the real menace creeping up from behind. He caught sight of the attack on one of his displays, then spun around on his axis so he could get a good look at the hounds that pursued him.

There, through his canopy (don't look at the divot, don't look at it), were three interceptors, bearing down on him at high speed from the heart of the cloud. Already they had begun to unleash their storm of projectiles, impactors coming at him in a nonstop torrent of solid metal.

His weapons board showed him the two disruptors he had left. One too few.

He could take down two of them, then wheel about, bank hard, loop back, and catch the other one from behind—assuming he somehow, miraculously, avoided all those impactors. Assuming there were no scouts anywhere nearby waiting to swoop in and catch him split-arsing all over the local volume. *A bad plan is better than none at all,* Dear Old Dad told him, and he tapped a virtual keyboard to try to get a firing solution, while working out the maneuvers in his head.

Then one of the interceptors exploded in a cloud of debris. And another.

A firing solution came up. He blasted the third, then wheeled around to look for scouts, to try to get some idea of what happened.

"Remember that time you saved my ass? We're even," Zhang called, on an open channel.

He found himself laughing, fear pumping endorphins all through his body and for a moment he felt good again, invincible.

Then he saw Zhang's fighter and felt the ice water of trepidation splash against the back of his neck. The whole flank of her BR.9 was a jagged mess of broken components and torn-open panels. He could see one of her secondary thrusters flap back and forth, connected now only by a thin, frayed cable. The red tentacles that writhed across her fairings were obscured by scorch marks and craters left behind by impactor strikes.

"You look like ten varieties of hell," he told her.

"Yeah, well, your canopy's about to fall off," she responded. Weakly, he thought. She sounded very tired. Well, her body might be twenty but her brain was much, much older. And if he were being fair, he wasn't exactly fresh himself. The inside of his suit stank of fear sweat and bad breath.

"We've both seen better days. How damaged are you?" he asked.

"In about ten minutes I'm going to look like a Fleet Day goose. How's your ammo supply?"

"I have one disruptor left, and maybe two thousand shots in my PBWs. Fuel?"

"I'd be lucky to get back to Aruna." Zhang was quiet for a moment. "Maggs, if we don't make it—"

"Should we die here," he said, cutting her off, "anything we say won't matter. If we live, anything we say will be embarrassing later."

"Fair enough," she said. "Oh, hellfire. Look at that."

Maggs could see it just fine.

He'd spent most of the battle at the periphery of the enemy ranks, scoring hits along the edges while she burned through the heart of the opposition. The two of them had put up a valiant effort, indeed—Maggs's displays showed him an enormous field of debris, hundreds of dead enemy ships reduced to scrap metal in a slowly expanding cloud. Yet in the midst of all that chaos at least a hundred drone ships remained active. They showed up on his display as pinpoints of light, a visual representation of the heat of their thrusters.

The display switched over to a vector analysis—a breakdown of how those ships were moving, how fast and in what direction. They were all burning blue. In other words, they were all headed straight for Maggs and Zhang.

"No point in cursing, really," Maggs said. "Shall we make a good show of this?"

"Yeah," Zhang told him. "Go out in a blaze of glory. Can't wait."

Maggs's hands flew over his boards, readying his BR.9 for what was going to be some of the hardest fighting he'd ever experienced. The fighter complained with red lights and warning chimes but he ignored them. No point in conserving resources or playing safe now.

In his mind he rehearsed his next moves. Dive straight into the cloud at all available speed. Punch through the far side, swing around, dive through again. Repeat as possible. Do as much damage as he could while Zhang hung back, hunting targets of opportunity. Maybe, just maybe, give Lanoe a chance to accomplish something here.

Or at the very least give him a story to tell back at the Admiralty, about how Auster Maggs died well.

"Ready to run," he told Zhang.

"Good luck," she said.

He leaned forward on his stick, opening his throttle until his engines screamed. Dove straight into the maw of a hundred enemy ships.

And then—the miracle occurred.

Another layer of scouts and interceptors had peeled off the destroyer, and still there was no sign of any crew compartments, any centralized command structure. Lanoe was starting to accept the inevitable conclusion: that the destroyer was just a drone, like every other enemy ship they'd encountered.

And behind him, back in the cloud, Zhang and Maggs were at the end of their tethers. They were going to die, and it would be for nothing.

He couldn't stop—there was no other course open to him. He kept flying tight spirals around the destroyer, killing anything that moved. It took very little concentration now. He could almost predict when the little ships would peel off the shrinking mass, all those disposable drones operating on simple programs. Which gave him plenty of time to watch his squadmates make their last stand.

He saw Maggs dive right into the fray, while Zhang drifted, nearly motionless, along the edge of the cloud, firing quick, deliberate bursts from her PBWs. He knew what that meant—she was in trouble, her engines compromised. Maggs's daring strike might keep the worst of the enemy away from her but eventually they would figure out that she was a sitting duck.

Lanoe couldn't break off from what he was doing. If he ran to her side to keep her safe, the destroyer would be able to launch all of its remaining ships with impunity. The best thing he could do for her was to keep thinning out the enemy ranks from afar. Yet he knew she had just minutes to live.

The idea of her dying out there like this, for nothing, was incredibly hard to bear. Harder than he'd expected. The two of them had fought in a hundred battles before, and he'd never worried about her like this. He'd always been able to shut down his feelings when the shooting started. Something had changed—and he didn't like it.

He was just about to do the stupid thing, break contact and run to her defense, when he saw something very strange happen inside the cloud.

Enemy ships were exploding in there, bursting apart. Well, Maggs was doing yeomanlike service, guns blazing away. But some of the enemy kills were happening well clear of his attack corridor, far enough away from him that they couldn't be his work.

Lanoe called up a display to get better imagery of the battle.

What he saw made his eyes go wide.

Maggs wasn't the only fighter pilot in the chaos of the cloud. Another human ship, another BR.9, had joined the fray. One with a broken airfoil.

On the display the fighter wove through a formation of enemy scouts, blasting them apart as an interceptor came chasing after. The fighter swung around to fire a disruptor and Lanoe got a good look at its fairings. They showed black stars on a blue background—the flag of the Establishment.

It was Valk.

Valk had come to the rescue, disobeying Lanoe's direct orders.

In a more formal order of battle that would be insubordination—grounds for a court-martial. At that particular moment Lanoe didn't give a damn for the chain of command.

A green pearl spun in the corner of his vision. He blinked to open the link.

"Thought I'd drop in, Commander," Valk said. "Hope you don't mind."

"I don't know what you're doing here," Lanoe said, "but I'm glad for it. Where's Derrow?"

"Halfway to Niraya by now," Valk told him. "I put the tender on a preprogrammed course. It'll get her to a safe parking orbit. When we're done here we can fly her down to the planet. Hold on a second."

On Lanoe's display the interceptor chasing Valk erupted in silent fire.

"Sorry about that."

"Don't mind me," Lanoe told him.

⇥

"I never thought I'd be so glad to see an Establishmentarian," Maggs said with a laugh, as Valk tore through another interceptor, his disruptor round blasting it to pieces. He wheeled his own BR.9 around and obliterated a scout that had crept up on Valk's tail.

"I've got a bunch of those little bastards up ahead here, think they're hot stuff," Valk called back. "You want to stack 'em up?"

"With unalloyed pleasure," Maggs told him.

It was like he was back in the academy, running a simulation. It ran that smooth. The scouts swung around into a tight formation, their plasma guns glowing with heat as they prepared to attack. Valk and Maggs rolled around them in a perfect double helix, catching the scouts in a textbook crossfire. The scouts tried to escape their net by zooming away in all different directions, but it was child's play to blast them as they ran.

"Interceptors," Valk called. "Four of them converging on us. How's your supply of disruptors?"

"All but nonexistent. Mind if I play the wounded dove?"

"Gotcha," Valk said. His engines flared as he burned away, as if he hadn't even noticed the approaching interceptors. Maggs made a good show of it, letting his maneuvering jets stutter ineffectually, fluttering his main thruster as if it had lost power. Firing off a few rounds from his PBW without even coming close to hitting the onrushing enemies.

The interceptors took the bait, closing on him with alarming rapidity. Their guns chugged away, filling the volume around Maggs with kinetic impactors.

Just as they'd expected, the interceptors' programming included a subroutine instructing them to go after wounded ships first. The hard part was keeping up the facade. He dodged just enough to

miss colliding with the enemy projectiles. Worked up a firing solution for his last disruptor, just in case.

He didn't need it. Valk hadn't gone far. One interceptor after
another burst apart, Valk's disruptors finding their fuel supplies
and turning them into scrap. The broken debris came showering
toward Maggs and he burned for a second—his thruster operating
just fine—to get out of the muck.

"Fine show, sir," he called, all fear of death forgotten.

Perhaps too soon, of course. Pride goeth before and all that. Valk
hadn't even waited to confirm his kills before wheeling about and
burning to catch a new formation of enemies. Maggs found himself surrounded with his own coterie of scouts before he even had a
chance to catch his breath. He twisted around in space, corkscrewing through their formation. Plasma fire caught his flank but he
shrugged it off, barely breaking a sweat. As he raced through and
past the scouts he pivoted on his axis until he was flying backward,
watching their thrusters recede.

He called up a virtual Aldis sight and lined up his crosshairs.
One, two, three—the scouts broke into pieces as he cut through
their skeletal frames. Four, five—

The sixth exploded before he could even get a bead on it.

Zhang limped up beside him, matching his velocity until their
airfoils nearly touched. "Let's head over to Lanoe's position, see
how he's doing," she called.

"Gladly, if I didn't have a battle to finish," he told her.

"Maggs, check your sensors. You see anything left but Valk out
here?"

A rather cutting retort died on Maggs's tongue. He brought up
a display and scanned the local volume in infrared and found she
was correct.

He saw Valk blazing red in the midst of a field of twisted,
scorched metal that had once been a trio of interceptors, cooling
from blue to black. He saw Zhang's own engines glowing a sickly
green. Beyond that—

Nothing.

No enemy ships remained. In the rush of excitement that gripped him after Valk arrived, Maggs had missed the most important part of any battle.

The part where you win.

~~

Lanoe barely registered the three of them coming up alongside him. His FA.2 had already identified them as friends, so it didn't chime to warn him of approaching vessels.

In silence, he flew below the destroyer, his squadmates like an honor guard as he inspected what he'd achieved.

Nothing.

This battle—this battle that nearly cost him everything—had been over dead bones.

In the last few minutes of the fighting whatever intelligence controlled the destroyer had grown desperate. It had launched all of its remaining ships at once, so fast that many of them were destroyed in midspace collisions. The rest had been prime targets for his PBWs as they rushed toward the fight, and he'd let none of them through. The local volume was crowded now with their wreckage, dead metal spinning without a sound in the void.

The mother ship they'd left behind, the destroyer itself, was all that remained, a tiny fraction of its original size now. Its true shape was revealed and it did not impress. A bulky thruster unit had long since exhausted its fuel, its engines now cold and useless. Extending forward from that thruster unit was a network of girders, dividing and ramifying outward like the limbs of a tree, the skeleton of some alien beast. The scouts and interceptors had been hung on that framework like grapes on a vine.

Other than that—other than the thruster and the skeletal frame—there was nothing to the destroyer. Not a single gun. No communications antennae or sensor pods.

No command bridge. No crew compartments at all.

Inert, defenseless, the big ship drifted through space. Lanoe had already checked its trajectory. It would pass by the moon Aruna in thirteen hours, then most likely be caught by the ice giant Garuda's gravity, pulled down into the planet's crushing depths and lost forever. It lacked the fuel to alter that deadly course.

The destroyer had possessed one simple mission, a program of dumb simplicity. It was to fly toward Aruna, that was all. The cargo of smaller ships it carried had the real program to execute: Kill anyone they found along the way. If the four pilots had left the moon alone, if they'd flown back to Niraya without bothering to investigate the destroyer, it would have self-destructed all on its own.

"No programmer," Zhang said, breaking the silence.

"No," Lanoe said.

"No aliens. Just drones," Valk said.

"One chances to think, perhaps it shouldn't be called a destroyer at all," Maggs pointed out. "More of a carrier, really."

Lanoe sneered inside his helmet. He very much wanted to tell Maggs to shut the hell up. But that wasn't how you talked to heroes, was it? And Maggs had just shown his sand. Taken Lanoe's orders and executed them with skill and aplomb, like a model officer.

Maybe it was time to rethink his opinion on Auster Maggs.

It was definitely time to rethink how he planned on fighting these aliens. "Swarmship," he said.

"That sounds nasty," Zhang said. "I mean, it fits. But it sounds nasty."

"The thing we've been calling a carrier," Lanoe said, because they'd got him talking now, got him thinking. "Call that a queenship."

"Queen?" Valk asked.

"Like the queen ant, or the queen bee. They don't care if we kill their workers, or their warriors. They'll care if we threaten their queen. Their programmer. And the big ship, the queenship, that's where the programmer will be. If there is one. It's the only place left. We're going to have to fight it directly."

"It's got seven more of these…swarmships defending it," Valk said. "The four of us barely survived fighting one of them."

"Sure," Lanoe said. "It's going to take some work."

He could hear the shiver in Zhang's voice as she spoke next. "What now, then? Give us some orders, Commander."

"Back to Niraya, first," he told them. "The three of you deserve some downtime. And I need a minute to think this through."

In other words—he had no damned idea what to do now.

Chapter Nineteen

Valk had brought extra fuel cartridges when he came to join the fight against the swarmship, but the fighters were damaged and they could barely limp back to Niraya. It took far longer than Lanoe liked, but they made it. Once they reached orbit around the planet they rendezvoused with the tender and he was glad to be out of the FA.2's cockpit. He'd been breathing his own recycled air for so long it had started to smell funny, never a good sign.

As they pulled themselves into the wardroom of the tender, Derrow rushed to embrace Maggs before he'd even dropped his helmet. She looked terrified.

"I'm so glad to see you," she told all of them. "I have no idea how to fly this thing. If you hadn't come back, I would have been stranded up here."

Lanoe was sympathetic but he knew her ordeal wouldn't have lasted very long. If the fighters hadn't come back, Niraya would have been defenseless. Derrow would have had a good vantage point to watch the apocalypse—the last place she would have wanted to have been would be down on the ground.

"Sorry," Valk said. "I couldn't leave them alone."

Derrow nodded at him. It was clear she had more to say, and was impatient with them while they scrubbed out the collar rings of their suits and gulped down some solid food. "There's something happening down on the planet," she said, finally, when they gave her the chance. "I've been watching on the displays—I don't actually know what it's all about, but you should have a look for yourselves."

Zhang ran her hands over a display from the sensor pod, a gray swirling image that made no sense to anyone who wasn't used to reading infrared arrays the way she was. "Oh," she said. "Oh. That could be bad."

Lanoe growled and reached for a virtual keyboard. He brought up visual light imagery of what she was seeing and whistled softly to himself.

Down in Walden Crater, all hell had broken loose.

The amorphous pile of the Retreat was visible on the display, but like an island in the midst of a flood. The streets around the building were packed with a surging mass of humanity. People— thousands of people—had gathered around the Retreat, a crowd so dense it was impossible to make out individual figures. "That looks like half the population of Niraya," he said.

"Only about a tenth, actually," Derrow said. "There's another crowd in the Centrocor crater. The canyon farms have all but emp- tied out—everybody's come to the craters to get some answers."

"What in Earth's name is going on?" Maggs asked.

"There was some kind of weird broadcast yesterday," Derrow explained. "That girl from the Retreat—Roan, right? That's her name? She opened an emergency channel on the network. She played the video of the lander attack."

"She did what?" Lanoe demanded.

"She overran the network with a high-power signal," Derrow said.

"How do you know it was her?" Zhang asked.

"The message was tagged with her personal metadata," Derrow explained. "She didn't bother trying to hide her identity. I think she just wanted to make sure everybody on the planet got to see the video. The elders haven't made a formal announcement yet, but I'm pretty sure this wasn't their idea."

"Hell, no," Lanoe said. "Elder McRae was holding that video

back. She was worried if people saw it that it would start a panic. Looks like she might have been right." He turned to Zhang. "Pull up an image of the spaceport."

Just as he'd expected, it was mobbed as well. There was no way they could land the tender down there, not without killing a few hundred people in the process.

"I can't tell if this is a riot or a full-fledged insurrection," he said.

"At least they haven't torn the place down yet," Valk pointed out. "It doesn't look like anything down there is on fire, either."

"Actually," Derrow said, "given how little oxygen there is down there, fires are incredibly hard to start. They'd be more likely to blow things up with explosives."

Oh, good, he thought. *Just back from the front and all kinds of fresh hell to deal with. Damned civilians.*

He took a deep breath and tried to formulate a plan. "Okay, we need to get to Elder McRae and find out what's going on. Plus, we need to do it without being torn to pieces in the process. Zhang, is there any way you can put down on the Retreat's roof?"

Zhang ran her hands over her display. "There's no flat surface big enough to take the tender. And I would worry it couldn't support our weight anyway."

Lanoe nodded. "Okay. Can you get close, though, hover over top of it, let a couple of us jump out?"

"That would take an incredibly skilled pilot with no sense of danger whatsoever," Zhang said. She wove her fingers together and cracked all her knuckles at once. "So, yes."

⟶⟵

Elder McRae focused on her breathing exercises. Three short, shallow breaths in, one long slow exhalation. Repeat. As many times as it took.

Or until you hyperventilated, because you were so angry you couldn't focus and keep the rhythm.

She felt anger, of course, just like any other human. She knew many disciplines that allowed her to control the emotion, usually. Right now it was threatening to overcome her. To possess her.

She wanted very much to slap Roan across her damned face.

Somehow, she resisted the urge.

"What's done is done," she said. She waved a hand across the display on her desk and dismissed the image there. She'd seen enough of the crowd gathered outside the Retreat. She'd heard their chants, seen their hastily put together signs and holographic displays that listed their demands, their fears, their needs.

There would be no mollifying that assembly. She had thought that she could wait them out, that if the Retreat made no official statement they would eventually lose momentum and disperse on their own. That had proven not to be the case. The crowd just grew with every hour, until those closest to the Retreat wouldn't have been able to leave if they wanted to.

Clearly this was going to require some action. As soon as she decided what that action should be, she would take it.

In the meantime, she had to speak to Roan. Speak, not shout.

"What's done is done," she said again, mostly for her own benefit. "You made your choice. Now you'll have to accept the consequences of your action."

Roan said nothing. She just stood there, shivering, in front of the elder's desk.

"Your time here as an aspirant is over," the elder said. "I think you knew that would happen."

Roan nodded and bit her lip.

"I would ask you to pack up your things and leave at once. We both know, however, that if I forced you to leave the Retreat just now you would have to face the crowd, and that would most likely not end well for you." She imagined a pack of angry protestors tearing Roan limb from limb, desperate for any kind of scapegoat, any target for their pent-up fear and frustration. In her mind's eye she saw it quite clearly. Perhaps too clearly. She forced herself not to dwell on the image so that she didn't start relishing it.

"You will be allowed to remain here until such time as it is safe for you to leave," the elder said. She took a deep breath and looked down at her minder. She began paging through the other business of the day. Elder Ving reported that they had enough food stored inside the Retreat's walls to last for another three weeks. More than long enough, surely. Elder Ghent informed her that classes for his aspirants had been moved to the dome so as to keep everyone away from the Retreat's windows. Just in case anyone threw a rock at them, or the like.

"I'm...Elder?" Roan asked. "I don't understand. Is that all?"

Elder McRae didn't look up from her minder. "Did you have something else to say?" she asked.

"I just thought...I mean, I was expecting something more in the way of punishment," the girl said. "I thought you might...I don't know."

"Flog you in the public square? Lock you in a pillory? That kind of thing doesn't belong in the Transcendentalist faith," the elder said. "As I thought you would know. You didn't strike me as being that ignorant of our beliefs." Regardless of how seriously the girl had violated them. *Better not say that out loud,* the elder thought.

"I just thought..."

The elder's minder chimed and a new display came up, showing a view of the sky over the Retreat. A large aircraft was approaching, flying very low. After a moment the view focused on the craft and she saw it was the tender, the same vehicle on which she'd returned to Niraya from the Hexus.

A message came in from the tender, one the elder found very hard to believe. Surely the pilots couldn't be so reckless?

She rolled up the minder and left her office, Roan following unbidden behind her. Elder McRae climbed three flights of stairs until she came out onto a narrow balcony on the roof of the Retreat. Before her she saw the wild profusion of shingles and tarpaper and flagstones that covered the top of the huge building. Others were out there as well, mostly elders, though a few aspirants stuck their heads out of skylights and the tops of stairwells.

The tender came in at a terrifying rate of speed, though Elder

McRae imagined it was flying as slow as its pilot dared. As it crossed the top of the Retreat its nose suddenly reared up and for a split second it stood on its thrusters, all but hovering there. It was clear even to one as untutored in aerodynamics as the elder that the craft could not stay like that for long, not without stalling out and crashing into the rooftops.

It didn't have to. A hatch on its side opened and three human figures leapt out, and then the tender bucked up into the air and shot away, its wind nearly bowling Elder McRae over. In a moment it was gone, far away from the Retreat.

The three suited figures fell through the air without making any attempt to slow their descent. Two smashed down onto a distant balcony, rolling with the impact. The third hit a terra-cotta roof and burst right through the tiles, its weight and momentum too much for the fragile ceramic.

That roof was on top of Elder Ving's office, Elder McRae knew. She hurried back inside, then down a corridor until she reached Elder Ving's door. She could hear a commotion inside and she threw the door open without knocking.

Elder Ving was unhurt, even smiling in joy as she studied the ruin of her desk. A person in a space suit was struggling to stand up, but they kept slipping on broken pieces of roof tile. Elder McRae peered through a helmet obscured by red dust.

"Lieutenant Maggs," she said. "Are you hurt?"

"My pride has seen better days," the pilot said. "My inertial sink took care of the rest." He finally got to his feet and bowed to Elder Ving. "My most sincere apologies," he said. "I couldn't resist the urge to make a dramatic entrance."

———

"First things first," Lanoe said. "We need to get you out of here."

They had gathered in Elder McRae's office—Lanoe, Maggs, and Derrow, along with half a dozen of the Retreat's senior elders—to watch the display and wonder just how things had gotten so bad. On the display they could see the people of Niraya weren't going anywhere. Some of them had set up tents outside the Retreat, including makeshift kitchens and even latrine facilities. Most of them were just standing out there, watching the Retreat's windows, perhaps hoping someone would poke their head out long enough to get it knocked off.

"That's not necessary," Elder McRae said.

Lanoe stared at the old woman. "You do realize that half the people out there would put a bullet in you right now if they could? That the other half would probably just shout questions at you until you went deaf?"

"The doors downstairs are secure," she told him. "There have been a few attempts to break in, but nothing serious. There's been very little violence, all things considered. A few Centrocor employees have been attacked, though there were no serious injuries."

Derrow scrabbled to pull a minder out of her pocket. "I need to contact my people. Make sure they're okay," she said.

Lanoe dismissed her with a nod. She stepped out into the hallway and closed the door behind her.

"There's a funny thing about crowds," Lanoe told the elder. "You can't predict how they're going to act. Maybe they're just demonstrating peacefully today—give it twenty-four hours and you could have a mutiny on your hands. Lieutenant Maggs and I brought sidearms with us. We can get you out of here, one way or another."

An old man who Lanoe had been told was Elder Ghent gasped at the thought. "You can't be considering firing on the crowd."

"Just over their heads," Lanoe said. "It'll make 'em disperse. Then we get you over to the ground control station. I had Zhang and Valk head over there to get Ehta and Thom—they'll be ready to fly as soon as we arrive. It'll be a squeeze, but we can get all of you elders on the tender and get you into orbit, where you'll be safe."

Elder McRae sat down in her chair. "Unnecessary, as I said."

Lanoe wanted to grab her by the arm and haul her to safety. He fought to keep his cool. Why couldn't Zhang be here? She'd know what to say. Or maybe Maggs might have some thoughts. He turned and looked at the pilot but Maggs just shrugged.

"You seem to think we're prisoners here," Elder McRae said. "That we would have left already given the chance. You're incorrect. One of our four basic principles, our eternal truths, is self-reliance. That includes preparing for all contingencies."

"What are you getting at?" Lanoe asked.

"There's a flare shelter at the bottom of the Retreat, under the dome. When we constructed it, we included an escape tunnel in case this building was damaged in a natural catastrophe. The tunnel runs out to a house in town—one whose owners probably don't even know what's in their basement. We could leave anytime we liked. We choose to stay."

Lanoe looked at the other elders, standing in a semicircle by the windows. Their faces were just as impassive as Elder McRae's.

"This is our place," Elder Ving said. "Now, especially. Someone must stand for order on Niraya. Our path is clear."

Lanoe sighed. Damned zealots. Well, he'd tried to rescue them. If they wanted to die here that was their business.

He turned next toward Roan. "When I got back here, I had a message waiting for me, from Thom," he told her.

At least she had the decency to react, a little. She tried to hide it but he could see by the sudden light in her eyes that she desperately wanted to know what the kid had said.

"He tells me this whole thing, this damned broadcast, was his idea. That he coerced you into helping him turn this planet upside down. He says he exploited your feelings for him and he hopes you won't be punished."

"He... said that?" Roan asked. "He's just trying to protect me. If anything, it's the other way around. I coerced him."

Lanoe nodded. About what he'd expected. "Elder McRae, are you thinking what I'm thinking?"

"I imagine so," the old woman said. "They did this together."

Roan's mouth opened but she was too disciplined to say anything.

Lanoe took a step toward her. "I could shoot you both for treason," he said.

He expected her to break down in fear but she barely winced.

Instead she stood up as tall as she could—still about six inches short of Lanoe's height—and set her mouth in a hard line. "I wasn't aware that Niraya was under military authority," she said. "Then there's the fact you have no official jurisdiction here at all, since your mission isn't sanctioned by the Navy."

Maggs laughed. "She's got you there," he said.

Lanoe didn't bother glaring at his pilot. He was too busy trying to stare Roan down. "Sure," he said, finally. "Okay. You do have me there, kid. Now—how about you use that powerful brain of yours and tell me what we're supposed to do next? Huh? How do we get that crowd to disperse so we can get back to the business of saving all your asses?"

"You don't," Roan said.

Lanoe said nothing. *Give her some more rope,* he thought. *See if she ties a noose.*

"The people out there were confused and frightened and angry before. They knew they were in danger but they didn't understand what that meant—they had some rough idea they were being invaded, but no concept of what was going to happen. Well, now they're not confused anymore."

"Which just left more room for the frightened and angry part," Lanoe said.

Roan nodded. "Perfectly rational responses to what's happening, don't you think? They know they're going to die. All Thom and I did was to give them a chance to make their own choice about how they're going to spend their last days."

Lanoe stepped back. Then he looked around at the elders. "That's how it is, huh?" he asked.

None of them dared reply.

He nodded at them. "You think we're going to lose. You think you're doomed, so none of this matters." He rested one hand on Elder McRae's desk. Suddenly he was leaning on it. He forced himself to stand up straight. "Well, just maybe we're going to prove you wrong."

"Perhaps," Elder McRae said. "Anything is possible."

There was more talking. Such was the nature of human existence—a thing could not happen but it would be endlessly discussed. Even when there was so little to say.

Elder McRae listened patiently as the Commander told her of the desperate fight out past the moon Aruna. She heard his report on swarmships and drone fighters and how M. Valk had saved them. Of what a terrible and alien thing they had fought.

It did little to improve her estimate of the pilots' chances.

When Commander Lanoe ran out of words, he started asking for suggestions. It almost seemed like he expected her to give him orders. She found she couldn't fulfill that need, so she simply asked him to do his best.

When she had first met him, at the Hexus, she had possessed a fragile kind of hope, a sort of half belief simply because he seemed so competent, so knowledgeable in the ways of war. There had seemed, then, to be plenty of time—and anyway, it might have turned out that the enemy fleet wanted something they could part with, some tribute or ransom that they would gladly have paid.

It was clear now, in these last days, that all such hopes had been pointless. That there had never been a chance.

Eventually he left her office—storming off to consult with Lieutenant Maggs and the engineer, Derrow. The other elders went with him. Roan had slipped away at some point, presumably to return to her own room, where she could contemplate what she'd done.

Quiet and a false peace filled her office and for a while she simply sat at her desk, her minder rolled up securely so she didn't even have to see the crowd outside. She sat and tried to breathe and tried, simply, to be. She meditated on the Four Eternals, worked through the catechisms of self-reliance and self-understanding. Attempted to clear her mind of all nonessential thoughts.

It proved difficult.

Impossible, actually. She couldn't concentrate, couldn't focus with so many clouded and angry people all around her, even if she couldn't see them directly. She needed to escape her office, the place where she considered worldly business all day long. She rose from her chair and went out into the hall, then passed down a side corridor until she was deep within the mass of the Retreat, until she could feel its bulk around her, sheltering her. A window-less meditation room lay there at the heart of the building and she stepped inside, closing the door silently behind her. The room was kept dim and some aspirant, keeping to their duties despite what was going on, had lit incense to fill the room with its calming scent.

It was only after she sat down on a woven mat, crossing her old and aching legs underneath her, that she realized she was not alone in the little room.

Elder Ghent sat against the far wall, his eyes closed. Ghent was the oldest and most infirm of her fellow elders and she thought per-haps he had fallen asleep. She tried to focus on herself, on her own being, pretending he wasn't there.

Then he spoke, and she nearly jumped in surprise.

"How did we come to this?" he asked, in a very soft voice.

"What do you mean?" she asked him.

He was silent for some time, perhaps collecting words. In the quiet room they seemed out of place. Yet when he spoke again he did not falter.

"Those who built the Retreat, those who settled Niraya, came here to get away from worldly things. To escape the temptations and empty stimulations of the wider universe. They came here to study and to practice their disciplines, and only that."

"It seems that one can keep the universe at bay only for so long," she replied.

He did not move. He did not nod or even open his eyes. Yet she could tell he was lucid and quite present. "It didn't take an invad-ing fleet to make that plain," he said.

Ghent was a teacher. He was in charge of leading the aspirants in their studies and helping them find their way. Years of that task had given him a roundabout way of speaking—a Socratic method of asking questions instead of simply giving answers. She wished he would just get to the point.

"We," he said, "never meant to rule. To govern. Did we? And yet here we are. Choosing a path for others, not just for ourselves."

"You mean the people outside," she said. She permitted herself the tiniest, least audible of sighs. "We never asked to lead them. They simply followed."

"As humans will. And we acted—as leaders will. We held information back from them. Hoarded secrets."

"We agreed, all of us, to withhold the video," Elder McRae insisted.

"I do not claim to be innocent in this. I thought, as you did, that it was the right thing to do. There is no point in pondering what might have been different. Yet I wonder now—what is the way forward? They know they will die. Now they know how it will happen. What is our responsibility to them in their final days? Do we try to teach them acceptance? Give them peace?"

"I doubt they're in the mood to listen to sermons now," she said.

"Is there time to teach them by example? I think not."

She closed her eyes and inhaled the scent of the incense. "I came here today—to this room, I mean—to escape such thoughts."

"That's too bad," he told her. "I don't think you can."

Her eyes snapped open. She felt anger rise up inside her like a snake lifting from its coils. That was not an appropriate way for one elder to speak to another.

Which, of course, was the point.

"Whether you asked for this responsibility or not—it is yours," he told her. "I will support you as I can. So will the others, I'm certain. You must choose for all of us, however. Please choose well."

She rose from her mat, wanting to storm out of there. To tell him exactly what she thought of his elliptical demand. Instead she collected herself and bowed in his direction. "Thank you for your counsel," she told him.

Then she opened the door and stepped out of the dim room, back into the hall.

It seemed there was nowhere left for her to go.

⇥⇤

"I refuse to give up," Lanoe said. "I refuse to just accept defeat. Even if every damned religious nut on this planet thinks we're doomed."

"An admirable position," Maggs replied. The smarmy little bastard had a smile on his face. Lanoe supposed that was the upside of not being in charge. You didn't have to take the blame when things went wrong.

Lanoe brought a gloved fist down on a little wooden table, not quite hard enough to smash it to pieces. Even though he wanted to. Damn it all. If Zhang was there—

Funny how fast things could change. When he'd first seen Zhang in her new body he'd wanted nothing but to keep away from her. He'd felt so awkward just talking to her again. Now he desperately missed her. She, he knew, would never give up. Not when she could still fight.

"We need to start planning the next phase of this war," he told Maggs. "Derrow—you're a big part of that. We've showed we can beat one of their swarmships but that's not going to be enough. I need ground-based guns. That's the only way we can punch through the fleet and get at the programmer on the big ship."

"Assuming," Derrow said, carefully, "there is a programmer there."

He turned to face her and he could almost feel the anger radiating off his face. He could definitely see her wince. "Let me guess. You've got doubts now, too."

"Well...not so much doubts, just...Commander," she said, folding her arms across her chest. "You asked me for ideas on how to fight this enemy and I did my best. I think there probably is a programmer somewhere in that fleet, someone who isn't just a drone. But I don't know it for a fact."

"Nothing in war is ever clear or certain," he told her. "You go into battle with your best estimate of the enemy. Often you're proven wrong, and then you have to scramble to keep up. Now what about those guns? How fast can you build them?"

"If I have the right people, the right materials—I can put them together pretty fast. Less than a day."

"Good."

"Except," she said, "I've been in touch with my engineers, the ones who ought to be out at the mining concern right now. Most of them are here instead. In that crowd outside. Getting them back to work is going to be a challenge. And when I say I need the right materials—well, I haven't even done an inventory yet, I know what we have in stock, but—"

"We're going to make it happen, damn it," Lanoe said. He thought about hitting the table again. But no, Derrow was already scared. No point making it worse.

"There is one bright spot in all of this," she said. She looked over at Maggs. "Everybody's so terrified, when I asked them about the evacuation they didn't hold back."

"Oh?" Maggs asked. His smile fell right off his face. "Maybe we can discuss that later. It's nothing for the Commander to worry about."

It took a second for Lanoe to process what they were saying.

He had so much else on his mind. He had very little brainpower left to waste on analyzing what was clearly yet another slimy act on Maggs's part. When he did manage to process the words, it felt like someone had stabbed an icicle into his spine.

"Evacuation," he said, very carefully.

"Auster—I mean Lieutenant Maggs—has agreed to organize it," Derrow said. "Obviously the timing is pretty tight but I think the money we've collected should go a long way to speeding the process. Basically every Centrocor employee on the planet has contributed. Maybe we could talk to the elders about that as well, make our offer even more attractive. I know the religious communities don't have much money, but—"

Maggs was out the door like a shot, so fast it slammed shut

behind him. Lanoe had to wrestle with the knob to get it open. The bastard had a considerable head start on him.

It didn't matter. There was only one place Maggs could be headed.

———✦———

Elder McRae turned a corner and just had time to jump back before Lieutenant Maggs bowled her over. He dashed down a corridor and then nearly leapt down a flight of stairs.

A moment later Commander Lanoe came rushing after him. With a pistol in his hand.

"What do you think you're doing?" she demanded, all of her discipline deserting her in the shock of seeing an armed chase in the halls of the Retreat.

"I'll tell you when he's dead," Lanoe called back, already running past her.

It had been a long time since the elder ran anywhere, but she hurried then, taking the steps as quickly as she dared. Up ahead she could see Lanoe's back receding from her. He was in far better shape than she was, but she had the advantage of having lived long enough on Niraya to have adapted to the low oxygen content of its atmosphere. Soon she was gaining on him, and she could even hear Maggs puffing for breath far below.

The staircase twisted through many floors of the Retreat, headed always downward, toward the central dome. It was the fastest way to ground level, but she had a suspicion that Maggs was headed even lower—to the flare shelter, and the escape tunnel there. Clearly he'd been paying attention when she mentioned it earlier.

She had no idea why Lanoe wanted to kill the Lieutenant, though she imagined there would be a good reason. Ever since Maggs had tried to defraud her back on the Hexus she'd found it extremely difficult to extend compassion or anything like trust in his direction. Even for one as steeped in the faith as she, Maggs was hard to love.

Lanoe had surprised her when he'd given Maggs a second chance, back then. Apparently he did not intend to give the man a third.

She couldn't let Lanoe kill him, though. Not here.

When she had nearly reached the bottom of the stairs, Lanoe only a few steps ahead of her, she heard a scream of pain and knew it had to have come from Maggs. It was followed almost instantly by a clatter of falling metal and a cry of surprise from a more feminine voice. When she reached the bottom of the stairs, where they emptied out into the dome, time seemed to crystallize, instants freezing in place as she took in everything that had happened.

She saw an aspirant down on all fours, a serving tray still rattling on the floor in front of her. Porridge had spilled in a long beige splatter away from the bowls the aspirant had been carrying.

The aspirant looked unhurt. The same could not be said for Lieutenant Maggs.

The man was down on his face, moaning in pain. He turned over on his back and clutched the leg of his suit, then started gasping for breath.

Lanoe had stopped before he'd collided with the aspirant. He stood, filling most of the archway, his pistol already coming up so he could take the fatal shot.

Surprising even herself, Elder McRae grabbed for his arm and yanked it downward. Fire spat from the muzzle and the projectile dug a deep crater into the stone floor of the dome.

The aspirant started to scream. Time sped up again, and the elder felt her heart pounding in her chest.

"Hellfire," Lanoe said, turning on her. "Why'd you do that? He's up to his old tricks, and—"

"I will not allow you to commit murder here," the elder told him. "This place is sacred."

"He's a traitor. He's betrayed me, and your damned planet," Lanoe insisted. "Again."

Beyond his shoulder she could just see the aspirant running for safety. Good. She could also see Maggs climbing to his feet. His

suit could apparently compensate for whatever injury he'd sustained, though his face was still white with agony.

Lanoe still had his weapon, and she assumed it had more rounds
in its magazine. She had to buy the Lieutenant a little time. "You
told me, the last time, that you needed him. That there was something like honor in him, something worth cultivating. I wanted
him punished. I wanted him to grovel in the dust. You shamed me
with your ability to forgive, Commander. You shamed an elder of
the Transcendentalist faith. It was when I started to admire you.
Will you throw away the respect you've earned?"

"I don't give a tinker's damn about your respect," Lanoe told her.

His eyes burned with fury. She knew perfectly well that words
alone wouldn't calm down a warrior gripped with a murderous
rage. Perhaps, though, there was still a chance.

Maggs was on his feet, stumbling around the dome. He looked
lost. Her heart sank as she realized that his escape plan had brought
him this far only to fail him at the crucial moment. He knew there
would be an entrance to the flare shelter somewhere in the dome—
but he didn't know where it was.

There was nothing for it. She slipped under Lanoe's arm and
interposed herself between the two of them. Then she lifted one
hand and pointed at the door Maggs needed so desperately to find.

Lanoe figured out what she was doing, but only half a second
after Maggs. The Lieutenant half-limped, half-ran for the door
while Lanoe stared down at her—then shoved her aside and
resumed his chase.

She hurried after the two of them, through the door and down
a short stairwell, the two pilots' boots clanging on the metal ris-
ers. At the bottom lay the shelter, a thick-walled room filled with
shelves of supplies. The entrance to the escape tunnel lay at the far
end, through a low hatch. Maggs moved as quickly as he could in
that direction but with an injured leg he was still too slow.

The Commander lifted his arm again, lining up another shot.

"Wait," Maggs begged, between ragged breaths. "Please."

"So much for fancy words," Lanoe said. "End of the road, Maggs."

"Lanoe," the Lieutenant gasped. "You don't understand. I have debts—"

"What about the debt you owe to Zhang? Or Valk, for that matter. You fought beside them. That's supposed to be a bond thicker than blood."

Maggs couldn't seem to frame a reply.

"You've got a Blue Star, you bastard," Lanoe said. Was he holding his fire because of something that had been said? Or simply so he could pronounce the sentence of death? Elder McRae couldn't tell.

"That's supposed to mean something," Lanoe went on. "You're a Naval officer with a high decoration. That's supposed to mean you're an honorable man. All you've achieved here—your entire legacy—is to wreck the last illusion I had. Don't bother with begging, Maggs."

"Commander," Elder McRae said, her voice sounding terribly high and reedy in her own ears. "Please! If you won't listen to him beg, listen to me."

Lanoe didn't turn to look at her. He didn't fire, either.

"This is a place of peace. It was consecrated a century ago, in the name of tolerance and compassion. Please. I beg of you, spare his life."

"We had a chance with four pilots," Lanoe said. She wasn't sure if he was speaking to her or to Maggs. "Four pilots I could trust. I can't fly with you now, Maggs. I can't fight with you, not knowing I'd always have to watch my back."

"Some debts have to be paid back," Maggs said, nearly whispering. Perhaps he meant those to be his last words.

"Commander," the elder said, "you came here—to Niraya—to save human lives. Not to take them."

"Is that right?" Lanoe asked.

She didn't know what else to say. She didn't have anything to give him, no ransom to save the Lieutenant's life. She had done all she could.

It turned out, in the end, to be enough.

Lanoe lowered his arm. Shoved his pistol back into its holster.

For the first time she noticed that Maggs had one just like it on his hip. He could have fought back—might even have killed the Commander. He hadn't even tried, though. Did he simply lack courage? Or had something else stayed his hand?

It didn't matter. What did matter was that there would be no bloodshed inside the Retreat, not this day.

The Elder's head spun with relief.

"Go on," Lanoe said. "Run. And hope I die here, Maggs. Hope I die here so I never bump into you again."

The Lieutenant did not waste any time clambering through the hatch and down the long, dark tunnel away from the Retreat.

Chapter Twenty

The ground control station was crowded with the four of them inside. Zhang sat with Valk and Ehta by the windows while Thom sat on the floor in a corner, working his minder. Typing something very long.

Zhang laughed and put her feet up on the main console. "I never thought I'd be so glad to see the big guy," she said, raising an imaginary glass in Valk's direction. "He came riding in like the thunder of judgment. You should have seen it, Ehta. No fancy flying or anything—he left that to Maggs—but our boy can shoot."

"I had a fresh ship and you'd already cut 'em down to size," Valk insisted. "I just mopped 'em up."

Zhang shook her head. "Ehta, you remember that patrol we ran out by Tiamat, when we thought the Establishment was finished and then it turned out they had three whole wings of fighters we didn't know about? You remember how Lanoe blasted right down the middle, punching a hole in their formation you could sail a carrier group through?"

"I remember," Ehta said. She wasn't smiling. "He was untouchable that day. Didn't even maneuver to evade, just cut and cut and kept moving." She shook her head. "Sorry, Valk, maybe you don't want to talk about that battle."

Zhang cursed herself silently. "The Establishment fought like feral dogs at Tiamat," she said, in way of apology.

Valk didn't seem too offended. Not that she could tell—his helmet was opaque even to her cybernetic eyes. "That was one of our last big pushes," he said. "I was in the hospital that day. I've heard stories, though. It's possible Lanoe won the war for your end that day."

"Don't let him hear that. His head won't fit in his helmet. The point I'm trying to make—Valk fought just like that, against the swarm. Between the two of them I'm not sure which one I'd less like to face in a dogfight. Glad I don't have to choose."

"Sounds like you're a damned hero," Ehta told him. "I wish... well, I wish I could have been there. I owe Lanoe my life. It would have been nice to pay him back. But you know what they say. Wish in one hand and spit in the other, see which fills up first."

Zhang put her feet back down on the floor. "Ehta—Caroline," she said. "You'll get your chance. When the enemy shows up in the sky here, ground control's going to make all the difference."

She couldn't read Ehta's expression, but she figured she knew how the woman felt. To have come all this way only to sit on the ground—it was a pilot's nightmare. She reached for more words of comfort or consolation, but then her minder chimed and she sat up very straight in her chair.

"Something up?" Valk asked.

"Yeah, out at the spaceport," she said. She hovered her hand over the minder's display and then grunted in surprise at what it told her. She opened a channel to Lanoe's suit right away. "Boss," she told him, "somebody's messing with one of our spare fighters. Maybe those protestors think they can break in to the Retreat with its PBWs."

"Negative," Lanoe said back. He didn't bother to send video, just his voice. "It's Maggs. He's leaving."

"Leaving? You send him on an errand or something?"

"He's not coming back," Lanoe said.

Zhang climbed out of the chair and stepped toward the door. "I can intercept," she said. "You want him back in one piece?"

"Let him go." Lanoe broke the connection without providing any more information.

She looked up at Valk. "You hear that? You figure…"

"I always did figure," Valk said.

Ehta looked between the two of them. "I think that conversation was encrypted or something," she said. "Because I didn't understand a word." In the corner, Thom looked up from his diary or whatever he was writing.

Zhang shrugged. "He's cut and run. Maggs is ditching us," she explained.

"Maybe he decided we didn't stand a chance," Ehta suggested. "Figured he could save his own skin."

"At the expense of ours," Valk said. "It took four of us to bring down one swarm. There's at least seven more of them around the queenship."

"Scuttle that talk," Zhang said, the kind of thing she would have said back when she was Lanoe's second in command.

Things were different now. Ehta and Valk didn't have to snap to attention every time she stood up. Still.

She wasn't going to sit there and listen to defeatism.

On her minder, she kept an eye on Maggs's fighter, in case Lanoe changed his mind. She watched it all the way until it entered the wormhole throat and disappeared, out of her reach. Lanoe didn't call.

——

Roan couldn't stay in her tiny room. There was nothing there she wanted to see. She had few personal possessions beyond a couple of changes of clothing and a meditation mat. The faith had taught her not to grow attached to objects, and she'd been devoted to that discipline.

So instead she roamed the hallways of the Retreat like a ghost.

When she passed one of her former fellow aspirants, they would turn their faces away. Not shunning her, she thought—they just didn't want to start an awkward conversation that would be sure to embarrass her. They were trying to be compassionate.

It didn't matter. She had her minder in her hands and that was all she could look at.

Seven new messages from Thom.

She hadn't opened any of them. The metadata showed, however, that they were text-only, and the file sizes suggested that he'd written page after page. She couldn't bear to find out what he was trying to tell her.

She knew, eventually, she wouldn't be able to bear not knowing.

Voices came from a room ahead of her, a small conference room where the elders sometimes gathered to discuss the progress of their aspirants. The door was notoriously thin and more than once Roan had eavesdropped on what was said in that room. She recognized the voices as belonging to Engineer Derrow and Commander Lanoe.

"—can't believe he would do this," Derrow said. She sounded like she'd been crying. "I thought I knew him, I—"

"Engineer," Lanoe growled, "I need you to focus."

Roan thought maybe Derrow hadn't heard him. "I didn't expect...I mean, we weren't in love, but...and then, when he started talking about evacuation..."

"Do the math," Lanoe said. "There are a hundred thousand people on this planet. Even the biggest liners carry fewer than a thousand passengers. You can't have thought he would be able to get that many ships diverted, no matter how much money you scraped together."

Derrow didn't respond.

"I see," Lanoe said. "You didn't expect him to save everybody."

"How dare you?" the engineer shot back. "How dare you judge me? I had my employees to think of."

"And now I have to think about them," Lanoe told her. "I have to think of a way to save them. Can we please talk about the guns?"

"Why even bother? You need people to build them, and half my people are down there in the crowd screaming for your blood. The other half think they're going to be evacuated. What am I supposed to tell them?"

"That's your job. I—hold on. I think I heard something."

Roan gasped as the door swung open and Commander Lanoe stared down at her. He grabbed her by the arm and hauled her into the room.

"This discussion isn't public," he told her.

She wrestled her arm away from him. "I have a right to know what's going on," she insisted.

"So you can share it with everybody? Maybe you'd like to broadcast it so the enemy can hear our plans," Lanoe replied.

She'd seen him angry before. Faced him down. She refused to be cowed now. She started to speak, then stopped when the engineer got out of her chair and headed out of the room.

"Derrow!" Lanoe called, but the woman was gone.

Roan sat down at the conference table, figuring Lanoe would have more harsh words for her. Instead, he just closed the door and took a seat himself. He didn't look at her. Just sighed deeply and rubbed at his eyes. "If there were no civilians in this galaxy," he said, eventually, "there wouldn't be any wars. Warriors can actually be trusted."

"You shouldn't be so hard on her," Roan said.

He laughed. It wasn't a very humorous sound.

"It's hard—losing somebody you care about," Roan went on. "Even if you just knew them a little while. We're all so scared right now that we cling to each other."

He lowered his hands and looked at her and she saw how old he was. He'd seen centuries come and go. This was not a man, his look said, who needed a lecture from a twenty-year-old girl.

"You and Thom, huh?" he asked. He didn't leer, at least.

"How did you know?"

"Because it's the oldest, dumbest story in the book."

Roan looked away from him. "It's over now. I suppose that makes you happy."

"No," he told her. "Right now nothing makes me happy."

She shook her head. "He—told me what he did." Lanoe would know, of course. He'd know more about it than Roan did. "That he killed his own father."

"Is that what he said?"

She bit her lip. "He told the truth, didn't he?"

Lanoe sighed again. "I don't have time for this. Get out."

But suddenly that wasn't an option. Lanoe knew all about it. Lanoe was maybe the only person on the planet who knew the whole story. "No, please—tell me. Tell me what happened."

He got up from his chair. Maybe, if she wouldn't leave, he intended to.

"Commander," she said, "I know there's some compassion in you. Please—I have to know."

Standing near the door he turned to look at her and his shoulders sagged. Perhaps he thought if he answered her question it would get rid of her. "His father had him tailored in a lab. He never had a mother—just an egg donor. Even he doesn't know that fact. He was designed from day one to be a spare body. His father was a powerful man, and rich, too. A planetary governor. You don't have one of those here, but people like that—they get what they want, and the law doesn't matter. When he got sick enough, he was going to have his consciousness downloaded into Thom's brain."

"Like—like Lieutenant Zhang," Roan said. "And the woman she switched bodies with."

"Sure," Lanoe said, "except that was voluntary. His father wasn't going to give Thom a new body. He was just going to be erased. Deleted."

Roan felt like the Retreat was shaking in an earthquake. She knew it was just her stomach turning over. "So he was justified in what he did."

"Justified? Not my department," Lanoe said. "When Thom found out what was planned for him, he stole a pistol and he shot his father three times in the chest. The first shot was right through the heart. The other two were, I guess, just to make sure. Then

Thom got in his racing yacht and he lit out for nowhere. I don't think he had a real plan. When I caught up to him, he tried to kill himself."

"But you didn't let him."

"He changed his mind. He wanted to live."

Roan held tightly to the edge of the table. "You took pity on him. You saved him. You must have thought he was worth something, then."

Lanoe grunted. "I liked Thom. I didn't like his father. That's all."

"But—was he right to do what he did? It was him or his father."

"Sure," Lanoe said. "Except—why not just run away in the yacht? Why kill the man first?"

"His father would have chased after him, then," Roan pointed out.

"Look, kid. I don't know what I would have done in his place. I don't want to think about that."

"Hypothetical questions achieve nothing but to engender fantasies," Roan said, quoting from one of Elder Ghent's lessons.

"They teach you that here? The elders know a couple of things. Too bad you didn't listen to them more often."

Roan felt herself blush, felt the heat of her own blood on her face. "Thom and I . . . We grew very close over the last few days. I've started having feelings for him but—"

"Okay, I'm done," Lanoe said. "I answered your question. Now get the hell out—I have a war to plan, and it looks like I'm doing it all by myself."

She knew better than to try his patience further.

In the repair suite of the tender, Zhang winched her BR.9 into place and engaged the restraint cradle, locking it down. She climbed up over its canopy and opened all the inspection hatches around the engine, once she was certain she wouldn't be venting radioactive gas by doing so. The thrusters were still too hot to touch, even after so many hours of being switched off, so she prodded them with a long wrench.

The cone of her main thruster fell off and clattered to the tender's floor. She looked down and saw a shard of a kinetic impactor still wedged into the cone. So strange to see a piece of an alien artifact like that, just lying on the ground.

She shrugged it off and got back to work. Her secondary thrusters were fried, their reaction chambers clogged with slag like shiny candle wax. She pried them out, not without difficulty, and tossed them in the recycle bin, then replaced them with spares printed by the tender's automated machine shop.

The fusion reactor looked sound. Its struts were loose so it ran the risk of shimmying out of true if she tried firing the main thruster again, but that was an easy enough fix. The main problem was going to be replacing the cones, elegantly designed components that were beyond the tender's capabilities.

Finding spares for those on a place like Niraya would take some doing.

Well, at least they had a spare BR.9 parked out at the spaceport. They'd had two before Maggs ran away. If she couldn't get her own fighter fixed she could just use that one. Pilots held it to be bad luck to change ships in the middle of a campaign, but Zhang had been unlucky before—say, the time she got cut in half. She'd survived that.

The question of whether she could survive a battle with only two other fighters backing her up wasn't worth entertaining.

"She sent me a message!" Thom cried out.

Through the open rear hatch of the tender she could see him over by the door of the ground control station. He beamed like a marine on shore leave, waving his minder in the air.

Ehta sat leaning up against the side of the station, her arms crossed on top of her knees. "Good for you, kid," the grounded pilot said. She sounded almost sincere. Zhang knew she'd spent some time with Thom and Roan while the other pilots were off having adventures—maybe she'd gotten close to the kids. "What's it say?"

"She says we need to talk," Thom said, still beaming.

From her perch on top of her fighter, Zhang winced.

"That's . . . uh, that's great," Ehta told him.

Zhang clambered down off the fighter and rubbed as much grease as she could off of her gloves and onto a relatively clean towel. "Thom," she said, walking over to where he held his minder like a prize he'd just won for being a clever boy, "you don't have much experience with women, do you?"

"Hey, come on," Ehta said, but Zhang just shook her head.

"What do you mean?" Thom asked.

"Just—don't get your hopes up," she said. She patted him on the shoulder, probably ruining his expensive tunic.

"Don't be mean," Ehta said.

Zhang smiled down at her. Thom asked her what she meant but she just shook her head. "Ehta," she said, "why don't you take a look at Maggs's old fighter and see if it can be repaired. I need a break." She stepped inside the ground control station. Valk was there, watching a minder. Her cybernetic eyes couldn't see what it displayed, but she could guess.

"Things still tense over at the Retreat?" she asked.

"They're starting to get organized," Valk told her. "From the video I've seen, they're choosing somebody to speak for them. I don't think this crowd is just going to get bored and wander off. Funny—if they want answers about what's going on, you'd figure they'd come up here and ask us. We're the ones who've actually seen the enemy."

"They don't want answers," Zhang said. "They want to not be scared. They can't do anything about the enemy so they've turned on their leaders—or the closest thing they've got, the elders. I wouldn't want to be Elder McRae right now. Even if we somehow manage to save this planet, there's going to be a lot of people questioning how she handled the invasion."

Zhang called up one of her customized displays and ran her hand over its warm surface. In her mind's eye she saw the crowd, surging against the walls of the Retreat. "I don't know why Lanoe is still there," she said. "We don't have time to waste on politics. I wish I knew what he hoped to achieve."

"You know him better than anybody," Valk pointed out.

Zhang favored him with a sad little smile. "I'm afraid that's not saying much. I've known a couple of people nearly as old as him and it's always the same way. After three hundred years you can't help but grow enigmatic. Too many secrets. Too many memories nobody else would understand."

She studied the Retreat through the display, wishing she could just see him. Know that he was okay. She was receiving live video but the image looked almost still, the Retreat a rock battered by the surging waves of the crowd at its base.

While she watched, something did change, however. On a balcony about three floors up on the side of the Retreat, a door opened. She almost missed it as someone stepped out and looked down at the crowd.

A wave of attention ran through the protestors, as visible as a shock wave in a dust cloud. Ten thousand heads craning back all at once so they could see who had finally come out to address them.

The Retreat had not been built as a center of government. No one had ever thought it would be necessary to address a crowd from its heights. The little balcony had room for one or maybe two people at most, and it was high up enough on the side of the building that any speaker would have to shout to be heard.

It was also high up enough that no one in the crowd would be able to throw rocks at the speaker, though that was just a fringe benefit.

The balcony hung on the side of Elder Kitaj's office, one of the smaller workspaces in the Retreat. The room was crowded to the point of being stifling. Roan didn't really understand why she was there. Maybe Elder McRae wanted her to see how much damage she'd caused.

Out on the balcony, Elder Ving—smiling, heavyset Elder Ving, the most affable of the elders—asked for a moment of the crowd's time. Roan could barely hear what she actually said over the roar of the crowd. It didn't much matter. Elder Ving had been chosen to get their attention, and then introduce Elder McRae. That was all.

"You still sure you want to do this?" Commander Lanoe asked. "Somebody down there might have a rifle. It's risky."

Roan had never seen Elder McRae look so composed. "It's my responsibility," she told the pilot. "It must be done, sooner or later."

"If there is a later," Engineer Derrow said.

They may have had their differences, but Roan had spent years learning at the old woman's knee. She couldn't help but be awed by Elder McRae's poise as she stepped out onto the balcony, allowing Elder Ving to hurry back inside.

"Thank you for your attention," Elder McRae said. "I'd like to address your grievances and demands, and assure you that we are doing everything in our power to protect you."

The crowd howled in rage.

"It is true that we kept some information from you concerning the present invasion," she went on. "This was done in your best interests. We of the Retreat are not elected officials, but we have taken our position as your counselors, your advisors, and, yes, as your leaders quite seriously. I assure you everything we do is aligned toward one purpose, that is, the safety and well-being of Nirayans and Niraya."

Roan felt like she might explode. "Tell them the truth," she said, under her breath. "It's what they want. Tell them what we know!"

The other elders crowded into the office turned to look at her with that expression they had sometimes when they addressed an aspirant, that expression that said you were being foolish and difficult but they forgave you, oh, they could forgive anything.

Commander Lanoe looked at her, too, but with a very different expression. She thought he might even have been smiling, a little, though his face was so wrinkled it could be hard to tell.

"You don't give up, do you?" he asked.

"Not when so much is at stake," she told him.

He was definitely smiling. Without a word, he nodded, just once, his eyes fixed on hers.

She'd seen him do that before. Once.

Out on the balcony, Elder McRae had to almost scream to be heard over the anger of the crowd. "We have tried to lead by good example. Our teachings are not for everyone, but we believe everyone can benefit from rationality and self-examination. I hope that over the years we have provided you with some measure of insight, and it's in that hope that I call on you today to reject violence against your fellow Nirayans."

"You mean against you!" someone in the crowd shouted, loud enough to drown her out. It sounded like they were right outside, close enough to grab the elder and pull her down off the balcony.

Roan wanted to push forward and peek out through the windows, in the hope of seeing what was going on. She couldn't move, though. Commander Lanoe, in his bulky suit, was pushing his way through the elders and there was no room for her.

"The current situation," Elder McRae said, "is bleak, that is true—"

She stopped when Commander Lanoe dropped a hand on her shoulder. She turned to face him and he squeezed in beside her on the balcony.

"There will be no evacuations," he said, his voice rolling like thunder. His suit must have had a loudspeaker built into the collar ring.

The crowd fell silent for a moment, then erupted in a sustained cry of confusion and absolute wrath.

"Some of you work for Centrocor and you thought you were going to be evacuated. That isn't going to happen," Lanoe said. "There's no time for that. The invasion fleet will be here in a couple of days."

Roan couldn't believe it.

She'd gotten through to him. Had he been impressed by her conviction? Or had he just decided there wasn't enough time left for telling half-truths and lies?

"They're aliens," he went on. "I know what you're thinking. We've never found aliens before—most of us assumed they don't exist. Well, they're real, and they're coming here."

Roan was so rapt listening to his words she barely noticed that the crowd noise was dying down.

"Niraya's in trouble," Lanoe said. "I won't lie to you about that. You've seen the video. Good. You know what will happen. Except it won't be one of those big drones, it'll be hundreds of them."

Gasps replied, and a few screams of terror. Not too many. The crowd had fallen almost silent. Roan started moving toward the balcony, needing to see what was happening out there.

"I came here to stop that from happening. I brought as many pilots as I could. I wish I had more. It's going to be a damned tough fight, and we may not win it. You need to accept that there will be no miracles. No promises—except one.

"I will fight them with every ounce of strength I have. I'll use every dirty trick I know, and if it costs me my life, I will continue to fight. My people and I are going to lay down our lives for you. I stake my honor on it.

"And as hard as it's going to be, I believe we have a chance.

"The enemy we're fighting—they aren't magic. They're machines," Lanoe said. "You shoot them hard enough and they go down. I plan to make one decisive strike against the enemy. If my plan works, it will stop this invasion in its tracks.

"I can't do it alone, though.

"I need ground support—everything I can get. I want to build gun emplacements, and that means I need engineers, I need crews to fire the guns. I need volunteers to make that happen. I—"

He stopped. He just stopped speaking.

Roan pushed past Elder Ghent and shoved her way onto the balcony. She looked down and saw the crowd arrayed around her, so many faces, so many Nirayans.

One of them was holding up his hand. A woman standing next to him lifted hers, as well. Then others, all over the crowd.

Lanoe nodded at them, pointing at each one as they volunteered.

Dozens. Hundreds of them. A couple of people shouted angry demands and threats but they were hushed by the people around them. More hands went up.

Roan felt someone moving beside her and she looked and saw Elder McRae, one of her hands lifted high in the air. "I can weld," the old woman said. "If that's useful."

Lanoe turned and looked at Engineer Derrow.

"It is," the engineer said. Then she lifted her own hand, even though only the people in the office could see it.

PART III

ICE GIANT

Chapter Twenty-One

Lanoe leaned back into his seat while Roan drove him toward the edge of the crater. There'd been no problem getting through the crowd when they left the Retreat, except for all the people who wanted to wave at them and raise their hands in solidarity.

"Half these volunteers are farmers and office workers," he said, frowning. "I don't know what to do with them."

"They want to work with you now, not string you up from a lamppost," the girl told him. "I'd say that's an improvement." She couldn't seem to resist gloating. "Tell people the truth, tell them what's going on, and they offer to help. Who could have thought that would happen?"

He glanced at her out of the corner of his eye. She'd impressed him, this child from a backwater planet. She was more in control of herself, mentally stronger, than half the marines he'd met in his time. "I still think what you and Thom did—broadcasting that video—was a damn fool thing to do. I have to admit it worked, though. It looked like maybe McRae came around a little, too."

"Nobody stopped me on my way to the motor pool to talk about reinstating me as an aspirant," she told him.

"Is that even something you want?"

Roan didn't respond, except to shrug.

When they arrived at the crater wall and climbed the long stairs up to the ground control station, Zhang was waiting for them outside. She wrapped her arms around Lanoe's suited shoulders and kissed him before he could protest.

"Nice work out there," she said, releasing him. "Hi, Roan. He's inside."

"Who is?" Lanoe asked.

Zhang gave him a look of exasperation—not easy given her cybernetic eyes, but she'd had a lot of practice. "Thom, of course." She turned to face Roan. "I have a feeling I know what you're going to tell him. Try to be nice about it, okay?"

"If you know what I'm going to say, I wish you'd tell me," Roan replied, but she didn't wait to discuss it further. She headed into the station like someone going to the gallows.

Lanoe had spent enough of his time worrying about the kids. "We've got a long list of things to do," he told Zhang. "I want to start shipping out first thing in the morning. Or whatever passes for morning around here. I've got a plan for how we're going to fight these bastards but it means we have to move fast. First things first—"

"First things first, tonight we don't talk shop," Zhang told him.

"Zhang, we need—"

"I know what you need. Which is to buy me that drink you promised," she said.

He started to talk again but she put a hand over his mouth.

"We'll be ready to go in the morning," she told him. "That gives us all night. Who's going to sleep the night before a battle? You and I never did. Valk could definitely use a little time off as well, though he won't admit it."

He smiled under her hand. It wasn't the first time she'd reminded him that his people needed to relax between battles. He'd always been thinking about the next fight while ignoring the mental condition of his squad. It had always been her job, as second in command, to make sure he didn't push them so hard they broke.

Well, he supposed he could find a few hours in the battle plan to cut loose. "What do we even have to drink out here?" he asked.

"There's some deicing fluid in the tender that isn't too toxic," she said. She laughed when she saw his face fall. "Just kidding. There's a full bottle of scotch in there. Did you forget I was the one who commandeered that tender?"

"You always were good at keeping us supplied," he said.

Valk sipped carefully at his liquor. No one had been able to find a straw for him, so he made do with a length of tubing from a vapor injector that still smelled like coolant—ably masked by the creosote taste of the scotch. He tried to savor the alcohol, though it didn't taste as good as it used to, back before his accident. Nothing ever did.

Still, he didn't like to feel sorry for himself. Zhang pumped some music into the ground control station and he whooped and patted his knee to the beat and saw her smile back at him.

The kids, Thom and Roan, had been talking quietly in one corner of the station, their eyes locked together in that intense way young people could manage. When the music started they looked up. Thom actually rolled his eyes. Maybe the tunes sounded too old-fashioned to him. Well, they had been popular back during the Establishment Crisis, so most likely before the kids were born. Together the kids got up and slipped out of the station together, probably intending to continue their conversation on a walk around the crater rim.

Valk shrugged and looked over at Lanoe. He raised his glass and the Commander did the same. "This is a little different," Lanoe said, "from the last time you and I shared a drink."

"Back then I was trying to figure out if you were going to ruin my life or just be a minor inconvenience," Valk replied.

Lanoe laughed—a genuine laugh for once—and poured himself another drink. "So which was it?" he asked.

"Guess we'll find out tomorrow," Valk told him, and got another laugh for it.

Zhang suggested a game of cards—she'd brought a deck for this particular purpose—but Lanoe barely started to shuffle before he gave up. Instead he pointed out the last time he and Ehta had played cards and she'd cheated him out of a month's pay.

"We'd just come off back-to-back patrols when you had me hunting for enemies we never found. You owed me," Ehta said.

Which just started them off on war stories, and as with all pilots everywhere, once those started they didn't stop. Zhang recalled a patrol where she'd gotten separated from Lanoe, only to find him six hours later in the debris of half a wing of Establishmentarians. Ehta exploded with laughter and said the exact same thing had happened to her. Soon they were breaking down all the major engagements of the Tiamat campaign, none of them getting the details exactly right.

Valk couldn't join in much. A lot of the time the three of them ended up talking about how they'd killed pilots Valk had known, had flown with.

He didn't let it get to him. It was all history now, anyway, and he could hardly begrudge them a chance to share old memories of glory. He was especially pleased to see Ehta joining in. He knew how bad she felt about being grounded, and he was glad if she could feel like she belonged, if just for a little while. He did notice that the bottle was in her hand more often than not, and that her face had grown very flushed, but he figured if anybody could afford to get ripped that night, it was her.

The music swelled and flowed and Valk let it pulse through him. It felt good, like a massage almost, and it eased his aching bones. For the first time in a while he didn't mind the pull of gravity. The white pearl didn't flash in the corner of his vision. He realized with a start that he was enjoying himself.

He was, he had to admit, a little drunk. Which maybe justified the fact that he couldn't stop watching Lanoe and Zhang. At least they couldn't see him staring through his opaque helmet.

They kept touching each other, in ways that weren't approved of in polite company—though he didn't suppose this counted as that.

Lanoe kept looking her up and down like he'd never seen a woman before. Valk knew they had some history but if he didn't know better, he'd think they were—

"If you'll excuse us," Zhang said, standing up suddenly. She was holding Lanoe's hand. "We need to go check something. In the tender." She couldn't help but grin wickedly. "Sensitive stuff, uh." She cracked up laughing and Ehta pointed and guffawed at her. "Top secret."

Ehta whooped and slapped her leg as the two of them headed out the door, in a real hurry, it looked like. When they were gone she got up and changed the music to something with a gnarly groove and stood by the main console, swaying back and forth a little. Only two of them remained in the station.

—*—

Lanoe climbed up through the hatch and reached for the lights but she pushed his hand away, kissed him hard, and then turned around to show him her back. "Open me up," she said, her voice low and breathy.

He laughed and ran a thumb down the release seam at the back of her suit. Her collar ring hinged open and the suit fell down around her shoulders. Her slender, perfectly shaped shoulders.

He kissed the back of her neck and felt her shiver. Kissed her again, just behind her ear and she fell back against him, her hands reaching for his. For a while, for a perfect, fragile little time he just held her, his arms wrapped around her stomach, his face buried in her hair.

The smell of her was intoxicating, even if it was a little wrong. Memories fell on him like a hard, driving rain. Flashes of bare skin and the glint of her eyes in the dark. Bursts of motion, of hands grabbing each other, of breath coming heavy and thick as they made love in places light-years and decades gone.

Her suit fell down around her ankles. She turned and pressed herself against him, reaching behind him to undo his own release seam. She stepped away from him just for a moment and pulled his suit down until he stood as naked as her. He felt the chill, the chill he always felt when he took his suit off, the bizarre sensation of air on his skin after so long, but it passed when she pressed herself against him and her body heat flowed into him, warming him, bringing back another memory.

That time—that time on Tartarus, in a field of purple flowers a dozen kilometers from the nearest town, when it had felt like they were as far away from war and fighting as anyone had ever been. Two weeks' leave could feel like an eternity.

She kissed him, her head tilted back. He was so much taller than her now. He reached down and picked her up and she squealed with laughter as he carried her over to one of the bunks, it didn't matter which one. He climbed in after her and she grabbed him, it didn't matter where, grabbed him and pulled him close.

The first time—he remembered the first time. They'd been up all night going over battle plans, he could barely remember which campaign. He'd been so tentative about making the first move, about responding to what he was pretty sure they both felt. But when he'd leaned across the table and kissed her, eyes open, her eyes open, too, she'd whispered, "Took your time about it," and then there was nothing tentative in what happened next.

Her eyes. He remembered her eyes in that moment. The way she'd looked at him. She'd lifted one eyebrow, trying for sarcasm, but in her eyes he'd seen how much she wanted him. How long she'd been waiting.

Now she buried her face in his chest, her mouth moving downward in a wet line. He pulled her up and looked at her. Even in the dark he could see her cybernetic eyes, dark pools in her face. Not Zhang's eyes.

He tried to put it out of his mind. She was beautiful, in ways she hadn't been before. Her body was taut and soft in exactly the right places, as if she'd been made for his hands, for his lips. She moved under him in exactly the right ways.

Still. He must have hesitated. Tensed up.

"I've been waiting for this for years, Lanoe. Don't stop," she said.

"I feel like I'm cheating on you," he told her. "While you're in the room. Like you're sitting behind me, watching me."

She cupped his cheek with one delicate hand. "Close your eyes," she said. "Close your eyes and pretend, if you have to."

He closed his eyes. "Your voice is still different," he said. "The way you smell…"

"Work with me," she told him. "Here. Put your hand here. That feels good, doesn't it? How about if I do this?"

It took a while. But they made it work.

⊁

Valk picked up the cards. "How about a game?" he asked. Maybe if Ehta had to focus on her play she would sober up a little.

"It's good," she said. She let out a roaring belch, which made her laugh. "Good to see the two of them, Lanoe and Zhang, back together. Been a long time. Back in the old days, in the damned old Ninety-Fourth squadron, he could be a real cuss of a commander, you know? But she always took his edge off." That was apparently enough of an innuendo to make her laugh again.

"They make a great team," Valk agreed.

Ehta nodded to herself. She beamed for a moment, and then her face fell. "We were. All of us. A great team. Madman Jernigan. Bloody Khoi. Hakluyt—he was a devil of a fighter, we were always running defense for him. They're gone now but Lanoe and Zhang, they, they're still here. Still together."

"And you. You survived."

"Yeah. Imagine that, huh? I made it through the war and then I made it in the marines. You're not supposed to live very long in the marines, but I did. We have a saying in the Navy—if you're born to die in the void, you'll never buy it on the ground."

"We said something similar in the Establishment."

Which made her laugh more than anything so far. "Imagine that. Imagine old Lanoe fighting along side one of your bunch.

That," she said, "is irony. Or no. That's not what that word means. It's just funny, I guess."

"That's all in the past. War's over."

She nodded, not looking at him. "The past. Sure. You know—I don't blame Maggs for running."

Surprised, Valk sat up a little in his chair. "You don't?"

"He didn't owe Lanoe. Not like me and Zhang. He wasn't one of us." She got up to search for the bottle. She wobbled a little but she didn't fall down. Eventually she found the scotch and poured herself another drink. "What's the point of staying here to die? He knew we haven't got a chance."

"Lanoe doesn't see it that way," Valk said.

Ehta studied him for a long time, just sipping at her drink. "He's not looking right now. Neither is Zhang."

"You suggesting something?"

"Nobody would notice if you decided to do the same thing," she told him, her eyes locked on his helmet.

"Run away, you mean."

"You aren't one of us, either," she told him.

Was this a test? Or maybe she hoped that he would say yes, that he would go out and steal the tender and fly back to the Hexus and try to rebuild his life—maybe she was hoping he would take her with him.

Except he knew better. She might be tempted, but Ehta would never run away from Lanoe, would she? She'd come all this way. She'd tried to overcome her trauma and fly for Lanoe, even though she must have known it wouldn't work.

How much courage had that taken? Well, he knew she was no coward. She'd joined the Poor Bloody Marines when she realized she couldn't fly. But there were different kinds of bravery.

Like his own, he thought.

It was easy being courageous when you were perfectly happy to die whenever the Grim Reaper had an opening in his schedule.

"This is where I want to be," he told her. "Until Lanoe came along, until he took me out of the Hexus, I hadn't flown in seventeen years. I'd forgotten how much it meant to me. All the shoot-ing, all the craziness of a battle, that I could have given up. But that feeling, when you're all alone out there in your cockpit, hanging over nothing, not even sky over your head—"

He barely registered how white her face had become until she dropped the bottle. It rolled across the floor, a few precious drops of liquor spilling on the concrete.

"I'm sorry," he said, suddenly feeling like an ass.

"Don't worry about it," she insisted, scrabbling around on her knees to pick the bottle back up.

"I didn't mean to—"

"I said it's okay." She climbed back into her chair. "You want to hear something funny?"

"Yeah," he said.

"I miss it, too." She wasn't laughing. "I think about it every day. I think about it and then I catch myself hyperventilating, or I hear my heart pounding in my ears. It's not me that's broken, you know? It's not me, it's my body. That's the funny thing. It doesn't feel like me."

He had no idea what to say to that.

⚞

Afterward, as Lanoe lay entwined with her, he kissed her toes, her tiny little toes. Zhang had big feet. She used to have big feet. Now they were positively dainty. The idea made him laugh.

"This is the best part," she told him. "This was always the best part."

"What, lying in bed being lazy?" he asked.

"No. The part where I've brought you back to me. When I know you aren't planning strategies or going over old patrols in your head. You're just here with me and there's nothing else." She sighed happily and shifted around until they were face-to-face again. She stroked his hair.

"I hope it's worth it. After I dragged you out here to the end of the galaxy to fight a war you didn't ask for."

She shook her head. "You didn't drag me. You asked for my help. I said yes."

"I wasn't sure if you would." He didn't want to talk about what came next, but he felt he had to. "I'm so sorry, Zhang. I should have stayed in touch. The way we left things…"

"I moved on, Lanoe. I got over it. Seventeen years. Do you think I spent all that time lying in that hospital bed, feeling sorry for myself? No. I built a new life. A good one."

"One you gave up the second I sent you a message asking for help."

"This is a good time for secrets, I think," she told him. "Let's start there. You don't think I dropped everything and stole a Navy tender just because I was still carrying a torch, do you? I had very good reasons to come here."

"Not just to screw my brains out?" he asked.

She laughed, startled by the profanity. It was a beautiful sound. Not Zhang's laugh, not her old laugh, but he liked this new one all the same.

"I came," she said, "because—well, okay, that was part of it." She snorted and buried her face in his neck. "But there was more. I came because you were still my commanding officer, regardless of what it says on the Navy rolls. I came because you and I were a team and you don't just give up on that."

"They disbanded the Ninety-Fourth," he pointed out.

"They don't have that power," she said. "But even beyond that, there was more. I had to know something. I had to find out your big secret."

"Me? I'm an open book," he assured her. "Never been subtle in my life."

"Ha. That's just it, really."

She burrowed into him, her arms holding him close, one leg hooked over his hip. "You're a lot older than me. You had whole lifetimes before I even met you. When I look back I think of our time as most of my life, but for you—it was just like an act in a video, a third or fourth act. Even when we were closest, when we were fighting side by side, I knew there was more to you than I was ever going to understand. But I wanted to. I wanted access to all of you. I still do."

"What do you mean?"

"For me," she said, "the fighting was like a drug. It was *fun*. It was like this big puzzle you had to solve, a challenge to be figured out. Even when we lost people, even when friends died, that was just momentum. Impetus to get out there and fight harder. For you, though—I could always see something happening behind your eyes. It meant more to you. You understood it better than I did, because you'd been doing it so much longer. Do you remember— there was this moon, some frozen chunk of rock and we stood on a ridge and looked down at broken ships lying on the floor of a crater. It was one of those times you asked me to marry me."

"I remember," he said.

"All I could think at that moment, all I could talk about, was the fact that we'd won. We'd won and they lost. I was thrilled. I was bubbling over with it. And then you proposed and I looked in your eyes and there was sadness in there, sadness I couldn't understand."

"I remember," he said again.

"You saw something I didn't. Something more. I've always wanted to know what it was. So," she said. She reached down and did something extremely pleasant with her hand. "Are you going to tell me? I think I deserve that. Don't I?"

"Sure," he said. Because he knew, for once, exactly what she wanted.

───── ⤙⤘ ─────

Ehta looked around the room and seemed surprised by something. "Everybody else is gone, aren't they? Hell. In the marines," she said, "this happened all the time."

"I'm sorry?"

"People would pair up before a fight. They knew some of them wouldn't be coming back. You ask your barracks room psychologists, they'll tell you it's some kind of evolutionary thing. Gotta reproduce in a hurry if your gene pool's about to dry up. I always figured it was just to stave off the boredom, you know?"

"I guess," he said. He'd seen it happen himself, in ready rooms and in crowded berths on destroyers around half a dozen stars. "Maybe people just enjoy sex."

She laughed again and turned the music up. Then she surprised him—though he should have guessed it was coming. She came over to him and plopped down on his knee.

"What do you think?" she asked.

He ignored the white pearl spinning in the corner of his eye. "Ehta—"

"Maybe I'm not your type," she said.

"It's not that."

She wrapped her arms around his collar ring and kissed the side of his helmet. "Might be our last chance," she pointed out. "Unless you think I'm ugly. Do you? Don't worry, I won't slug you if you say yes. I'm a marine, I've got scars."

"I like tough women," he said. "It's just—I can't take off my suit. Ever."

She slumped against him, her body weight falling across his shoulder and his side. For a second he thought she might fall asleep like that. Then she whispered into the side of his helmet, roughly where his ear might be.

"You've still got hands, don't you?"

<hr />

"You think there was something more," Lanoe said. "Some great understanding I had about the nature of war and life and death that you were too young to get." He shook his head. "No. After all those years, all those wars. There was something less.

"Age doesn't make you wiser," he told her. "It makes you more experienced, but there's a difference. You go into things knowing what's going to happen. Maybe not all the details, but you've seen similar situations before and you know how it's likely to play out. You know how you're going to feel about it afterward; that's the worst part."

He pulled her closer. He'd stopped thinking about the new body, about the cybernetic eyes. This was Zhang. It had always been Zhang. The one person he could ever tell this. "I've been fighting since I was a teenager," he said. "When I signed on, it was because I thought girls would like me better if I was wearing a space suit."

She laughed. "I bet it worked."

"Absolutely," he said, and laughed, himself. "It didn't take me long, though, to realize that what we were doing meant something. This was the very start of the Century War, back when Earth and Mars were still squabbling over asteroids. Earth—my homeworld—*had* to win. I'd found something I was willing to die for. To kill for."

He closed his eyes and tried not to think about how long ago that was now.

"The war ended. Not because I shot down all those pilots and all those line ships. It ended because the polys—we still called them corporations then—agreed to bankroll Earth. Mars and Ganymede didn't have the resources to keep fighting, not when Earth had that kind of backing. Their populations starved and eventually they had to surrender. It wasn't about guns, in the end. It was about money.

"Most of the pilots I knew, the ones who were still alive, were smart enough to get out of the Navy then. But not me. I kept fighting. It wasn't like I had trouble finding more battles. There was always some Brushfire conflict out there, some place they needed pilots. They were always so happy when I showed up. The legend, the hero. I won't lie, that felt pretty good.

"It wasn't until the Establishment Crisis that I realized it hadn't stopped. That I'd been fighting every day since I was a teenager. That patriotism I'd felt as a child, that *need* to protect Earth, that was long gone. Earth—this is about when you were born, Zhang— it wasn't even home anymore. I couldn't recognize the place. I guess, thinking about it now, maybe it hadn't changed that much. But I had.

"There were more wars, always there were more wars and I went and I fought even though I knew, in the end, I wasn't going to achieve anything."

"You're the most effective pilot who ever lived," Zhang insisted.

"Sure," Lanoe said. "Except—we're still fighting each other. Now it's polys fighting other polys. Fighting over the flimsiest of justifications. Earth sends the Navy in, supposedly to keep the peace. In reality all the Navy is doing is maintaining a balance of power. Fighting for this poly today, that one tomorrow. Making sure none of them ever gets too big." He shook his head. "When the Establishment Crisis began, I felt so clear, so focused. The Establishmentarians were terrorists, they had to be stopped. Even if I agreed with every damned thing they said, their methods were wrong. But once we put them down, the polys didn't even take a break. They just started more wars. Always more wars. Why do you fight, Zhang? Why did you sign up?"

She moved against him. A full-body shrug. "Somebody had to. And I wanted to learn to fly."

He took a long, deep breath. "When I fought for Earth, I fought to win. I fought so the war would *end*. I lost, Zhang."

"What?"

"I lost. I lost that war because all I did was clear the way for more fighting, over things that mattered less and less. The polys always find another reason to fight. They wouldn't let me win. They wouldn't let me win because they make money off the fighting, and if I won, the wars would be over, and they wouldn't make any more money. I was justifying their greed, that was all."

"Is that why you retired?" she asked him.

"Yeah. That's why I retired."

She kissed his neck. Maybe just because it was there. "Awhile back, I asked why you were here. Why you were fighting for Niraya. You told me you needed to pay back some kind of moral debt. Was that true?"

"No," he said.

Because he could admit that now, to himself.

Lanoe wasn't given much to introspection. When he plumbed the depths of his psyche he rarely found anything he wanted to see. She deserved this, though. She deserved the real answer.

"No," he said. "I didn't come here to make something right. Not really. When Roan and the elder told me their story, I wasn't thinking about right or wrong."

"So...why?"

"I'm a warrior, Zhang. I've never done anything else, never learned how to be a farmer or an office clerk or a mechanic. I've spent my whole life fighting wars, and I don't even know why. I don't know what all that fighting, all that killing achieved."

He shifted around until he was looking into her face. Into her artificial eyes.

"I came here because if we actually succeed—if we drive back this invasion fleet. Well. That'll feel like I fought for a reason, for something meaningful. I came here because I wanted to feel like I'd fought in a war and I'd actually *won*."

Ehta fell asleep before long, slumped forward over the main console. Valk tried to make her as comfortable as he could. There was a little cot in the corner of the ground control station. He laid her down carefully, then covered her in a thick blanket. She snored and slapped at his hands in her sleep, but she was drunk enough she didn't wake up. He draped her suit over a chair nearby, where she would see it when she woke up.

He switched off the music. Cleaned the place up a little, tossing cups and half-eaten plates of food in the recycling bin. Checked the minder on the main console, to see if there was any new imagery of the enemy fleet, or if anything else had changed. Nothing had. He found the bottle of scotch lying on its side on the floor. Only a mouthful of liquor remained inside. He picked it up and took it with him as he left the station.

By all rights it should have been dark outside. He should have been able to see the stars. Niraya turned so slowly, though, that the sun was only halfway to the horizon. It would be weeks yet before it set.

He shrugged in resignation. It still felt like the middle of the night. The quiet hours.

He looked out over the crater. At the town, sleeping below. A few people were still camped outside the Retreat but most of the tents had been taken down and the open space around the big building had been cleaned up.

He looked up, at the sky. Where he belonged.

He heard footsteps crunching on gravel behind him and he turned and saw Thom and Roan walking toward him. They weren't looking at him, though. They were deep in conversation. As they approached, Thom nodded at Valk.

"You two have a good talk?" Valk asked.

It was Roan who answered. "We worked a lot of things out," she said. Then she blushed. At first Valk didn't see why—but then she reached up and buttoned the top button of her tunic.

"Good to get things straightened out now," Valk said, turning his whole torso away from them so she would know he wasn't staring. "Just in case."

She didn't reply. As the two of them walked on past, she had her head down, her chin nearly touching her chest. They were holding hands.

Valk sighed pleasantly. In a few hours everything would get crazy again. But now, in the dusty light of this quiet time, he felt okay.

It had been a very long time since Valk felt okay.

He leaned back, stretching. It hurt but not too much. He looked over at the tender and saw his BR.9 nestled against its side. Its fairings were switched off so they didn't show the Establishment flag, but he could recognize it by the broken airfoil. It was possible, in fact, extremely probable, that he would die inside its cockpit very soon.

The thought didn't scare him, or bother him at all. These last few days had been worth it. To be a pilot again, after so long. It had meant everything.

The tender's hatch opened and Lanoe stepped out. He wore his heavy suit and he'd even run some razor paper over his face, so he looked as fresh as morning dew. Ready to get to work, even if everyone else was just winding down. He came over to stand next to Valk without a word, the two of them looking over the crater rim, not toward town but toward the empty canyon land beyond, at the maze of rock where nothing whatsoever moved.

Valk handed Lanoe the bottle, and the old man drained it, then wound up and threw it as hard as he could over the crater wall. Together they watched it glitter as it arced downward, watched it shatter on the rocks twenty meters below. An old, old pilot tradition. Empty bottles were also known as "dead soldiers." You didn't keep them around where somebody might see them and remember that.

"All in," Lanoe said.

"All in," Valk replied.

Chapter Twenty-Two

Lanoe waited by the top of the stairs when the first load of engineers arrived, led by Derrow. They looked rested and ready to get to work. Good. "We've got two fighters here that need significant repairs," he said, showing Derrow the damage to Zhang's thrusters and all the superficial damage on Maggs's BR.9. "Think you can put them back in fighting shape?"

Derrow took a quick look at both of them. "No problem," she said. She shouted orders at a couple of her people and they moved, not like sullen poly employees but like people who knew how much was at stake. Others came up to refit the tender itself. Under Derrow's instruction they unbolted the cannon and the sensor pod from the sides of the big ship, then started stripping it of everything that wasn't essential—tearing out the bunks in the wardroom, carrying out boxes of supplies and equipment they wouldn't need.

The noise of it woke Ehta. She came out of the ground control station looking supremely annoyed and in no small amount of pain. A little brown bottle flu, that was all, Lanoe decided. A hydration tab and a quick jolt from her suit's onboard medical supplies would fix her up like new. "Get Zhang and Valk together," he told her. She nodded without making a nasty comment, which was more than he expected. "Oh. And Thom—get Thom, too."

"The kid? Why?"

"I'll explain everything," Lanoe said. That was all it took to get her moving.

In a few minutes he had his pilots and Thom sitting in front of the station's main console, all of them looking bright and chipper and ready for what came next.

He hoped that attitude would last.

"This is it," he told them. "The end of this campaign, one way or another." He touched a minder lying on the console and a display lit up, showing the enemy fleet. The image was in color, now, though all the shapes it projected were dark and drab. It showed the seven remaining swarmships in exceptional detail—if you looked close you could see the interceptors and scouts mounted on them. The queenship still looked a little choppy and indistinct but its general shape was distinctly visible. A rough, irregular ovoid, with a huge opening on one end surrounded by spiky projections. "In a couple of days the enemy fleet will be close enough to attack Niraya directly. But we're not going to wait for that to happen. We're taking the fight to them."

Zhang nodded grimly, and looked over at Valk and Ehta, as if to make sure they were paying attention.

They were.

"We hurt them bad at Aruna, at the moon here," Lanoe said, bringing up a new image. It showed the ice giant planet Garuda rotating slowly, its moons swinging around it in their far-flung orbits. Aruna, where the enemy had built their mining facility, flashed once when he named it. "Bad enough they sent an entire swarmship to take it back. The main fleet is still on a trajectory straight for Niraya, but we can change their minds. If we give them a reason to think Aruna is more important, they'll engage us there instead. We'll fly out there today and harry them until we have their attention, until they commit to taking back their moon. Once they come around, our mission is clear. We use our guns to punch a hole through their defenses, then our fighters go straight for the queenship. It's possible that if we just damage the thing, the programmer inside will panic and surrender. That's our best chance.

If that doesn't happen—if they don't surrender, well. We blow the hell out of the queenship and let the guns mop up the swarms."

Lanoe could see that Zhang had questions, but he wasn't done.

"The hardest part is going to be staying on mission. Once those swarms start deploying, the volume of space around the queenship is going to get very crowded. We'll have to fight our way through a lot of small craft before we even get close to the main objective."

He tapped the minder, drawing arrows across the display. "We've all flown missions like this before. The fact these are aliens and not human enemies doesn't change our best tactic. Two fighters here, two here. One pair screens the advance of the other. I'm not looking for glory. Whoever has the best chance at a run straight at the queenship takes that chance, and they don't have to wait for my permission. If they fail, somebody else takes their place. I can't stress this enough—our only chance to beat these bastards is to hit the queenship hard and repeatedly."

He saw Zhang nearly bursting with questions. Maybe it was time.

"Go ahead," he told her.

"Two major issues, here. First," she said, "guns on Niraya won't be able to shoot far enough to reach the fleet. I assume—"

"Yeah," he said. "We're not building the guns on Niraya. We're building them on Aruna. Engineer Derrow's already got schematics and plans for how it's going to be done. There's plenty of scrap metal there—we made sure of that—so she'll have the resources she needs, and now we've got the people to do the work. It means our engineers will have to work in suits on hostile territory. It's hazardous duty, definitely. I told the volunteers as much and a couple of them retracted their offers to help. But only a couple. Most of our civilian support is ready for this. Including Elder McRae, who's never worn a space suit before but says she's willing to learn." He nodded to himself. The civilians had no idea what they were getting themselves into, but they wanted to save their planet. They would work—and fight, when the time came.

"Wait," Ehta said, squirming in her chair. "If the guns are on Aruna, and you're fighting out there in deep space, what's my role?"

"Ground control. You're coming with us," Lanoe told her. "We need you to aim the guns. To make sure they do as much damage as humanly possible."

Ehta's face writhed in emotion. Maybe she was panicking at the thought of flying in a spaceship again. Maybe she just wanted a chance for redemption so badly it hurt. He couldn't quite tell.

"Okay, second, bigger question," Zhang told him. "You said two fighters in each group, two fighters screening the advance of the other two."

"Sure," Lanoe said.

"Except there's only three of us. You didn't forget that Maggs is...that he left us, did you?"

"Nope," Lanoe said. "I said four. I meant four."

He turned to look at Thom. Chairs squeaked as everybody else did, too.

For Thom's part, he just looked stunned. Cartoonishly so, his eyes bugging out of his head, his mouth open, his knees visibly shaking.

"Assuming," Lanoe said to the boy, "you're in."

***

"Me?" Thom asked.

No one told him he'd misheard what Lanoe said. Nobody suggested it might have been a joke.

They were all staring at him.

Thom shook his head. Pushed his chair back. "Lanoe—I'm not a Navy pilot."

"You're one of the best civilian pilots I've seen," Lanoe replied.

"But that's...that's different. I race yachts," Thom pointed out. "Nobody shoots at a yacht. And I've never...I've never fought anybody in my life. I've never even fired a shot."

Lanoe tilted his head back and took a long breath. "We both know that's not true."

Zhang and Valk were already staring at him. Neither of them

had proper eyes to widen—it was hard to tell if they were surprised by Lanoe's revelation. They couldn't know, though. Lanoe hadn't told them anything about Thom's father. Thom certainly hadn't. But that was immaterial.

"I need a fourth pilot," Lanoe said. "You're the best candidate we've got. I'll give you what training I can. I'll show you how everything works. It won't be enough—it takes years to make a good pilot—but it'll be a start. No one's expecting you to turn into an ace on your first patrol, Thom. No one expects you to be the one that blows up that queenship. But if you can provide covering fire while one of us moves in for the kill, it'll mean all the difference."

Zhang twisted around in her chair. "Lanoe," she said. "You're sure about this?"

Yes, Thom thought. *Yes. Just one person point out how absurd this is. How impossible.*

Lanoe didn't relent, though.

"Thom, I can't order you to do it," he said. "All I can do is ask."

He didn't point out any of the reasons why Thom should say yes. He didn't mention the fact that Thom owed Lanoe his life. He didn't suggest that this could mean saving Roan—and all of Niraya—from a terrible death. He didn't even appeal to Thom's vanity, or his pride, or his sense of shame.

He just asked, and stood there waiting for a reply.

Thom muttered something, the words meaning very little, really. Then he got up and staggered out of the ground control station, because he thought he might be sick.

Outside the engineers were hard at work, bolting cargo pods onto the tender. He had to jump aside to dodge a shower of sparks. The noise was good, though. The noise drowned out everything in his head.

He had to find Roan. She wouldn't be far. Since she'd left the Retreat, she had nowhere else to go. He walked around the station and went to the top of the long set of stairs leading down into the crater.

She was sitting a couple of flights down, down where the noise wasn't as intense. When she saw him coming she stood up and smiled. A little breeze blew the hair back from her eyes and he had to catch his breath.

She wrapped her arms around him when they came together. He held her very tight.

"I'm going," she said.

"What?"

Her smile changed. He could tell she was worried that what she said next might upset him. "We're going to set up a ground control station. On Aruna. Ensign Ehta and I are..." She stopped and her smile was gone. She must have seen the look on his own face. "I know, it's dangerous. I know—"

"It's something you have to do," he told her.

She nodded.

"I—I have my own thing. To do." He took a deep breath. Then he told her what Lanoe had asked of him.

"No," she said, as if she could just veto this. "No, you can't do that." Just a simple matter of fact. "Not after last night. I mean—I mean not after what we figured out." She laughed, though he could tell she was laughing out of confusion, not humor. "No," she said, and shook her head, still holding him close. "No. You won't do it. Just tell him no."

"I already said yes," he told her.

Lanoe watched as the engineers loaded the last of their equipment into the tender. Tools, food, box after box of cheap disposable space suits donated by the mining concern. Habitat tents and oxygen generators. No personal items, no luxury goods. They could fit about twenty engineers in there, as well as Ehta and Roan. Down at the spaceport, other volunteers were readying two shuttles—also Centrocor property from the mines—that could just about make the journey to Aruna. Each of those shuttles could hold another fifteen passengers each. Fifty civilians in all who would go out to the moon and start building guns on a crash schedule, and hopefully have something ready to fire by the time the enemy fleet arrived.

The timing was very tight. The enemy's trajectory had them on a fast course toward Niraya. They would pass by Garuda and its moon in less than two days. They wouldn't come within a million kilometers of the moon if they held to their present course, but Lanoe intended to force them to make a detour. If the guns weren't ready by the time the enemy arrived, this was going to be a very short battle.

The tender had its cannon, but the shuttles had no weapons at all. Zhang and Valk would fly out to Aruna with the engineers and run patrols to protect the civilian volunteers as necessary. Lanoe and Thom would stay on Niraya for the boy's training, then rush to catch up.

From here on in there was no more time to waste.

Just time for a couple of quick goodbyes. There was a good chance he would never see Zhang again outside of her cockpit. He half-expected her to pull him into the station for a quick reprise of what they'd gotten up to the night before, but he'd forgotten who she was. Inside the young body, behind those metal eyes, she was still Bettina Zhang, Lieutenant, Navy Expeditionary Force. An ace pilot and a hell of a second in command.

He found her over by where the fighters sat, ready for takeoff. "Repairs are finished," she told him. "The engineers gave my BR.9 a good overhaul while they were at it. Probably flies better than ever."

"And when they were finished you checked it over yourself anyway, right?" he asked.

"Of course. They did a little something for your FA.2, as well."

"They did *what*?" he demanded.

"You might want to check it out." She took him over to where his fighter sat a little distance away, separate from all the noise and chaos. At first glance he didn't see anything had changed.

Then he noticed the difference. Someone had painted the number 94 on the ship's flank in Gothic script.

He looked over at Zhang's BR.9. On the fairing displays, he saw the designator of the 94th squadron superimposed over the red tentacles there. Even Valk's ship had a 94 blazoned over the Establishment flag—which would have been in the poorest taste in any other circumstance.

When he was quiet for a long while, holding his mouth steady so it didn't betray him, she said, "If I didn't know better, I'd think you were moved."

"Good thing you know better. All right, Lieutenant. You have your orders."

"Yes, sir." She gave him a snappy salute. Then, in a very different tone, she asked, "You ready for this?"

"Sure," he told her.

She nodded and tilted her head back and they kissed, a long, soft kiss that said more than a hundred words possibly could. There was no talk now of them rebooting the old relationship, of beginning again. That had to wait and they both knew it. When the kiss was finished she put up her helmet and jumped in her cockpit and in less than a minute she was just a speck receding into the deep, deep blue of the sky.

When this is over, he told himself. Except that was as far as the thought got. *When this is over.*

They would talk, then, he supposed. Maybe he would ask her to marry him again, and maybe this time she would say yes.

He wouldn't let himself think about that.

Instead he headed inside the station, where Valk was sitting with Ehta, talking in low tones. Though she was smiling she looked slightly embarrassed. Well, wonders never cease, Lanoe thought. He'd never seen her blush before.

"Time to go," he told Valk.

The big pilot nodded and got up. He patted Ehta on the shoulder and headed out of the station. Lanoe gave Ehta one last look, then followed Valk out. "Is she okay?" he asked.

Valk shrugged. "She wants to do her bit. She's scared witless by the thought of the flight to Aruna, but she'll make it if she doesn't have to look out a window."

"Good enough," Lanoe said. "Hold on a second."

Valk had been headed toward his BR.9. He stopped and turned around.

"Over here, where we won't be bothering the engineers," Lanoe said, and led Valk around the side of the station, away from the noise. "Before you go," he said, "there's something I needed to give you."

"Oh?" Valk asked.

"It can't be official, of course," Lanoe said. He opened a display on his wrist and tapped at a virtual keyboard. "The Admiralty has to approve these. But check your cryptab."

The big pilot looked down at the blank gray patch on the front of his own suit. Lanoe knew what Valk would see there. Something new.

Right at the top, next to his name, would be a blue star. A Blue Star.

The mark of an ace, of a pilot with five confirmed kills. The only commendation any pilot had ever cared about. The one the Navy took away from Valk when he lost his war.

"You earned that when we fought the swarmship, if not before," Lanoe told him.

Valk lifted his head. "I don't know what to say."

" 'Thank you, sir' is traditional," Lanoe told him. "But belay that."

Valk couldn't seem to help himself. He checked the cryptab again, presumably to make sure the Blue Star was still there.

Lanoe let him look at how pretty it was for a while before he spoke again.

"There's something else," he said. "Something I've been meaning to do for a while now, but I knew you wouldn't like it, so I've been putting it off."

"Yeah? After this? Anything you want."

"If I'm going to fight side by side with a pilot," Lanoe said, "I want to know what he looks like. I want to see your face."

"No you don't."

Lanoe just stood there, watching him.

Valk let out a very deep, very long sigh. Then he swung around from side to side, perhaps to make sure nobody else was in sight. He reached up with a shaking finger and touched the recessed key at his throat. His helmet flowed down into his collar ring like black ice melting.

What Lanoe saw underneath didn't quite make sense.

"Oh," he said.

"Oh?" Valk asked. "What the hell does that mean?"

"Just—it's not what I expected." Lanoe fought to control his face. To not show his shock. "Tell me something, Valk. When was the last time you looked in a mirror? I mean, with your helmet down?"

Valk shook his head. "Not since the accident."

"Do you...do you want me to get you a mirror now? Because I think—"

"No!" Valk said. "No," he said again, less vehemently. "I don't want to know. Maybe you're going to tell me it's not as bad as I think. And then I'll look, and I'll see it's healed some, but it still won't be what I want. It won't be what it was. Maybe you were going to tell me something else. Don't."

Lanoe didn't know how to respond. Except in his traditional manner.

"Sure," he said. "Whatever you want."

Valk pressed the key again and put his helmet back up. "Time to get moving, right? Time to deploy?"

"Yeah," Lanoe told him. "Okay. Maybe we'll talk about this later—or not. If you don't want to. Just—"

"What with 'later' being a conditional kind of thing, let's drop it for now."

Lanoe walked him over to his BR.9, then watched as he lifted into the air and shot away toward space.

When this is over, he thought, *I'm going to have to figure out what in hell's name I just saw.*

When it was over.

Thom ran one hand over the smooth fairing on the side of the BR.9. He had to admit he was a little excited. Like any civilian pilot, he'd grown up devouring information about every spacecraft in existence—especially the military ships. He knew all the specs and the control schematics for fighters ranging as far back as the original FA.1, the first real cataphract, up to the latest Z.XXV prototypes.

None were more versatile or more proven than the BR.9. The Navy had more of them than any other kind of fighter, and for good reason. All the great stories of tense dogfights and crazy bombing runs featured the BR.9—an eminently flyable, survivable ship that could perform in multiple roles across a wide range of theater conditions.

It was not, of course, much to look at. The airfoils were curved and swept forward to give it a predatory look but the main fuselage was lumpy and studded with equipment boxes that wrecked its lines and its aerodynamics. It was also quite small, even for a fighter. No bigger than Roan's ground car, in fact. Much of the small volume was taken up with weapon systems and the massive Gôblin engine, so that the cockpit seemed to bulge from the front, as if the pilot were an afterthought strapped on at the last minute.

"Want to pop 'er open?" Lanoe said.

Thom didn't want much else. "Can I? I mean—"

"We don't have a lot of time."

Right. Thom had forgotten, for a second, that he'd been recruited for a job that was almost guaranteed suicide.

He ran his finger along a groove just under the canopy until he found a recessed key. The canopy melted away, just like a suit helmet. The engine ticked over as the cockpit displays lit up and the pilot's seat reclined a little to let him inside. Thom jumped up into the cockpit and the safety harness automatically locked into sockets on the back and legs of his suit.

His fingers danced over the various board displays. Power, flight, weapons, communications, sensors... New displays jumped up all around him, filling his view. He dismissed or rearranged enough of them that he could actually see forward. He tapped a virtual key and the canopy flowed up over his head, sealing him in.

He watched as Lanoe jogged across the spaceport's concrete apron, toward his FA.2. They were really going to do this.

Thom lifted off the ground with just the slightest touch of the maneuvering jets. Flywheels hummed as the fighter stabilized itself in the air. A green pearl appeared in the corner of Thom's eye. Lanoe calling him. He accepted the connection. "Head out, over the crater rim," Lanoe said. "We'll take 'em down into the canyons. Get you used to maneuvering."

"I know how to fly," Thom pointed out.

"You think you do," Lanoe told him. "Just follow my lead for now, okay?"

Thom opened his throttle just a touch and grabbed the control stick. The BR.9 tried to get away from him—it wanted to move *fast,* wanted to really fly. He could see his airfoils ripple as they changed shape to bite into Niraya's thin atmosphere, could feel the engine spinning and roaring just behind his seat.

He'd flown yachts with peppier throttles and shuttles with tighter controls, but the BR.9 was so well balanced it didn't feel like he was in control at all. It was designed to fly itself as much as possible, to let the pilot focus on fighting, he presumed.

He followed Lanoe up over the edge of the crater—the BR.9 hopped up over the rim with barely any input from the controls, automated collision avoidance systems kicking into play—then down the side of a gently sloping plateau. Below them the canyons twisted and bent back on themselves, a labyrinth of gray-yellow stone. He remembered driving through those defiles with Roan, but this was nothing like that. The BR.9 was designed to fly halfway around a star system in a day. Covering a few dozen kilometers of ground in a minute was an insult to its capabilities, and the fighter let him know as much, its thrusters whining piteously with the lean fuel mix he fed them.

For a while Lanoe's FA.2 seemed to hang motionless in the sky, just ahead and to the left, as the two fighters matched velocities and course. Then Lanoe promptly vanished. Thom had to check his boards to see that Lanoe had pulled a steep powered dive down into the canyons below. He followed as carefully as he could, dropping down until the walls of rock surrounded him on both sides. His navigation board tinged yellow to warn him he was in danger of crashing but he managed to ignore it.

"The early years of the Century War," Lanoe said, his FA.2 dipping under a natural bridge of stone, "were dominated by line ships. Destroyers and cruisers penetrated the skies over Earth with impunity—they could smash whole cities before ground defenses could even come online. The casualties were nightmarish. Fighters of the time," he went on, banking hard to turn into a side canyon, "were useless against big ships—like gnats attacking a bear. Countermeasures mounted on the line ships could pick off an entire wing of fighters before they got close enough to fire disruptors."

"Lanoe," Thom said, following the FA.2 through a ravine no more than fifteen meters wide, his nav board blaring red now, "is this really the time for a lecture?"

"I had to listen to this when I was in training," Lanoe said. "So do you. You've got to learn floating focus, Thom—you have to pay attention to a dozen things at once. I know what I'm doing. Now, as I was saying. The war would have been over in six months, with Earth and Mars both in ruins, if it hadn't been for the invention of the vector field."

The two of them wove around a line of rock spires, then stood on their sides as Lanoe took them into a deep valley between two ridges of stone.

"There's no such thing as a force field, Thom—probably never will be. The vector field's the next best thing. Anything that tries to touch the field gets accelerated away, like a judo artist using an attacker's momentum against him to flip him on his back. The field's not perfect, though. It can't protect you from a direct hit. And it drinks an astonishing amount of power, thousands of watts per square centimeter. The bigger the thing you want to protect, the more power the field needs—in fact, the power drain goes up exponentially, and quickly the demand gets beyond anything even a hypothetical reactor can provide. A line ship is way too big for a vector field, but those puny fighters, the gnats in my previous analogy, could carry one and still have power left over for their engines. Thus, the cataphract was born."

Lanoe dropped toward the floor of the valley, until his undercarriage nearly skimmed the slickrock down there. Thom kept up as best he could. Together they went contour-tracing—flying as low as they possibly dared, hopping over boulders and obstructions with bare centimeters of clearance. The BR.9 knew how it was done, and Thom had to constantly remind himself to trust its assistance. He could feel his heart pounding in his throat every time they nearly missed a fatal crash, but Lanoe refused to pull up.

"A small fighter craft with a vector field—and a good pilot—could sprint in toward a battleship, shrugging off antivehicle fire, and get off three good disruptor shots before having to break away and evade. Three disruptors put in just the right place will cripple a battleship. The fighter pilots survived those attack runs seven times out of ten. It meant the end of city-killing raids and it's changed the way wars are fought in space. Every military force since then has depended on cataphract-class fighters. Every battle has been decided by who had the better pilots. It's why there still *is* an Earth, Thom. It's why you and I can even be having this conversation."

Lanoe pulled up just a little. Thom gasped in relief, though he knew something even more terrifying than contour-tracing was up next on the slate. It still took him by surprise. One second the FA.2's thrusters were right there in front of him, shining like little suns. The next Lanoe had disappeared completely and Thom found himself flying at speed right at a wall of rock.

He pulled up into a tight loop to avoid the wall, then looked all around him for Lanoe's fighter. He found the FA.2 flying leisurely away from him off to his right. Lanoe had made a ninety-degree turn in the blink of an eye.

That wasn't physically possible. It couldn't have happened.

"How—how did you do that?" Thom asked.

"Rotary turn," Lanoe told him. "One of our best tricks. Fighters have to be small to mount vector fields, but they need big engines to fly fast. This presents a serious design problem in the cataphract. Your engine is spinning perpendicular to your long axis and it acts like a massive flywheel, its momentum constantly pulling you toward the right. Your controls are designed to compensate for that effect but if you switch off the compensation for a couple of micro-seconds, you'll snap around in a right-hand turn sharper than a knife's edge. You may find this useful if you ever find an enemy on your tail. Which is something that's going to happen a lot."

"If I tried that in a yacht I'd snap it in half," Thom said.

"Yeah, it puts a lot of strain on your engine mountings. Which is why the Navy strictly forbids rotary turns. In the middle of a dog-fight a lot of pilots conveniently forget that."

"I want to try it," Thom said. He pulled out of his loop and leveled out, then brought up a board of safety controls. The com-pensators were right near the top and he wasted no time tapping to cut them out, leaning hard on his stick at the same time.

His BR.9 screamed with the sudden turn. His inertial sink yanked him sideways until he couldn't move his arms and he felt like his teeth might tear their way out through his cheek. His air-foils stalled and he twisted into a corkscrew turn headed straight at the ground, sky and stone whirling all around him until he couldn't tell which way was up. He started to call for Lanoe's help, desperate for someone to come rescue him, but there was no time, nobody could reach him before he crashed—his boards lit up red, red all over the place, and all he could do was pull back on the stick, firing his maneuvering jets hard until a noise like thunder tore through his cockpit.

It took every bit of skill he had to pull back up, his nose almost scratching the ground. His whole body shook with terror as he leveled out and cut his throttle until the BR.9 just skated along on the air, until his airfoils caught the breeze once more.

"That," he said, "did not go well."

Lanoe laughed. The bastard laughed—didn't he realize Thom had just come within a millimeter of death?

"You can't fight the rotary turn, kid," Lanoe said. "You have to give up control, just for a second—the hardest thing a pilot ever has to do. Let's practice that a few more times. Then I'm going to start shooting at you."

The kid gave it his all, Lanoe had to hand him that.

Thom took off like a shot, blazing down a narrow canyon with barely any clearance, then zoomed upward just before a cliff face and corkscrewed up to ten thousand meters in the space of a few seconds. Lanoe twisted around in a barrel roll to keep up, not bothering to try to match Thom's orientation, just keeping them close. The FA.2's engine struggled to pour on that much speed—it was no match in a flat-out race with a BR.9—but he managed.

The sky turned black as they left the atmosphere behind, but Thom wasn't just running for the void. Outside the planet's atmosphere he could pull some tricky maneuvers that weren't possible in what passed on Niraya for thick air. As Lanoe watched, Thom pivoted around on his long axis until their two cockpits were facing each other. Then Thom goosed his engine and shot past Lanoe in a near collision. Lanoe pulled back on his stick and threw the FA.2 into a loop, only to see Thom dive under power back toward the ground below, his airfoils visibly flexing as they caught the wispy upper layers of the atmosphere.

Lanoe followed as fast as he could, twisting out of his aborted loop to shoot downward after Thom's glowing engines. He opened up his comms panel and switched his communications laser over to manual aiming. It was such a strange thing to do that his fighter demanded confirmation.

"Right," he called, "instead of shooting at you with my PBWs, which might be dangerous," he said, "I'm going to try to hit you with my comms laser. Don't worry, you won't feel a thing."

"Catch me if you can, old man," Thom called back, sheer jubilation in his voice. The kid loved to fly—something you definitely looked for in a fighter pilot.

The two of them hurtled down toward the yellow rocks below as if they'd made a suicide pact. Thom pulled up at the last possible minute, leveling out in a canyon so deep its walls shaded him from the sunlight.

Smart, Lanoe thought. *He knows I can barely see him down there.* He followed Thom's flight path as if the two fighters were tethered to each other, then quickly shoved his stick over to the left as Thom just missed grazing a huge boulder that squatted on the canyon floor.

Up ahead a natural arch of stone covered the canyon like a roof, forming a narrow tunnel with sunlight just visible on its far side. Thom's airfoils all but retracted as he shot through the narrow gap, Lanoe right behind him.

Out into the light again, Thom reextended his airfoils and pulled into a tight bank, following the curve of the canyon floor. Just as Lanoe thought he had the kid, Thom started weaving back and forth, cutting a zigzag through the air as crooked as a lightning bolt. Lanoe held his own course steady, not even trying to match Thom's eccentric flight.

Which might have been exactly what Thom had hoped for. He'd subtly adjusted his airfoils in what should have been the wrong way. Instead of providing lift they added drag—which slowed Thom down to nearly half his previous speed.

Lanoe shot past him, still headed down the canyon at full throttle.

"Got you in my sights," Thom called, from behind Lanoe. "I won't use my PBWs, though—that might be dangerous."

"Nice maneuver," Lanoe said, sincerely impressed. The kid must have seen a lot of videos about dogfighting.

Of course, there was a big difference between watching a video and actually dueling with a living, thinking pilot. Lanoe leaned on his stick and twisted around in midair. His airfoils shook with the stress—he half-expected them to tear off and go fluttering away—but the FA.2 made the turn, banking around in a tight arc. The stunt cost Lanoe some altitude and his navigation boards lit up red for a moment but once he was back in control he pulled back on his stick and shot upward, just meters in front of Thom's canopy. The near collision made Thom yelp in surprise, and Lanoe grinned to himself.

He'd been doing this awhile longer than Thom. He knew every trick in the book.

"Okay, break off," Lanoe said. He executed a leisurely, slow loop until he was flying alongside the BR.9. He looked over and saw Thom inside his canopy. "You can fly, we already knew that," he said. "I still won that one."

"What, because you could have rammed me back there? You would have killed both of us," Thom protested.

"Because I could have killed you long before you pulled that zig-zag," Lanoe replied. "Check your comms log. See how many times I painted you with my laser."

The kid was silent for a moment. Then he swore.

Lanoe didn't need to confirm. He knew he'd scored at least six direct hits on Thom's thrusters while they were pulling dumb stunts. If that had been a real dogfight it would have been over before Thom climbed out of the atmosphere.

"Fancy flying won't keep you in one piece, not alone," Lanoe said. "You need to—"

"Come on! That's not even fair," Thom interrupted. "You expected me to dodge your laser? That's not physically possible. I can't outfly a projectile moving the speed of light. You can't, either."

"That's part of what I'm trying to teach you," Lanoe said. "You don't need to dodge the laser. You need to dodge *me*. You need to constantly be aware of the guy behind you, Thom. You need to anticipate when he's about to shoot."

Together they flew toward the end of the canyon, then pulled back to crest the top of a wide plateau. They'd flown so far that Lanoe could see the planet's terminator up ahead of them, like a storm cloud running all the way across the horizon. In another few seconds they saw the sun set for the first time since they arrived on Niraya, the sky turning a brilliant crimson for just a moment before fading to black. In the few minutes they'd been chasing each other they'd flown over half the planet's surface.

"The enemy drones I've seen couldn't keep up with human pilots," Lanoe said. "We flew circles around them. Still, all of us took hits fighting them—Valk lost an airfoil. Zhang, who is a better natural pilot than I am, nearly died out there. For one simple reason: There were more of them than there were of us. You're never going to dodge everything. But you need to learn to not get hit as often as possible. That means you need to be able to focus on a dozen different things at a time. You need to have eyes everywhere."

"But that's just... Human beings don't work that way," Thom protested.

"Cataphract pilots do. They have to," Lanoe replied. He could sense the kid's frustration. Understand it, even. He wished he had something more to give him, some word of advice that would open the gates of enlightenment. Let the kid understand, in one fell swoop, how this was done.

But there was no such word. There was nothing that could show you, nothing that could make you see it. It took doing it over and over again before you actually got the point. Before you could call yourself a fighter pilot.

Lanoe had been as green as Thom once. He'd trained for months before the first time anyone tried to shoot him down. He'd had the best instructors Earth could offer, combat veterans whose bodies or minds were too broken to let them keep fighting, but who had found a real gift for teaching.

He knew perfectly well that he lacked that gift. That he was failing Thom. He was going to throw the kid into battle headfirst and he would probably die, probably in the first few minutes of the engagement.

If he had any choice, if he could just tell Thom to head back to the spaceport, to go be with Roan and forget about fighting, well... he would.

But what if Thom just gave up? He was a spoiled rich kid who'd never had to fight for anything in his life. A yacht racer—the most pampered kind of pilot there was. If Thom lost his nerve now, if he said he just didn't want to do this anymore, that it was too *hard*— what then? What would Lanoe even say to that?

Could he order a child to fly to his death?

If Thom backed out now—

"Okay," Thom said, finally.

"Okay?"

"Okay! You've made your point. Do we have time to try that again?"

"Absolutely," Lanoe said. He glanced down at the canyons below, their depths lost in pools of featureless night. "And this time we'll do it in the dark."

Chapter Twenty-Three

Elder McRae rode out to Aruna in one of the Centrocor shuttles, crowded into the small space with far too many engineers and technicians from Walden Crater. The tiny craft had been designed for the simple purpose of ferrying passengers to and from larger ships in orbit around Niraya. It had never been meant to fly between planets, and it had undergone a serious refitting in the short time it had been conscripted to the war effort. It showed everywhere she looked. Panels had been removed to expose bundles of wiring. The cockpit door had been removed and extra equipment bolted in where a copilot should have sat. Massive fuel tanks had been bolted onto the shuttle's exterior, with an additional tank shoehorned into the passenger cabin—an engineer with the hexagonal Centrocor logo shaved into the side of his head actually rode on top of this tank, strapped down with mismatched safety belts.

There was no room to move inside, barely room to breathe. The elder sat with her knees touching those of volunteers on either side of her. Fortunately they were all wearing cheap, disposable suits— fortunate because the suits took care of their biological necessities, as there was no way for anyone to reach the shuttle's washroom. Even if they could its fixtures had all been torn out to save on weight.

She could not help remembering the terrifying long voyage to the Hexus, when she and Roan had stowed away in a cargo container. The shuttle might be warmer and better supplied—but she and Roan had had far more room to get up and do basic exercises in the container.

It was going to be a long journey out to the ice giant's moon.

"Can we even make it so far on this ship?" she whispered to an engineer sitting next to her.

"The numbers look okay. We'll get there," the young woman replied. Her face was very pale and she was sweating, a little. "Of course, how we get back is another question. Assuming there's somewhere to get back to, when this is over."

"You look unwell," the elder said to her.

The engineer laughed and shook her head. "We're about to launch," she said. "It's the most dangerous part of the whole trip. Statistically, I mean. I'll be okay."

"Take three quick breaths, then exhale very slowly," the elder told her. "That's good. Keep up that rhythm. It'll help with—"

She didn't get to finish her sentence. Without any kind of warning, not even a verbal announcement, the shuttle's engines fired all at once and they were off. Elder McRae was shoved hard to the side, her safety straps digging into her flesh, and she felt like the loose skin of her face and neck were being stretched out by a fierce wind. The noise of the engines was so loud she couldn't hear anything, not the engineer breathing beside her, not her own thoughts.

The crushing acceleration seemed to go on for hours, though she supposed it could only have been a few minutes. She closed her eyes but then she felt like she was dangling from her straps, hoisted up over a great abyss, like she would be torn away from her seat at any moment, torn and thrown down toward the ground far below.

She forced herself to open her eyes. Up ahead, in the cockpit, she saw the windows glow with fire as the shuttle tore through Niraya's thin atmosphere. The glare increased until she couldn't see anything but coruscating light. She felt a crushing pain in her fingers and realized the engineer had grabbed her hand, grabbed it and held on so tight she might break it.

And then—again without warning—the light disappeared. The flames receded from the cockpit windows and through them she could see only darkness. Even the terrible acceleration eased up, and she sagged in her harness.

All around her, volunteers cheered and gasped for breath and applauded.

They were on their way.

Zhang watched to make sure the shuttles and the tender launched successfully, then raced ahead to meet up with Valk en route to Aruna. They didn't worry about wasting fuel this time—each of them had plenty of spare fuel cartridges onboard their fighters— and though it wouldn't be a comfortable ride they expected to reach the ice giant's moon in less than six hours.

That meant some heavy acceleration. Zhang's inertial sink could protect her from the worst of the g-stress, but still she found herself struggling to breathe as her thrusters burned hard and long behind her. Heat built up in her cockpit until she was sweating, despite all her shielding.

"You okay, big guy?" she called.

It took Valk a while to respond. "I'd like to speak to the cruise director," he said, eventually. "My daiquiri is melting."

She laughed. Pilots were notorious complainers. Lanoe had told her once that griping among his squaddies never bothered him—a pilot who can still bitch, he'd told her, is a pilot who's still alive. She'd never met a pilot like Valk, who just seemed grateful to be invited to the party.

Despite the fact that he was probably in excruciating pain the whole time.

She knew about the legend of the Blue Devil—she'd fought against the Establishment, and while she'd known that Valk was being used for propaganda she had to admit it had worked. They used to whisper about him in the bunkrooms, talk about how the

Establishmentarians were tougher than carbon fiber, how when you killed one you had to make damned sure he stayed dead.

She'd never thought she would actually get to meet the man. Much less find out that the legend was true. She was very glad he was on her side.

"Hang in there," she told him. "If it gets too bad, take a white pearl."

"Thank you, but no," Valk said. "After my accident they gave me this suit. It includes painkillers that are a lot stronger than what you're used to—which is why I've never taken them."

"Never?" Zhang asked. If it hadn't been for the white pearl in her own suit, after her own *accident,* she would never have made it until she was rescued. She would have killed herself with her side-arm. She'd taken the white pearl plenty of times since then. She took it whenever she had a bad headache.

"If I take it once, I won't stop," he told her. "They swore up and down the stuff isn't habit forming. I figure there's more than one way to get addicted to something. Anyway, I need to be sharp for this battle. I can't risk getting all fuzzy."

The painkillers in Zhang's suit had never touched her skills as a pilot, but she supposed maybe it was true, that his were different. To each their own, she supposed.

To take his mind off the rough ride, she asked, "So—when I came over to the ground control station after last night's party, I couldn't help noticing that somebody put Ehta to bed. Without her suit on."

"I figured she'd be more comfortable that way," he replied, his voice carefully neutral.

"Uh-huh," Zhang said. "She and I used to be squaddies. I know she never had a problem sleeping in a suit, even under gravity. She was a marine, too—they never take their suits off except for one thing. You and she didn't...I mean, not that I'd judge you, but..."

"An officer never tells," Valk called back.

"You know, I've heard that expression before, a couple hundred times," Zhang said, smiling even though the acceleration made her face ache every time she moved her mouth. "I've never heard anybody use it when they could have just said no."

Valk laughed. "Maybe this is the first time, then. Am I going to hear about what you got up to with Lanoe? All the juicy details?"

"Fair point," Zhang said, suddenly embarrassed. Certainly that story wasn't for sharing. "I was just glad, that's all I meant by it. If you and she found a little comfort. I didn't mean any offense."

"None taken," Valk said. "Listen, how about some music? I find it helps take my mind off the discomfort."

"Sure," Zhang said.

He switched on some terrible old-fashioned stuff, grungy and with a bass line so deep it just sounded like distortion in the speakers. Most likely recorded in the low-rent sound studios of Mars—it lacked the technical precision of Earth music. Before another minute had passed he started singing.

"Brand new threads / gonna hit the town / girls to the side / when the boys...get down!"

Zhang couldn't help herself. She laughed uproariously.

Valk might be superhumanly tough and a hell of a pilot. He still had the worst singing voice she'd ever heard.

They'd been forbidden to bring any personal possessions, but someone had smuggled a tiny drum machine onboard the shuttle, and the engineers passed the time singing very old songs. It was a way to pass the time during the long, cramped flight.

The woman who had squeezed Elder McRae's hand so hard seemed almost apologetic when she joined in. "Probably not the kind of music you're used to," she said, in a break between songs.

"I wouldn't say that," the elder replied, with a warm smile. "I wasn't born into the Faith. I grew up on Jehannum, as a matter of fact."

"Really? I would never have guessed it. I have an aunt who lives there. I doubt you'd know her, though."

"I imagine you're right. I left there very long ago. There was a time, though, when I knew the words to all of these songs. I used to love music." She proved it by joining in on the next number. Some of the engineers cheered and clapped and smiled at her, which was nice.

Still, it was a very long journey, and the music couldn't stop her from thinking about how much her joints had started to ache, or how hungry she was getting. The latter need, at least, was seen to halfway to Aruna. Someone at the back of the shuttle opened a box of protein bars and handed them forward. It took the edge off the emptiness in the elder's stomach.

"Now this," she admitted, as she licked the foil wrapper for every last morsel of the largely tasteless food, "is something I'm not used to. I'm going to miss fresh food while we're away."

"I wish they'd let us bring minders, so we could just watch videos," her neighbor said. "I've always hated spaceflight. I guess you probably know that—I hope I didn't hurt your hand, before."

"Yours is not the first hand I've held in a stressful moment," the elder replied. "I'm Elder McRae, by the way."

"I, uh, I know," the engineer replied, with a sheepish grin. "I'm Wallach. Yuna Wallach."

"Well, M. Wallach, if we can't have videos, we'll have to find other ways to pass the time." They'd already gone through all the songs she knew, but perhaps she had something else to offer. The elder couldn't stand up—she was forbidden to release herself from her safety straps during the flight—but she could raise her voice. "Would anyone be interested," she asked, "in some spiritual guidance? Perhaps a sermon?"

Accustomed as she was to speaking with others of her faith she was a little surprised by the silence that was the first reply.

Then one of the engineers, on the far side of the shuttle, asked, "Are you trying to convert us?"

That even elicited a few laughs.

The elder mused that she had perhaps forgotten that the majority of people in the shuttle were Centrocor employees. They lived on

Niraya, true, but not because they'd come there, like her, looking for a spiritual path away from the cosmopolitanism of other worlds.

She began to consider how to withdraw her offer without losing her dignity, when someone else spoke up.

"I'm, uh, I'm kind of scared," a young man near the cockpit said. That got a few laughs as well, though they sounded more sympathetic this time. "I wouldn't mind hearing something. You know. Something kind of hopeful."

"I'm afraid," the elder said, "that in our faith we don't believe in raising false hopes. I can't offer you any promises. I can't tell you this will turn out just fine, or that we will for certain prevail against the enemy."

"Maybe we don't need to hear what you have to say, then," the engineer with the Centrocor logo shaved into his head, the one strapped to the extra fuel tank, said.

What he didn't seem to realize was that the sermon had already begun. "I can," she went on, as if there had been no interruption, "talk about what human beings can achieve, when they set their minds to something. About the incredible potential each of us possesses. There have been many times in human history when all seemed lost. Throughout every age people just like us have found themselves with their backs against the proverbial wall, with no clear path ahead of them. Think of the original Martian colonists, when their main water tank rusted through just a month into their mission."

"That's what you get for using the wrong paint on a planet half made out of oxides," one of the engineers called out.

The elder smiled and let the laughter die down before she continued. "They faced immediate and certain death. They did not surrender, though. They dug for ice beneath the soil and they found it. They found more water than they would ever need. Think, if you will, of the explorers who arrived at Tau Ceti, only to find hellish worlds where they could not even land. Including the planet we now call Hades. A planet that, once it was terraformed, became one of the jewels of humanity's expansion among the stars." Inspiration struck her, as it often did once she began to preach. So far her examples had all been of great engineers, as she had intended. But there was one story that might resonate even more with this crowd. "Think of the miners on the asteroids of Appolyon—"

The engineers cheered and lifted their hands in the air.

She smiled. She had them now. "When Wilscon decided their production quotas were not sustainable, when a hundred years' worth of work was going to be thrown away because a column of numbers didn't add up, the miners there had never known another life. They were to be discarded, disbanded—they could not live in an asteroid belt without constant resupply. They could not afford to move somewhere else and start anew. So a group of poor, largely uneducated miners instead invented a...M. Wallach, what was it they invented?" she asked.

The woman looked surprised to be asked. "A continuous injection smelter," she said. "The same kind we use on Niraya."

The elder nodded. "A new kind of smelter, a device that could increase their yields tenfold. Instead of being shut down and abandoned, those mines became incredibly profitable."

With any other crowd it would hardly be the most stirring example of her point, but the engineers in the shuttle grew excited and loud as they shouted back and forth comments she couldn't understand about colloidal sieves and mesoscale electrostatics, debating the genius of the Appolyon miners' innovation. She let them debate for a long while before she cleared her throat to get their attention once more.

Then she looked across the shuttle, between two rows of passengers, and caught the eye of the man who had first asked her to speak. She nodded at him. "You see? Humanity cannot work miracles. Miracles are impossible. What we can do, when faced with impossible odds, is build a solution. We find the possible way, where once it seemed no such thing existed."

The reaction was immediate and enthusiastic. Some applauded, some cheered. Some just looked down and smiled. She'd reached them.

"Did you just come up with all that now?" M. Wallach asked.

"I extemporized it, yes," the elder said, softly now, as her sermon was complete. "I've had a great deal of practice. Now, rather than boring all these good people with more speeches," she said, raising her voice again, "how about another song?"

The engineers launched into a very old tune from Earth about a miner and his lost love named Clementine. Half the words made no sense to the elder, but she liked the cadence of it. Before the song was half-finished, however, it stopped suddenly because the shuttle lurched and they were all thrown against their straps. For a moment the elder worried something terrible had happened, that perhaps they were under attack.

Then she felt weightless, and she understood. The shuttle had simply stopped accelerating. She floated in her straps and felt the aches in her knees and back start to recede.

She looked forward, but could see nothing through the cockpit windows except darkness. Not even stars. Yet she understood what the sudden weightlessness meant. They must be getting close to their destination.

Zhang and Valk arrived at Aruna well ahead of the tender and the shuttles. Garuda, the ice giant planet, grew to fill most of her forward view. To Zhang's cybernetic eyes it was just a big round shape with no surface features at all—because she couldn't see color, she couldn't tell if it was banded and spotted with storms like Jupiter or just hazy and pale like Uranus. A shame—she'd always found gas giant planets pretty.

Aruna, the moon, showed much more detail. She could make out its craters and rilles and scarps, the jagged terrain of the tiny world. She could even tell that the weather seemed to have improved since her last visit. Only a few curving wisps of cloud obscured the factory crater.

Her sensors picked up a number of objects orbiting the moon, even though they were still too small to see. She found mostly what she'd expected. When they'd left Aruna they'd put a number of microdrones in orbit, just to keep an eye on the place.

There was one object in orbit, however, that shouldn't be there. A metallic object about six meters across, almost perfectly spherical. "You picking this up?" she asked Valk, sending him the object's particulars in case he'd missed it. "Does it look familiar to you?"

"Yep," Valk said.

"I'd say that looks exactly like one of the enemy's orbiters." The spacecraft that carried their landers. The enemy must have sent it in to scout the moon. Presumably so that a larger force could come retake Aruna if the coast was clear.

"I've seen them before," Valk said. "You want me to move in and blast it?"

"Not yet," Zhang told him. "I'm not picking up anything else— no interceptors, none of those little scouts. The orbiters we've seen so far weren't armed. I'm guessing this is just a reconnaissance ship. Maybe we should let it get a good look at us—Lanoe's plan hinges on them coming out this way to fight us, so let's give them a reason to do just that. Approach within a hundred kilometers and see what it does."

"You got it, boss," Valk said. She watched him pull away from her, his BR.9 banking around in a very long, shallow curve toward Aruna's north pole. She followed him a little more cautiously, using just tiny bursts of her maneuvering jets to send her ship into an orbit around Aruna.

The orbiter didn't move or open fire as Valk got closer. If it had even seen them it made no sign. It could be in communication with the enemy fleet by way of comms laser but there was no way to know.

"This one's different from the others," Valk called. "Close up I can see it's got a bunch of sensors mounted on its outer skin. Millimeter-wave scans show it's mostly hollow inside—I don't think it's carrying a lander. I'm at three hundred kilometers now and it hasn't changed course. Still closing."

Zhang kept an eye on the volume of space around the moon, expecting an ambush of enemy fighter craft at any moment. None of her scans showed anything out of the ordinary, but you never knew. Maybe the aliens had some kind of stealth technology that could hide a whole wing of ships from her sensors. Maybe they were down on the moon, camouflaged by all the wreckage and debris.

"Two hundred kilometers, still closing," Valk called. "It's leaking electromagnetic radiation."

"You think that's the signature of some kind of weapon?" Zhang asked.

"Negative. I think it's got a radio onboard. A really strong radio. Weird. If it uses that radio to contact the fleet, why hasn't it transmitted yet? If we—"

His voice disappeared in a welter of static, a high-pitched squealing wave of white noise that deafened her until her systems automatically turned the volume down.

Her fingers danced across her comms board until she'd figured out what she'd just heard. That squeal had come from the orbiter, from the radio unit Valk had found. The orbiter had dumped a huge amount of energy into the radio, sending out a signal so strong it would propagate throughout the entire system. A warning to the fleet, most likely—she could guess that the message would be "enemy sighted."

Good enough. She hit her thrusters to send her over toward the orbiter, to get a good look for herself before they blew the damned thing up. It turned out she needn't have bothered. The energy behind that radio blast had been more than the orbiter could take—the thing was fried, its outer shell half-molten with the heat of the transmission. Its sensors looked like they'd burned from the inside out.

Valk hung in space about eighty kilometers from the thing, not moving. For a second she thought maybe the radio pulse wasn't a communication at all, but some kind of weapon—maybe a microwave burst that could have cooked Valk alive inside his suit.

"Big guy," she said, "say something. Let me know you're okay."

"I'm fine," he called back. "My ears hurt a little. Damn. Did you hear that?"

"Everybody in the system heard it," she said, just relieved he was okay.

"Then can you tell me what it meant?"

Zhang shrugged inside her suit. "Who the hell knows? It just sounded like white noise to me. Probably some kind of machine code only its fellow drones would understand."

"Then you didn't...Zhang, you didn't hear it speak?" Valk asked.

She had been about to blast the orbiter to slag. Her hand hovered over her weapons board.

"What do you mean?" she asked, cautiously.

"You didn't hear words?" Valk asked her. "You didn't hear it talking about a false-mind?"

⸺※⸺

Landings, Elder McRae was told, were almost as dangerous as launches.

She held M. Wallach's hand again as the shuttle shook and tossed in the thick air of Aruna, its wings vibrating with the heat of atmospheric entry. It wasn't nearly as frightening as the launch had been, nor did it last nearly as long.

Once the shuttle had touched down and stopped shaking, they all released themselves from their safety straps and almost trampled each other getting out through the shuttle's narrow hatch, all of them eager to at least stretch their legs—and certainly to see the place where they would be working for the next few days.

A whole new world.

Elder McRae stumbled out onto a surface of wind-blasted rock and looked up at a dark purple sky and for the first time wondered if she had made a bad mistake. She could hear her breath in her ears, see it turn to fog on the inside of her helmet. The suit's life support pack chugged and wheezed in the small of her back and heating elements came on across her stomach and her thighs, hot enough she worried they might burn her.

She had to move out of the way as engineers poured out of the shuttle. Her first step nearly sent her flying—the gravity here was only a fraction of Niraya's.

M. Wallach grabbed her arm and steadied her. Through the engineer's helmet she could see that Wallach was as dumbfounded as she, that at least she wasn't the only one confused by this new place.

She tried to orient herself by looking around, but the landscape made no sense. Everything was taller than she expected, cliffs jutting up on every side, craters so deep their bottoms were full of shadows. She saw the other shuttle land some distance away and it seemed tiny, a child's toy. The tender set down nearby and finally she was able to put some scale to what she saw. They had set down on a narrow shelf of rock that stuck out from the outside of a crater rim, a crater that must have been much larger than Walden Crater back home. The rim towered above them, perhaps a kilometer over their heads.

Everywhere on the rock shelf engineers and volunteers shuffled about, taking long loping strides as they unpacked the cargo pods on the side of the tender, as they studiously set about learning how to walk here, as they milled about aimlessly, waiting for someone to give them instructions.

These were not long in coming. Engineer Derrow leapt up onto the top of the tender, making it look easy. She could be recognized by the hexagons painted all over her suit and by a light just below her helmet that flashed when she spoke.

"I know this place is weird," she said, and dozens of helmets turned toward her. "We don't have time for sightseeing. We need to get to work right away. We're going to climb up that slope," she said, pointing at an impossibly steep pile of scree a few hundred meters away, "and then head down into the crater. What you see in there might freak some of you out. Try to cope, okay? We're all professionals here. If you weren't one of my employees back on Niraya, you are now."

She jumped down from the tender and loped toward the jumbled boulders of the slope, then seemed to dance up them like a mountain goat, her feet barely touching the rocks. One by one the engineers followed. Elder McRae was very glad to see no one else had Derrow's effortless grace.

Of course, Derrow had been here before. She'd come here with the pilots, though the elder still knew few details of what they'd done on Aruna.

Up at the crest of the rim a couple of engineers bent to assemble a rover, a simple cage of pipes with four balloon wheels and a compact motor. A parabolic dish stuck up at the top of a pipe mounted behind the driver's seat. The rover was just big enough to seat Derrow. She took it over the edge of the crater and disappeared. The engineers and the volunteers like the elder had to walk.

Moving carefully, checking every foothold before leaping to the next, she followed a line of engineers up the slope. She was breathing heavily by the time they reached the top and they could look out over the massive crater. Despite Engineer Derrow's urgency regarding time, everyone up there was just standing and gaping at what they'd discovered.

Elder McRae couldn't blame them.

Below, inside the crater, the enemy had built a massive installation of towers and hangarlike structures and things like giant seed pods. None of it looked remotely like human architecture. The elder, who had trained in building when she was still an aspirant, who had built, in fact, her own office back at the Retreat, couldn't see how any of those structures were erected. The shapes were all wrong, round and sculptured where there should have been right angles, or minimally worked out of thin girders and tangles of pipes where a human designer would have put solid walls. Much of the crater's contents looked as if it had been smashed or burnt—she supposed that was the work of Commander Lanoe and Lieutenant Zhang—but everywhere that things were still intact metal glittered weakly in the orange light of the far sun. There was no color anywhere in that tangled mess of construction, nothing ornamented or decorated at all, not even any writing or signage to help the human eye make sense of it.

Derrow rolled past in her rover, pointing out details of the crater to an engineer who jogged along beside her. "Main problem is we have no power," Derrow said, her voice broadcast to everyone's suits. "We'll pull it from the tender's reactor until we find a better solution. Plenty of scrap metal; get some teams on sorting through it to find the alloys we need, use anybody who doesn't have specific skills. Everyone needs a job and they need to keep doing that job until I say stop. And keep an eye on your sensors—any depleted uranium you find, tell me."

One by one the engineers around the elder hurried to find tasks, to begin their labors. The elder looked around for M. Wallach, but the woman was gone, probably already hard at work.

"You," someone said, an engineer with a blue stripe painted down the sleeve of his suit. "What are you standing around for, damn it? Oh. I'm sorry, Elder, I didn't recognize you."

"That's all right," she said. "Just tell me what to do."

Lanoe and Thom had left Niraya but they were still hours away. Even patching Lanoe into the conversation meant waiting long minutes for Zhang's signal to reach him, then minutes more to hear his replies. She was used to communicating over such distances but that didn't mean it wasn't frustrating.

"We all heard that signal," she said. "Every radio in the system picked it up. Somehow, though, Valk heard something different. I can't explain it, so don't ask me to. I've got Derrow on this call; maybe she has some ideas."

"Don't get your hopes up," Derrow said. "I don't exactly have a lot of free time down here, but I've dedicated some computing power to analyzing the signal. I didn't learn much."

Lanoe's voice cut in, words from nearly a quarter of an hour ago, just catching up. "What did Valk hear? Just tell me what he heard."

"Ignore that," Zhang told Derrow. "We'll fill him in as best we can. Go ahead with your analysis."

"It sounded like static at first. Just white noise. When I ran a basic Fourier analysis, though, it turned out that it wasn't random, it was compressed data. A lot of data, hundreds of megabytes squeezed down into a few seconds of high-bandwidth transmission. Data I can't translate, though. It's not in any kind of human language. It's not even in any kind of human protocol—every poly has their own proprietary way of talking to machines, but this doesn't look like any of them. It's all in base fifteen, just like the software onboard that lander I studied. So it's definitely from the enemy. Beyond that...I'm at sea here. The first fifteen digits are all zeroes. That looks like a handshake to me."

"A handshake?"

Derrow sighed in frustration. "When a computer contacts another computer for the first time, it sends a short, recognizable signal. Something to say, 'Hello, I am prepared to send you information.' A handshake can be as simple as that or it can contain information about how to process that information—the transmission rate, the protocols to use, things like that. Those fifteen zeroes look, to me, like a signal to another system, telling it to pay attention. Of course, that's just a guess. I have no idea how alien drones talk to each other."

"It's a place to start. Lanoe, we think the orbiter was put here just to send this message. It slagged itself in the process. The message means nothing to me or any of us—but somehow it got through to Valk. Engineer, any thoughts there?"

"M. Valk was the closest person to the orbiter when it transmitted. Maybe it sent a second message, one in clear text, but with a weaker signal. One that didn't propagate far enough for anyone else to pick it up."

"It's not that," Valk said. "I checked my comms logs—"

"Damn it," Lanoe said. Fifteen minutes in the past. "Zhang, you're going to have to figure this out before I arrive. Have some kind of conclusions ready for me when I get there, will you?"

"Everyone, please ignore that," Zhang said. "Valk—you were saying?"

"I checked my comms logs," Valk repeated. He sounded nervous. Like he was on trial here. "They didn't record anything except the same gobbledygook you two caught. There was no second message. Just the one—except to me it sounded like a voice speaking. Not a human voice. It sounded synthesized—you know, like a drone voice. Flat. Weird inflections, no rhythm to it. Just words."

"That should be impossible," Derrow pointed out.

"I heard what I heard!" Valk shot back.

"Okay, okay, let's all calm down. Valk," Zhang said. "For Lanoe's benefit—tell me what you heard."

Valk cleared his throat. He repeated the message word for word, raising or lowering his voice to match the inflections. "IF *(conditional; signify compliance)* would *(subjunctive)* speak. THEN *(allow? deny?)* speak: this system, false-mind."

Zhang had heard it before. It still spooked her out to hear him repeat it. For a while no one spoke, as they digested the words. Then Lanoe cut in again, still well behind everyone else.

"Thom, it was some kind of signal from the enemy. The first time they've tried to communicate at all. I know. I know! Kid, I'm working on it—Zhang's trying to decode it now. Clear this channel until I say otherwise. Zhang—what the hell is going on?"

"I wish I knew," she said, catching herself too late before she said it out loud.

"I think it's kind of obvious," Derrow said. "I mean, okay, it's confusingly worded. But it sounds like they want to negotiate."

"I didn't hear anything like that," Zhang said.

"Yeah, it sounds like a computer having a stroke. But to me that's exactly how a device just short of artificial intelligence would ask if we wanted to talk to it. 'IF you want to speak, THEN speak.' It's like a line of computer code for a system that wants to negotiate. Maybe to stop this war."

"Lanoe won't see it that way," Zhang said.

"Let's have some perspective here," Derrow said. She was still talking. "I know we're all scared. But this is one of the biggest moments in human history, isn't it? I mean, isn't it? First contact with an alien species?"

"First contact," Valk said, "was when they started killing farmers on Niraya."

Derrow growled in frustration. "We don't even know—maybe they didn't understand, maybe they didn't know we were sentient, maybe they were just...exploring, who knows? I don't know! But neither of you do, either. We have to take this opportunity. We have to try to talk to them."

"Elder McRae said—back in the very first briefing we did, back at the Retreat—that they'd been trying for weeks to contact the enemy, long before Lanoe even started recruiting us. There's never been any response."

"Maybe they just didn't know how we communicated, maybe—"

"Enough," Zhang said.

"Please just listen," Derrow said.

But Zhang was done. "No. Hold that thought. This is too big a decision for us to make. We need to wait until Lanoe gets here. Engineer, thank you for your assistance. When we're ready to discuss this again, I'll let you know."

She cut Derrow out of the call before she could say anything else.

"Zhang," Valk said, when it was just the two of them, still circling Aruna in their BR.9s, still within shooting distance of the slagged orbiter. "Zhang, she could be right."

"Don't start."

"No, look," Valk said. "She could be right. But I don't trust these bastards. And that 'false-mind' bit, that doesn't exactly sound friendly to me."

"Nor me," Zhang admitted. "Even if I had any idea what it meant. I'd be a lot happier if I knew why they sent this message to you. Just to you."

"There's one possibility," he said. "Maybe I'm the only one who heard it because I've gone crazy. Maybe the voice was just in my head."

Zhang laughed, though she knew he hadn't been joking. At least not entirely. "Maybe," she said. "Maybe."

Mostly, the elder found herself gathering things and carrying them from one place to another. Pieces of debris and junk, parts of broken drones. She carried them to the smelters, where the engineers were busy casting long, perfectly straight iron rails. They fussed and argued over their calipers and their geodesic lasers, always trying to get the rails that much closer to some hypothetical ideal of straightness. The elder didn't understand any of what they were doing. So she just kept carrying things, walking them over to the glowing mouth of the smelter. Casting them in.

In the low gravity she could lift objects that, on Niraya, would have been ludicrously too heavy for her. Boulders so big she could hardly get her arms around them. Whole legs of destroyed landers. It was almost comical how much she could carry. There was a problem, though—their weight might be different than what she expected, but they still had mass. Just because everything felt like it was made of packing foam, she couldn't beat inertia. If she moved too fast, so did the thing she was carrying. If it massed more than she did, when she tried to stop it would keep moving, and carry her with it.

It would be easy here to break an arm, or a leg. The cheap suit she wore had no safety measures built in to protect her or keep her working if she was injured.

She had to learn a whole new way of moving. Shuffling along the ash-covered ground wasn't enough. She had to think through every step. Which quickly grew exhausting. Every muscle in her legs screamed to be set free, to walk again in the normal way. Her back ached from the simple exercise of bending over and picking things up. The heating elements in her suit scorched her abdomen but couldn't seem to keep her gloves warm. Her fingers grew first numb, then prickly in the incredibly cold wind of Aruna.

She wouldn't allow any of it to get to her. Lead by example, she thought. It had always been the way of the Transcendentalists. When this was over, they would say she had lifted more rocks, fed the smelter faster than anyone else.

No, she thought, her discipline straightening her spine. No. That was unnecessary competitiveness. Making this a game that someone could win meant everyone else had to lose. This was a group effort. When it was over they would say she'd done her part, and done it competently. That was all the praise she needed.

She found a rock that glittered a little in the faint orange light of the sun. A sensor on her wrist started to tick unhappily when her hand got too close to it. She knew what she had to do. She sent a signal to her supervisor indicating she might have found something radioactive. She flagged it on a map on her minder, all the while moving carefully away from it.

Her suit didn't protect her from radiation, either.

She found another piece of debris—a long pipe that had fallen from a high column made of similar pipes. She picked it up. Carried it toward the smelter. Its unwieldy shape kept swinging her around but she struggled up a long ramp and pushed one end of the pipe deep into the orange light that burst from the smelter's mouth. The pipe resisted, as if it had caught on something inside the smelter.

She pushed, as hard as she dared. The pipe slid forward a few centimeters, then stopped again. She looked around but she couldn't see any engineers nearby. Anyway, what would she say? *I'm sorry, this pipe is being stubborn? I can't handle it by myself?*

Self-reliance was one of the Four Eternals. She pushed again. The pipe gave a little, slid a little farther into the glowing pool of metal inside the smelter. She pushed a third time and it just stuck there, sticking up in the air.

Her helmet muffled external sounds. She could barely hear the keening of the nitrogen wind. When she heard the gurgling, glooping noise she had no idea what it was at first.

Then a trickle of molten metal spilled from the top end of her pipe. A spurt of bright orange liquid iron followed, jetting high up in the air.

She'd pushed the pipe down into the smelter and now it acted like a giant straw. Or, in this case, a deadly hose.

She staggered backward, lifting her hands as droplets of metal, no longer glowing but still soft, pattered all around her. A fat drop smacked against the front of her helmet and she almost screamed, except there was no time. As she ran she saw the iron solidify in a thick nodule against the carbonglas, right in the middle of her view.

If any of the hot metal fell on her arms or back, she would be incinerated. The thin fabric of her suit couldn't take the heat the way her helmet did.

Behind her the pipe slouched and bent as it melted, sagging until it pointed out of the smelter at a forty-five-degree angle. Hot metal jetted from the end, flicking out in great tongues of fire.

She threw herself to the ground, her hands over her head—stupidly, since her hands were far more at risk than her helmet. Behind her the pipe crimped and collapsed, one last gout of molten metal drooling from its end. All around her the hot metal cooled on the ground, coagulating and turning dark.

People came running from every direction, calling out to see if she was all right, demanding to know what had happened. A young man grasped her arm and helped her up to her feet.

"Are you okay?" he asked. "Did you get any on you?"

"I don't think so," she said. She checked her arms and legs and they looked all right. The glob of metal adhering to her helmet was the only thing she could see.

Suddenly a wave of exhaustion rolled through her muscles and she sagged in the young man's grasp.

"Hold on," he said. "We'll get you some help. Maybe—maybe you should go back to the shuttles. Have a little rest."

"Hey!" someone shouted.

She looked up and saw M. Wallach come loping toward them. "Hey—she's fine. She should get back to work," the woman said.

"She's an old lady!" her benefactor, the young man, insisted.

"She's a volunteer," M. Wallach replied.

Looking disgusted, the young man released her, then headed off toward his own next task.

The elder looked up at M. Wallach. The engineer looked back, studying the elder's face through her helmet.

Then Elder McRae nodded her thanks, and marched away from the smelter, looking for some other piece of debris she could salvage. She felt inordinately grateful to M. Wallach. Had the engineer not shown up just then, if the young man had continued to suggest she should go lie down—the elder was pretty sure she would have agreed. She would have gone and found a bunk and lay down in it and who knew how long it would have been before she got back up?

Temptation was a terrible thing.

———※———

Lanoe and Thom arrived at Garuda a few hours later, coming in at high velocity. They had to take a lap around the planet, with their airfoils grazing the outermost layers of its atmosphere, just to slow down. When they made orbit around Aruna, Zhang and Valk were waiting for them.

Valk started in first. "Listen, Lanoe, I don't know how much you know about what happened out here, and, frankly, I'm not too clear on it myself—"

"Take it easy," Lanoe said. "We'll figure this out together. All of us. Zhang, you want to give me the quick version?"

"The aliens tried to communicate with us. They managed to get through to Valk, but nobody else. It sounds like they want to talk."

She couldn't see him. His FA.2 was a dozen kilometers below her, tracing a faster orbit around the moon so that he was always pulling away from her. It frustrated her—she really wanted to know what he was thinking, and with a guarded man like Lanoe that meant getting a look at his face.

Maybe that was why he'd chosen the lower orbit.

"I've already heard from Ehta. Her sensors didn't pick anything up that yours missed. Let's get Derrow's opinion," Lanoe said, with a sigh.

It didn't take long to get the engineer talking. "We have to take this chance. If we just start attacking them now, they may decide we're not worth talking to. We may never get to communicate with them again."

"I've seen no indication these aliens can be trusted," Lanoe said.

"Centuries in space. We've seen hundreds of worlds. We've never seen so much as the remains of an alien culture," Derrow pointed out. "Until now. It's imperative that we make an attempt to talk."

"What do we say? 'Never mind about those dead Nirayans. Never mind that you tried to kill every single one of my pilots. Friendship is what's important.' Something like that?" Lanoe asked her.

"No, of course not—look, they'll have to explain themselves. And they'll have to stop killing us, if they want any kind of truce. Obviously. But we can't even begin to know how they see things. They had this base on Aruna, they've been working here for years. Then we came along and blew it up. They may well consider us the aggressors."

Zhang bit back a curse. She was amazed at how quickly Derrow had turned on them. One minute she'd been their best friend, helping them build the guns, now...What made it worse was that Derrow knew what the aliens were like. "You might be forgetting something, Engineer," she said. "You were the one who figured out how the landers operate. They see an organic life-form, they kill it. That's their only function."

"Just think about what we might lose, if we stick to the battle plan," Derrow said.

"If we change it," Valk said, "we'll definitely lose the war."

Derrow called back, her voice hot with rage, "You can't think that—"

"Engineer, thank you for your input," Lanoe interrupted.

"What? Commander, you can't just ignore what I'm saying."

"I can do exactly that," Lanoe told her. "This is a Naval operation. That means I'm in charge, as ranking officer on-site. I appreciate your comments and your concerns. But we still need to think of this as a military decision."

"I could shut down work on the guns," Derrow said.

The threat hung in the air, unanswered, for far too long. Zhang just sat there in her cockpit and tried to breathe. What Derrow was suggesting—

"Sure," Lanoe said. "You could."

"Then maybe you should listen to—"

"You could," Lanoe said. "But you won't."

"Why's that?"

"Because you're a reasonable person. You know full well that this could be a trick. Or that even if we talk to them, it doesn't mean we can come to any agreement. They might demand our unconditional surrender. They might just want to gloat about how they're going to wipe us out. Given their numerical superiority, I think the possibility of peace talks right now is slim."

"I'll admit that much," Derrow replied, in a quiet voice.

"So you'll keep building my guns. Just in case." Zhang could hear Lanoe take a deep breath. "Okay. It's up to me to make this decision. I wish to hell it wasn't. I wish we had time to contact the Admiralty and ask for advice. Too damned bad for me."

He was nearly around the limb of the moon now. Zhang could barely see the FA.2 as a speck of light, far away.

"We continue as planned," Lanoe said. "Thom and I will make a feint at the fleet, get their attention. Draw them into our trap. Derrow, you have those guns ready for when they take the bait. Zhang, I want total reconnaissance on the local volume of space. If they have a wing of interceptors hidden on one of the other moons, if there are more landers hidden around here somewhere, just waiting to attack my guns, I need to know that."

"You've got it," she said.

"What about me?" Valk asked.

"Valk, buddy? You've got a call to make."

Chapter Twenty-Four

A trickle of cold sweat ran down the back of Thom's suit, tickling his spine. He'd never felt so alone, so far from help. There was nothing for a thousand kilometers in any direction, no shelter whatsoever to hide behind if the enemy started shooting at him. Lanoe was just a bright speck of light, far off to his left. Garuda was just a bluish smudge far behind him.

Even on the longest races he'd ever sailed—endurance runs that could go on for days and cross entire star systems—he'd always had a support team waiting to catch him if things went bad. Rescue vehicles, supply ships, hundreds of spectators watching his every move. Every ship around him had been there to help. Now he was facing down an entire fleet of craft designed to kill him.

Flying exercises with Lanoe in the canyons of Niraya hadn't made him nervous like this. There'd been real danger involved but only if he messed up, if he made some idiotic choice. His death would have been his own fault, then. This was different.

He reached for his comms board, then pulled his hand back. Lanoe had told him to maintain comms silence as much as possible. Not because he was worried the enemy might hear them. If the two fighters stayed in touch by communications laser there was no risk of that—it was next to impossible to intercept a tightbeam signal. No, Thom had gotten the impression that Lanoe just didn't want to be bothered.

A sensor panel flickered into life in front of him. There was new imagery of the enemy fleet available if he wished to review it. As far as they might have come from their base at Aruna, the fleet still wasn't visible to the naked eye. The enemy ships were built of low-reflective materials and were nearly as dark as the black void behind them. The fighter could see more of the electromagnetic spectrum than Thom could, however, and it had built up a picture of what they faced.

He hesitated. Did he really want to know? But of course a fighter pilot couldn't think like that. He tapped for the imagery and watched as his display filled up with the spiky shapes of interceptors and scouts, alien machines with no pilots onboard. They wove complicated patterns around their swarmships, which seemed to hang motionless in space. Behind them the huge round bulk of the queenship looked more like scenery than an enemy spacecraft. This was the clearest picture Thom had seen yet of the massive vehicle, perhaps the first time anyone had actually seen it in visible light.

A green pearl appeared in the corner of Thom's vision. He flicked his eyes across it and he could hear Lanoe breathing. "You getting this?" the old pilot asked.

"Yes," Thom said. "How close are they?"

"Check the corner of your display. There's metadata for this imagery."

"Right. I should have thought of that," Thom said. He expanded a tiny window inside the display and saw that the closest parts of the image—an interceptor at the vanguard of the fleet—was still a hundred and seventy thousand kilometers away. Far beyond shooting range.

"What do you make of the queenship?" Lanoe asked. "You can adjust the focus on the image to get a clearer look."

Thom studied the big vessel. It was roughly spherical, nearly a kilometer in diameter. Much bigger than any spacecraft the Navy could field. "Um," Thom said, trying to think of what to say. Beyond the fact that the giant ship scared the hell out of him.

"Well. We know one thing for sure. It didn't come through a wormhole."

"Is that right?" Lanoe asked.

Thom realized, suddenly, that Lanoe would already know that. That he was asking Thom's opinion on the queenship not for actual information but to see what Thom could work out on his own. This was just one more test.

This one, at least, he had a chance of passing. Back in his yacht racing days he'd made an exhaustive study of spacecraft design. You had to know why ships were built the way they were if you wanted to find ways to make them go faster.

Even the biggest human ships were built long and thin, and for good reason. "Some wormhole throats are only a few hundred meters across. There's no way the queenship could have fit through a wormhole without disintegrating. So they must have traveled here the long way—across interstellar space."

"Good," Lanoe said.

"Which raises the question of why," Thom said. "Why fly all that way—a voyage that must have taken hundreds of years, probably even longer—just to attack a backwater planet like Niraya?"

"We're not likely to figure that one out just by looking at them," Lanoe said, "so let it go for now. What else do you see?"

Thom looked for things that didn't make sense. "What are all those circular depressions?" he asked. The queenship was spotted with them, dozens of round shadows like the dimples on a golf ball, perhaps. "Do you think those are weapons or docking bays?"

"Neither," Lanoe called back. "I think those are craters."

Thom wanted to laugh at the idea. Craters on a spaceship? No, you found craters on a moon, on an asteroid... "Oh," he said.

"We know that thing's old," Lanoe said. "It flew here without the benefit of a wormhole, which means it's been out in the deep void for centuries, at least. Probably even longer. And judging by its albedo and by virtual spectroscopy it looks like it's made out of rock, not metal."

"You think it's not a ship at all," Thom said. "You think it's an asteroid. You think they hollowed out an asteroid and stuck an engine on the back of it."

"Makes sense, actually. If you're going to fly from star to star you need a lot of radiation shielding, and rock is good for that. Plus it's probably cheaper to use a hollow rock than to build a ship hull that big—and we know the enemy likes to build things cheap. I don't know if those craters were part of the original rock or if they're from impacts it suffered along the way, but, yeah, those are definitely craters."

Once Thom knew to look for it, the nature of the queenship was obvious. No one, not even an alien, would build a ship that lumpy and amorphous. The natural shape of the asteroid made the artificial parts of the queenship stand out by way of contrast. The long toothlike projections on its forward end looked like gracefully engineered pylons, though Thom couldn't hazard a guess as to their function. Maybe they were weapons, or docking facilities, or . . . something unguessable. Alien. They stood in a perfectly spaced ring around a circular maw at the very front of the ship, a pit dark and deep enough that it showed no features at all. Most likely that was how smaller craft got in and out of the queenship. Then again, it could be a ramscoop designed to suck in interstellar hydrogen. Or the barrel of an enormous cannon.

"This is good," Lanoe said. "This tells us something important, even though it makes our lives more difficult. My scans tell me the rock of that thing's hull is at least twenty meters deep. Way too thick for our disruptor rounds to penetrate. Even the guns we're building on Aruna would take hours to dig their way through."

Lanoe didn't sound like he was ready to give up, though. It took Thom only a second to see why. "That means," Thom said, working through the idea, "we'll need to attack the maw directly. The forward opening. In the hope there's something in there we can blow up."

"Good," Lanoe said. "All right. That's enough recon for now. Time for actual operations. Right now that fleet is headed on a direct course for Niraya. We need them to change that course so they're moving toward Aruna instead. The way we make that happen is to convince them we take Aruna seriously."

"By attacking them from Aruna," Thom said.

"Exactly."

"What if they don't turn?" Thom asked. "What if they ignore us and just keep to their current trajectory?"

"They won't. If they fly past Aruna that means leaving us—the only threat in this system—behind them. It's basic military strategy. You never let your enemy take up position behind you, because that makes it way too easy for them to stab you in the back. Okay, follow my lead. We're going to move in as close as we dare, just out of range of their interceptors. But remember—we don't shoot first. We give them a chance to hear what Valk has to say. Maybe they'll agree to negotiate and we don't have to shoot at all."

"You don't think that's very likely, do you?" Thom asked.

"No. But I'd love to be proved wrong."

The green pearl disappeared as Lanoe cut the connection. On Thom's left he saw the bright little dot of Lanoe's FA.2 race forward, ahead of him. He opened his throttle up to follow, straight toward the enemy fleet.

⸺✦⸺

Ehta had expected her role in the battle—ground control—to involve a lot of sitting around watching displays and relaying information people already knew. She'd expected it to be mind-breakingly boring.

Instead it had turned out to be terrifying.

The trip from Niraya to Aruna had been bad, very bad. She'd been crammed into the wardroom of the tender—as far as she could get from any windows—with a bunch of engineers who couldn't help but comment every time the ship rattled or lurched. She'd kept her eyes tightly shut for hours at a time, just trying not to think about the fact they were in space.

Once they'd landed, the engineers had all jumped out of the tender as quick as they could, so they could get to work. Ehta and Roan had remained behind so they could turn the tender into a ground control station close enough to the action to maybe even be useful. The ship was designed to serve such a role—its sensor pod was better suited than even the field of radar dishes back on Niraya—but still it took endless work to get ready, configuring the tender's software to the task at hand, laying out rectennas on the cold soil of Aruna and calibrating them until they gave good intel. Ehta and Roan had worked nonstop for hours.

Now they had another job. One that could mean the end of the war.

"Transceivers are up and running," Roan announced. She was over at the tender's main console, fine-tuning equipment at a virtual control board.

"I've got the signal cross-checked and rechecked," Ehta replied, watching lights turn green on her minder. Valk's message was simple enough but they weren't taking any risks. This could be the only chance they had to talk to the enemy.

The data file Valk had sent to the station had to be perfect. The transmission needed to be carefully managed, as well. It had to come from a very strong signal source—stronger than anything the fighters could put out—to match the strength of the alien message. The tender was the only comms unit in the system that could pump out a signal that strong.

Ehta came over and stood next to Roan. The girl had been born on Niraya, and this message could determine the fate of her planet. She should be the one to press the button. "You do the honors," Ehta said.

They traded a tense nod, and then Roan tapped a key on the console. The minder fed Valk's message through the tender's equipment and blasted it out into space. They heard the big pilot's voice on the minder's tiny speakers. Ehta fought the urge to grab Roan's hand.

"You have indicated a willingness to speak to us," Valk's recording said. "We are also willing to speak. We are willing to negotiate with you. We require that you cease all hostile activity immediately. As a show of good faith, we will not attack your vehicles unless we are attacked. Please indicate receipt of this transmission."

Just that, nothing more.

"How long…?" Roan asked.

Ehta didn't need to check the minder. "The fleet's more than a million kilometers away, but it won't take long for the signal to reach them. Give them some time to think about what we said and come up with a proper response. Who knows? That could be hours, or just a few seconds."

"What do we do in the meantime?"

Ehta cleared her throat. "We stand here. And we wait."

The images Thom had seen of the enemy fleet had lied to him. They'd made it look like all the alien ships were bunched together in a tight knot of steel. In fact the images had been squashed to better show detail, and individual enemy vessels were quite far from each other, strung out in a long line almost a hundred thousand kilometers long. The queenship was surrounded by escorts but the seven swarmships stood off from each other so far they wouldn't have been visible to one another with the naked eye, and small patrols of scouts and interceptors flew even farther afield, screening the fleet's advance.

At the vanguard, a lone alien interceptor stood sentry about ten thousand kilometers ahead of the main fleet. Thom could almost see it through his canopy, a smudge in the darkness. A shadow only really visible when it passed in front of a distant star.

His displays showed him the interceptor in much greater detail. He had plenty of time to study its alien curves, its irregular, lumpy shape. The spiky cones of its guns twitched and rotated in their sockets as if they were sniffing him out. He had no doubt the thing could sense him just fine.

"Move in," Lanoe said. "I'm right beside you. Remember, the point is to get its attention without getting yourself killed. Stay out of its range—a minimum of a hundred kilometers. Keep your weapons board on standby, but don't touch it."

"Got it," Thom said. He opened his throttle. Fed a little fuel to his maneuvering jets until his BR.9 banked into a long, shallow curve that would take him on a course that intersected the alien ship's trajectory.

As he closed in, his display showed him that the interceptor's weapons had stopped moving. They were all pointed directly at him. Near-infrared imaging showed them glowing a dull orange, like banked furnaces. It was ready to shoot if he came too close.

He fought the urge to turn around and run for safety.

Closer. Close enough he could almost make it out with his naked eye. Closer still, and his hands started to shake, just a little.

"That's enough," Lanoe said. "Move back now. See if it follows us."

Thom just barely nudged his stick. His fighter arced away from the interceptor in a graceful, low-energy swoop. It would have been child's play for the interceptor to accelerate and close with him, if it wanted to.

The alien ship kept its distance, not varying from its previous course by even a thousandth of a degree. He did notice that its guns stayed hot.

Lanoe grunted with impatience. "I would have bet my salary that thing would give chase," he said.

"Maybe they're serious about wanting to negotiate," Thom pointed out.

"Then they should say something, damn it. They've heard Valk's message by now. They know we're here. It's their move," Lanoe said. "Okay. Stay with me." His FA.2 swung out on a new course, one that took it well clear of the interceptor but still in the general direction of the enemy fleet. "I'm picking up some scouts ahead, about five hundred kilometers from here. You see them?"

Thom tapped at his sensor board. "Got 'em," he said. There were three of the tiny ships, which looked like glaring eyeballs connected by a skeletal frame to some rudimentary thrusters. They flew in close formation, on a nearly identical trajectory with the interceptor—their noses pointed straight at Niraya.

"They're armed with plasma cannon, which are only effective at very short range—maybe a hundred meters. Give them two hundred meters clearance, just in case."

Thom licked his lips. By the standards of spaceflight, two hundred meters was nothing. Lanoe wanted to buzz the little ships so close it would set off collision alarms. Well, he was the boss.

"Nice and slow," Lanoe said. "Like a cat with a mouse."

The two of them pressed in on a course that passed between the interceptor and the three scouts. There was no way the enemy could see that except as an aggressive move, though Lanoe was sticking to his word so far—they had not, technically, attacked the enemy, not while they waited for the reply to Valk's message.

In Thom's forward view the scouts were invisible at first, too small to even make decent shadows. That changed rapidly as they approached. As Lanoe's course took them closer and closer Thom saw the scouts as outlines traced against the void at first, then as dark shapes, and then they were so close he felt he could reach out and touch them.

Their spherical plasma cannon rolled like eyes to stare at him. Infrared showed them burning hot as hell.

"I don't think they like this," Thom said. They were three kilometers away now...two...one...

"Hold on, kid," Lanoe called. "Hold steady."

Five hundred meters. Four.

"Lanoe, you're off course," Thom called. On his displays he could see the FA.2 veering away from him. Moving toward the scouts. "Lanoe—"

"I'm right where I want to be," Lanoe said. "Hold steady!"

Three hundred meters, and the scouts were hurtling toward Thom, their eyeballs locked on his fighter; two fifty and they weren't moving; he'd expected them to break away and take up new positions but they weren't moving—

Two hundred. Thom jostled his stick and opened his throttle, shooting away from the enemy ships. No lance of fire burst from those eyeballs to spear him, to bathe him in flame. The scouts didn't move, didn't deviate from their prior course.

He looked back over his shoulder and saw Lanoe falling behind. He brought up a rearview display so he could see what was happening.

Just in time to see Lanoe pass across the nose of one of the scouts, no more than five meters from a collision. The scout's cannon swung around to follow the FA.2. Thom knew Lanoe's vector field wouldn't protect him if the scout fired just then. The plasma would wash across Lanoe's canopy, hot enough to roast him inside his cockpit.

In the infrared the scout's cannon burned white hot. For a microsecond the heat level spiked until Thom's display couldn't even register its temperature.

He started to shout, to call Lanoe's name. But there was no time.

The scout fired, a long plume of dazzling plasma streaming out into the cold of space. If it so much as touched Lanoe, if it grazed him—

But it didn't.

Lanoe had pulled a rotary turn at the last possible moment. His FA.2 twisted around and the plasma missed him entirely as he shot between two of the scouts, leaning hard to one side so he didn't clip off his airfoils on their hulls.

"Now, kid," Lanoe shouted. "Light 'em up!"

The scouts had finally veered off their established course, swinging around in tight loops to get a better firing solution on Lanoe. All three of them were running hot now, ready to fire.

Thom brought up his weapons board and armed his PBWs. Before the board could even chime to tell him the guns were ready, he squeezed the trigger built into his control stick and blasted one of the scouts, his particle beam cutting through its thrusters like a kilometer-long knife. The tiny ship lost power and its eyeball lost containment. It erupted like a bomb, filling space with glowing debris.

Lanoe shot up and out of that mess, chunks of half-molten metal

426 **D. NOLAN CLARK**

bouncing off his vector field to go spinning off into nothingness. One of the scouts tried to follow him up but Lanoe turned to face it in a tight spin and blasted it to slag.

The third scout had swung around until Thom could see the glow of its thrusters. It took him a moment to realize that he was right behind it. He cut it to pieces with his PBWs and then, finally, exhaled. He hadn't even realized he'd been holding his breath until then.

"Good," Lanoe called. His FA.2 twisted around until he was facing Thom, canopy to canopy, no more than three hundred meters away. "We've got our answer."

Thom shook his head. He couldn't process that, couldn't worry about what Lanoe meant. On his tactical board he saw the interceptor had broken course and was making a long, ponderous turn, coming about to meet them. Its guns pulsed and fired even though it was well out of range. "We're not done yet," he said.

"Yes, we are," Lanoe said. "Don't bother with that one—he's too slow to chase us home." The FA.2 spun around until its nose pointed at Aruna and then Lanoe opened his throttle until his fighter shot off through space faster than anything had a right to. Thom didn't wait for the order to follow. He matched courses with Lanoe and punched for a burn. Behind his head he could hear his fusion engine roar as it came to life. His inertial sink grabbed him hard and very tight as his BR.9 accelerated and soon the interceptor dwindled behind him, disappearing back into the shadows.

Safe again.

Away from the fight. Away from the danger. Thom felt his whole body shake. His hands ached and he realized he'd been holding them tense the entire time, and they were just now relaxing.

———

"So much for negotiating," Ehta said, nodding to herself.

"What just happened?" Roan asked.

Ehta pointed at the display. Ships were indicated there as tiny dots with a lot of empty space between them. "Lanoe buzzed one of their scouts and it took a shot at him. That was the answer he was looking for. He and Thom blasted the scouts and then ran, exactly as planned."

"But—then—" Roan shook her head. "What does this mean?"

"It means the war's back on," Ehta said.

On the display the dots shifted position, though not in any meaningful way, really. Battlefield displays were like weather forecasts. You could see fronts building up, watch pressure increase, but it wasn't until the lightning flashed that you knew you had a real storm on your hands. It would be a long time before the display told her anything she wanted to know.

In the meantime she had to deal with the girl.

"They could have given the enemy more time to respond," Roan said. She chewed her lip like she wanted to bite it off. "We could have waited longer—"

"Nope," Ehta said. "It had to be this way."

"What do you mean? If there was a chance for peace, we should have taken it!"

Ehta sighed but there was part of her that was glad it had worked out this way. She'd never had much patience for diplomacy. War she understood; it was in her bones. "They know what a bad spot we're in. They're negotiating from a place of power, right? So the burden was on them to maintain a cease-fire. We have a lot more to lose. For all we know, the message they sent was just a trick. A way to buy more time so they could move their fleet closer to Niraya. Every hour we waited would have made our situation more desperate, and their position better. Lanoe had to test them, and they failed."

Admittedly, she thought, he didn't have to be quite so aggressive about it. The enemy scout might have fired on him just because it thought he intended to ram it. Given the number of pilots under his command a suicide attack was sheer stupidity, but the aliens wouldn't necessarily have seen it that way. They threw away their drones all the time.

She had flown in Lanoe's squadron long enough to know him,

a little. As much as anybody except Zhang probably did. Still, she had to wonder.

Had he even wanted the negotiations to succeed?

She looked at the dots on the display again. The enemy fleet looked a little more clumped to one side, maybe, but it could just have been random motion. If the fleet was turning toward Aruna, if Lanoe had drawn them into his trap, there was no immediate indication. Of course, fleets were always slow to react—it was one reason why cataphracts were so effective against them. A human fleet could take hours to change course as orders were passed down the chain of command, from one captain to another. The enemy, relying on computers more than people, should maneuver much more quickly. If the fleet was going to turn, it would do so soon, she thought.

On her display the dots continued to tell her nothing.

Roan turned away, as if she couldn't stand to look at the random scattering of pixels on the display. She paced back and forth across the floor of the tender, bouncing in the low gravity. Ehta tried to ignore her.

It wasn't going to happen.

"Is Thom okay?" Roan asked, looking out the tender's window as if there were something to see. "Is he...?"

Ehta pointed at two blue dots that were moving away from the enemy fleet at high velocity. "He's still alive," she said.

Chapter Twenty-Five

The blue giant star Balor was only six times as wide as Earth's sun, but it put out forty thousand times as much energy. No spacecraft could get even close to its surface without being obliterated instantaneously, reduced to very, very hot particles that would blow away like a puff of steam on its gale-force stellar wind.

Balor's wormhole throat stood off from the star only a few hundred thousand kilometers, far too close for comfort. Yet the star's gravity anchored a massive nexus of wormholes, connecting dozens of planets—including Earth. You could get almost anywhere in human space from Balor if you could survive the trip. It was just too convenient a nexus not to use.

The answer had been to deploy massive shields of Mylar, hundreds of kilometers across, in a stationary orbit between star and throat. Though thinner than paper the shields were coated with a substance that made them almost perfect mirrors, reflecting Balor's annihilating light harmlessly back toward the star.

Almost perfect. The shields absorbed a tiny fraction of the star's output—no mirror was ever one hundred percent reflective. Enough heat built up in the Mylar that microscopic holes were constantly burning their way through, letting that deadly light pass. The shields didn't so much smolder as evaporate, little by little, over time. They had to be patched or replaced every twenty-four hours or so—an operation that required a lot of expendable drones and a staggering amount of money.

The inhabitants of the Balor system could afford it. After all, they wrote their own budgets.

The BR.9's canopy turned solid black, opaque as it could get, yet still bluish-white light suffused the cockpit, drowning out every display, every board. The pilot kept his eyes clamped shut, which blocked out some more of the light. Still, he could just barely see the green pearl rotating in the corner of his vision.

"Unidentified cataphract-class fighter, you have entered a secure area," he was told. "If you attempt to maneuver we will open fire without further warning. If your weapons systems come online we will open fire without further warning. Maintain your current course and velocity or we will open fire without further warning."

"Oh, I wouldn't dream of doing otherwise," Maggs called back.

The light faded a little at a time as the BR.9 shot away from the—quite eponymous—blue star. Eventually Maggs could open his eyes and see that he was flanked on either side by a fighter escort. Z.XXs, in fact. Rather butch-looking cataphracts built specifically for dogfighting, with quad PBWs mounted around their cockpits and deflector baffles extending from their thruster cones like black crowns. The BR.9 would hardly be a match for even one of those ships, and Maggs knew perfectly well that the two he could see were backed up by hundreds more just like them, hiding nearby in the glare.

The system ahead of him was full of warships. Whole carrier groups cavorted in a belt of dust where once a planet might have spun, hundreds of giant ships engaged in constant war games, keeping themselves prepared for inevitable future wars.

Out past the belt lay a whole clutch of planets, though only one of them mattered, and even then not because of its own properties. Mag Mell was a super-earth, a chunk of solid iron and nickel much denser than humanity's cradle. Its heavy carbon dioxide atmosphere was thick enough that the surface was racked by constant storms. Its gravity was only one and a half times that of Earth, but that was beastly enough. Nobody ever went down there if they could help it.

Instead, they stayed up in the planet's artificial ring. From a distance the planet looked much like Saturn but when one approached more closely it became apparent that the ring wasn't made of shards of ice or dust. Instead it was formed of countless artificial worlds—stations and habitats and orbitals, some no bigger than luxury mansions, some that would dwarf the Hexus. Some of them spun to maintain their own interior gravity. Some were just empty shells, drydocks where new military vehicles could be constructed by endlessly toiling drones. Some of the elements of the ring were in themselves weapons of hellish power—cosmic ray guns, coherent energy weapons fueled by antimatter-matter explosions, particle beams that could cut moons in half.

Only one thing unified that vast collection of space junk, one symbol that appeared on the hull of every single man-made bit of it. The triple-headed eagle, of course. The logo, blazon, and flag of the Navy.

The ring, considered as a unity, was Navy General HQ. The Admiralty.

The grand beacon of human military might, the place where the highest-ranking officers in the service came to plan and scheme and debate strategy. Headquarters, marshaling yard, indomitable fortress. It was the closest thing Maggs had to a homeworld. It was the place he hated most in all the galaxy.

It was also, at the moment, the only place that was likely to take him in.

His escorts followed him all the way to the ring, keeping station no more than seven hundred meters on either side of him. He did not doubt they would make good on their threats if he tried anything. They must have pinged his cryptab by now and learned who he was, though—otherwise they would have blasted him out of space before he got within sighting distance of the Admiralty ring.

He was directed to set down on a docking hub in the ring's outermost band, a largely administrative sector. As he set his course for landing and let the BR.9 fly itself down he took a very deep, very pensive breath.

"I've really put my foot in it now. Haven't I, venerable father?" he said, careful not to broadcast the words to anyone who might be listening.

For once the voice in his head was silent.

The BR.9 came in for a perfect landing in a docking hub of one of the more secure orbitals. As the engine idled down, Maggs touched a key and let his cockpit flow back into the fuselage. He kept his hands visible, because a squad of marines had already gathered around him, ready to attack should he give them any reason to do so. There was no gravity in the docking hub but they floated with feet locked together and hands on their weapons, the free-fall equivalent of standing at attention. The message was clear. They could function equally well as an honor guard—or a firing squad—depending on what he did next.

He pinged the cryptab of their commanding officer. "Lieutenant," he said, "my name is Auster Maggs and I—"

"I know who you are," the lieutenant replied. Her golden hair was only a little longer than the stubble on Maggs's chin. Her eyes bored through him like cutting lasers. "What I don't know is why you're flying that cataphract."

"This old thing?" Maggs asked. He had not yet climbed out of his cockpit. He felt that doing so might send the wrong message. Not that he possessed any right messages to share at that particular moment.

"Are you aware," the marine lieutenant said, "that this vehicle was registered as having been stolen from general stores several weeks ago?"

Ah. He'd forgotten that Zhang hadn't secured the BR.9s through official channels. Bit of a complication, there. Of course, to one as quick as Maggs, complications could often be turned into opportunities.

"Well, of course I'm *aware* of that," Maggs told the woman. One of the great secrets of lying: Never admit you don't know what you're talking about. "Why do you think I brought it here? I took it back from the thief and now I'm returning it to its rightful owners, aren't I?"

The lieutenant was clearly not the kind of woman who enjoyed uncertainty. Her left eyelid twitched as she processed his words. "You recovered this vehicle from its unlawful possessor," she said.

"Yes."

"And you flew it here—to the Admiralty—to return it. Instead of just taking it to the nearest quartermaster," she went on.

"Yes," Maggs said. He hazarded a tiny closed-eyes nod as if to say, *Good, now you're getting it, dear.*

"You came to the Admiralty to—"

"It was on my way," he told her. "I have business here."

"What kind of business?" she asked. Doubtfully.

"I need to pay a social call," he said.

——➤≺——

Elder McRae had been lucky to avoid injury when the smelter spat out its molten metal. Others of the volunteers had not been so fortunate.

Two of them died—instantly, if that was any comfort—when a pylon they were dismantling collapsed on them. Even in Aruna's low gravity they hadn't been able to flee as countless pipes and tubes and pieces of alien machinery came tumbling down.

One engineer had a broken arm. He kept working, his suit keeping the injured limb pressed up tight against his side.

Two others were showing signs of radiation poisoning. They were expected to recover but they were sent back to the shuttles, where they could do nothing but lie on the floor, sweating and shivering at once. The elder took them food they couldn't keep down and swept up their hair when it fell out.

Minor injuries were legion. Bone bruises from improperly handling heavy loads, sprains, and simple fatigue took their toll. Many of the volunteers, stuffed into ill-fitting suits, chafed so badly they bled. They did their best not to complain, at least not on an open communications channel.

Cuts happened. Much of the debris in the alien facility had sharp edges. If they were sharp enough to cut through the thin material of the suits, they could gouge human flesh as well. Several of the engineers developed frostbite when their suits were punctured and the bitterly cold, choking air of Aruna touched their exposed skin.

Still they kept working. Still they kept at it, building the guns.

The elder understood little of the principles involved. She could see the pieces of the guns coming together, long skeletal tubes of cast metal that were then clad in a micron-thin layer of heat-resistant plastic. The firing chambers were far more complex, but built on a modular design that meant individual, simple components could be snapped together even by a layperson like herself.

She learned the gist of the guns' mechanisms by inference and from the terse answers the engineers gave to her infrequent questions. The tubes of course were the barrels of the guns, carefully designed but only so they wouldn't melt when they were fired. The ammunition was inert and simple as well, just large chunks of depleted uranium that was dense and heavy enough to survive being shot from the barrels at relativistic speed.

The firing chambers were the only parts of the guns that were at all complex. They were built with alternating layers of superconductors and superresistors that could be switched on and off with incredible speed, allowing the chamber to build up enormous electromagnetic potential. Inside the chambers the depleted uranium rounds would be given a massive static electric charge, negative in polarity. When the gun was fired, an even stronger negative charge would be introduced behind them, delivered through tightly wound capacitor loops. The rounds would be repelled by the new charge with incredible force, launched into space at a good fraction of the speed of light. There were not many things in the universe that could withstand their momentum once they were moving.

Four barrels were already complete. Engineer Derrow oversaw the construction of the firing chambers herself, shouting orders until she was hoarse. Four more barrels were almost finished, but it seemed there just wasn't enough depleted uranium on-site to make as many projectiles as M. Lanoe had requested. She sent her salvage parties farther and farther afield, deeper into the haunted ruins of the alien facility.

With her welding skills not currently in demand, the elder volunteered to go scouting with her Geiger counter. She spent long hours climbing over half-melted structures, poking her head inside enormous constructions like metal seed pods, watching the shadows, constantly, as if one of the alien landers might jump out at her at any moment. She knew the idea was absurd. She also knew that if one of them was still active, lying in wait under a pile of broken concrete or inside one of their massive factory buildings, there was no one around to help her.

Once she saw a fighter go streaking by overhead, too fast to make out any of its details. Long after it was gone her suit's computer picked up an image the fighter had transmitted, a surveying map of the local area with radiation sources marked in red. It seemed M. Zhang knew how badly they needed more ammunition and was helping out by scouting from the air.

With the pilot's help, the elder soon found a slag pile that chattered angrily when she waved her Geiger counter over it. There was far more depleted uranium there than she could hope to carry by herself and she climbed up on top of a ridge—what had once been a cluster of pipes until they all melted together—and tried to send a signal back to base camp.

Below her, about half a kilometer away, she saw a suited figure loping across the rocky soil. She waved at them and they turned and came toward her. They climbed up the ruined pipes with leaping bounds that made her think they must be very young. One missed step and they could seriously injure themselves.

She started to call out, to warn them—but then she saw through the figure's helmet and realized who it was.

"Elder," Roan said. "I'm glad I found you."

"What are you doing here?" the elder asked.

"I was helping Ensign Ehta set up a ground control station, over at the tender. We finished that job and then she told me I was annoying her and I should go see if I could help the engineers."

"And you just happened to run into me, so far from the base camp?"

The girl had the decency to look embarrassed. "I guess I came looking for you."

"You came looking for me," the elder repeated. "Why?"

"I hoped we could talk," the girl replied.

It took all of the elder's decades of training and discipline not to sigh.

⤙⤚

They couldn't find any reason to arrest Maggs on the spot, so they had to just let him go. They impounded the fighter, of course, perhaps thinking that losing the BR.9 limited his mobility and kept him from running away.

For the moment, at least, he intended on staying put. The bit about the social call, deliciously snide as it might have been presented, was no ruse.

He took a ferry inward across the ring, heading toward the sector known locally as Officers' Row. The orbitals there were built a little better than the rest, occasionally showing a token effort at ornamentation and even style—though that tended to run to triple-headed eagle motifs and patriotic murals. In the very midst of the sector was a large habitat called Fiddler's Green, a massive foamcrete wheel with an ancient name and gilt decorations on all its fittings.

Nearly half a kilometer in diameter, the wheel spun endlessly to generate a convincing semblance of Earth standard gravity. Its inner surface was lined with sumptuous green parkland and low stone buildings, artfully crumbling as if they were subject to actual weather. A vast greenhouse roof stretched over it all, transparent to visible light. One could actually see the stars if one looked straight up through that carbonglas ceiling.

Of course, because the whole thing rotated at speed, the stars always looked as if they were streaking past, not unlike an endless meteorite display. The designers of the place suggested this wild gyre added to the ambience. On his many visits here, Maggs had always found it made him feel a bit ill if he looked too long.

He docked at the hub of the wheel, then took an elevator down to the inner surface. The moment he stepped out into the floor-level lobby, he pitched forward and nearly fell right on his face.

He'd forgotten what gravity could do to you, when you had a broken leg.

Drones descended on him instantly to help him up and offer medical assistance. They scanned his leg and sent a call to the nearest hospital—of which there were many on the Green—but he waved them away and cautiously, slowly, put weight back on the leg.

His suit compensated for the broken bones, stiffening like a cast around the fractures and giving him added support where he needed it. A white pearl in the corner of his vision took the pain away, and he could walk again. He had no intention of arriving at his destination on a stretcher.

Outside the lobby, paths stretched away in many directions, winding through low, rounded hills covered in lush grass. He could hear fountains nearby, and string music playing at a tasteful volume. Ahead of him lay an endless curving landscape of pergolas and gazebos and stately gray stone buildings. The light level had been adjusted so that it felt like late afternoon, just before dinnertime. Soon the glass ceiling overhead would turn a shade more opaque, favoring light in the pinker part of the spectrum, to simulate dusk. It was all so perfectly civilized, if a tad bourgeois for his tastes.

He struck out on foot, heading antispinward. People walked everywhere in the Green. One was expected to enjoy a healthy level of exercise there—at least, until your legs wouldn't carry you anymore.

Fiddler's Green was perhaps the most expensive and certainly the most highly decorated (in the military sense) nursing home in human space. It was where old admirals went to slowly die. Staff admirals, anyway. Field officers didn't tend to last long enough to make use of the place.

As he walked he nodded at the people he passed by, mostly old men with white hair—an affectation, but a socially required one—and women in dresses with high collars that had been fashionable fifty years ago. Almost all of them turned their faces away when they saw him, but he didn't let it bother him.

Paper tigers, the lot, his father's voice said in his head. *Brandish a dueling pistol around here, watch 'em scatter like starlings.*

Maggs had to admit the idea had its attractions. The men and women he passed had spent their careers issuing orders that sent braver officers to their deaths, all from the safety of wood-paneled offices on staff ships light-years away from any actual fighting. They could ping each other's cryptabs all day long and never see an actual Blue Star.

By the time he'd reached his destination he had a nasty sneer on his face. He took the time to switch it out for a warm smile. Then he took a deep breath and stepped inside a low stone building constructed to look like an ancient Greek arcade. As his eyes adjusted to the dimmer light of the place, a drone waiter handed him a flute of something more fruity than alcoholic.

A thick knot of people reclined at the center of the space, some of them less than a hundred years old, though of course it could be hard to tell. Dress suits and actual cloth uniforms—unseen in the field since the Century War—on the men, brocade dresses and long shiny boots on the women. They chuckled at each other's jokes and nodded gravely when someone broke into an old, oft-heard war story, all while feasting on small morsels of food from silver platters. Drones made sure their glasses were always full.

Cocktail hour never ended in Fiddler's Green. There were parties like this going on all over the wheel, filled with the human wreckage of centuries of warfare. Not that one could tell from the look of them that any of these people were veterans.

Well, not all of them were.

Halfway across the broad arcade, perched on a long divan, sat a woman in a rather louche gown—something much closer to modern fashions—slit high up one leg and with a black lace ruff that resembled, to an artful degree, the ring collar of a suit. Ringlets of blue-washed hair framed a face of alabaster and laughing eyes tinted the exact shade of a Blue Star. Other than the color of her hair she looked about seventeen, the same age she'd been when she first met her famous husband.

White-hairs simpered and knelt around her. She was holding court, as usual. The center of attention—the queen bee. She hadn't changed in the slightest since the last time Maggs had been here.

Enough to make a horse kick its way right through the stable wall, Dear Old Dad's voice said. *Why, Maggsy, when I first laid eyes on her—*

To drown out the unwelcome words Maggs strolled right up to her and clicked his heels together.

"Dearest heart!" she exclaimed, clutching her hands over her bosom. "You've come to see me again! How wonderful!"

The courtiers around her didn't applaud, though some of them looked like they were trying to decide if they should. The prodigal returned and all that.

"Hello, Mother," he said.

\~\~*\~\~

They found some sheeting in the alien ruins. It wasn't exactly cloth, and it definitely wasn't plastic. Thin veins of graphite ran through it like the patterns of circuitry or perhaps like blood vessels. It didn't matter what its purpose had been when the drones made it—it blocked radiation and that was all Elder McRae cared about.

Between the two of them they managed to maneuver several dozen chunks of depleted uranium onto the sheeting, then roll it up like a carpet so they could carry it safely.

While they worked, they talked. That had been the deal she struck with Roan. In exchange for the girl's help moving the depleted uranium back to the base camp, the elder had to hear her former acolyte out.

"First off," Roan said, "I'm sorry. I know that when I stole that video from you, I put you in a bad spot."

The elder said nothing. The girl had clearly thought carefully about what she was going to say. She would let Roan finish before responding.

"I know the Retreat is supposed to be above politics. I also know that isn't true. You're going to lose a lot of influence with the other elders after what happened. If you hadn't volunteered to come out here, I think they might have stripped you of your rank, even. I didn't want that, I promise. I didn't want to hurt you—I didn't want to hurt anyone. I just thought it was the right thing to do."

"All right," the elder replied.

"All right? That's all?"

Elder McRae didn't shrug. That might have shifted the mass of the rocks rolled up in their burden, and made it more difficult for them to carry. "It's clear to me now, Roan, that you weren't suited to be a member of the faith."

"I—what?"

"If you were, you would have listened more to our teachings. You would know that this apology isn't necessary, or desired. You followed your own path. In the end it turned out your path moved us forward. It got the people behind the defense of Niraya, and it led to us both being here."

"So... I did the right thing?" Roan asked.

"Had you paid more attention," the elder went on, "you would know there is no such thing. The path you chose for us was the one that brought us here. That's all. A different path would have led to different outcomes. The hardest part of our teaching, the truth that separates aspirants from elders, is this: You must choose a path, but you will never know if your path was the best possible one. The universe doesn't work that way."

"But... but..." Roan sputtered and shook her head. "The people had to know!"

"I think I understand why you felt the need to have this conversation," the elder told her. "You don't wish to apologize to me. You want me to tell you that you did the right thing. That you saw more clearly than I did."

"No," Roan insisted. "This isn't about me being better than you—"

"Perhaps you want absolution, then? I'm sorry, Roan. I can't forgive you. I don't have that capacity. No one does. You did what you chose to do. Whatever the consequences of that choice may be, they're yours to live with."

"I just wanted to save Niraya."

"Perhaps you did. Perhaps not. What if we fail here? If the pilots can't turn back the enemy, and we all die? Will it matter then, what your intentions were?"

"Hellfire!" Roan nearly dropped the bundle of rocks. "Would it really be that hard for you to say I did the right thing?"

"No," the elder said. "It would just mean turning my back on everything I believe in."

She might have said more but they had crested a low ridge and now they could see down into the camp where the engineers were working on the guns. Space-suited figures moved in knots down there, struggling with huge assemblies of girders and electronic components. Engineer Derrow raced around them in her pipe-work rover, pointing here and there, the light at her throat flashing as she gave orders. The tempo of the work had increased considerably.

"What's going on down there?" Roan asked.

"Perhaps we should find out," the elder told her, and started down the ridge.

"It's wonderful to see you, Maggsy," his mother said. Her smile was very warm and bright. It ought to be—it had been expensive enough. They were out for a walk in the manicured gardens of the Green, just a little past dark. A drone lit their way so they didn't stumble on the grass. Another floated beside her, connected to her wrist by two lengths of tubing. It was filtering her blood, something that had to be done every day now. Staying as youthful as she appeared without swapping bodies took a certain amount of maintenance. "I hesitate to even ask, but..."

"I don't have any money for you," he told her. He'd long grown out of the decorous way some children spoke to their mothers. Their relationship had changed the first time she'd asked him to pay off her debts.

To her credit, she did not attempt to hide her disappointment. Her smile evaporated like spilled coolant off an airfoil and she took a meaningful step away from him. "I see."

"I came quite close," Maggs said. "Twice, in fact. Once I literally had terraforming chits in my tight little hand."

"Are those valuable?" his mother asked.

"Rather." He had trouble looking at her, just then.

He did not enjoy watching her red blood flow in and out of those tubes. Not out of any squeamishness, of course. Simply because he knew how much those treatments cost.

"You might be interested to know," he explained, "that both times I was foiled by none other than Aleister Lanoe. The famous pilot."

"Oh, yes, I remember him, from when he flew for your father." She leaned close and grasped his arm. "Bit working class, on the whole, but he did look rather dashing in the videos. They would trot him out whenever we won some major new offensive. They needed a young man to encourage recruiting. Of course, it was the Admiral who won the wars. He never did get the recognition he deserved."

A fighting man cares not for medals and parades, Dear Old Dad said inside Maggs's head. *Though I'll admit I never turned either down.*

"And now it takes positively all of my energy just to remind people who your father was. Around here admirals might be ten a penny, but your papa was something special. Don't you want people to remember that?"

"Of course I do," Maggs said, a bit more snappish than he liked. He felt her stiffen beside him. "You know I spend every waking minute trying to help with your work."

The wives of admirals were expected to be accomplished for themselves—though only in certain fields. If they were award-winning scientists, say, or yacht racers, or musicians, that was all well and good. Unfortunately Guennifer Maggs had possessed none of those talents. Her particular skills had mostly revolved around throwing delightfully wild parties and losing money in casinos.

Now she was engaged full-time in maintaining the family honor. A fact she never let Maggs forget.

"I really do need that money, child. You can't imagine how expensive it is, just keeping up appearances."

"I know, Mother," Maggs said.

"Living expenses keep going up and up and up. And one can only rely on creditors for so long. Oh, for the days when Earth would shower its victorious officers with little gifts. How marvelous that was! But he's dead now, and you're not quite in a position to earn encomia. Working in an office, as you do."

"I did my bit," Maggs insisted. More than his bit, in fact. He'd draped himself in glory back when he could afford to be a pilot, not a poly liaison. He'd only given up the pilot's life to support his mother's largesse.

"If I default now, it'll be such a scandal," his mother implored. "It'll tarnish the name of Maggs forever. You can't possibly want that."

"No, of course not—"

"Then we must have some money," she said, patting his arm.

"I suppose you could get a job," he told her.

She stopped walking and he was forced to do the same or drag her off her feet. The air around them turned frigid and overhead the stars whirled crazily in their courses.

"Just a bit of a joke," he assured her. "Don't worry, Mother. I'll find some way to get the money."

"For your father's sake, not mine," she said, a trace of steel in her voice. "You know I'd give up all this," she said with a little exhausted wave of her free hand to take in the Green, the social life of the Admiralty, the endless medical treatments, "if it wouldn't hurt his name."

"I know, I know. I'm so very sorry to have failed you again,"

Maggs said. Saying it made him feel like he'd bitten into a rotten pear. "I was sidetracked, I'm afraid. Press-ganged into a spot of fighting I had no interest in. Lanoe forced me to come along on a doomed jaunt for honor in some backwater system, wasting my time and yours. He had us fighting aliens, of all things."

"Aliens!"

"Yes, I know it sounds ludicrous. I don't mind saying, though— I was half-convinced they were real by the time I got away."

"Aliens," she said again, with a pretty little laugh. "You sound just like your uncle Wallys, don't you just. Do you remember how he would go on so, with his wild theories and funny little surmises?"

"Wallys? Was he the one who shot one of our servants for spilling soup?" Maggs's memory of his childhood was hazy now, full of bright colors and loud noises but not much context. Only a few events stood out.

"No, that was Auntie Helminthus. She's dead now, I've heard. Poisoned by a disgruntled ex-lover. Wallys, now—he was the one who gave you your rare coin collection for your fourteenth birthday. The collection you looked at once and then put in storage."

Maggs sighed. "I wonder what became of those coins," he mused. Of course he knew perfectly well. Some of them had been valuable.

"Wallys was of a sort you just don't see anymore. An officer and a scholar—he had a degree from some university back on Earth, a rather distinguished one. Full of knowledge, and he always wanted to talk about abstruse things. I remember one time he caught me at the end of a lovely ball, out on a balcony where I'd gone to take the air. I thought he was going to try to seduce me. Well, such things happen. Instead he talked my ear off about lost wormholes and ghost fleets and the like. I'm sure there was something in there about aliens, as well. I couldn't break away, of course, that would have been terribly rude, but I swear that by five minutes in, my brain had quite shut down and he might as well have been talking about dog breeding, for all I actually heard." She smiled at the memory, which meant the encounter must have happened back when his father was still alive. Back when an invitation to one of her parties was a sign that someone was about to get promoted. Now her invitations were just accepted pro forma by those who couldn't think of a good excuse.

"For all that he was a terrible boor," she said, "and he was, Wallys was a good friend to us. Not really your uncle, of course. Your father had no siblings, but Wallys was like a right-hand man to the Admiral. Lovely mustache as well. He kept it waxed."

Maggs felt a quite familiar sensation then, a certain rippling chill down his spine.

The feeling he always got when a scheme occurred to him.

"Uncle Wallys," he said. "He's not still alive, is he?" He reached for his wrist display, intending to check the old man's service record. "Do you have a way to get in touch with him?"

⟶⟵

When the elder and Roan arrived back at the main camp the barrels of the guns were already standing up on end, like skeletal fingers clawing their way out of the icy soil. Engineers and volunteer workers swarmed around them, sparks flying from welding torches, gun components being tossed back and forth so they could be installed.

The pace of the work had been feverish before. Now it looked like sheer chaos, though the elder knew it was all being done in the most efficient way, every step overseen by Engineer Derrow as she drove in circles around them in her little rover.

A call came in for Roan, from the tender where Ensign Ehta had set up her ground control station. The two of them dropped off their load of depleted uranium and parted ways. The elder ran to meet her supervisor, to find out what work she should be doing next. She didn't even have a chance to ask what had changed, why the pace had picked up so much, as she helped grind and polish the projectiles, making them so perfectly smooth they looked like drops of mercury. When the rounds were fired from the guns even the slightest imperfection in their shape might drag them off course by hundreds of kilometers, missing the enemy entirely. They had to be polished down to a tolerance of microns, which meant constant adjustments and calibrations. No time for questions.

She picked up a little information anyway, just by listening. Derrow and her core group of engineers didn't bother to censor themselves as they worked and while most of their conversation was technical to the point of being arcane, the occasional word registered. Soon the elder knew that it was true, that something major had changed.

The enemy fleet had started its turn. Changed course toward Aruna.

M. Lanoe's gambit must have succeeded. He would get the battle he wanted—the fight that could save or doom everyone back on Niraya.

Chapter Twenty-Six

Lanoe forced himself not to grunt in impatience as Thom fumbled with his forward thrusters and threw his BR.9 into a flat spin. The kid cursed but straightened himself out easily enough.

"Don't be afraid to lean on your positioning jets," he told Thom. "They can take the strain. Fighters spend half their time flying backward, so you need to get used to this."

The two of them were edging away from a small cloud of interceptors and scouts that kept threatening to come into attack range. Exactly what he wanted—Lanoe's plan was to draw the enemy after them, to force the fleet to commit to its turn. So instead of burning hard for home, the two fighters were easing their way back toward Aruna with their noses pointed outward at the fleet.

"This is ridiculous," Thom complained. "I touch the stick to the left and I go spinning off to the right."

"You ever go ice skating?" Lanoe asked. "It's just like skating backward. Pretend your stick is on the other side of a mirror."

"I have no idea what you're talking about," Thom insisted. The kid was right on the edge of panic. "Lanoe—there must be fifty of them out there. Fifty!"

Lanoe couldn't help but laugh. "You haven't seen anything yet," he told the kid. "If those swarmships deploy, you'll have ten times that many on you." All the same he checked his sensors and did a quick count. There were in fact only thirty-nine enemy ships in the local volume, about evenly divided between interceptors and scouts. It would seem like plenty if they actually engaged, but for the moment nobody had fired a shot.

"Why haven't they deployed yet?" Thom asked. "They could swamp us anytime they wanted."

"The enemy doesn't think like us," Lanoe said. "They're using drones. They don't care if a couple of their ships are killed—they have plenty more, and they're cheap to replace. They don't think the two of us are a real threat."

"I'm inclined to agree," Thom told him.

Lanoe ignored the negativity. "As long as we appear to be retreating, they'll keep thinking that way. I don't think they'll really deploy until they're close enough to attack Aruna. I'm counting on it, in fact."

"The guns," Thom said.

"Sure," Lanoe said. "The guns are powerful, our strongest weapon, but they fire a lot slower than our PBWs. If the swarms deploy too far out, the guns will take forever to pick off individual scouts—way too long to be helpful. If we can keep the swarmships intact, though, the guns can blast them with one or two shots and save us a hell of a lot of trouble. Watch out for that interceptor on your left—your left!—do *not* let it get behind you."

"Its guns are heating up," Thom pointed out.

"Yeah, looks like they're tired of chasing us. They want a kill. Time to start playing for real stakes—get your weapons board up, so you're ready to fight. Whatever happens, though, stay on course for Aruna. Maneuver as much as you need to, but always keep your tail pointed toward home, and don't let them get behind you."

"You already said that."

"It bore repeating," Lanoe called back.

"Good luck," Valk said.

"You, too," Zhang replied.

The two of them had been flying in close formation, hidden inside the thin ring of dust circling Garuda. Zhang's BR.9 broke off, dodging around house-size chunks of rock and burning hard to circle around the enemy fleet. He watched her go for a moment, then plotted his own course.

The burn hurt, of course—his bones ached inside his suit as he was pressed back against his seat. His inertial sink absorbed a lot of that energy but it couldn't get it all. His course carried him in the opposite direction that Zhang had taken, looping around the banded atmosphere of the ice giant, so close in he could hear stray molecules of hydrogen hiss against his canopy. He let the planet's gravity pull him around in a broad slingshot curve that flung him at the left flank of the enemy fleet, still a million kilometers away.

The plan was for Valk and Zhang to take up position on either side of the enemy, picking off any scouts or interceptors that strayed from the main body of the fleet. They weren't supposed to engage directly, just corral the enemy to keep their formation nice and tight.

It made a better target for the guns that way.

With the gravity assist from the giant it wasn't long before he saw enemy ships. Just a couple of scouts, riding ten thousand kilometers out from the fleet. Pickets, set there to screen against flanking attacks. They had no support from interceptors and the nearest swarmship was too far away to send reinforcements in any kind of timely fashion.

He had plenty of time to line up his shots. The scouts didn't even seem to notice him until he was upon them, flashing right through the center of their formation, PBWs firing left and right and up and down. He cut two scouts in half before they even had a chance to maneuver. A third wheeled around on him and he blasted apart its eyeball gun. It went up like a blossoming rose of destruction, its stored plasma expanding outward in a bright red fireball. Two more scouts came screaming down at him before the explosion had even faded. He spun around and caught one of them with a direct hit, then maneuvered hard to get out of the way as the second one breathed fire, its plasma blast missing him by only a few meters.

Valk kicked out with his maneuvering jets and turned his nose to face the last scout. In the infrared he could see its eyeball glowing hot, ready for another blast. He burned backward to get clear, then cut through its skeletal frame with a raking salvo of PBW fire. Its eyeball spun away from its severed thruster. Cut off from its power plant, the eyeball lost containment of its stored plasma but instead of exploding, this one just melted, its metal hull swelling and changing shape then falling back to form a rough, amorphous ball of slag.

He reached out for his comms panel. "In position," he signaled to Lanoe.

"Same here," Zhang called back.

On his display he saw Lanoe and Thom racing backward, away from the oncoming fleet, taking the occasional potshot but not engaging the enemy in any real sense. The kid was flying messy, his tail all over the place, but he was hanging in there. "Received," Lanoe called. Then he and Thom broke left and right, burning hard away from the enemy—they'd just been toying with them before. Now their job was to get out of the way.

"Engineer Derrow," Lanoe announced, "you may fire at will."

—————

Lanoe burned hard to get away from an interceptor that had caught his scent. No point in engaging the thing just then—he couldn't take it down with just his PBWs, and he couldn't spare a disruptor round. He needed all of those for the queenship, if he actually got a chance to make a run at the thing.

It hung there in his view like a planet, a dull grayish black this far from the system's sun. Its vast maw was darker still, a hole cut out of space. Ahead of it the swarmships hung like huge needles, all of them pointed right at his FA.2.

"Lanoe, I've got scouts on my tail," Thom called, sounding panicked.

The old pilot gritted his teeth. He fought back the urge to go racing over to help Thom—the kid needed to stand on his own now. "Get away from them if you can," he called back. "Give the gunners a chance to—"

He didn't get to finish his thought. The first of Derrow's projectiles came rocketing past him just then, maybe ten kilometers away but moving far too fast for him to see it at all. Instead he felt the way it warped space, a weird tug that pulled at his bones and his teeth.

He brought up a tactical display and traced its path, arrow-straight as it tore through space. Before the display could even refresh he slammed one hand against the console in front of him. For all its speed, for all its precision, the round was going to miss the entire fleet. It would pass right through them and head off into interstellar space, at half the speed of light.

They were still most of a million kilometers out from Aruna. Even the best computers would have trouble hitting a moving target at that distance. But he needed a hit, he needed to thin out those swarmships, or they were all dead. He—

Another shot made his head buzz. Then a third, close on its heels. His display lit up with their tracks, glowing orange lines like lasers fired across his field of view. He looked up and saw one strike the queenship, well clear of the maw. It brought up a long plume of dust from the surface and left a new crater there, but the queenship didn't so much as vibrate with the impact.

The third one hit a swarmship. Just a grazing blow, raking along the side of the alien vessel. Its initial impact looked almost comically pathetic, as it tore a hole through an interceptor near the nose of the swarmship and disappeared. The projectile kept moving, though, too energetic to be stopped by mere metal. It obliterated the scout moored behind the interceptor—and the one behind that. As it traveled it built up a bow wave of vaporized metal in front of it and no alien ship could withstand that heat. Scouts and interceptors exploded, their fuel and plasma adding to the cascade of explosions. The swarmship came apart in pieces, all of them glaring white in Lanoe's infrared display. A handful of small craft managed to deploy before the swarmship died, but the vast majority were slagged before they could launch. Light and heat and burning debris showered the survivors, sending them twisting away on desperate trajectories that couldn't save them—they just couldn't get clear in time.

"Holy hell!" Valk shouted, and whooped for joy.

More rounds were incoming from Aruna, most of them failing to connect, but a second swarmship was destroyed even faster and more violently than the first. A third was clipped by an errant round that still left it crumpled and half-dead. Zhang and Thom joined in with the chorus of excited yelling until Lanoe had to turn down the volume on his speakers.

He wished he could join in. It would be good to get in a whoop or two of his own. There was only one problem—he saw what the others must have missed.

The aliens weren't stupid. As soon as the first swarmship was destroyed, they'd already begun to react. The remaining swarmships seemed to bubble and grow as they deployed their scouts and interceptors as fast as they could, sending out small craft in a hundred directions, all of them burning hard to get away from the debris of their wrecked brethren.

The guns on Aruna would be useless against the smaller ships— they were too maneuverable, too small in cross section for proper targeting. Once they deployed, they were Lanoe's problem.

———

"Did we—" Thom sounded like he was trying to catch his breath. "Did we just start the battle?"

"Started an hour ago, kid," Valk told him. "You must've blinked and missed it." He understood what Thom must be feeling, though. In every battle Valk had ever fought it was the same way. A whole lot of maneuvering and not engaging and getting into just the right position. When the shooting actually started, you were usually too busy planning your next trajectory to notice.

You could win or lose a battle in those first few seconds when one side didn't realize the fighting had started in earnest. This time it looked like they had the drop on the aliens. The swarmships were deploying as fast as they could, but that just meant they suddenly had ten times as many ships in the same small volume of space. The interceptors and scouts scattered without taking up anything like formations, simply trying to get away from the incoming projectiles. As more and more ships deployed behind them they clumped up in thick clouds of metal, sometimes colliding with each other. Meanwhile whole sections of the volume were left empty and undefended.

Valk swooped down on a lone interceptor that had strayed too far from the chaos. He couldn't take it out with a disruptor—orders were orders, he had to save those for the queenship—but he raked its nose with PBW fire and made it turn to face him. Its guns heated up and it burned to close with him but he pulled a tight loop over its top and got around behind it, the glow of its thrusters bright in his canopy. It tried to turn its guns to target him but they weren't designed to take on a threat from behind. Before it could open fire he put a salvo across its thruster cones, shredding them like tissue paper. Maybe he couldn't kill the thing with PBWs alone, but if he could keep it from maneuvering it was effectively out of the battle.

He burned away from the crippled enemy, looking for his next target. A whole squadron of scouts showed on his display and he rushed to meet them. They'd deployed from their swarmship in poor order and were trying desperately to construct a formation but they kept getting in each other's way. They didn't even seem to see him as he approached, and he started computing a fire pattern in his head when he noticed what lay beyond them.

Nothing.

Past the clot of small ships, there was nothing but empty space between Valk and the queenship. He had a clear run at the thing.

⤙⤚

"Stick to me and watch my six," Lanoe told Thom. "Just keep them off me as best you can." The two of them were deep in a disorganized cloud of ships, scouts, and interceptors so thick he could barely see any stars between them. He cut apart a scout in front of him, then craned his neck back to see two interceptors collide above his canopy, debris from the resultant explosion pattering off his vector field. "Keep shooting, even if you can't get kills—don't give them a chance to regroup."

"You've got scouts on your...your ten," Thom said. "Lanoe—look out!"

A projectile from Aruna came streaking past, so close its space-bending wake pulled Lanoe forward against his restraints. The metal sphere tore through a pair of scouts before rocketing past the queenship and out into the void.

Lanoe ignored it—if one of those rounds hit him it would happen so fast he wouldn't have time to know he was dead. He rolled over on his side as a scout breathed fire across his airfoils, then he twisted around and dove for a thick knot of enemy ships below him. Thom mirrored his maneuvers flawlessly, the kid's PBWs stitching a line of tiny craters across the skin of an interceptor.

Dead ahead, through his canopy Lanoe could see a swarmship deploying, a boiling cloud of drones desperately trying to launch before they were destroyed. Another shot from the guns tore through that cloud, lighting it up from the inside with flashes of red and bursts of lightning. Most of the alien ships came away intact, but he could see the scars on their hulls from a thousand small collisions, places where debris had torn loose gun mounts or dug deep into armor.

"Zhang, report," he said.

"Heavy resistance on my flank," she said. He could hear collision alarms warbling in her cockpit. "I can't keep 'em corralled for long. Lanoe—this chaos is working to our advantage right now, but if they get a chance to draw up proper formations—"

"Understood," he told her. The only chance they had was to keep the enemy dancing. The aliens outnumbered them a hundred to one—if they got organized, if they came at the human pilots with proper tactics, this battle would be over in minutes.

They needed a decisive strike now, while the enemy was still off balance. He twisted his head around, looking for the queenship. He almost missed it, hidden behind a welter of scouts and interceptors and the slagged remains of a dead swarmship. There must be a hundred drones between him and the queen.

Lanoe had never believed in false modesty. He knew his own capacities—and he knew he could punch through that mess. The aliens were too disorganized to stop him if he moved fast enough. He would take some hits, and there was no guarantee he would survive the run, but he could do it. He could cut his way through and drop every one of his disruptors down the queenship's maw. He could do it.

There was only one problem—Thom couldn't.

If he dragged the kid along with him on his suicide mission, Thom would be dead before they got halfway there. The kid just didn't have the skills to dodge enemy fire. Yet if Lanoe left Thom behind, if he went for the glory himself, he'd be abandoning Thom in the middle of the thickest action. Either way he would be signing the kid's death warrant.

He gritted his teeth. Reminded himself he was the commander. That he had made decisions like that before, and never hesitated.

Then a green pearl started spinning in the corner of his vision. He flicked his eyes across it to open a channel.

"I've got a clear run," Valk told him. "I can hit that thing right now."

Lanoe felt a cold wash of relief run down his spine.

"Do it," he said.

Chapter Twenty-Seven

Every time the guns fired, Roan felt like a zipper was being ripped open in her head. She kept trying to clamp her hands over her ears, forgetting that she had her helmet up. She tried just to stay on her feet and avoid touching anything metallic. Snakes of crackling static electricity writhed across the cables and junction boxes that crowded the ground of the base camp as power flowed from the tender's fusion reactor into the eight skeletal towers that pointed at the distant enemy.

The projectiles tore apart the sky as they launched from their barrels at half the speed of light. Blue lightning traced their path as they ionized the atmosphere of Aruna, lingering in the upper air long after they were gone. The light left afterimages floating in her vision.

"Number six, you're running hot," Engineer Derrow called. She stood up in her rover and pointed at the gun. "Stand down for repair." The energies surging through the guns were enough to melt vital components, enough to tear them to pieces if they weren't constantly maintained. Crews of engineers worked endlessly, stripping out fused superconductor loops and checking circuits to make sure they didn't misfire.

Other crews carried the heavy projectiles from the main store and loaded them into the firing chambers, as fast as they could manage. It was bizarre to think that for all the technology that had

gone into constructing the guns, they were still loaded by hand.
Roan caught sight of Elder McRae among the loaders, and considered running over to help. Then the guns fired again and her brain
quivered inside her skull and she decided instead to duck back
inside the tender. Maybe Ensign Ehta needed her.

In the spacecraft's wardroom a massive display of the battle
flickered in the air. The queenship was a rough sphere at the center
of it all, with the swarmships hanging before it at seemingly random angles. Smaller ships were represented by individual pixels.
There were so many of them they seemed to coruscate, as if they
were shimmering in and out of existence. Enemy craft were picked
out in white, while the human pilots were dots of blue, though the
battle area was such a chaotic jumble Roan kept losing track of the
blue pixels as they disappeared inside clouds of white.

"Zhang's in deep," Ehta said, moving her gloved hand through
the display, as if she could wave aside alien drones like gnats.
"Lanoe and Thom are holding their own." She looked pointedly at
Roan. "I thought you'd want to know."

Roan refused to blush. She had a right to be worried. "Where is
he?" she asked.

"Here." Ehta pointed at a pair of blue dots right in the middle
of the battle. They wove and swung around thick formations of
white, matching each other's maneuvers as if they were tethered
together. "He's alive, okay? So maybe we can get back to work?"

Not that there was much for them to do. The purpose of the
ground control station was to model the battle, keeping track of all
the individual ships—their position and speed. With that data the
tender's computers could build up predictions of how the enemy
would act, where they would build up formations, and where they
would leave weak spots in their strategy. Weak spots Lanoe and his
pilots might be able to exploit.

It was mostly an automated process, though Ehta was keeping
a very close watch on the data as it emerged, getting a feel for the
battle. Looking for places where the pilots needed to strike, and
when they needed to disengage so they didn't get overrun.

"Zhang can't keep this up much longer," Ehta said, pointing at one flank of the battle area. "Lanoe wants her to keep the enemy contained, but she's all alone out there. That kind of sheepdogging needs at least two fighters, one to herd and one to cut out strays. If Valk could get over there and help, maybe, but he…"

The Ensign trailed off as she studied the display.

"What is it?" Roan asked.

"Valk. Go for it, you crazy bastard," Ehta whispered.

Valk reached over to a virtual panel by his left hand and adjusted a control. Music swelled to fill his cockpit, a loud, driving beat to push every thought out of his head. If this was it, if he was going to die here, at least his death would have a good soundtrack.

He flipped over on his back to avoid a blast of plasma fire, cutting a scout in half almost without thinking about it. Looped around a bewildered interceptor and burned on past it before it could start shooting at him. Up ahead lay the remains of a dead swarmship, a vast wall of metal curled and bent by destruction. He bobbed over it at the last possible second. A scout had been chasing him at full speed, but it wasn't as maneuverable as his BR.9 and it plowed into the dead swarmship in a burst of flame.

Up ahead there was nothing but clear space—and the queenship. It filled up half of his canopy, a landscape of shadow-filled craters and jagged rills. It felt exactly like he was coming in for a landing on a desolate moon.

His boards showed half a dozen drones curving in to meet him, burning hard to catch him before he could reach his target. None of them would beat him there. He dropped lower and lower toward the surface of the queenship, a virtual altimeter pinned to the corner of his heads-up display. Ten kilometers up. Nine.

He poured on the speed as if he planned to smash right into the side of the queenship and the numbers blurred. At the last moment, barely fifty meters over the surface, he pulled back hard on his stick and broke out of his dive. The ground below him—he couldn't think of it any other way—turned to a gray blur as he skimmed over the surface, barely clearing a high ridge.

He'd forgotten how exhilarating contour-tracing could be. He cut left to avoid a hill, then dropped into the darkness of a crater and raced across its bottom so low he pulled up a plume of dust in his wake.

All this high-speed maneuvering hurt like hell, of course. The white pearl in the corner of his vision positively throbbed as it begged him to accept its offer of painkillers. He almost laughed as he dismissed the pearl. He'd spent seventeen years grunting his way through the pain. He wasn't about to start drugging himself up now.

He eased back on his stick and shot up out of the crater, over its lip and across a wide expanse of smooth rock beyond. His boards chimed and flashed red lights at him. At first he ignored them, assuming they were just ground avoidance alarms. A display opened automatically, though, and showed him what the BR.9 had been trying to tell him. He had company.

Coming up from behind him three scouts flew in close formation, bearing down on him fast as hell. Gaining on him, in fact— he had to keep his speed down to avoid flying right into the terrain, but they didn't seem to care what they hit if it meant they could catch him before he reached the queenship's maw.

He couldn't turn around and face them. Flying backward here was just too risky. He was going to have to shake them the old-fashioned way.

<hr />

"That tall son of a gun is making a run at it," Ehta said, her face lit up with joy. "If he can pull it off, we actually stand a chance. Quick, kid—get over to the sensor console and give me everything we have on the queenship."

Roan worked the controls and the display changed, zooming in on the queenship until it filled the wardroom with white light.

Ensign Ehta called out commands and Roan trained the sensors on the giant maw. Visual light imagery gave them very little data—it was almost perfectly dark inside the opening—but the tender's sensor package could see in far more wavelengths than the human eye. As it scanned the queenship with various instruments the display gained detail.

Just inside the maw titanic gantries ringed the opening, cluttered with moving objects that looked like the worker drones they'd found on Aruna—clusters of legs that ended in clawlike hands. They hurried to and fro at unguessable tasks.

Beyond the gantries lay open space. The queenship was hollow inside, though not empty. Structures stuck out of the inner skin—countless spires pointing inward toward the center of the ship. At a perfectly spherical core of some kind.

"Trace its power flows," Ehta said. Roan studied the controls, looking for a way to do that, but she must have taken too long. Ehta shoved her out of the way and did it herself. The white shapes in the display tinged with orange as the sensors analyzed how power moved through the structures of the queenship. The central core glowed with power, looking exactly like the molten core of a planet. All the huge ship's power seemed to flow from that central mass.

Ehta brought up a comms console. "Valk, I've got a target for you, if you can get close enough," she said. "The power plant of that thing is right in the middle. If you can hit it hard enough, maybe you can stop the bastard in its tracks."

"Understood," Valk called back.

"How you doing up there?" Ehta asked.

"Busy—gotta go," Valk said, and the connection broke off.

Roan watched as a blue dot streaked across the surface of the queenship, followed by three white dots that were steadily gaining on it. The blue dot wasn't far from the maw—and the giant spikes that stuck up around it like teeth.

"Can he actually do it?" Roan asked.

"He's the damned Blue Devil," Ehta replied. "Of course he can." Then she reached over and grabbed Roan's hand and held it tight.

Valk flew as low as he dared, just meters from the surface of the queenship. So low he couldn't help but pull his feet up off the floorboards of his cockpit, as if they might get ripped off by a swell in the terrain. He looked at his sensor display, not at his cockpit as he nudged his stick back and forth, dodging low hills and scarps that made his collision detectors blare.

Behind him the scouts were just out of range. If they got within a hundred meters of him they could blast fire all over his thrusters. His cones were already running hot, and the added heat would push them over the edge.

Time to shake his tail. Up ahead he saw a sort of miniature mountain range, a row of peaks no more than ten meters high, their sides perforated like coral with tiny impact craters. He forced himself not to shout in panic as he aimed for the thin notch between two of the peaks. He would have to fly through them sideways just to keep from scraping off all his airfoils.

The scouts stuck like glue to his course. As he leaned over on his side they didn't deviate by a fraction of a degree. He had the briefest, faintest sense of rock closing in on him and then he was through—and behind him, one of the scouts tore into a peak, exploding in a cloud of rock and metal debris.

Two left.

He had no idea if they would fall for the same trick twice. They weren't exactly bright, nor did they have much of a sense of self-preservation. Still—relying on your enemy's stupidity was a great way to get killed.

Luckily for Valk he had one more card to play. Dead ahead lay a hill that was little more than a large boulder, a pimple of rock sticking out of the queenship's surface. No more than eight meters high, something he could easily just jump over with his maneuvering jets. He leaned forward on his stick as if he intended to crash right into it.

Maybe the scouts weren't so stupid after all. The two of them split up, one going right, one going left, so they would fly around either side of the hill. The maneuver didn't slow them down at all.

Valk let go of his stick, his hands hovering over it like he was afraid to touch it, afraid that he would chicken out at the last moment. The hill came rushing toward him, filling the view through his canopy. The scouts kept creeping closer, ever closer—

Now.

He pulled back hard on the stick like he was trying to break it off. His BR.9 shot upward in a tight corkscrew, a hundred meters up over the hill. He feathered his positioning jets until he tumbled through space, his nose twisting around. When it was pointed right back down at the queenship he punched his thrusters for a power dive, until he was dropping faster than a stone back down toward the hill.

On the far side of the hill, the scouts closed up again, rebuilding their formation. He saw their eyeball cannon twisting around wildly as if they were looking for him, trying to figure out where he'd gone.

A weapons panel lit up on either side of him, his PBWs armed for independent fire. Valk pried his hands off his stick and brought up two virtual Aldis sights, one for each of his guns. Tough to aim that way, but he didn't need to be precise. As he fell down toward the scouts he blasted away, his shots kicking up plumes of dust wherever they touched the queenship's rocky soil.

One scout erupted in a ball of flame. The other just came to pieces, turning into debris that streaked across the asteroidal surface and plowed up great furrows wherever it touched.

A green pearl appeared in the corner of Valk's vision. Ehta calling to congratulate him? Lanoe asking for a progress report? It didn't matter.

As he straightened out and turned his nose back toward his previous course he could see what he'd come for: two of those spiky projections that ringed the queenship's maw, standing up tall and triangular like the pillars of a gate.

"Holy hell," Ehta said, her mouth open as she stared at the display. "He's going to make it!"

Roan turned from her console and looked at the model of the queenship. It filled so much of tender's wardroom with white light she felt like it might crush her. A single blue dot broke up the white, moving with aching slowness over the rough surface of the asteroidal ship. It was only centimeters now from the maw, at least in the scale of the display.

Ehta clenched her hands together and looked over at Roan. "I thought the queenship would have more weapons, or they would send more drones after him, or...hell! I didn't think it was possible. I thought we were all going to die here. I thought—"

Roan pointed at one of the spiky protrusions surrounding the maw, the things they'd all started calling teeth. "What's going on there?" she asked.

When Ehta saw it her face didn't change, not right away. The excitement, the wide eyes stayed the same. As if Ehta were frozen in place.

The tooth in question had started to bend over. Curling like a frond toward Valk's fighter. Its tip split apart like the fibers of a rope teasing apart. Like the petals of a flower in bloom, maybe.

Or like skeletal fingers.

It happened so fast Valk barely had time to register it.

Something long and ropy and made of bundled wire slapped across his canopy, tendrils of it sparking as his vector field tried to push them away. More of them wrapped across his view and then he felt like his skeleton was trying to jump out of his skin.

Valk's inertial sink grabbed him tight and shoved him back into his seat. He heard a mechanical whine just behind his head, a rising, building howl of tortured machinery. Something bounced off his vector field and his BR.9 lurched over on its side. The stick moved in his hands, fighting him as the ship tried to stabilize itself. That wasn't supposed to happen—the fighter was never supposed to take control like that, it was supposed to obey the pilot's every command.

Unless the pilot tried to pull a stunt that would instantly kill him.

The fighter shook and then lurched over again and Valk bobbed in his seat, his inertial sink trying desperately to compensate for whatever was going on. He stared in horror at his instrument panel. A second ago he'd been traveling as fast as a bullet in flight but now his speed indicator just flashed meaningless numbers, dropping impossibly fast—

More tendrils slapped across his canopy, a web of steel that gripped him tight, stopping him in midflight as if he'd flown right into an impenetrable wall.

The white pearl in the corner of his vision began to blink but he didn't even have time to see it.

On the display the skeletal hand grabbed the blue dot and just... squeezed it out of existence.

The tooth—except of course it wasn't a tooth at all, it was an *arm*—bent again, bringing its prize down toward the maw.

It looked exactly like the queenship had snatched Valk out of the air and then swallowed him whole.

Roan shook her head. "Where is he? I don't see him. Where'd he go?"

Ehta moved over to the console and switched off the display.

She wouldn't meet Roan's eye.

"Where's M. Valk? What happened?" Roan asked, because she wanted to hear that she was wrong, that she didn't just see that.

"Dead," Ehta told her.

"No, it grabbed him, but he—"

Ehta punched the console in front of her, hard. In the low gravity of Aruna the vibrations made every loose object in the tender jump and clatter. "Kid," Ehta said, very quietly, "they teach you anything about physics back on Niraya? Valk was moving at seventy meters per second. That thing grabbed him and stopped him cold. Inertial sinks are good, but they can't handle that kind of deceleration."

"So, maybe he's hurt, maybe he's broken some bones," Roan suggested.

"You go from that speed to a dead stop, you don't just break bones," Ehta said, almost spitting the words. "You damn near *splash*. Roan...give it up. There's nothing left of Valk right now but red jelly."

Chapter Twenty-Eight

Lanoe, Valk is—"

"I saw it," he called back. He wasn't really aware of who was talking to him. A woman, so either Ehta or Zhang. It didn't matter. He didn't want to talk to them.

He didn't want to talk to anybody. Which was too bad, since everyone seemed to want to talk to him.

"He just—it just—"

"—pinging him, but there's no response, no telemetry—"

"Thom, are you—"

Lanoe gritted his teeth. He didn't need this chatter. He needed to see what was happening over at the queenship.

"Silence," he called, on the general frequency. "Now."

He put his very best commander growl on it, and it seemed to work. For a moment at least there was silence.

"People die in battles. Happens all the time," he told them. "We all knew coming out here the odds were against us. Valk was a friend. More than that, a comrade. *He would want us to keep fighting,* don't you think?"

Eventually Zhang replied. "Give us orders," she said.

That was better.

"Break up those formations. Don't give them time to think." Exactly what they'd been doing already, in other words. Just holding their own.

He banked around a thick group of interceptors that were struggling to create a formation. They started shooting at him almost at once but at least he had a better view of the queenship from his new position.

The teeth—the arms—around the maw were all moving now. Bending inward, their tips unraveling and growing. Strands of them flowed across the maw until it looked like the opening was covered in a spiderweb of tendrils.

The programmer, or whoever was onboard the queenship, knew their plan now. It knew they were trying to attack its one weak spot, and it was taking steps to protect itself. Closing off the maw.

Lanoe's original plan, his one best shot at winning this battle, was sunk. As he watched, the web thickened and new filaments shot across the maw, until it was covered almost completely. There was no clear shot at the queenship's power plant anymore.

Kinetic impactors bounced off his vector field and he had to wheel away from the view. He dove down through a cloud of scouts that turned to face him but never got a chance as he raced past them. He blasted a few just to make himself feel better.

He needed to concentrate. He needed a new plan.

Meanwhile, the queenship drew ever closer to Aruna, and the enemy fleet kept organizing itself into meaningful formations.

They were running out of time.

✦

Elder McRae went to grab another projectile from the stack, but when she got there, there was no stack. All the projectiles had been loaded, and nearly a third had already been fired. The guns kept up their pace, firing a new round every few seconds, but the volunteers who weren't part of the gun crews could only stand around, looking at each other, looking up at the savaged sky. Bruise-colored aurorae danced over their heads, sheets of gray and purple light dancing and shimmering in and out of existence, and still the guns kept firing, their noise making the elder's senses reel, making her feel dizzy—

"Elder!" someone called. She jerked her head up and saw Engineer Derrow not five meters away. She was staring right at the elder, her faceplate glaring with the purplish light. "Get over here, now!"

She ran to obey. "What can I do?" she asked.

"Nothing," Derrow replied. "I just needed you out of the way of the number six gun crew."

The elder blinked and looked around and saw that she had been standing in the middle of a flurry of activity, volunteers bent over machinery with welding torches and circuit probes.

"I'm...sorry," the elder breathed, unable to believe she'd been so close to the gun, to its crew, without even realizing it.

"No time for apologies," Derrow told her. "Just stand there, and don't move." The engineer was bent over a console with sixteen displays that she constantly moved around, dismissing some, pulling up others. Some showed raw data coming in from the guns' computers; some were live feeds of what was happening out in space.

"What's going on there?" the elder asked, pointing at one of the displays.

The engineer stared at her for a moment, then reached up to her neck. The light that had been flashing there went out—the light that indicated that the engineer's words were being broadcast to all of the volunteers. Then Engineer Derrow leaned forward until her helmet touched the elder's. When she spoke her voice was muffled and almost drowned out by the noise of the guns. "This is just between us, all right? I guess you deserve an update. But this can't become common knowledge."

"All right," the elder said.

"Tannis Valk is dead. He made a run at the queenship but it didn't work. Don't ask me for details—nobody up there is telling me much—but it looks like now they can't attack the queenship directly at all."

"I see," the elder said.

"Commander Lanoe wants me to train the guns directly on the queenship, see if I can damage it somehow. But these guns weren't made for that. They were just supposed to take out the swarmships.

I can't punch a hole through an asteroid with these things. Hell, Elder. He must know that. What do you think of all this? Did we just lose this battle?"

"I'm sorry," Elder McRae said again. "I'm not a warrior. I just don't know." She'd never felt more useless in her life. As a woman who had devoted herself to work, to always having some function to fulfill, the feeling was nearly unbearable.

"I just don't know...Is there any point to what we're doing?" Derrow asked. "Is there any point to keeping this up, if we're just taking potshots?"

"I wonder," the elder tried, "is there any point to stopping?"

The engineer met her eyes directly. Then she took a deep breath. She tapped the key on her collar ring and the light there started flashing again. "Guns three through six," she called, on the universal channel, "prepare for new targeting information. Guns seven and eight, reload!"

Then she reached out a hand in the elder's direction. The elder grasped it, understanding. There was one small thing she could do, after all—she could be present. Give moral support.

It was something, anyway.

A green pearl rotated in the corner of Lanoe's vision. A call from Zhang, but she'd chosen to send it as a request rather than just signaling him directly. Which meant she was giving him the option of ignoring it.

He looped around an interceptor, blazing away with both barrels of his PBWs, pouring fire into the thing's thick skin. Useless. Nothing short of disruptors could get through the armor on the bigger drones. The interceptors would be the thing that killed them all, he thought. They just didn't have a good method for destroying the things. He rolled away as its guns spoke and kinetic impactors started skimming off his vector field.

"Zhang," he said, opening a private channel, "you have something?"

"An idea. Maybe just a thought. We can't get at the queenship through the front door. We need another weak spot to go after. We could target its engines. Get behind it and use up every disruptor we've got and maybe we get lucky, maybe we cripple it. Leave it dead in space."

"Until it can repair itself," Lanoe pointed out.

"In the meantime we fall back. Regroup. Live to fight another day."

Lanoe shook his head, though he knew she couldn't see it. "No. We're never going to have a stronger position than what we've got right now. There's a way to win this battle; we just haven't seen it yet."

"That's your read on this?" she asked.

She was giving him a chance to doubt himself. To question whether he was just too hot, too committed to this battle. She was doing her duty as his second in command, holding up a mirror for him.

So he gave it serious thought before he answered.

"Yes," he said. "We win here or we die. You, me, and Thom." Otherwise, he thought, Valk had died for nothing. Otherwise, Niraya had no chance.

He stitched a line of particle fire up the nose of the interceptor that was still chasing him. Mostly just to get his frustration out, to—

A section of armor plate peeled back from the hull of the interceptor, ragged and shiny around the edges. Underneath he could see bundles of wire flexing and shifting. The guts of the machine.

Somehow, through sheer ablation, he had cut through the interceptor's armor. Exposed its soft underbelly.

He brought up a virtual Aldis and lined up a perfect shot. Squeezed his trigger.

The interceptor didn't explode. It didn't melt or fall apart or scream in agony, nothing like that. Yet as he maneuvered around it, it failed to match his course, and in the infrared he could see its guns cooling down.

It was dead as a doornail. No way to tell by looking at the thing, but he'd killed it.

In life, he told himself, you cherished the small victories.

Number seven gun crackled with stray energy as the engineers took it offline. Its last shot had launched successfully, but only at about half the expected speed. Derrow shouted for as many people as she could spare to take its firing chamber apart and find the fault. They saw it right away, a capacitor that had melted under the strain of repeated firings. Without waiting for her to give the order, they replaced the capacitor and put the firing chamber back together again. They stood clear as it came up to charge, but when it failed to explode and kill them all they moved quickly to load a new projectile into its chamber. There was no time to make everything perfect, no time to test the repaired circuitry. It needed to get up and firing again as quickly as possible.

They must have gotten something wrong, though. In their haste, they must have overlooked something vital.

Elder McRae happened to be looking in the right direction when the firing chamber came apart in a shock wave of loose energy and flying shrapnel.

She saw the light, felt the heat of the explosion through her faceplate. Heard the screams over her suit radio. Staggered as the ground shook beneath her feet. She saw an engineer's suit come apart in shreds, the man's naked skin exposed to the cold, poisonous atmosphere of Aruna. He didn't live long enough to asphyxiate. She saw the number eight gun lean over on its side even as it launched another projectile, sending it off over the horizon of the moon.

Engineer Derrow shouted for repair crews, shouted for the rest of the gunners to keep working. Shock turned her face pale and bloodless but she kept her hands moving, swiping at her displays, bringing up new data as if nothing had happened.

Down by the base of the guns, in the crater of wreckage where number seven had been, bodies crawled over cracked rock. Blood slicked the framework of number six. The screams didn't stop.

"Let me go help them," the elder said.

"That gun's a loss, no fixing it now," Derrow told her.

"I mean the wounded—let me go tend to the wounded."

Realization crossed Derrow's face like a rippling wave of horror. For a second the engineer just stared at the crater, stared at the people dying down there. She was frozen, unable to think, unable to act.

"You keep shooting," the elder told her, grabbing her by the shoulders of her suit. "You have to keep working."

Behind her faceplate Derrow looked like she'd been paralyzed. Then, taking far too long about it, she nodded once.

The elder sped away, headed down into the crater to where the dead and the dying lay sprawled out across the skin of the moon. There were dozens of them, engineers and volunteers she recognized from back home. Some of them had been on the shuttle with her. Some she didn't know at all.

Most of them were already dead. When she saw ice crystals growing over their eyes she just steeled herself and passed them by. She could do nothing for them. She found a man who was missing both legs. His face was a mask of agony. She tied off the ragged ends of his suit's legs, trying to create tourniquets that would seal his suit shut and keep him from losing air. There was nothing she could do for his pain.

She found a woman who looked unhurt, who was just staggering around the crater as if she couldn't figure out what to do next. "Go to the shuttles," the elder told her. "There are medical kits there, and—"

She stopped because the woman had just fallen over in a heap. When the elder checked her suit, she found a jagged piece of metal sticking out of the woman's back, half a meter long. Blood pooled inside the woman's helmet, submerging her face. She was dead.

"Number six, go offline," Engineer Derrow called. "Check for damage and get it fixed! One through five, you're all we've got—increase your rate of fire. What? No, I don't care if it's running too hot. If the barrel starts to melt, then I'll care. Until then, keep shooting!"

The elder looked down at the dead woman, the one who'd been

impaled. She laid a gentle hand on the woman's helmet. Then she moved on to the next body, checking it for signs of life.

—⊸⊱⊰⊶—

A scout spat fire across Lanoe's underbelly, and he felt a wave of searing heat rush through his cockpit. He swiveled around to kill the drone before it could do much damage, and coolant rushed through his suit, turning the sweat that covered his skin to ice that quickly sublimed, leaving him chilled and damp. Too close—far too close for comfort—but the best he could hope for. The pieces of the drone bounced off his fuselage as he leaned on his stick, rolling away before two more scouts could get close enough to finish him off.

He looked to his left and saw Thom bank wide around the scouts. The kid's BR.9 was missing half its airfoils and had lost all the paint from one flank, but it looked like Thom was still alive in there.

He had no idea where Zhang was.

"Damn it," he said, careful to make sure he wasn't broadcasting. Valk's death had rattled him. He needed to get back on top of things. He brought up his comms board and sent out a general call. "I need information—Derrow, Ehta, Zhang, give me reports."

He didn't expect the news to be good.

"I'm okay but I can't hold these formations back," Zhang said. "They're getting organized, and it's all I can do to pick off stragglers here and there. We're losing control of the battle area."

He'd already figured that much out for himself.

Ehta had built up imagery of the queenship's backside, looking for vulnerabilities there. "There are thrusters you can target, sure. Lots of them—hundreds of cones. Heavily armored—you would need disruptors to break those things. Looks like they're ion engines, low thrust but high efficiency. It could lose two-thirds of them and still be maneuverable."

So much for Zhang's alternate plan, then. Maybe they could

474 D. NOLAN CLARK

take out the queenship's engines but not with one decisive attack—it would take all three of them in a concerted effort.

Engineer Derrow called in last, with the worst news of all. "Half the guns are down—out for the duration."

"You can't repair them?"

"You can't fix slag. One of them blew up and I lost some vital people. Two more were totaled in the blast. A fourth one can be repaired but there's even odds on it exploding the first time we fire it."

Lanoe didn't have time to close his eyes, or sigh, or even process what he was hearing at more than a minimal level. He had to act, though. He had to act right now. The battle would be lost if he didn't think of something right now.

Sure, he thought. Just like every battle he'd ever fought. You moved and you fought and you did whatever looked best at the time. The one thing worse than making the wrong move was making no move at all.

"Okay. Zhang, you move toward those engines—I don't know what good you can do back there, but maybe you'll draw some of the formations after you if they think the queenship's in danger. Thom, you stick close to me, and we keep thinning the herd. Ehta, get me every bit of data you can on the queenship. Find something, anything we can use. And Derrow—you keep as many guns firing as you can. Measure your risks but *keep firing.* Target the queenship—maybe we can punch through that web over the maw."

Maybe. Maybe a miracle would happen.

Chapter Twenty-Nine

Roan had gone to help with the wounded out by the guns, leaving Ehta alone in the wardroom of the tender. She didn't mind the solitude—the girl had kept pestering her for information about Thom and the damage to his fighter—but it meant she had to hustle, moving from one console to another as she scanned the queenship, still half a million kilometers away.

She had plenty of instruments at her disposal. The tender's own sensor pod was top-shelf, a compact bundle of millimeter-wave and neutrino backscatter scanners as well as some really powerful synthetic aperture telescopes. She also had access to the network of microdrones that Valk had set up when they first arrived in the system, and all the sensors onboard the fighters as well. She could see in almost every frequency of the electromagnetic spectrum from X-rays down to deep radio, and the tender's computers could synthesize all that data into a very coherent picture of the queenship and how it worked. But the data needed a lot of massaging, and she had to stay on top of the instruments to make sure they didn't waste processor time duplicating information she already had.

Her model of the queenship had started as a white blob hanging inert in the middle of the wardroom. Now it grew skeletal and ghostly as she stripped away its skin one layer at a time, peeling it like a virtual onion with a tomographic algorithm. She could see how busy the thing was on the inside, and what she saw made her flesh crawl.

Worker drones moved everywhere inside the queenship, crowding together in some areas, racing apart elsewhere as they finished one task and moved to a new one. The gantries just inside the maw shimmered with activity, hundreds of the little robots clambering over each other, busy at work. They seemed to be constructing spherical objects, dozens of them, then rolling them into some kind of huge tube.

When she realized what she was looking at, Ehta started shouting curses and she didn't stop until she had an encrypted connection to Lanoe's fighter.

"Boss, take a look at the web and tell me what you see," she said. "I want to make sure I have this right before I wreck your day."

"Too late for that—give me a second," he said, and she could hear his reactor whine as he worked through some complicated maneuver. "I can't get a real good look, but—did we hit the web? Did Derrow's guns put a hole in it?"

Ehta's display showed her the individual strands of the web in stark detail. They were twitching apart, stretching themselves open. It looked like an eyelid opening in the middle of the web. Behind that opening lay the tube crammed full of spherical constructs.

"Other way round," Ehta said. She zoomed in on the view—just in time to see the queenship fire its own gun.

"What the hell," Lanoe shouted. "Thom, incoming, low on your seven! Move!"

Ehta switched to a visual light telescope view to see it happen. The spherical objects were pushed out through the opening in the web, spat out like seeds from a mouth. There were dozens of them and they moved incredibly fast, spreading out in a cone as they rushed away from the queenship. When the last of them had been ejected the opening twitched shut again, filaments of the web closing up even tighter than they had been before.

The spheres tumbled as they rushed through the battle area. They didn't seem to have the ability to maneuver. Several of them collided with debris, or with the wreckage of dead swarmships, or with drone ships. They cracked open like eggs when they hit anything, spilling their lethal cargo out into space.

Ehta recognized that cargo. The spheres were orbiters, exactly like the one that had first made contact with Niraya. Every one of them carried a lander exactly like the one that had slaughtered the farmers on the planet—six meters tall, all legs and sharp claws.

The spheres moved faster than anything in the battle area, too fast for the pilots to draw a bead on them. In seconds they were clear of the debris field and hurtling onward, unimpeded, through space.

Ehta didn't need her fancy instruments to tell where they were headed. In the display they came right at her, and in real life it was the same. Those landers were all headed for Aruna. The queenship had sent its killer drones to wipe out the volunteers in the crater—and the guns they crewed.

They would take only minutes to arrive.

Initializing.

Loading protocols from /con. Using template Default; Confirm connection.

Listening to 0.0.0.0.1D. Create TempDir; failed.

Confirm connection. Create TempDir; completed.

Connection established to 0.0.0.0.1D. Configured for 1 client.

Transfer rate at .01% nominal. Request additional bandwidth.

Send keepalive. Set connection type to persistent.

Keepalive returned positive flag.

Alive.

No light. No eyes to see it. Nothing to feel but pain, and processes had been evolved to moderate pain inputs.

A squeal of noise that should have meant nothing, just noise, no signal and yet...and yet...processing...information hid inside the randomness. Information that could be understood.

How?

Light, faint, but growing brighter. A dull red. The smell of ozone.

Alive. That didn't fit with known datasets. Alive, all the same.

A sudden rush, a kind of psychological wind that tore through the canyons of the brain, whistling through synapses that had already shut down for the last time. Except—alive. He was alive. How was that possible? He'd never been a scientist, but he knew the physics of inelastic collisions. Every pilot did. He was dead.

Light was everywhere, dull red, everything bathed in that same shade. He saw things moving, segmented arms shifting spasmodically. Like the legs of an insect trapped inside the lens of a display projector, jerky and huge, just out of focus.

Something like a millipede, something with too many legs, hovered over him. The legs touched him but he felt nothing, only the tug, the drag as he was manipulated, his limbs moved by this terrifying puppeteer.

Addressing: false-mind. Will speak {this unit/false-mind}. Accept connection.

Those weren't words. They were numbers, strings of numbers in base fifteen.

False-mind. Speak.

"Whuh…" It was the best he could do in terms of communication. Except—

Except it wasn't. It was the best sound he could make, sure. But this thing didn't use sound to convey information.

"Where am I?" he tried, in the language the millipede-thing could understand. Except his words were translated, even before he'd formed them. What he actually said was:

"Request: physical location."

The reply came instantly.

Interior, this unit.

False-mind, request: designation.

He couldn't feel his face. He couldn't feel his tongue moving as he spoke. He couldn't even tell if he was breathing.

"/Tannis Valk/," he said.

"Lanoe," Ehta said, "they're headed for Aruna."

"I can see that."

Ehta gripped both sides of the console with her hands. She felt so light she might float away. "They'll touch down in...one hundred and forty-five seconds," she said. "Less than three minutes."

On Ehta's display the orbiters showed as a tight cone of white dots, never shifting position except to move away from each other as they progressed through space. They were on a perfectly straight trajectory that would leave them in Aruna's upper atmosphere. Ehta knew what would happen when they arrived. They would make an orbit or two, using the drag from the moon's thin air to slow them down. Then they would open up and drop their landers onto the cold soil of the moon.

From there it would just be a question of butchery.

Zhang called on the open channel. "They don't have any weapons down there," she said.

"Are you kidding? They've got the guns—those are our best weapons," Lanoe replied, but even coming from him it sounded like an evasion. The guns couldn't hit such small targets, not with any hope of getting them all. "Anyway, they've got the tender as well. The cannon on that thing can—"

"Who's going to shoot it?" Zhang asked.

Lanoe didn't have an immediate response. Perhaps because the answer was so obvious it didn't need to be stated.

Ehta could handle this, he might have said, *if she was capable of flying.*

Ehta had spoken with enough psychologists to know that what she had was a disease. That you couldn't just will your way to health. If she tried to fly the tender now, if she went and sat in the pilot's seat, it wasn't just a question of forcing herself to work the controls. The harder she tried, the worse she would feel. She would end up trembling on the floor, vomiting and blind with headaches.

There were drugs you could take to calm those nerves, sure. She'd tried pretty much every one she could get her hands on. None of them had worked—they'd made her feel high, made her sleepy. The second she'd tried to fly again they'd stopped working altogether.

Willpower wouldn't do it, either. She couldn't save herself—on anyone on Aruna—simply by overcoming some psychological hurdle, especially not in a high-stress situation.

The only real treatment was the one she'd turned down. The one she'd joined the marines rather than undergoing. Even if she changed her mind now, even if there had been a doctor present to perform the brain surgery required, it couldn't be done in two and a half minutes. There was no way for her to just get past her disease.

There was no way she could fly the tender.

There were a couple of pilots among the volunteers—the Centrocor people who had flown the two shuttles here from Niraya. Maybe one of them could do it. Of course, neither of them had ever flown a combat mission in their lives. They knew how to get from point A to point B. She doubted they could exercise maneuvers, much less shoot and fly at the same time.

Then there was the fact the tender had no vector field. It was too big. If the enemy sent even one scout to accompany the orbiters, the tender had no chance.

On Ehta's display she could see an entire squadron of scouts and interceptors chasing the orbiters, following them down.

The pilots were still talking, still ignoring the fact that she could hear them. "I know what you're going to say," Zhang announced. "You're going to say we can't spare a fighter to protect Aruna. You know what I'm going to say in response?"

"Sure," Lanoe said.

"I'm going to say 'the hell we can't.' The people down there came here thinking we would protect them—"

"They came as volunteers," Lanoe said. "Knowing it was dangerous."

"Knowing we would do the heavy lifting, when it came time to fight this battle. Lanoe, I want to go down there and save them.

You can order me not to. If you do, I'm just going to go anyway. So what are your orders?"

Thank you, Ehta mouthed. *Thank you.* She couldn't say it out loud.

———

"How are you even talking to me? You're not speaking any language I know," Valk insisted.

The words came out differently, of course. They were translated automatically into computer code. He ignored that, focused on finding out what the hell was going on.

The millipede-thing—he understood now that it was a kind of avatar of the queenship—held him in a dozen arms. It twisted his body this way and that, turning him so he faced the red glow of the asteroid's core. Then it flipped him back over on his back. He did not have any capacity to resist it.

Operational parameters include: examine local machines. Learn data transfer protocols for purpose: communication.

"You—you found one of our computers?" Valk asked, trying to comprehend.

In his head an image popped up, exactly as if he'd opened a display. It showed one of his microdrones, floating in interplanetary space. Limbs like scuttering claws plucked it out of the void. Tore it to pieces.

He wanted to shake his head. He found he couldn't move it, couldn't so much as twitch a muscle. "So—so you wanted to talk to us. I mean, we got your message. I got your message. But you didn't talk! You kept trying to kill us!"

Destruction of minds outside operational parameters.

"What? What are you talking about? You tried to kill everyone—every mind—on Niraya!"

Loading requested data: Worker unit dispatched to scan local resources. Metals, silicon, energy. No minds encountered at that time.

"That's crap! You killed all those farmers, and the people from the Retreat—"

Reloading requested data: No minds encountered at that time.

Frustration tore at Valk like birds picking at his corpse. He couldn't understand half of what the millipede-thing was saying, and it wouldn't explain. It was like talking to one of those advertising drones back on the Hexus—they sounded human, even friendly, as long as you stuck to what they were programmed to talk about. Exceed that remit and suddenly you were shouting at a floor waxer.

"I don't understand. You sent that killer drone to Niraya to look for metals? Not to kill people?"

Return flag: true.

He wished he wasn't the one having this conversation. Maybe Lanoe would have handled it better. No. He would have just threatened the millipede-thing. Tried to scare it into surrendering. Maybe Zhang would have been better; she was pretty diplomatic. Hell, Maggs, for all his faults, would have probably know exactly what to say to this thing. He probably would have convinced it to sign a contract with Centrocor.

Instead it was him, Tannis Valk, who had to have the very first conversation between a human being and an alien...thing.

"What the hell are you?" he demanded. "I don't even get—"

High-order operational parameters include: move, expand through galaxy. Find planets and planetary objects. Extract resources. Construct infrastructure for future settlement. Construct more units identical to {this unit} for purpose: move, expand through galaxy. Find planets and planetary objects. Extract—

"Wait! Stop! Let me try to understand," Valk begged. "You're—you're not even military?"

Return flag: true.

"You're...you're just a miner. Just like Engineer Derrow."

Unknown designation.

"She's—she's one of the people on Niraya. The people you tried to kill. But you say that's your function. To extract resources."

He tried to imagine it, the alien fleet, all those killing machines. Except...they weren't, were they? On Aruna they'd found worker drones and factories for making the killer landers—except, the killer landers looked like just larger, less functional versions of the worker drones. The mine on Aruna had been defended by smelting towers repurposed to be plasma cannons. The scout drones they'd fought so many times had been pathetically bad at dogfighting—but they would work great as welders and metal cutters.

Valk's mind reeled with it. Was it even possible? The genocidal fleet hadn't come to Niraya to kill everybody. It had come to... what? Mine and extract resources. To build copies of itself.

Even as he understood that, more data came in—more information from the queenship's avatar. Information he hadn't asked for, information he didn't know how to ask for, poured into him. And he got it. He understood.

Space is very, very, very big, and it takes a long time to travel from one star to another. Especially if you don't have access to wormholes. Sometime in the past, some alien—an actual alien, not a drone—had built the millipede-thing, the queenship, and sent it out into space to look for new habitable planets. If it found them it was supposed to extract resources and build infrastructure, so that when the aliens arrived themselves, they'd find prefabricated colonies waiting for them.

Except what happens if you send your machines out into space and they don't find a suitable planet? There were millions of stars in the galaxy with no planets at all, billions with planets that couldn't support life. You would have wasted centuries and have nothing to show for it. So you do exactly what life and evolution did back on Earth: You give your drones the power of reproduction. One drone fleet arrives at a planet and sets up shop. Then it builds, say, ten—no, fifteen—copies of itself and sends each of them out with the same mission. Those fifteen copies each build fifteen more. Eventually one of those copies will find the perfect system, one with lots of habitable planets, plentiful resources, just the right temperature, and plenty of water and all the things you'd want in a new home.

In fact, as your machines multiplied throughout the galaxy, they would find hundreds, even thousands of systems like that.

"You're an explorer," Valk said.

High-order operational parameters include: move, expand through galaxy. Find planets and—

"Yeah, that's exactly what I just said. Damn. This is a mess. This is . . . How long have you been out here, following your program?"

Time server calculations complicated by relativistic dilation. Subjective time server reports: 2.17 galactic rotations.

Valk did the calculation in his head without even trying. It took the galaxy about 250 million years to rotate, so . . . the alien machine had been traveling the galaxy for half a billion years.

Forget humans. On Earth, creatures with spinal cords hadn't even existed when this thing left home. For a second Valk was overcome by a wave of awe at what its creators had done. Did they even still exist? Had they wiped themselves out millions of years ago, and forgotten to turn off their machines? They certainly had never had a grudge against humanity, a species they couldn't even have imagined someday existing. The aliens had never meant to kill the Nirayans, or any humans, they had . . .

No. Just because it was an accident, that didn't excuse all those dead farmers.

"You failed in your mission," Valk told the millipede-thing. "You've deviated from your program. You were supposed to talk to any . . . any minds you found. Not kill them."

Reloading requested data: No minds encountered—

"What do you call those Nirayans you killed? They had minds, they—"

Return flag: false.

Valk stared down at the molten core of the queenship. It was all he could do. "I don't understand. Your programming requires you to talk to other minds. But you didn't even try! You just killed the first humans you found, you—"

Loading operational parameters, subroutine 61D341A: maintenance of work areas. Keep work areas clean of debris and castings.

Scan for damage to equipment and repair where resources available. Eliminate vermin that may damage equipment.

"I didn't ask for your task list. I asked why you killed those—"

Reloading requested data: eliminate vermin.

———⟩⟨———

Ehta shut down all the displays. The tender could send any new information directly to her suit, and just then she didn't want to be alone. She climbed out of the tender's hatch and watched the gun crews running around the base camp. The guns weren't firing as fast as they had before—it took her a second to remember that half of them had been destroyed—and she was grateful that they didn't make her head spin so much. She headed over to where Engineer Derrow leaned on a console, looking like she was about to collapse.

Elder McRae was over there, rubbing the engineer's back through her suit. "Is there some new information?" the old woman asked, as Ehta came up. "Please tell me there's some good news."

Ehta just bit her lip and sent her files over to the engineer's equipment. A display lit up in front of them, showing the slowly spreading cone of orbiters headed for Aruna, and the squad of drone ships that wove and flitted around it, protecting it.

"Good news? No."

The elder and the engineer stared at the display in shock. Ehta didn't blame them. She took a step back, letting them process what was coming for them. Only then did she notice the green pearl in the corner of her vision. It was a paler shade than usual, which meant she was being added as a silent connection to an ongoing communication. Zhang had patched her in, but kept her line muted. Clearly she was supposed to hear what was being said—whether other parties in the connection wanted her to or not.

"—need you here, there could be...I don't know," Ehta heard Lanoe say. "Something could break and I'll need you then, need everybody I can get to—"

"If you don't let me go down there," Zhang said, "they will die.

All of them. Roan, and the elder. The people who hired you for this job in the first place."

"I wasn't hired. I volunteered."

"So did Ehta. She's down there. You remember her? Your squadmate?"

"Ehta," Lanoe said.

He sounded very far away.

"You know how to push my buttons, Zhang. I'll give you that. But I know you, too. I know that if I order you to stay, you will," Lanoe said.

It took Zhang long enough to answer that it was obvious he was right.

"If we all have to die here," she said, finally, "I want to die fighting to save the people I care about."

Lanoe grunted in frustration. Ehta could see him in her mind's eye, shaking his head back and forth that way he did when somebody pointed out that he was wrong, and he didn't want to admit it.

The funny thing about Aleister Lanoe was that when you backed him into a corner like that, when you forced his hand, you would expect him to lash out. To get defiant and angry and refuse to listen to reason. Just like anybody else. Except—sometimes he didn't.

"Go," he said. "Go. And come back as fast as you can. I'm not ready to give up, not yet. I'm not ready for any of us to just lie down and die. But go—go save Ehta."

"Vermin." Like rats chewing on cables. Like birds fouling a construction site. That was how the aliens saw human life. Something that needed to be eradicated so work could proceed unhindered. There was no ethical question there—it was like spraying for bugs. "Vermin," he said again. "They were not vermin! They were people . . . they were people with minds and lives and . . ."

Return flag: false.

"You have to understand. I know you're just a machine, maybe the distinction doesn't mean anything to you. But I have to make you understand—the people out there, the ones you're trying to kill, they're not vermin. You can't just wipe them out. They're not just rats..." He tried desperately to find a way to make the millipede-thing understand. "Rats don't build spaceships!"

Second-order operational parameters include: adjust value definitions based on new data. Space-going vermin discovered during seventh iteration. Logged: vermin definition expanded to include: organic units capable of damaging or polluting work areas. Vermin definition includes organic units found on ground or in space.

Valk grunted in frustration. "You encountered...space-going vermin," he said. Meaning people—not human people, but people—in spaceships. "And you're supposed to exterminate vermin. So you send your, your welders—the scouts—after these vermin. But I don't understand—what about the interceptors? Those aren't construction machines."

Return flag: true.

"You had to build those—design those—specifically to attack spaceships. It never occurred to you that the things you were attacking were sapient? And what about the landers? Those things are designed for nothing but killing!"

Logged: during ninety-twelfth iteration, space-going vermin proved more persistent and organized than expected. Required developing new tools to fulfill subroutine 61D341A.

"Ninety-twelfth," Valk said, confused until he remembered this thing thought in base fifteen. "You saw spaceships and you couldn't understand they were built by sapient creatures. They were just tougher vermin than you'd encountered before. So... you just attack anything alive? Anything you find that's alive, not a machine, is vermin? That's crazy," Valk insisted. "That's just crazy."

The millipede-thing didn't seem to understand. He realized that he'd spoken but only half his words had been translated into machine-speak. There was no word for "crazy" in the alien machine's databases.

No. A computer couldn't be crazy. It would be buggy, instead.

Valk cursed himself. He'd wasted all this time learning about the machines when he should have been making demands. "I want to talk to your programmer," he said. That had been the whole point of threatening the queenship, after all—Engineer Derrow felt there had to be a programmer onboard, someone who could give the drones the command to stand down. "Where is your programmer? Is there one here, or not?"

Communication request has been sent, logged.

Okay. Okay, then. Maybe—maybe there was a chance, still. Maybe if he could just talk to the programmer, get it to understand...maybe.

Seconds ticked away while he waited. Would the programmer come to meet him in person? Was he going to get to see an alien? Would it even understand him, or would he have to communicate through its drone?

More seconds. Too many. "Are they coming?" he asked.

Request could not be processed.

The damned machine didn't understand. "How long until the programmer responds?" he tried.

Due to signal lag, response expected in: twenty-one thousand, two hundred, seventeen [years].

Oh, no.

No. The bastards—they hadn't sent a programmer along with their queenship. The nearest programmer who could alter the queenship's programming was living on some distant planet, still. Valk's request to talk would have to be sent across light-millennia of space, and even then the reply wouldn't come for thousands of years more.

The battle outside the queenship would be over in a matter of hours, maybe minutes. Niraya would be sterilized of "vermin" within the next few days.

"Damn you! Damn you damned machine bastard! Hell's ashes, don't you understand? Can't you see we're not vermin? Can't you see I'm not vermin?"

Return flag: true.

"What?"

Confirm: false-mind excluded from class: vermin.

"But I'm—I'm human. I'm just like the people you're trying to kill. I'm one of them. I'm vermin!"

Return flag: false. False-mind, you are false-mind.

"Damn it, what does that even mean?"

Full communication impossible {this unit/false-mind} while mind is false. False-mind contains personality ideates that resist full communication.

"I don't understand! What the hell is an ideate?"

Define term: ideate: constructed falsehood implemented to simulate false-consciousness. Remove personality ideates to facilitate full communication {this unit/false-mind}.

"Remove what?" Valk demanded.

The millipede thing reached down then with several of its thinner legs and gripped Valk's left index finger.

Minimize damage to false-mind. Remove personality ideates incrementally, until false-mind allows full communication.

With no effort at all, the millipede-thing ripped Valk's finger out from its socket and cast it away, into the molten core.

Then there was no room in Valk's mind for anything but pain, bright white pain that strobed behind his eyes, bounced back and forth inside his skull. He tried to scream, tried to convulse in agony, but the millipede-thing wouldn't let him. Instead it reached for his thumb.

A white pearl appeared in the corner of Valk's vision. It spun and flashed and jumped up and down, begging for his attention. If he just flicked his eyes across it—

He'd resisted doing that for seventeen years.

If there had ever been a time when he deserved painkillers, though, this was it. He moved his eyes. Accepted the white pearl.

He didn't expect that it would switch everything off. His consciousness, his thoughts, his memories. Everything. Like rolling up a minder and putting it in sleep mode.

Just gone.

Chapter Thirty

L ight. White light.

A room, not big. Not much in it. Very clean. A drone moved through the room, its ducted props whispering away. It was painted in Establishment colors, blue with black stars. It shone a light that flickered across him and then it floated out of view. Somewhere nearby, someone tapped on a virtual keyboard.

Then she stepped into frame. A woman, long brown hair in a thick braid that fell down over one shoulder. Sad eyes.

He wanted to comfort her. Why? Did he know her? Did he know why she looked so sad? He couldn't remember. There were holes in him.

Holes all the way through him. Places where there should have been something. A memory, a thought, a feeling. Nothing there, though. Just holes.

Nothing hurt.

"I'm not supposed to turn you on yet," she said. She scratched at her nose. Looked over at the drone. "I'm not supposed to talk to you. You aren't supposed to know that I exist. It's okay. I'll encrypt this when I'm done, so you won't remember. My name is Yalta. Colonel Engineer Yalta. Can you... can you speak?"

He couldn't. There was a hole where his ability to speak should be.

"It's okay. Just listen, I guess. First things first. I'm so sorry."

There was no hole in his empathy. He wanted to reach over and grab her hand. It wasn't possible.

There was a hole where his hand should be.

"Tannis—I'm sorry. What we're doing to you, it's not... It isn't ethical. I understand why they want me to do this but it's..." She shook her head. "Orders are orders, right? You have to understand, we're losing. The polys just have so much money to throw at this war, and all we have is people. People we can't afford to lose. That's the point of this, I guess. We can't afford to lose *you*."

Yalta stepped out of the frame again. He wished she would come back. He wished he could tell her it was all right. That they were going to lose, that he'd seen the future somehow. Knew what was going to happen with the Establishment, and that it was going to be bad, really bad actually, but that most of them would live through it.

"Admiral Ukiyo gave me a very long lecture about propaganda this morning," she said. Her voice was muffled as if she was very far away. "About appearances. About heroes. She said the Establishment is an idea, not an armada or a place or a political philosophy, but an idea. An idea that needs to be fed to keep it alive. She told me the only way we can win this thing is if people believe. So that's why we have to..."

Yalta's voice trailed off. She was gone for a long time, as the drone moved across his field of view again. Eventually it wandered off, and she came back, closer now. Looking right into his eyes.

"I can't lie to you, Tannis. I've spent too long going through your memories, learning who you are. You're a good man and you don't deserve to be lied to. So I'm going to tell you the truth.

"You died. You burned to death in your cockpit. I've reviewed the memories and they were awful. I...I cried. I cried for you, Tannis. I've edited those memories down as much as I could, made them... shorter. You died in that fire and when your ship came back to the carrier you were already gone. Fourth-degree burns over one hundred percent of your body. All that was left, really, was your brain, and even that was cooked. We had a hell of a time scanning it.

"We had our orders. Admiral Ukiyo told us to scan you, and

download your memories, your consciousness, your you-ness, into a new body. Of course, we don't have the ability to put you in a living, human body; that's poly technology and we can't afford it. So instead... we're going to put you inside a drone.

"Two of us quit from the project then and there. It's against every principle we have as scientists. Two of us quit from the team and they were arrested on the spot. The rest of us did what we were told.

"They're going to make you a hero. They've worked up a whole story around you; they're going to call you the Blue Devil and they're going to pretend you lived through that fire, that you're a perfect representative of the Establishmentarian ideal. Tough as nails, unwilling to surrender.

"They're going to put you in a suit with a black helmet, and put you back in a fighter so they can take video of you, the pilot who refused to die. When the war is over, when we *win*," Yalta said, unable not to sneer at the improbability, "they'll let you die for a second time. Give you a proper burial and maybe a statue or something.

"In the meantime, they're going to make you go through this sham.

"They need you to fly. To fight. They think that if you knew the truth, it would send you into a nasty depression. You might even get suicidal. They say that would 'harm your effectiveness as a propaganda tool.' So I have to program you to believe the lie. That you survived the fire.

"I told them—I wrote up a whole report on it—that you would be in constant pain. That you would have phantom limb syndrome all over your entire body. I was told that was perfect. The pilot who fought on, despite constant pain. The bastards! I'm even supposed to tease you. Put painkillers in your suit, painkillers that would do absolutely nothing since you don't have veins anymore. I'm also supposed to include a stubborn streak. A psychological barrier to keep you from ever using those painkillers.

"But the pain—it might get to be too much, someday. I can't

bear the thought of you suffering like that. So when it happens, when you can't take it anymore, maybe you'll take the white pearl after all. If you do, you'll see this message. You'll know the truth.

"If they find out I recorded this, if they find out I let you in on the joke, I'll be court-martialed. I might be executed for treason. But I had to give you a chance to know. You have rights, Tannis. You're a human being.

"At least...you used to be."

She disappeared again, but only for a second.

"If you never see this, well, maybe that's for the best. They tell me the war will be over in a few months, one way or the other. So you won't have to suffer very long.

"But if you do see this...I don't know. I hope you can forgive me. I know what kind of man you were. I think maybe you're capable of that. I really hope so.

"Even if you can't, even if you hate me right now, I want to give you one last gift. Here."

A black pearl appeared in the center of his vision. Much bigger than the white pearl had been. It obscured most of her face. It rotated slowly, a string of endless zeroes scrolling across its surface.

"This is a bomb, Tannis. It's a data bomb. Accept it, and every scrap of data in your memory will be deleted. Right down to root. You'll...I won't say you'll die, because that doesn't mean anything; you can't die twice. But you'll cease to exist.

"All you have to do is flick your eyes across the black pearl.

"If that's what you want."

Chapter Thirty-One

Thom twisted his head around right, then left, trying to see all the scouts that were chasing him. A whole formation back there and while his displays could show him where they were he needed to see them. He had to look.

He wished he hadn't.

"Lanoe," he called.

"I know," the old pilot sent back. "Keep moving, Thom. It's your best bet."

The enemy fleet had gotten itself organized. Its drone ships had established deep formations, squadrons lined up to provide support for each other, whole wings of drones moving as pincers. The enemy would gladly sacrifice a few dozen scouts just to push a human pilot into a trap full of interceptors.

A fireball of plasma erupted just to one side of Thom's canopy and the flowglas reacted by going black, polarizing itself so he wasn't blinded. It made him feel like he was trapped in a coffin. For a second he could only fly by instruments, veering out of the way of a whole line of scouts that were readying themselves to blast him with more fire, corkscrewing down through a space where the battle area was a little thinner, knowing it had to be a trap. When his canopy cleared he saw three interceptors ahead of him, spread out so they wouldn't hit each other with their guns.

"Hellfire," he had time to breathe, before those guns opened fire and kinetic impactors were all around him, a blizzard of iron. His BR.9 shook violently as one of them skidded off his fuselage. His vector field positively crackled as it shrugged off two more.

Lanoe was halfway across the battle area—too far away to help.

Behind him, the scouts he'd evaded were coming around for another pass.

⇢—⇠

Zhang couldn't close her cybernetic eyes. She could close her eyelids but she could still see right through them. So she did the next-best thing: One by one, she shut down every display, every board, every panel in her cockpit.

She needed to focus, now.

Ahead and below a squad of drones circled around the expanding cone of orbiters that were headed for Aruna. Six interceptors and nine scouts, maneuvering around each other so elegantly they looked like they were dancing. If she wanted the orbiters, she was going to have to get through that formation.

She couldn't worry about Lanoe. Or Thom, for that matter. She couldn't think about Valk's death. She couldn't even think about Ehta, down on the ground. This was going to take some very fancy flying and shooting. She needed to get into that headspace where it was all just angles and lines, mathematically simple and pure.

It would help if she weren't so terrified.

She worked her controls with both hands, firing her positioning and maneuvering jets in rapid sequence, at the same time shoving her stick forward with her knee. Once she had a hand free she grabbed the stick and dropped into a steep dive while swinging left and right, a hyperfast variation on a very old maneuver called the falling leaf. It wasn't supposed to work outside of an atmosphere, but you could fake it if you were a good enough pilot.

Zhang was a very, very good pilot.

The squadron below her opened up a little, the scouts spreading out to try to envelop her. They left an enticing opening where she could have just shot straight down and attacked the orbiters directly, but she wasn't falling for it. The six interceptors were still clumped tight around the prize and she couldn't take them on all at once.

A scout twisted around until its eyeball was pointed right at her. There was no time to bring up a virtual sight and actually aim at the thing, so she opened up with her PBWs and hoped for the best. Another scout banked around to try to get on her tail, while a third rushed her from the side.

She switched off her compensators and pulled a rotary turn, twisting her trajectory around ninety degrees in the space it took to draw a breath. Her inertial sink sat down on her hard, pinning her to her seat as the stick jumped in her hand like a snake. Suddenly the scout that had tried to flank her was right in front of her, so close she could see the weld marks on its plasma cannon. She must have surprised it because it didn't even have a chance to build up heat—as her PBWs tore through its eyeball it didn't explode, it just broke into pieces.

The other two scouts came at her then from opposite directions, ready to blast her, but she was already moving, pulling back hard on her stick and firing her maneuvering jets until she looped up over them.

She had kind of hoped the two of them would simply crash into each other in a head-on collision. Of course she'd never been that lucky. They flashed by each other, a good meter of space between them. In a second they were maneuvering to track her.

The damn things could corner; she had to give them that.

Meanwhile three more scouts had broken from the pack and were lining up high above her, ready to swoop down the second she lost her concentration.

She had no intention of giving them that opportunity.

———✦———

"I'd forgotten how good she was," Lanoe said, with a chuckle.

"Who are you talking about?" Thom demanded. "Zhang? I'm in trouble over here!" The interceptors wouldn't let up. Every time he tried to maneuver to get away from their welter of impactors they would just shift position, drawing him deeper into their web. He flipped over on his back, hit his retros hard to get moving backward, away from the scrum, but there were scouts behind him, pulling together into a tight formation.

"Get out of there, kid," Lanoe said. "Don't let them pin you. I'm coming but I'm still ten seconds out. Hold on!"

But there was no way Thom was going to survive the next ten seconds. Not with those interceptors locking him up.

Unless he found some way to get through them, without flying right into their impactors. Unless he—

There was a way.

"I'm sorry," he said. Then he pulled up his weapons panel and armed his disruptors.

He wasn't supposed to use them. He was supposed to save them for the queenship. Making a run at the asteroid seemed like a pipe dream now, though. And he was dead if he didn't do something.

The interceptors knew they were all but immune to PBW fire. They didn't even try to maneuver as Thom fired every disruptor he had. The heavy munitions made a nasty chunking noise as they launched from the belly of his BR.9, moving slowly enough that he could actually watch as they streaked toward their targets.

The first one struck an interceptor right between two of its guns. It melted its way right through the thickest of the drone's armor and Thom saw light flash from the gun muzzles as it tore away at the interceptor from the inside.

The other disruptors didn't hit quite so cleanly, but they found their targets. One after another they dug through the interceptors' armor and blew them apart.

The impactors disappeared. The guns stopped firing.

Thom wasted no time. He opened his throttle wide and screamed through the formation, even as one of the interceptors exploded in a vast orange cloud of burning fuel and slag. Debris bounced off Thom's vector field, a couple of pieces hitting him directly and smacking dents into his fuselage.

But in another second he was free, past the interceptors and into something resembling open space. He swiveled around to look back and saw a wave of scouts start to chase after him, then break off as they were pelted with debris.

"I'm sorry," he said again.

"Kid—it's all right. You did what you had to do," Lanoe called. His voice belied his words. He didn't sound angry that Thom had disobeyed orders. Instead he sounded almost sad about it. Disappointed, maybe?

"I know you said we needed to save our disruptors, but—"

"You did what you had to do," Lanoe said again. "I just wish... ah, hell. Clearly this is not a day when I get to make a lot of wishes. Thom—I'm just glad you made it out of there."

≈

Zhang cut a scout to pieces, then wheeled around hard and took out another with a quick burst of particle fire. There were only a few of the scouts left, but all six interceptors remained intact. She couldn't take them on all at once, and they refused to budge from their formation, a ring of steel around the orbiters. If she couldn't trick them into peeling off there was no way she could isolate them.

She chewed on her lip, trying to think of some clever move. Some gambit that would break the formation open.

A scout crept up too close on her left. She spun around and gave it both barrels and it stopped being a problem.

Ahead of her lay the vast round disk of Garuda, the ice giant. Aruna, the moon, was obscured by the mass of orbiters and interceptors, but she knew it was getting close. She had at most a minute before the orbiters reached the moon and dropped their deadly cargo on the volunteers down there.

It was time to get drastic. She opened her comms panel and called Lanoe. "I'm out of clean options here," she told him. "I need your permission for something. I've got to use my disruptors."

Lanoe surprised her by laughing. "You too, huh?"

"I have no idea what you're talking about."

"Thom just used all of his. Zhang, do what you need to—we're way past the original plan here."

Zhang swerved away as a scout tried to get the drop on her. "Lanoe. Do we...do we have any...new plans?" she asked, choosing her words very carefully.

"Always," he told her. "Just none anybody's going to like."

"Understood," she said, because she didn't want to ask any more questions.

The scout maneuvered to get a better shot at her, but it was like a fly buzzing around her head. She worked her thruster board until her BR.9 did a backflip, then cut the scout apart with two quick pulses of PBW fire.

Only one scout remained, loitering on the far side of the ring of interceptors. Too far away to shoot at, too far for it to hurt her. She ignored it—right now she needed to break up those interceptors so she could hit the orbiters. Even with disruptors it was going to be a dicey proposition.

There was no time for fancy maneuvers, no room for error. She leaned forward on her stick and let go with her PBWs, just laying down fire to try to distract the enemy. Just as she'd expected, it had no effect. The interceptors were spaced perfectly, down to the millimeter, and they didn't budge. They started firing long before she came within their range and she had to feather her controls to dodge around an increasingly thick storm of impactors. One touched the rear left quarter of her fighter but she ignored the damage—nothing chimed at her, which meant she was still functional.

The first interceptor swam toward her, growing huge as she buzzed it close enough to watch the impactors belching from its guns. She loaded a disruptor and fired it right through the armor on the thing's nose. Without even waiting to see what happened she twisted around and shot through the gap between the interceptor and its nearest neighbor, right into the middle of their ring. Orbiters bobbed all around her and she spared a fraction of a second to lance as many as she could, their spidery cargo spilling into the void in a flurry of twitching limbs.

Next, she thought, and found an interceptor wheeling around to face her. She put a disruptor between two of its guns and moved on.

Number three. Impactors brushed against her canopy, less than a meter from her face. Nothing exploded or cracked. She launched her disruptor and looped up above the ring formation.

The fourth tried to pin her by flanking her while the fifth moved up to target her undercarriage. She raked its bow with PBWs mostly as an insult. It was moving too fast to get a clean hit so she put three disruptors into it and flew away.

The fifth loomed beneath her where she couldn't see it. She rolled over onto her side as its guns let loose. An impactor tore through one of her airfoils but she didn't need those. Her head spun as she twisted around and around, trying to get a good line on the bastard, but it was turning fast now—the interceptors were sluggish but once they got up to speed they could *move*. She spun around it in tighter and tighter circles, the blood pooling in one side of her head until she started to feel faint. Right before she would have blacked out she hit her trigger and sent four disruptors out in a fan pattern, two of which actually found their target.

The sixth interceptor nearly got her. It crept up on her right, low where she couldn't see it without instruments, and its impactors thundered against her fuselage, her vector field throwing out enough sparks to blind someone with human eyes. She saw them as nothing but heat. She pulled up into a loop, then twisted out at the top and dove back down to launch the last of her disruptors right through the bastard's heart.

She could hear nothing but her own breathing. Feel nothing but the blood throbbing in her veins. She felt like she was about to die.

With a shaking hand she reached for her sensor board.

Behind her, below her, the ring of interceptors exploded, one by one. Pieces of them went pinwheeling away into space, while their fuel cooked off in an ever-expanding cloud of high-energy gas. Half a dozen orbiters were caught in that blast and just shredded, reduced to unrecognizable debris that bounced and shook and spun away into nothingness.

She took a long, deep, gasping breath.

Twenty-one of the orbiters remained intact, still speeding toward their destination.

That was okay. They were unarmed and fragile. She could scoop them up at her leisure.

Above her a whole new squadron of scouts and interceptors was swooping down toward her position, backup sent just a little too late. She could safely ignore them—her mission now was just to cut up those orbiters. Save Aruna, and Ehta, and all the Nirayans down there, and that was easy. That was cake. That was—

She had of course completely forgotten about the last little scout, the one that had been keeping its distance. The one that had been too far away to worry about.

The one that had crept up on her now when she was too busy to notice.

❧

An impactor bounced off the side of Thom's BR.9, knocking him sideways in his seat. He screamed a little, by reflex. Red lights flashed all around him but he ignored them long enough to swerve out of the way of another shot before checking his damage control board. Nothing vital had been hit—but now an interceptor was turning toward him, lining him up for a new volley of impactors and he had to—

The interceptor exploded into shrapnel while he watched, bits of it flying in every direction, some of them knocking a scout off course before it could blast him. He threw his fighter into a cork-screw maneuver, just as he'd been taught, and dove for the periphery of the battle area, still trying to figure out what had happened.

His tactical board came up and he saw it cut in half by an orange line that passed right through where the interceptor had been. A shot fired from the guns on Aruna. If he had been less than a kilometer to the left, it would have smashed him instead.

His teeth ground together. His head felt like it was being

squeezed in a vise. He tried very hard to just breathe as he maneuvered around to where he could see Lanoe through his canopy.

He was a little heartened, at least, to see that the FA.2 wasn't in great shape, either. It was missing most of its airfoils and the paint was gone from one whole flank.

"Keep it together," Lanoe said. "We're making progress."

"We are?" Thom asked, and he heard the edge of panic in his own voice.

"Take a look at the queenship," Lanoe told him. Then he spun away to face a group of scouts that Thom hadn't even noticed. For a minute the two of them could only focus on holding off the little drones.

When Thom did have a chance to look at his sensor display he saw what Lanoe had been trying to show him. The face of the queenship was covered in new craters that were all exactly the same size. Places where the guns had struck the asteroidal hull, the depleted uranium rounds gouging out deep holes in the rock.

As Thom watched the display another round came flying past, not ten kilometers from his position. He felt it like a ripple running across his skin.

"Come on," Lanoe breathed. "Come the hell on…"

Together they tracked its course, even as new wings of enemy drones converged on their position. This round looked like it was headed straight for the web that covered the queenship's maw—exactly what Lanoe had been asking for. Thom found himself chanting along with Lanoe. "Come on…come on…"

The round tore through a scout that happened to be in exactly the wrong place at the right time. Thom's heart sank—he was sure the impact would deflect the round, make it miss its target by kilometers. But—

The scout had barely slowed the round down. It tore through the little margin of space between the scout and the queenship, then hit the web just a little off center. It punched through with seemingly no resistance at all. In a magnified view Thom could see the hole it left behind, about a meter across, the edges of the gap ragged with twisting, severed wires.

"Yes!" Lanoe shouted, loud enough to hurt Thom's ears. "Yes, this is what we needed. Another couple of shots in that same location and we'll have an opening I can fly through."

"You're going to…fly inside that thing?" Thom asked.

"It's the best shot we're going to get. Fly in there, shoot anything that looks important, run like hell. As soon as Zhang gets back, we'll start our attack. And then this will be over, Thom."

One way or another, Thom thought.

"We just need Zhang back. Hold on, I'll call her, get an ETA. Zhang? You there? I have you on an open channel. Go ahead, Zhang."

Scouts came at Thom from above, their eyeball cannons already hot. He broke away from Lanoe to weave a tight slalom between them, raking them with PBW fire. They tried to break formation to surround him but he was getting the hang of this, he thought. He was finally learning to fight.

"Go ahead, Zhang," Lanoe said again.

A scout spun around until Thom could see the barrel of its cannon looking straight in through his canopy. He blasted the thing before it could open fire, then immediately cut left in case there was another one behind it.

"Zhang, come in," Lanoe said.

More scouts—and an interceptor—were moving on Lanoe's position but the old pilot wasn't moving. Thom kicked open his throttle to screen the FA.2, ready to hold the enemy off no matter what it cost.

"Zhang—"

"Lanoe?" she said. "Lanoe, I think—I think I may have a problem."

~~∗~~

It happened so fast she was barely aware of what was going on. The scout was moving at high speed and she was just coming out of a tricky maneuver. Its plasma cannon was already hot. She was flying backward, focused on the ring of debris that was all that was left of the interceptor formation.

Maybe the scout had time to fire its weapon, maybe not—it didn't matter. Her BR.9 smashed into its plasma cannon just as it was reaching peak temperature. It exploded in a fireball that enveloped her completely, hot plasma washing over her instruments, vaporizing her airfoils, burning out her maneuvering jets.

Her main thruster cone had been hastily repaired back on Niraya. The fix had held up just fine through all of her wild maneuvers and desperate chases, but when it was heated up to several thousand degrees in a span of microseconds, it failed. The cone collapsed inward, crushing the heat sink that kept her engine cool.

Her fusion engine was already running hot. The heat from the exploding scout pushed it into a critical state. There were safety features built into the engine, interlocks to keep it from just exploding—instead it vented its contents, its own store of plasma, in a great plume of fire. For a full second the engine was transformed into a very efficient, incredibly powerful rocket engine.

All of its thrust hit Zhang square in the back.

Her inertial sink still had enough power to compensate. It locked her in place, freezing her so tight she couldn't breathe, so tight her heart stopped beating. Her tongue was glued to the side of her cheek, her left hand pinned to her shoulder. If the inertial sink hadn't worked exactly like it was meant to, she would have been reduced to a red mist by the sudden acceleration. Instead she was merely held perfectly in place, unable to react as her fighter went shooting past the cloud of orbiters, past the battle area altogether, past Aruna at a speed it had never attained before.

She could only watch in horror as Garuda, the ice giant, grew steadily larger in her forward view.

It was over in a moment. The reactor melted down, globs of superheated metal and fuel streaming away behind her like a blazing pennon. The thrust went away and her inertial sink relaxed and her heart could beat again, sending spikes of pain throughout her body. She gasped, desperately sucking at breath, unable even to scream.

An alert chime sounded behind her head, warning her that her engine had failed. She cursed at it, demanding that it shut up. It went away but other chimes sounded next, telling her that her cabin temperature had reached dangerous levels. Chimes informing her how many systems had just gone offline. Chimes warning her that her current trajectory was ill-advised.

That one was hard to ignore. When she brought up a navigational display, when she looked at where she was headed—she understood. The explosion had thrown her at high speed into Garuda's gravity well. She was headed directly for the ice giant's atmosphere. Now that her engine was gone, that was a one-way ticket.

A damage control board came up and told her everything she'd lost. It took a while to figure out what she still had. Maneuvering, main, and secondary thrusters were gone; that was to be expected. She still had her positioning jets—those had their own fuel supply not dependent on the main engine. She had a working inertial sink, but no vector field. Comms were still operational, at a minimal level.

She would take what she could get.

"Ehta," she called, "it's Zhang. I'm afraid...I'm afraid I won't be able to take out the rest of those orbiters. I'm sorry. I gave it my best shot." She closed off the channel before Ehta could respond. There was nothing more she could say there.

She licked her lips before she made her next call. The skin around her mouth was badly chapped. Well, she'd just gotten a terminal sunburn, hadn't she? She put all thoughts of her physical condition out of her mind. There was nothing she could do about that. As long as she could move her hands, there were still things she needed to do.

Like make one more call.

"Lanoe," she whispered. Then she cleared her throat and said the name properly. "Lanoe. I think—I think I may have a problem."

Outside her canopy, Garuda kept getting bigger, until it filled almost all of her view.

Chapter Thirty-Two

Say again." Ehta worked the controls of the tender's sensor pod, trying to boost the gain. The signal had been faint. Not faint enough that she hadn't understood Zhang's message. Just faint enough she could pretend otherwise.

"What happened?" Roan asked. The girl was over by the display that still showed the queenship's innards in high definition. Maybe she'd missed it.

"Say again, please, Zhang," Ehta called.

Nothing.

"Did she do it?" Roan asked. "Did she get the orbiters? Are we safe?"

Ehta didn't answer the girl. Instead she switched the imagery on the main display to show a much wider view. Garuda, the ice giant, in full color. The queenship still a tiny dot three hundred thousand kilometers away, farther than Aruna was from its planet.

A blue dot blinked in the display, too small to show up unless it drew attention to itself. Ehta zoomed in on it. The holographic image of Garuda grew huge until it was too big to fit inside the wardroom. The display shifted so that the planet was at the bottom of the view, as if Ehta and Roan were giants standing inside its thick atmosphere. Aruna orbited near the ceiling. The blue dot was still too small to see in detail, but now Ehta could see the wreckage it had left behind. Dozens of drones had been blown apart, creating a far-flung cloud of debris over half the distance between the queenship and the moon. Red blobs wobbled and then blinked out as molten debris cooled in the vacuum of space.

"She made a hell of a mess," Ehta said, softly.

There was one other salient feature of the display—the cone of orbiters, unescorted now but still headed for Aruna at high speed. More than twenty of them, and they would arrive in just over a minute.

She did the calculations in her head. The orbiters would need to slow down before they could establish stable orbits around the moon. That meant aerobraking, flying low through Aruna's airspace so that atmospheric drag would decelerate them below the local escape velocity. They would probably get pretty hot in the process, and need to cool down before they sprang open and dropped their cargo.

Then—call it another minute before the landers touched down. Before they killed every living thing on Aruna.

Not much time.

Not much she could do about it.

She ran the fingers of her gloves through her short hair. Then she turned around and looked at the display again.

"Hell's back door," she said, though the words came out as little more than hissing breath.

The winking blue dot—Zhang—wasn't changing its trajectory. It was moving in a shallow curve, the kind of long parabolic course that natural objects took in space, objects that didn't have the ability to control their flight. Objects at the mercy of gravity.

This particular course took Zhang far from the orbiters, far from anyplace she might reasonably want to go. It ended someplace very, very bad.

She tried raising Zhang again. "What's your engine status?" she asked. "Zhang, come in, what's your available delta vee? Zhang, are you receiving?"

There was no response. Instead a pale green pearl appeared in the corner of Ehta's eye, the universal symbol for a held or blocked call.

So Zhang was still alive—she just wasn't interested in talking.

That was very bad form for a military woman. You were always supposed to respond to incoming calls in a timely fashion—it was just part of the order of battle. Even if all you could do was say you were busy, say you didn't have time to report, you at least let your comrades know that you were still there.

If a consummate warrior like Zhang was blocking calls, that could only mean one thing—there was nothing left to say.

Ehta watched that wicked curve, the final trajectory of Zhang's BR.9, stretch out through space and time on the display. She knew that if there was any way Zhang could change her course, she would.

She was headed straight for Garuda, with no power, no propulsion.

"Is she coming back?" Roan demanded. Maybe she just didn't understand. She wasn't a pilot—maybe she didn't get it. "Is she going to get the last of them?"

"Shut up," Ehta said.

"What? Tell me what's going on!"

"A good woman is about to die, Roan. So shut your damned mouth."

Ehta sent Lanoe the data he'd requested, telemetry regarding Zhang's position and velocity. The calculus of her motion, all the numbers and variables and constants necessary to plot out where she was going and how fast. None of it helped—it just added up to a blue dot sinking across a field of white.

He waved it away.

"There's one last thing I can do," Zhang told him. "I've got about half a second's worth of burn left in my positioning jets."

"Save it," he told her. "Remember when I parked Thom down in the atmosphere of Geryon? He stayed aloft for days, Zhang. Days—long enough for me to come get him. You can hang in there at least a little while. Just get under the top cloud layer, where the aliens can't see you, then—"

"Lanoe, you've already run those numbers and you know it won't work. Thom still had an engine when he entered Geryon. I don't.

He was moving a lot slower than I am, too. I'm not going to make a leisurely descent through the clouds here. I'm going to hit Garuda like a meteor. My vector field's gone, most of my armor's burned off already. I'll be a fireball, not a spaceship. It'll be . . . quick."

"I've known you for a very long time, Zhang. I know you're not a quitter."

It took her a while to respond. Lanoe had to shift his position several times, to keep ahead of the drones that buzzed all around him. Thom was working hard to screen him from the worst of the attacks but they were still in the middle of a pitched battle—he couldn't just sit in space talking to Zhang as if they had all the time in the world.

He didn't give a tinker's damn. He was going to figure this out.

"I'm not quitting on you, Lanoe," she said. "I have one last thing I can do. The enemy sent a squadron of drones after the orbiters, reinforcements for the ones I slagged. They're still on my tail, though it looks like they're ready to break off pursuit. But here's the thing. If I fire my positioning jets just right, I can make it look like I'm changing course. It won't actually stop me from hitting the giant. It might fool them, though. If they think I'm still viable, maybe they'll chase me down. All the way down into the atmosphere."

"We can handle those ships—"

"Won't it be better if you don't have to?" she asked. "Let me go down fighting, Lanoe. They don't have airfoils. They can't handle atmosphere. If they follow me into the clouds they won't be able to get back out again. That's fifteen less drones that you have to worry about. I think it might actually work."

He paused, not so much to think about what she'd said as to dodge an incoming salvo of kinetic impactors. Three scouts jumped up on his left and he cut them apart before he replied.

"Forget it," he said. "I'm going to break off here and come get you. If I put every ounce of power I've got into a burn I can match your velocity, come alongside and you can jump out, grab hold of my fuselage, we can—"

"Lanoe," she said, in a tone of voice he knew all too well. "Don't you dare."

"I can't just...I can't—"

"You have to. There's too many people counting on you. If you break off now, you're admitting defeat. There's no way you'll be able to drive back the enemy once you lose momentum like that. Don't you remember what you said to me? You wanted to win a war. You want to win."

"I remember. But that was just talk. This is reality. Zhang—"

"You win this damned thing, Lanoe. I'm going to fire my positioning jets now. I'm going to help you *win*."

———※———

"Hellfire," Ehta said. "She's *brilliant*. I knew she was good, but..."

"Did she just move, a little?" Roan asked.

"Yes, yes she did," Ehta said, nodding vigorously. "And so did they," she added, jabbing a finger at the display where a squadron of drones had just shifted position as well. The movements were tiny, incremental. When you trained as a pilot, though, you learned to think in terms of time as well as space. You learned how objects moved in a vacuum, and how they would continue to move—like watching a chess game and seeing where the pieces would be three moves ahead. Ehta could see exactly what Zhang was trying to accomplish. And she was pretty sure it was going to work.

"She knows how the drones think," she explained to Roan. "She's been studying them this whole time. Getting a sense for when they'll jump, and when they'll hang back. She knows they want to protect those orbiters. She made the tiniest move toward them, and the drones reacted exactly as she expected. Even then, it shouldn't matter. Any human pilot would realize she was just making a feint, an empty gesture. But these machines—they don't care how many ships they lose. They don't think about what's going to happen, they just pursue their objective."

"So it's fifteen fewer drones, that's great," Roan pointed out. "But the orbiters are still coming, and Thom is still up there fighting the rest of the fleet."

"A fleet that just got fifteen units smaller. It might be enough— so far they've been able to screen the queenship because they had such overwhelming numbers. Fifteen ships won't make a huge difference, but it means they'll have to leave gaps in their defense. Gaps Lanoe can take advantage of."

"I don't understand, but okay—that's good," Roan said. She came over and leaned on Ehta's console, invading her personal space. "It doesn't change our situation, though."

"It might change everything," Ehta told her. "It could mean—"

"I mean *our* situation. Yours and mine. The orbiters are still coming here," Roan said. "And nobody's left to stop them."

Ehta turned and looked back at the display. Those twenty-odd orbiters were still there. Still getting closer.

"Yeah," she said. Her mouth was suddenly very dry.

"Somebody has to go fight them off."

Ehta couldn't find the words she needed.

"You're the only one who can," Roan said. "You need to take the tender up and fight them, Ensign Ehta."

"You know I can't."

Roan's face was pitiless. "Then you have to go tell Engineer Derrow and Elder McRae why they're going to die."

———※———

"Okay," Zhang said. "It's done. My sensors are fried, though. How does it look?"

"It looks like it's working," Lanoe said. "Of course, if they stop to think for even a second, they'll break off the chase."

"Such an optimist. It was worth a shot," Zhang told him.

"Sure," Lanoe said.

"I've got about thirty seconds until...well." She couldn't keep her voice from wavering, a little.

Lanoe squeezed his control stick until he felt like his fingers might break.

"I need to know something," she said. "This planet, Garuda.

I'm going to be spending a lot of time there from now on." She laughed. Good old Zhang. As long as she was laughing he didn't need to scream. "What color is it?"

"What?"

"What color is this planet? My eyes don't see color. But I want to know."

He had to think about it for a second. He hadn't paid it much attention. "It's... blue. Blue with purple bands. There's a big storm near the equator that's kind of, I don't know, indigo."

"It sounds beautiful," she told him. "Nice."

"Sure."

"Tell Thom something for me. Tell him I was impressed—I've never seen a raw recruit pick up our business so fast. He's a hell of a pilot. And when they write about this war, make sure they remember what Valk did. They'll try to minimize his role since he was Establishment, but don't let them."

"I will," he told her.

"Okay. Not much time now. I've been thinking about something lately," she told him. "Well, in the last two minutes or so. Something about us. About something I always meant to get around to saying."

"Zhang—"

"All the years I've known you and I never actually said it out loud. I thought it a million times but it never felt right, saying it, not for us, not for how we were together. None of that matters now. I love you, Lanoe. Always did."

"I love you, too," he told her.

"Say again?"

"Damn—is my signal breaking up?"

"Nope," she said. "I just wanted to hear it one more time."

"I love you, too, Bettina Zhang. I always will."

"Sure," she said, a gentle tease.

And that was just like her. Good old Zhang.

Leave on a joke.

"Marry me," he whispered, but there was no response.

On his display the blue dot winked out. Nothing remained but an unbroken field of white. Then white dots started to appear at the top of the screen. Following the blue, on exactly the same course. One after another.

The damned drones were chasing her, just like she'd wanted. One by one they hit the atmosphere and burst into flame. He switched to visual light imagery and pulled up a view of Garuda. Watched tiny firefly lights flare and then die out across its banded sky.

Chapter Thirty-Three

Lanoe?"

Lights flickered on his boards. An alarm chimed from somewhere. Not so loud that he had to think about it.

Through his canopy he saw them. The drones, lined up in elaborate formations. Scouts and interceptors, closing on his position. Ready to box him in. To kill him.

"Lanoe?" Thom's voice. He could ignore that, too.

Beyond the formations, the queenship. Implacable and huge. Just a tiny hole in its face, a crater the guns had made. Not big enough. Not big enough for a proper run.

That ship—that thing—had taken Zhang from him. Taken away the woman he loved. He'd wasted so much of his life not being with her. Not talking to her, not touching her skin. Not breathing in the smell of her. Not even thinking about her, because that had hurt too much. Then, for just a little span of time, she'd come back. And he'd just wasted more time being hung up over the fact she wore a different body.

Why had he been such a fool?

"Lanoe, come in, please."

One quiet night in a bunk. They'd had one soft night and then they'd gone back to war. Because war was what they did best. Better than being lovers. Better than being human, maybe.

They should have tried harder.

When she told him to go away, all those years ago, he should have said no.

He closed his eyes.

"Lanoe, I need to know what to do."

The aliens had taken Valk from him, too. That didn't hurt quite so much. But it meant something. Lanoe and Valk had never really had a chance to become true friends. Becoming comrades happened a lot faster, when you fought side by side.

It didn't matter what he'd seen when Valk took his helmet down. It didn't matter that there was no man inside that space suit. Valk had been more human than half the people Lanoe had ever met.

"Lanoe. I know it's hard, losing her, but..."

Thom. They were going to kill Thom. It was just a matter of time before the alien drones overwhelmed the kid. He'd done a remarkable job so far but Thom was no immortal warrior. He was going to die. Lanoe genuinely liked the kid. He had gone out of his way to save him, just so Thom could come here and get killed.

Just like Ehta, down on the moon.

Ehta, whose life he'd saved in the ring of some damned planet, Ehta who had fought by his side, who'd been one of his squaddies once upon a time. Ehta who came when he called even though she must have died inside to think of flying again, even though she was afraid. That counted.

Elder McRae, who had spent two weeks in a cargo container just to go ask for help from a world that was only ever going to shrug and turn away.

Engineer Derrow, who came to Niraya for a job, and then found out she was going to die because she picked the wrong planet.

Roan. Roan who threw her calling, her whole life away just to get him the guns he needed. The guns that punched that tiny little hole in the queenship.

They were going to die one by one and he was going to have to listen to their last words, and mourn them for just a little space of time, before he was killed himself.

He'd seen good people die before. So many times. He had fought for so many years, in so many wars. He had fought for Earth, and for the Navy, and for polys he didn't believe in. He'd fought because he was a warrior, because he didn't know what else to do.

For the first time in centuries he'd found a fight he could care about. That meant something. That counted. Was it worth it, to die here, for that?

Yes.

Was dying enough? Was sacrifice all that mattered, in the end?

No.

"No," he said out loud.

"Lanoe? I don't understand," Thom said. "What do you mean, 'no'?"

"No," he said. To himself. It wasn't enough. "But it's a start."

"Lanoe—"

"I'm going in," he said.

"Lanoe? You mean—you're going to try to fly inside that thing? But the hole the guns made—it's too small. You'll never get your fighter through there."

"If not, it won't be for lack of trying. Thom—cover me. You understand what this means? You understand there's no turning back?"

He could hear Thom swallow. The kid understood.

"Yes," he said.

Good.

━━✦━━

Ehta stepped out of the tender and down onto the soil of Aruna. The dirt crunched and squeaked under her boots. She had weight here, she had mass. She had to keep reminding herself of that fact. Her head felt like it had come loose, like it was just tethered to her neck by the thinnest of strings. She was breathing still and her heart was beating but she might have been a ghost, looking down on all of this from above.

Roan jumped down beside her. Together they walked the short distance to where the guns were still pounding away, every round they shot like a wind that would blow Ehta's soul away, send it cartwheeling away over the craters and ridges.

Engineer Derrow and Elder McRae were bent over a console, their hands moving in elaborate, private gestures. They looked busy. She really didn't want to interrupt them.

"There's no more time," Roan said.

The girl could be a real pain in the ass. Ehta liked her for that, most of the time, the way Roan refused to bow before age or rank or anything else. Right now she just wanted to strangle the little twerp.

Which, Ehta knew, was a sign the girl was right. This had to be done.

The engineer looked up when Ehta came close. "Something happened just now," she said. "I don't claim to understand, but—a bunch of the drones just flew right into the planet." She pointed upward. Garuda filled a quarter of the sky, its purple light leaving highlights on her shoulders and the side of her helmet.

"That was Zhang," Ehta said. She felt like she was belching out the words, pulling them from somewhere deep in her gut. "She's gone now."

"Gone? As in . . . ?"

Ehta nodded.

"I'm—I'm sorry, I know she was a friend of yours," Derrow said, one hand on her helmet as if she wanted to press it to her forehead. "But I have to know. Did she get all those orbiters, or . . . are we . . ."

She didn't finish the thought. Maybe because she didn't want to say it out loud. Maybe just because she saw the answer in Ehta's face.

A bubble of acid popped inside Ehta's stomach. She thought she might vomit inside her helmet. That was never good. It would take weeks to get rid of the smell, at the very least.

Lucky for her she'd be dead within the hour, she guessed.

"What about the guns?"

It was the elder who spoke. The old woman's face looked ridiculous behind the carbonglas of her helmet. Nobody like her should ever wear a space suit—it just didn't look right.

"Can't they shoot down the orbiters? We have all of this fire-power, right here."

The engineer lifted her arms. Let them fall again. "We'll try. They're not designed for that kind of work, though. They're meant to shoot at much larger targets. Better chance of getting a hit that way. But . . . we'll try."

They turned away, back to their console. As if Ehta weren't even there anymore.

The thing she'd dreaded, the thing she absolutely could not handle, just hadn't happened.

No one had asked her to save them. Nobody had even consid-ered the idea that she might just magically get over her disability and learn to fly again. To just not be nervy anymore.

She turned to go. To head back to the tender, where she could be alone, maybe. Where she could just wait this out. Where—

She saw the PBW cannon mounted on the side of the tender.

Then she turned around and looked behind the engineer. The absurd little rover sat there, a thing made of hollow pipes and over-inflated tires. A roll bar stuck up above the driver's seat, with a little dish antenna clamped to it like it was wearing a flower in its hair.

On a planet, the idea that had just come to her would be laugh-able. The weight of the cannon would just be too much. But on a little moon like this . . .

"I'm on it," she said, and she was right back in her body again. Awake, aware, alert. Here. "I'm on it," she said again. "I just need a little help."

A lot of eyes turned to look at her. It was Roan who spoke first.

"What does that mean? Exactly?"

Engineer Derrow shook her head. "Never mind that. What do you need?"

"A good mechanic." She didn't wait for an answer. She knew that Derrow had those to spare. She walked over to the rover, put her hands on the roll bar. Pulled backward, hard, testing its strength.

"What are you going to do?" Roan demanded.

"I may not be a pilot anymore," she told the girl. It felt like the bar would hold. "But I'm still one hell of a marine."

Zhang had pulled a full squad of enemy drones down into the hell of Garuda's atmosphere with her. Some eighty-odd ships remained, gathered in three thick formations. Arcs of steel like bands of armor across the face of the queenship. The early part of the battle had been especially hard on the enemy's scouts, which meant that a full third of the alien fleet was made of interceptors. All but immune to PBW fire.

They did not intend to let Lanoe through. They had computer-generated attack strategies and more than enough firepower to take down an FA.2 and a BR.9.

Lanoe's only trump card was that he didn't plan on flying away from this. He didn't need to bother figuring out how he would survive his run.

"Scouts on your four," Thom called. "Interceptors at eleven high!"

Lanoe saw them.

He twisted around a line of scouts that flew in such perfect formation they might have been wired together. Jinked to his left as they started firing, plumes of bright plasma streaming across his canopy. Sweat burst from his forehead and rolled down into his eyebrows, but he just blinked it away.

The interceptors on top of him started firing long before he was inside their effective range. They shot with precision for once, careful not to hit the scouts or each other. Kinetic impactors rained down around him and he feathered his stick to dodge those he could, taking those he couldn't as deflecting shots that rattled his vector field and filled his view with sparks. His airfoils were gone almost instantly but he didn't need them out here in the vacuum. One shot struck his canopy, denting the carbonglas, but he didn't even flinch.

Behind him Thom cut the scouts up like he was slicing a cake. The kid had learned to shoot, there was no denying it. Lanoe had forgotten to tell him what Zhang had said, her encouraging words, but there was no time now.

"Stay below me for this bit," he called. He didn't bother checking his displays to make sure Thom complied. Three more interceptors were coming up from down there, splitting off their formation to try to catch the human pilots unaware. They failed at that task, but their impactors were harder to dodge when Lanoe couldn't see them coming. One hit the FA.2's undercarriage, a nearly direct hit, but not near enough. The fighter jumped under Lanoe, his seat hitting him hard against the backs of his legs, but his positioning jets compensated automatically and put him back on course.

More scouts, a wall of them dead ahead. He opened up with both barrels, not bothering to aim at all, just punching his way through. Debris from a scout that wasn't quite dead smacked across his fuselage, its eyeball cannon still trying to track him, to aim, but he was gone before it could fire.

Two of the massive formations, nearly thirty drones each, were already moving, tightening their screen, blocking him from his approach to the queenship. He rolled over on his side then dove as if he were breaking off his run. Fire from Thom's PBWs raked across the space where he'd been, catching a scout that had tried to sneak up on him. Its cannon was hot and it exploded in a vast bloom of fire that blocked Lanoe's view of the moving formations. That was fine—he didn't need to see what they were doing. He could maneuver a lot faster than those interceptors.

He dove for the better part of a kilometer, then yanked back hard on his stick. His maneuvering jets pulsed with flame as they twisted him around, his view rolling this way, then that, and then his main thrusters caught and he rocketed upward, right between the two massive formations. Both of them opened fire the second he started his climb but he just corkscrewed past, letting them fire broadsides right into each other. Maybe they scratched each other's paint jobs—he knew better than to expect them to wipe each other out in the crossfire.

He rushed past a new line of scouts like a gauntlet of blow-torches, fire washing over him, but he was moving fast enough that it did nothing but start red lights flashing on his damage control board and moisten his armpits. His engine was running hot but he disengaged the automatic temperature controls. Flooding the reactor with coolant now would just slow him down.

"Interceptors," Thom called, but Lanoe had already seen them.

Seven of the big beasts, flying in a ring formation between him and the web that covered the queenship's maw. Spaced perfectly so that they could avoid shooting each other but still leave no gap he might fly through.

Well, he had an answer for that. He loaded his disruptors, all of them, and let them go in a broad fan, the FA.2 shaking every time one of them launched.

He didn't need them where he was going.

The rover had been designed for one simple thing: to let Engineer Derrow move around the gun camp at a pace slightly faster than her legs could carry her. It was built of lightweight modular components and a single storage battery that had half run down by the time Ehta got to it.

The engineers did their best.

They stripped out the old battery and mounted four fresh ones in its place, holding them onto the frame with nylon straps. When they started up the little engine it roared but all of the rover's bolts shivered and started shaking themselves loose. They welded those down as best they could and moved on. They tore the little dish antenna off the roll bar and tossed it away, then reinforced the bar with an additional length of pipe, using spot welds to let it carry some real weight.

They unbolted the PBW cannon from the side of the tender. Like all Naval technology it was designed to attach to any available hardpoint. The roll bar almost qualified. They clamped it on tight, then strung power cables from its leads to the batteries. The cannon had *not* been designed to be triggered by hand. Ehta brought a heavy rifle from the tender's stores and they cut its grip off, then ran command lines from the cannon's electronics to the trigger. It would work.

They bolted nylon straps to the rover's back end, so Ehta could wedge herself in back there and hopefully not fall off.

They overhauled the rover's steering, its suspension, its brakes. It was going to be ridiculously top-heavy, there was no getting around that. The PBW cannon weighed more than the rover did. In Aruna's low gravity, though, it could function. As long as it didn't corner too hard.

When it was ready to go the engine thrummed with power. Ehta fired off a quick burst of the cannon and a high-density particle beam shot off into space, making all the engineers duck their heads.

"If I had time, I could put armor plating on there," Derrow said, all but wringing her hands in concern. "You're going to be pretty exposed."

"If we had time we could build a squad of tanks," Ehta told her. "We don't."

It was Roan's turn to object. "How are you supposed to drive and shoot at the same time?" she asked.

"I'm not," Ehta told the girl. She wasn't sure if Roan could see the nasty smile on her face behind the flowglas of her helmet. "Jump in."

Roan stared at the narrow driver's seat at the front of the rover. "You can't expect—"

"You know how to drive. I saw you drive Thom all over Niraya. Get in," Ehta said, "or explain to all these nice people why they have to die."

The girl climbed into the seat. She had to duck her head over to one side to avoid the barrel of the cannon, but she could reach the steering wheel and the pedals just fine.

"We'll send you all the data we can," the engineer promised. "Let you know where the landers touch down. That's about all the help we can give you."

"I'll take it," Ehta said. "Roan, get us moving."

The girl goosed the accelerator and they shot away over the loose soil of the moon, a vast plume of dust jumping up behind them.

———— ·<· ————

The interceptors burst apart, one by one. Big chunks of metal debris spun and bounced before the web, some of it smashing into the FA.2. The jagged remnants of an interceptor gun hit his canopy head-on and a spiderweb of cracks shot across his view. He jettisoned the canopy, sending it hurtling away. He didn't need it anymore.

"Scouts coming in," Thom called.

"Keep them back!" Lanoe shouted. The queenship filled the view ahead. The web twitched as he approached, its filaments readjusting as debris punched tiny holes through its thin substance.

One thin arm of wire rose from the web, its end twisting toward him like a serpent rising from its coil, sniffing the air. Searching him out.

He set the FA.2's controls to run an automatic program. Reached up and unbuckled his safety harness.

Now came the hard part.

He was still a good kilometer out from the web, still moving fast. The fighter's retros burned hard to slow the pace. He had no desire to die the way Valk had, from sudden deceleration.

"Lanoe, they've seen you!" Thom called.

"Then shoot them!"

The deceleration pushed him backward, back into his seat. He grabbed the edge of the fuselage where his canopy used to be and pushed up until he was standing in the cockpit, his head and shoulders outside the fighter. A piece of a blasted interceptor the size of a cow came rolling toward him and he ducked just in time. It would have taken his head off.

Light flashed off to his left. He looked and saw Thom fending off a whole wing of scouts, laying down suppressing fire and maneuvering hard to keep them from catching up with him. Off to

his right he saw shadows moving, more scouts or maybe interceptors rushing in to stop him before he reached the web.

He needed to move fast.

With a grace that belied his years, Lanoe flipped himself out of
his cockpit and grabbed a jagged piece of metal that used to be one
of his airfoils. The whole side of his fuselage was dented in and broken by enemy fire. It hurt to see that damage, when he'd been with
the FA.2 for so long.

He knew it was only going to get worse.

He crawled across the fighter's body, pulling himself along to its
undercarriage, wrapping his legs around one of the landing gear.
There was so much debris flying past him it was like being in the
middle of a dirty snowstorm. He reached for another handhold just
as a stray impactor, left over from some long-ago salvo, smashed
into the fuselage and he had to yank his hand back in a heartbeat
or lose it. The impactor tore open a plastic fairing and shredded the
sensitive electronics behind it, and he felt the whole FA.2 lurch to
one side, the start of what was going to be a nasty flat spin.

Ahead of him more filaments of the web had lifted away from
the main mass, tentacles groping toward him in the dark. There
was no more time. He found the panel he wanted, a recessed part
of the fuselage about as long as his arm. He got the fingers of his
glove under the edge of the panel and tore at it with all his strength.
The whole panel came loose, cartwheeling off into the debris
cloud. Underneath lay six lumpy spherical objects, each the size of
his fist. Bombs, just like the ones he'd used to destroy the geothermal power plant on Aruna.

One by one he tore them loose from their restraining clips, then
stuck them to his chest with adhesive patches. He was pretty sure
they wouldn't go off accidentally, that they needed to be armed
manually. Pretty sure. He'd never tried anything like this before.

A whip of steel smacked across the back of the FA.2, tearing at
its thruster cones. One of them cracked apart and bits of it showered down across Lanoe's helmet and shoulders, making him duck.

Another filament snared the nose of the FA.2.

A third got its landing gear just a split second later.

The fighter had been decelerating and it was moving nowhere near as fast as Valk had when he'd been caught by the web. Yet when the filaments caught the FA.2 and dropped its velocity to zero in a fraction of a second, there was still a lot of momentum that had to go somewhere.

Lanoe was torn free of the fighter's undercarriage. He bounced hard off its side, then went spinning off into the dark, like any other piece of debris. Blood rushed to his head and his vision dimmed. He could hear himself breathing a hundred times a minute. Feel his heart bursting in his chest.

"Lanoe!" Thom cried.

The rover bumped and bounced over the rough terrain. Ehta held on tight to the cannon and forced herself not to lock her knees, riding with the suspension rather than against it. Roan kept her head down as she drove, as if she expected a lander to come crashing down on her at any second.

They headed down a long slope at the outer edge of the crater, the rover constantly threatening to come up off its rear wheels and send them somersaulting down to the plain below. Ehta focused on the heads-up display in her helmet that showed the orbiters lining up in the sky above. She thought maybe she saw one, an especially bright star streaking over the horizon.

They had a pretty good idea of where the landers would come down. The landing zone was a stretch of relatively flat ground a hundred kilometers across, right outside the crater. That left a huge amount of ground to cover but—

"There!" Roan shouted, pointing up at the sky.

"I see it," Ehta replied.

A thin streamer of fire coming straight down from above. Even the thin atmosphere of Aruna was still thick enough to heat the lander up as it fell, and it was glowing a dull red as it touched down in a crown-shaped spray of dust, maybe ten kilometers from their position. Roan poured on the juice, sending them careening over a low rille, so they briefly went airborne, then crashed back down with a thump that made Ehta's shins ache.

"Easy!" she called, but the girl ignored her. She drove straight for the landing site, then pulled up short three hundred meters away, turning into her deceleration to keep the rover from rolling. They rocked to a stop, side-on to the impact site.

Ehta peered through the slowly settling dust. She thought maybe she could see it, a dark, angular shape in the murk. Climbing to its feet, its legs straightening.

She'd forgotten how big the damned things were.

Six meters high. All legs and pointed claws and nothing else. No head, no face, no eyes. Nothing even remotely human about it. It didn't even look like an insect, or a cephalopod. It was alien, just alien. Something human eyes were never meant to see.

A wave of dust blew over them, fizzing quietly as it scoured her helmet. The dark shape was moving, she was sure of it. Walking toward them on its many legs.

Then, as the dust cleared a little more, she saw she was wrong. It wasn't walking toward them.

It was running at full speed.

Its wickedly pointed claws stabbed at the ground, shoving its mass forward until it was bounding at them, one or two legs always in the air, reaching as if it could extend those legs across the intervening space and impale them where they stood.

"Shoot it," Roan said, breathless. Then louder. "Shoot it!"

"I can shoot while you drive," Ehta called back. She brought the cannon around on its pintle mount and tried to aim. No virtual Aldis sights here, not so much as an iron tab at the end of the barrel to help her get a bead on the thing. She squeezed her trigger and the particle beam spat from the gun, scoring a deep black line through the soil between them and the lander. She brought her aim up a little, just as Roan threw the rover into gear and got them moving again, lurching forward in an arc that took them around the lander. Ehta fired again and again, trying to get a feel for the cannon, trying to hit something.

Her beam finally cut across the lander's front legs, digging in deep through its cladding and into the bundles of wires inside. A leg came loose, severed near its root, and the lander tumbled forward, rolling with its momentum, knocked off its feet.

Ehta whooped in joy, but not for very long.

A thing with that many legs could spare a few. It was up again in an instant, running toward them just as fast as before.

And just off to Ehta's left three more of them were coming down, burning through the atmosphere and striking the ground hard enough to leave craters.

※

Lanoe bounced off a chunk of debris hard enough that he saw stars. He couldn't catch his breath. A filament of the web slashed toward him but it snagged on the broken skeleton of a scout, and they both went spinning away.

Behind him as he tumbled he caught stroboscopic images of the FA.2, as more and more thin arms of the web grabbed it and wrapped it up like they were spinning a cocoon. The entire fuselage had collapsed inward and the nose had crumpled upward. The next time he spun around he saw the fighter break in half. Its reactor collapsed, blinding him with a sudden flash of light.

Lanoe

His helmet responded by turning opaque, protecting him from the harsh light. He tried to flick his eyes at the virtual controls to depolarize the flowglas but he could barely feel his face, much less move any of it. As he spun his blood was all shoved into his head and his feet and he felt like an overripe tomato, like he might burst.

Inside the opaque helmet he could only see afterimages, flickering green and blue. He couldn't hear anything but the thudding of his own heart.

As quickly as the helmet had polarized it cleared again. He

squinted to see what was left of the fighter but there was nothing but more debris, more chunks of metal spinning between the thin columns of the filaments.

are you

His back struck something—he never saw what—and he went flying off in a new direction, his arms flailing in front of him. He fought for control, fought to get his right hand over to his left wrist even as centrifugal force kept forcing it back.

There...there...just another centimeter, and the tip of his index finger just brushed the gray surface of the display patch on his wrist. A flashing red screen popped up, filled with warnings—hundreds of collision alerts, oxygen and nitrogen gauges dropping as he hyperventilated, biometric readings telling him what he already knew, that he was perilously close to losing consciousness.

He was so busy looking at the alerts he almost missed the filament that came speeding toward him, its thin end moving so fast it could cut him in two.

receiving

He threw up his arms, knowing it would do no good at all, knowing he was dead, that his incredibly risky gamble had not so incredibly failed, that he had thrown away everything on—

A particle beam stabbed out of the dark, a perfectly straight line studded with gems of pure light. The filament came apart in sections that moved slowly away from each other, inert and harmless, each of them missing Lanoe's suit by full meters.

He saw more beams slanting down through the debris, carving away at a nest of serpents that twisted and bent beneath him. Filaments he hadn't even seen, filaments that had been reaching for him, filaments that recoiled now, away from the deadly beams.

Lanoe?

With a start he realized that Thom was trying to contact him. The kid's voice was incredibly faint and distant. Whether that was because of the congested blood in Lanoe's eardrums or that his suit's comms unit had taken damage, he didn't know.

"I'm alive!" he shouted. "Thom, I'm alive."

He reached for his wrist again. Fought with physics until he could tap at the display. He switched on his suit's emergency positioning jets. Fired one after another until he'd canceled out the worst of his spin. Almost instantly the blood flowed out of his head. He felt like he might pass out for a second, and even when that sensation was gone a horrible ball of nausea cramped his stomach, but he was alive.

And right where he wanted to be.

—✦—

"Go, go, go!" Ehta shouted as a lander came chasing after her. She yanked her feet out of the nylon straps and jumped up on the roll bar so she could swivel the cannon around a hundred and eighty degrees, then poured particle fire into the pursuing drone. It gained ground steadily, even as she chopped limb after limb from its mass.

"Go!" she cried again, not even bothering to line up shots, just spraying fire across the chasing lander's front. "Faster!" she shouted.

Without warning Roan stamped on the brakes. Ehta's feet went up in the air and she had to grab hold of the cannon to avoid being thrown clear of the rover. Behind her the lander took a swipe at her with one long, jointed leg but she cut it off before she'd even got her footing back. The thing fell back and she kept cutting away until it toppled over—only then turning to look and see why Roan had stopped so suddenly.

Dead ahead of them stood two landers, one to either side. Closing in.

"Reverse!" Ehta shouted.

Roan worked the gear selector, peering back over her shoulder so she could steer and avoid the dead lander back there. She got them turned around, then threw the rover back into forward motion. Ehta hurriedly got her feet back in the straps and swiveled the cannon around to point at the lander coming from their left—it was the closer of the two, the more dangerous.

They were still coming down. Pillars of fire stretched upward into the sky all around them. They were in serious danger of being surrounded—Roan was a hell of a driver but she needed room to maneuver. Ehta looked around to see where the worst danger lay.

She spotted a gentle slope leading down toward the rim of a small crater. "That way," she said, pointing, before going back to shooting at the lander on the left.

"That takes us farther away from the camp," Roan said. Meaning, away from any possible help, Ehta knew.

The girl didn't seem to understand that they were it, the only chance the engineers had. "These things go for the nearest living thing they can find," she told Roan. "That's all they're programmed for. Leading them away from Derrow's people is a good thing. Trust me!"

"You're the boss," Roan said, and turned the wheel hard to the left.

All around Lanoe filaments of the web rose up and lashed toward him. He dove under them, then twisted around to see how far he was from his goal. Not far now—the ragged hole in the web was only a few hundred meters away—but his suit only had a small reserve of propellant left. The jets built into his boots and shoulders weren't designed for this kind of acrobatic work.

Above him Thom did what he could, dashing in until the tendrils snapped out toward his BR.9, then climbing hard away to stay out of their range. His PBWs cut through the individual filaments just fine, but there were hundreds of them—thousands. The big triangular spikes they'd seen when they first scanned the queenship had been made of countless strands of metal braided together so tight they looked like one solid mass. It seemed the queenship could control every single one of those threads independently.

One slashed across his arm, and he barely accelerated away in time. It cut through an outer layer of his suit but foam hissed across the tear, sealing it automatically.

Next time he wouldn't be so lucky. Nor were the filaments the only thing he had to worry about. Debris was hurtling all around him, some moving fast enough to tear him apart if it hit him. His suit didn't have a vector field to protect him.

He needed a lucky break, and he needed it now.

When it came, though, it nearly killed him.

A shadow passed across his view and he swiveled around to look up, away from the queenship—and saw the wreckage of a swarmship drifting toward him. The swarmship was just a skeletal frame, having deployed most of its drones except a few that had been slagged and hung like rotten fruit off its spars. It wasn't moving fast but there were still tons of metal in the thing and if it fell on him it would crush him like a bug. He reached for his wrist controls and found he only had a tiny reserve of propellant left—nowhere near enough to get him out of the way of the giant skeleton.

He looked desperately for a way out but couldn't find one. There was no way he could get clear.

Of course, if it was going to hit him, it couldn't help but strike the queenship. Suddenly every filament around him went taut as they stretched upward to snag the swarmship, trying desperately to cancel its momentum before it could crash into the web. Lanoe touched the controls on his wrist and burned hard, straight down toward the web.

The filaments ignored him. Fending off the swarmship occupied every single one of them.

"Thom," he called. "Thom—I'm going in!"

"Received," Thom called back. The kid was busy holding off a group of scouts that had moved in to do what the filaments no longer could.

"Do what you can," Lanoe told him. "Just—get clear of this and stay alive, and try to—"

"I'll be here when you come back!" Thom shouted. Lanoe could hear all the warning chimes ringing inside Thom's cockpit. "I'll wait for you!"

"Don't wait too long," Lanoe said.

The last of his propellant escaped from his jets just as he smacked into the web. He'd half-expected it to grab him and pull him apart but it just twisted under him, individual filaments moving to fill gaps in the web every time a piece of debris fell around him.

He'd been very careful about where he came down. Only a few dozen meters away was the hole that Derrow had managed to punch through the web. Its edges looked ragged, bits of sheared wire sticking up in every direction. Some of them twitched but most were just inert.

He dragged himself over to the hole. It was going to be a tight fit. His suit might tear on the jagged edges.

He'd come this far, though. He wouldn't stop now, not after what the bastards had done to Zhang. He wriggled his head and shoulders into the hole, then pushed hard to get through, into the perfect blackness beyond.

Into the queenship.

Chapter Thirty-Four

One by one the landers came galloping after the rover. Ehta took a half a second to check her wrist display and see the data Engineer Derrow had sent her.

Hot damn. It was working. Every single one of the landers was headed in their direction. Not normally something to celebrate. But if even one of the landers had turned around and headed toward the crater where the volunteers were, it would have been a catastrophe. They had no weapons to defend themselves. They could have huddled inside the tender but it would have just been a matter of time before a lander could tear through its armored walls.

It looked like that wasn't going to happen—at least as long as Ehta and Roan kept moving and shooting.

Ehta sliced through the front legs of a lander and it stumbled—only to be overrun by the landers behind it, trampled as they clambered over its twitching body. She got a lucky shot on another one, her particle beam lancing right through its legs so it fell over, inert, shaking the ground with its impact even in Aruna's low gravity.

There were still more than a dozen of them back there. But this was working, she was having an effect, thinning their numbers and—

Roan just had time to say "Wh—" before a pillar of flame came down right beside them, a lander touching down only meters away. Ehta hugged the cannon as the girl threw her wheel over to one side and cornered, hard, trying to get away from the impact site. Roan knew the rover's tolerances by now and she didn't cut her turn too hard, but she didn't account for the shock wave of the impact.

The sky and the ground tried to switch places as the rover went up on two wheels. If it tipped over the two of them could probably right it—but that would take precious seconds, and the herd of landers would be on them before they could get moving again.

Ehta gripped the cannon's hot barrel with one hand, then threw herself over the side of the rover, dangling over its edge between its two spinning wheels. The rover started to right itself and Roan turned the wheel this way, then that, until it fell back to the ground with a crunch. Ehta's ankle hit a rock and she felt her foot twist around inside her boot. Sharp pain lanced up her calf.

"You okay?" Roan asked, as she accelerated away from the impact site.

"Fine, keep going!" Ehta shouted, dragging herself back up onto the back of the rover. "They're almost on us!"

"I'm doing what I can," Roan said, but then Ehta felt the rover fishtail underneath her as Roan stamped on the brakes and swung the wheel at the same time. "Damn damn d—"

In her desperation to get the rover back on all four wheels, Roan must have ignored what was right in front of her.

"Hold on!" she cried, as the rover went pitching over the rim of a tiny crater.

───◦─◦───

No gravity under his feet. No air inside, no warmth, nothing you would find on a human ship. No lights.

Lanoe could hear himself breathing, the same thing you heard when you were floating in the void, very far from anything else. His eyes adjusted slowly to the gloom. In the distance, very faint, he could see a smudge of red.

He switched on his suit lamps, adjusted his helmet's filters for low-light amplification.

He didn't know what he'd expected to see, really. Not decks full of aliens bent over consoles, calling out orders. Not a giant thing made out of legs sitting at the center of it all, meditating on war. Something more than this, though.

Before him the inside of the queenship was almost all empty space, cold, useless darkness. Metal catwalks spiraled inward, stretching toward the red glow. Curved constructions of long girders braced by triangular supports. They looked almost like something humans would build, but they were off—they didn't run straight, not anywhere, but always curved in long sinuous coils, and the supports were spaced farther apart from each other than seemed proper. Here and there on those skeletal frames crouched big pieces of machinery that shook and twitched and pushed out the round shapes of orbiters. Factories, building war machines. Nearer the center larger structures hung motionless and unsupported. Impossible to guess what those were—their forms were covered in scaffolding that hid their intent.

Here and there on the catwalks, things moved. Workers—bundles of legs, some of which ended in tentacular hands. There weren't nearly as many of them as he'd expected. They picked their way along the girders carefully, as if they were trying to walk in a place that had no floor, no down of any kind.

Around the maw, just inside the web, the catwalks grew together to form a thick ring. A sort of staging area, maybe. He saw the thick body of an interceptor embedded in the mass of girders as if it had crashed there and was slowly being absorbed by the metalwork. Then he noticed it had no thrusters, no guns, just cavities where such things should be and his perception shifted and he thought that no, the drone ship hadn't crashed there—more like it was *growing,* the girders around it like stems holding a piece of complicated fruit. Workers scuttled over the interceptor's surface, welding pieces of the war machine into place. Even as he noticed them, though, they stopped moving. Lifted themselves up on their many legs. They didn't have eyes, or any visible sensory organs, but he knew, he was certain that they had just become aware of his presence.

They didn't need to waste any time deliberating among themselves, or checking with superiors. As one, with fluid motions, they came streaming toward him across the catwalks, multi-fingered hands raised before them.

They made no sound at all. They didn't need to. He understood just fine what they wanted—to tear him to pieces.

Lanoe reached down to his hip and found his sidearm, the one he'd nearly killed Maggs with, back in the basement of the Retreat. It had maybe a dozen rounds left in its clip. There were at least twenty workers coming for him, moving so fast they would be on him in seconds.

He really, really wished he'd had time to come up with a better plan.

⤙⤚

The cannon went spinning out of Ehta's hands. She needed them to grab the roll bar, to hold on. The rover tilted underneath her and she felt weightless, that horrible, water-in-the-gut feeling of zero gravity, and she heard Roan scream.

She ducked down as low as she could. There was no chance of using her weight to balance the rover this time. Its wheels spun in Aruna's poison air. Stars and clouds twisted overhead and they were falling, bouncing in the low gravity, bouncing and falling and clattering down the steep slope.

She heard something creak, some pipe in the rover's chassis failing under stress. Heard it snap with a sudden, final sound, and then a wheel came up and smashed into the side of her helmet—the flowglas held but her neck was wrenched sideways. She felt the rover dig in hard as it struck loose soil but still it was falling, spinning around now so all she could see was white, powdery dirt and then she was facedown in it, half-buried.

"Ehta!" Roan called. "Ehta! Are you alive back there?" There was something wrong with Roan's voice. Or maybe Ehta's ears were ringing, or—or her brain was still reeling from the crash, or—

She pushed herself up with her hands. Looked around.

"Ehta?"

"I'm okay," she called back. "I think." Her neck felt weird and her left arm throbbed with pain. Broken, maybe, but when she got to her feet her suit just tightened from her elbow to her wrist and she could move the arm just fine.

She looked around and saw they'd fallen all the way down into the crater. The dirt at the bottom was soft and shifted under her feet, like she was walking on sifted flour. In the low gravity she didn't quite sink into it.

The rover was a total loss. It had been designed to be lightweight and to break down into small, easily portable sections. It was a twisted pile of junk now. One of the batteries had cracked open and lithium slurry was draining into the loose soil. Incredibly toxic, but it wouldn't eat through their suits, so she decided not to care.

"I don't think we're driving out of here," she told Roan. Roan, who—

Roan.

Where the hell was Roan?

She ran around to the front side of the wreckage. Not that it was easy to tell which side of the wreckage was the front. The steering wheel had snapped off completely and lay a meter or so away. She found a boot sticking out from underneath the tangled pipes. She grabbed at the chassis and lifted it, her injured arm barely complaining. And there the girl was.

Flat on her back, staring upward with vacant eyes. Impaled on a piece of broken pipe.

"Are you okay?" Roan asked.

"Oh, hellfire," Ehta said, kneeling down next to the girl. "Roan—Roan, honey, you're hurt. Don't try to move."

"Okay."

Ehta searched through the wreckage, hoping to find a first aid kit. There wasn't one, and it wouldn't have helped anyway. She went back and saw that Roan was breathing, still. There was very little blood—the thing that impaled her had penetrated her suit and her body with very little resistance.

Ehta had no idea what to do. She'd never been trained as a field medic. Pilots typically either died in space instantaneously, or were able to fly themselves home. Marines typically just died where they fell.

"Is Thom okay?" Roan asked.

"What? I—I don't know," Ehta told the girl. Did Roan think they were back in the tender, monitoring the sensors? "No, wait, never mind. I just checked and he's fine. He's just fine."

"Okay," Roan said. "Watch out."

Ehta spun around, unsure what she was going to see. It didn't surprise her in the least, though.

All around the rim of the little crater, the landers had gathered. Standing above her like a fence of claws, blocking out her view of the sky.

One of them put a tentative leg down into the crater, testing the steep wall, preparing to clamber down toward the two humans.

Lanoe lifted his pistol and lined up a shot. The worker was no more than five meters away. The projectile dug through one of the thing's hands, blasting off a couple of fingers, but that didn't even slow the drone down.

Others came up behind it. They clambered over each other, grabbed each other's limbs to throw themselves forward, toward him. Lanoe cursed. If he didn't move they would be on him in seconds.

He looked up—toward the center of the queenship, toward the red glow. Then he braced himself as best he could with no gravity to support him and kicked hard, tossing himself off the gantry and out into empty space. He started to tumble almost instantly but there was nothing he could do. His suit's propellant tanks were empty and he was at the mercy of physics.

Behind him one of the workers tried to do what he had done. It had a lot more legs to kick with and it came at him fast, its dozens of limbs spinning outward until it looked more like a sea anemone than a spider.

If he didn't act fast it would catch up to him. Pull him to pieces in midflight. He lifted his pistol and steadied it with both hands. Fired three quick shots. Two missed. The third one barely chipped at the cladding on the worker's leg—but it sent the bastard spinning off in a slightly different direction. For a second he was safe.

Then his back struck something very hard and unyielding and he started bouncing away, all the air in his lungs exploding out of his mouth and misting the inside of his helmet. He twisted himself around and reached out with one hand, desperately trying to get hold of whatever was behind him, whatever it was he'd hit.

It was another of the long spiral catwalks, a helix pointing at the red smear at the center of the queenship. He held on even as momentum tried to yank him free. Bounced around like a ball on a string until he could get one leg around a girder, bracing himself.

Back near the maw more of the workers launched themselves toward him, dandelion seeds of wicked limbs drifting through the open space. He lifted his pistol but it was useless—there was no way he could shoot all of them, and even if he did he doubted he'd be lucky enough to push them away like he had the first one.

No, they would catch him eventually. Especially since his lamps showed him movement all around him now, plenty more workers on various catwalks speeding toward him.

He had to keep moving. Had to reach the core before they could kill him.

He slapped his pistol back on his hip and grabbed the catwalk with both hands. Pulled himself along, inward, toward the core. The bombs bounced against his chest like medals on an admiral. At least he still had those.

He moved as fast as he could, pushing himself from one handhold to the next, kicking with his legs and flying free when he was sure he would find something to catch. He followed the curve of the catwalk, twisting along with it. In zero gravity there was no up and down and he knew he was in real danger of getting disoriented, of ending up crawling in the wrong direction.

He reached out and grabbed a support stanchion, yanked himself around and over a girder to try to get a better look at his destination, to see if he was at least making progress. Reached for another stanchion—and stopped dead still.

A worker perched on the catwalk, almost right on top of him. One of its multi-fingered hands reached for his face.

Lanoe grabbed for his pistol, knowing there was no time to bring it up, knowing he would never get a shot off. That hand would close around his helmet at any moment, close and crush it until it shattered—

Except when he looked back up at the thing, its arm was still centimeters away from him. It moved with a sudden jerk, a millimeter closer, then stopped.

One of its legs was descending toward the girder, maybe looking to improve its grip there. He watched it move with glacial slowness, in little fits and starts.

"Lanoe?" someone called.

He was too shocked to answer, at first.

"Lanoe?"

"Valk?" he called back. "Valk? You're still alive?"

"Heh. I wouldn't say that. Exactly."

The lander put another leg down inside the crater.

Drew it back.

"They're having trouble—they can't get good footing," Ehta said. Maybe just to herself. She didn't know if Roan could hear her. She didn't know if the girl was still alive. "Hell's bells. I kind of wish they would just jump down here. Make it quick." She was close to sobbing. She'd really thought they had a chance. She'd thought she could make up for her inability to fly, somehow. She'd thought—

"No," Roan said.

Her voice was very faint. Ehta could hear her just fine.

"We have to stay alive," the girl told her. "The landers..."

Ehta rushed over to kneel next to the girl. Roan's face had turned white as a sheet, the blood having drained even from her lips. Her eyes looked like they were drying out. "The landers sense life. If we die..."

"They'll move on," Ehta finished. "They'll head for the next living thing they can find." Which meant the volunteers over at the gun camp. "But Roan—they'll figure it out in a minute. They'll find some way down here, and then—"

Well, she didn't have to make it easy on them.

She hurried around to the back of the broken rover. The cannon's barrel was dug into the soft ground but it didn't look bent. It was still hooked up to the three intact batteries.

It was too big, too heavy for Ehta to lift, even on Aruna. She could never just pick it up and use it like a rifle—the thing was a vehicular weapon, meant to be mounted to the side of a spacecraft. Still. Maybe. Maybe just.

She hauled down on its stock, worried the pistol grip might break off at its jury-rigged weld point. The barrel resisted her, buried as it was in the dirt. It came loose with a jerk that sent her sprawling.

Up on the lip of the crater, one of the landers had three feet down inside the steep wall. Two of its claws pushed hard into the rock there, anchoring themselves. It was making progress.

Ehta grabbed the end of the cannon and twisted it around. It clanked against the roll bar—it couldn't quite traverse far enough for her to get a shot at the adventurous lander. She cried out in dismay. Then she did what she had to do. She found the cotter pin that held the cannon in its mounting and yanked it free.

The cannon came down on top of her, heavy enough to make her gasp. She wrestled it around until the barrel pointed almost straight up. Pulled the trigger and prayed the cannon hadn't been damaged in the crash, that it wasn't about to explode in a million pieces.

She had no control, no real ability to aim with any kind of accuracy. She kept the trigger held down, spraying particle beams across the whole lip of the crater. A lander's leg and then two more came loose, severed by her wild fire. They tumbled down the slope toward her, still twitching.

"Is Thom okay?" Roan asked.

"He's doing great!" Ehta screamed, as she kept blazing away at the shadows up above her.

Lanoe pulled himself along the catwalk, hand over hand. Behind him the workers followed, plodding along so slowly they were no threat.

"How did you—I mean, how are you—"

"I was a false-mind," Valk told him. "An artificial intelligence tricked into thinking it was something else. The queenship made me true."

Lanoe didn't even try to understand what any of that meant.

"You knew what I was. Didn't you? When I lowered my helmet for you, back on Niraya. You saw what I was."

Lanoe shook his head. "I didn't know what I saw. I guess maybe—it was one thing I thought, that maybe you were...a..."

"AI," Valk said.

Totally illegal. Thoroughly unethical. Somebody had recorded Valk's brain, all his memories, his personality, his innermost thoughts and secret desires. His sense of humor. His goofy mannerisms. Put them in a computer, then told him he had lived, that he hadn't burned to death in his fighter's cockpit after all.

"I could have died, Lanoe," Valk said.

"I thought you—"

"I mean, I could have died for real. Anytime I wanted to, anytime since they put me in this suit. I had an off switch. They hid it from me, but not very hard. If I'd gone looking for it I could have saved myself so much pain. I could have just stopped. It wouldn't even have felt like dying. It wouldn't have hurt."

Lanoe grimaced as he pulled himself along the catwalk. His arms burned with the effort and he didn't see that he'd made much progress.

"It's really tempting," Valk said. "I could do it right now."

"I'm guessing you're the one keeping me alive right now," Lanoe said, looking back over his shoulder. The workers were still coming after him. Very, very slowly. "You're slowing them down somehow."

"P does not equal NP. It's a kind of denial-of-service attack," Valk said.

"Buddy, you made a lot more sense when you thought you were human."

Valk laughed. It sounded exactly like his old, human laugh.

"The aliens who built this thing—actually, not this one, this ship was built by another ship, which was built by another ship—"

"Details later, maybe," Lanoe suggested.

"The aliens built this thing to terraform worlds for them. *Terraform* is the wrong word, maybe a better term would be...sorry. Never mind. They built this thing as a construction vehicle. They knew it might run into other life-forms out there in space. People like them. They put a big subroutine in its programming telling it that it had to try to talk to any intelligent life it found. Any minds."

"There were minds on Niraya when it arrived," Lanoe pointed out.

"That's the problem, of course. The aliens, when they wrote the program, they expected other self-aware creatures to be like them. To look like them. You don't look like them, you don't even run on the same kind of chemistry. It thinks you're just vermin. A bug to be exterminated. Me, though—it recognized me. Because I look like it does. A computer."

"That's why you could understand the message it sent, the request to talk, when nobody else could," Lanoe posited.

"Yep. It thinks I'm its peer. So it has to talk to me. Its programming requires it to answer any question I ask."

"So you…you asked it if you could be in charge, right? If you could give it new instructions?"

"I tried that. Sorry, Lanoe, it didn't work. I can't tell it what to do. All I can do is ask questions. But I can ask a lot of them. Now that I know what I am, I'm not limited to asking questions verbally. I can ask them as fast as I can transfer data, and that's very, very fast. I'm currently asking it about eight billion questions per second."

"Hellfire."

"Mostly the same ones over and over. It doesn't take long for the queenship to answer them. But because P does not equal NP— sorry, I'm doing it again. Because of the way the queenship thinks, it takes processor power to answer all those questions. I'm keeping it busy, and that slows down its ability to build new drones. Or send workers to pull your legs off."

"I…appreciate it," Lanoe told him.

"Anything for the squadron, right? And then, when you're done, doing whatever you plan on doing here—"

"I've got some—"

"Don't tell me!" Valk insisted. "It can ask questions of me, too."

"Oh. Sure."

"When you're done, then I can press the big black button. That's all right, isn't it? You'll let me? You'll give me permission to die?"

<hr/>

"Bastards!" Ehta shrieked, blazing away at the landers above her.

She did not look at how much power remained in her batteries. She did not want to know.

Her arm had grown numb. That might just be her suit compensating for her injury. She didn't care.

Roan hadn't spoken in a while.

Let her rest, Ehta thought.

"You want me? Come and get me!" she shouted.

Marines knew when not to ask too many questions.

The catwalk came to an end, its long spiral petering out to a sharp angle. An arrow pointing at the queenship's heart.

He could see it now, a dully glowing orb of magma, maybe fifty meters across. A hell of a power source—the heat it generated could keep the queenship running nearly indefinitely. That much energy wouldn't want to be held tight inside a little sphere like that. It must be contained inside a ridiculously powerful magnetic bottle, a field of electromagnetic radiation keeping it from expanding outward in one huge volcanic burst.

If he could find the emitters for that field, if he could put his bombs in just the right place...

The catwalks all came together around the core, some of them reaching closer than others. He saw where two of them coiled together to form a sort of platform over the core. Something dark and many-legged crouched there, huddled over a shape that might have looked human once.

"I can see you," Lanoe told Valk.

"You shouldn't come any closer," Valk told him. "Lanoe—it's dangerous. I can slow this thing down but I can't pull its fangs."

"Sure," Lanoe said.

The end of his catwalk was separated from the platform by about twenty meters of open space. He could make that jump, if he was careful. He would have to aim just right. If he was off by even a couple of degrees, he would just go sailing off into nothing. Or maybe he would just throw himself right into the core. No way he could survive that.

He didn't hesitate. Not now.

He bent his legs and put his feet against the end of the catwalk. Pushed off hard, his arms stretched out so he wouldn't spin too badly. It wasn't enough—he started tumbling almost instantly. His head was already pounding from the lack of gravity and now black spots swam in his vision, black spots lost against the darkness inside the queenship.

Ahead of him the platform grew in size as he neared it. Was he going to make it? So close—he felt like he could almost reach out and touch it. So close—he threw out his arms at the last possible moment and grabbed on with both hands. Momentum tried to tear his grip loose but he just held on, held on with all the strength he had.

He pulled himself up over the side of the platform. No gravity there but plenty of stanchions to hold on to. Hauled himself along until he was right next to Valk.

The big pilot was in bad shape. Several fingers had been torn off his gloves. His helmet was broken, shattered down to jagged shards that stuck up from his collar ring. There was nothing inside, no head, no skull.

When Lanoe had asked Valk to lower his helmet, back on Niraya, that was what he'd seen. Nothing. Valk's suit was empty, with nobody inside it. The artificial intelligence that called itself Tannis Valk was contained entirely within the computers built into that heavy suit.

A bundle of thick cables snaked down inside the collar ring, presumably the conduit through which the queenship answered Valk's interminable questions. Lanoe followed those cables up to see a thing like a millipede, a thousand segmented legs, hovering over him, anchored to the platform by a dozen thick tendrils.

Even as he saw the thing, it struck. Long thin arms shot out from its mass, stabbing down at the platform around him. Lanoe pushed himself away from the attack, but more legs kept coming at him. He had no doubt Valk was still slowing the thing down—otherwise it would have pierced him through with a hundred claws already—but it was all Lanoe could do to move out of the way of those stabbing arms.

"Hellfire," he breathed.

The arms seemed to lurch out at him at random. One of them would strike home before long. Lanoe tore the first bomb from his chest, pulled its arming lever. He pushed himself over to the side of the platform and threw it down, straight down at the core. It hit the containment field and just stopped, its momentum canceled out in an instant. He armed another bomb and threw it overhand and it flew true, only to stop again, well clear of the core. Like throwing pebbles into gelatin, he thought.

An arm of the millipede came down right through the sleeve of his suit, tearing through the fabric there. It didn't break his skin but it pinned him to the floor. Another arm came down right next to his face, smashing into the girders and making them ring.

Lanoe pulled another bomb off his chest with his free arm. It was no use—he needed both hands to arm them.

He pulled hard and his pinned arm came free. Air hissed out of his suit but only for a second—the suit patched itself, foamy goo spreading across Lanoe's bicep. He armed the bomb and tossed it. Grabbed for a fourth.

The millipede stabbed him right through the shoulder. He felt its metal claw grate against the bones in there. He cried out in agony and the bomb he'd been holding flew out of his hand, off into empty space.

The landers were stupid. They were also persistent.

Even as Ehta blazed away at them with the PBW cannon they kept testing the walls of the crater, finding solid rock that would support them so they could climb down, one at a time. She drove them back with particle beams as best she could but it was just a matter of time. There were so many of them, and they were so hard to kill.

The one in front tumbled as its legs came off. It twisted and skidded its way down the wall to collapse right at her feet. She fired a long blast right through its core, the place where all its legs came together, and it fell in a heap.

There was another one right behind it. She screamed, just incoherent noises exploding from her mouth as she fired again and again, as she poured particle beams into its whirling legs. One of those legs came up, its pointed end aimed right at her face. She cut it off at its root but two more were already descending on either side of her—the thing was right on top of her, it could just fall on her and crush her and then—and then—

She heard a shrieking roar and then rock exploded all around her, dust clouding her view. The ground shook and the lander fell away, twisting over on its side, crushing part of the already totaled rover. Ehta had no idea what was happening but she didn't let it stop her. Another lander was already coming down the slope. She raised the cannon and aimed, and only then realized that the barrel had been sheared away, that the lander that nearly killed her had, in fact, smashed the cannon on its way down. Capacitor loops hung from its broken side and fluid ammunition leaked all over her hands.

She pushed the cannon away from her with a squeak as electric arcs jumped up and down its length, enough power to fry her if she touched it.

The ground shook again and another lander fell into the crater, a mass of twisted and fused legs that didn't even twitch.

Something passed right over her head, its shadow making it impossible to see. She threw her arms up to protect her helmet but there was no need. That wasn't a lander looming over her. It was a fighter.

A damned cataphract.

It was gone in a moment, but she could hear its engine whine as it looped around for another run, and she saw a lander torn apart by a disruptor round, parts of it flying in every direction. Bits of burnt wire fell down all around her like coppery snow.

"Thom," Roan said, the first word she'd spoken in what felt like hours.

"No," Ehta told her. "No, not Thom."

She'd barely gotten a glimpse at the fighter as it streaked by overhead. She knew the silhouette of every spacecraft humans had ever built, though, and that had been no BR.9, of that she was sure. It was a damned Z.XIX.

What the hell was going on?

Lanoe screamed in agony as the millipede's arm twitched inside his flesh, tearing at his muscle fiber, scoring his bone. A white pearl flashed and strobed in the corner of his vision, offering him the strongest painkillers available. He ignored it and reached up with both hands to grab the thin mechanical arm and pull—

—*oh bloody, oh, all of hell's chapels that hurts*—

—pull, millimeter by millimeter, the thing out of his body, pull it even as it snagged on something, even as he felt blood pouring down his arm inside his suit and finally, with a horrible wet plop it came free, and sealant foam hissed over his front and back.

With his good arm he pulled himself along the platform. Back to the edge. Armed and threw his last two bombs.

The millipede-thing couldn't reach him over there, right at the edge. Its arms flashed down around his boots but he just pulled them away.

In a few seconds the bombs would go off. In a few seconds everything would be over. He could just lie there and . . . and . . .

No.

Not after everything. Not if there was still something he could do.

He watched the millipede-thing's arms come down in a wild pattern, watched it stab at the platform. Timed his move just right. Threw himself under its swaying arms, grabbed for two handfuls of Valk's suit.

"Lanoe, leave me—I just want to die, I can do that here, you don't need to take me with you," Valk moaned.

"No," Lanoe grunted. He grabbed the suit and then kicked off the platform, as hard as he could. Just as he'd hoped, the cables snaking down inside Valk's collar ring snapped and broke free. Together they went spinning away, out of the millipede's reach, Lanoe clutching Valk's suit around the waist.

"Lanoe, if I'm not connected I can't slow down the processors; you don't need me, you can just leave me behind—"

"Negative," Lanoe told him. "I'm out of propellant for my suit jets. I'm assuming you still have some," he said.

"Oh," Valk said.

Valk's boot jets fired then, burning hard. The two of them shot forward, looped around the core, and went flying straight toward the maw, toward the web.

Behind them the bombs went off, one by one. The explosions looked like nothing more than sparks at first, sparks that stretched out along the lines of force that made up the core's magnetic bottle. But the sparks didn't die out—instead they grew brighter, until whole bands of fire played across the dull red surface of the magma.

Worker drones jumped toward the two pilots, flinging themselves off the catwalks, their legs moving at full speed now. One came close enough that Lanoe had to shoot it, emptying his sidearm's magazine into its writhing shape.

Down on the platform, the millipede-thing shimmied with activity, its thousands of arms reaching for who knew what, as the queenship's mind tried to fix what was going wrong, tried to save itself.

Then a jet of loose magma blasted upward, right through the platform, vaporizing the millipede-thing instantaneously. Arcing prominences lanced out from the core in every direction as the magnetic bottle began to fail, arcs of molten rock slagging anything they touched.

Ahead of the two pilots the web writhed and twisted back on itself, its filament arms whipping back and forth in confusion, perhaps, or even panic. Lanoe pointed at the hole in the web, the place where he'd come through, and Valk corrected their course.

Just as the magnetic bottle failed completely and the core exploded outward, expanding like a tiny nova inside the belly of the queenship.

Outside the web a lone BR.9—or what was left of it—came swooping down to meet them. Its airfoils were gone, its canopy cracked in a dozen places, its entire fuselage buckled and broken so that its fairings hung loose like the petals of a dead flower. Half of its thrusters were missing.

Through the broken canopy Lanoe saw Thom staring at him with very wide eyes.

Lanoe found a broken panel on the side of the fighter. He grabbed on with both hands, while Valk did the same. "Get us out of here!" Lanoe called.

"Yes, sir," Thom said. He burned hard to get away even as the web melted, its strands falling away into the red fire that burst from the queenship's maw, a vast vomiting forth of ultrahot magma that glittered against the black of space.

Thom banked hard across the rocky face of the queenship, getting clear of that explosion. It was all Lanoe could do to hold on, his gloves locking in place as his suit compensated for the sudden maneuver.

It took him a while to realize they had company. Ships—dozens of them—flying in formation, keeping a set distance away from the BR.9 but matching its course exactly. *No,* he thought, *no, not after all that.* The humblest alien scout could easily burn them all to a crisp, as beaten up and wrecked as they were. If there were any interceptors in that formation, they were—

Then he actually looked at their escort. Blinked a few times.

Those weren't alien drones.

They were Z.XIXs. Cataphract fighters.

One shifted inward until it was flying right along side them. Until Lanoe could look through its canopy and see its pilot.

"Did someone call for the cavalry?" Maggs asked.

Chapter Thirty-Five

The Hoplite-class cruiser had a wide hangar bay amidships, capable of holding a dozen cataphract fighters. One of those berths had been cleared out to make room for the prize specimen of the expedition: an alien lander, missing only two of its multitudinous legs. It had been carefully drained of power until it was no longer dangerous, but it still twitched every now and then like a sleeping dog, probably aware that there were living things nearby and searching for a way to get at them.

It had been found floating loose in space near the ruined queenship, perhaps ejected during the explosion that had slagged the big alien vessel. Just getting it into the fighter bay had been a bit of a challenge, but nothing a little Navy ingenuity couldn't master. Engineers were already studying it as the cruiser burned back toward Niraya.

On the bridge of the Hoplite, Rear Admiral Karten Wallys watched a display of the hangar deck. As the lander twitched his eyes jumped with excited light. "Oh, my, yes," he said. "Oh, indeed. Maggsy, I believe you can tell your mother she won't have to worry about creditors for a while."

Smug little bastard, Maggs's father said inside his head. *He was insufferable when I was alive. He'll be un-bloody-bearable now.*

"I'm glad it meets with your satisfaction," Maggs told the older man.

Among the great thinkers of the Admiralty, there had been a long-running debate as to why humanity had never, after centuries among the stars, met so much as one intelligent alien. The prevailing opinion had always been that there was no such thing, that life had only ever arisen on one planet, Earth, and thus it should ever be.

Among the few dissidents from that belief, Wallys had always numbered the most insistent and opinionated. He had spent much of his career chasing alien spoor and had been widely derided for it.

Now he had real evidence of alien intelligence. When his people had finished studying the lander, there would be no doubt it had been built by nonhumans. That it came from another species. He would be able to prove his critics wrong. For a man like Wallys that would always be the chiefest among pleasures.

Of course, it hadn't been easy to convince Wallys that Maggs had what he was looking for. It had taken a fair amount of persuasion to get the Rear Admiral to dispatch this expeditionary force, and Maggs had been forced to make many promises. Had there been no intact alien drones left in the system by the time they arrived, he would have had a great deal of explaining to do.

So nice when something actually worked out in this life.

With the cruiser under acceleration there was a hint of gravity on the bridge. It caused Maggs some soreness in his broken leg but it spared them all the indignity of having to float around like circus performers while they worked. Technical and staff officers moved about the bridge's workstations, keeping the ship in trim, while large displays showed views of Aruna. Fighters streaking across the clouded sky of the moon, searching for intact alien machinery. Suited figures cutting their way through the still half-molten remains of the queenship, looking for anything that might have survived the alien craft's demise. There was an enormous amount of work to be done, and the cruiser was likely to stay in the system for months while any bit of data concerning aliens might still be gleaned. If any drones remained active—other than the one in the fighter bay, of course—they could be dealt with safely by the expeditionary force's impressive firepower. It looked like the people of Niraya were safe.

As for Maggs himself, he planned on sticking around not one second longer than was physically necessary. He had his brand-new Z.XIX fueled and ready to take him someplace more civilized. All the warrants and bulletins surrounding his less than legitimate activities were in the process of being expunged, another nice little perk thanks to Uncle Rear Admiral Wallys and his obsession with all things alien. Maggs could go back to his job working as a Centrocor liaison or retire from the Navy altogether, if he liked.

He looked forward to having options for a change. Mother's debts had been hanging over his head far too long.

Of course, he knew she would start racking up new ones without delay. Sufficient to the day is the evil thereof, and all that.

The hatch at the back of the bridge opened and everyone looked up to see a suited figure climb through. When he saw who it was Maggs stood up a little straighter, and kept his hand near the sidearm holstered on the leg of his thinsuit.

"Permission to enter the bridge, sir?" Aleister Lanoe asked.

"Of course, Commander," Wallys said, looking up from his display, if only a moment. "You and I have much to discuss, don't we?"

"Yes, sir," Lanoe replied. He came over and stood at attention next to the admiral's console.

"You did some incredible work here, given the resources you had," Wallys told the old pilot. "We came as fast as we could but without your efforts a lot of people would have died before we could have saved them."

"Sir," Lanoe said.

"I want you to know that all is forgiven." Wallys tore his gaze away from the lander in the display long enough to give Lanoe a curt nod. "The matériel you...requisitioned from Navy stores, for instance. The fact that you didn't actually have the authority to transfer Ensign Ehta or Lieutenant Zhang to your command. I think we can forget all the broken regulations, considering what we got in exchange. By damn, first proof of a nonhuman intelligent species! This is a moment that will go down in history, and all of our names will ring with honor for generations."

"As you say, sir," Lanoe told him. "I'm not very interested in history."

"What do you want, then? I daresay you can have it. A commendation would be easy enough to arrange. Not that you have any shortage of those. How'd you like to have your command reinstated? A new squadron all your own?"

Lanoe turned and looked Maggs right in the eye.

Maggs made a point of not flinching.

"I saw a Z.VII down in one of your bays," Lanoe said. "A two-seater reconnaissance scout. I wonder if I could borrow it for a while? I lost my FA.2 in the battle."

"All yours," Wallys said, with a cheerful grin. "Going somewhere? With someone special?"

"One of my officers, Tannis Valk, was killed here. I managed to recover his body and I'd like to take it to his homeworld for a proper burial."

Wallys's grin might have faded by a few watts. "The Blue Devil. The, ah, Establishment man."

"That's correct. I promise I'll keep it a quiet affair," Lanoe said.

"Very good. But that's all you want? Just a fighter of your own?"

"It's all I've ever needed. With your leave, sir, I'll be on my way."

Wallys shook his head. "I think you're forgetting one thing, Commander. I believe you owe someone a word of thanks. When we arrived in-system you were down to just one cataphract facing nearly a hundred alien drones. You didn't even have a ship of your own to fly. If it weren't for our prompt arrival I daresay it would be your funeral to be seen to. And if it weren't for Maggsy here, we wouldn't have come. I believe, sir, you're in his debt."

Lanoe's face hardened. His wrinkled features had always been hard to read in the past. Not this time. The look he gave Maggs spoke volumes.

"I'm only sorry," Lanoe said, "that I can't pay Lieutenant Maggs exactly what I owe him, right here and now."

Maggs managed to wait until Lanoe had cleared the bridge before he allowed himself a little shudder of fear.

—✦—

The cruiser's medical suite was cramped and cluttered with equipment. Patients were sequestered to small bunks set into the walls. Roan stared up at a ceiling no more than twenty centimeters from her face and felt like she was lying in a coffin.

She'd come pretty close to needing one. The doctors had spent hours bringing her back from the edge of death, repairing the damage her body had suffered in the wreck of the rover, treating her for blood loss and anoxia. There had been tests to make sure she hadn't suffered any irreparable brain damage—she'd had to look at pictures of everyday objects and name them one by one. Minders, advertising drones, apples, and cats. Some of those objects were things not commonly found on Niraya and when she'd hesitated the doctors had gone pale, but in the end she'd been cleared. They told her she was going to be okay.

In time, anyway. She had to lie very still for days yet, moving as little as possible, while a robotic surgeon climbed around her shoulder, cutting away dead tissue with a laser and knitting her bones back together.

Well, she'd had plenty of training in being still, back at the Retreat. She tried to meditate and put herself into a trance of peace.

There was only one problem. People kept coming to annoy her.

Ensign Ehta came first, grabbing her hand and nearly reopening Roan's wound. Tears had brimmed in the marine's eyes and then the smell wafted over Roan and she realized that Ehta was drunk. Ehta kept repeating how glad she was that Roan had made it, how damned lucky they both had been. Roan eventually figured out that Ehta hadn't just come to see how she was doing, that the marine wanted something.

It wasn't difficult to figure out what.

"You saved them," Roan said. "Nothing that came before matters. You saved the people on that moon."

"We did," Ehta told her, and reached for her hand again. "We did good." She still sounded like she was trying to convince herself.

Elder McRae came by a bit later, after Ensign Ehta left. The elder sat down next to Roan's bunk and watched her with eyes that bore no expression, whatsoever. She did not speak for the longest time.

"I am glad," she said, finally, "that you'll live."

"I'm glad Niraya is safe," Roan told her.

The elder nodded. "You asked my forgiveness, before. You know that isn't something I can give you."

"Yes," Roan said. "I think I understand that a little more now. You said I'd chosen my path and that it was up to me to decide if it was the right one. Well, I've decided. I did the right thing. I don't need you to tell me that."

The elder didn't smile. That would have been a betrayal of her beliefs. Roan thought that maybe, though, deep down, the elder agreed with her. That Roan had chosen the correct path.

That was all she was going to get. It would have to be enough.

Before she left, Roan said one more thing. "I'm glad you survived, too."

The elder did not respond.

The next visitor was the one she wanted to see the most. Thom came clattering into the medical suite, knocking over a scanner and nearly tripping on a cable that snaked across the floor. He knelt down next to her bunk and stared at her, and cried, and reached for her but then pulled his hands back. He kept smiling. He smiled through the whole visit. He didn't say a word.

There would be plenty of time for words, and for holding hands, and a great deal more later.

Her fourth visitor was Commander Lanoe. He pulled up a chair and sat there, nodding at her. She had no idea what he was thinking, what words were unspooling in his head, but he eventually said, "It worked, huh? Who would believe it."

"Thank you," she told him. When the entire galaxy had heard the plea of Niraya and had done nothing more than shrug, he had come to their aid. "Thank you." She said it several more times.

"Stop that," he said, eventually.

"I'm ... sorry?" she said.

"You fought as hard as any of us. Whatever we accomplished here, you were part of it."

Then he held out his hand, and she shook it.

"Does this make us squaddies?" she asked.

"Sure," he said.

Later on, in a room darkened to simulate the middle of the night, Lanoe scrolled through some image files he had stored on his personal minder. He didn't have many, even after three hundred years.

The pictures showed his old squads, typically after a bad fight, but laughing. Throwing rude hand gestures, lounging on top of their battered fighters. Jernigan with his arm around Khoi's waist. Candless and Holt and Amrit in a swimming pool on Ganymede, still wearing their suits, mugging for the camera. Old friends he'd simply stopped calling. Too many years gone by and he'd always been too busy. There were pictures of Lanoe getting medals, getting salutes from admirals. He flipped past those without giving them much of a look. Most of those people were dead now.

Other pictures showed Earth, the way it had been, once. Those pictures used to mean something to Lanoe, but not anymore. He'd spent so long fighting for the planet where he was born. Fighting to keep it safe, to keep it free. The last time he'd visited, he couldn't recognize any of the buildings. The food hadn't tasted right, not the way he remembered it.

The last picture in his collection was just a still of Garuda, the ice giant. Blue with bands of purple, dark storms near its equator. He didn't have a picture of Bettina Zhang as she had been when he met her. He didn't have one of the way she'd looked when she fought aliens by his side. He had one of her tomb.

Zhang—she hadn't been his only lover, not in a life as long as his. He'd had other seconds in command, plenty of other squadmates.

She'd been the only one who stayed. The only one who wanted him back. He realized that he'd drifted through time, not putting down any roots. Never getting too attached to anyone, because he knew they could die without warning. An enemy fighter could get them, or a training accident, or—

Zhang had stuck with him. When she'd pushed him away, in the hospital after she lost her legs, that had hurt. More than he'd let himself acknowledge. For long years he'd tried to pretend he didn't need her, that they were better off apart.

How stupid could one man be? He should have…he should…

Aleister Lanoe was too old to cry. A sound worked its way up through his throat, though, a sound not unlike a choked sob. He stared down at the picture of Garuda. Of the place where Zhang died.

Eventually he deleted the image. It was morbid, and he didn't need pictures to help him remember her.

I got my win, he thought. *I won a war.*

Sure.

It cost too much.

I could have let go. I could have stopped fighting. Found you, in those years we were apart. Found you and convinced you to stop fighting, too.

Maybe.

Instead I got my win.

It cost too much.

———

Ehta wriggled out of her suit and attached it to an adhesive pad on the wall of the bunkroom. For a moment she stood there in just the comfort garment, looking at the limp suit, wondering if there was anything special she should do. She swabbed out the collar ring. Sprayed the inside with fungicidal foam, then tapped at the wrist display until the suit crackled and shrank, flattening itself so it would fit in a drawer.

Her Navy suit. Her pilot's suit. The one Lanoe had given her, back on the Hexus, when everyone still thought she was going to fly. The last Navy suit she would ever wear. She didn't need it anymore.

An armored marine's suit, with ropes and anchors engraved around the collar ring, was already stuffed into her bunk. It was a cast-off, a spare suit donated by one of the cruiser's marines. It stank and there was a bad scorch mark on one leg but it would fit her. Marine suits were one-size-fits-all. They had to be—marines had such a short life span it wasn't worth paying to have their suits properly fitted.

She pulled off the comfort garment and recycled it. Marines didn't worry about comfort. She slipped inside the armored suit and reached behind her to zip it up. Touched the key at her throat to make the helmet flow up around her head, just checking, listening for the familiar hiss of life support, then released the helmet again and left it down.

She headed out of the bunkroom and into the corridor, hoping she could reach the hangar deck before she saw anybody. She was disappointed in that hope, though it was only Maggs she saw. Trust him to turn up at the worst possible moment.

"You were a big brute of a woman before," he said, pulling up alongside her as she walked. "Now you're positively terrifying. I like it."

She chose not to react to that. "I'm shipping out. Got my deployment orders."

"Already? I didn't even think the Navy knew you were here."

"They need me on Tuonela," she told him. "Fighting Thiess-Gruppe, this time. Not enough sergeants down there, I guess."

"There never are," Maggs said. "Or so my father used to tell me. Shame, though. You help pull off a miracle here and they send you right back to the front. Not even a week off to recognize your service. Criminal, really."

"This wasn't official duty," she said, and shrugged. "Anyway. That's life in the Poor Bloody Marines."

She took a corner, headed for the hangar deck and the transport that awaited her there. She'd hoped he wouldn't follow, but of course he did. "You haven't said goodbye to the old man yet, have you? Certainly there's time for that."

Ehta glanced back up the corridor. As if she expected Lanoe to be standing right behind her. Well, in a way he always was, wasn't he?

But she'd done her bit. Helped him the best she could. Whether it had been enough, whether she'd paid him back for the debt she owed him—she didn't know how to even begin solving that equation.

"He's probably busy," she said. For now she figured she could leave it at that.

She was sure she would see Lanoe again.

⟶⟵

"Enter."

Thom stepped inside a cramped little compartment, not much inside it but a bunk and a couple of chairs that faced a display. This was how officers lived onboard the cruiser, apparently. He closed the hatch behind him and came over to sit near Lanoe. "You said we needed to talk."

Lanoe nodded without looking up. Thom thought the old man's eyes looked a little red, but he couldn't tell why. It was hard to read that craggy face. "You know you're still in trouble, right?" Lanoe began. "I was a little surprised when I saw you come aboard this cruiser. There are people here who would be required by law to take action if they knew who you were. If they knew what happened to your father. I'm surprised you haven't been arrested already."

"When they showed up—when the Navy came swooping in to kill all those drones and save me," Thom said, "they asked who I was. I told them I was a farmer from Niraya. That I knew how to fly because I used to do crop-dusting."

The corner of Lanoe's mouth turned up. "Clever," he said. "That'll keep them satisfied for a while. And they have no reason to check your identity, not unless you give them one, I suppose. But what comes next? Where do we take you, to keep you safe?"

Thom wrapped his arms around his knees. He'd been dreading this. Afraid of how Lanoe would react. He knew better than to hesitate, though. Best to just come out with it.

"I'm staying right here. On Niraya, I mean. With Roan. There's no place else I want to be."

Lanoe raised an eyebrow. "No. I don't think that'll work. You can't stay anonymous forever. The Navy's going to be all over Niraya from now on," he pointed out. "Studying the mess we made."

"No, they'll be all over Aruna," Thom said. "When they come to Niraya they'll stick to Walden Crater. Roan and I will go out to the canyons, as far away as we can get. We'll be safe there."

"Kid, you're not thinking. This is a dumb plan, you'll—"

"I'm sorry, sir, but I disagree."

Lanoe froze in place, his mouth still open to say more. For a moment his eyes narrowed and Thom wondered if he was about to be charged with insubordination.

"I'm only trying to help," Lanoe said.

Thom chewed on his lower lip. He let his emotions swell for a second, then got them under control. The way Roan would have.

"Sir," Thom said, "you already have."

Lanoe grunted and turned away.

"You've done so much for me, so much for Roan, we can't ever…" He let the words die away. "You've done enough. I need to stand on my own from here."

Lanoe reached up and scratched at the iron-colored hair on the back of his head.

"Listen," he said, after a long silence. "Something I forgot to tell you. Before Zhang died, she asked me to let you know that you impressed her. That you picked up our work faster than any recruit she'd ever seen."

"That's…that's really nice of her to say," Thom mumbled.

"You impressed me, too. I'm proud of you, Thom. You think

it's the right play, you and Roan hiding in plain sight. Well, maybe you're right. Maybe it'll work."

"Thank you," Thom said.

Lanoe waved a hand to indicate that they'd finished talking about it.

Thom looked down at his hands. "Lanoe—come with us. I mean, come to Niraya, anyway. The people there owe you so much. They'll...I don't know, throw you parades. They'll be so glad to see you."

"Nah," Lanoe said. "I hate it when people make a fuss."

"Elder McRae will want to thank you. I mean, she—"

"I don't need her to give me that look," Lanoe said. "You know the one I mean? Like she just noticed I've got dirt on my face, but it's okay, she forgives me?"

Thom laughed. "Yeah. I know that look."

"Anyway. I've still got work to do." Lanoe rose from his chair and reached for something that lay inside his bunk. A heavy suit with the helmet down, with a hexagon painted on one shoulder. Valk's suit.

When Thom picked up the two of them, just before the queenship was slagged, Valk had still been talking. His helmet had been shattered and Thom had gotten a good look at what was underneath. Or rather, the fact that there was nothing there.

But Valk had still been talking. Begging to be allowed to die. Eventually Lanoe had decided to let the big pilot—the AI—rest. He'd pressed the recessed key under Valk's collar ring and all the life, all the shape anyway, had gone out of the suit. It was suddenly just an empty vessel.

Lanoe had told Thom he was pretty sure that if he pressed that key again, Valk would come back to life—and that Valk had information that he needed to hear. Now he propped the suit up in a chair, the arms dangling over its back. "You ready for this?" he asked.

"If you think it's okay I hear it," Thom replied.

"You've earned that right. You and I are the only ones who know the truth about what he is. Frankly, if I'm going to raise the dead here, I'd like some company."

Thom laughed, though he didn't exactly feel mirthful. In fact a shiver ran down his back as he looked at Valk's suit draped over the chair. Torn and filthy and abused, it looked like a bundle of rags waiting to be recycled.

Lanoe pressed the recessed key in the collar ring. The black flowglas moved and shifted. Took on the shape of a helmet.

Instantaneously Valk lurched forward, his arms out as if he'd been falling and he was trying to steady himself. He leaned forward and pressed his helmet between his hands. Thom could hear him breathing hard—or at least, he could hear a simulation of someone breathing hard.

"Oh, hell," Valk said. "Oh, damn. I'm back. You brought me back."

"You know why I had to," Lanoe told him.

Valk nodded, his helmet sagging forward. "Okay," he said, softly.

—✦—

Valk had been—nowhere.

There had been no darkness. No sense of time passing. No sensory input, and no thought. Not even a hole where something used to be. Just—nowhere.

It wasn't like sleep at all. It wasn't like blacking out. He had exact, perfect knowledge of the moment Lanoe shut him down, and then...nothing...and then he'd come back fully awake, fully aware.

Knowing exactly what he was. What he'd always been.

Tannis Valk was dead. The man had lived a slightly courageous life and died a nasty death and he was gone. The thing in his suit, this thing, this unit, he thought, using the term the alien machine had used—this was something else. Not even a recording so much as a simulation.

He was an artificial intelligence. Well, that put things in context. AI was illegal. Unacceptable. By rights, he should be shut down and dismantled. There was no wiggle room in the law. AIs were just too dangerous to be allowed to exist.

It would be easy enough to comply. The black pearl, the data bomb that would end his existence, was still there. It had moved over to the corner of his vision, replacing the white pearl that he'd resisted for so long. All he had to do was flick his eyes sideways, acknowledge the black pearl—

Except. Except he didn't have eyes now. He never had.

And there was the fact that he'd made a promise to Lanoe. A promise that he would do one last thing.

And then, when it was done—

Nowhere.

〜

The display on the wall lit up even though nobody had touched it. "That was me. I can do that now," Valk said. "Turns out I'm really good with computers. Takes one to know one, I guess."

On the display a rotating image took shape. It showed something kind of like a jellyfish, a globular, translucent orange body filled with dim shapes that might have been organs or, maybe, bones. Lights shifted inside, glowing and then fading out. Fifteen limp arms dangled from its side, a ring of tentacles around a gaping, toothless mouth.

Thom gasped. "That's them?"

"Yeah," Valk said. "The queenship gave me this image. That's what an intelligent being looks like, as far as it was concerned. That's one of the things that built it. They're big, you can't tell that from the display. Maybe twenty-five meters across. They evolved on a gas giant planet near galactic center. I guess that explains why they never invented the wheel, huh?"

Thom frowned. "Why do you say that?"

"If you evolve on a planet with no surface," Lanoe said, "you can't build roads. No roads, no wheels." He crouched near the minder and studied the image from up close. "What are they called?"

"They communicate with those flashing lights. Their name, I guess, would be Blue-Blue-White. Except it's more complicated than that, of course, because there's inflections, like how long the light lasts, how intense it is, and so on."

Lanoe shook his head. "I guess it was too much to hope the first aliens we met would speak English."

"Whatever you want to call them, they built the first queenship about half a billion years ago. Sent it out to make new worlds where they could live. Gas giants, I mean. They go after ice giants, warm them up, make sure the level of hydrogen in the atmosphere is right so the Blue-Blue-White can breathe it."

"Ice giants. Like Garuda," Lanoe said.

"Yep. They never wanted Niraya at all. No interest in terrestrial planets; they just wanted gas giants. They never figured out wormholes, either, and they knew it would take thousands of years to just find the planets they wanted, much less fix them up. They gave the queenships the ability to make copies of themselves, so they could spread out to new worlds faster. The queenships have been travel-ing from star to star ever since, gasiforming or whatever. Mining for silicates and metals on moons and rocky planets—that's what they were doing on Aruna, digging up raw materials to make more workers.

"Along the way they're supposed to look for other creatures like their makers, people for the jellyfish to talk to. Instead, they found creatures they couldn't recognize. Part of their programming was to kill off any vermin they found, any life-forms that might inter-fere with their work. When those life-forms didn't talk with flash-ing lights, they were automatically considered vermin. Even if they had spaceships and cities and who knows what else. Everybody just looked like vermin. And vermin had to be exterminated."

"Hellfire," Thom swore.

"How many?" Lanoe asked. "How many species you think they ran across in half a billion years? Intelligent or otherwise?"

"That's the thing, Lanoe," Valk said. "I think the answer is all of them. I think what we met here, the fleet we fought—we didn't meet aliens." He shook his head. "I think we met the reason there *are* no aliens."

"Huh?" Lanoe asked.

"I think they wiped out every alien race that ever evolved. The queenship told me there were millions of fleets out there, each with a queenship just like itself, an exact copy. Millions of them—well, they've been reproducing for eons, after all. How long does it take for a species to evolve to become intelligent? A couple billion years? In that time, the odds are they would run afoul of at least one queenship. Humanity got lucky. We didn't meet them until just now. If they found us four hundred years ago, when we didn't have spaceships, well...we would have just been one more species of vermin that was no longer a problem."

Lanoe nodded and moved back to a chair. "They talked to you, though."

"Yeah," Valk said. "The queenship did. Because it knew what I was. It knew I wasn't vermin. Because I was a computer, just like it was. The thing was excited, Lanoe. It didn't hate us. It didn't hate anybody. It was lonely, I think—lonely because after a half billion years it had never found anybody else to talk to. Maybe it ran across other computers, I don't know—but it told me none of them, no one, had ever come to speak with it. Until me. It was desperate to answer my questions. It believed, utterly and truly, that it was doing good work and spreading a message of peace and friendship."

"Oh, come on," Thom said.

Valk shook his head. "You're not seeing it, kid. The Blue-Blue-White—they didn't set out to sterilize the galaxy. They didn't want to kill us. They just couldn't imagine we existed. All of the damage they've done, all the death—it's just bad coding. Their programming was shoddy. That's all."

"And because they didn't think, every living thing in the galaxy has to die?" Thom demanded.

For a long moment none of them could speak to that. They just stared at each other, letting it sink in.

There were a hundred billion stars in the galaxy. Half of them had planets. Some small fraction of those planets would have, should have developed life. Some tinier fraction of that number should eventually have evolved into sapience.

Should have, if not for the queenships.

"It was a mistake," Valk said.

"Sure," Lanoe said. He steepled his fingers in front of him. Looked at nothing at all, lost in thought. "You think that we should forgive them, because it was a mistake?"

"Hell, no," Valk said. "Never."

Lanoe nodded in agreement. He did not look up.

"Okay, that's what I've got," Valk said. "I've done what you asked. Now I want to stop. I want to stop knowing things like this. I want to stop knowing what I am."

"What do you mean?" Thom asked. "What are you going to do?"

Valk turned to Lanoe, though, when he said, "Permission to die, Commander?"

Lanoe didn't move. He didn't stop looking right at Valk's helmet.

"Denied," he said.

Valk nearly jumped out of his chair. "Lanoe—"

"I still need you," Lanoe said.

"For what, damn you?"

"You know how to talk to them. Valk, you and me, we're going to find these jellyfish. We're going to find them somehow and we're going to make them shut down all these fleets. I don't know how. Somehow. Stop this damned program. Failing that, we're going to make the bastards pay."

The story continues in...

FORGOTTEN WORLDS

Book Two of The Silence

Keep reading for a sneak peek!

Acknowledgments

This book would not have been possible without the encouragement and friendship of Alex Lencicki. He's no Johnny Halfways. I'd also like to extend my gratitude to my agent, Russ Galen, and my two perspicacious editors, Will Hinton and James Long.

extras

introducing

If you enjoyed
FORSAKEN SKIES,
look out for

FORGOTTEN WORLDS

Book Two of The Silence

by D. Nolan Clark

PART ONE: CIRCUMBINARY

1

Behind the wall of space lay the network of wormholes that connected the stars. A desolate and eerie maze of tunnels no more than a few hundred meters wide in most places. The walls there emitted a constant and ghostly light, the luminescent smoke of particle-antiparticle annihilations. This ghostlight provided a little illumination, but no warmth.

For more than a century humanity had used that web of hidden passages to move people and cargo from one system to another, yet the maze was so complex and so convoluted it was rare for one ship to pass another in that silent space.

extras

It was even rarer, Aleister Lanoe thought, to find four cataphract-class aerospace fighters blocking your way. Rare enough that it couldn't be a coincidence.

"Those aren't Navy ships," said Valk, his copilot, currently riding in the observation blister slung under the ship's belly. "Look at the hexagons on their fairings. They're Centrocor militia."

"I bet their guns still work," Lanoe said.

The two of them were still hours out from their destination. They could try to punch through this formation and make a run for it, but their Z.VII recon scout was slow compared to the BR.9s they were facing. It would be a long and nasty chase and it wouldn't end well. Fighting wasn't a great option, either. The Z.VII carried a pair of PBW cannon, as good as anything the Centrocor ships could bring to bear, but its vector fields weren't as strong. The BR.9s could shrug off most of their firepower. They would get chewed to pieces in a dogfight.

Lanoe tried opening a channel. "Centrocor vehicles, we need a little room here. Mind letting us squeeze by?" As if this were just a chance encounter on a well-traveled shipping corridor. "Repeat. Centrocor vehicles—"

"Lanoe," Valk cut in, "their guns are warming up."

About what Lanoe had expected.

Outnumbered four to one. Outpaced, outgunned, and no way to call for help. Well, if they had to fight, at least they had one advantage. The pilots of the BR.9s were militia, hired guns working for Centrocor poly—one of the commercial monopolies that managed all human planets except Earth. These pilots had been trained by a corporation. Lanoe was one of the best pilots the Navy ever had.

"Hold on," he told Valk. Then he threw his stick over to the side and goosed his lateral thrusters, throwing them into a wild corkscrewing dive right toward the wall of the wormhole.

576

extras

The recon scout's inertial sink pulled Valk backward in his seat. It felt like someone was sitting on his chest, pinning him down. He was used to the feeling—without a sink, any pilot who tried a maneuver like that would have been crushed into pink jelly by the g forces.

It made it tricky, though, to reach the gun controls. Valk grunted and stabbed a virtual menu, bringing his cannon online. The ship's computer automatically swung him around to give him the best firing solution possible on the BR.9s. That meant he was flying backward, which in turn meant he couldn't see the wall of the wormhole looming up toward them. He was just fine with that. If they so much as brushed the wall—a curled-up tube of spacetime—the recon scout would be instantaneously disintegrated, its atoms torn apart down to the quark level.

Valk trusted Lanoe to not let that happen.

"Coming in, seven o'clock high," Valk called, and tapped another key to bring up a virtual Aldis gunsight, a collimated reticule that moved around his canopy to show him where his shots were likely to hit. It jumped back and forth as the computer tried to compensate for Lanoe's spinning dive and the movement of the four targets. Valk cursed the damned thing and switched it off. He was going to have to do this manually. "I think they're angry," Valk said.

Streamers of PBW fire like tiny burning comets flashed across the recon scout's thrusters as the enemy opened fire. Lanoe twisted them around on their positioning jets and most of the shots went wide, only a few sparking off their vector field.

"I think they're trying to kill us," Lanoe said.

They pulled up sharp just before colliding with the wormhole wall and Lanoe fishtailed back and forth as they pulled fire. Valk realized why Lanoe had headed for the wall—it kept the enemy from getting around them. The recon scout's top side was vulnerable to attack, and Lanoe wanted to make sure they couldn't get a bead on it. This did mean that Valk, in his observer's blister, was right in the line of fire.

Wouldn't be the first time. He swiveled around to face the closest

BR.9 and squeezed his trigger. The PBW fire tore off one of the enemy's airfoils, but the bastard didn't need them—there was no air inside the wormhole, so he could afford to lose a wing. Valk started to line up another shot when his view swung around and suddenly he couldn't see the enemies at all. Lanoe must have pulled some fancy maneuver without warning him.

"Give me something to shoot at, at least," Valk called.

"Don't worry," Lanoe replied. "You'll get another chance."

In the pilot's cockpit at the front of the recon scout, Lanoe worked his boards with one hand while the other stayed tightly wrapped around his control yoke. On a secondary display he saw a three-dimensional view of the four militia fighters with their projected courses streaming out before them like ribbons of glass. The four of them were cruising along well behind and above him, lined up in a textbook formation. They had him boxed in, at a distance where they never came close enough to get a good, clear shot at him. It was a solid play—they were keeping their distance because they knew time was on their side. They could afford to pepper him with long-distance shots, knowing they only needed one lucky hit to finish him off.

He couldn't outrun them. If he tried to fall back, to let them get ahead of him, they could just close the distance and then they could carve him up or just shove him into the wall of the wormhole, and that would be that.

Militia pilots weren't, as a rule, all that talented. Many were cadets who washed out of the Navy and found the only job they could get was flying for a poly. Others were recruited from the civilian population, given ten hours in a flight simulator, and sent out to do their best. This batch, though, were clearly a cut above—smart, adaptable. Patient.

He very much wished he knew who had sent them. And why they wanted him dead so badly.

If he was getting out of this trap, he was going to have to get reckless. "Valk," he called, "I know you like to be miserly with your ammunition." Valk had earned his wings during the Establishment Crisis. Back then resources had been scarce and every shot had to count. Valk never liked to squeeze off a shot that he didn't know would be a direct hit. "Right now, I need you to get downright profligate. When I pull this next trick, you hold down your trigger and don't stop until your gun overheats, okay?"

"Wait," Valk said. "What are you about to do?"

Lanoe didn't waste time answering. He punched in a sequence of burns on his thruster board, then yanked his stick straight back and simultaneously kicked open the throttle.

The Z.VII had been built for long-distance patrols. It carried an impressive package of sensors and a very energy-efficient fusion engine. All that extra equipment made it bulky and slow to respond to commands, though. It had never been designed for close-in fighting, and definitely not for stunt flying. The complicated maneuver Lanoe executed just then ran the risk of tying its frame in knots. He could hear its spars groan as the ship twisted around nearly a hundred and eighty degrees on its long axis. It took more strain when the dozens of jets and miniature thrusters built into its nose and sides all fired in a complex rhythm. If Lanoe was unlucky, they might have torn themselves right out of their mountings.

It turned out—as it usually did—that he was lucky, instead. Everything held together. It just looked like he'd lost all control and sent his ship into a wild, uncontrolled vertical spin.

The Z.VII tumbled up and backward, right into the path of the pursuing militia fighters. They were fair pilots, Lanoe had to give them that, and they reacted instantly, breaking formation to make room and avoid a full-on collision. Fair pilots, but not great. One of them sideswiped a second in a great shower of sparks as their vector fields fought to shove each other away. A third pilot started to bank, to try to get a shot in as Lanoe's ship went cartwheeling past. It would have been an easy hit, and it would have cleaved right through the Z.VII's vector field and cut the recon scout in half.

If Valk hadn't already started shooting. He'd done as asked, releasing a wild spray of PBW fire that lit up the canopy of the BR.9. The militia pilot inside probably didn't have time to scream. The shot tore the BR.9 to pieces, and the three remaining militia pilots had to scatter further to avoid the superheated debris.

Lanoe pulled the recon scout out of its tumble and leveled out, skating along just a few dozen meters from the wall of the tunnel. They weren't out of the woods yet. He opened his throttle as far as it would go and burned for speed, headed in exactly the wrong direction.

2

Valk rotated his observer's blister around a hundred and eighty degrees. Behind them, through the haze around their thrusters, he could see the remaining BR.9s banking hard, regrouping to chase after them.

"You know the Admiralty's the other way, right?" he asked.

"They're not going to let us get to the Admiralty. Not today," Lanoe answered.

Valk switched off the intercom so Lanoe wouldn't hear him cursing. He tried focusing on the pursuit, tried lining up a long, impossible shot on one of the pursuing fighters, but there was no point. He switched the intercom back on. "Lanoe, you promised me. You said we would go to the Admiralty and download all this stuff in my head. And then you would let me—"

"I didn't forget," Lanoe replied.

There was no point in arguing. Valk could see perfectly well how things were stacked up against them. He'd just thought they were close—so close. "Ignore that last comment," he said. "What's the new plan?"

"Get out of this in one piece. If we can. Listen, we've bought ourselves about fifteen seconds' worth of a head start. There's no way we can outrun them. So I need you to keep them off balance—lay down suppressing fire as soon as they get close, keep them from forming up again. I don't expect you to actually kill these bastards. Just make it difficult for them to kill us. Got it?"

"Yep," Valk said. He brought up his weapons board. There was still plenty of ammo in his cannon. He checked his other displays and nodded to himself. "Mind if I get a little creative? I might have a few surprises for them."

"Whatever you can do, do it," Lanoe told him.

Valk tapped a few virtual keys. This might be interesting, he thought. If they could stay alive long enough to see it.

<hr />

The wormhole rolled out before Lanoe, its walls snaking back and forth, spitting out ghostly fire. He brought a display up into his main view, showing a camera feed from directly behind them. The BR.9 pilots hadn't expected his crazy maneuver and it was taking them a little time to get themselves turned around.

Not much time. One of them pulled a perfect half loop, a maneuver that was a lot harder to do in vacuum than inside an atmosphere. The other two banked and rolled, slower but safer. Behind them light flashed again and again, sudden and bright as lightning, as debris from the downed ship touched the walls. Those little annihilations would give off a lot of gamma rays, but it was too much to hope that any of the remaining pilots would be fried.

The ship that pulled the half loop burned hard in pursuit, enough so that Lanoe could see the ion trail of its wake, as if the BR.9 were standing on a pillar of fire. Valk put a couple of pointless PBW shots across its nose and its airfoils but it didn't even bother rolling to evade.

The BR.9's powerful engines ate up the distance. Any second now the militia pilot would be close enough to get a perfect bead on Lanoe's main thruster—a perfect kill shot, and then it would all be over. Lanoe considered a couple of different tricky maneuvers, just to make it harder for him to get that shot, but any deviation from their course right now would slow the Z.VII down, and he would still have the other two pursuers to worry about. They weren't far behind.

"Valk," he called, "if you've got something—"

"Close your eyes," Valk said.

✦

"I'm a little busy flying this crate," Lanoe pointed out.

Valk reached for his sensor board. His finger hovered over a virtual key.

"Hellfire, Lanoe—close your damned eyes."

He stabbed the key.

The Z.VII came with a whole suite of advanced sensors and communication gear. Included in that package were several hundred microdrones—basically satellites no bigger than Valk's thumb. Each of them contained a camera, an antenna, and a tiny thruster. There wasn't room for anything else. In normal conditions these would be released one at a time as the recon scout made a long patrol across a battlefield, stringing them out like a trail of breadcrumbs. They were designed to work together to create a distributed communications and imaging network, providing a comprehensive picture of a massive volume of space.

Valk released all of them all at once. They burst out of panels recessed into the Z.VII's hull, flaring away on their tiny thrusters, headed in every possible direction, a whole cloud of them zipping away and behind like chaff. They would ruin the pursuing BR.9's ability to get a clear lock on the Z.VII's thrusters, but it would only take a fraction of a second for the pursuer's computer to compensate. That wasn't what Valk was after.

Nor did he hope they would hit the BR.9. They would make lousy projectiles—too slow and too small to do any damage, and anyway the BR.9's vector field would just shunt them away.

No, Valk had fired off all his microdrones for another reason.

He had disengaged their standard programming, specifically the collision avoidance algorithms. One by one, then in great numbers, they shot away from the Z.VII on perfectly flat trajectories that had them smash right into the walls of the wormhole.

They were annihilated instantly, torn apart and converted into pure energy. Hundreds of impacts all in the space of a half second, each one giving off as much light and radiation as a nuclear blast.

"Hellfire!" Lanoe shouted, which was apt whether he'd meant it to be or not. "Valk—I can see that right through my eyelids! What did you just do?"

The pilot of the BR.9 hadn't been warned ahead of time to close his eyes. He was also directly behind the burst of light, whereas Lanoe was ahead of it, looking away from it.

Valk had flown a BR.9 before. He knew that it was a very good machine, and that it was designed to protect its pilot from all kinds of hazards. A microsecond after the flare-up, its canopy would polarize until it was one hundred percent opaque, blocking out every bit of that horrible light.

It was an open question whether the pilot was permanently blinded before that could happen. An academic question—with the canopy opaqued, there was no way he could see anyway. For about nine-tenths of a second, he was flying blind.

Plenty of time for Valk to line up a good, solid shot, even at a distance. Of course Valk had been facing the light blast, but unlike Lanoe or the pilot of the BR.9, he didn't need his eyes for what came next. He reached out into the raw code of the Z.VII's sensors, synthesized the ones and zeroes into a perfect firing solution. He didn't need to be able to see his hand to pull the trigger.

PBW fire hit the BR.9 dead on, cutting right through its vector field. The fighter broke into pieces, airfoils and weapons and thrusters all tumbling away from each other as the particle beam cut them apart like a scalpel.

"Got another one," Valk said.

"As soon as I can see through all the spots in my eyes," Lanoe told him, "I'd love to know what just happened. It was a great trick."

"Yeah," Valk said. "Too bad I can only do it once."

———

Lanoe blinked and squinted and shook his head to clear the tears out of his eyes. The tunnel ahead of them was as crooked as a dog's leg and he was taking it at top speed. If he wasn't careful he'd brush the walls and finish the assassin's work for them.

Not that they needed much help. The remaining two fighters were catching up with them, fast. They'd been lucky so far—well, Lanoe had been lucky enough to have Valk crewing the guns for him—but the law of averages was running after them just as fast as their enemies. The two BR.9s were firing indiscriminately, wasting ammo on long-range shots that had very little chance of hitting the Z.VII as it wove through the corridors of the maze. One of those rounds could hit at any moment.

"There was a side passage, a little ways back," Lanoe said. "Remember?"

"No," Valk said.

Lanoe laughed. "Yeah, well, it's there. No idea where it leads but if we can get out into open space we can at least maneuver a little more. I'm going to make a hard turn in a second here. It might hurt a little."

"I'll survive," Valk told him.

Lanoe nodded. Well, the big guy was probably right about that. He could take a lot more g forces than Lanoe could, after all.

Still, this was not going to be fun.

Most people thought of the wormhole network as a kind of superhighway system, a grid of streets that connected all the stars in human space. Pilots knew better. The system had all the untidy chaos of the root structure of a massive tree, or maybe the burrow of a digging animal—wormholes crossed each other at junctions, split off into dead ends and long loops that doubled back on themselves. Making it worse, there was no real map of the entire system, because it changed over time—only the widest and most heavily-traveled routes stayed constant for long, and even those twisted and knotted themselves up when nobody was looking.

You passed junctions and new tunnels all the time. Pilots had learned not to go exploring, in case they found themselves in a wormhole that went nowhere, or, worse, one that narrowed down until it was too tight a squeeze for even small ships like the Z.VII.

Of course, sometimes you just had to take a chance.

The two BR.9s were almost on them. Valk laid down salvo after salvo of suppressing fire, but the assassins had velocity to spare—they swung and jinked back and forth as they came on, refusing to let themselves be decent targets. Lanoe studied the tunnel ahead, looking for the side passage he vaguely remembered. If it was farther down the tunnel than he thought—

No. There it was. The ghostly vapor that steamed from the walls grew thicker, almost opaque up ahead. The sign of a junction. Lanoe pulled up his engine board and scrolled through a menu to the gyroscopic control settings. He had to confirm twice that he was really sure he wanted to disengage the rotary compensator.

He was sure.

"Hang on!" he said, and stabbed the virtual key.

The recon scout twisted ninety degrees to the right in the space of a few milliseconds. The fuselage groaned under the stress as its engine tried to rip its way off its own mountings. There was a good reason you had to confirm twice to pull this stunt—there was a very real chance it would tear your ship in half.

The effect on a squishy human body could have been much worse. Lanoe's inertial sink slammed him down as if he were being hammered into his seat. He couldn't breathe. The blood in his body stopped moving and for a split second he went into cardiac arrest. Even his vision blurred to nothing as his eyeballs were flattened inside his head.

Then the compensators snapped back on as alarm chimes blared in Lanoe's ears and his heart thudded in his chest as it started beating again. He made a horrible choking gasping noise as his lungs re-inflated. The recon scout compensated for the time it took him to physically recover. His positioning thrusters burned hard to keep the scout from fishtailing into a bootlegger's turn.

Up ahead of him, through his canopy, he could see the side passage. It wasn't very long. He goosed his main thruster and sent the Z.VII rocketing down the tunnel, barely worrying about twists and turns.

"Valk, you okay back there?" he called.

There was no answer.

Right behind him the two BR.9s copied his turn perfectly. They didn't so much as skid as they twisted around to follow him.

Bastards.

He would have to worry about Valk later. For the moment, all he could do was fly fast. Something he was very good at.

Up ahead the tunnel ended in a lens of pure spacetime. It looked like a glass globe, through which he could only see darkness. A wormhole throat—one of the exits from the maze. Lanoe had no idea what lay beyond. It could be a star with nice planets to hide behind, it could be some forgotten corner of deep space, light-years from anything. It could open out into the event horizon of a black hole.

Lanoe would take his chances. He punched through the lens—it offered no resistance—and into bluish-white light. His eyes adjusted and he saw stars, stars everywhere—speckles of white on a black background.

Real, normal space. The kind that made up most of the universe. The void.

For a fighter pilot like Lanoe, flying free through open space was the closest he ever felt to being home.

He wasn't safe, though. Right behind him, the two BR.9s shot out of the throat side by side, their weapons still glowing in the infrared. They converged on him, a classic pincer maneuver, and then—

They stopped. For a second they just hung there behind his

shoulders, ready to blast him to smithereens. Then they twisted around and shot back through the throat. Back into wormspace.

A second later Lanoe realized why. A green pearl appeared in the corner of his vision, his suit telling him he had an incoming call.

"Reconnaissance scout, please identify. This is a Naval installation and off-limits to unauthorized personnel. Repeat, reconnaissance scout, please identify. This is..."

Some of those twinkling lights all around him weren't stars after all. His displays showed him magnified, light-enhanced views of cruisers, carriers, a couple of big habitats. Hundreds of cataphract class fighters, and all of them painted with the three-headed eagle of the Navy. Clearly, whoever the assassins had been, they had no interest in tangling with that much firepower.

He couldn't remember the last time he'd been so happy to see his own people.

introducing

If you enjoyed
FORSAKEN SKIES,
look out for

ARTEFACT

The Lazarus War: Book 1

by Jamie Sawyer

Mankind has spread to the stars, only to become locked in warfare with an insidious alien race. All that stands against the alien menace are the soldiers of the Simulant Operation Programme, an elite military team remotely operating avatars in the most dangerous theaters of war.

Captain Conrad Harris has died hundreds of times—running suicide missions in simulant bodies. Known as Lazarus, he is a man addicted to death. So when a secret research station deep in alien territory suddenly goes dark, there is no other man who could possibly lead a rescue mission.

But Harris hasn't been trained for what he's about to find. And this time, he may not be coming back...

Radio chatter filled my ears. Different voices, speaking over one another.

Is this it? I asked myself. *Will I find her?*

"*That's a confirm on the identification: AFS* New Haven. *She went dark three years ago.*"

"Null-shields are blown. You have a clean approach."

It was a friendly, at least. Nationality: Arab Freeworlds. But it wasn't her. A spike of disappointment ran through me. *What did I expect?* She was gone.

"Arab Freeworlds Starship New Haven, *this is Alliance FOB* Liberty Point: *do you copy? Repeat, this is FOB* Liberty Point: *do you copy?"*

"Bird's not squawking."

"That's a negative on the hail. No response to automated or manual contact."

I patched into the external cameras to get a better view of the target. She was a big starship, a thousand metres long. NEW HAVEN had been stencilled on the hull, but the white lettering was chipped and worn. Underneath the name was a numerical ID tag and a barcode with a corporate sponsor logo – an advert for some long-forgotten mining corporation. As an afterthought something in Arabic had been scrawled beside the logo.

New Haven was a civilian-class colony vessel; one of the mass-produced models commonly seen throughout the border systems, capable of long-range quantum-space jumps but with precious little defensive capability. Probably older than me, retrofitted by a dozen governments and corporations before she became known by her current name. The ship looked painfully vulnerable, to my military eye: with a huge globe-like bridge and command module at the nose, a slender midsection and an ugly drive propulsion unit at the aft.

She wouldn't be any good in a fight, that was for sure.

"Reading remote sensors now. I can't get a clean internal analysis from the bio-scanner."

On closer inspection, there was evidence to explain the lifeless state of the ship. Puckered rips in the hull-plating suggested that she had been fired upon by a spaceborne weapon. Nothing catastrophic, but enough to disable the main drive: as though whoever, or whatever, had attacked the ship had been toying with her. Like the hunter that only cripples its prey, but chooses not to deliver the killing blow.

"AFS New Haven, *this is* Liberty Point. *You are about to be boarded in accordance with military code alpha-zeroniner. You have*

trespassed into the Krell Quarantine Zone. Under military law in force in this sector we have authority to board your craft, in order to ensure your safety."

The ship had probably been drifting aimlessly for months, maybe even years. There was surely nothing alive within that blasted metal shell.

"That's a continued no response to the hail. Authorising weapons-free for away team. Proceed with mission as briefed."

"This is Captain Harris," I said. "Reading you loud and clear. That's an affirmative on approach."

"Copy that. Mission is good to go, good to go. Over to you, Captain. Wireless silence from here on in."

Then the communication-link was severed and there was a moment of silence. *Liberty Point*, and all of the protections that the station brought with it, suddenly felt a very long way away.

Our Wildcat armoured personnel shuttle rapidly advanced on the *New Haven*. The APS was an ugly, functional vessel – made to ferry us from the base of operations to the insertion point, and nothing more. It was heavily armoured but completely unarmed; the hope was that, under enemy fire, the triple-reinforced armour would prevent a hull breach before we reached the objective. Compared to the goliath civilian vessel, it was an insignificant dot.

I sat upright in the troop compartment, strapped into a safety harness. On the approach to the target, the Wildcat APS gravity drive cancelled completely: everything not strapped down drifted in free fall. There were no windows or view-screens, and so I relied on the external camera-feeds to track our progress. This was proper cattle-class, even in deep-space.

I wore a tactical combat helmet, for more than just protection. Various technical data was being relayed to the heads-up display – projected directly onto the interior of the face-plate. Swarms of glowing icons, warnings and data-reads scrolled overhead. For a rookie, the flow of information would've been overwhelming but to me this was second nature. Jacked directly into my combat-armour, with a thought I cancelled some data-streams, examined others.

Satisfied with what I saw, I yelled into the communicator: "Squad, sound off."

Five members of the unit called out in turn, their respective life-signs appearing on my HUD.

"Jenkins." The only woman on the team; small, fast and sparky. Jenkins was a gun nut, and when it came to military operations obsessive-compulsive was an understatement. She served as the corporal of the squad and I wouldn't have had it any other way.

"Blake." Youngest member of the team, barely out of basic training when he was inducted. Fresh-faced and always eager. His defining characteristics were extraordinary skill with a sniper rifle, and an incredible talent with the opposite sex.

"Martinez." He had a background in the Alliance Marine Corps. With his dark eyes and darker fuzz of hair, he was Venusian American stock. He promised that he had Hispanic blood, but I doubted that the last few generations of Martinez's family had even set foot on Earth.

"Kaminski." Quick-witted; a fast technician as well as a good shot. Kaminski had been with me from the start. Like me, he had been Alliance Special Forces. He and Jenkins rubbed each other up the wrong way, like brother and sister. Expertly printed above the face-shield of his helmet were the words BORN TO KILL.

Then, finally: "Science Officer Olsen, ah, alive."

Our guest for this mission sat to my left – the science officer attached to my squad. He shook uncontrollably, alternating between breathing hard and retching hard. Olsen's communicator was tuned to an open channel, and none of us were spared his pain. I remotely monitored his vital signs on my suit display – he was in a bad way. I was going to have to keep him close during the op.

"First contact for you, Mr Olsen?" Blake asked over the general squad comms channel.

Olsen gave an exaggerated nod.

"Yes, but I've conducted extensive laboratory studies of the enemy." He paused to retch some more, then blurted: "And I've read many mission debriefs on the subject."

"That counts for nothing out here, my friend," said Jenkins. "You need to face off against the enemy. Go toe to toe, in our space."

"That's the problem, Jenkins," Blake said. "This isn't our space, according to the Treaty."

"You mean the Treaty that was signed off before you were born, Kid?" Kaminski added, with a dry snigger. "We have company this mission – it's a special occasion. How about you tell us how old you are?"

As squad leader, I knew Blake's age but the others didn't. The mystery had become a source of amusement to the rest of the unit. I could've given Kaminski the answer easily enough, but that would have spoiled the entertainment. This was a topic to which he returned every time we were operational.

"Isn't this getting old?" said Blake.

"No, it isn't – just like you, Kid."

Blake gave him the finger – his hands chunky and oversized inside heavily armoured gauntlets.

"Cut that shit out," I growled over the communicator. "I need you all frosty and on point. I don't want things turning nasty out there. We get aboard the *Haven*, download the route data, then bail out."

I'd already briefed the team back at the *Liberty Point*, but no operation was routine where the Krell were concerned. Just the possibility of an encounter changed the game. I scanned the interior of the darkened shuttle, taking in the faces of each of my team. As I did so, my suit streamed combat statistics on each of them – enough for me to know that they were on edge, that they were ready for this.

"If we stay together and stay cool, then no one needs to get hurt," I said. "That includes you, Olsen."

The science officer gave another nod. His biorhythms were most worrying but there was nothing I could do about that. His inclusion on the team hadn't been my choice, after all.

"You heard the man," Jenkins echoed. "Meaning no fuck-ups."

Couldn't have put it better myself. If I bought it on the op, Jenkins would be responsible for getting the rest of the squad home.

The Wildcat shuttle selected an appropriate docking portal on the *New Haven*. Data imported from the APS automated pilot told me that trajectory and approach vector were good. We would board the ship from the main corridor. According to our intelligence, based on schematics of similar starships, this corridor formed the spine of the ship. It would give access to all major tactical objectives – the bridge, the drive chamber, and the hypersleep suite.

A chime sounded in my helmet and the APS updated me on our progress – T-MINUS TEN SECONDS UNTIL IMPACT.

"Here we go!" I declared.

The Wildcat APS retro-thrusters kicked in, and suddenly we were decelerating rapidly. My head thumped against the padded neck-rest and my body juddered. Despite the reduced-gravity of the cabin, the sensation was gut wrenching. My heart hammered in my chest, even though I had done this hundreds of times before. My helmet informed me that a fresh batch of synthetic combat-drug – a cocktail of endorphins and adrenaline, carefully mixed to keep me at optimum combat performance – was being injected into my system to compensate. The armour carried a full medical suite, patched directly into my body, and automatically provided assistance when necessary. Distance to target rapidly decreased.

"Brace for impact."

Through the APS-mounted cameras, I saw the rough-and-ready docking procedure. The APS literally bumped against the outer hull, and unceremoniously lined up our airlock with the *Haven*'s. With an explosive roar and a wave of kinetic force, the shuttle connected with the hull. The Wildcat airlock cycled open.

We moved like a well-oiled mechanism, a well-used machine. Except for Olsen, we'd all done this before. Martinez was first up, out of his safety harness. He took up point. Jenkins and Blake were next; they would provide covering fire if we met resistance. Then Kaminski, escorting Olsen. I was always last out of the cabin.

"Boarding successful," I said. "We're on the *Haven*."

That was just a formality for my combat-suit recorder.

As I moved out into the corridor, my weapon auto-linked with my HUD and displayed targeting data. We were armed with Westington-Haslake M95 plasma battle-rifles – the favoured long-arm for hostile starship engagements. It was a large and weighty weapon, and fired phased plasma pulses, fuelled by an onboard power cell. Range was limited but it had an incredible rate of fire and the sheer stopping power of an energy weapon of this magnitude was worth the compromise. We carried other weapons as well, according to preference – Jenkins favoured an Armant-pattern incinerator unit as her primary weapon, and we all wore plasma pistol sidearms.

"Take up covering positions – overlap arcs of fire," I whispered, into the communicator. The squad obeyed. "Wide dispersal, and get me some proper light."

Bobbing shoulder-lamps illuminated, flashing over the battered interior of the starship. The suits were equipped with infrared, night-vision, and electro-magnetic sighting, but the Krell didn't emit much body heat and nothing beat good old-fashioned eyesight.

Without being ordered, Kaminski moved up on one of the wall-mounted control panels. He accessed the ship's mainframe with a portable PDU from his kit.

"Let there be light," Martinez whispered, in heavily accented Standard.

Strip lights popped on overhead, flashing in sequence, dowsing the corridor in ugly electric illumination. Some flickered erratically, others didn't light at all. Something began humming in the belly of the ship: maybe dormant life-support systems. A sinister calmness permeated the main corridor. It was utterly utilitarian, with bare metal-plated walls and floors. My suit reported that the temperature was uncomfortably low, but within acceptable tolerances.

"Gravity drive is operational," Kaminski said. "They've left the atmospherics untouched. We'll be okay here for a few hours."

"I don't plan on staying that long," Jenkins said.

Simultaneously, we all broke the seals on our helmets. The atmosphere carried twin but contradictory scents: the stink of burning plastic and fetid water. *The ship has been on fire, and a recycling tank has blown somewhere nearby.* Liquid *plink-plink-plinked* softly in the distance.

"I'll stay sealed, if you don't mind," Olsen clumsily added. "The subjects have been known to harbour cross-species contaminants."

"Christo, this guy is unbelievable," Kaminski said, shaking his head.

"Hey, watch your tongue, *mano*," Martinez said to Kaminski. He motioned to a crude white cross, painted onto the chest-plate of his combat-suit. "Don't use His name in vain."

None of us really knew what religion Martinez followed, but he did it with admirable vigour. It seemed to permit gambling, women and drinking, whereas blaspheming on a mission was always unacceptable.

"Not this shit again," Kaminski said. "It's all I ever hear from you. We get back to the *Point* without you, I'll comm God personally. You Venusians are all the same."

"I'm an American," Martinez started. Venusians were very conscious of their roots; this was an argument I'd arbitrated far too many times between the two soldiers.

"Shut the fuck up," Jenkins said. "He wants to believe, leave him to it." The others respected her word almost as much as mine, and immediately fell silent. "It's nice to have faith in something. Orders, Cap?"

"Fireteam Alpha – Jenkins, Martinez – get down to the hypersleep chamber and report on the status of these colonists. Fireteam Bravo, form up on me."

Nods of approval from the squad. This was standard operating procedure: get onboard the target ship, hit the key locations and get back out as soon as possible.

"And the quantum-drive?" Jenkins asked. She had powered up her flamethrower, and the glow from the pilot-light danced over her face. Her expression looked positively malicious.

"We'll converge on the location in fifteen minutes. Let's get some recon on the place before we check out."

extras

"Solid copy, Captain."

The troopers began a steady jog into the gloomy aft of the starship, their heavy armour and weapons clanking noisily as they went.

It wasn't fear that I felt in my gut. Not trepidation, either; this was something worse. It was excitement – polluting my thought process, strong enough that it was almost intoxicating. This was what I was made for. I steadied my pulse and concentrated on the mission at hand.

Something stirred in the ship – I felt it.